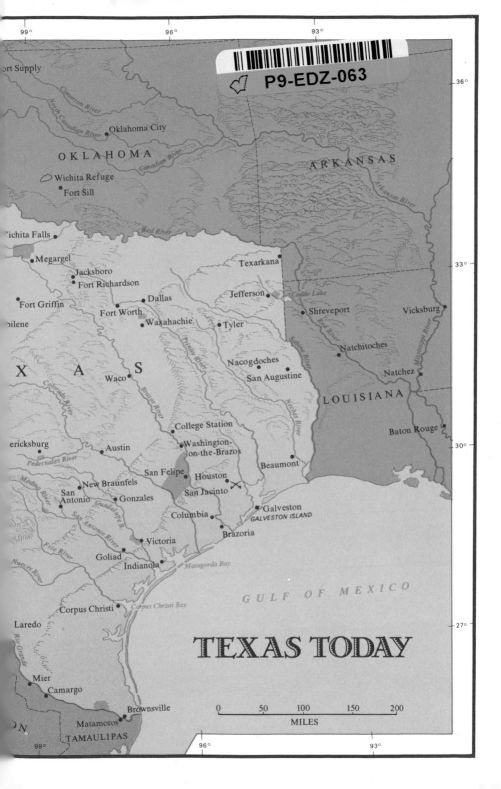

99° 96° 93°

36°

ort Supply

OKLAHOMA

Cimarron River

North Canadian River

Oklahoma City

Canadian River

ARKANSAS

Arkansas River

Wichita Refuge

Fort Sill

ichita Falls

Red River

Megargel

Jacksboro

Fort Richardson

Texarkana

Jefferson

Caddo Lake

33°

Fort Griffin

Fort Worth

Dallas

Waxahachie

Tyler

Shreveport

Red River

Vicksburg

bilene

Nacogdoches

Natchitoches

Mississippi River

X   A   S

Waco

Colorado River

Brazos River

Trinity River

San Augustine

Natchez

Sabine River

LOUISIANA

ericksburg

College Station

Pedernales River

Austin

Washington-
on-the-Brazos

Neches River

Baton Rouge

30°

Medina River

San Felipe

New Braunfels

San
Antonio

Gonzales

Guadalupe R.

Houston

San Jacinto

Beaumont

Columbia

San Antonio River

Victoria

Galveston

GALVESTON ISLAND

Frio River

Brazoria

Goliad

Indianola

Matagorda Bay

Nueces River

GULF   OF   MEXICO

Corpus Christi

Corpus Christi Bay

27°

Laredo

Rio Grande

TEXAS TODAY

Mier

Camargo

Brownsville

0   50   100   150   200

MILES

ON

Matamoros

TAMAULIPAS

99°

96°

93°

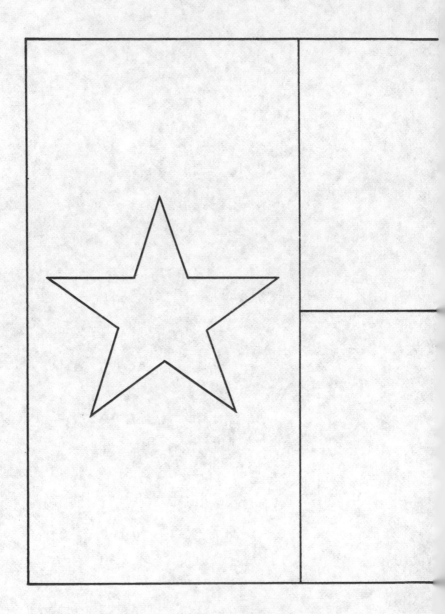

TEXAS

JAMES A. MICHENER

RANDOM HOUSE   NEW YORK

VOLUME 2

FACT AND FICTION

This novel strives for an honest blend of fiction and historical fact, and the reader is entitled to know which is which.

IX. Loyalties: Edisto Island, Social Circle and Jefferson are real; the families occupying them are fictional. Events at the siege of Vicksburg are historical, as are the various behaviors of Sam Houston. The cotton trade to Bagdad was historical, as was the now-vanished Bagdad. The massacre of the Germans and the hangings along the Red River were historical.

X. The Fort: Fort Sam Garner and its military occupants are fictional. Visiting officers Sherman, Grierson, Miles, Mackenzie and Custer were historical. Chief Matark, Earnshaw Rusk and Emma Larkin are fictional, but each is based upon real prototypes. Quakers did administer the Comanche camps, but Camp Hope is fictional, as is Three Cairns. Rattlesnake Peavine is fictional.

XI. The Frontier: All citizens in Fort Garner are fictional. The architect James Riely Gordon was real, and the famous carvings on his fictional Larkin County Courthouse can be found today on his real courthouse in Waxahachie. The Parmenteer-Bates feud was fictional but it could have been modeled after any of a dozen such protracted affairs. The trail to Dodge City was historical, but R. J. Poteet is fictional. So is Alonzo Betz, but the impact of his barbed wire was historical. The destruction of Indianola happened as described.

XII. The Town: All characters are fictional, including the revivalist Elder Fry, but the church trial of Laurel Cobb is based upon a real incident whose details were provided by a son of the accused. The Larkin oil field is fictional, but its characteristics are accurate for that part of Texas. Ranger Lone Wolf Gonzaullas was real. Details regarding the Fighting Antelopes are fictional but are based upon numerous real teams of that period. Politics as practiced in Bravo and Saldana County are fictional, but prototypes abound and some still function.

XIII. The Invaders: All characters and incidents are fictional, but the Larkin tornado is based on real and terrifying prototypes.

XIV. Power and Change: All characters and incidents are fictional, except that the summer storm of 1983 was real.

CONTENTS

IX
LOYALTIES

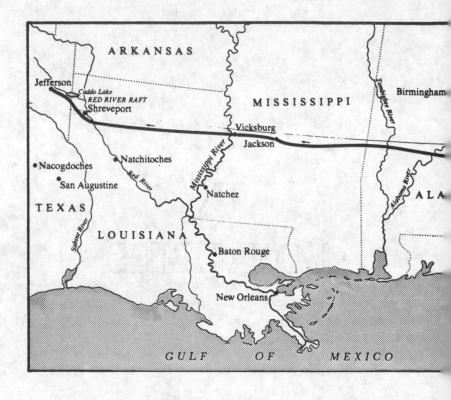

A S SOON AS IT WAS CONSONANT WITH HIS UNDERSTANDING OF MILITARY
honor, Persifer Cobb resigned his commission in Vera Cruz, but when he
submitted his papers to General Scott's aide, Brigadier Cavendish of Virginia, the latter tried to dissuade him: 'Colonel Cobb, since the days of Washington we've always had a Cobb among our leaders. We can't let you leave.'

'I will never again accept the humiliation I've had to suffer in this war. Deprived of a rightful command. Sentenced to work with those Texans.'

'Are you aware that we've sent your name up for promotion?'

'Too late.'

'You mean you won't accept it if it comes through?'

Cobb was polite but resolute: 'No, sir.' He thanked Cavendish for his concern
and was about to leave when the brigadier pushed back his chair, rose, and took
him by the arm: 'Perse, my dear friend . . .'

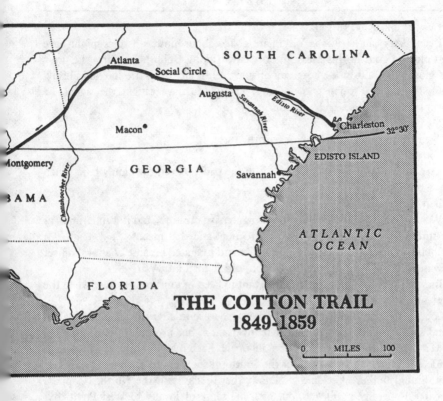

THE COTTON TRAIL
1849-1859

0   MILES   100

In the formal discussion it had been 'Colonel Cobb,' as was proper, and this sudden switch to the familiar unnerved Persifer, who mumbled 'Yes, sir' with the respect he always accorded superior rank.

'Could we walk, perhaps?'

'Of course, sir.'

In the public park that fronted the sun-blinded Gulf of Campeche the two officers stared for some moments at that bleak fortress out in the bay, San Juan de Ulúa, where Mexican prisoners sentenced in Vera Cruz rotted in their dark dungeons. 'How would you like seven years in there?' Cavendish asked.

'I have much different plans.'

'Then you won't change your mind? You're definitely leaving?'

'I decided that two years ago . . . at least.'

'And I understand your bitterness. But do you understand why we cannot lose you?'

'I can think of no reasons.'

'I can.' Very cautiously the Virginian looked about him, as if spies might have been planted even in this Mexican port city. Taking Cobb by the arm, he drew him closer and said in a conspiratorial whisper: 'Many of us are looking ahead.' Then, fearing that Cobb was not alert enough to have caught the signal, he continued: 'We're on a collision course.'

'Meaning?'

'Two irresistible forces—South, North.'

'You think . . .'

'I see it in signs everywhere. I read it in the papers. Even my family hints when they write.'

'Is it that bad?'

'Worse. The North will never stop its aggressive pressure, and if it intensifies, as I'm sure it will, we'll have to leave the Union, and that means . . .'

Cobb had not interrupted. The brigadier had hesitated because as a loyal officer he was loath to utter the word, so Cobb said it for him: 'War?'

'Inevitable. And that's why it's important to keep in uniform. Because when the moment of decision comes . . .'

Cobb, reluctant to contemplate another war so soon after finishing one he had found so distasteful, tried to end the conversation, but Cavendish, having parted the veil that hid the future, kept it boldly open: 'Each man in uniform will have to decide. Men like me, we'll fight for the South till snow covers Richmond sixty feet deep. Stupid bullies like some we know, they'll stay with the North. I suppose men like Robert Lee will, too, out of some sense of loyalty to West Point. But really able men like Jefferson Davis, Braxton Bragg, Albert Sidney Johnston, they'll give their lives to defend Southern rights. And you must be with us.'

'I'm still sending in my resignation,' Cobb said, and he returned to his quarters, where packing had to be completed before reporting to the waiting ship.

When he stepped ashore at New Orleans, a civilian, and saw the mountain of cotton bales ready for shipment to Liverpool, where world prices were set, he was eager to hurry back to his family plantation on Edisto Island and assume command of its cotton production. Prior to enrolling at the Point he had known a good deal about cotton, for the Cobb plantation had for many decades produced the best in the world: the famed Sea Island, with the longest fibers known and a black, shiny seed which could be easily picked clean even before the invention of the gin.

As soon as he had located a hotel and arranged for his journey northeast, he asked the way to the offices of a journal which his family had read since 1837 and to which cotton growers looked for guidance. When he introduced himself to the editor of *New Orleans Price Current,* a scholar from Mississippi, he was warmly greeted: 'A Cobb from Edisto. Never expected to see one in my office. You are most welcome, sir.'

'I'm returning home after military service and wanted to learn how things are going in the trade.'

'Never worse.'

'Do you mean it?'

The editor slid his yearly report across the desk, and before Cobb had finished the third paragraph he grasped the situation:

> The commercial revolution which had prostrated credit in Great Britain, and which subsequently spread to nearly all parts of the Continent of Europe, and to the Indies, put a sudden check to our prosperous course . . . A still more severe blow was given by the startling intelligence of a revolution in France, and the overthrow of the monarchy. This movement of the people in favor of popular rights rapidly spread to other countries of Europe, and in the tumultuous state of political affairs, commercial credit was completely overthrown and trade annihilated . . .

> All this produced a more rapid depreciation in the price of cotton than we remember ever to have witnessed. At Liverpool sales were made at lower rates than were ever before known for American cotton . . . Many English mills simply shut down, while others were compelled to resort to part-time working . . .

Cobb, feeling his mouth go dry, asked: 'How bad is it?' and the editor handed him the price report for Middling as sold at New Orleans: 'Here's how bad it is.'

As Cobb took the paper he asked: 'What do you figure it costs to raise and deliver a pound of cotton these days?' and the expert replied: 'With care, seven cents.' When Cobb saw the record he felt dizzy: 3 September 1847, 12⁵/8¢ and a modest profit; 26 November, after the first flood of bad news, 7¹/2¢, right at the no-profit level; 28 April 1848, when Europe was falling apart, 6¢, which meant a cash loss on each sale.

'Do you see any relief?' Cobb asked, and the editor pointed to his explanatory notes for this dismal year:

> . . . The Royal Bank of Liverpool suspended business.

> . . . Numerous business houses of great antiquity and reputation closed.

> . . . Many contracts with American shippers voided without recourse.

> . . . Forced abdication of King Louis Philippe from throne of France.

> . . . All Europe in worst condition since 1789.

   . . . Angry mobs of Chartists threaten the peace in England.

   . . . Population of Ireland in an unruly mood.

'Surely,' Cobb protested, 'our marvelous victory in Mexico must have affected the market favorably,' but with his ruler the editor pointed to a minor note at the very end of his gloomy report: 'This shows how the rest of the world evaluated your war. "Our own war with Mexico was brought to a successful close by Mexico's cession of California &c. to the U.S." '

'What can be done?' Cobb asked.

'You long-staple Sea Island men, you don't have to worry.' He showed Cobb his summary: South Carolina short staple, 280,671 five-hundred-pound bales, 7⁹/16¢; they lost a fortune on that. Sea Island long staple, 18,111 bales, much of it from Edisto; price held reasonably firm, 19¹/2¢.

And there was the difference: short staple, eight cents; long staple, nineteen cents, and Edisto grew only the long. Other plantations, of course, would have grown Sea Island had their land permitted, but it did not, and they were condemned to growing the more difficult and less profitable short.

'Haven't you a brother in Georgia who grows short?' the editor asked, and Persifer smiled: 'A cousin. My father's brother became insulted over some fancied grievance years ago, about 1822 if I recall, and off he trundled to Georgia, predicting that he'd make a fortune. But of course he couldn't grow Sea Island up in those red hills. He was stuck with short, and he's never done too well with it.'

'Why didn't he return to Edisto?'

'When a Cobb leaves, he leaves.'

'Did you say you were leaving the army?'

'I did.'

'But in case of trouble . . .' The editor paused exactly as Brigadier Cavendish had paused.

Cobb, who had refused to consider such a possibility in Vera Cruz, now responded as an honorable soldier would: 'If real trouble threatened the Union, of course I'd report. So would you.' A long silence ensued, and it was obvious that neither man wished to be the one to break it. Then the editor surprised Cobb by switching subject matter dramatically.

'Your cousin in Georgia should study this,' and he shoved a provisional report into Cobb's hands. 'I was going to print it in this year's summary, but I wanted to verify some of the amazing statistics.' And Cobb read:

AVERAGE YIELD PER ACRE (ACTUAL)
OF COTTON CROP IN NINE STATES

Florida	250 pounds
Tennessee	300 pounds

South Carolina	320 pounds
Georgia	500 pounds
Alabama	525 pounds
Louisiana	550 pounds
Mississippi	650 pounds
Arkansas	700 pounds
Texas	750 pounds

'Could these figures be real?' Cobb asked, astonished by that last line. 'We think so,' the editor said, 'but we're going to double certify. If they prove out, we'll print them. So you and your cousin both ought to move to Texas. Looks as if it's to be our major cotton state.'

When Cobb started to ridicule the idea, the editor returned to his gloomy summary, tapping it with his pen: 'The lesson, Cobb, is that cotton prospers, and you and I prosper, when things around the world are kept in order. Why would the French throw out a perfectly good king? Why would the damned Chartists raise trouble in England, along with those idiotic revolutionaries in the Germanys and the Austrian Empire? For that matter, you tell me why the abolitionists are allowed to rant and rave in this country?'

'They'd better not rant and rave in South Carolina.' In swift, inevitable steps Persifer Cobb had progressed from being against any war, to defending the Union in case of trouble, to championing the South.

'The world would be so much better off,' the editor said, 'if only people would remain content with things as they are. Tell me, in Texas did you hear any agitation against slavery?'

'In Texas I heard nothing except the buzz of mosquitoes.'

'I envy you that plantation on Edisto. One of the world's best.'

'I aim to keep it that way.'

Edisto Island was a low-lying paradise formed in the Atlantic Ocean by silt brought down the Edisto River, a meandering stream that wound its way from the higher lands of South Carolina. An irregular pentagon about ten miles long on the ocean side, the island's highest elevation was six feet and its dominant physical characteristic large groves of splendid oak trees, some deciduous but most live, which were decorated with magnificent pendants of Spanish moss. Its fields were miraculously productive, with soil so soft and even that it could be plowed with a teaspoon.

About fifty white people lived on the island's great plantations, and fifteen hundred black slaves. Except for small family gardens and some acreage of rice, the only crop grown was Sea Island cotton: sown in March, ginned in September, shipped to Liverpool in Edisto ships in January.

Every white family who owned a plantation home on Edisto—handsome affairs, with white pillars supporting the porch—also maintained a grander home along The Battery in Charleston, twenty-four miles away. In that congenial city the spacious life of the Carolina planter unfolded, and Cobb was most eager to renew his acquaintance with it. Both his father and his wife would be in Charleston, and he longed to see them, but he felt it his duty to report first to the plantation, where his brother would be in charge.

He liked Somerset, four years younger than himself, and had felt no qualms about turning the plantation over to him when he enrolled at West Point. His letters from the Mexican War had testified to their continuing rapport—they were more like those of a friend than of an older brother—and he was impatient to see Sett, as the family called him.

He therefore ended his homeward journey at a road junction some twenty miles west of Charleston; here the Cobbs maintained a small shack in which lived an elderly slave whose duty it was to drive members of the family down the long road to the ferry that would carry them across to Edisto. This slave bore the extraordinary name of Diocletian, because an earlier Colonel Cobb had loved Roman history, believing the gentlefolk of the South to be the descendants of Romans. He had named all his house servants after the emperors, except his personal servant-butler-valet, whom he invariably called Suetonius, on the logical grounds that 'Suetonius was responsible for all we know about the first Caesars. He wrote the book. So you, Suetonius, damn your hide, are responsible for all the Caesars in this house.' He usually worked it so that he had twelve house servants, which permitted him to make the joke: 'My Suetonius and his Twelve Caesars.'

Diocletian, an artful onetime house slave who knew that his welfare depended upon keeping various masters pacified, created the impression of being deliriously happy at seeing the colonel home from the wars. 'Get dem horses!' he shouted at his sons. 'We gwine carry Gen'ral Cobb to de ferry!' But when he was alone with his aged wife he predicted: 'Ol' Stiff-and-Steady back with his big ideas. Don't look good for Somerset.'

Rapidly a buggy was prepared, and with Cobb holding the reins, he and Diocletian started the pleasant nine-mile ride to the ferry. As they rode, the slave spoke of events on the island, and since he had for some years served as a house servant, he could speak English rather well, but he was basically what was called a Gullah Nigger, and as such, used the lively, imaginative Gullah language, Elizabethan English spiced with African Coast words. Since Cobb had learned it as a boy, he encouraged Diocletian to use it as they talked of familiar things:

'E tief um.'	*He stole it.*
'Ontel um shum.'	*Until I saw her.*
'Wuffuh um sha'ap?'	*Why is she so smart?*

'Hukkuh im farruh ent wot?'	*How come his father isn't*
	worth much?
'Um lak buckra bittle.'	*He likes white man's food.*
'Bumbye e gwine wedduh	*By-and-by it's going to rain*
pontak Edisto.'	*upon Edisto.*

But now, as they passed the interminable wetlands whose lazy waters and wind-blown reeds pleased Cobb, for he had not seen them in five years, Diocletian switched subjects, and as he spoke of Cobb affairs he used English: 'You wife, Miss Tessa Mae, she never better. Sett's wife, Miss Millicent, she not too well, two chir'ns now.'

'Boys, aren't they?'

'Boy 'n' a girl, bofe fine.'

Diocletian said that he himself had 'two gramchir'n, bofe fine.' When the buggy approached the ferry, he began to shout and snap the whip, which he had taken from Persifer, and in this way he roused the boatman, who also gave the impression of being delighted to see the colonel after such a long absence.

'How dem Mexicans?' he wanted to know. 'Dem Mexican womens, dey all dancey-dancey like dey say?'

The three men discussed the war, after which Diocletian bade his master farewell: 'We hopes you bees here long time, Colonel. Dis yere's you home.' In fluent Gullah, Persifer thanked the slave for the pleasant ride and immediately thereafter boarded the ferry, allowing its keeper to pole him across the shallow North Fork of the Edisto River.

Before the little craft landed, slaves on the island side had saddled a horse for the colonel, dispatching one boy on a mule to alert the big house that Persifer was about to appear after his long absence. Down the tree-lined roadway the boy sped, kicking his mule in the sides as he shouted to everyone he met: 'Colonel Cobb, he come home!'

It was about seven miles from the ferry landing to the gracious two-story white house in which Somerset Cobb, as plantation manager, lived with his wife, Millicent, and their two children, and as the ride ended, it became apparent that the messenger had spread his news effectively, for everyone inside the house, and from outlying work houses too, had crowded beside the long lane leading to the colonnaded porch, prepared to give him the kind of enthusiastic welcome he expected. Ten whites and about fifty blacks stood waving as he and his attendant cantered through the spacious gateway. Modestly but with no excessive show of subservience, the slave slowed his horse and stopped it by the side of the roadway while Persifer rode on ahead, wearing the uniform of his country but with no insignia marks to show that he had once been a colonel.

He stopped and gazed in surprise, for from the porch came someone he had expected to be in the more salubrious climate of Charleston. It was his wife, Tessa Mae, daughter of a leading Carolina family, a slim, self-possessed young woman who rarely said anything thoughtlessly, and for that reason commanded his attention as well as his affection. 'Darling,' he cried. 'How wonderful to see you!' Easily he swung his right leg free of the saddle, leaped to the ground and took her in his arms.

Over her shoulder he saw his brother, a bit heavier now but with the same manly appearance he remembered so well. He was dressed, Persifer was glad to see, in expensive boots from England; trim trousers, made to order by a Charleston tailor; an open-neck shirt, of good French cloth; and a soft beige scarf from Italy, tied loosely about his neck. He was a fine-looking fellow of thirty-one, rather retiring in disposition, who appeared to have managed plantations all his life and intended continuing. Although he was quiet, there was about him none of the softness which so frequently attacked second sons of planter families when they realized they would not inherit the family estate and life goals became indistinct. It was also apparent that he liked his older brother very much, and he now waited for a proper chance to show it.

'Somerset!' the colonel cried, moving on to his brother. 'I've thought of you and this house whenever I sent you a letter.'

'How wonderful they were!' Millicent Cobb interrupted as she moved forward to receive an enthusiastic kiss. 'You should be a novelist, Persifer. I could see your Panther Komax coming at me through the woods.'

'That would be a very bad day for you, Lissa, when that one came at you.'

'Did he wear a panther cap?' the Cobb boy asked, and Persifer said: 'Indeed he did, and he smelled like a panther, too.'

Turning to his wife, he asked, 'And where are our children?' and she replied: 'At school. In Charleston.'

It was quickly agreed that the four older Cobbs would leave at once for Charleston to go to the great house on The Battery, and orders were sent to the plantation ferry—a much different one from the general ferry which Persifer had used to get to the island—to prepare the boat and the rowers for the delightful voyage to that golden city of the southern coast. But now Millicent, who seemed frail in everything but determination, put her foot down: 'We shall not go today. Persifer is tired, whether he realizes it or not, and we can go just as well in the morning.'

However, the brothers felt that servants should be sent ahead in a smaller boat to alert their father of his son's return, and Millicent saw nothing wrong with that: 'I'd have preferred a surprise, and so would Father, I judge. But let it be.'

Talk turned to cotton prices, and Persifer reported what the New Orleans editor had said about how adverse conditions in Europe affected them.

'What the German barons ought to do,' Persifer said, 'is line those agitators up and spread a little canister about.'

'Give them time, they will.'

They both thought it unfair for peasants in Europe and especially in Ireland to be causing disturbances which unsettled the Liverpool market, and Somerset was astounded when his brother informed him of the collapse of Liverpool's Royal Bank: 'Good God! Rioters tearing down a great bank! I was damned pleased, Persifer, when you told us how your Texans handled those rioters in Mexico City. What they need in Europe is about six regiments of Texas Rangers.'

'Please!' the colonel said. 'Don't send them anywhere. Not even to the Ottoman Empire.'

Later in the evening, when the brothers were alone, each realized that he should speak openly of the altered situation on the plantation now that Persifer had resigned his commission, but each was loath to broach this delicate question, so Persifer raised one of more general significance: 'In New Orleans men spoke openly . . . well, not directly, but you knew what was on their minds. They spoke of a possible rupture between our oppressors at the North and ourselves. Have you heard any such talk, Sett?'

'There's been constant talk since I can remember. But only by the irresponsibles who seem to flourish in this state and Georgia. Men like you and me, we'd surrender many of our advantages if we broke with the North.'

'Have we any advantages left?'

'Cotton. Every day I live, every experience I have, proves anew that the rest of the world must have our cotton. Cotton is our shield.'

'Even when it can drop from twelve and five-eighths to . . . ? What price did you say our upland people got? Four cents plus? That's a two-thirds drop in three months.'

'And we'll see it back to twenty cents as soon as peace is regained and the mills resume weaving.' He leaned forward: 'If a man grows Sea Island, he worries far less, and we grow Sea Island.' On that reassuring note the brothers went to bed.

They rose early, walked down to the plantation landing, entered their long, sleek craft, its six slaves already in position, and started one of America's outstanding short voyages. When they left the pier they had a choice of two routes. They could head east and soon enter the Atlantic Ocean, where a rough thirty-mile sail would carry them to Charleston. Or they could head west and enter a fascinating inland passage that would take them to the same destination, except that on this route, protecting islands would hold off the Atlantic swells, making the voyage a sea-breeze delight.

If the brothers had been sailing alone, they would surely have taken the open-sea route for its challenge, but with their wives aboard, they chose the inland passage, moving through vast marshes until they saw above them the headland on which rested the beautiful homes and imposing trees of Charleston.

Now, with the wind gone, they dropped sail, and the slaves, their back muscles glistening in the sun, leaned on the oars, their voices blending in a soft chantey as they moved the boat toward its docking place near The Battery:

> 'Miss Lucy, don't you bake him no cornbread,
> Don't you feed him like you done feed me.
> Miss Lucy, don't you dare bake him no cornbread
> Till I comes home wid your two possum.'

When they broke out of the narrow channel and into the glorious bay which made Charleston so distinctive, they could see dead ahead the glowering walls of Fort Sumter, unassailable on its rock; and while the sails were being hoisted again, Persifer told his listeners of San Juan de Ulúa, a comparable fortress set in another part of the same great ocean.

With deft moves the black helmsman brought the craft about and landed his four passengers on The Battery, one of the nation's majestic streets. It stood on a hill so low it scarcely merited its name, but so pleasingly high that any house atop it caught a breeze off the sea. The stately houses were not positioned like those of any other American street; because a house was taxed according to how much of the precious Battery it took up, the Charleston mansions were not built with the long axis facing the sea, which would have been reasonable, but with the shortest end possible facing east and the longer sides running far back into the town.

'Charleston has always looked sideways at the world,' Persifer said as he saw once more those homes in whose pleasant gardens he had spent the better hours of his youth. There was the Masters mansion, in which he had courted Tessa Mae, and farther along, the Brooks house, where he and Somerset had gone so often to visit Millicent Brooks and her sister, Netty Lou; for almost a year it looked as if the two Cobb boys were going to marry the two Brooks girls, but then Netty Lou met a dashing boy home from Princeton, and Persifer had to settle for the Masters girl. Out on the great plantations and along The Battery it seemed as if a Charleston man did not marry a specific young lady on whom his fancy fell; he married the heiress to some other plantation, some other mansion along the seafront.

The Cobb mansion, which at the present had no girls to marry off, but which soon would when Somerset's daughter matured, was, from the street, a modest red-brick structure of three stories, with two ordinary-looking windows on each floor but no door for entrance. A stranger to Charleston's ways, seeing this plain façade for the first time, would glean not the slightest indication of the quiet grandeur hidden behind the plain walls. But let him move slightly to the left and enter the beautiful wrought-iron gate, set between two very solid brick pillars, and he would come upon a fairyland of exquisite gardens, elegant marble statues from Italy and brick sidewalks wandering past fountains, all enclosed by the long, sweeping, iron-ornamented porch on the right and the high brick wall on the left.

The wall, about ten feet high, was a thing of extraordinary perfection, for its bricks were laid in charming patterns which teased the eye along its immense expanse, and it was finished at the top in graceful down-dipping curves whose ends rose to finials on which rested small marble urns. On a hot afternoon one could sit on the long porch sipping minted tea and study the variations in the wall as one might study a symphony or a painting.

The porch was the masterwork of this excellent house, for it ran almost thirty yards, was two stories high, and was so delicately proportioned, resting on its stately iron pillars, that it seemed to have floated into position. Wicker chairs, placed about round glass-covered tables, broke the long reach into congenial smaller units that could be comfortably utilized by any number of visitors from one to twenty. Flowers adorned the porch, some planted in beds along its front, some in filigreed iron pots hanging decorously from the posts, but its salient characteristic was its sense of ease, its promise of shade on a hot day, the glimpses it provided of the nearby bay, and its constant invitation to rest.

When the Cobb brothers came through the gate they saw, resting on this porch at one of the smaller enclaves, their father, Maximus Cobb, seventy-two years old, his two canes perched against an unused chair. White-haired, with a prim white goatee but no mustache, he was dressed wholly in white, from his shoes to the expensive white panama resting on a table which also held his midmorning tea.

He did not rise to meet his sons, for to do so would have necessitated use of his canes, but he did extend his hands to Persifer, holding on to his older son for some moments with obvious delight and love.

'Suetonius!' he called. 'Come see!' But Suetonius, a slave now in his late sixties and weighted down with dignity, did not appear. In his place came a moderately tall, handsome black man in his early thirties, very dark of skin, with close-cropped hair, flashing eyes and a constant smile that showed extremely white teeth. He was not amused by the life about him, for he was painfully aware of being a slave, but he did prefer easing each day along with a minimum of difficulty, and had found that the simplest way to accomplish this was to smile, no matter what absurdity was thrown at him. Now, although he spoke good English, he used the dialect expected of him: 'Suetonius, he workin' wid de cook.'

'Trajan!' Colonel Cobb cried as soon as he saw the graceful figure appear in the doorway, and the slave, having been forewarned by yesterday's messenger that the young master of the plantation was to arrive, smiled with genuine affection and stepped forward to clasp the extended hand.

Three years younger than Persifer, a year older than Somerset, Trajan had grown up with them, had played with them at wild games along the marshes of Edisto and, at their suggestion, been brought into the Charleston mansion and given a Roman name. He had always liked the boys, finding in them not a single mean streak that the young men of Charleston sometimes displayed in their treatment of blacks, and he had never quailed when one of them became momentarily angry in some game, shouting at him: 'You damned nigger! I'll break your kinky head.' When they had tried, he had fended them off with ease, knocking them about until everyone collapsed with laughter.

Under their tutelage he had dropped his Gullah to acquire proper English, and under his teaching they had learned Gullah, which helped them enormously in dealing with the field hands. He now looked approvingly at the almost emaciated body of his friend Persifer, so debonair in his military uniform, and cried: 'He come home!' These simple words, spoken so obviously from the heart, touched Persifer deeply, and he gripped his slave's hand more tightly.

Maximus Cobb felt, with some reason, that he had only a limited time to spend in any day—for he required long naps—or in the passage of life itself, so with no embarrassment he asked Trajan to tell Suetonius to have the slaves rearrange the porch and move four chairs near his. Then, when the slaves were gone and the two couples faced him, he launched right into the heart of the problem that faced the Cobbs: 'When our ancestors settled Edisto, English law required that family estates be handed intact to the eldest sons. In South Carolina that's no longer the law, but we Cobbs and other families of ancient repute still honor it. Just as my father turned the plantation over to me rather than to Septimus, so that I could perfect the Sea Island cotton which has made it flourish, so now it must go to Persifer, who will make the decisions that will enable it to prosper in the new decades.' He nodded to Persifer, who nodded back, taking at the same time Tessa Mae's hand in his.

'When responsibility was given me,' he said slowly, looking now at Somerset, 'my younger brother Septimus felt that a great wrong had been done, and as you know, he hied himself off to Georgia, a terrible self-banishment. I could never persuade him to return, and there he rotted, in the wilderness.' Tears of regret did not come to his eyes, but he did wipe his lashes, for he knew that tears might come at any moment.

'Somerset, I know this must be a difficult situation for you, because you had reason to suppose that your brother would spend his life in the military. That was not to be. He's home, and the responsibility becomes his. I know you'll accept it gracefully, and I do not want you to scuttle off to Georgia like your uncle Septimus. I beg you to stay and assist your brother in running our very large plantation. He needs your help, and so do I.'

Neither Somerset nor Millicent volunteered any response; from the time they received that letter, more than a year ago, in which Persifer first suggested that at the end of the year he was going to quit the service, they had known that this day of decision would inevitably be upon them, and they had often discussed it quietly between themselves, never letting Tessa Mae or the old man know how deeply concerned they were. They had even gone so far as to send Cousin Reuben in the hill country of Georgia a secret inquiry: 'What is the quality of land in your district? And how difficult is it to grow short staple?' He had replied enthusiastically—which they had to discount, because everything Reuben did was marked

with disproportionate enthusiasm—that a man was a darned fool to waste his
energy on worn-out Carolina plantations making three hundred pounds an acre
when his good fields in Georgia were making five hundred and fifty. He had
added a paragraph which bespoke ancient grudges:

> A man is stupid, insanely stupid, to believe that he is somehow socially
> superior if he grows a few pounds of long-staple cotton with its easy
> black seed while his neighbor in Georgia grows an immense crop of
> short staple with its difficult green seed. The world of cotton is domi-
> nated by the short-staple men, and if you have any sense, you'll become
> one of us.

But such gnawing decisions were relegated to the shadows that evening when
Maximus Cobb entertained the Charleston elite in his home by the sea. Now the
big gates at the rear were thrown open: six slaves in blue livery guided the
broughams and phaetons as they deposited the plantation gentry at the long
porch; Suetonius, in gorgeous attire suitable for a French palace, greeted each
guest by title and name; and Trajan, in similar garb, led them to the punch table
for their beginning glass.

An orchestra played. Couples danced quietly both in the large room and on the
porch. Candles in the glittering chandelier from Bohemia and refined whale oil in
the lamps along the brocaded walls cast a soft light on the fine faces. Everyone
seemed glad to have Persifer back home where he belonged.

The two Cobb boys, as they would always be called while their father lived,
passed among the guests, treating each with lavish deference, aware that one day
soon they must find husbands and wives for their children from the families here
represented. No Cobb within memory had ever married anyone not from Charleston. But if the Cobbs had to be polite to the guests against the day when they
would have to seek marriage alliances, so did the guests—especially those with
smaller plantations—have to be especially attentive to the Cobbs, for their children would represent the best catches in the 1850s.

The evening was one of the most festive that the Cobb mansion had known in
years, and it was capped when Maximus banged on the floor with one of his canes
to announce: 'We welcome home our son Persifer, mentioned in dispatches from
the various battlefields in Mexico. Tomorrow he resumes stewardship of our plantations, and we wish him well.' Glasses were raised; toasts to Persifer's success
were drunk; and in every carriage that pulled out of the circular driveway at
midnight, someone asked: 'And what will young Somerset do now?'

Young Somerset was the gentlemanly kind of man who would never challenge his
brother's assumption of the Cobb plantations, but he was not allowed to surrender

because his wife, Millicent, one of the sagest women in Charleston, would not. Under her coaching, he spent the closing months of 1848 outwardly calm, apparently preoccupied with the job of instructing Persifer in the complexities of the big plantation on Edisto, and inwardly contemplating a score of practical alternatives which Millicent kept placing before him.

'You must see, Sett,' she said with unwavering determination. 'We really have to leave. And I think it ought to be done before this year ends.'

'No, I'd never quit before the next crop is planted. But go we shall.'

They had six sensible choices, which Millicent reviewed whenever they talked, keeping them in strict order of preference: 'First, buy our own plantation near Charleston, but have we the money? Second, take over the Musgrave place, which their old people have suggested from time to time . . . not directly, of course, but they have intimated. Third, manage one of the great plantations, of which there seem to be many, but I wouldn't care for that, and I'm sure you wouldn't, either. Fourth, with Persifer leaving the army, you could join, but it could only be in the militia, and you'd have to start so low. Fifth, join your cousin Reuben in Georgia, but that sounds so desolate after you've known Charleston. Sixth, pull up stakes and move to fresh new land, new friends in Mississippi.'

Unemotionally, and always willing to explore even the more distasteful alternatives, they analyzed the positives and negatives of each solution and found themselves on dead center, almost equally doubtful about each of the options. They were hindered in making a decision because they could obtain no clear understanding of how much money they controlled. Sett had a private bank account, of course, but it contained only eight thousand dollars; he had never received a wage and had no land of his own to sell. He had always assumed that when his father died, there would be ample cash to distribute between the two sons, but then again, there might not be, because a great plantation family like the Cobbs often had 'much land, many Nigras, no cash,' as the saying went.

But now another Cobb woman entered the debate, never openly, never betraying her plot to anyone but her husband in the secrecy of the night. It was Tessa Mae, daughter of a family that had prospered only because it adhered tenaciously to one rule: 'Get possession of a good plantation and never borrow money against it.' In the darkness she whispered: 'Persifer, I'm glad you chucked the army. I needed you here at home. We must do everything to make Sett and Lissa get out.'

'I wouldn't do anything . . .'

'Perse, it's them or us. Mark my words, if quiet Sett stays around long enough, he's going to lose that modest charm and become a real bastard.'

'Tessa!'

'Keep applying pressure on him. I'll work on Lissa. But let's get them out of here.'

In early 1849, Millicent saw that any continued co-occupancy of the Cobb plantations was impossible: 'Sett, that Tessa Mae's a wily witch. Three times now she's suggested in various clever ways that we might be moving to Georgia. And mealy-mouthed Persifer, so tall and proper, he throws barbs at you. I'm fed up. I want to hear from your father himself what your financial prospects are, and I want to hear it now.' So, much against her husband's wishes, she marched down to the jetty alone, climbed into the longboat, and had the six slaves take her to The Battery, where she clanged her pretty way through the gates and confronted Maximus as he sat on the porch.

'Somerset and I need to know what money arrangements we can expect, Father.'

The old man harrumphed. He had never discussed such matters with women, not even with his wife, one of the Radbourne girls. Now he equivocated: 'Well, with Edisto . . . our income from all that land . . . he has no cause to worry.'

'But if we wanted to purchase a plantation of our own . . .' Millicent said boldly.

'That would be foolish in the extreme, wouldn't it?'

'We don't think so,' she said bluntly.

'Well, I do,' and he would discuss the matter no further. He did invite her to stay for lunch, and though she was strongly disposed to reject the courtesy, because he was a lonely old man hungry for companionship, she did stay, but that was a mistake, for when the slaves were gone from the room she said bluntly: 'Father, you really must explain to Sett and me what our position is going to be . . .'

'When I die?'

'I didn't say that.'

'But you meant it.'

'I did not mean it. I meant that my husband is a grown man of thirty-two and you're treating him like a boy of thirteen.'

'Why do you need to know about money? Haven't you always been cared for?'

In a moment of anger she snapped: 'Because we might want to move to Georgia.' As soon as the words were out she regretted them, for at the reiteration of a name which had given him much grief he seemed to wilt, as if his long-absent brother, now dead, had thrown at him once more the word *Georgia*.

'You would go to Georgia?' He uttered the word as if it represented some leprous site denied the graciousness of Carolina, and Millicent was prepared to retract, but before she could do so, Trajan came in to clear the table, and it was in that moment, seeing this impeccable black man, that she thought: When we go we must take Trajan with us.

Upon her return to the house on Edisto, which they now shared with the Persifer Cobbs, she very quietly told Sett: 'Your father practically dismissed me. Would tell me nothing. On Edisto we're millionaires. On the streets of Charleston we're paupers. Now I want you to find out in exact dollars how much we have.'

When Somerset, as an obedient son, learned that his wife had actually revealed their conversations about going to Georgia, he was aghast, for he appreciated how deeply this must have hurt his father. Still, he had long realized that sooner or later the possibility of such a move must surface, and when Millicent's unemotional review of the situation ended, he concluded that perhaps she had accomplished something desirable in clearing the air. Next day they posted a letter to Cousin Reuben in Georgia, asking him to come down and give advice.

In such speculation, whether family or public, Sett remained so passive that some considered him slow, especially when his wife's opinions were so pertinent, but it was genteel reserve rather than lack of comprehension which prevented him from airing his opinions. So he allowed her to pose the options, Georgia or Mississippi, with her favoring the longer jump west and he the shorter. However, each was willing to adjust to the other's preference.

On a fine summery day in June, when the cotton was well established and hoed, Reuben Cobb and his wife, Petty Prue, each twenty-six years old and brimming with vigor induced by the Georgia uplands, roared into Charleston and pretty well blew the place apart. Reuben was six feet tall, slim and fine-looking like all the Cobb men, but with fiery red hair, which none of the others had. He wore long mustaches, also red, which he liked to twirl when disputing a point in a powerful voice which rode down opposition. At the first big dinner in his honor, given grudgingly by his uncle Maximus, he was out on the porch arguing cotton, when his loud exclamations penetrated the room inside as he boasted, to the disgust of certain gentlemen who specialized in Sea Island: 'Short staple is king. Those Manchester mills can't get enough of it. And whether you're ready to believe it or not, the man who rules short staple is goin' to rule this country.'

The eye of the Georgia hurricane was Petty Prue, the tiny, winsome daughter of a Methodist clergyman who had never planted a row of cotton in his life but who had taught his little girl all she needed to know: 'To get along in this life, you got to please people.' She was five feet one, weighed not over a hundred pounds, and had cultivated such an excessive Southern drawl that she could pronounce even the briefest word in three syllables. With her, *more* became *moe-weh-err,* delivered in a high, lilting voice. She looked directly at anyone who spoke to her, smiling ravishingly at women and men alike, as if each in turn were the prettiest or wittiest in the room. She was a giddy little bird, all gold and silver, who engulfed the normal reticence of Southern decorum in an irresistible enthusiasm which bubbled unceasingly from her pouting lips.

Two women, watching the visiting Cobbs from a corner, observed: 'You can tell they're not from Charleston.' But they were clearly eligible to belong had they wished, for they were charming, volatile and, according to Georgia standards, well bred, and at every critical moment they assured listeners of their undeviating loyalty to the South.

'Our men could sweep the field, if it ever came to a test of arms,' Reuben boomed from his position near the punch bowl. 'Ask Persifer. In the Mexican War hardly a single Northern officer measured up to the best of ours. Don't lecture me about railroad mileage and factories that belch smoke. It's character that counts.'

By the time that first noisy evening ended, the ladies and gentlemen of Charleston were satisfied that the Cobbs of Georgia were not only acceptable but also downright enjoyable: 'Shame he ever left us. We need men like him.' And as for Petty Prue: 'Clearly not gentlefolk, and rather loud, but she has a quality that melts the heart. Let's have them over.'

However, it was on the plantation that the Georgia Cobb revealed his true merit, for Reuben had the rare ability of looking at evidence and quickly reaching sound conclusions, a skill that few men commanded: 'Your soil's failing, Persifer. Per nigger, there's no way you can do well on this plantation.' And when Persifer said that he could always import fertilizer, Reuben said loudly: 'Waste half your profits. At your age, with your skills, you ought to get out of here.'

'And go where?' Persifer asked with obvious disdain. 'Georgia?'

'No. It's doomed, too. Yield per nigger way down.'

'Where then?'

'Texas.'

At the sound of this unfortunate word, Persifer Cobb winced; that any man in his right mind might wish to leave the cultivated paradise of Edisto Island and emigrate to the savage wilderness of Texas was so improbable that it did not even deserve comment. But Sett Cobb, to whom such a proposal had never before been suggested, was intrigued.

Now Reuben took from his pocket a clipping from a Louisiana newspaper, and when Persifer read it, echoes of an earlier discussion began to vibrate: 'I saw these figures at an office in New Orleans.' And there they were: South Carolina, 250 pounds of cotton per acre. Texas, 750.

'And you believe these figures?' Persifer asked, and with almost trembling excitement Reuben replied: 'I've written to the experts. They assure me that for the first years, virgin soil and all that, these results have been proved time and again.'

'But for how long?' Persifer asked, and Reuben replied: 'Long enough to make a fortune. By then you'd be ready to move on to fresh land. Damn, this could be the most exciting adventure in America. Perse, Sett, let's all go west.'

The idea that a Cobb would exchange Edisto for Texas was so repugnant to Persifer that he dismissed it haughtily, but when Reuben and little Petty Prue were alone with the Somerset Cobbs, the discussion continued: 'Sett, Lissa, we must all go to Texas, really. We're used up in Georgia. You're obviously used up in Edisto. We can buy land, the best bottomland, for two dollars an acre. Take our wagons, our niggers, money enough to start a new paradise.' He stopped abruptly and asked: 'Sett, how much hard cash could you scrape together?'

'Now that's difficult to say. I have a few thousand saved but . . .'

'Don't tell me "a few thousand." How much?'

'I have eight thousand, and I suppose Father would want to give me something.'

'Don't count on that. His father gave my father nothin'. But you could take your slaves with you?'

'Lissa and I have about six each, personal. We could surely take them.'

'Hell! Excuse me, ma'am, but I'm talkin' about fifty, sixty. Surely you could talk your family into at least fifty.'

Obviously he had for some months been reviewing the possibility, for he took from his pocket a carefully tabulated list of things he and Petty Prue could provide for such an expedition, and the Cobbs were amazed at its completeness: 'I'll provide the cotton gin, because it has to be the best. I'll provide the cotton seed, the best Mexican strain, tested on land like we'll find in Texas. I'll take the blacksmith shop.'

'How many wagons are you thinking about?' Somerset asked.

From another pocket Reuben produced a list of wagons, each specified as to size, the numbers of mules or oxen required to draw it, and its order of contents. Thirty-seven were numbered, at which Millicent asked: 'But why the frenzy? You don't have to move. We do.'

And then little Petty Prue, in her high-pitched voice and delightful accent, revealed her real reasons: 'Georgia's changed. Old men makin' new rules. What we seek is a new life where we can invest our money and our energy and build our own paradise.'

Millicent was startled to hear this giddy child speaking so boldly: 'You'd be willing to take such great risks?'

'I want to take them. I'm bored with Georgia.' When she pronounced the word *boe-we-edd* it sounded amusing, but when Millicent saw the hard set of her chin, it wasn't funny at all. Now Petty Prue hammered at Lissa: 'After all, you sent the letter, we didn't. And you sent it because you knew you were finished here. It was one of your best ideas.'

But when the three Cobb families dined together on the second night, some of the things that motivated red-headed Reuben began to surface: 'Another reason I'd like to be in Texas, I'd like to keep my eye on the northern part of the Indian Territory that they're calling Kansas.' The word had never been mentioned before in Edisto, and it sounded strange the way Reuben said it, as if it carried terrible freight: 'Great decisions are going to be made in Kansas, and I want . . .'

'What decisions?' Millicent asked.

'Slavery. If those swine in the North can prevent us from carrying our slaves into open territory like Kansas, they can halt our entire progress.'

'Will Texas remain slave?' Somerset asked, and his cousin cried: 'Without question. They fought Santa Anna because he wanted to end slavery. They know how to protect their rights.'

'I would not care to bet on anything, where Texas is involved,' Persifer said, but Reuben stopped this reasoning bluntly: 'Where are Texans from? Tennessee, a slave state. Alabama, Mississippi, Georgia, all slave. Texas will be there when we need her.'

'Will we need her?' Persifer asked, and a hush fell over the candlelit room. The long silence that followed was broken only by the chirping of crickets in the warm night air, until finally Reuben stated his beliefs: 'I've met a few abolitionists. Sneaked into Georgia. Fine-looking men, but absolutely corrupt at heart, coming here to steal our property. They'll never surrender. But men like us three won't ever surrender, either. There must come a testing.'

'I should think you'd want to be here,' Persifer said, for he had heard that his Georgia cousin was a violent man.

'In Georgia, each good man will count for one. In Texas, he'll count for two.'

'Why do you say that?'

'Because many of the big decisions will be reached there. Control of the West. Control of Kansas. And a role in helping to control the Mississippi. I want to be where I'll count double.'

The men now went onto the porch, where Somerset tried quietly to explain that he believed the real disparity between South and North was not slavery, but the callous way in which the North profited from Southern raw materials and then imposed through Congress excessive tariffs which prevented the South from obtaining the goods it needed from Europe.

Millicent, listening to an argument she had heard before, indicated to Petty Prue that she wanted to pursue further their abbreviated table discussion, so when Tessa Mae took herself to bed, the two younger women sat in the light of a flickering candle and discussed the tremendous matter of moving a civilization west for more than a thousand miles. 'Does it frighten you?' Millicent asked, and Petty Prue said brightly: 'Not a bit. Thousands are going to California all the time. If they can do it, we can easily reach Texas.' She sought for a word and said: 'It'll really be like a great picnic . . . that lasts for a hundred days.'

'A hundred days!'

'Yes, Reuben has it all worked out, from Edisto—'

'He seems sure we're going.'

'And so am I.' With never a faltering doubt, the little Georgia woman, in her mid-twenties and already the mother of three, said: 'The time comes, that's all I can say. It's like when a young man of twenty and a young girl of eighteen . . . the time comes, and everything that seemed so tangled falls into place. It's time for you and Sett to get out, and that's that.'

In the days that followed, when it became generally accepted that the Somerset

Cobbs were going to withdraw gracefully from any competition for the Edisto plantation, both Persifer and Tessa Mae became wondrously generous. No decision had yet been voiced by their father as to how much money Sett could take with him, but word on that would come in due course; for the present, Persifer said: 'You can take twenty of our Edisto field hands, no question.'

'Trajan belongs on Edisto, really. But I'd want him.'

'Trajan you shall have. I'll explain to Father.'

Millicent nominated nine of the best female house slaves, women who could sew dresses and shirts, and they were surrendered too, with Tessa Mae adding two others that she knew Lissa favored, making thirty-two in all. Persifer, looking far ahead, said: 'Western Alabama and Mississippi, those roads were never solid. You'll need the best wagons,' and he started his wheelwrights and carpenters to mending nine wagons already in existence and building seven new ones, but when the first provisional lists of gear were compiled, it was obvious that Sett would be wise to buy another three in Charleston.

Maximus Cobb made petulant protest over the loss of Trajan, whom he had been breaking in nicely as a house servant, but on this point his sons were adamant, with Persifer leading the fight: 'A Carolina gentleman is entitled to at least one perfect servant. It lends him distinction, and for Sett, Trajan is ideal.' When his father continued to demur, Persifer said: 'They were like brothers,' and to this the old man had to assent.

When the time came that discussion of money could no longer be deferred, Maximus said: 'I'll tell you one thing. If you were going to Georgia, like my brother Septimus, you'd get not a nickel. Not a nickel. But if you're going to Texas, to help preserve our Southern way of life . . . to spread goodness and justice . . .'

He fumbled with his ivory-headed cane, and tears came to his eyes: 'Why do young people feel they have to leave? What have we ever done to wrong you, Somerset? Tell me, what?'

'The time comes,' Somerset said, and his father seemed to accept this, for he took from his pocket a letter—a copy of one, the original having already been mailed to a New Orleans bank—and before delivering it to his younger son he said, with evident sadness: 'It's my gift to you and Lissa in your new life.' It was a draft for twenty thousand dollars.

On Sunday, the last day of September 1849, the Cobb brothers, their wives and their five children gathered at the mansion in Charleston, where an Episcopalian minister had been invited to say prayers, after which a fine feast was managed by Suetonius and three of his Caesars: Tiberius, Claudius and Domitian. Trajan was overseeing the four wagons that would leave from Charleston in the morning to meet up with the fifteen others that would be crossing the Edisto ferry and coming up to the main road.

It was a beautiful day, and in the late afternoon the two couples with their children walked along The Battery, looking out to Fort Sumter in the bay. At night singers came from a mansion nearby, and various families who had once thought of allying their children with Somerset's dropped by to say confused farewells, for they were losing prime candidates for future marriage alliances.

At dawn everyone was alert. The four wagons with their borrowed horses were ready for the taxing ride to where the heavier wagons coming directly from Edisto would be waiting. Kisses, tears, embraces and prayers were exchanged, and finally old Maximus waved one of his canes, and the Somerset Cobbs bade farewell to one of the most gracious houses in Carolina and to the best of the offshore islands. G.T.T. (Gone to Texas) could have been painted on their four wagons, for like thousands who preceded them, they had watched their fortunes at home slowly decline.

But it was at dusk on that first day when the true farewells were said, because as the little caravan approached the spot where the ferry road from Edisto joined the main road, the Cobb children riding in the lead wagon shouted back to their parents: 'Oh, look!' And there ahead, waiting as shadows deepened, stood the other fifteen wagons. Around them clustered not only the slaves who would go with them to Texas but also some hundred others who had trudged up from the island to say goodbye.

There was not much sleeping that night, for groups clustered here and there, exchanging little gifts, whispering in Gullah, and savoring the precious moments of friendships that would be shared no more. For as long as anyone could remember, no Cobb of Edisto had ever separated a slave child from its parents, and none were being separated now—for example, Trajan and his wife were taking their boy Hadrian with them—but inevitably, adult brothers and sisters were seeing each other for the last time, and many others were being separated from their old parents. There was sorrow, but as the night waned, there was also singing, soft hymns chanted in Gullah.

'Oh, I shall never see you again!' a young woman cried to a man she might have married had he stayed on Edisto, and at dawn the caravan of nineteen wagons moved on to Texas, four white people and thirty-two slaves, plus three babes still in arms.

On this second day of October 1849 the plodding trek westward began, with Trajan's wagon in the lead as the mules and oxen shuffled along at their own measured pace. By noontime the drivers had learned how much distance to leave between wagons so that dust did not engulf them. By late afternoon, when the first stop occurred, the line of wagons covered about a mile and a half, and there was much joking among the slaves as the last one pulled in.

As soon as the wagons carrying the Cobbs and their private gear halted, male and female slaves sprang into action, pitching the masters' tents, arranging for baths, and starting the evening meal. On this first night it was a noisy game, with cooks unable to find pots and maids not knowing where the bedding was, but with stern prompting from Trajan, things were straightened out, and the expedition assumed some kind of rational order.

It was a hundred and thirty-four miles from Edisto to the South Carolina line opposite the city of Augusta, and Somerset had calculated that the distance could be covered in not more than twelve days, but on Saturday, when they were about halfway across the narrow part of the state, Millicent announced with some finality that she did not intend traveling on Sunday. When he started to protest, he found that all the slaves supported his wife, most vociferously: 'We ain't never work Sundays. Ain't proper.' With Mrs. Cobb it was a matter of religion, but with the slaves it was religion-cum-custom, with the latter weighing the heavier: 'Work six days, God says so. Even He work six days. But come seven, no more, neither God nor man.' Trajan was a leader in this rebellion, so at sunset that first Saturday, Sett Cobb ordered the tents pitched securely, for nothing he could say or do was going to change the fact that they would stay beside this rivulet for two nights.

On the second Saturday night the enforced halt irritated him even more, because the caravan had now reached the Carolina shore of the Savannah River, across which the buildings of Augusta could be clearly seen. 'We could get up tomorrow at dawn and be in the city in time for morning prayers,' he argued, but Lissa would not listen: 'The Sabbath is God's holy day, and if we profane it at the start of our trip, what evils will He pour down upon us in the later days?' Sett said that he doubted God was paying much attention to one small group of wagons on the Augusta road, but Millicent prevailed.

They entered Augusta very early on Monday, October fifteenth, and spent the next two days making purchases of things they had discovered they needed. Sett figured that this shopping would please his wife, but when he returned to the wagons at dusk on Tuesday, he found her looking across the river and weeping: 'I shall never see Carolina again. Look at it, Sett, it's the gentlest and loveliest state in the Union.' He remained with her for a long time, staring back at that lovely state in which he had been so happy and of which he was so proud.

The next week was hard work, a slow, slogging progress along the bumpy roads of northern Georgia, and for three solid days, enduring a considerable amount of rain, they pushed their way west through the little towns of Greensboro and Madison, and by Thursday morning, when the sky cleared, Sett was in fine spirits. At breakfast he said: 'Everybody watch closely today and tomorrow. May be a big surprise.'

So the two children rode forward with Trajan, peering ahead like Indian scouts, and about noon they were rewarded by seeing a lone rider, a very large black man, coming toward them on a mule. As he drew closer he began to shout: 'You de

Cobbs fum Edisto?' and when Trajan waved his whip enthusiastically, the big man reined in his mule, lifted his arms in the air, and began shouting: 'Halley-loo, I done found you.'

He was Jaxifer, prime hand of the Georgia Cobbs, dispatched along this road to meet the caravan. He had acquired his name in a curious way. Reuben Cobb, seeking to retain a sentimental tie with his cousins on Edisto, had named him Persifer, in honor of the family's soldier-hero, but in Gullah the word had been quickly corrupted to Jaxifer. 'My job, show you de way home,' he explained, and after the wagons fell in behind him, he pranced his mule and shouted: 'Halley-loo, we on our way to Texas!'

He rode with them all day on the twenty-sixth, shouting to everyone they passed: 'Halley-loo, we for Texas!' and that night he told the children, who had by now adopted him, for he was just as vigorous and loud as his master: 'Tomorrow we home. Finest town in Georgia.'

'What's its name?' the children asked, and he replied: 'Social Circle,' and they said: 'That's no name for a town,' and he corrected them: 'It be the name of dis town, and dis town is Queen of Georgia.'

Early on Saturday he led them along the last dusty roads to Social Circle, an attractive village which boasted two cotton gins, warehouses for the storing of finished bales and a beautiful old well right in the middle of the main street. Waiting there, as men and women had waited for many decades to greet their friends, were Reuben and Petty Prue, who provided ladles of cool water for the travelers.

'Our town had another name, once,' Petty Prue explained, 'but since everyone gathered about this pump for local gossip, it became Social Circle.'

After so many days of dusty travel, twenty-seven of them, the Edisto Cobbs were delighted with the five days they stayed over in Social Circle. The main street was lined with nine large houses, each with handsome white pillars supporting fine balconies that opened out from the upper floors, each with flower beds and finely graveled turnarounds for the carriages.

'Somebody's making money here,' Sett cried when at the end of this first parade of tall mansions he saw another six of somewhat smaller size.

'Everybody is . . . for the moment,' Reuben said. 'These men know how to grow cotton, how to work their slaves.'

Sett was especially interested in the cotton gins, for as a grower of Sea Island, he had never worked short-staple and for some years had believed that no one else could, either, so Reuben took him to a gin owned collectively by all the Cobbs of the region, a sturdy wooden building of two stories, with the bottom one mostly open so that slave boys could lead two pairs of horses around and around in a perpetual circle. The horses were harnessed to long wooden arms projecting outward from a central pillar, which revolved slowly but with great force.

The pillar reached well up through the second floor, where its constant turning provided motive power for an Eli Whitney gin of fifty saws. The bolls of filmy white cotton passing these saws had their tenacious green seeds removed, the latter falling down a chute to the ground after wire brushes caught their filaments.

'Not much different from what we do by hand with Sea Island in Carolina,' Somerset muttered while studying the wonderful effectiveness of the gin. As it continued its work, handling the fractious seed so competently, he had a vision of that endless chain of which he had always been a part: the land tilled, the seed sown by slaves, the tender plants chopped to eliminate weeds and weaklings, the bolls gathered, the seeds removed, the bales sent to the rivers, the ships loaded, the cotton delivered to Liverpool, the spun thread delivered to Manchester, the cloth woven, the clothing made, civilization enhanced—and every man in the chain earning a good living from this miraculous fiber. Cotton was surely a king among crops.

The slave, Cobb reflected, lived well under the loving care of kind masters; the planter watched his lands flourish; the owner of the gin extracted his fee; the shipper his, and the Liverpool merchant his pounds and shillings. The weaver seemed to earn most, with the manufacturer of clothes not far behind. 'Wait!' he called to the busy gin as if to correct some misapprehension under which it toiled. 'The one who makes the most is the damned banker who finances it all.' In his many years of supervising the vast fields on Edisto Island, Cobb, unlike Tessa Mae's family, had never once planted with his own or his family's money. Now he thought: It was tradition to use the bank's money. Always they got their share first. He supposed that in Texas it would be the same.

Reuben nudged him: 'Wonderful machine, eh? How simple. How difficult it was to work cotton before it came along.' Rather ruefully he added: 'You know, Sett, we Southerners dreamed about a gin like this for a hundred years. Even worked on crude designs now and then. A damned schoolteacher from Massachusetts comes down here on vacation or something, studies the problem one week, and produces this.' With profound admiration he watched the gin as it ceaselessly picked the fiber from the seed; as long as the boys below kept the horses walking, and the central pole turning on its axis, so long would the miraculous gin do in an hour what a thousand nimble fingers in Virginia once took a month to complete.

'This gin ensures the South's domination,' Reuben said, almost gloatingly. 'The world needs clothing, and it can't afford wool.' Grabbing a handful of lint, he apostrophized it: 'Get along to Galveston, and then to the mills in Lancashire, then as a bolt of cloth on some freighter headed for Australia. The world has to have what you provide, and if the North ever tried to interrupt our cotton trade, all the armies and navies of Europe would spring to our defense.' Patting the gin, he said: 'You are our shield in battle.'

Then he laughed: 'How ironical history can be, Sett. Maybe the greatest invention of mankind, certainly of our South, and the genius who made it earned not a penny.'

'I didn't know that. Of course, gins aren't that important to Sea Island.'

'Whitney lost his patent. Never really got it, because the gin was so vital that everyone moved in and simply copied it. Lawyers, you know.'

As Reuben said these words, his cousin noted that he was looking at the gin strangely, as if trying to remember each element of its movement so that it could be duplicated in Texas, but this seemed odd, because a good commercial gin could be bought from many sources for less than a hundred dollars. Powered by one of the new steam engines, it might cost a hundred and a half, so that any important cotton plantation could afford its own.

For five days the citizens of Social Circle entertained the emigrants in one big mansion after another, until Millicent cried at one dinner: 'You have certainly proved your right to your name. This is the socialest circle I've ever been in,' and a banker responded with an apt toast: 'To the Cobbs, the first group ever to leave Georgia for Texas without the sheriff chasing them.'

On the morning of Thursday, November first, the Georgia Cobbs moved their wagons into line, and as they did so, Millicent, to her amazement, counted thirty-eight. 'Good heavens, Prue, are you taking everything you own?' she asked, and Prue replied: 'Yes.' So the caravan was formed: Edisto wagons, nineteen, Georgia, thirty-eight; Edisto slaves, thirty-two, Georgia, forty-nine; Edisto whites, four, Georgia, five; plus one Bible from Edisto and certain remarkable items from Georgia.

On Friday, Sett discovered how remarkable the items were, for when one of the wagons mired in the mud, he saw that it contained the metal parts of the disassembled gin which he had been studying only a few days before. He recognized the splashes of yellow color and especially the saw mechanism, which carried in iron letters the name of the manufacturer. Reuben Cobb, on that last night when the banker was extolling his honesty, had been busy stealing one of the town's two gins.

'Oh, it belongs to me, you might say,' he explained. 'It's a Cobb gin, that's for sure, but it belonged to the other Cobbs. They owed me a lot, and they can get another.' However, Sett noticed that despite his bravado, Reuben followed a most circuitous route around Atlanta, keeping a rear lookout posted in case sheriffs tried to recover the gin.

Once when the lead wagon was well and truly mired in the mud of Mississippi, the Edisto Cobbs caught a glimpse of their cousin's darker nature, for after minutes of bellowing at Jaxifer to get the wagon moving, Reuben lost his temper and thrashed the struggling slave with a whip he kept at hand. Seventeen, eighteen times he lashed the big, silent man across the back, and it would have been difficult to guess who was the more appalled by this performance, the Edisto whites or the Edisto blacks, for during his entire stewardship of the island planta-

tion Sett Cobb had never whipped a slave. He had disciplined them and occasionally he threw them into the plantation jail, but never had he whipped one, nor
had he allowed his overseers to do so.

Although the whites and blacks may have been equally appalled, it was the
latter who suffered in a unique way. You could see it in the way Trajan cringed
when the strokes of the whip fell; you could hear it in the gasps of the Edisto
women, for this incident in the swamps of Mississippi demonstrated what slavery
really meant: when one slave was whipped, all slaves were whipped.

When Trajan, quivering with outrage, sought to move forward to aid Jaxifer,
Sett reached out a restraining hand, and without words having been said, Trajan
knew that his master was promising: 'We Edisto people will never do it that way.'

It was an ironclad rule of the cotton states, broken only by fools, that one white
master never reproved another in the presence of slaves, and Somerset Cobb was
especially attentive to this rule, so that when the thrashing ended he felt ashamed
of himself for having revealed his feelings to his slave Trajan, and he attempted to
assuage his conscience by going quietly to Reuben that evening and saying: 'You
were having a hard time with Jaxifer. That wagon was really mired.'

'Sometimes boys like Jaxifer require attention.'

'They really do, Reuben, they really do.' Then he added, almost offhandedly:
'At Edisto we never whipped our niggers.' And he said this with such calm force
that Reuben knew that whereas he might beat his own slaves, he must never touch
Sett's.

A genteel Southern family traveling anywhere seemed always to have waiting in
the next town a cousin or business associate who had left the Carolinas or Georgia
some time back. In Vicksburg, that important town guarding the Mississippi
River, the Cobbs visited a delightful pair of spinsters, the Misses Peel, whose
parents had left Charleston some forty years earlier to acquire a large plantation
bordering the river.

The sisters, unable to find in Vicksburg any suitors of a breeding acceptable to
the elder Peels, had languished, as they said amusingly, 'in unwedded bliss.' They
were charming ladies, alert, witty and given to naughty observations about their
neighbors.

Their gracious home was located on a bluff at the north end of Cherry Street,
and so situated that it overlooked the great dark river below. 'The Mississippi isn't
the first water you see,' one of the Misses Peel explained. 'That's the Yazoo
Diversion. It's a canal that makes our town a riverport. But beyond, out there in
the darkness . . . when there's a full moon the Mississippi glows like a long
chain of pearls.'

'It's good of you to entertain us so lavishly,' Petty Prue exclaimed, 'because
when we leave Vicksburg we separate.'

'Oh, dear! You're not parting?'

'Only temporarily. Somerset and Millicent, they're taking a riverboat down to New Orleans and then up the Red River. To make all the arrangements in Texas before Reuben and I get the wagons there overland.'

One of the Peels said with great enthusiasm: 'Millicent, you and Somerset don't have to sail all the way to New Orleans. Twice when I've gone, our big boat has stopped in the middle of the Mississippi while a small boat came out from the Red to take passengers from us. How romantic, I thought, changing ships in midocean, as it were. How I wanted to quit my cabin and join that small boat to see where it might carry me.'

'But, Lissa, you wouldn't want to miss New Orleans,' Petty Prue cried in her high, lyrical voice. 'All those shops.'

'I have little taste for shopping,' Millicent said. 'I'm impatient to reach our new home.'

The Peels now turned to Petty Prue: 'Surely, you're not going to ride those rough wagons across Arkansas when you could sail to Texas in a big riverboat!' But the saucy little Georgian snapped: 'I ride with my husband. Where he goes, I go.' Miss Peel said: 'But the boat would be so comfortable,' and Prue replied: 'After three months of wagons, my backside's made of leather.' And she helped supervise the loading of the wagons Reuben would be taking, placing them just so on the rickety ferries which would carry them across the Mississippi to start them on their way to Texas. She waved goodbye to the Edisto Cobbs: 'We'll overtake you about the first of February. Have our lands selected, because Reuben will want to plant his cotton.'

And so the two families separated, one leading a slow caravan cross-country to Texas, the other going by swift riverboat down the Mississippi to a romantic halting place in midriver, where a much smaller steamer waited to receive passengers bound for the Red River. When heavy planks were swung to join the two vessels, the four Cobbs, seven of their slaves, two disassembled wagons and six horses were transferred. Then, as whistles blew, the emigrants started one of the more surprising journeys of their lives.

The Red River ship was small; it smelled of cows and horses, and the food was markedly less palatable than that on the larger boat. But the river itself, and the land bordering it, was fascinating, a true frontier wilderness with just enough settlement scattered haphazardly to maintain interest. The Cobb children were delighted by the closeness of the banks and the variation in the plantations. 'These aren't plantations,' their mother said with equal interest in the new land. 'These are farms. White people work here.' She was seeing a new vision of America, one she had not known existed, and she was impressed by its sense of latent power.

'Will we have a farm like these?' the children asked, and she laughed: 'For a year, maybe, yes. But at the end of two years we'll have a plantation just like Edisto. Cousin Reuben will see to that.'

Near Shreveport the Cobbs made their acquaintance with one of the marvels of America, as explained by two red-faced men who were conveying a passel of slaves for public auction in Texas: 'Dead ahead, blockin' things tighter'n a drum, what we call the Great Red River Raft.'

'What could that be?' Somerset asked, and with obvious delight the two men told of this natural miracle: 'First noted by white men in 1805, and what they saw fairly amazed them. Centuries past, huge trees, uprooted by storms, floated downstream and were trapped by bends in our sluggish river.'

The second slaver broke in: 'Happens in all rivers, but in the Red the trees carried so much soil in their matted roots, they provided choice growin' ground for weeds and bushes and even small trees.'

'Like he says, more big fallen trees trapped in the river meant more small trees growin' in the mud. There! Look ahead! A whole river shut down.'

And when the Cobbs looked where he pointed, they saw a major river, one capable of carrying big steamboats, closed off by this impenetrable mass of tree and root and tangle and lovely blooming flowers. 'How far does it reach?' Cobb asked, and the answer astounded him: 'Ah-ha! That first report in 1805 said: "We got a Raft out here eighty miles long. In places, maybe twenty miles wide." So officials in Washington said: "Break it loose," and they tried, for it converted maybe a million acres of good farmland into swamp.'

'Why couldn't they break it up?' Somerset asked, and the men cried gleefully, each trying to convey the story: 'They tried. Army come in here and tried. But for each foot they knock off down here, the Raft grows ten feet up there. Last survey? One hundred and twenty miles long, packed solid, no boat can move.'

'Then why have we come here?' Cobb asked, and the men gave a startling reply: 'Miracles! Bring your children up here and they'll see miracles.'

So the four Cobbs stood beside the slavers as their steamboat headed right for the Red River Raft, and when it seemed that the boat would crash, it veered off to the left to enter a bewildering sequence of twists, turns, openings and sudden vistas of the most enchanting beauty. The boat was picking its way through a jungle fairyland stretching miles in every direction.

The slavers seemed to take as much delight in this mysterious passage as did the Cobbs: 'Nothin' anywhere like it! The Raft backs up so much water that these private little rivers run through the forest. But the best is still ahead.'

They were correct, for as they emerged from the watery forest, a grand lake, mysterious and dark, opened up. 'It's called Caddo,' the men said. 'After a tribe of Indians that once lived along its shores.' The lake had a thousand arms twisting and writhing inland, a hundred sudden turns which allowed the boat to keep moving forward when passage seemed blocked. The live oaks that lined this vast swamp especially pleased the older Cobbs, because from all the lower branches hung matted clumps of Spanish moss; Caddo Lake was virtually identical with the swamps of Edisto, and when they consulted a map they saw that the two locations, so far apart, were on almost the same latitude, about 32° 30'.

After intricate maneuvering, the steamer broke out of Caddo Lake, and on 24 January 1850, entered a small cypress-lined creek and blew its whistle as it steamed into the wharf at Jefferson, Texas: population 1,300; distance from Edisto, 997 miles.

When Somerset and Trajan met Reuben Cobb and his wagons a week later in Shreveport, they had exciting news, and Trajan told the other slaves: 'Land almost de same. First class fo' cotton. Carpenters already buildin' us homes.'

Somerset was more specific: 'Reuben, you led us to a treasure,' but before he could say more, his cousin interrupted: 'Sett, I want to talk with you and your boy Trajan,' and Somerset was perplexed, because he could not imagine what might have happened which would involve both him and his slave.

Reuben's words were grave: 'First day west of Vicksburg we come upon this man, his slaves in bad shape. He was in bad shape too, damn him. Begged me to lend him one of our slaves to drive his wagon for the rest of that day. Out of the goodness of my heart, I loaned him Hadrian.'

'Where is my boy?' Trajan cried.

'Gone. The son-of-a-bitch stole him. It was a trick.'

'Gone?' Trajan wailed.

'Yep, stole clean away. But we propose to get him back.' He suggested that he, Jaxifer, Trajan and Somerset mount their horses, arm themselves and fan out to catch that swine, so for two days the Cobbs searched the countryside, looking for the kidnapper, questioning everyone they met.

Somerset had never seen his cousin so furious: 'Damnit, Sett, to steal a boy like that. To take a boy that age away from his father. Trajan, if we catch him . . .'

They did not find him, then or ever. When it was clear that they were not going to recover this promising boy worth three hundred dollars, Reuben Cobb's fury increased, and on the night they abandoned the chase both brothers spoke with Trajan. Somerset said, tears moistening his eyes: 'As long as I live, Traje, I'll search for your son. I'll find him for you. I'll find him.' Reuben, clasping the slave by the shoulder, said: 'We got ourselves an orphaned boy, good lad I believe. Not your son's age, but would you consent to care for him? I'd pay you a little somethin'.' But the boy himself, Trajan's son, was never found.

The putting together of the Cobb plantation at Jefferson became an act of high comedy, because whereas Somerset in his first days had found some three thousand acres exactly to his liking, it was settled land with a good portion of the fields already cleared, and it was priced at three dollars and seventy-five cents an acre, which Reuben believed to be excessive. The land lay just south of town and belonged to an enterprising Scotsman named Buchanan, who had accepted four hundred dollars as down payment on the deal.

Reuben, assured that he could find better land for much less, roared into the home of the astonished Buchanan like a wayward tornado, demanding a refund of the four hundred dollars on grounds that the Scotsman was a thief, a perjurer and a scoundrel who had viciously misrepresented both the land and its value. When the startled Scotsman said there was no chance that he would return the money, Reuben warned him that he, Reuben, was a practiced attorney from Georgia, well versed in land law, and that if Buchanan did not hand over the deposit immediately, he was going to find himself in a court of law charged with even worse offenses than those so far enumerated.

The four hundred dollars was returned, whereupon Reuben directed the workmen who had been building the slave shacks on the Buchanan land to tear them down and save the lumber. When asked where the shacks were to be built, Reuben said: 'I'll tell you in three days.'

He now became tireless, rising before dawn in the tiny rooms the family had rented in the home of a Baptist minister, riding back and forth along all the dusty roads so far opened and looking at fields near and distant which might be for sale. At the end of four days he had settled upon three thousand acres a few miles east of town and situated nicely on the north bank of the stream which connected Lake Caddo with Jefferson. The land was owned by a widow who felt that she could not handle it by herself, now that her husband was dead, but realizing that it was favorable land, she wanted three dollars an acre, which again Reuben still considered excessive.

He therefore paid ardent court to the widow, explaining that the best thing for her to do was sell the land, which would require an enormous amount of effort to clear, and hie herself to New Orleans, where she could live in comfort for the rest of her days. When she replied that she had never been in New Orleans and knew nobody there, Reuben assured her: 'I know people of excellent reputation. The day you sell I'll put you on the steamer with your money and letters of introduction, and you'll thank the day you met me.'

When Somerset heard of the negotiations, he said flatly: 'I'll not cheat a widow,' and since he liked the new land very much, acknowledging that Reuben had found better than the first lot, he wanted to pay the asked-for three dollars. But this Reuben would not permit.

'I'll tell you what,' he told the widow. 'If you persuade Mr. Adams, who owns the land adjoining yours, to sell it to me for a dollar an acre, I'll give you two twenty-five for yours,' and when Mr. Adams demurred, Reuben promised him: 'If you can get me that two thousand acres of bottomland owned by Mr. Larson . . . obviously floods every year and is worth almost nothing . . . if you can get him to sell it to me for twenty cents an acre, I'll give you a dollar twenty-five for yours.'

He now had three owners involved, and was dickering with a fourth, a Mr. Carver, for the purchase of eight hundred acres of the best cleared fields he had ever seen, contiguous to the rest, for a flat three dollars an acre when it was obviously worth at least four.

When the pot was bubbling, with the four owners pondering their parts in the intricate sale, Reuben rode from farm to farm one afternoon, warning each of the people that his offer was good only till noon of the next day, and he came to his quarters that night satisfied that he and Somerset were going to get possession of their land by next nightfall: three thousand of the widow's acres, four thousand of Mr. Adams' uncleared acres, two thousand of Mr. Larson's useless bottomlands, and eight hundred of Mr. Carver's prepared fields. It was a massive deal, one which would exhaust much of the cousins' cash, but he was convinced that this was the way to acquire a major land holding in Texas.

He went to bed pleased with his manipulations, but at four in the morning he sat bolt upright, catching for breath as if someone were strangling him. 'The Raft!' he told his wife, and he ran across the hall to waken Somerset: 'Don't you see, Sett? They're willing to sell because they know the Great Raft is going to be removed.'

'What are you talking about?'

'The Raft! The Raft! The minute it's removed, we lose all the water in our river. No boats will ever get to Jefferson. This land won't be worth fifty cents an acre.'

In real anxiety he threw on his clothes and dashed out to where the Cobb horses were stabled, and calling for Jaxifer, he leaped into the saddle. 'Meet with them,' he shouted back to Somerset. 'Tell them I'll be back in five days. Appendicitis.' When his own lead slave could not be found, he pressed Trajan into sleepy service, and off they went to inspect the Raft.

Somerset was embarrassed to visit with the four sellers, but decided to explain to each that his cousin had been called urgently to Shreveport to handle a large amount of money being forwarded from Georgia, and when the widow who was selling the first parcel asked if it was true that the other Mr. Cobb had influential friends in New Orleans, he found himself assuring her: 'He'll take care of your interests, believe me.'

Five days later Reuben returned, tired but happy and fully prepared to go ahead with the four purchases. When Sett asked about the Raft, he said: 'Even God couldn't remove it.' The water at Jefferson seemed guaranteed for all time.

The Cobbs got their nine thousand eight hundred acres for the prices that Reuben had wanted, but even when they had them safely in their possession, he wanted two hundred more to make a round ten thousand, and he uncovered a wispy little fellow who owned four hundred of the most miserable bottomland, underwater twice each year, so he bought the whole batch for ten cents an acre.

The Cobbs were finding that Jefferson, settled by responsible immigrants from the Southern states, was almost indistinguishable from a town of similar size in Alabama or Georgia, but what made it especially attractive was the fact that it combined the best features of each of those states, for this corner of northeast Texas was a flowering paradise. 'No wonder they call it the Italy of America,' Millicent cried one February morning when she saw the stately trees on their new land, the wealth of casual flowers beginning to appear on all the fields.

Reuben, always with an eye to future business, had been enumerating the trees which awaited the ax: 'We have six kinds of oak: live, black, post, water and the two tough types, white and red. I've seen elm, hundreds of good ash, maple, sycamore and two that are going to be damned valuable for shingles and fencing, cypress and red cedar. But I want you all to see a real wonder.'

He led them to a tree they had not known. It grew abundantly but not in height and produced thorns of immense size. 'They call it two ways,' Reuben said, 'bois d'arc or Osage-orange. You can see a few of last year's oranges up there.'

'Are they palatable?' Millicent asked, and her cousin said: 'Not even for cows. But I want you to look at the wood,' and he sliced off a small branch of the Osage to show the women the bright yellow color, wood and sap alike. 'It's very hard, and what I like about it, if we plant two rows, side by side with the trees of the second row filling in the gaps in the first, within three years we'll have fences that no cattle can penetrate. You're going to see a lot of Osage-orange on Lakeview.'

Reuben had insisted that the name of the plantation be Lakeview, and when Sett objected: 'But there's no lake,' the determined redhead said: 'There will be.'

Even when the Cobb plantation was finished, the cousins would plant only a relatively few acres of cotton; the major part would be held in woods, or used for cattle and hogs. But as soon as that first small stand of cotton was planted, and before their homes were built, Reuben put all the slaves plus six hired men from town with their mules and iron sleds to work digging out to the depth of four feet an immense sunken area immediately adjacent to the river.

'Leave a dike wide enough to keep the water out,' he ordered, and as the depression deepened he worked as strenuously as any of the men, digging deeper and deeper and moving a huge amount of earth to be piled along the rim of the future lake. When everyone was exhausted, he gave the crew two days' rest, then brought them back to finish off the bottom and dig a six-foot channel from the river to the place where the future plantation wharf would be built.

The men dug this channel in an interesting way. The hired hands from town hitched their mules to a heavy iron implement that looked like a very large sharp-edged dustpan, except that it had higher sides and two handles instead of one. When the mules strained forward they dragged this huge pan behind them, so that the man holding the handles could tip the edge forward and slice off a huge wedge of moist earth, which stayed in the scoop as the mules moved faster, dragging it aloft to the sides of the depression.

When the channel was well dug, wide enough to safeguard a boat coming in from Lake Caddo, Reuben announced: 'Now for the fun!' He directed the slaves to pare the top of the dike, which kept out the river, down to the very water's edge. He then dug holes in the remaining walls, filled them with explosives, and warned everyone to stand back. When he detonated the charges, the dike crumbled and waters from the bayou rushed in to fill the man-made lake and the channel leading to where the wharf would stand.

From the side of the slight hill on which the Cobb mansions would one day be erected, the women and children watched with delight as their lake came into being. 'How beautiful!' Petty Prue cried, and Millicent, less openly enthusiastic, agreed. It was a splendid lake, which would be even lovelier when the trees which Reuben proposed planting were established.

The Cobb men were not foolish. They never believed for an instant that two families as distinct as theirs, or two men as radically different as they, could own a plantation in common, and as soon as the purchases of the land were completed they consulted a Jefferson lawyer—there were three to choose from—who drew up a most detailed schedule of who owned what: 'Now, as I understand it, Somerset is to have the initial three thousand acres purchased from the widow, plus four hundred of the very fine acres of the Carver land. Reuben is to have clear title to all the four thousand acres bought from Mr. Adams, plus all the bottom-lands from whomever.'

'That's my understanding,' Sett said. 'And mine,' agreed Reuben.

'But the entire is to be called Lakeview Plantation?'

The Cobbs looked at each other and nodded: 'That's what we want.'

'Most unusual. Two plantations, one name.'

'Doesn't seem unusual to me,' Reuben said, and the lawyer coughed.

'Now, the lake, and ten acres of land about it, plus access to the river, that's to be held in common, owned by no one specifically, and with each of your two houses to have equal access and equal use, in perpetuity.'

'Agreed.'

'And that also includes any wharf that will be built there, and any cotton gin or storage buildings which might be called warehouses.'

'Agreed,' Reuben said. 'We'll build them with common dollars and have common ownership. But I wish you'd put in there not only the gin but also any other kind of mill we might want to operate.'

'And what kind would that be?' the lawyer asked.

'That's to be seen,' Reuben said.

So before even the wharf was built, or the family houses well started, he was preoccupied, along with Trajan and Jaxifer, in laying out the kind of mill complex he had long visualized. Because no running stream passed through the land, he could not depend on water power, and he did not want to go back to the old-style gin operated by horses walking endlessly in a circle. Instead, he hired three skilled carpenters from the town—one dollar and ten cents a day, with them supplying all tools and nails—and working alongside them, he built a two-story gin building, traditional except that on the ground floor he left only a small open space.

When Trajan warned: 'No horse kin walk there!' he explained: 'Somethin' a lot better'n a horse,' and he had the slaves erect a rock-based platform on which a ten-horsepower steam engine would rest; he would purchase this from Cincinnati, where it seemed that all the good machinery of this period was manufactured.

But the gin was only a part of his plan, for when a heavy leather belt was attached to the revolving spindle of the engine, it activated, on the upper story, a long master spindle from which extended four separate leather belts. There would not be sufficient power to operate all the belts simultaneously, but any two could function. One, of course, led to the gin, and it drew down little power; another returned to the first floor, where it operated the massive press which formed the bales that would be shipped down to New Orleans for movement to Liverpool. It was the third and fourth belts which led to the innovations of which Reuben was so proud, and one might almost say that these accounted for the material growth of Lakeview Plantation.

The third belt carried power to an enlargement of the gin building that housed a gristmill, a massive stone grinder which revolved slowly in a heavy stone basin, producing excellent flour when wheat was introduced between the stones or fine meal when corn was used. The fourth belt powered a sawmill, and it required so much power that it could run only when the press and mill were idle.

Cotton was ginned and pressed less than half the year; the gristmill and sawmill could be utilized at any time, and it was these which determined the plantation's margin of profit. The gin, using less power than any of the other three, provided the great constant in Texas commerce, the lifeblood, but with this assured, the quality of life depended upon what was accomplished additionally. Only a few geniuses like Reuben Cobb realized this interdependence; the great majority of Texans never would—and from generation to generation producers and their bankers would believe in turn: 'Cotton is King. Cattle are King. Oil is King. Electronics are King.' And always they would be deceiving themselves, for it was the creative mix of efforts, plus the ingenuity and hard work of the men and women involved, that was really King.

The four combined mills at Lakeview Plantation constituted an early proof of this truism, and one aspect of the operation was startling: after the buildings were constructed and the machinery installed, Trajan was in charge. He had mastered the technique of mending the leather belts when they tore; he knew how to guard the water supply to the engine; he knew what types of wood to cut for stoking the engine; and he, better even than Reuben, appreciated the subtle interlocking relationships of the four components. The building and its contents had been put together only by the ingenuity of Reuben Cobb, who had learned by studious apprenticeship in Georgia what was needed, but it was managed successfully by Trajan—no last name—who had that subtle feel for machinery which characterized many of the ablest Americans.

The lake had been so judiciously placed that the Reuben Cobbs could build their home on a promontory overlooking it, while the Somerset Cobbs could place another house on their rise and obtain just as good a view. But in the actual construction of the two houses, there was a vast difference.

The cousins had learned from the building of their slave quarters and the dredging of the lake that skilled workmen could be hired in Jefferson for around a dollar a day, and good husbandry advised the Cobbs to pay the fee and use these craftsmen. A good slave shack, caulked to keep out the rain, could be built by these artisans for less than fifty dollars, and an entire house, dog-run style for white folks, could be put up for six hundred dollars. The Somerset Cobbs built such a house, hastily and with no amenities, fully expecting to tear it down and build a better in the years ahead.

Reuben, with a keen sense of his position in Jefferson, did not do this. Instead of the traditional four small rooms at the compass points, he built four surprisingly large rooms, and instead of perching them on piles of stone at each corner, he used slaves and employed townsmen to dig substantial footings, four feet deep, which he filled with stone and rubble and sloppy clay in order to establish a firm, unshakable base. It, too, was a dog-run, but the central breezeway was twenty-six feet wide and the roof was not thrown together; it was most sturdily built and covered with cypress split shingles hewn from Lakeview trees.

To everyone's surprise, Reuben paid little attention to the porch, accepting one that was both shorter and narrower than his cousin's, so that when the unusual house was finished, several people, including some of the workmen, said in effect: 'Hell of a big breezeway. Itty-bitty porch. It don't match.'

He did not intend it to, for as soon as the plantation began prospering he did three daring things: he boarded up the two open ends of the breezeway, paying great attention to the architectural effect of door-and-window; he built at each far end of the axis a stone chimney, tying the two halves of the house together; and he tore off the inadequate porch and installed instead a magnificent affair supported by six marble Doric columns shipped in segments and at huge expense from New Orleans.

The red-headed Cobbs, as they were called in the community, now had a mansion which would have graced Charleston or Montgomery. It was clean, and white, and spacious, and the happy combination of the two stone chimneys and the six marble pillars gave it a distinction which could be noticed when one first saw it from the steamboat landing down on the lake. But what pleased Reuben most, when he surveyed the whole, was the developing hedge of Osage-orange that enclosed and protected his grand new home.

When the mansions were livable, Sett, as the steadier of the two Cobbs and the more experienced in managing a sizable plantation, cast up the profit-and-loss figures for their enterprise, and when he displayed them to his partners, the wives declared that with Reuben's sharp purchasing and Sett's good management, the family was on its way to having a very profitable operation:

10,200 acres bought at various prices, total cost	$14,590
81 Carolina and Georgia slaves, less Hadrian stolen, plus 12 additional acquired en route means 92 at $425 per head, fair average	39,100
Cost of equipment for the slaves, plus cattle, hogs and fowl to keep the plantation running, at $62 per slave	5,704
Total investment	$59,394
Counting all slaves, each slave produces .89 bales of cotton per year times 92	82
Each bale contains 480 pounds times 82	39,360
Each pound sells at 10.8¢	$4,250
$4,250 divided by $59,394 yields yearly profit of	7.11%

'And remember,' cried Reuben when he saw the final figure, 'nine of us Cobbs had a good living from our land. Each year the value of our slaves increases. And I'm convinced cotton will sell for more next year when it reaches Liverpool.'

Cautiously, lest he excite too much euphoria, Sett added: 'We'll soon be showing substantial profit from our mills and gin,' and Petty Prue burbled: 'Hail to Cobbs! Best plantation in Texas.'

While the Cobbs were establishing themselves so securely, Yancey Quimper was taking his own giant steps down in Xavier County, for at the moment back in 1848 when he learned of Captain Sam Garner's death on the uplands of Mexico, he thought: He leaves a widow, damned nice, and two children. With all that land, she's goin' to need assistance.

Actually, Garner had not acquired a great deal of land: six hundred and forty acres because of his services at San Jacinto; some acres that his wife, Rachel, had managed to acquire; and a couple of hundred that he had taken over for a bad debt. Right in the heart of Campbell, the county seat, the Garner lands were worth having.

Keeping a watchful eye on the Widow Garner lest some adventurer sneak in ahead of him, General Quimper waited what was called 'a decent interval' and then swooped in, his colors flying. Actually, in a frontier settlement like Texas where women were scarce, the decent interval for an attractive widow to mourn after the sudden death of her husband was anywhere from three weeks to four months. Men needed wives; wives needed protection; and orphaned children were a positive boon rather than a hindrance.

When Quimper first began speaking to Rachel Garner about her perilous condition, he stressed only her responsibility for the rearing and education of her children, and in this he was not being hypocritical, for he liked the boys. 'These are children worth the most careful attention,' he told her, sounding very much like a clergyman.

But on subsequent visits he began talking about her problems with the eight hundred and forty acres with which she found herself: 'Today they're worth nothing, maybe a dollar an acre. But in the future, Rachel . . .' He now addressed her only as Rachel and always saw to it that one of her children was at his side as he spoke. He dwelt upon the difficulties an unmarried woman would face if she endeavored to manage so much property. He stressed the fact that the land lay half within the town, half out in the country, a division which trebled the complications.

On an April day in 1850, at the time the Cobbs were excavating their lake, he suddenly took Mrs. Garner's hands, her children being absent, and gazed at her as if overcome by a totally unexpected passion: 'Rachel, you cannot take care of a farm and two lovely children alone. Allow me to help.'

Everything he had been saying for the past months had made sense, indeed the only common sense she had heard for a long time. A preacher for whom she had little respect had mumbled: 'God always looks after the orphaned child,' but General Quimper had outlined practical courses of action which did not depend upon God's uncertain support, and she was now disposed to listen seriously to his next recommendations.

Having uttered the critical words, he retreated from her kitchen as if overcome with embarrassment and stayed away for two days, but on the third day he returned filled with apologies for his intemperate behavior during his last visit, and with great relief he heard Mrs. Garner say: 'No apologies are necessary. You were seized by an honest emotion, and I respect you for it.'

When the proposed marriage was announced, Rachel Garner was visited by an unexpected member of her community, a tall, shaggy, rough individual known unfavorably as Panther Komax, whom her dead husband had once described: 'An animal. Good with a gun, but an animal.'

Panther's message was blunt: 'Don't marry him, Mrs. Garner.'

'What are you saying?'

'He does nothin' withouten a plan.'

'What do you mean?'

'He plans to grab your land. He plans to grab ever'thin'.'

'My children need a father.'

'They don't need him.' In the silence that followed, Panther studied the neat kitchen, then said: 'You're doin' all right as it is. Captain Garner would be proud of you.'

At the mention of her husband's name, Rachel frowned, as if Komax had been unfair in bringing into the discussion that fine man, that unquestioned hero, but since Sam had been brought into the room, she said, as if for him to hear: 'Sam would want his children to have a father. He would understand.' Then almost aggressively, she turned on Panther and demanded: 'What has General Quimper ever done to you?' Komax, not wishing to compound a mistake which he now realized he had made, replied: 'Nothin'. I was only comparin' him and your husband. And when I do I get sick to my stomach.'

Actually, Quimper had been doing a great deal to Panther, and as soon as the marriage to Rachel Garner had been safely solemnized, with her children in attendance, the general directed his attention to a business matter which had been concerning him for some time.

Like the rest of Xavier County, he had watched in disbelief when Komax returned from Mexico in 1848 leading a chubby Mexican bootmaker named Juan Hernández, who proceeded to make the best boots the men of the county had ever seen. They were pliable, yet so sturdy that mesquite thorns could not penetrate them, and when three different users reported that rattlesnakes, 'and damned big ones, too, thick as your leg,' had struck the boots without forcing the fangs through the hide, Komax Boots began to be discussed favorably wherever men appreciated good leather.

In fact, Juan's boots became so popular that Panther could not supply all the men who sought them, even when he raised his price to four dollars a pair. Therefore, in December 1849, when hordes of prospectors were pouring through Texas to reach the California gold rush via the overland route through El Paso, Komax was embarrassed by the number of gold-seekers who offered him up to forty dollars for a pair of Juan's boots.

But embarrassment soon gave way to enthusiasm, and Komax told his boot-maker: 'Go down to Matamoros or Monterrey. Find five or six good cobblers. Bring 'em here, and we'll make a fortune if these California men keep comin'.' But before Juan set out, Lomax gripped him by the wrist: 'You promise to come back?' and the Mexican replied in Spanish: 'Amigo, I never lived so well. You are a man to trust.'

Soon Hernández was back in Xavier with five Mexican bootmakers, who, under his and Panther's tutelage, began to turn out boots of such remarkable quality that even when the California gold rush petered out, the demand from Texas men continued to snap up all that Panther could supply.

The price was now fixed at eleven dollars a pair, twelve if Hernández himself decorated the upper part with the Mexican designs he liked. He favored the symbol of his nation, the valiant eagle battling the rattlesnake, but most Texans rejected this: 'Damned vulture eatin' a worm,' they called it, and they asked instead for the Lone Star with crossed pistols. Juan could do either.

But the main advantage of a Komax boot was that it fitted properly, and in this respect it was unique. Up to this time, in both Mexico and Texas, shoemakers had been accustomed to make simply a boot: big, square, solid, but with the same outline for left foot and right. Such boots were so uncomfortable that a buyer sometimes had to wear them for six months before they adjusted to his feet, or vice versa. Juan Hernández changed this by drawing on a piece of paper the exact outlines of a customer's feet, properly differentiated as to right and left, and then shaping boots to fit. Men were apt to sigh when they first put on such boots: 'They fit!'

The lucrative trade which Komax had developed by his simple device of having befriended a weeping bootmaker about to have his neck slit attracted the attention of many Xavier men, who wondered why they had not thought of importing shoemakers from Matamoros, but no one paid closer heed than General Quimper, who said, one afternoon as a new rush of California-bound men clamored for boots: 'This dumb ox has a gold mine.'

It offended Quimper, offended him deeply, to think that a reprehensible man like Komax had stumbled upon such a bonanza, and he felt it his duty to see that the manufacturing operation, as he called it, was brought under honest control. He could think of no one better qualified to exercise such control than himself, for he spoke Spanish, knew men of property who could afford to buy the boots, and obviously was reliable, for he had both land and money.

To accomplish this transfer, General Quimper needed the cooperation of either a judge or a sheriff, and in frontier Texas both were available to a gentleman of good standing, especially if he came from Tennessee or Alabama and had some gold coins in his pocket. Yancey decided upon a three-pronged assault, so one morning Judge Kemper summoned Komax to his chambers: 'Panther, you could go to jail for bringing in those Mexicans.' There was no law forbidding this, for law-abiding Mexicans had always been free to cross the Rio Grande, but the judge's manner was ominous, and it was substantiated by a visit from Sheriff Bodger, who said: 'Us sheriffs in these parts got our eye on you, Panther, and your illegal operations.' The convincing blow, however, fell when six gunmen appeared at the workshop, threatening to shoot everyone in sight if they didn't get the hell out of Texas.

Quimper himself, terrified of a brute like Komax, did not make an appearance till the threats had softened up the wild man. Then he appeared, unctuous and reassuring, to deliver the good news that he could protect Panther and square things with the law by taking the offending Mexicans off his, Panther's, hands. By this simple but effective strategy, General Quimper obtained control of the boot-making operation, and it must be conceded that once he got it he knew what to do with it. Advertising in both Houston and Austin, he visited the many United States Army forts, peddling his excellent boots to the eager officers, and he established the designation 'General Quimper Boots' as effectively as Samuel Colt had made his name synonymous with good revolvers, or as John B. Stetson would make his with hats. In the great war that was about to erupt, generals and colonels fighting for both the North or the South were apt to wear the heavily ornamented Quimpers, as they were called; but very few enlisted men would have them unless they stole them from the bodies of dead officers. Yancey did not find it comfortable selling to enlisted men.

The Cobbs now had eleven thousand acres, Reuben having acquired eight hundred more of relatively useless river-bottom swamp, and to run it they had ninety-eight slaves, not all field hands. Since from long experience the owners had learned that one strong field hand could effectively tend only ten acres of cotton and six of corn, this meant that much of their land had to lie idle, and this was just what Reuben had intended: 'Today those bottom acres look like nothin', but time's comin' when they'll be priceless.' When someone asked why, he smiled, for what he had in mind was to dike them in, play farmer's roulette, and make enormous crops when the great floods stayed away, lose everything when they came. 'But even when floods do hit,' he told his cousin, 'we win because they bring down fresh silt from somebody else's place to enrich ours.'

The Cobb cotton fields were like no other in the area, for they were hardly fields at all, merely open spaces between tall trees, so that in early March a slave with a plow could never follow a furrow for very long before being stopped by one of the trees, and when in late March the plants showed their pale-green heads, they did not appear like proper cotton at all but rather like patches of green thrown helter-skelter. However, if the fields lacked neatness, they did carry signs that three years from now they were going to be masterpieces, because each tree which now prevented proper cultivation had been girdled and was dying; in two years it would wither, and in three it could be pushed down and the stump drawn.

Reuben did not propose to be girdled, not by nature, which he battled, nor by Northern abolitionists, who threatened his prosperity and his way of life, and he was more afraid of the latter than the former: 'Nature you can control. If the great flood comes, you hunker down and let it come, then use it later to your advantage.' At Lakeview there were three bottomlands: the low-bottoms, which were underwater much of the time; the middle-bottoms, which presented a reasonable gamble; and what might be called the upper-bottoms, which had been underwater centuries ago when the streams were powerful but which now were relatively secure against flooding. In these rich upper fields the Cobbs had planted their first crops and on them built their homes. Reuben was not worried about the ultimate worth of any of his fields, and since he had reassured himself about the permanence of the Great Raft he was satisfied that his water supply was guaranteed also.

It was his slaves about which he worried, for in a distant land like Texas, where replenishment was not easy, they were of considerable value, and if he should be deprived by Northern guile, he would lose not only his investment in them but also his capacity to work his plantation. The worth of an average adult male slave in Jefferson had increased to $900, a female, to $750, and since he and Sett had brought with them only the best, their investment, forgetting the children, stood at something better than $60,000. Since the value of a good slave seemed to rise steadily, he could anticipate that with natural increase by birth, which he figured at 2.15 percent per year, and the judicious purchase of new slaves from farmers going out of business, by 1860 he and Sett ought to have no less than a hundred and fifty slaves worth more than $1,000 each. This was property worth protecting.

He was therefore most attentive when a Northern newspaper writer named Elmer Carmody arrived in Jefferson. Carmody told everyone quite frankly what he was up to: 'I'm writing a series of essays on the New South—Alabama, Mississippi, Texas . . . We already know about the Old South. But Texas is of powerful concern to Northerners.'

He talked with anyone who would pause, and showed an intelligent interest in all details of plantation life, taking careful note of financial and husbandry details. As he went about in the small town he heard repeatedly of the Cobb brothers, as they were called, for the size and ambition of their plantation excited admiration: 'Mister, they have the best mill in the whole South, Old or New.' Several Jeffersonians volunteered to drive Carmody out to Lakeview, but he preferred to take things easy, and on the fifth day of his stay, Reuben Cobb did indeed drop by to see him.

'We hear you're writin' about us.'

'I propose to.'

'Unfavorable, I suspect?'

Carmody extended his right hand palm down, and rotated it, up and down, to indicate strict impartiality: 'I write as the facts fall, Mr. Cobb. And the facts I've been hearing tell me that you and your brother . . .'

'Cousin. He's from Carolina. I'm from Georgia.'

'Would I be presuming . . . ?'

'To my mind, you're presumin' by even bein' in this town. But if you want to see a plantation at its best, I'd be proud to have you ride back with me.'

Reuben was on horseback, and he naturally assumed that Carmody had a mount, and when the newspaperman confessed that he didn't, Cobb hastily arranged to borrow one from a grocer with whom he did business, and soon the pair were heading out to Lakeview.

'I hear that you have more than ten thousand acres. Why were you so willing
. . . ?'

Carmody rarely had to finish a question, for Cobb had such an acute interest in
everything, he could anticipate what data an intelligent man might seek. 'We
believe in Texas,' he said, turning sideways. 'We're willing to invest all our savings.'

'What did the land cost you, on the average?'

Cobb was surprised; no Southerner would dream of asking such a question of a
plantation owner. Forbidden were: 'How many acres?' 'How many bales?'

Next Carmody asked: 'How many bales do you hope to ship?' And before Cobb
could answer, he asked: 'Is it true you have your own wharf?'

By the time they reached Lakeview, Reuben actually liked Carmody, for in his
brash twenty-six-year-old way the young man asked probing questions without a
shred of guile, doing so in such a rational progression that Reuben wanted to
answer, and when the four adult Cobbs met with Carmody, who stayed with them
three days, the conversation became extremely pointed, with Reuben asking at the
beginning of the first session: 'Are you an abolitionist?' and with Carmody reply-
ing: 'I'm nothing. I look, I listen, I report.'

'And what are you goin' to report about us? Here in Texas?'

'That you are the last gasp of profitable slavery.'

'You admit, then, that we do make profits?'

'You do, but not for long. And at a terrible cost to your society.'

Reuben flushed, and there might have been harsh words, for he was a voluble
defender of the South and its peculiar traditions, but he also wanted to hear a
logical explanation of the Northern point of view, so he restrained himself and
asked: 'Why do you say our obvious profits exact a terrible cost?' and Carmody
launched into a careful analysis:

> 'Let us suppose two recent immigrants go, one, like you, to Texas,
> another, also like you, to Iowa—two states that joined the Union at
> about the same time. You each bring to your new location the same
> amount of cash, the same amount of intelligence and energy. I'm afraid
> that the man who goes to Iowa will in the long run have every advan-
> tage, and the cruel difference will be that he will not be encumbered by
> slaves and you will.

> 'This difference will manifest itself in every aspect of life, but principally
> in two vital ways, manufacturing of goods and self-government. Let's
> take manufacturing first. Because the Iowa man has no slaves, he can
> rely on no ready crop like cotton. He must work in many different fields,
> and when he does he builds skills. Pretty soon everything he needs to
> live on is available locally. If he wants a bricklayer, he can hire one. If he

wants an engineer, he can ask about the neighborhood, and soon he has produced a diversified society capable of supporting itself by the exchange of money for services.

'The man who comes to Texas with his slaves cannot do that, for he must apply all his own energies and that of his slaves to growing one cash crop, cotton. Now, the profits from cotton can be great. My studies satisfy me that even a poor farmer can produce his crop for seven cents a pound. But with good management you can bring it in for five and three-quarters cents, and then, even if you have to sell at seven, you prosper, and if you can get sixteen, you make a fortune. I know that in many years you do even better. But you must buy more slaves and more land. What happens when the land gives out? Your profits are not invested in the creation of a multiple society. Now and next year and for all the years to come, when you need something, you must send to Cincinnati to find it. You are not producing those useful things upon which a complex organization depends, and down the road a way you're bound to pay a terrible price for this neglect.

'Eight or nine times during my travels I've heard sensible men say: "We may have to go to war, some day, to protect ourselves from the Yankees . . . to protect our sacred way of life." And the speakers have convinced me that they mean it and that their young men are the bravest in the world. But, Mr. Cobb, if the North has all the production, all the railroads, all the arsenals, all the shipbuilders, it must in the long run prevail, no matter how gallant your young men prove to be.

'And before you argue me down, let me say that the gravest price you pay for your slave economy is the tardiness it encourages in the building up of government, of education and of the good agencies of society. You have no public schools because half your population, the Negro half, does not need them. Your friend in Iowa will soon have libraries and publishing houses, and you will not. He will have lively politics, divided between reasonable factions, and you will have only the party dedicated to the preservation of slavery. This is the terrible cost of your peculiar institution. You ought to abandon it tomorrow.'

Each of the four Cobbs had a dozen points on which to debate Carmody's thesis, and he proved responsive to all of them, listening sagely, nodding his head agreeably when they scored and shaking it when they indulged in fantasy, not fact. He really was seeking information, and they believed him when he assured them that he was not an abolitionist: 'I truly have no preconceptions. I've studied

Adam Smith and have learned from him that economy governs a great deal of human effort, and the more deeply I probe into the economy of the South . . .'

'What is this word *economy?*' Petty Prue asked.

'It means everything we do at work and trade. For example, the most interesting thing I've seen at Lakeview, and let me tell you, this is an impressive plantation and you're impressive people . . . No, you guess what's been most interesting.'

The Cobbs guessed that it was their manufactured lake where none had been before, their multipurpose mill, perhaps the girdling of the trees and letting them stand in the midst of the cotton. 'No,' Carmody said, 'it's that slave Trajan. He runs your mill, you know. Gin, press, grist, saw, he does it all. Frankly, he's a better mechanic than any I saw in Iowa. And you must have in these fields around Jefferson . . .' He threw his arms wide to include all this part of Texas. He had become so excited that he lost his line of reasoning; ideas cascaded through his mind with such rapidity that this sometimes happened.

'Tell me,' he said, 'is that Great Raft I saw at Shreveport, is it there forever?' When the Cobbs assured him that it was, he said: 'Remarkable. But then, a great deal in this part of the world is remarkable.'

For two more days he talked with the Cobbs, and on the evening before his departure Reuben said: 'You know so much about us, I'd like to hire you as manager,' and Carmody replied: 'You've almost convinced me that plantation life can work,' and Somerset asked: 'But you leave here still unconvinced?' and he said: 'Yes. This way of life is doomed. Its economy must deteriorate.'

'Now, that's where you're wrong!' Reuben cried, leaping to his feet. 'If we can keep moving our slaves westward, we can maintain the paradise forever.'

Carmody stiffened, visibly, and Petty Prue wished her husband had not spoken so openly, for she knew the young visitor must respond; he was the kind who did: 'Mr. Cobb, the nation will not permit you, will never permit you, to carry your slaves even ten miles west of Texas.'

Reuben flushed and his neck muscles grew taut, whereupon Petty Prue said blithely: 'I've prepared a small libation in honor of your departure, Mr. Carmody,' and the tempest was avoided, but just before retiring for the night Carmody said something which caused Reuben to fall silent: 'Up on the Red River, I met this Methodist preacher, man named Hutchinson, not a very good preacher, if you ask me, in the pulpit I mean, but a man of profound wisdom. He told me that he's been teaching slaves in that district to read and figure, and he's found that some of them were distinctly clever.'

On the day that Elmer Carmody left Jefferson, Reuben Cobb and two neighbors rode north to the Red River, a distance of only sixty miles to the Indian Territory, and there they made quiet inquiry as to the comings and goings of this Methodist minister Hutchinson. When they had him well spotted, they enlisted the aid of several local plantation owners, and in the dark of night they apprehended the lanky, weepy-eyed man and tied him to a tree. Warning him that if he continued preaching insurrection to slaves in the district, they would kill him next time, they then lashed him till he fainted. Leaving him tied to the tree, they returned to their homes.

Just before Christmas 1850, the Cobbs met General Yancey Quimper, and were at first impressed by the man's bearing and his obvious patriotism, although they differed as to the amount of support they wished to give him. Reuben, always on the hair trigger where Southern rights were concerned and looking far forward in his defense of slavery, thought that Quimper made a great deal of sense in his opposition to Henry Clay's notorious Compromise of 1850, which restricted the spread of slavery, and he supported Quimper with special vigor when the general objected to the part of the compromise which delineated the boundaries of Texas.

'Look at this map, what they did to us,' Quimper cried as he explained how Congress had stolen immense areas of land from what should have been Texas. 'We won all this territory from Mexico, won it with our guns.'

'Is it true that you led the infantry at San Jacinto?' Somerset asked.

'Most powerful sixteen minutes in the history of Texas,' Quimper said. 'In those flaming minutes we won all this land, and now Congress takes it away.'

His map was compelling, for it showed the original Republic of Texas in 1836, bordered on the west by the Rio Grande in such a way that Santa Fe was part of Texas, and there was also a panhandle which stretched all the way into what would later become the states of Colorado and Wyoming, encompassing much of the good land of New Mexico and Oklahoma. 'If we'd of kept this,' Quimper stormed, 'we'd of been one of the major nations of the world.'

Somerset tried to placate him: 'General, you forget that Congress paid us ten million dollars for our rights.'

'No honest Texian would ever sell his birthright for a mess of potatoes.'

'We call ourselves Texans now. The old days are gone.'

'Ah-ha!' Reuben cried. 'Did you hear that, General? First time my cousin used *we* when speakin' of Texas. Always before it was *you*, like he was a visitor here.'

'I feel myself to be part of Texas,' Sett confessed, 'and while I can't see the other states allowing us to hold all that land, especially up in the North, I do think we ought to have had the upper reaches of the Rio Grande as our western boundary.'

'Exactly!' Quimper shouted. 'Then we'd have Santa Fe as a counterbalance to El Paso.' With a broad and generous hand he gave away Colorado and Wyoming, but with hungry fingers he drew Santa Fe back into the Texas orbit.

The cousins were at first charmed by this affable man with the very attractive wife. The general was now thirty-eight years old, fleshy, clean-shaven, and often prophetic when peering into the future: 'Worst mistake Texas ever made, gentlemen, was when we sent Sam Houston to the United States Senate. Hell, he don't represent the interests of true Texans or the future of the South.'

'Wait a minute,' Somerset interrupted. 'I've seen pamphlets in which you and Houston fought side by side in getting Texas into the Union.'

'We did, that we did. Even a habitual drunk can sober up sometimes and do the right thing. But he's a man who cannot be trusted, never could be.'

Reuben said: 'They tell me you had a chance to shoot him in that duel, and that as a gentleman, you shot off to the side.'

'Worst mistake I ever made. Sooner or later, somebody's goin' to have to handle that old drunk.'

When Quimper left Lakeview, the Cobb cousins remained confused because so much of what he said was true, so much of what he did was false, and it was during these days of review that Reuben and Sett began to draw apart in their judgment of the man. Reuben, always thirsting for action, was eager to associate himself with Quimper and was uneasy lest the tall-talker initiate some campaign without including him, but Sett, a cautious judge of men, grew more suspicious of Quimper the more he thought about the man's behavior. In this he was abetted by Millicent, who said simply, when they were alone: 'He's a fraud. Couldn't you see that?'

'I did see it, but I also saw that he makes great sense when he talks about South and North.'

'Easy. Listen to him when he talks, but leave him when he begins to act.'

In 1854, Yancey Quimper rode back to Jefferson with a band of nineteen Southern patriots who were determined to move Kansas into the slave column, and he was not only prepared to march them right into that area but also to help them in disciplining any Northerners who might have slipped across the border. He was so excited, so persuasive, that Reuben Cobb rode north with him.

They entered Kansas quietly, in three separate groups, and spent two weeks listening to accounts of Northern perfidy. For fifteen days they did nothing except scout the land and establish escape routes in case a superior Northern force attacked. Of course, at this time there was no Northern force, superior or inferior, but they did come upon a pair of isolated farms occupied by families from Illinois, and these they surrounded and attacked on their last night in the area.

'No killin'!' Quimper ordered as his men crept closer, and his command was obeyed, for the Texans ran at the houses shouting and yelling, and so swift were they in executing Quimper's commands, they had possession of the farms before the occupants could think of gunfire. The families were herded onto a hillside, where they watched as torches were applied to the rude homes they had built with painful effort.

'You go back where you belong,' Quimper warned them. 'Your kind is not welcome here.'

When the vigilantes returned across the Red River, recognized by Congress as the northern boundary of Texas, they learned that Reverend Hutchinson, the Methodist minister who had been punished before because of his incendiary work among slaves, was still up to his old tricks, so Quimper, Cobb and three others rode out to his parsonage and hanged him.

The group then separated, Cobb heading east to Jefferson and Quimper south to Xavier, but each carried a promise from the other: 'When the trouble starts, you can rely on me.'

When Elmer Carmody published his travel book, *Texas Good and Bad,* he could not have foreseen that his carefully considered judgment on two types of Texas community, English and German, would place the residents of the latter in mortal danger. First, his generalizations about the typical Texas town of that period:

> South of the Brazos, I stopped overnight at the hostelry of one Mr. Angeny, from parts unknown. He had four guests that night, but explained to us: 'I ain't got no food in the place, saven some cornbread and lard and sugar.' That's what we ate. He had no blankets, either, and his two beds in which four of us would sleep with all our clothes on for warmth were lice-ridden. He also had no hot water for shaving, no chamberpot for convenience, and very little hay for our horses. Charge, $1.50 for man, $.85 for beast.

In this frame of mind Carmody chanced to move west from Austin, which he considered a pitiful excuse for a state capital, 'worst in America, all spittoons and greasy beef,' and in his casual wandering he came upon Fredericksburg, which he extolled:

> It was with these gloomy reflections that I turned a bend in the Pedernales River and came upon the two beautiful stone houses of the Allerkamp family, and immediately I saw them, I realized that I was passing from barbarism into civilization.
>
> The trees were trimmed, as trees should be when they stand about homes. The lawn was green, and flowers were confined to neat beds upon which someone had spent considerable care. The well-designed houses were of stone, with no open spaces for the wind to enter, which I had been accustomed to on my Texas travels. And over everything there was a cloak of neatness, of respectability, of the very best husbandry.

As a practiced writer, Carmody realized that for an outsider to venture into a sensitive area like Texas and offer comment on its way of life was hazardous and bound to excite criticism, but even he did not appreciate how inflammatory it was to compare the Germans so favorably to the barbarians he encountered elsewhere. Especially dangerous were his comments about white cotton growers:

> I had been assured since entering Texas that the cultivation of cotton could be achieved only with the work of slaves and that no white man could possibly plant and harvest this demanding plant. I saw that the Germans of the hill country did very well with cotton. They grow it efficiently, bale it more carefully than others, then watch it bring a marked premium at Galveston, New Orleans and Liverpool. Fredericksburg proves that most of what Texans say about slavery is nonsense.

A writer has certain advantages. He can publish such evaluations, then scurry out of the country, but his words remain behind, generating bitterness, and in the years following the circulation of Carmody's *Texas Good and Bad,* other Texas citizens began to look upon the Germans as aliens who refused to enter the mainstream of Texas life, as cryptic abolitionists, and even as traitors to the fundamental patriotism of the state.

When General Quimper visited the Cobbs, he found them incensed at what Carmody had written about them, but they had not finished voicing their grievances when he interrupted: 'Gentlemen, it isn't only his infringement of your courtesy that should bother you. What can you expect of a writer? It's his praising of the Germans. And particularly what he says about slavery.'

He took the Carmody book and read with emphasis the passage about growing cotton without slaves: 'That's treasonous! The time could come when we might have to teach those Germans a lesson in manners. They invade our land and then try to tell us how to behave. If we catch them tamperin' with our slaves . . .'

He had touched upon one of the strangest aspects of Southern life: many slaveholders were convinced that their slaves, at least, were supremely happy in their position of servitude; but at the same time, the owners were desperately afraid of slave uprisings, or of Northerners inciting their slaves; there was a constant tattoo of hangings, beatings and terrible repressions whenever it was suspected that the 'happy' slaves might be surreptitiously preparing a general slaughter. Thus there had been fierce punishments meted out when it looked as if the slaves might rebel at Nacogdoches, and white clergymen had been hanged at the Red River on the mere suspicion that they had been 'tamperin' with our loyal slaves.'

Any serious consideration of punishing the insidious Germans was forgotten in early June of 1856, when word reached Texas of the insane behavior of John Brown and his sons in Kansas.

'They've murdered Southerners!' General Quimper cried as he carried the news from house to house, and before the details could be verified, Quimper and Reuben Cobb were back on the trail to Bleeding Kansas. With the nineteen men who accompanied them, they formed a powerful support for the Southern agents who were trying to ensure that if a plebiscite ever occurred, the vote would favor slavery. Of these twenty-one vigorous defenders of the Southern position, only four owned slaves—Quimper was not one of them—and only thirteen had come into Texas from Southern states, but all were willing to risk their lives in defense of the South. As Quimper himself explained, after a wild skirmish in which four abolitionists were slain: 'You have a strong feelin' that God intended things to be the way they are in the South. And any man can see that the welfare of Texas depends on our standin' shoulder to shoulder with our Southern brothers.'

When Cobb and Quimper reached home with the exciting news of their victories in Kansas—'Nine abolitionists killed without the loss of a Texan'—they started to try to whip up enthusiasm for some kind of vague action against the Union, but now they ran into the iron-hard character of Sam Houston, who was determined to protect the Union and keep his beloved Texas firmly within its protection.

Quimper, an able man where political savagery was required, led the fight to humiliate the 'old drunk,' as he still called him: 'He sits there in the Senate of the United States and does everything possible to humiliate Texas. Always he votes against our interests. He might as well be an abolitionist.'

His charges were partially true, because in these closing days of his life Sam Houston, now sixty-four, dropped the vacillation which had sometimes clouded his character and came out strongly and heroically in favor of preserving the Union, regardless of the offense to local preferences: 'I support the Union which has made us great, and if there are any temporary imbalances, they can be corrected.' When pressed, he admitted that he was now and had always been a strong pro-slavery man, but that slavery could be protected and even advanced within the existing structure, and he begged his fellow Texans to protect it in that constitutional manner.

In a time of threatening chaos, he was a constant voice of reason, and when others talked with increasing passion he became more conciliatory, imploring his friends, North and South, to retain the rule of common sense. When he had felt that to preserve the Union he must vote for the Compromise of 1850, because he saw it as the only way to prevent dissolution, he had been denounced as a traitor to the Southern cause, and when he spoke even more forcefully against the shameful surrender of the 1854 Kansas-Nebraska Act, he was vilified.

It was as a consequence of this general disfavor into which Houston had fallen that General Quimper devised a clever manipulation to show Houston and the rest of the state just how deeply Texas now despised its former hero. 'Let's show the old fool we mean business,' Quimper argued. 'Let's elect his replacement in the Senate right now.'

'His term has two more years to run. Such a rebuke has never before been given.'

'We'll do it, and he'll be the laughingstock of the nation.' And forthwith Quimper bullied his fellow Texas state senators into designating Houston's replacement while he was still in office.

But Houston was a fighter, and in 1859 he astounded Quimper and his cronies by announcing that since he was being denied his Senate seat, he would run for the governorship of Texas on a platform of preserving the Union. Aware that sentiment was veering against him on this point, he mounted an intensely personal campaign, crisscrossing the state and applying his unusual powers of persuasion. People swarmed to meet with him, listened, rejected his program but supported him personally. Some felt that the old Indian-lover could solve the Indian problems that agitated the western counties, and when the votes were counted, this man who swam against the tide had won, capping a career unmatched in American history: congressman from Tennessee, twice elected governor of that state, twice president of the Republic of Texas, United States senator, and now governor of the state of Texas. He had known more ups and downs than any other major figure in American politics, for after almost every victory, there had come defeat. Now, with the Union in peril, he would launch a heroic defense of his principles.

It was not going to be easy. General Quimper, encouraged by Houston's foes, dusted off his old anti-Houston pamphlet of 1841, the one written by another hand, and added a salvo of subsequent charges:

> We have known for many years that Houston is a drunk, a bigamist, a liar, a land-office crook, a despoiler of ladies and a coward who avoided battle and an honest duel whenever possible. But did we then know that he was also an enemy of the South, a betrayer of the interests of Texas, a cheap tool in the hands of abolitionists and a stealer of public moneys? That is the real Sam Houston, and he is powerless to deny even one of these charges, because the entire nation, and Texas in particular, knows they are true.

As the crucial presidential election of 1860 approached, Quimper maintained the drumbeat of charges against Houston, and the agony into which the nation was stumbling encouraged people to believe the accusations, so that within months of his surprising victory at the polls, the reputation of Sam Houston had fallen to new depths. He may have sensed that he was heading for the major role in a Greek tragedy of destroyed ambitions, but if he did, he still plunged ahead, his actions showing his belief that the preservation of the Union was more valuable to the world than the salvaging of a local reputation.

From the vantage point of Texas, the presidential election of 1860 can be quickly summarized but not so easily understood. The new Republican party nominated a former congressman from Illinois, Abraham Lincoln, whose very name was anathema to the South; when planters like the Cobbs were forced to speak it, they either spat or cursed.

The Democrats, split over the question of slavery, produced splinter groups that nominated three candidates whose combined popular vote smothered Lincoln, 2,810,501 to a mere 1,866,352. However, the peculiarity of the electoral system gave the Illinois lawyer the victory, 180 to 123, enabling him to become President of a nation already painfully divided on a vital issue, all of his electoral votes coming from the Northern states. In Texas he collected not a single vote, popular or electoral; he was not allowed on the ballot. But the most shocking fact was that in the Southern states, which he must now try to govern, he received less than 100,000 votes in all. Tragedy became inescapable, and men of all parties sensed it.

Everything Sam Houston had wanted to preserve, all the honorable things he had fought for, he had lost. But he was still governor, and from his powerful position he was determined to keep Texas on a sober course. There would be no impetuous acts while he was in control.

But to keep Texas in line he had to contend with hotheads like General Quimper and relative moderates like Reuben Cobb, who had been terrified by the various John Brown raids. As soon as the election results were known they and thousands like them began to shout: 'Immediate secession! Abe Lincoln is not our President!' Houston, ignoring the fact that this cry galvanized the state against him, vigorously opposed secession, reminding his Texans that the Union still stood, still protected freedom as in the past.

When South Carolina, always the incendiary leader, always first to defend its rights regardless of cost, voted to secede on 20 December 1860, Houston fought even more valiantly to prevent his state from following, whereupon Quimper and his fellow secessionists decided to make their own law: 'We'll assemble a convention of elected delegates and let them determine what course Texas shall take.' When it became clear that this revolutionary tactic was going to succeed, Houston bowed to the inevitable and sought to give the action a cloak of legality. Calling for a special session of the legislature, he allowed it and not Quimper's compatriots to summon the convention.

It was a fiery assembly, determined to break away from the Union, and when one fearless delegate tried to persuade his fellows to remain loyal, the gallery hissed, inspiring one of the great statements in Texas history: 'When the rabble hiss, well may patriots tremble.'

A plebiscite was authorized, and when the popular vote was counted, the men of Texas had decided 46,153 to 14,747 to secede, even if this resulted in warfare. The tally provided an interesting insight into Texan attitudes, because only one person in ten owned a slave, but nearly eight in ten of those who voted defended Southern rights, and when the test of battle came, nine in ten would support the war.

When these results were announced, General Quimper felt justified, for they proved that his ancient nemesis, Sam Houston, had been repudiated by the state he was supposed to lead. 'He should resign,' Yancey shouted. 'He has lost our confidence.' As before, Houston ignored such talk, arguing ineffectively with any who would listen: 'Yes, yes, Texas has withdrawn from the Union. But that doesn't mean we have joined the Confederacy.'

'What does it mean?' men like Reuben Cobb demanded, and Houston, not wishing to see Texas take arms against the Union he loved, proposed a pathetic alternative: 'The vote means that Texas is once more a free nation, strong enough to ignore both South and North. Let us now resume control of our own destiny.' But the majority were so hungry for war that his advice was rejected.

Houston, nearing seventy and failing in years, now fought his greatest battle. Still governor of the state, but scorned by all and calumniated by General Quimper, who once again challenged him to a duel, he sat in the governor's mansion in Austin and reflected on what he must do.

The new laws of Texas stated that if he wished to retain office, he must take an oath of allegiance to the Confederacy, and this would have been an easy gesture, except for one constraint: 'I have always been and am now loyal to the Union. My tongue would cleave to my mouth if I took a contrary oath.' He decided that when the test came, if men like Quimper forced him to deny his allegiance to the Union, he would resign.

But before he was forced to act, an escape presented itself. President Lincoln secretly offered to send Federal troops into Texas to assist Houston in retaining his governorship and thus keep Texas within the Union, and this was a most alluring temptation. But Houston could discuss it only with a man who would be honor-bound to respect the secrecy, so he sent for a man he had met only once, Somerset Cobb, the big plantation owner at Jefferson, and when the two men talked in Austin, Houston said: 'In the debate about secession, Cobb, you were a voice of sanity. How do you see things now?'

Cobb had not ridden so far to talk platitudes: 'War is inevitable. The South will fight valiantly, of that you can be sure, but we must lose.'

The two men sat silent, tormented by the problems of loyalty. Houston was loyal to the Union, that splendid concept so ably defended by Andrew Jackson when Houston was a young man learning to master politics. But he was also loyal to Texas, the state he had rescued from burning embers. God, how he loved Texas.

Cobb, for his part, would be forever loyal to the principles upon which he had been weaned in South Carolina, and if his natal state declared war, he must support her. But recent experiences had made him loyal also to Texas, and he saw that her present course was self-defeating. Even so, he must volunteer his services in a cause he knew would lose. Loyalties, how they cascaded upon a man, confusing him and tearing him apart, yet ennobling him as few other human emotions ever did.

'What should I do, Cobb?'

'Can you, in honor, take the oath of allegiance to the Confederacy?'

'No.'

'Then you must resign.'

'And Lincoln's offer of military aid? To keep me in power?'

Now the silence returned, for how could the governor of any state accept outside force to retain office when the people of that state had shown they rejected him and all he stood for? In his question Cobb had touched the vital nerve which activated the best men in these perilous days: Can you, in honor, do thus or so? Men like Cobb and Houston had been raised in that Virginia-Carolina tradition of honor; as boys they had read Sir Walter Scott and imbibed from his dauntless heroes their definitions of honor. They had fought duels to prove their integrity, and when Houston's first wife behaved in a peculiar way, his sense of rectitude prevented him from explaining his position. Now honor demanded that Somerset Cobb respond to the bugle calls, and honor required that Sam Houston refuse President Lincoln's offer of aid, which could bring only war to Texas. There was not a chance in ten thousand that Cobb would refuse to fight for the South; the odds were the same against Houston's accepting outside aid to hold grimly to a governorship he had already lost.

Twice in one lifetime, as a young man in Tennessee, now as an old man in Texas, Houston faced the moral necessity of surrendering a governorship, and surrendering Texas proved twice as bitter as the earlier debacle. On 15 March those state officials eager to fight on the side of the Confederacy, should war come, revoked their pledge of allegiance to the Federal Union and took in its place an oath to defend the Confederacy.

Sam Houston refused to do this, so he was commanded to appear at high noon on Saturday, 16 March, and pledge allegiance to the new government. That night the old lion read from the Bible, spoke gently with his family, then went aloft to his bedroom, where he stalked the floor all night in his stocking feet, wrestling with the monumental choices that faced him. When he came down for breakfast, gaunt and worn, he told his wife: 'Margaret, I will never do it.'

As noon approached, he retreated to the cellar of the capitol, where he sat himself firmly in an old chair, took out his knife, and started whittling a hickory limb. From the top of the stairs a messenger from the new government cried three times: 'Sam Houston! Sam Houston! Sam Houston! Come forth and swear allegiance!' Silent, he continued whittling, and thus surrendered the nation-state he had called into being.

Although Houston preferred exile in silence, there was such a public demand that he explain his unpatriotic behavior, he, against his better judgment, agreed to defend himself at an open meeting held in Brenham, a little town due east of Austin, and people gathered from far distances to hear his attempt at justification.

When General Quimper and other staunch Southern partisans learned of the meeting, they were infuriated: 'His views are downright treason!' and a half-dozen rowdies announced that they would shoot Houston the moment he appeared on the platform. Friends urged Houston to cancel the meeting, but to retreat under such circumstances was not his style: 'I shall speak.'

Millicent and Petty Prue rode south to hear the historic address, and were startled at how old Houston looked when he came onstage, six feet four, rumpled hair, his shoulders warmed by the Mexican serape he favored, his eyes sunk, but visible in every feature that old fire, that love of combat.

'Look!' Millicent whispered. 'He sees Quimper,' and indeed he did, for he looked directly at his would-be assassin and nodded.

'See those men!' Petty Prue cried loud enough for others to hear, and all looked to where six of Quimper's followers were moving resolutely toward the stage.

But then Millicent uttered a low 'My God!'—and when Prue looked to where she pointed, she saw that onto the stage had come the two Cobb men, pistols drawn.

'No shooting!' Prue whispered. 'Please God, no shooting.'

'We've gathered here tonight,' Reuben said quietly, 'to hear a great man try to justify his mistakes. Sett and I, we oppose everything he stands for. We deem his actions a disgrace to Texas, but at San Jacinto he saved this state and we propose to let him have his say.'

Some cheered, but it was Somerset who electrified the hall: 'If anyone makes a move to interrupt this meeting, Reuben and I will shoot him dead.' And he pointed his two guns directly at Quimper while his cousin covered the others.

'Let him speak!' people began to shout, and when the noise subsided, the old warrior stepped forward, drew about his shoulders the tattered serape, and said:

> 'I love the plaudits of my fellow citizens, but will never sacrifice my principles in order to gain public favor or commendation. I heard the hiss of mobs in the streets of Brenham, and friends warned me that my life was in peril if I dared express my honest convictions.'

At this point Quimper and his men started to move forward, but Sett Cobb raised his pistols slightly and whispered: 'Keep back.'

'Never will I exchange our Federal Constitution and our Union for a Confederate constitution and government whose principle of secession can be only short-lived and must end in revolution and utter ruin.'

This blunt rejection of the Confederacy, to which almost every man in the audience had pledged his loyalty and his life, outraged the listeners, the Cobb brothers included, but the old fighter plowed ahead. Now, however, he threw a sop to the Southerners, for he rattled off that impressive list of great leaders provided by the South:

'Our galaxy of Southern Presidents—Washington, Jefferson, Madison, Monroe, Jackson, Taylor, Tyler and Polk—cemented the bonds of union between all the states which can never be broken. I believe a majority of our Southern people are opposed to secession.' (Loud cries of No! No!) 'But the secession leaders declare that the Confederate government will soon be acknowledged by all foreign nations, and that it can be permanently established without bloodshed.' (Cheers, followed by the thundering voice of prophecy) 'They might with equal truth declare that the foundations of the great deep blue seas can be broken up without disturbing their surface waters, as to tell us that the best government ever devised for men can be broken up without bloodshed.'

Now he called upon his wide knowledge of war and politics, and like the great seer he was, he hammered home a chain of simple truths: 'Cotton is not King, and European nations will not fight on our side to ensure its delivery.' 'One Southern man, because of his experience with firearms, is not equal to ten Northerners.' 'The civil war which is now at hand will be stubborn and of long duration.' 'The soil of our beloved South will drink deep the precious blood of our sons and brethren.' And then the tremendous closing of a tremendous speech, the mournful cry of an ancient prophet who sees his beloved nation plunging into disaster:

'I cannot, nor will I, close my eyes against the light and voice of reason. The die has been cast by your secession leaders, whom you have permitted to sow and broadcast the seeds of secession, and you must ere long reap the fearful harvest of conspiracy and revolution.'

The crowd was silent. Quimper and his rowdies stood aside to let him pass. The Cobb brothers put down their guns. And Sam Houston left the stage of Texas politics.

What contribution could Texas make to the Confederacy? It was far removed from the fields of battle and possessed no manufactures of significance: if it wanted to arm its men, it had to forage through Mexico to find guns and ammunition.

It had only a sparse population—420,891 white persons, 182,566 slaves and 355 freed blacks—most of whom lived in communities of less than a thousand. Only two towns, Galveston and San Antonio, had as many as five thousand people.

Nor could the Confederacy look to Texas for large numbers of recruits, since the state was heavily agricultural and required its men on its farms. Also, it offered an insane number of exemptions from military service: Confederate and state officers and their clerks, mail carriers, ferryboat operators, ship pilots, railroad men, professors in colleges and academies, telegraphists, clergymen, miners, teachers of the blind or any kind of teacher with more than twenty students, nurses, lunatic custodians, druggists—one to a store—and operators of woolen factories. Matters were further complicated in that any man chosen for military duty could purchase a substitute and stay home. Also, most Texans wanted to fight as cavalry, and in extension of the rough-and-ready rules of the Mexican War, they wanted to enlist for brief, stipulated periods and then fight only under Texan officers whom they elected.

It was a rule of thumb in all the armies of the world that a civilian population could never be expected to provide more than ten percent of its total population to a draft. Texas, with less than half a million white persons, should at best have provided about fifty thousand soldiers to the Confederacy. Despite all the exemptions, it sent between seventy-five and ninety thousand.

Reuben Cobb, as the operator of a cotton gin, was specifically excused from military service: 'The Confederacy will survive only if its cotton continues to reach European markets, for then we'll bring in the money we need for arms and food.'

But Reuben would have none of this, and on the first day that volunteers were accepted he enrolled, telling his wife: 'Trajan and Jaxifer can run the gin as well as I can,' and off to war he went, never doubting that the two trusted Negroes would keep his plantation prospering.

Cobb was welcomed as a proven fighter, but it was judged that he would be most useful not in the east with General Robert E. Lee, well regarded in Texas for his frontier wars against the Comanche, but as a member of a force defending the Red River approaches to the state. Elected by his troops as their captain, he roamed his command, assuring the safety of the Confederacy in that underpopulated quarter; he would have preferred more active duty and put his name in for either the Mississippi campaign or what General Quimper called 'our attempt to recapture Santa Fe,' but to his disgust he was left where he was.

His post had one advantage: he could at various times ride south to visit Lakeview and his family. His two sons, of course, were in uniform, one with the Texas Brigade, one with fellow Texan Albert Sidney Johnston; and his wife, Petty

Prue, was more or less in charge of the plantation, assisted when possible by Cousin Sett. Somerset Cobb, too, could have claimed exemption under a '20-slave owner' rule, but he had quickly volunteered at the first news of Fort Sumter. The government had then decided that he was more needed at home, supervising the movement of cotton that brought the Confederacy wealth when delivered at New Orleans, which remained open at the moment. There brave rivermen sneaked it through the blockade to waiting English and French ships.

'Are we winning?' Sett asked during one of his cousin's unannounced visits.

'You know more than I do.'

'Any trouble along the Red River?'

'A great deal, if the truth were known. We suspect rebellion in that quarter. Watch it closely.' Flicking dust from his handsome General Quimper boots, he asked solicitously: 'How are the women? Is Petty Prue able . . . ?' His voice drifted, indicating the concern he felt about leaving a woman in charge of a major plantation.

'We give her what help we can.'

'We?'

'Yes, Trajan and I. He really runs things, you know.'

'The mills, yes. But surely he doesn't . . .'

'Reuben, we have to use every hand we have. You know, I'm going off, first chance I get.'

'You're needed here, Sett.'

'I cannot have my son in uniform, my two nephews . . . What do you hear from the boys?'

'John tells me that the Texas Brigade has seen more battle than any unit in the army. Wherever they go, major combat. If it's critical, Lee calls for Hood.'

'He hasn't been wounded . . . or anything?'

'God looks after brave men. I believe that, Sett. If two men march into battle, it's the coward who dies first.' He reflected on this, then asked: 'And how's Millicent?'

'Poorly. But she was never strong, you know. The absence of the boys, mine and yours . . .'

'You mustn't let her grieve. I ordered Petty Prue not to grieve just because she has two sons in service. Fact is, Sett, we should all be celebrating. Lee and men like Jeb Stuart, they're pushing the Yanks about.'

Very carefully Sett asked: 'Do your men, the sensible ones, that is, do they still think we can win this war?'

Reuben leaped to his feet. 'What an awful question! In my own house!' When his temper cooled he said: 'We've got to win. The entire fate of the South . . .'

'But *can* we win?' Sett hammered, and Reuben avoided an answer: 'I'm puttin' in for duty in the east . . . with Lee.' He submitted his papers and was accepted.

When the Texas plebiscite on secession was broken down by counties, it was found that eighteen out of a total of 152, of which 122 were organized, had signified their desire to remain in the Union: seven along the northern border, where Southern traditions had not been able to prevail because of the constant influx of settlers from the North, ten among the German counties in the center of the state, where abolitionism had gained root, and one, Angelina, which stood alone and unexplained; its vote defied logical explanation. Equally dangerous, eleven other counties had come within ten percent of voting for the Union. Texas had not been nearly as unanimous in its support of the South as the Cobbs had predicted.

In the hill country, fiery abolitionists were visiting German settlements and trying to inflame the residents with talk about opposing slavery. When they reached Fredericksburg they awakened response in certain families who felt that slavery was an intolerable wrong, but they accomplished little with the Allerkamps or with their daughter, Franziska, whose husband was down along the Nueces pursuing Benito Garza. However, they did enlist the vigorous support of three families, who put them in touch with like-minded Germans to the south.

After a careful evaluation of that area, the abolitionists returned to the Allerkamp settlement with a persuasive proposal: 'We all know that slavery is wrong. We know it debases the man who practices it and the man who suffers it. What we propose is nothing radical. It injures no one. It can raise no opposition among those who support the Confederacy.'

'And what is that?' Ludwig asked, because he had for some time now been seeking just such a solution to his confusion.

'We shall leave Texas for the moment. We shall quit all the wrongdoing, all the killing. And we shall go quietly down into Mexico, hurting no one and seeking refuge there until this senseless war is over.'

On 1 August 1862, sixty-five Germans, including Ludwig Allerkamp and his son Emil, headed west, then south, to escape the war.

General Yancey Quimper, feeling himself responsible for the safety of the Confederacy whether the threat came from the Red River or from Fredericksburg, had infiltrated into the latter area a spy named Henry Steward, who reported to Quimper:

> Fifteen hundred fully armed and rebellious Germans have been meeting secretly at a place in the hills near Fredericksburg, where not a word of English is spoken, at a secluded spot called Lion Creek. I know that these men are plotting to terrorize towns like Austin and San Antonio,

then cross the Rio Grande into Mexico, from where they will sail to New Orleans in hopes of joining the Northern army.

When Quimper, keeping an eye on Northern sympathizers along the Red River, read this report and visualized a contingent of fifteen hundred effectives joining the Federals, he became determined to thwart them and wanted to leave immediately to engage them in battle before they could reach the Rio Grande. But when he presented the details to Major Reuben Cobb, the latter said: 'This is the word of one spy, and not a reliable one, if what I hear of him is true,' so the dash south was postponed. In further discussion Cobb pointed out several weaknesses in the story: 'How do we know they intend enlisting in the Northern army? What proof have we that they're doing anything but escaping into Mexico?' Three days later the spy Steward was found with his throat cut.

Infuriated by this attack, Cobb became even more eager than Quimper to punish the Germans, and together they rushed south to place themselves under the command of a mercurial Captain Duff, who had been dishonorably discharged in peacetime but allowed back in war. Duff's ninety-four mounted men sighted the sixty-five Germans fleeing on foot at the banks of the Nueces, a river accustomed to violent deeds, and less than fifty miles from Mexico. 'We must not let them escape,' Quimper whispered to Duff, who replied: 'They ain't goin' to.'

On the night of 9 August 1862, with safety in Mexico near at hand, Ludwig Allerkamp was most uneasy when the men commanding the German escape decided to spend a relaxed evening under the stars rather than forge ahead to the Rio Grande. 'We should get out of Texas immediately,' Ludwig argued, but the commander lulled him with assurances that no Confederate troops would bother them, or even care that they were heading for Mexico.

It was a lovely summer's night graced with fresh-shot turkey, the inevitable choral singing and even several bottles of San Antonio beer used to toast homes in Texas: 'Till we come back in peace.' And of course, when the eating ended there were the inevitable formal discussions which Germans seemed to need; a man from Fredericksburg served as chairman for 'Crushed Hopes in Germany,' and a doctor for 'Health Problems We Will Encounter in Mexico,' but at the conclusion of the meeting Ludwig suggested: 'I think we should post sentries tonight,' and when asked why, he responded: 'We are of military age and we are leaving the country. We could be arrested as deserters.' The others laughed at his fears.

General Quimper said as the sun set: 'We were damned lucky to have overtaken them,' but he was grievously disappointed to find that instead of the fifteen hundred Germans his spy had reported, there were fewer than seventy. 'Not many Germans,' Quimper told Duff, 'but they form a dangerous body,' and every precaution was taken to see that none escaped.

The Confederate troops were astonished at how close to the Germans they were able to move without detection, and the contingents that waded across the Nueces to cut off any rush to the south splashed water when two men fell in, but even this did not alert the sleepers.

At three in the morning Ludwig Allerkamp awakened and grew uneasy when Emil did not answer his call. He started to look for him, but before he could find the young man he stumbled into a nest of soldiers, who fired at him indiscriminately; they missed him but killed his son, who had leaped to his feet when the firing started.

Now the shooting became general, and terribly confused, with the Confederate soldiers firing their deadly Sharps directly into the terrified mass of Germans, who tried to establish a defensive line from which to return fire. Some fell, shot dead; some splashed back across the Nueces and fled north; most stood firm and fought it out against vastly superior odds. Allerkamp, raging because his son had been slain in such a senseless battle, was one who stayed, and in the heat of morning he saw that others he respected were with him too. Cried one: 'Lass uns unser Leben so teuer wie möglich verkaufen!' (Let us sell our lives as dearly as we can.) And this the man did, blazing away until he fell.

Three soldiers in gray charged at Allerkamp, stabbing at him with their bayonets and shouting their battle cry 'For Southern Freedom.' When the bloody skirmish ended shortly after dawn, there were nineteen Germans and two Confederates killed in one of the least justified actions of the war.

There were also nine wounded Germans who, seeing no possibility of escape, surrendered. And it was what happened to them that caused the battle at the Nueces to be so bitterly remembered, for while they lay helpless in the morning sunlight, Captain Duff asked Quimper to help him drag them off to one side. When Major Cobb heard about this he cried automatically: 'Oh Jesus!' but he was too late to interfere, for as he ran to halt whatever evil thing was afoot, he heard shots, and when Duff and Quimper returned they were smiling.

'What in hell have you done?' Cobb shouted, and Duff said: 'We don't take prisoners.'

When Cobb checked the battlefield, he found that twenty-eight Germans had been slain and thirty-seven had escaped. Eight would be killed later trying to cross the Rio Grande, nine others were killed elsewhere, one crept back to Fredericksburg, and the rest escaped either into Mexico or California, where, as Quimper had feared, some of them joined the Union army.

On the way back to the Red River, Major Cobb pondered this extraordinary act, and as a partisan of the South he felt obligated to find an excuse, if there was one: If the Germans had escaped into Mexico, certainly they'd have run to New Orleans or Baltimore to fight against us. . . . We've instituted a legal draft, and they refused to comply. . . . This is war, and they killed some of our good men. But no matter how he rationalized Quimper's actions, he could construct no justification. Damn it all, no gentleman that I know would shoot nine helpless prisoners.

As a result of this self-examination, Cobb made two major decisions. The first was inevitable: I shall no longer place my honor in the hands of Yancey Quimper. He disgusts me. The second, representing his growing maturity, was reported in a letter to his wife:

> I've been thinking about honor and battle a good deal recently, and especially those fine talks we had with the Peel people in Vicksburg. I'm fed up with second best. I love the people in Walter Scott's novels and want to conduct myself like them. I made a terrible mistake when I named our plantation Lakeview. Means nothing. From here on, with your permission, it's to be Lammermoor. That sings to the heart.

On the night before they reached the Red River, with Major Cobb encamped as far from General Quimper as he decently could, another soldier embittered by events at the Nueces told him: 'You know, Major, I've heard that Quimper was never a real general, and his behavior at San Jacinto . . . he talks so much about it, maybe it wasn't the way he says.' If such rumors were true, Cobb thought, they would explain a lot.

Cobb refused to ride with Quimper when they headed north to duty along the Red River, and he suspected that when they met, there would be a certain tenseness. But the big, flabby fellow was as sickeningly jovial as ever: 'Great to have you back, Reuben. Important work up here.'

Trying to mask his dislike, Cobb temporized: 'Yancey, the way you handled those German prisoners . . .' Quimper leaned in to forestall criticism: 'We did all right. But now we're onto something much bigger.'

And on the very next day Cobb was with Quimper when two spies came before them to report:

> 'Evil elements have slipped down from Arkansas. They've accumulated massive arms and have conspired with Texas citizens to stage a vast uprising. Our slaves are to cooperate when the signal is given and kill all white men in the district, women and children too.'

Cobb, remembering that Quimper's other spy had detected fifteen hundred Germans in motion when there were actually fewer than seventy, was reluctant to accept this new call to frenzy, but when he quietly initiated his own inquiries, he learned to his dismay that there was a plan for insurrection and that nearly a hundred participants were incriminated. So once more he was thrown in with

Quimper, whether he wished it or not, and now began one of the startling events of the war, as far as Texas was involved.

The frightened defenders of the Confederacy placed their security in the hands of General Quimper, who, with considerable skill, arranged for a coordinated swoop upon the plotters. This move bagged some seventy conspirators, and there was serious talk of hanging them all. General Quimper loudly supported this decision, but Major Cobb rallied the more sober citizens, who devised a more reasonable procedure. A self-appointed citizens committee, hoping to avoid any criticism of Southern justice through the accidental hanging of the innocent, met and nominated twelve of the best-respected voters of the area, including two doctors and two clergymen, to serve as a court of law—judge, jury, hangman— and these twelve, following rules of evidence and fair play, would try the accused.

It was this laborious process which Quimper wanted to by-pass with his waiting nooses, but men like Cobb insisted upon it, so on the first day of October 1862 the drumhead court convened. Its first batch of prisoners was quickly handled:

'Dr. Henry Childs, in accordance with the decision of this Court you will be taken from your place of confinement, on the fourth day of October '62 between the hours of twelve and two o'clock of said day, and hung by the neck until you are dead, and may God have mercy on your soul.'

The executions were held in midafternoon so that townspeople could gather about the hanging tree, a stately elm at the edge of town from whose branches three or sometimes four corpses would dangle. No observers seemed dissatisfied with the hangings, for the victims had been legally judged and the verdicts delivered without rancor. There was, moreover, considerable interest shown in the manner with which each of the condemned met his death, and those who did so in ways deemed proper were afterward applauded.

On and on the fearful litany continued: Ephraim Childs, brother of the above, hanged; A. D. Scott, hanged: 'He viewed calmly the preparations for his execution. And when the last awful moment arrived he jumped heavily from the carriage; and falling near three feet, dislocated his neck, he died without the violent contraction of a single muscle'; M. D. Harper, hanged; I. W. P. Lock, hanged: 'His conduct throughout revealed all the elements of a depraved nature, and he died upon the tree exhibiting that defiance of death that usually seizes hold on the last moments of a depraved, wicked and abandoned heart.' His crime, and that of the others: he had preferred the Union to the South.

After twenty festive hangings had occurred, Major Cobb was sickened by the illegality of such actions, for he had reason to believe that several men clearly innocent had been hanged. He spoke with certain humane men on the jury, advising against any further executions, and his arguments were so persuasive—

'Excess merely brings discredit to our cause'—that the hangings were stopped, and nineteen additional men who would otherwise surely have been executed were to be set free, an act which most citizens approved, for they had wearied of the ringing of the bell that announced the next assembly at the hanging tree. Quimper, however, railed against what he called 'this miscarriage of justice.'

'Hang them all!' he bellowed so repeatedly that the rougher element in town began to take up the cry, and he would have succeeded in organizing a mob to break down the jail had not Cobb and others prevailed upon the men not to stain their just cause by such a reprehensible act. That night, however, someone in the bushes near town—who, was never known—shot two well-regarded citizens, partisans of the Confederacy, and now no arguments could save the men still in jail. Quimper wanted to hang them immediately. Cobb insisted that they be given a legal trial, and they were, fifteen minutes of rushed testimony and the embittered verdict:

> 'C. A. Jones known as Humpback, James Powers known as Carpenter, Thomas Baker known as Old Man, and nine others tried on the same bill, all found guilty and sentenced to be hung, the evidence having revealed a plot which for its magnitude, infamy, treachery and barbarity is without a parallel in the annals of crime.'

So thirty-nine men guilty only of siding with an unacceptable moral position were hanged; three who had nebulous connections with the Confederate military were tried by court-martial and hanged; two others were shot trying to escape. But this was not a lynching or a case of mob frenzy; it was an instance of the heat of warfare in which men dedicated to one cause could not see any justification in the other. Even in its fury the jury endeavored to maintain some semblance of order, and of the accused men brought before it, twenty-four were found not guilty and set free.

Cobb, a tempestuous man who had always fought his battles openly, was now thoroughly revolted by the hangings, and in a letter to his wife, posted on the last day of the executions, he wrote:

> There was a man in jail who was charged with being a deserter from the Southern army, and a horse thief. When the jury on this day failed to furnish any Northerners to hang, the bloodthirsty men outside took that man from the jail and hanged him.

Two days later Cobb left his post at the Red River without permission, rode south to his plantation, and announced that he was organizing a unit for service with General Lee. Among his first volunteers was his cousin Somerset, who apologized to his ailing wife: 'Lissa, it tears my heart to see you in worsening health, and I know it's my duty to stay with you, but I simply cannot abide in idleness when others die for our cause.' The brothers' first flush of patriotism waned when they learned that they would be serving not in the cavalry with Lee, but in an infantry unit, for as Reuben exploded: 'Any Texan with a shred of dignity would ride to war, not march.' But march they did, to Vicksburg.

The hinge of victory in the west would be Vicksburg, and as the Cobbs moved toward it, always striving to join up with their parent regiment already in position at Vicksburg, they could hear their soldiers grousing: 'We still ain't got no horses, and that's a disgrace. And we still ain't got enough rifles, and that's a disaster. And we're bein' led by a Northerner, and that's disgusting.'

Yes, the army which was to defend Vicksburg was commanded by a Philadelphia Quaker who despite his pacifist religion had attended West Point, where he had acquired a fine reputation. Marrying a Southern belle from Virginia, he considered himself a resident of his bride's family plantation, where he became more Southern than Jefferson Davis. A man of credibility and power, he had not wavered when the great decision of North or South confronted him; he chose the South of his wife's proud family and quickly established himself as one of the abler Confederate generals. Now General John C. Pemberton had a command on which the safety of the South depended, and his men, who had been born in the South, did not approve.

'With all the superb soldiers we have,' Reuben growled, 'why do we have to rely on a Northerner of doubtful loyalty? If Vicksburg falls, the Mississippi falls, and if that river goes, the Confederacy is divided and Texas could fall.' He lowered his voice: 'And if Texas falls, the world falls.'

He was also having trouble with a new officer assigned to his unit, Captain Otto Macnab, who had reported to the bivouac area with guns and pistols sticking out in all directions. Some men in Cobb's force had Enfields of powerful range, some had the old Sharps that could knock down a house, and a few had old frontier single-shot rifles which their grandfathers had used against Indians.

But there were nearly two dozen in the company who had no armament at all, and Major Cobb fumed about this, dispatching numerous letters to Austin begging for guns. None were available, he was told, and so he moved among his men, trying to find any soldier who had more than one, and of course he came upon Captain Macnab, who had an arsenal, but when he tried to pry guns loose from him, he ran into real trouble: 'I don't give up my guns to anybody.'

'If I give you an order . . .' Cobb suddenly remembered from Macnab's enlistment papers that he had been a Ranger, and Somerset had warned: 'Reuben, never tangle with a Ranger. My brother Persifer had Rangers in his command and he said they were an army of their own, a law to themselves.'

'They're in my command now,' Major Cobb had replied, 'and Macnab will do what I say.'

'Don't bet on that,' Sett had said, and now when his cousin tried to take one of Macnab's guns, the red-headed warrior met real opposition.

'Isn't it reasonable,' Cobb began, 'that if you have two rifles and the next man has none . . . ?'

'I know how to use a rifle, maybe he don't.'

There might have been an ugly scene had not Somerset intervened: 'Aren't you the Macnab who served in Mexico with my brother?'

'Colonel Persifer Cobb?' Macnab asked, and when Sett nodded, Macnab said: 'He knew how to fight. I hope he's on our side now,' and Cobb replied: 'No, he's tending our family plantation in Carolina.'

A month before, that statement would have been correct, for Persifer Cobb, like many of the great plantation managers throughout the South, had been asked to stay at home, producing stuffs required for the war effort, but as the fortunes of battle began slowly to turn against the South, men like him had literally forced their way to the colors, sometimes riding far distances to enlist, and as a former West Point man, his services were welcomed.

So now three Cobbs of the same generation were in uniform: Colonel Persifer in northern Virginia; Major Reuben in charge of replacement troops for the Second Texans; and Captain Somerset. There were also five Cobb sons from the three families, while at the various plantations the wives of the absent officers endeavored to hold the farms and mills together: Tessa Mae at Edisto, Millicent at Lakeview, and Petty Prue at the newly christened Lammermoor. The Cobbs were at war.

Major Cobb wisely withdrew his attempt at forcing Macnab to surrender one of his guns, but he was gratified when his tough little officer came into camp one day with seven rifles of varied merit which he had scrounged from surrounding farms. 'They'll all fire,' he told Cobb. 'Not saying how straight, but if you get close enough, that don't matter.'

When the contingent crossed over to the east bank of the Mississippi, Major Cobb saw that his Texans would have to fight their way into Vicksburg, for a strong Union detachment was dug in between them and the town. He could have been forgiven had he turned back, but this never occurred to him. Acting as his own scout and probing forward, he identified the difficulties and gathered his men: 'If we make a hurried swing to the east, we can circumvent the Northern troops, then dash back and in to Vicksburg.'

'What protects our left flank if they hear us and attack?' Macnab asked, and Cobb said: 'You do.'

'Give me a couple dozen good shots and we'll hold them off.'

Through the dark night Otto coached his team, and at two he said: 'Catch some sleep,' but he continued to prowl the terrain over which they would fight.

Just before dawn a Galveston volunteer asked: 'If we do get in to Vicksburg, can we hold it, with a general like Pemberton in charge?' and Otto gave him a promise solemnly, as if taking a sacred oath: 'When we set up our lines at Vicksburg, hell itself won't budge us.'

This reckless promise did not apply to the battle next morning at Big Black River, for Grant was moving with such incredible swiftness that he overtook the Confederates before dawn, and launched such a powerful attack that he drove them right across the deep ravines and back to the gates of Vicksburg.

In previous battles and skirmishes Captain Macnab, now a man of forty-one and extremely battlewise, had not in even the slightest way tried to avoid combat —that would be unthinkable—but he had thoughtfully picked those spots and developing situations at which he could do the most good. However, this battle degenerated into such a hideous mess that plans and prudence alike were swept aside, and he found himself in such a general melee of Grey and Blue that in desperation he lashed out like a wild man, casting aside his rifles and firing his Colts with such abandon that he himself drove back almost a squad of Yankees. In those moments he was not a soldier, he was an incarnation of battle, and when because of their tremendous superiority the Northern troops began to sweep the banks of a little stream which the Texans were struggling to cross, he shouted to his men: 'Don't let it happen!' When by force of ironlike character he had driven away the Northerners so that his troops could complete their escape, he contemptuously remained behind, searching the field the Yankees had just deserted, even though their sharpshooters still commanded it.

'Macnab!' Major Cobb shouted from a distance. 'What in hell are you doing?'

'Looking for my guns.' And when he saw where he had discarded his rifles during the chase, he calmly stooped down, retrieved them, and headed into Vicksburg.

On 19 May, General Grant brought 35,000 Union soldiers before the nine-mile-long defenses of Vicksburg; there he faced 13,000 Confederate troops well dug in, with 7,000 in reserve. The Northern battle plan was straightforward: 'Smash through the defenses, take the town, and deny the Mississippi River to the Confederates. When that happens, Texas will be cut off from the Confederacy and will wither on the vine.' So every Texan fighting at Vicksburg knew that he was really fighting to defend his home state.

As soon as his massive army was in position, Grant ordered a probe of the Confederate lines, and to his surprise, it was thrown back. For the next two days he prepared the most intense artillery bombardment seen in the war so far. It would utilize every piece of ordnance—hundreds of heavy cannon—and it would start at six in the morning.

On the night of the twenty-first he assembled his commanders and issued an order which demonstrated the mechanical strength he proposed to throw against the Southerners: 'Set your watches. At ten sharp, the artillery barrage will cease. And your men will leave their positions, attack up that hill, and overwhelm the enemy.' For the first time in world history, all units along a vast front would set forth at the same moment.

'There's bound to be some ugly skirmishing,' an Illinois captain warned his troops, 'but before noon we should have their lines in our hands. Then an easy march into Vicksburg.'

That last night, as the two armies slept fitfully, General Grant's order of battle was awesome, studded as it was with distinguished names: the 118th Illinois Infantry; the 29th Wisconsin Infantry; the 25th Iowa; the 4th West Virginia; the 5th Minnesota; and then two names that symbolized the fraternal agony of this war: the 7th Missouri, the 22nd Kentucky. Their brothers would be fighting the next day as Confederates: the 1st Missouri, the 8th Kentucky.

To reach the Confederate lines, the Union soldiers had to sweep down into a pronounced valley, then climb a steep hill and charge into the teeth of cleverly disposed fortifications. These were of three types: the redoubt, a large square earthwork easy to hold if there were enough men; the redan, a triangular projection out from the line to permit concentration of fire upon an attacker; and the smallest of the three, the lunette, a crescent-shaped earthwork, compact, with steeply sloping sides and not easy to capture.

Tough Louisiana swamp fighters occupied the major redan. Detachments from various parts of the South held the Railroad Redoubt, and the 2nd Texas Sharpshooters, a name recently bestowed because of their great accuracy with rifles, held the key spot in the line, a lunette guarding the main road back to town. Here Major Cobb's replacement detachment finally joined up with their fellow Texans.

During the furious cannonading on the morning of 22 May, Cobb's men took what shelter they could, doing their best to survive until the attack began. 'Why can't our side fire back?' a frightened boy of seventeen asked, and Cobb said bluntly: 'Because they have the cannon and we don't.'

At ten minutes to ten, all the Yankee batteries fired as rapidly as they could, in order to provide their troops with as much last-minute cover as possible. At ten o'clock the fiery monsters fell silent, and in that first awful hush bugles began to sound, first one and then another, echoing back and forth until the valleys facing the redoubts, the redans and the lunettes reverberated with their clear and stirring sounds.

Then came the infantry attack, down slight inclines at first, then across level ground, then straight up the steep flanks protecting the Confederate line. It required about eighteen minutes for the thousand or more blue-clad troops assigned to take the Texas lunette to advance across the open land, and to some who watched the solemn approach from inside the fortification, it seemed as if the Northerners would never reach their goal, as if they would march forever like dream figures across a timeless landscape. But quickly enough for both attacker and defender, the ominous blue line reached the steep flanks, scrambled up, and broke into the lunette, where a wild, confused struggle took place. With rifles, pistols, revolvers, even with bayonets and clubs, the Texas defenders threw back the Union attackers, South and North falling upon each other in bloody fury.

The struggle went on for an incredible number of hours, with the dogged Texans repelling first one assault, then another, then countless others. Each time the Yankees surged forward, up those steep final flanks, they did reach the top, and they did kill defenders, and always they seemed to have victory just within their grasp. 'Follow me!' shouted a lieutenant, waving his blue cap until a Texas rifle ended his charge and his cry and his life.

Otto Macnab kept his men from panic by constantly moving among them with gestures of encouragement—he used few words—and by leaping into the breach whenever a perilous weakness showed. Indeed, he stifled so many nearly fatal assaults that his survival was a miracle.

Well into the afternoon the Yankee assault on the lunette halted, to enable the batteries encased in the hills behind to throw down a savage curtain of fire, hoping thus to dislodge the weakened Texans, but when the cannonade stopped and the men in blue resumed their charge, the indomitable 2nd Texas repelled them yet again.

The slaughter now became obscene, a grotesque expenditure of life, Grey and Blue, on the sloping edges of a lunette which could never quite be taken. Loss came closest at about two-thirty, when a determined captain from Illinois led a charge with such bravery that he carried right into the lunette, with some nine or ten Yankees following, and had even a dozen more succeeded in joining him— and they tried, desperately—the Texans would have been subdued and Grant would have had the one foothold he needed to break the line.

But at this moment, while Macnab was engaged with a mighty assault on his little sector and Reuben Cobb was involved on his, Captain Somerset Cobb, with a courage he had not known he possessed, leaped directly at the Illinois leader and drove a sword clear through his body. The man staggered forward, thinking victory still within his grasp, clutched at the air and fell back, and the crucial charge faded.

But now a young boy, not over fifteen, ran screaming into the lunette from the southern stretch of the trench line: 'Railroad Redoubt's fallin',' and when the Texans looked across the short distance to the big fort on their right, they saw that the messenger was correct. This redoubt, big and loosely constructed, was pro-tected by a much less severe slope than the Texas lunette, and against it the Yankees were having real success. Some were already in the fort and others seemed about to break through. If Northern guns occupied the redoubt, the Texas lunette was doomed.

It took Major Cobb and Captain Macnab about five seconds to see and to appreciate the peril in which the Confederate line stood, and without consultation these two plus some fifty of their men ran like dodging, frightened, low-clinging deer across the open space between the two projections. They arrived just in time to meet the day's most furious battle, Blue and Grey in one tremendous tangle, with the former on the knife edge of victory.

'Stop them!' Major Cobb shouted to the men following him. 'In there!' Macnab never uttered cries in battle; he was always too busy managing his deadly guns, but this time the peril was so great that even he shouted: 'Here!'

He and some fifteen others leaped directly into the foremost Yankee guns, and although several of his men went down in the dreadful fusillade, their sheer weight carried them forward. But as soon as this breach was stabilized, Otto saw that Federal troops were streaming in through a larger break farther on.

'Cobb!' he shouted, and the red-haired major, his cap lost in the battle, swung about to face some new enemy when a musket discharge caught him full in the face, blowing his head apart.

'Men!' Macnab cried, and his high voice was so compelling, so unique among the battle sounds, that his men formed behind him, and in a surge of slashing and firing, repelled the attackers from the wavering line.

Grant had been denied his victory. The Confederate lines had held firm, all the way from the Railroad Redoubt at the south, which Major Cobb and Captain Macnab had saved at the last moment, to the bloodied Stockade Redan at the north. Now the long, cruel siege would begin.

The terror of Vicksburg lay not in those wild charges of that first day, for then men from both sides fought in white heat, and death came so explosively, so suddenly that there was no awareness that it had struck until a companion fell silent amid the roar. The real terror began on that night of 22 May, because in the open space between the two battle lines lay several thousand Union wounded, and for reasons which have never been explained, General Grant decided to leave them there rather than allow the customary battle truce for the removal of the dead and the rescue of the wounded. Perhaps he thought that on the next day the Confederates would be so exhausted that his men could gain an easy triumph, and he did not want to give the enemy any respite. At any rate, he left his dying exposed to the cold night air; but what was worse, he left them there all during the next day, that fiercely hot May morning, that blazing May afternoon.

Now some of the men dying on the dusty field were so close to the lunette that the Texans could hear them pleading for water, and others were so near the Federal lines that Union men could hear their companions' pleas, but all across the vast battlefield the order stood: 'No truce.'

Night brought no release, for now the battle wounds, some of them forty hours old, had grown gangrenous from the day's prolonged heat, and both the pain and the smell were unbearable. It was unspeakable, the agony that came as a result of this hideous decision not to clear the battlefield. 'If I ever see Grant,' a Texan shouted into the night, hoping that some Northern soldier would hear, 'I'll shoot his bloody eyes out.'

At about two in the morning Otto Macnab, who had seen a great deal of war and who knew how men should die, could stand no more. Leaving the lunette, he went out among the dying, and when he found a Northern soldier in the last shrieking pain of gangrenous agony, he shot him, and in doing this he attracted the attention of a Missouri man who was doing the same from his lines. Meeting in the dark shadows, neither soldier entertained even the most fleeting idea of shooting the other.

'That you, Reb?'

'Yank. What unit?'

'Texas. You?'

'Missouri.'

'We have Missouri men on our side. Good fighters.'

'You know a sergeant named O'Callahan?'

'I don't know many.'

'Should you come upon him . . .' The man was a schoolteacher.

'I'll tell him.'

'My brother. Good kid.'

When Otto crept back to the lines he went to all parts of the lunette and even back to the Railroad Redoubt, shaking men awake and asking if they'd seen a Missouri man named O'Callahan.

On the morning of 24 May, in response to a plea from the Confederates, General Grant relaxed his inhumane order, a truce was agreed upon, and men from each side moved out upon the battlefield to look at the bodies of those who might have been saved had it come earlier. When the truce ended, the soldiers returned to their respective lines, the war resumed, with General Grant bitterly acknowledging that he was not going to capture Vicksburg by frontal assault. He would have to do so by siege, which he promptly initiated. Not a man, not a scrap of food, not a horse would move in or out, and the last bastion on the Mississippi would fall.

But during the truce soldiers from each side had met with their opponents, and a respect had developed, so that invariably in the quiet evenings the men began to fraternize and sing. The Northern troops refrained from insulting their friends with the 'Battle Hymn' while the Southerners rarely sang 'Dixie.' Always, in the course of the night, some group of Southerners would begin the song they loved so deeply, and Northerners would fall silent as the winsome harmony began:

'We loved each other then, Lorena,
More than we ever dared to tell;

And what we might have been, Lorena,
Had but our lovings prospered well.'

The song had a wonderfully rich sentiment which sounded elegant in the stillness, and some from the North almost chuckled at it, but toward the end, even the most indifferent hushed when a strong high tenor sang solo of death and life hereafter:

'There is a future, O thank God,
Of life this is so small a part,
'Tis dust to dust beneath the sod;
But there, up there, 'tis heart to heart.'

Otto did not care for such songs, too much about death, but he did stop his battlefield wandering when Northern troops sang one song he had not known before. 'Aura Lee' spoke of love as he recalled it, and sometimes when the singing ended he found himself humming the tune to himself or mumbling the words:

'Aura Lee, Aura Lee,
Maid with golden hair,
Sunshine came along with thee
And swallows in the air.'

He thought of Franziska in those terms. He could see her bringing sunshine, and it was not preposterous to think of her as attended by swallows.

In the following weeks, when starvation clamped its iron claws about the innards of the Texans, both Somerset Cobb and Otto Macnab took short, dreamlike excursions: Cobb, into Vicksburg to meet with the Peel sisters he had stayed with while on his way to Texas in 1850; Macnab, out into the battlefield at night to compare situations with O'Callahan of Missouri.

The Peel sisters still had their house at the north end of Cherry Street, but since it was exposed to artillery fire from Federal warships in the Mississippi below, they lived, like so many others, in hillside caves. Lucky for them the caves were available, for their house had already taken two hits, and had they been sleeping upstairs, they would probably have been killed.

Like all the citizens of Vicksburg, the Peels had started out confident that Grant would be forced to withdraw, but as the foodless weeks passed they began to see the inevitability of defeat. However, they would not speak of it.

'You mean that fine young man who traveled with you from Carolina . . . ?'

'From Georgia, ma'am. My cousin.'

'And he was killed on the first day?'

'Most gallantly.'

'I remember his reading to us from *Ivanhoe.*'

'He loved Scott. We named our Texas plantation Lammermoor.'

'That's nice. That's very nice.'

'Miss Emma, I wish to God we had food in the lines to share with you.'

'No, Major. We wish we had food for you.'

Miss Etta Mae said: 'Is my sister right? You're a major now?'

Before he could answer, the cave in which they were meeting was shaken by a violent attack of shellfire from the warships, and as soon as it stopped, a cluster of explosions from the batteries inland rocked the area. 'They hold us in a crossfire,' Miss Emma said. 'It's murderous. Three slaves on this street killed this week.'

The Peel sisters did not leave their cave except for sunlight on quiet days, and even then they never knew when a stray shell from the river or from the battle line might kill them and everyone else in sight. They were wraithlike, each weighing less than a hundred pounds, but they maintained high spirits in order to encourage the soldiers who stopped by to see them.

On the evening of July first, Otto Macnab, suffering from the acute hunger which had attacked him viciously that day, wandered through the battlefield during the customary informal truce, and when he saw how close to the Texan lunette the Yankee sappers had brought their trenches, he gasped. Starting to pace off the tiny distance that would separate the two lines when battle resumed next day, he was interrupted by a voice he was delighted to hear. It was O'Callahan.

'Distance is seven feet, Reb.'

'You could spit into our lunette.'

'Spittin' even a foot with you Rebs is difficult.'

The two men sat side by side on the edge of the fatal trench, and each knew that when it progressed a few feet farther, the Texas position could be blown to hell with dynamite charges.

'You 'bout starved out, Reb?'

'Well, now . . .' The posturing was ended. Macnab could joke about death, and the Union failure to consolidate, but he could no longer joke about starvation. 'One hell of a way to end a battle.'

'Only way you left us, you stubborn bastards.'

As they parted for the last time, the Union man looked about swiftly, then moved toward Macnab: 'I could be shot. If they catch you, say you stole it.' And into Otto's pocket he stuffed two pieces of bread and a chunk of Wisconsin cheese.

Back in the lunette, Macnab knew that as a human being and especially as an officer, he ought to share his unexpected treasure with his men, but this he could not do. Surreptitiously he gnawed at a tiny piece of the cheese, and he believed that he had never tasted anything so delicious in his life; he could feel the nourishment racing through his body, as if one organ were shouting to another: 'Food at last! Sweet Jesus, food at last.'

He had slowly, secretly consumed one of the pieces of bread and much of the cheese when an orderly passed by: 'Colonel wants to see you.'

When he reported, his stomach reveling in the food it had found, the colonel, a medical doctor from Connecticut and a Yale graduate but now the defender of a lunette on the Mississippi, said: 'I suppose you've heard about Major Cobb?'

'What?'

'Visiting his two old ladies. Smuggling them food, I suppose. Came out of their cave just in time to meet a Union shell head-on.'

'Dead?'

'Left arm blown off. The slave who ran out here said they thought he bled to death.'

'May I go in?'

'You're needed here. You're Major Macnab now, and your job is to hold off those sappers at the foot of our lunette.'

'Yes, sir.' All day on the second of July, Macnab devised tricks for rolling giant fused bombs down into the Northern trench only a few feet away, and once when he was successful, blowing up an entire length of the trench and all its occupants, his men crowded around to congratulate him. That was the last major event at the Texas lunette, for that night the soldiers of each side, without orders from General Grant or anyone else, quietly decided that this part of the war was over.

'Pemberton sent Grant a letter,' a Northerner said. 'I spoke with the orderly.'

'I think Pemberton wants to surrender right now,' a Rebel reported. 'But Grant, he'll want it for a big show on the Fourth of July.'

'For us it ends tonight.'

Otto searched for O'Callahan, but no one had seen him, so, still a professional, he walked to the daring sap which had carried the Union lines so close to his. 'Six more days,' he told a Northern soldier, 'you'd have made it.'

'We'd of made it today, but some clever Greycoat dropped a tornado on us.'

'You know a man named O'Callahan?'

'One of your rolling bombs got him this afternoon.'

'Dead?'

'Probably alive. I saw them drag him away.'

In the distance there was singing, 'Aura Lee' from the Northerners, and then, as an act of final Confederate defiance, 'The Bonnie Blue Flag,' whispered at first by the defeated Southerners and then bellowed, with many Northerners joining in:

> 'We are a band of brothers
> And native to the soil,

Fighting for the property
We won with honest toil.'

Along the Vicksburg line that night there was not one Negro in uniform, on either side. The fight had been about him but never by him. One Confederate trooper, who operated a cotton gin at Nacogdoches, summarized Texan thinking: 'No nigger's ever been born could handle a gun. They'd be useless.'

The month of July 1863 was one of overwhelming sorrow at the Jefferson plantation, for tragedy seemed to strike the Cobbs from all sides. Petty Prue, in the big house at Lammermoor, knew that her husband was dead at Vicksburg and her older son at Gettysburg. Her younger boy was fighting somewhere in Virginia. On some hot mornings she doubted that she could climb out of bed, so oppressive was the day, so oppressive was her life.

But she had a plantation to run, some ninety slaves to keep busy, and cotton to be handled for the Confederacy, so at dawn each day she was up and working just as if her husband were absent for a few weeks and the crop promised to some factor in New Orleans. What perplexed her as the cotton matured in its bolls and the picking began was how to handle the crop when it had been harvested, for the Yankee blockade of all the seaports prevented open shipments of fiber to Liverpool. Cotton was being grown but it was not being moved, and there was always the danger that if the bales accumulated at a spot like Jefferson, so near the border, Union forces might rush in and burn them, and the plantations, and set free the slaves. Now, with the entire Mississippi River in Union hands, the possibility of such a foray grew, and a lone woman like Petty Prue, somewhat flighty in peacetime, faced problems she could scarcely solve.

The dismal news affected Millicent too, for in mid-July word was received via the telegraph to New Orleans that Colonel Persifer Cobb of Edisto, that erect, formal gentleman with his West Point education, had died at Gettysburg. The telegram had ended: SON JOHN ALSO DIED WILL YOU ALL COME BACK AND SUPERVISE PLANTATION TESSA MAE

Millicent, weakened by the privations of war, was incapable of grappling with the changes contained in this message. Vaguely she remembered that it had been sweet-talking Tessa Mae who had encouraged the expulsion of the Somerset Cobbs from Edisto, and Millicent could not imagine any terms on which they might consent to return. But such selfish considerations vanished when she thought of Tessa Mae's double bereavement and of how distraught she must be trying to manage that vast plantation. During the better part of a morning she wept for the lone widow on Edisto and for all the other widows this war was making.

This led her to thoughts about herself, and her head sagged, for she could not be sure that Somerset was alive. All she knew for certain was that in the final days of Vicksburg a Yankee shell had ripped off his left arm. At first he had been reported dead from loss of blood, but then soldiers from his unit, now in prison camp in Mississippi, had sent word that Major Cobb—'not the red-headed one'—had been taken in by two elderly women in the town and nursed. 'And you can thank God for that,' a fellow officer wrote, 'because if he had fallen into one of our hospitals or into a Yankee prison camp, he'd be dead.'

Perhaps he was dead. Perhaps her son Reverdy was dead, too. Perhaps the Yankees would invade Texas and set the plantations aflame, as they were doing in other parts of the Confederacy. The possibilities for disaster were so overwhelming that she could not face them, and her health, never good, began to deteriorate badly. As the heat of summer increased she found difficulty in breathing, and on one extremely hot afternoon she felt she must apologize to her energetic cousin: 'Petty Prue, I am not malingering. I want to help but I'm truly sick, and I'm frightened.'

'Stay in bed, Lissa. I'll manage.'

Prue could not have done it alone, but like many women all over Texas who had to manage large holdings while their men were absent, she learned that she could rely on her slaves, especially Jaxifer from Georgia and Trajan from Edisto. With no white master to berate him, and sometimes beat him, Jaxifer assumed a more important role, issuing orders to other slaves and seeing that they were carried out. It was he who kept a small herd of cattle hidden in the brakes, away from government agents who would have impressed them for military use. Occasionally he would butcher one of the precious steers in the dark of night and mysteriously appear in the morning with small portions of beef for all: 'We got meat.'

Trajan was even more ingenious. He found the honey trees which provided a substitute for sugar. He tracked down a bear now and then, knowing that when smoked, this made bacon almost as tasty as a hog's, but when he first placed it on the table, Millicent whispered: 'One can hardly eat this without salt.' Trajan heard, and although store salt was absolutely unobtainable, he had the clever idea of digging up the soil where meat had been cured in peacetime and boiling it until salt could be skimmed off. It was dirty, but it was good.

His major contribution to Petty Prue was the substitute he devised for coffee: 'Now, this here is parched corn and this is charred okra, you mix them just right, you got . . .'

'It tastes . . . well . . .'

'Well, it ain't coffee, and it don't taste like coffee, but it looks like it.'

Often during that dreadful July, Petty Prue wondered why her slaves did not run away, for with no master to check them they could have, but they stayed, without restraint, to keep the two plantations running. 'It's because,' Prue explained to her neighbors, 'they're happy here. They like being slaves when the master is kind.'

In whispers, when she attended church on Sunday, she asked the older people: 'Do you think the slaves know what Mr. Lincoln's done?' The white folk were aware that on the first day of January 1863 he had tried to put into effect his Emancipation Proclamation freeing slaves, and by the most rigid controls the whites in remote areas like Jefferson prevented this news from reaching their slaves, so that men like Jaxifer and Trajan worked on, legally free but actually still slaves.

'Tell them nothin'!' Petty Prue warned Millicent and the two Cobb daughters, and when an elderly white man from the village came to visit and refresh himself with the good food raised at Lammermoor, he gave them reason to keep silent.

'Emancipation Proclamation! Rubbish. The most cynical thing that evil man in the White House ever did.'

"Some day the slaves will have to be freed,' Millicent protested.

'Many would agree with you,' the old man said. 'Economically?' He shrugged his shoulders. 'That young fellow who stayed with you—Carmody, who wrote the book about us. He made some points. But the slaves will never be freed the way Lincoln said.'

'What did the gangling fool say?' Petty Prue asked, for she was willing to believe anything bad about Lincoln, author of so many tragedies.

'It isn't what he said. It's what he didn't say.'

'Tell me, please.'

'Duplicity. Total duplicity. He has freed the slaves in all those parts of the former Union over which he now has no control. And he has not freed them in the areas which he does control.'

'I can't believe it,' Prue snapped.

'You better. Your slaves here in Texas—where his words don't mean a damn, thank God—are freed. So are they in Carolina and Georgia, and the rest of the Confederacy. But in Maryland, and Kentucky, and Tennessee and even in Louisiana, where the Federals control, they are not freed, because Good Honest Abe does not want to irritate his Northern allies, God damn their souls.'

The four Cobb women had a difficult time digesting this immoral Northern charade, but the old man made it simple: 'Where he can, he won't. And where he can't, he does. Some patriot with good sense ought to shoot him.'

The owners of plantations had extra reason for caution, because once the slaves learned that they were free, they would surely desert and the cotton would rot in the fields. But by extreme caution they continued to keep news of emancipation, fraudulent though it might be, from their slaves, and it was well known that anyone who divulged the information, or even hinted at it, would be hanged.

But now the problem arose as to what to do with this new crop of cotton which could no longer be sent to New Orleans, and Petty Prue, as the one who had to make decisions, pondered this for a long time, and the same old man, a furious patriot, came out from Jefferson to counsel with her.

'If I was younger, ma'am, you can be sure I'd be tryin' to sneak this cotton through the blockade to Liverpool. But I'm not young any more, and no woman by herself could do it.'

'What can I do?'

'Keep your voice down,' the old man said conspiratorily as he led her to the gin, 'but this cotton is the lifeblood of the Confederacy. We have no manufacturing, as your book-writing fellow said. And we have few railroads. But by God we have cotton, and the world needs it.' Picking at the edge of a bale, he fingered the precious fiber he had spent his life producing. 'On this wharf it's worth a cent and three-quarters a pound. Aboard ship to Europe, it's worth a dollar-sixty a pound. With Vicksburg gone and Lee thrown back at Gettysburg, we must get it on board some ship somehow.'

'I'll try anything,' Prue said.

The old man looked at the bayou to which boats ought to have been coming, and tears showed in his eyes: 'By water, no hope. Even if you could get it overland to Galveston, the Yankees would still intercept it when you tried to ship.' Then his eyes brightened with the thrill of old challenges: 'But, ma'am, if you could somehow work your bales far inland and then drop down to the safety of Matamoros in Old Mexico, you'd have a market as big as the world.'

'I do not understand,' Prue said, and the old man explained: 'Abe Lincoln's warships keep us bottled up everywhere. Oh, a few blockade runners slip in and out of the Atlantic ports, but not many. They've tied up Texas, too. For a while Brownsville was kept open, but Abe corked that real quick. So what does that leave us? Matamoros, just over the Rio Grande from Brownsville.'

When he told her that sometimes as many as a hundred ships lay off Matamoros, hungry for cotton, she asked: 'Why doesn't Lincoln sink them?' and he cried: 'That's the arrow that we have in our quiver. What one thing could win the war for us tomorrow?' When she said she didn't know, he explained: 'If England and France jump in on our side to ensure safe delivery of cotton. Lincoln doesn't dare antagonize Europe. So he's got to let English and French ships come to Matamoros and load up.'

Petty Prue walked up and down her wharf, studied the accumulating bales, then snapped her fingers: 'I'm taking ours to Matamoros.'

Once the decision was made, she never looked back. With an energy that would have alarmed her husband, who had known her as a little wren of a woman, she worked almost without sleeping, and her enthusiasm ignited the imaginations of her slaves.

'There are two ways we can go,' she said at the beginning of the discussions with Jaxifer and Trajan. 'We can cut west to Waco, where they're assembling shipments, and sell to the government. Lose half our profit. Or we can drop in a straight line down to Matamoros, and sell our bales for maybe eighty cents a pound.'

The two men listened, then Jaxifer asked: 'You goin' wid us?'

'It's my cotton. My responsibility.'

A plan was devised whereby four extra-stout carts would be loaded, each with five bales of five hundred pounds each. If they could deliver the cotton to the Mexican side, it would bring eight thousand dollars, a gamble worth taking. But one night as she concluded the final plans for the bold journey, she had a frightening doubt, and ordering her carriage to be readied, she had Jaxifer drive her to Jefferson, where she asked the old man one question: 'When we get to the Rio Grande, how do we get the bales across to Mexico?' and he said: 'If cotton is so valuable, they'll work out a way.'

'But they say there's no bridge. No ferry could handle all the bales you speak of.'

'If the world needs cotton, they'll find a way.'

'I'll risk it, then.'

The old man grasped Prue's hands: 'I wish I had a daughter like you,' but this farewell was dampened by the agitated arrival of a horseman from Lammermoor: 'Missy, hurry! Miss Lissa, she sick bad.'

The old man insisted upon accompanying Prue to the plantations, and when they reached the kitchen at Lammermoor they found that Millicent had been working there with the slaves, making jelly and preserving fruit in the last moments before she died. Prue, looking at the scene she had shared so often with her cousin, did not weep or cry out. Slowly she slipped to the polished floor, and there she stared at the uneven patterns, for life had become too complex for her to unravel.

The old man proved to be most valuable, not because of anything he did, for he was frail and nearing his own death, but because of the sensible advice he gave and his shrewd analysis of alternatives: 'Of course you could go with your cotton, Miss Prue, but what happens to the plantations if you do? What makes you think Somerset will ever return, if his wound was as bad as they say? With you gone, Jaxifer gone, Trajan gone, crows will tend cotton on this farm.' Patiently he led her to the only sensible conclusion: 'Would to God I could volunteer to manage your place while you go, but I'm too old.' He fought back tears. 'I won't live to see the end of this war. If I did take charge and died while you were gone, chaos, chaos.'

'What must I do?'

'You have two treasures. These valuable bales. These valuable plantations. Surely, the second is more important than the first.'

'But I'm going to protect both,' she said stubbornly.

'The only way, send your cotton south with Trajan and Jaxifer.'

'Can I trust them?'

'What choice have you? You've got to stay here, with that trustworthy slave Big Matthew. And pray for the best.'

Again, once the decision was reached she did not flinch. Inspecting the four wagons, she was satisfied from what Jaxifer told her that they would withstand the load and the six-hundred-mile trip. She watched as the men loaded each wagon, three bales crossways on the bottom, two perched on top, and satisfied herself that each wagon carried heavy grease for the axles, and when all was ready she asked the old man to deliver to each of the four slaves who would be driving the wagons a copy of a letter he had had the local judge prepare:

Jefferson, Marion County, Texas
21 July 1863

To Whom It May Concern:

This will certify that the bearer of this note, the slave known as TRAJAN, is on official duty for the Confederate government, delivering cotton to Matamoros in Mexico and returning home to his plantation, as above. The government will appreciate any consideration and protection you may give him while he is discharging this important assignment.

Henry Applewhite
Judge of the County Court

To travel six hundred miles to the Rio Grande with the heavily laden wagons was a journey of at least two months, for rivers had to be forded and forests negotiated. Also, the route had to be painstakingly deciphered, with rascals on every hand to belay and betray, especially when the men in charge were slaves. But Trajan was resourceful, forty-seven years old and afraid of very little, and with Jaxifer's help he proposed to deliver this cotton to Mexico and earn his mistress a fine penny for doing it.

They had been on the trail about a week when Trajan saw, joining them from the west, a remarkable sight: two wagons, well loaded with bales but without drivers. 'What can this be?' he asked his fellow drivers in Gullah, and they could not guess, so he left his own wagons and started walking toward the mystery, but as he drew close he heard a child's voice crying: 'Don't you come no closer,' and when he looked up he found himself facing a very big gun in the possession of a very small boy. On the second wagon, with his own gun properly pointed, sat an even smaller boy.

'What you doin'?' Trajan asked, indicating that the boys should put up their guns.

'One more step!' the first boy warned, and Trajan realized that he meant it, so he stopped, held out his empty hands, and asked: 'What you doin', boys?' And after a pause in which the first boy looked back to the second, they confessed that they were taking their family's cotton to Galveston.

'Where's your father?'

'Dead at Vicksburg.'

'You got no uncles?'

'They're at war.'

'Your mother?'

'She's workin' the farm.'

'Galveston is not the best—'

'Don't you take a step. They told me people would try . . .'

And then Trajan saw that the two boys were near to exhaustion, for the one in back had begun to cry, at which his older brother shouted: 'Stop that, damnit. We're bein' held up.' But the younger boy could not stop; these days had been too long and cruel, and now to be accosted by a bunch of slaves who intended cutting throats: 'I want to go home.'

'Course you do. So do I.' And something in the way Trajan spoke softened the heart of the boy in front, and now he, too, began to cry.

'Now, you hold on to your guns, boys. But you got to get some rest,' and hardly had he led the two wagons to his four than the two young fellows were sound asleep. Trajan lifted them onto his wagon, and as they slept, the most powerful and confusing emotions swept over him, for the boys were about the age his son had been when he was stolen. Endlessly he had brooded about his lost son, wondering where Hadrian could be, and now he asked himself: Was he as brave as these two youngsters were in defending their bales of cotton?

When the boys at last awakened, aware that they were at the mercy of the strange Negroes, Trajan did his best to comfort them, but whenever he tried to explain why they must not go to Galveston, where the Federal ships prowled trying to steal Confederate cotton, they suspected trickery, so always the slave said: 'All right, all right. We'll go as far as we can together. Then you hie off for Galveston and the enemy.'

The oldest boy, Michael, was eleven, and old enough to think that there might be something most suspicious about Trajan and his three companions, especially Jaxifer, who looked very black and ferocious.

Trajan himself had no clearer view of things, for he knew that in delivering cotton to Matamoros, he was aiding the Confederacy, which was determined to keep him a slave forever, and therefore what he was doing was stupid, but he also knew that through the years he had lived in moderate decency with the Cobbs of Edisto, and that they had not changed for the worse in moving to Texas. He suspected that within his lifetime all slaves would be set free, for he had heard through rumors and the surreptitious teaching of Methodist ministers that there were large parts of the nation where blacks were free and where food and clothing and medicine were just about as available as in Texas.

He had known perhaps a dozen slaves who had tried to escape to Mexico; most had been recaptured quickly with the aid of tracking dogs; others had returned of their own will, unable to cross the great expanse that seemed to encircle the little green paradise at Jefferson; and he had seen both groups savagely whipped for their attempt to escape bondage, but he also knew that a handful had either made it to freedom in Mexico or died in the attempt. He had never felt impelled to run away from the Cobbs, for they were about as decent as the system provided, despite Reuben's hot temper at times, but he did know that if the new masters who might be taking over at Lammermoor proved brutal, he would flee.

Why, then, did not he and the other three plan at that moment to get as close to Mexico as practical, take the money for cotton, and run for freedom? They were restrained because all they knew, all they loved, centered on Lammermoor. In Trajan's case there was another factor: he had been given a responsibility, and as a man of honor he must discharge it.

He was considering these conflicts, answers to which could determine his chance for freedom, when he was faced by a more immediate problem. 'We want to go to Galveston,' Michael said one morning as he and his brother faced the four slaves. 'We think you're kidnapping us and stealing our cotton, and we want our guns back.'

'You have them,' Trajan said. 'You've always had them.'

'Then can we go to Galveston?'

'You're going to Galveston. That's always been understood.'

'Where is it?'

Now Trajan asked the boys to sit with him, and as they perched beside the road, he had to confess: 'I don't know where it is. But the first person we meet on this road, we're goin' to ask.'

The boys could not believe that Trajan was telling the truth, and they wanted desperately to draw apart and discuss the trap into which they had fallen with their mother's cotton, but they were afraid to do so lest the slaves kill them right there. So they were overjoyed when they saw coming at them from the south a group of riders, and they were especially relieved to see that they were white.

But when the riders reined in at the lead wagon, they were far less pleased, for the leader was a terrifying man, very tall, covered with hair, dirty, mean-looking, and topped by a panther pelt which he wore with the tail hanging down the left side of his face. 'Sergeant Komax, Confederate army. On duty with these men to gather all cotton wagons headed for Matamoros and bring them in safely.'

'Which way is Galveston?' Michael asked very politely.

'Don't matter. Ever'body goes to Matamoros. You niggers, what you doin'?'

Very carefully, very politely, Trajan directed Jaxifer to show the paper which the judge had written; he certainly did not propose to show *his* copy lest the soldiers keep it. When Komax had one of his men read the safe-passage to him, he grunted: 'We find a lot of slaves takin' their plantation cotton south. Join up.'

Komax had little trouble convincing Trajan to agree, but when he turned to the two boys he found himself looking into the same cumbersome rifles that had stopped the slave. 'We're goin' to Galveston,' Michael said in his quavering voice, and he was supported by his brother, who cried: 'You come closer, we shoot.'

To Trajan's surprise, the big, hairy man halted immediately and withdrew: 'Do somethin' with them kids!'

'You act as if they's gonna shoot.'

'At their age I'd of shot.'

So once more Trajan had to convince his two charges that going to Galveston was not only impractical but also forbidden. With the gravest foreboding that they might be slain or their cotton taken from them, the boys lowered their guns, but during the rest of this dangerous journey they remained close to Trajan, for Panther Komax terrified them.

By the end of that week three other wagons had fallen in line, and during the week after, four more. The plodding caravan had now passed Victoria and was about to skirt the dangerous port city of Corpus Christi, blockaded by Union ships. By the time Komax was ready to ford the shallow Nueces River, other Confederate scouts had rounded up a dozen or more creaking wagons, and Panther gave stern orders: 'Yonder, the Nueces Strip. We keep together for three reasons. Benito Garza and his bandits might attack. Union troops comin' at us from the sea might attack. And if you fall behind, you will perish for lack of water. Git!'

It was about a hundred and forty miles, in the hottest time of the year. The draft animals sometimes staggered in the blazing heat, and men fared little better, so that even the slaves, who were supposed to be impervious to heat, sweated and groaned. At times there seemed to be not a single living thing on the vast coastal plains, so flat they were, so devoid of pleasant vales and cool streamlets. The drivers wrapped rags across their faces and looked like ghosts gray with dust, but still the dreadful heat assailed them.

Water was rationed, and at the worst of the journey exhausted men and animals simply lay on the ground during the sunlight hours, sweating and jabbing at insects; there was no shade except under the wagons. It seemed stupid to be lying bathed in sweat, but the brief rest enabled the teams to travel through the cooler night. And then the miracle of Texas happened, because wherever in this vast state one traveled, arid and forbidding land finally ended and green pastures appeared. Komax had brought his caravan safely into the valley of the Rio Grande, that fragile paradise where a few industrious farmers were beginning to coax the waters of the river inland to produce the finest fruits and dairy cattle in this part of the world. Rarely were travelers more delighted to find shade and cool water.

At Brownsville the difficulty that Petty Prue had foreseen eventuated. Overland convoys like the one Panther Komax had brought through safely were arriving constantly, and with only one small, overworked ferry available for carrying the bales across the Rio Grande, a swirling confusion developed. Men with the loudest voices and the roughest manners preempted the ferry, and even though Panther was strong in both departments, he had learned that he had little chance of forcing the cotton of these slaves and their two small boys onto that precious craft.

'Why wait?' he said to Trajan. 'You can swim it acrost.'

'Me?'

'Yes,' Panther explained. 'You lug them bales to that river's edge, and then you shoves 'em in and you follow. And you kick your feet like a puppy dog, and pretty soon you're on the other side.'

'Not me!'

'If you don't do it, it ain't gonna get done.' He showed the slaves how to muscle the bales right down to the river, and then he demonstrated how Trajan must jump in after the bale and push it to the far side, but Trajan was terrified.

'Cotton don't float, and Lord knows, I don't float.'

'But it does float. Enough air locked in there, makes it a boat.'

'Water hit cotton, it's ruined.'

'It's packed so tight, water don't penetrate quarter of an inch.' Carefully Panther explained that perfect safety prevailed: 'Cotton floats. You float. Nothin' gets wet but your black hide. You ride back on the empty ferry.'

If Trajan was scared of the water, Jaxifer and the other two were paralyzed, and there seemed no way that the Cobb bales were going to be delivered to the people on the south shore who were eager to pay a fortune to get them. So, cursing all black men in words which ought to have shriveled Trajan's skin but which affected him not at all, for he was not going into that river, Panther shed most of his clothes until he stood a forbidding, hairy ape at the side of the Rio Grande. Instructing the slaves how to get the heavy bale into the water, he swore and plunged in after it, but he had taken only the first few kicks when off to his right he heard a boyish shout: 'It's easy!' and Michael was steering across the first of the many bales he would manage that day.

Swearing a new set of oaths, Komax crawled out of the water, grabbed Trajan by the neck, and thundered: 'If he can do it, you can.' And Trajan, trembling like an aspen, edged into the water, kicked, and found that it would require fifty strong men to sink that bale of air-filled cotton.

On the next trip, even the smaller boy, Clem, swam his bale across, but no one, not even Komax with all his profanity, could get Jaxifer and the other slaves into that river.

Returning on the ferry after each trip, Trajan and the boys got their entire cargo across, and then the slave offered the lads a proposition: 'Clem, you the littlest, you swim over to the other shore and mind our cotton. Jaxifer, you stay here. Michael, you and me is gonna earn a fortune.' And they did. Well practiced now in swimming, they invited cautious owners to shove their bales into the water, where they took charge, maneuvering them to the Mexican shore.

They charged for this service, and so jammed were the supply lines that after several dripping days, they had accumulated quite a few dollars and would have been willing to continue the traffic indefinitely, for as Michael said: 'After you been without water in the Strip, this is fun.'

But now problems of a much different nature confronted them, because they must arrange a deal for their cotton and see that it reached some waiting cargo ship off the Mexican shore, and this threw them into the tremendous chaos of Matamoros, which stood twenty-seven miles inland from the Gulf. More than sixty small sailing craft crowded the river, clinging meticulously to the Mexican half, with each owner screaming: 'I'll carry your bales out to the big ships waiting in the Gulf.' And if one did elect one of these boats, greater confusion followed, for when the open sea was reached, the pilot must turn immediately south and take refuge in Mexican waters, where two hundred ships from all the ports of Europe posted seamen on their decks who bellowed: 'We'll take your cotton to Liverpool.' Off to the north, sometimes less than a hundred yards away, hovered warships of the United States Navy, never leaving American waters but always ready to pounce upon any ship laden with cotton that moved even a foot north of the international line.

Day after painful day the comedy was played out. Cargo ships owned by supposedly loyal Northern merchants in New York sailed blithely to some British or French port—or to any neutral port—where they were instantly issued papers by European powers hungry for cotton. Then, as privileged ships of that nation, they sailed to join the fleet waiting at Matamoros, hoping to acquire a load of cotton. In exchange they would give the Confederates shot and shell, muskets and hardware, cloth and food. If the Confederate government could move its cotton onto a European ship, it could acquire in exchange almost anything it needed.

But how, in this welter of thievery, chicanery and murder, could a slave like Trajan or two boys like Michael and Clem hope to get their bales from Matamoros to the waiting fleet? There was a way. The Confederate government had assigned a clever, manipulative man to Matamoros, and his job was to collect the cotton ferried or swum across the river and move it overland to the improvised Mexican seaport of Bagdad—a line of shacks along an open beach—and there turn it over to an even more ingenious Mexican conniver who saw to it that the bales got aboard ship.

The Confederate was big, jovial Yancey Quimper, dressed in full uniform, ideally qualified as an expediter and willing to pay any graft to accomplish his ends; the Mexican was a dapper man in a bright-red uniform laden with medals known as El Capitán. The two connivers were well matched, with Quimper's military rank as spurious as El Capitán's medals, and together they controlled the movement of cotton to the world markets.

The finances of this sleazy operation were interesting; cost of growing, 7¢ a pound; value on an interior Texas plantation, 1³/4¢; value delivered on the north bank of the Rio Grande, 22¢; on the south bank, 37¢; delivered by General Quimper to Bagdad, 49¢, of which he pocketed 6¢; delivered to a waiting ship by El Capitán, 89¢, of which he pocketed 7¢; placed on the dock at Liverpool, $1.60, of which the shipowner retained a large portion.

Since thousands of pounds were being moved daily, it was obvious that the two expediters were getting rich, but so were many other patriots who managed to escape battle. There could have been unpleasantness over the fact that the captain was stealing a penny more per pound than the general, but Quimper also had a neat plan working whereby he bought for his own account, and not the government's, five or six bales each day if he could force some unfortunate seller to unload them at bottom price. These bales he disposed of through a special, undocumented arrangement with a Russian ship captain.

One praised a man like Major Reuben Cobb for being loyal to his theory of honor, or Sam Houston for being loyal to his theory of government, but it was also possible for a man to be loyal only to himself and to adjust quickly to every whimsical gale which affected his interests. Yancey Quimper saw in the Union effort to strangle the Confederacy a chance to make his fortune; every situation in which decent men exalt noble sentiments is used as a chance to profit by those who look at such sentiments cynically.

One Confederate soldier assigned to help Quimper in his work, a veteran who had fought at Shiloh, summarized it well: 'This is a rich man's war, a poor man's battle.' Quimper, evaluating the same evidence, said: 'When bugles blow, wise men know.'

How had this man of no character and limited talent found himself in so many theaters of the war: at the Kansas preliminaries, at the massacre of the Germans, in charge of the hangings along the Red River, and now supervising operations in the cotton exchange, not to mention months spent tracking down draft evaders hiding in the Big Thicket northeast of Houston? Two reasons: the war was appallingly prolonged, with the nation's best men dying year after hideous year, and this provided time for those left at home to pursue many activities; indeed, a man like Quimper was forced into them. He was in Brownsville because the Confederacy needed him there. Also, when good men like Somerset Cobb and Otto Macnab were engaged in battle, only the dregs were left to manage scandalous operations like those along the Rio Grande.

It was highly improbable that naïve cotton handlers like Trajan and Michael could bring their bales into Quimper's maelstrom and end up with any money at all, but they had one advantage: Panther Komax had grown to love Texas, and this meant that he hated Abe Lincoln and the North, and if he had brought his convoy so far, he was determined to see that his bales, at least, reached their proper destination. More important in the present situation, he had once watched helplessly as Yancey Quimper stole his bootmaker, Juan Hernández, so when he overheard the general trying to pluck off the cotton of his charges, he suddenly leaped from behind a stack of bales, gun drawn and shouting: 'Quimper! You'll take these bales to your Russian captain, and you'll pay nobody, not even yourself.'

Terrified and sweating, with the gun at his belly, Quimper took the boys and their cotton out to Bagdad, waved away El Capitán with the warning 'This is special,' and concluded a deal which gave the amateurs an honest profit. And Komax and the boys watched from the beach as the Russian ship raised sail and started for Europe.

In Brownsville, Komax arranged for their funds to be transferred by a letter of credit on an English bank: 'So they don't steal them from you on the way home.' The boys did not trust this, fearing that Panther would cheat them the way General Quimper had tried to, but Trajan, who had seen letters of credit at the mill, although he could not read them, assured the boys that Komax was telling the truth: 'The money be waitin' for you when you gits home. Gemmuns do bidness this way.'

But now he had his own problem. From his tireless work swimming the bales across the Rio Grande, he had accumulated more than a hundred dollars, and he knew that if he appeared at the plantation with such funds, he would be accused of having stolen them. So he asked Komax if he, Panther, would write him out a statement explaining that the money really was his. 'I cain't write,' Panther said, but he found one of his men who could, and the precious document was executed:

Brownsville, Texas
9 November 1863

To Who It Concerns:

This sertificate pruves the Slave Known as Trajan erned $139.40 by swiming cotton acrost the Ruy Grandee. The money is his, duttifully erned, and I sware to said.

Johnson Carver
Confederate Army

Trajan had been so preoccupied with financial arrangements for himself and the boys that he failed to notice a development in his group. Now Jaxifer came to him, no longer the noisy young clown whom Trajan had met on the approach to Social Circle, but a powerful man, mature and thoughtful: 'Micah, he done gone.'

And Trajan realized that Micah had found the temptation of freedom in Mexico too powerful to resist, and was no doubt already in Monterrey.

This presented difficult choices for the three remaining Lammermoor slaves, who discussed them, using the deepest Gullah. When such slaves used their fragmentary English they came up with constructions which sounded funny, like *He done gone,* but when they spoke in Gullah they had a complete language for the expression of complete thoughts, and there was nothing amusing about it.

'Why should we three go back to slavery?' Jaxifer asked.

'Micah did no wrong,' Trajan replied evasively. 'If he felt he had to be free . . .'

'How about us?'

'There Mexico is, spit across the river. You'll never be closer.'

'If I go, will you try to stop me?' Jaxifer asked, for it was obvious that the third slave, Oliver, would not make the attempt.

Trajan pondered Jaxifer's question a long time, for it cut to the heart of black-white relations, and also to the core of his own behavior: 'A man wants to be free, that's maybe the biggest thing in life. If you feel it in your heart, Jaxifer, go.'

'How about you?'

'Well, now. No man wants freedom more than I do. I lost my son because people knew they could steal from a slave, no trouble. I lost my wife, worked to death.'

'Then join me.'

'No, I want to be free, more than any of you. But freedom is surely coming in Texas.' He hesitated before making a point which for him weighed most heavily: 'Better to work hard for freedom in a good place like Texas than accept it easy in a place not so good like Mexico.' Before Jaxifer could respond, he added: 'At night I say to myself: "Trajan, you built Lammermoor as much as any Cobbs. It's your place too." I do not want to give up a place I built.'

'But up there you'll always be a slave.'

'Not always.'

'Do you believe that?'

'If I didn't, I would cut my throat.'

Jaxifer asked: 'If I cross the river, will you send soldiers after me?'

'Oh, Jaxifer! How can you ask?'

'Then why don't you come with me?'

Again Trajan thought a long time before answering: 'I promised Miss Prue and the old man—I'd get the cotton south, I'd collect the money, and I'd bring it home.'

'But it went home by the bank, you said so.'

'The money's home, yes. But now I have to go. Jefferson is where I belong.'

At the edge of the Rio Grande, Jaxifer stared in silence at his longtime friends Trajan and Oliver. Then, turning his back upon them, he strode to where bales waited and pushed one into the river. Terrified though he was, he plunged in, grasping a corner of the bale with both arms and kicking his feet frantically as the cotton carried him to freedom.

It was chance, an intervention of fate, which led Panther Komax to get his homebound convoy on the road when he did, because in early November, Federal troops launched a determined invasion that captured Brownsville, thus terminating the Matamoros-Bagdad trade. To prove that they meant business, the troops also ranged inland at isolated spots, attacking any southbound convoys and burning the cotton, or bursting the bales and scattering it across the landscape until snow seemed to be falling on the brushy plains.

One evening such a foraging party came upon Komax and his stragglers. Panther shouted to the slaves and the boys: 'Run! Hide!' but when he and his men turned back to fight off the attackers, a sudden fusillade of Union bullets ended his violent life.

Major Somerset Cobb did not return to Lammermoor until after Lee's surrender at Appomattox. Then, his left arm gone, his weight not more than a hundred and twenty, he came up the Red River from the hospital at New Orleans, with the doctor's benediction: 'God must have saved you, Cobb. We did damned little.'

At Shreveport he was pleased to see that the Great Raft was still in place, and his heart expanded and he felt something close to joy when the limping steamer, one boiler gone, edged into Lake Caddo and he saw once more the knobby cypresses and the Spanish moss hanging in lovely festoons from the live oaks that crowded the shore.

As always, the steamer sounded its whistle as it approached Lammermoor, and he saw with fresh pleasure that slaves aboard the craft were preparing to unload at that wharf called the Ace of Hearts. With pulsating enthusiasm he explained to a first-time passenger: 'Our slaves can't read, you know. We mark shipments Spades or Clubs, showing where parcels go. We're Ace of Hearts.'

The little vessel docked and the pain of return took command. He saw fields rotten with weeds, buildings unpainted. But the mill still stood, and here came Trajan, best slave a man ever had. Cobb leaped ashore, his empty left coat sleeve pinned up, and embraced him.

'It's good to be home, Trajan.'

'Been a long war, master.'

Slowly, for Sett was very tired, they walked up the slope toward his house, and now a small, fearfully thin woman came to greet him. It was Petty Prue, much smaller than he remembered, much more worn by the last years of war than he could have imagined.

Reaching for his one hand, she said: 'It was always stupid to have two planta-tions here. I've joined them, Sett.'

She had joined not only the land, but also their lives.

On 23 June 1865 there was great excitement in Jefferson, for a Union captain attended by fourteen soldiers marched in, ordered a bugle to be sounded, and informed the white citizens who assembled: 'I am here to address your former slaves, too. Call them.' Stiffly he waited till the latter were gathered, then signaled for another blast on the bugle. A sergeant shouted 'Silence!' and the fateful words were spoken:

> 'Citizens of Jefferson! On the nineteenth of June instant, General Gordon Granger of the United States Army issued at his headquarters in Galveston General Orders Number Three. All slaves are free. This in-volves an absolute equality between former masters and their slaves. The new connection between white and black is that of employer and hired workman.' (Here he turned specifically to the Negroes.) 'You freedmen are advised to stay at your present homes and work for wages. You are informed, and most strongly, that you will not be allowed to collect at military posts and you will not be supported in idleness. You must find work to do, and it would be best if you continue to work for wages at your present jobs.'

The captain stepped back, pleased with the impression he had made, then signaled his sergeant, who cried: 'Former slaves! You are free!'

There was a rustle, more of confusion than of comment.

'Slaves, you are no longer slaves,' the captain said. 'You are as free as I am or . . .' He looked about for some white person, spotted Cobb, and pointed at him: 'As free as this man.'

An old slave in the front rank fell to his knees, raised his hands over his head, and shouted in a feeble voice: 'I lived to see it. Praise God A'mighty, I lived to see it.'

When the reality of what had been announced struck home, there was no wild outcry, no jubilant dancing in the square, and white men were surprised that the former slaves took word of their freedom with such composure. But there were scenes which epitomized that crucial day in Jefferson history. One black woman, obedient to impulses no one could later explain, grabbed her seven-year-old boy and shook him violently, shouting at him: 'You ain't no more slave. Now will you mind?' And she wept.

Major Cobb had come to the meeting anticipating what might happen, and he moved among his former slaves, assuring them that what the stranger said was true: 'Yes, you're free,' but his attempt at conciliation failed when Big Matthew ran up to him, shook a fist in his face, and shouted: 'Don't work for you no more.' When a laundry woman asked Matthew: 'What I do wid your clothes?' he roared: 'Burn 'em.' And again he shook his fist at Cobb: 'Don't work for you no more. Don't work for your bitch no more.'

Instinctively, Cobb raised his right arm, but a Union soldier prevented any further action.

The meaning of true emancipation—not President Lincoln's false gesture of some years before—was brought home to Lammermoor the next afternoon when amidst the clamor about freedom, Trajan appeared at the mansion, a place he had rarely entered, knocked politely at the door, and asked to see the master. Standing respectfully, he said: 'Major Cobb, you got the plantation under control, I'se leavin'.'

'What?' The statement was like the explosion of a bomb.

'I wants a place of my own. I got no more taste for livin' in slave quarters here at Lammermoor.'

'But you helped build this place. You're part of it.'

'Always I builds for someone else. Now I wants to work for myself.'

Cobb called for his wife, and when Petty Prue heard of the former slave's unexpected announcement, she echoed Sett's reaction: 'Haven't we always treated you decently?'

Trajan would not be sidetracked by any discussion of past conditions. Standing very erect, as he had been taught to do when reporting to a master, he said: 'I come home from Mexico, two years ago, money I earned swimmin' the river.'

When he saw incomprehension on the faces of the Cobbs, he produced the paper signed by Johnson Carver during those days of high adventure with the two boys. And there in the silent room, when he thought of those daring lads, so like his son, he hung his head and the terrible grief of this war and these tangled years overcame him. He could not present his case, and the Cobbs let him go, thinking that emancipation had unsettled him.

Next day Major Cobb and his wife invited their former slave to meet with them, in the same room, and this time they asked him to sit down. 'Trajan, we suppose that with your money . . . And congratulations on having so much. I know many white families who would—'

Petty Prue, suddenly the more masterful of the Cobbs, broke in: 'Don't spend your money on land. You've been so faithful and we appreciate you so profoundly . . .' She choked and seemed not so masterful after all.

'What we propose,' her husband said, 'is to give you five acres of your own. That land against the oak trees.'

Trajan rose: 'All these years I got my eye on a nice strip of land, edge of Jefferson. Last night I bought it.'

'A slave? Buying land?' The words had slipped away from Petty Prue, who was immediately sorry she had said them.

'I bought it. I paid dollars and I'm leavin' this mornin', and your maid, Pansy, wants to go with me.'

'But, Trajan,' Petty Prue cried in real confusion. 'You were so wonderful, helping me. Taking that cotton down to Mexico and coming back home.' She looked at him in near-despair: 'We thought you liked it here.'

Trajan moved to the door, determined not to be swayed by any argument these good people might advance. With tall dignity he told them: 'You can say I was faithful, because I was. And you can say I come back when I could of run away, because I did. And you can say I was respectful, because I liked the way you handled this plantation with the men gone, Miss Prue. I tried to be a good slave, but don't never say I liked it.' And he was gone.

Not long after, Major Cobb and his new bride entered their carriage, old now and needing refurbishing, and rode in to Jefferson, where on the edge of town they found the small cottage for which their former slave Trajan had paid twenty-two dollars and fifty cents, including an acre of land. The spring flowers were fading, but the Cobbs could see where the summer beauties would soon be peeking out.

'We've come to make you a proposition, Trajan.'

'I been expectin' you.'

'How so?' Petty Prue asked, accepting the chair her former maid Pansy offered. The others would stand, for there was only the one.

'Because you need me. You goin' to need me bad, to run your gin, your mills.'

'You're right,' Cobb said. 'We do need you.'

'We miss you,' Petty Prue said, 'and we trust you.'

'What I'd be willing to do,' Cobb said enthusiastically, 'is buy this house from you. Give you the land I spoke of, and you could—'

'This is my house,' Trajan said. 'Pansy and I, we live here. You want us to work for you, we walk to work. But when work's over, we come back here.' He said this so forcefully that the Cobbs were stunned; they could not imagine that a black man would surrender such an obvious financial advantage in defense of a principle.

There was silence, broken by a practical suggestion from the major: 'We'll give you a mule so that you can ride to the mill.'

'I would like that,' Trajan said. Then he added a suggestion of his own: 'To run the mill right, we ought to have Big Matthew back.'

Cobb noticed Trajan's use of *we,* as if he were once more in charge of things, but the suggestion that Big Matthew be forgiven for his intemperate behavior was too much. 'No,' Cobb said gravely. 'Matthew tried to strike me, and that I cannot forgive.'

'Don't you think he got a lot to forgive?'

Cobb studied this sensible question for some moments, then asked: 'Will he work?'

'He ain't been workin' and he ain't been eatin'. Big Matthew, he ain't dumb.'

When Cobb reluctantly agreed to hire the big man, Trajan brought forth a most unexpected request: 'Major Cobb, Miss Prue, I knowed you would be comin' and I knowed what you was goin' to propose this mornin'. And I knowed I would accept, because I loves Lammermoor. But I had to jump the gun a little.'

'You borrowed money?'

'No!' He broke into an easy laugh. 'Smart man like me don't throw money around. I still got all but what I paid for the land.'

'What then?'

'Union officers been houndin' us. In a nice way, but they say all us former slaves got to take last names. They come to me yesterday, very forceful. This is the one they give me'—he hesitated—'at my suggestion, if you ain't mad?'

He presented the Cobbs with a card bearing his new name: TRAJAN COBB, and Petty Prue said: 'We welcome you to freedom.'

. . . TASK FORCE

The *Washington Insider* almost wrecked our two-day May meeting in which we were to discuss the effect on Texas history of Southern immigration from states like Georgia and Alabama. Three days prior to our session the magazine revealed in a long think-piece the secret deliberations of a committee that had been assigned the task of selecting a new director of the Smithsonian Institution. The names of the four finalists were disclosed not in alphabetical order but according to their position in the betting, and the committee was astonished to find my name given last but with the notation 'May be the dark horse. Apparent favorite of the board's intellectuals.'

Before we could open our meeting in Dallas, a pulsating city whose vitality excited me, members of the press wanted to interview me, and when they were through, our own committee took over.

'It's a big job,' I said, but immediately I corrected my phrasing: 'Make that "It would be a big job . . . for whoever gets it." '

'What are your chances?' Rusk asked, cutting as usual to the crucial question.

'You saw the story. Last in line but still fighting.'

'Do you want it?'

'Anyone like me would want it, Ransom. Best job of its kind in the nation. But my chances—'

He cut me off, asked for a phone, and within eight minutes had spoken to his Texas friends serving in Congress, telling them, not asking, to get on the ball and see that I got the appointment. He put in a special call to Jim Wright, the representative from Fort Worth, majority whip in the House, asking him for special help.

Much of our first day was wasted in aimless discussion about the possibility of my going to Washington, but the situation was placed in its proper perspective by the arrival in the late afternoon of a senior editor from the *Insider*, who asked to have cocktails with us and who divulged in the course of our chatting the actual situation: 'I hate to say this, Barlow, but I have reason to believe that the selection committee threw your name in the hopper only to avoid the charge of parochialism. Most of the leading candidates were from the Northern and California establishments and they wanted the news stories to carry at least one Southern or Western name, and you covered both Texas and Colorado. To provide a respectable balance.'

'Wait a minute!' Rusk protested with that automatic defense of Texas which made men like him so abrasive. 'You don't use a Texan for window dressing. Damnit, we'll soon be the most powerful state in the Union—'

'But the University of Texas! A national committee would never—'

Now Quimper broke in to defend the school on whose board of regents he sat: 'Our university takes a back seat to no one.'

'In academic circles it does. That miserable show you people put on some years back, that regent Quimper going around firing everyone he didn't like.'

'That was my father,' Quimper exploded, 'and you're right. Some people condemned him as a meddler. Those who knew him considered him a genius. At any rate, Texas now has two first-class public institutions.'

'Which two?' the visitor asked, and I was astonished by Quimper's answer: 'Texas and A&M.' Often at our meetings he had joked about the latter school, denigrating it horribly, but now he was defending it; the difference was that when he joked, he was doing so to fellow Texans; when an outsider presumed to criticize, he became defensive.

'They're decent schools,' the Washington man conceded. 'Of the second category.'

'What the hell are you sayin',' Quimper asked, his face growing red and his pronunciation more Texan. 'The university has Stephen Weinberg, Nobel winner, and A&M has just signed up the great Norman Borlaug, also a Nobel winner for his work on grains.'

'Yes,' our visitor concluded, 'but you hire them long after they've done their best work elsewhere. It's doubtful you'll ever produce a Nobel winner of your own.'

'You Washington know-it-alls make me puke,' Quimper said, retiring from the conversation. But the rest of us accepted the challenge, and in a series of short, impassioned statements we defended the intellectual honor of our state.

Miss Cobb was most effective: 'You must remember, young man, that power is flowing into Texas at an astonishing rate. More congressmen with every census. More industry. More of whatever it is that makes America tick. You unfortunate people in the North will be spending the rest of your lives dancing to a Texas tune. You should accustom yourselves to it.'

'There are rules of quality which cannot be evaded,' the editor, a graduate of Amherst and Yale, said. 'Texas will have the raw power, yes, but never the intellectual leadership. You'll always have to depend on the areas and the schools with higher standards.'

'That's the sheerest nonsense I've heard in a long time,' Rusk grumbled. 'In the fields that matter these days, Texas is already preeminent . . . and we'll stay that way.'

'What fields?' the Washington man asked, and Rusk ticked them off: 'Petroleum, aviation, silicon chips, population growth.'

'When your oil wells dry up,' the editor said, 'you become another Arizona. Colorful, but of little relative significance.'

Rusk leaned back and looked at the young expert: 'Son, of a hundred units of oil in the ground in 1900—take any well, any field you want—how much do you suppose we've been able to pump out so far? Go ahead, guess, if you're the last word on petroleum.'

'What? Seventy percent taken out, thirty percent still underground?'

'We've taken out twenty percent. The limitations of present techniques prevent us from taking any more. So eighty percent of Texas oil, and that's a monstrous reservoir, is still hiding down there, waiting for some genius to invent a better pump, a better system of bringing it up to where we need it. And you can be sure we'll invent some way of doing just that.'

Now Quimper snapped back: 'And the man who figures it out is gonna get his own Nobel Prize.'

Since the discussion had centered on me originally, I felt obligated to make a contribution: 'I wanted the Smithsonian job. Anyone would. To shepherd the material record of the nation. But in a way, these two men are right. That's a museum job. The past. The great struggles of the future are going to be fought out here in Texas. Even more than in California.'

The young man had excited our minds so thoroughly that Rusk suggested: 'Some of the things you say make a lot of sense. Have dinner with us.'

During the meal the visitor made two points which kept the pot of agitation bubbling: 'Texas will accrue power, that's obvious, but two deficiencies will hold you back. Because you produce no national newspaper like the *New York Times* or the *Washington Post,* you'll not command serious intellectual attention. *Newsweek* losing its Texas editor, that hurts the opportunities of other Texans like Barlow enormously.'

Before either Rusk or Quimper could leap to defend the young man who had left *Newsweek*, the editor made a humorous evaluation which ignited the basic fires of patriotism: 'And because your diet is so very heavy and unimaginative, you'll lose ground to California, which eats so sensibly.'

This was too much for Quimper: 'A good chicken-fried steak smothered in white gravy, or a big slab of barbecue with baked beans and potato salad, that's man's food. That keeps the blood circulatin'.'

'And the cholesterol raging.'

'I wouldn't be surprised,' Quimper said, 'if quiche and endive salad don't destroy California, grantin' it's still there after the earthquake hits.'

As the night wore on, Professor Garza asked seriously: 'So what are the chances that our boy will land the Smithsonian job?' and our visitor said: 'Nonexistent. They'll have to have someone with more prestige, and from a more acceptable locale, but even listing Barlow was a vote of confidence. Twenty more years, if things progress as Miss Cobb suggests, someone from Texas will be acceptable.'

'At that point,' Rusk said firmly, 'we'll be sending our young people to see Washington and New York the way we send them now to see Antwerp and Milan. Interesting historical echoes but no longer in the mainstream.'

When we convened in the morning we found that our staff had provided us with a professor from Texas Christian University, who offered a genteel antidote to the heated argument of the night before: 'I must warn you right at the start that I'm a Georgia woman who did her graduate work at South Carolina, so I'm imbued with things Southern, and the more deeply I dig into our past, the more respect I feel for Southern tradition. So please bear with me as I parade my prejudices.'

She delivered one of those papers that flowed along amiably, making subtle points whose veracity became self-evident as she marshaled her data; if the *Insider* man had dealt with the turbulent future, she led us seductively into a gallant past: 'When I was a student, Southern professors made it a point to avoid what they called "that unfortunate phrase *the Civil War*." They claimed it was never a civil war. They said that implied that in a state like Virginia, half the families sided with the North and took arms to defend that cause, while the other half favored the South and fought for it, with blood from two members of a given family mingling as it ran down some country lane in Virginia. They argued that that did not happen, not even in fractured states like Maryland, Kentucky and Missouri. "No," they said with great emotion, "this was a war between states, Massachusetts versus Alabama. And when those Missourians who did favor the North fought their fellow Missourians who sided with the South, they did so at outside places like Vicksburg and Shiloh, never in Missouri itself." For them it was a war between sovereign states, and in our papers we had to refer to it as such. But now, for historians South and North, it's the Civil War.'

Having instructed us on that important point, she proceeded to the heart of her statement: 'While I find it impossible to describe Texas as a true Southern state, I do not ignore the profound influence that Southern mores have exerted. In 18 and 36, Texas had principally a Northern cast, as installed by people from Connecticut and Ohio who had laid over in Kentucky and Tennessee. But within the next twenty-five years, say to 18 and 61, the influence of the South became overwhelming.'

'The vote on secession,' interrupted Rusk, who was always surprising us with his command of relevant data, 'was more than three-to-one—forty-six thousand to fourteen thousand—in favor of quitting the Union and fighting on the side of the South.'

'Far more important was the cultural domination. The few Texas children who had schoolteachers tended to have Southern ones. Children able to go away to college often went to Southern ones. Books by Southern authors were purchased from Southern stores. Southern newspapers were read.'

Turning to Garza, she said: 'You won't like this, Professor, but recent studies are beginning to suggest that the Texas cowboy derived not primarily from Mexican prototypes, but from the habits of drovers coming in from the Southern states.'

She cited a score of challenging statistics and illustrations showing that the impact of the South on Texas custom was pervasive, but as so often happens in such discussion, three of her almost trivial observations aroused far more interest than those of a graver nature: 'Food! Here the traditions of the South dominated. The Texan's love of okra, for example. One of the world's great vegetables, not native to Texas and unknown in states to the north, but a staple in the South. One could claim that the finest contribution we made to Texas life was the introduction of okra.

'Corn bread the same. Iced tea, which is practically the national drink of Texas, especially with a touch of mint or lemon. And I'm particularly fond, as many Texans are, of dirty rice.'

'What's that?' Garza asked, and the lecturer looked at him as if he were deprived: 'You don't know that gorgeous dish? Rice steamed in bouillon, with chicken giblets and chopped onions and pepper? Professor Garza, you ain't lived!'

Her second point was more serious: 'The most lasting influence may have been the language. The famed Texas drawl is nothing but the Deep South lingo moved west. You never say *business*. It's *bidniss*. And I am very partial to the dropping of the *s* in words like *isn't* and *wasn't*: "Iddn't today glorious and wuddn't yesterday a bore?"''

It was her third assertion which generated most comment: 'I sometimes think that the major importation from the South was a sense of chivalry—a dreamlike attitude toward women. The men coming west really had read their Walter Scott. They did see themselves as avatars of the heroic age. They lived on the qui vive, always ready for a duel if their honor was in any way impugned. They had exaggerated interpretations of loyalty, and were ready to lay down their lives in obedience to those beliefs. Passionately devoted to freedom, they sacrified all to preserve it. And like champions of old, they were not afraid to defend losing causes.

'Texas today is Carolina of yesterday, and in no aspect of life is this more apparent than in your attitude toward women. You cherished us, honored us, protected us, but you also wanted us to stay to hell in our place. In no state of the Union does a woman enjoy a higher social status than in Texas. She is really revered. But in few states does she enjoy more limited freedoms. If I were, and God should be so generous, nineteen years old, with an eighteen-inch waist, flawless skin and flashing green eyes, I'd rather live in Texas than anywhere else, because I would be appreciated. But if I were the way I actually was at that age, thirty-one-inch waist, rather soggy complexion and an I.Q. hovering near a hundred and sixty, Texas would not be my chosen residence.'

Quimper took vigorous exception to this: 'No state in the world pays greater deference to women than Texas.'

Our speaker proceeded: 'Texas has its own peculiar set of laws, and they stem directly from the tenets of Southern chivalry. But this also has its drawbacks. Because Texans prize freedom so highly, they refuse to burden themselves with the obligations which other less wealthy states have assumed. In public education, very tardy in establishing schools, very niggardly in paying for them. In public services, except roads, among the least generous in the nation. In health services, care for children, care for the aged, provisions for prisoners, always near the bottom.'

This was too much for Rusk and Quimper, who battled to see who would refute her first; Rusk won: 'But does not Texas stand, when all's considered, as one of the best states in the Union?' and she said: 'Unquestionably.'

Then Quimper asked: 'Wouldn't you rather be working in Texas than in Carolina?' and again she said: 'Of course.'

'Then what's this beef against chivalry? I'm proud of the way I treat women,' and she said: 'Chivalry is a man's determination of how he should treat women. It's his definition, not hers. I would like to see a somewhat juster determination of the relationship.'

'You ain't gonna like it when you get it,' Quimper warned. 'I got me a dear little daughter, comin' on sixteen. I would like nothin' better for her than to build a good life here in Texas. Maybe a cheerleader at the university. Find herself a good man, maybe a rancher or an oilman out on the firin' line. Ma'am, that's true chivalry. That's Texas.'

'I'm willing to grant that,' the speaker said, 'but I'm trying to make two points.

One, the values you've just defended are essentially Southern. Two, it's easier to maintain them, Mr. Quimper, if you have nine ranches and nineteen oil wells.'

Il Magnifico startled our visitor by swinging the conversation around to where we had started the night before: 'Did you know, Dr. Frobisher, that our boy here, Travis Barlow, is bein' denied a major job up North because he's Texas? Because he ain't from Harvard or Chicago?'

'I find that difficult to believe.'

'It's true. It's what we Texans have to fight against. And much of the stigma comes from the fact that like you said, we adopted all those Southern rules and customs.'

'I suppose that's right,' she said. 'I sometimes see the next fifty years as a protracted effort by the South to reestablish its leadership of the nation. We Carolinians and Virginians aren't powerful enough to do it by ourselves. So we're going to use Texas as our stalking horse. With your strength, your duplicity, we have a chance of winning.'

'Ma'am,' Quimper said, 'you've made a heap of sense this mornin'. You did us great honor in comin' here to share your views with us.' He was growing more Southern by the minute.

'I'll tell you something,' she said to all of us as she gathered her papers. 'I stay here at TCU because I love Texas. I've been invited back to four different schools in Carolina and Georgia. Sometimes I long for that easier life, that civilized custom, but I stay here for one good reason. I want to be where the action is. I love the skyline of Fort Worth . . . the noise, the vitality, the wheeling and dealing, the expensive shops, the good restaurants.'

Rusk interrupted this song of praise with a blunt question which any of us might have asked: 'Are you classifying Texas as a Southern state?'

'Definitely not. It has none of the basic characteristics of Mississippi or Virginia.'

'It's Southwestern?'

'No. It lacks the qualities of Arizona and New Mexico.'

'What is it, then?'

'Unique.' Jamming her papers into her briefcase, she smiled: 'When you reach the age of forty-seven, if you have any brains, you awaken to the fact that the race is going to be over much sooner than you thought. So if I have only one life to live, only one dent to make, I want to make it where it counts, in Texas.'

X
THE FORT

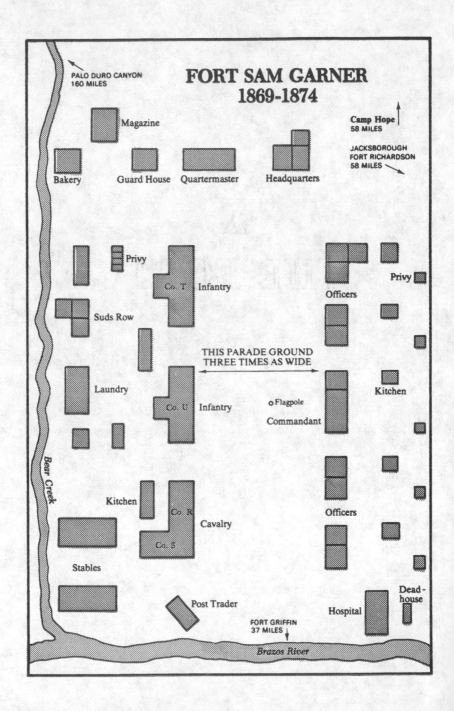

FORT SAM GARNER
1869-1874

PALO DURO CANYON
160 MILES

Camp Hope
58 MILES

JACKSBOROUGH
FORT RICHARDSON
58 MILES

Magazine

Bakery

Guard House

Quartermaster

Headquarters

Privy

Co. T

Infantry

Officers

Privy

Suds Row

THIS PARADE GROUND
THREE TIMES AS WIDE

Laundry

Co. U

Infantry

o Flagpole

Commandant

Kitchen

Bear Creek

Kitchen

Co. R

Cavalry

Officers

Co. S

Stables

Post Trader

Hospital

Dead-
house

FORT GRIFFIN
37 MILES

Brazos River

WHEN ULYSSES GRANT, ONE OF THE BLOODIEST GENERALS IN UNITED STATES history, assumed the presidency in 1869, his fellow officers serving in the West were jubilant: 'Now we can settle with the Indians once and for all!' and they made preparations to do so.

To their astonishment, Grant initiated a thoughtful, humane and revolutionary Peace Policy, which he believed would lure the warring Indians into some kind of harmonious relationship with the white settlers who were increasingly invading their plains. His proposal had several major aspects: instead of allowing the army to govern Indian affairs, the churches of America would be invited to nominate from their congregations men of good will who would move west to the reservations, where they would be in control. Their task would be to win Indian allegiance by kindness, by distributing free food and by setting an example of Christian brotherhood. Funds would be provided from the national treasury to support the new plans. In return, all Indians would be expected to live peacefully on reservations, where they would be taught agriculture and where their children would attend schools that would Christianize them and teach them to wear respectable clothes instead of deerskin and feathers.

When Captain Hermann Wetzel, a veteran of both the Prussian army and the Civil War, and now serving with the 14th Infantry on occupation duty in Texas, read the new orders he threw them on the table: 'The General Grant I knew never signed such garbage,' an opinion shared by most of the army, which saw its freedom to act diminished and its prerogatives shaved. Like Wetzel, many officers were determined to sabotage what they considered General Grant's misguided order.

The religious group most eager to supply civilian personnel for the new system was the one whose principles were most antithetical to army methods, the Quakers of Pennsylvania, one of whose major tenets was pacifism; in this Indian challenge they saw an opportunity to prove that friendly persuasion produced better results than military force. Indeed, they called themselves Friends and their church the Society of Friends. They were a small group, concentrated mainly in Pennsylvania and New Jersey, but they had gained notoriety throughout the South for their vigorous opposition to slavery. Loyal Texans like Reuben Cobb and Yancey Quimper had characterized the Quakers as 'damned fools and troublemakers,' a view generally held throughout the state, for those who had fought against the Indians, especially against the Apache and Comanche, could not imagine how the peace-loving Quakers intended handling them: 'It's gonna be a shambles when Comanche like Chief Matark go up against them Bible pushers.'

One of the first men to be considered for this challenging task was a young farmer from the tiny village of Buckingham in Bucks County, Pennsylvania. His place of residence reminded people of George Fox, the founder of Quakerism, who had had powerful associations with Buckinghamshire in England. 'Earnshaw's a fine Quaker,' they said of him, so when the letter from President Grant arrived, asking the local Quakers to nominate men qualified for this critical new assignment, the elders naturally thought of Earnshaw Rusk, twenty-seven years old and unmarried: 'It's as if he were designated by God to carry on the good works of our founder, the saintly Fox.' Without alerting Rusk, they sent his name forward.

Rusk gave the impression of being saintly, for he was tall, very thin, diffident in manner and rumpled in appearance, with the detached behavior of some minor Old Testament holy man. Even as a young boy he had seemed gawky and apart, his trousers ending eight inches above his shoetops, his sleeves, seven inches from his wrists. His piety evidenced itself before he was nineteen, when in Meeting he was constrained to lecture his elders about what was proper in human behavior; and at twenty he ventured behind Confederate lines in Virginia and North Carolina, seeking to arouse the slaves in those states to demand their freedom. His innocence had protected him, for he had bumbled into three or four really perilous situations, only to find miraculous rescue. Once, south of Richmond, a black family whose members thought him quite irresponsible had hidden him in a cotton gin when a posse came searching for him, and in North Carolina a woman who owned slaves lied to the searchers about to arrest him, then told him when they were gone: 'Go home, young man. You're making a fool of yourself.'

But in the summer of 1865, when everything he had preached had come to pass, he returned to those slaves who had saved his life and to the good woman in Carolina, bringing them food and money contributed by the Philadelphia Quakers, and he had prayed with both the blacks and the whites, assuring them that God had ordained that they save him in 1862 so that he could return now to help them get started in a better life. The Carolina woman, whose farm had been burned by Sherman's rioting men, warned him once more that he was making a fool of himself, but after he had stayed with her for three weeks, helping to clear away the ruins and make space for a new home, she concluded: 'Rusk, you're a living saint, but you're not long for this world.'

The officials appointed by President Grant to receive nominations for the new posts were delighted to hear of a man who seemed to fill every requirement: 'He's vigorous. He has no wife to cause complications and expense. And he will love the Indians as he loved the slaves.'

There was a dissenting vote, for an older man who had made his living in

Philadelphia commerce, a harsh testing ground, feared that anyone as naïve as the recommendations showed Earnshaw Rusk to be was bound to have trouble translating his piety into positive action: 'I'm afraid that if we throw this young fellow into a place like Texas, they'll eat him alive.'

'He won't be going to Texas,' a member of the committee explained. 'He's ticketed for a location in the Indian Territory,' but the other man warned: 'That's pretty close to Texas.'

The committee, eager to announce its first appointment, overrode the businessman's objection and informed President Grant that 'Earnshaw Rusk, well-respected Quaker farmer of Buckingham, Pennsylvania, unmarried and in good health, is recommended for the position of United States Indian Agent at Camp Hope on the north bank of the Red River in the Indian Territory.' Grant, also quite eager to get his program started, accepted the recommendation: 'We've found the perfect man to tame the Comanche.'

Earnshaw was plowing his fields when a local newspaperman came running to him: 'Rusk! President Grant has appointed you to a major position in the government!' Unprepared for such news, Earnshaw asked to see verification, then stood, with the telegram in his left hand, reins in his right, and looked to heaven: 'Thee has chosen me for a noble task. Help me to discharge it according to Thy will.' But the reporter broke in: 'Says in the telegram that General Grant did the choosing.'

When confirmation reached Buckingham, Rusk felt inspired to address his final First Day Meeting:

> 'I must demonstrate to the army and to the nation as a whole that our policy of peace and understanding brotherhood is God's elected way for bringing the savage Indian into productive partnership. I deem it my duty to work among the Indians as I worked among the slaves, and I am satisfied the results will be the same.
>
> 'If William Penn could bring peace to his Indians, I feel certain I can do the same with the Apache and the Comanche. I seek your prayers.'

A cynical Quaker businessman who had traveled in Texas whispered to the man next to him: 'William Penn would have lasted ten minutes with the Comanche.'

As Rusk spoke his hopeful words in eastern Pennsylvania, the rambling family of Joshua Larkin was preparing to establish rude quarters on a site Larkin had scouted about sixty miles west of the newly established town of Jacksborough, Texas. Army officials stationed at nearby Fort Richardson warned the Larkins as they arrived that they ran serious risks if they ventured so far west, and Captain

George Reed, a gloomy man, was downright rude: 'Damnit, Larkin, if you stick your neck way out there, how can we protect you?'

'Six times in Texas we've moved west, always to better land. And six times we heard the same warning. The Waco will get you. The Kiowa will get you. And now you're sayin' "The Comanche'll get you." ' Larkin, whose lined face seemed a map of the frontier lands he had conquered, poked Reed in the arm: 'We ain't never been as afraid as the army.'

'And you ain't never battled the Indians, the way the army has,' Reed snapped, imitating Larkin's raspy whine.

'That's because we're smarter'n the Indians, and you ain't.'

'You're from Alabama, aren't you?'

'Sure am.'

'I learned twenty years ago, you can never teach an Alabama man anything.'

'That's why we conquered the world.'

'Up to a point,' Reed said, indicating his blue military sleeve.

'You had the big factories, the railroads,' Larkin said without rancor as he prepared his wagons for the final push. 'Any time we start even, we'll whip you Yankees easy.'

'Why you so eager to move west?' an older officer asked, and Joshua replied: 'There's two kinds of Americans in this world. Them as looks east and them as looks west.'

'Meaning?'

'East men look for stores and banks and railroads. They have dollars in their eyes. Us west men look for untamed rivers, deep woods, open prairies. In our eyes we have the sunset. And we'll keep goin' till we stand with our feet in the Pacific, lookin' at that sunset.'

'Aren't you afraid of Indians?' the officer asked, and Joshua replied: 'We Larkins been fightin' redskins fifty years. No reason to stop now.' But as soon as he had uttered this boast, he added: 'As for me, I never killed an Indian, never propose to.'

Next morning the sixteen pioneers departed: Joshua; his two married brothers; the three wives; an unmarried brother, Absalom; and nine children of all ages. 'There they go!' a soldier shouted as the wheels began to turn. 'Israelites pouring into the Land of Canaan.'

They would head slightly northwest along almost unbroken trails until they intersected the Brazos River, the aorta of Texas, coming at them from the left. 'And when we go along it a bit we come to Bear Creek, joinin' from the north. Prettiest little creek you ever saw, and where they touch, that's where we'll call home.'

It was a sixty-mile journey, and since experience enabled them to make fifteen miles a day, they planned to reach their new home at the end of the fourth day. Joshua kept his brother Absalom riding ahead as scout, and repeatedly the latter galloped back to assure the wagons that on the next rise they would see wonders, and they did, the great opening plains of West Texas, those endless, rimless horizons of waving grass and sky. Rarely did they see a tree, not too often a real hill, and never growing things on which to subsist.

Through various devices the Larkins had obtained title to about six thousand acres of this vast expanse, at a cost of four cents an acre, and they realized that it was no bargain, but it did have, as Joshua had reported after his scout, four advantages: 'Cattle unlimited, wild horses for the ropin', constant water, an open range for as far as a man can throw his eye.'

There was excitement when Absalom rode back to inform his relatives: 'Brazos River ahead! One more day's travel.' He was correct in his guess, and when the Larkins started their trip along its northern bank they felt as if they were once more safe. When they reached the confluence with Bear Creek they stopped on a small rise and surveyed their promised land: 'Ain't nothin' here but what we're goin' to build. All ours.'

They had brought with them a few domesticated cattle, a string of good horses and six wagons containing a bewildering mixture of whatever goods they had been able to amass: cloth and medicines, nails and hammers plus the lumber on which to use them, spare axles and wheels, a few pots, a few forks and two Bibles.

The Larkins were Baptists, Democrats, veterans of the Confederate army, excellent shots and afraid of nothing. The three wives came from three different religions, Baptist, Methodist, Catholic, but all knew 'The Sacred Harp,' that twangy religious music of the South, and now as they prepared to pitch their tents for the first time at their new home, they united in song. Their nine children joined in, and when the lilting hymn ended, Joshua cried: 'Lord, we made it. The rest is in your hands.'

To the three sod houses they were about to build they brought an arsenal of firearms: Sharps, Colts, Enfields, Hawkens, Springfields, and each child above the age of five was trained in their use. They did not anticipate trouble, since, as Joshua had boasted to Reed, they had edged their way five previous times into lands recently held by Indians and had invariably found ways to neutralize the savages, principally by trading with them, giving them a fair exchange. Of course, when Texas Indian policy had become expulsion or extermination, their bold forebears had helped in the former and applauded the latter. But this generation, probing into a more dangerous section of the state and up against a more dangerous type of Indian, hoped for peace.

They spent two days of hectic action gouging a large sod dugout in which all would sleep at first, and then Joshua turned to the second preoccupation of all Texans: 'The land is ours. The water we got to collect.' And he put all the men and boys, even the tiny lads, to the task of throwing across a gully a rude dam which would impound enough water to form what Alabamans called a pond but Texans a tank. 'With a good tank,' Joshua said, 'we can manage cattle and horses.

But now we got to get ourselves some ready cash,' and he divided his work force into two groups: one to rope wild horses and bring in stray cattle that could be sold in Jacksborough, the other to go out onto the plains with their powerful Sharps rifles to kill buffalo. They would be skinned, with the aid of horses that pulled loose the hairy hides and dragged them back to where they could be baled for shipment to markets in the East. The carcasses, of course, they left to rot.

It was miserable work, and as the buffalo began to withdraw westward, travel to the killing grounds became more onerous, but always Joshua spurred his brothers: 'Get horses. Get cattle. Kill the buffalo.'

His strategy was not accidental, for if the Larkins could assemble horses and cattle, they would possess the basis for a prosperous ranch, and if they could exterminate the buffalo, they would make the plains uninhabitable for the Indians. The Larkin brothers did not want to kill off the Comanche; they wanted to ease them onto reservations north of the Red River, leaving Texas as it was intended to be, freed of Indians.

'Give us three years of peace,' Joshua said at the end of one vigorous stretch, 'and bring soldiers fifty miles west to a new chain of forts, we'll have this land pacified.' He never said that Bear Creek would be their permanent home, for he and one of his brothers had already scouted more than two hundred miles west to where green canyons dug deep in the earth, with plenty of water and even some trees. Given time and persistence, the Larkins were going to own those canyons.

The particular tribe of Comanche led by Chief Matark, a forty-year-old veteran of the plains wars, had for many generations occupied the rolling areas west of Bear Creek, and from this sanctuary, had ranged two hundred miles north into Oklahoma lands and five hundred miles south into Mexico. They had ravaged competing tribes of Indians and plundered white settlements, including El Paso and Saltillo. Whole decades would pass without a major defeat, for under Matark's strategies the Comanche eluded pursuit by the army, avoided pitched battles, and struck whenever a position stood exposed. They were cruel and crafty enemies, well able to defend themselves and remorseless when an isolated ranch seemed unprotected.

In the autumn of 1868 the bold appearance of the Larkin clan at the confluence of Bear Creek and the Brazos troubled Chief Matark so much that he did an unusual thing: he convened a war council; it was unusual because customarily he made all military decisions himself.

'How many are they?'

'Four grown men, all good with the rifle. Three wives who can also shoot. Nine children, some old enough to use guns.'

'How do they dare move onto our land?'

'They expect the fort they call Richardson to protect them.'

'How far are they from the fort?'

'Their huts stand three days' walk to the west.'

'Three days!' the chief cried. 'In that time we could wipe them out.' But then he grew cautious: 'Could they have an arrangement with the soldiers there? Detachments hiding in the gullies? Waiting for us to attack?'

'No soldier has visited the three sod huts. Never.'

'But could there be a secret? Something we can't see?'

'There is no secret. If we strike now, as we should, the army cannot reach us in two days.'

Matark, not wholly satisfied with the reports of his younger braves, sought counsel from two old men who had seen many battles, and the older of the two, a man with no teeth who stayed alive by will power, said: 'It is not the army. It is not how many guns they have in the three sod houses. What will destroy us is the way they kill our buffalo.'

Said the second old man: 'With each moon the animals move farther away.'

'And fewer of them.'

'If they stay at Bear Creek . . .'

'And if more come, as they always do . . .'

'What shall we do?'

'Now, there we face trouble,' the first old man said. 'If we could only pray that the fort at Jacksborough would be the last . . .'

'Always they push the forts closer,' his associate pointed out. 'That's how it always has been. That's how it always will be.'

'Until we are pushed where?' Matark cried in what was for him close to desperation.

The two old men looked at each other, well aware of what must be spoken but each afraid to utter the doleful words. Finally the older spoke: 'We shall be pushed to the sunset death.'

'But not quickly,' Matark said, betraying the tragic strategy he intended following.

'No!' the younger of the two sages cried, happy to hear the courage in his chieftain's voice. 'It will be like the old days, when every hand was raised against us. Kiowa, Apache, Mexican, Texan. We shall strike them all.'

With these fighting words, re-creating the bravery the Comanche had displayed against all enemies, a grand euphoria filled the air and imaginary arrows whistled around the conspirators. The Comanche would strike again. They would strike again and again. They would battle the entire blue-clad army. They would protect their range, they would expel invaders, now and forever.

'We will destroy them!' Matark decreed, and with a mixture of fear and joy the old men ran out to reveal the decision to the braves. They knew that judged by the long years, this strategy must fail, but they also knew that it was a gesture which had to be made. The odds against them were tremendous, for they knew how few in number they were and how powerful that line of Texas forts could be, crammed with blue-clad soldiers. The Comanche could recite the fearful names: Fort Richardson in the north, the new Fort Griffin, Fort McKavett, Fort Concho where the many rivers met, Fort Stockton to the west, Fort Davis, strongest of all beneath the mountains, Fort Bliss at the Rio Grande, and a dozen more.

There were also forts in New Mexico, in Arizona and California, so placed that cavalry troops could strike at Indians from any direction. The old men knew they were doomed, but they also knew that they had no alternative but to defend their rolling plains as they had always defended them. And they were proud that a young chief whom they had helped train was willing to assume the burden. So they moved among the warriors, crying: 'It's to be war!' and they kept their voices strong to mask their fears.

One hundred and nineteen Comanche braves left their camp at the headwaters of the Brazos River and rode in three separate groups, quietly and with sullen determination, toward Bear Creek, and on the morning of the third day, just after dawn on 15 October 1869, they came thundering down upon three sod huts.

Catching Absalom as he tended his horses, they tomahawked him immediately and made off with about half the animals. They then struck the westernmost of the huts before the occupants could organize its defense, and with total superiority, overwhelmed it, killing the wife and her two children but saving the husband for ritual tortures.

With the second house they ran into real trouble, for here Micah Larkin and his wife were ready with a full arsenal, with which they held off the attackers for more than an hour. In the end the defenders were helpless; the Indians rode their horses right up to the walls and fired into the openings. Again, the wife was killed with her child but the man was spared for attention later.

At the somewhat larger home of Joshua Larkin the defense was formidable, with father, mother and two children firing guns with deadly result. Nine Indians died while circling this house, until finally Matark himself had to lead a charge which set fire to the grass roof, forcing the occupants out. When Joshua appeared, he was slain instantly, but the wife was captured alive. Of the six children in the hut, three were killed with tomahawk blows to the head, two were lanced, and the girl Emma Larkin, twelve years old, was taken alive to serve as a plaything for the younger braves.

Because the nature of Indian warfare on the Texas range must be understood if the history of Texas is to be appreciated, it must be recorded that during a span of about thirty years dozens of farmers and ranchers and traders were killed each year by the Indians, an awesome total. But it was the manner in which they were killed that enraged the settlers and made any peace with the Indians impossible.

At Bear Creek, two of the youngest children were grabbed by the heels and bashed against rocks, three were hatcheted and three were lanced. Absalom and a brother were tomahawked in what might have been called fair fight, and two of the wives were also slain in the heat of battle. But even the bodies of these four were sought after the slaughter and ceremoniously mutilated, appendages being cut off and sexual organs defiled in savage and repulsive ways.

It was the four living prisoners, three adults and a young girl, who suffered the real terrors of Indian warfare, because the two men were staked out in the embers of their burned homes, and living coals were edged about them while their extremities were painfully hacked off. Their genitals were amputated, dragged across eyes from which the lids had been cut away, and then stuffed into their mouths. Their eyes were then blinded, and slowly they were roasted to death.

The third wife was saved till last, and even the official reports of the massacre, compiled by Captain Reed from Jacksborough, refrained from spelling out in detail what she had suffered, for it was too horrible for him to write.

> Not one of the fifteen dead bodies was left whole. Heads were cut off. Arms and legs were chopped into pieces. Breasts were severed. Eyes were gouged out. And not even torsos were entire. From the evidence I saw, I must conclude that four adults were burned alive after the most terrible tortures.
>
> I cannot imagine that a chief as wise as Matark is supposed to be can think that by such actions he can frighten away our legitimate settlers or deter our army from retaliation. When I buried the fifteen bodies I stood beside their common grave and took an oath, which I required the men at Fort Richardson to take with me when I returned last night: 'I will hunt down this savage killer, even though he hides at the ends of the earth. These dead shall be revenged, or I shall die in the attempt.'
>
> But after the oath was taken, a soldier who had kept records of settlers passing through reminded us that the Larkin family had consisted of sixteen members, which meant that one must still be alive, and with help of my men who assisted at the burial, we reconstructed the family and concluded that a girl named Emma, about twelve years old, was not among the dead. She must be with them, and with God's help we shall win her back.

As he forwarded his report to Department headquarters in San Antonio, which in turn would send it along to Divisional offices in Chicago, the girl Emma was indeed alive. She was in a camp out toward the canyons, where she had already been raped repeatedly by young braves and where jealous women and sportive young men had begun the slow, playful process of burning off her ears and her nose.

The orders initiated by four-star General William Tecumseh Sherman in Washington for Captain George Reed, Company T, 14th Infantry at Fort Richardson near Jacksborough, Texas, were concise:

> You will proceed immediately to the spot where Bear Creek joins the Brazos and there establish a fort of the type common in Texas and the Indian Territory. You will take with you two companies of the 14th Infantry and two from the 10th Cavalry, plus such supporting cadre as may be required, not to exceed the authorized complement of 12 officers, 58 non-commissioned officers and 220 privates, 8 musicians and 14 auxiliary personnel (total 312). The fort is to be named, with appropriate ceremony, in honor of the Texas Ranger captain who distinguished himself so heroically at Monterrey, Sam Garner. Your mission is to protect American settlers, to establish working relations with the Indian reservation at Camp Hope in the Indian Territory, and to capture and punish Chief Matark of the Comanche if he strays into Texas.

At the end of October 1869, Captain Reed, thirty-three years old, crop-headed, clean-shaven, underweight, and the owner of an unblemished military record, led his contingent west. Symbolic of the condition in which he would find himself during the next three decades of his command, his paper allotment of 312 effectives was 66 short, including a Lieutenant Renfro, whose energetic and conniving wife, Daisy, had succeeded in gaining him a third extension of his temporary desk assignment in Washington. Since the conclusion of the Civil War, Renfro had avoided any frontier duty and seemed on his way to avoiding this stint as well.

Several aspects of Fort Sam Garner were noteworthy. First, it was not a *fort* in the accepted sense of that romantic word, for it boasted no encircling walls and provided no secure defense against an enemy. It was instead a collection of some two dozen buildings laid out neatly on a large expanse of open ground. Second, the buildings were not of stone or brick but of timber, adobe, fieldstone or whatever else might be at hand. Third, even these miserable accommodations were not in existence when the 246 effectives arrived on the scene; the enlisted men would have to erect them in haphazard fashion as time passed. Until then the men would live in tents, and since winter was approaching, the men worked diligently, requiring little urging from their officers, because until houses of some sort were slapped together, they were going to freeze at night, regardless of how much they sweated during the day. Fourth, when General Sherman assigned two companies of the 10th Cavalry to the fort, he knew that he was creating permanent trouble for Captain Reed, because the 10th Cavalry was an all-Negro regiment, which meant it would generate not only the customary animosity which existed between foot and horse soldiers, but also the more serious viciousness stemming from the difference in color.

One aspect of the typical Texas fort in 1869 would have surprised the Northern troops who built it had they known the facts. Their wall-less, adobe, unfortified assembly of buildings resembled strikingly the old presidio which the Spanish military had erected in San Antonio a century and a half earlier. Like sensible men, the Spanish and the American soldiers reacted almost identically to similar geographical and logistical problems.

But the outstanding characteristic of the fort was the nature of its officer cadre, as revealed by the roster:

OFFICER	BORN	WIFE	NATAL STATE	DUTY	PERMANENT OFFICIAL RANK TODAY	TEMPORARY BREVET RANK DURING CIVIL WAR
Reed, George	1836	Louise	Vermont	Co. T, 14th Inf. Fort Commander	Capt.	Brig. Gen.
Minor, Johnny	1839	Nellie	Wisconsin	Co. R, 10th Cav. Senior Cavalry Officer	Capt.	Col.
Wetzel, Hermann	1829	Bertha	German	Co. U, 14th Inf. Senior Infantry Officer	Capt.	Col.
Sanders, Tom	1840	Ruth	Maine	Co. T, 14th Inf. Adjutant	1st Lt.	Capt.
Harrison, Tom	1843		Iowa	Co. S, 10th Cav.	1st Lt.	Lt. Col.
Logan, Jim	1844		Ireland	Co. S, 10th Cav.	2nd Lt.	Major
Masters, Andrew	1845		Illinois	Co. U, 14th Inf.	2nd Lt.	Capt.
Toomey, Elmer	1849		Indiana	Co. R, 10th Cav.	2nd Lt.	
Renfro, Lewis	1838	Daisy	Ohio	Co. S, 10th Cav. Detached duty Washington	1st Lt.	Col.
Jaxifer, John	1827		Georgia	Co. R, 10th Cav. First Sergeant	1st Sgt.	1st Sgt.

One interesting thing to be noted was that none of the officers—and only an occasional black enlisted man—came from the South, because that region had recently been in rebellion, with even its West Point sons like Generals Lee and Davis rejecting their oath to defend the Union: 'You cain't never trust no South-'on, and we won't tolerate 'em in our army.' Of the many forts that would protect Texas in these years, none would be manned by Texans.

The presence of a German and an Irishman at Fort Garner was not unusual; thousands of such volunteers had served in the Union forces, usually with distinc-ion, and not infrequently it was these European veterans who formed the backbone of the frontier army. They were belligerent, sticklers for proper drill, and dependable. In Hermann Wetzel and Jim Logan, Fort Garner had two of the best: the former a Prussian disciplinarian in charge of all foot soldiers; the latter a daring, laughing horseman who worked with the black troops.

It was the last column of the roster that showed the heartache of a peacetime fort, because, as can be seen, all the officers except Lieutenant Toomey had enjoyed, during the Great War, a brevet or temporary rank considerably higher than what they now held. A brevet promotion could have been conferred in one of many ways: a new regiment would be formed, requiring colonels and majors, so officers much lower in rank would be temporarily promoted to meet the emergency, it being understood that when peace came, they would revert to their lower rank. A senior officer would be killed in battle, and a replacement would be breveted. Often in the heat of battle some extremely brave lieutenant would be breveted to colonel, and he would be addressed as colonel and treated like one, but his real rank would remain lieutenant. Now it was peacetime, and military personnel was savagely reduced—1,000,516 men in 1865; 37,313 now—and even the slowest-witted officer could foresee that he was going to remain in his lowered permanent rank for years and years. During the war an able soldier like Reed had almost leaped from second lieutenant to brigadier general, six promotions in heady sequence; he, George Reed, a schoolteacher from Vermont, had actually been a general in charge of a flank attack on Petersburg, and now he was a lowly captain, four demotions downward, with every expectation of remaining indefinitely at that level. During the war the leap from lieutenant to major had required, in his case, five months, for attrition had been great. In peacetime the slow crawl back to major would require at least a quarter of a century, if it was ever attained.

Yet all except young Elmer Toomey could remember when they had been officers of distinguished rank. Johnny Minor had been a full colonel and a good one, but now and for as long as he could see into the future he would be a captain in charge of one company of black troops, and he could not reasonably anticipate higher promotion, not ever. White officers who served with black troops were contaminated, and scorned by their fellow officers; to such men few promotions fell.

However, within the security of these remote forts, it was customary when speaking directly to an officer to award him the highest rank he had held as brevet, so although the adjutant, when reporting in writing to Washington, had to write: 'Captain Reed, Commanding Officer, Fort Garner, wishes to inform . . .' when that same adjutant addressed Reed within the fort he would say: 'General Reed, I wish to report . . .' It was a delicate game, where sensitivities were constantly exposed and where imagined insults rankled for years, and nowhere was it played out with richer variation than on the vast expanses of Texas. Actual duels were forbidden, but they sometimes occurred; what was more likely, some disgruntled first lieutenant who had once been a lieutenant colonel would nurture in secret a grudge against a lieutenant who had been only a brevet major, and on some hate-filled day would find an excuse to bring court-martial charges against him. This then became an affair of honor, dragging on year after year; often each officer would publish a small book giving his *True Account of What Transpired at Richards Crossing,* proving that it was his accuser, not he, who had been craven.

This was Fort Garner in 1869, a collection of makeshift and undistinguished buildings, but each laid out with that compass-point precision which would have prevailed had they been built of marble. Reed had insisted on this, and during the planning he had appeared everywhere with his chalk line, squaring walls and ensuring that buildings of the same character stood in orderly array: 'It may be an unholy mess now, but it won't always be.'

After consultation with Wetzel, who had a keen sense of tactics, he had decided that the fort would be built east of Bear Creek, so that any Indians coming at it from the west would have to attack across that stream or across the Brazos. To safeguard against flooding, he had his men spend two weeks deepening each stream, and then he strengthened the mud dam with which the Larkins had constructed their tank.

Fort Garner would stand fifty-eight miles west of Jacksborough, same distance south of Camp Hope in the Indian Territory. The five officers' buildings, each with detached kitchen and privy, would form the eastern boundary of the long parade ground; the enlisted men's quarters, the western. The northern limit was hemmed in by the service buildings, while the southern was defined by the hospital and the store run by the post sutler.

As if to give protection from the west, where the enemy roamed, the stables were located there as a kind of bulwark, north of which stood one of the curiosities of the western fort, Suds Row, where the hired laundresses, sometimes Mexican, sometimes reformed prostitutes, but most often the wives of enlisted men, washed uniforms six days a week. When the men of Fort Garner were at their home station they were a natty lot, especially the Buffalo Soldiers, as the blacks were called because their knotted hair was supposed to resemble that of the buffalo.

Buffalo Soldier, originally a term of opprobrium, had been adopted by the black cavalrymen as a designation of honor, and one fact about Fort Garner summarized that situation: the effective complement had begun at 246, but because of desertion, conniving to escape difficult duty and slow recruitment it would become only 232; but of the 134 black horsemen assigned to Fort Garner, only two would desert over a period of three years; of the white infantrymen, fourteen had already gone by the end of the first four months. To be a Buffalo Soldier was a sterling attainment. Many of these men had entered Union service in the darkest days of the war and they had served heroically, fighting both the avowed enemy at the South and the insidious one at the North. From the begin-

ning they had known they were not liked and were not wanted, and during peace
this dislike was hammered home in a hundred mean and malicious ways.

For example, the parade ground at Fort Garner had been in operation less than
a week when Wetzel came to Reed with a serious complaint: 'General, when the
troops line up at morning and evening review, the Buffalo Soldiers, as is proper,
stand at the south, before their stables. Could you direct Colonel Minor to keep
his niggers well removed from my men? We cannot tolerate the smell.'

When Reed broached the subject to Minor, the Wisconsin man showed no
animosity, nor did his cavalrymen when he jokingly asked them to muster 'just a
wee bit to the south, so we don't offend anyone.' The cavalrymen knew how
desperately they were appreciated when at the height of some offensive against the
Indians, they appeared at the critical moment to support infantry units pinned
down by Indian fire: 'We was there when you needed us and we'll be there next
time, too.' It was unpleasant, sometimes, being a Buffalo Soldier, but the work
provided moments of great satisfaction, and it was for these that the black troops
drilled so strenuously and served with such resilient humor.

A distinctive component of any frontier fort was the group of wives who managed
to stay with their husbands, often under the most appalling conditions, and Fort
Garner was blessed with two of the finest. The mud huts had scarcely been roofed
over when Louise Reed, the commander's wife, and Bertha Wetzel, wife of the
senior infantry officer, appeared in a cargo wagon which they had commandeered
at Jacksborough. Mrs. Reed brought her ten-year-old daughter, who reveled in the
ride across the plains, and such household gear as she and Mrs. Wetzel could
assemble, not only for their own families but for all the others at the fort.

When the two women drove onto the parade grounds, men cheered, for those
long associated with the four companies were well acquainted with the contributions such energetic wives made to soldiering, and within two days evidences of
improved conditions were seen. Mrs. Reed gave a tea at which the eight officers
and the four wives were present, and on the next day Mrs. Wetzel carried her
teapots to Suds Row, where she assured the washerwomen that if they had any
problems with the men, they would find support from her. She served them
sandwiches and called each by name.

The two women were remarkably similar. Each was a little taller than average,
a little thinner. Mrs. Reed was from her husband's state of Vermont; Mrs. Wetzel
had met her German husband when he was stationed at a fort in Minnesota. Each
had a strong affiliation with her Protestant church, and each was painfully aware
that her husband was probably going to remain in his present rank for as long as
he wore the uniform. They were about the same age, too, in their early thirties,
and whereas neither could ever have been termed beautiful, each had acquired
from years of service that noble patina which comes from dedication to duty and

the building of a good home. One enlisted man who had never spoken directly to the commander's wife said: 'The two good days at a new fort: when we put a roof over where we sleep and when Mrs. Reed appears.' In the postwar period she had helped make life easier at three different forts as the army moved resolutely west, and although this was the poorest site of the lot, she observed with pleasure that the land was flat and easy to manage and the water supply copious: 'The rest will come in due time.'

One factor at Fort Garner displeased her. Johnny Minor, one of the best leaders of cavalry and a man who already bore a heavy burden because he was required to lead black troops, had a pretty little wife named Nellie, who gave him much trouble. She despised his assignment and humiliated her husband's black cavalrymen by refusing ever to speak to them; to her they did not exist, except when she was talking with the other wives. Then she called the Buffalo Soldiers 'those apes,' and lamented that it was they who prevented Johnny from gaining the promotions he deserved.

Mrs. Reed would not tolerate such dissension and halted Nellie whenever it began, but Mrs. Wetzel, so admirable in other respects, shared her husband's deep distrust of colored troops: 'Colonel Wetzel tells me constantly when we talk at night of how irresponsible they are. He says it's bad enough to serve with cavalry . . .' At the most inappropriate times she would forcefully proclaim her husband's harsh theories about the cavalry: 'And I mean any cavalry, not just the unfortunate Negroes. The colonel tells me: "Horses require so much fodder, and this must be carried along in so many wagons that the cavalry winds up doing nothing but riding happily along, guarding its own train. In fight after fight, the poor infantry is far ahead, doing the dirty work, while the cavalry lags behind, bringing up its food." '

Mrs. Reed, wife of an infantry officer, believed that most of what Mrs. Wetzel said was true: 'The cavalry really is a most wasteful branch,' but she also knew that to keep peace in the fort, this constant barrage of criticism must be silenced, or at least muffled, so she cautioned her friend against blatant disparagement. For some days Mrs. Wetzel kept quiet, but she was a Scandinavian, well educated by her parents, who found it impossible to remain silent when she saw error, and one afternoon when most of the officers and all the wives were present, she erupted: 'It's a known fact that during the first days of a campaign against the Indians, the cavalry is most daring, dashing here and there. But we rarely encounter Indians during those first days, and soon the cavalry horses are worn down, so that they can barely keep up with the infantry. And by the end of the second week the horses are so tired, they cannot keep up. On all days after that, the foot soldiers have to make camp early, and sit there waiting for the cavalry to drift in. From the twelfth day on they're really useless, for not only are they exhausted, but they've also used up all their fodder.'

'Why do we bother with them?' young Andrew Masters from Illinois asked, and Mrs. Wetzel replied with more insight than she suspected: 'Because generals like to ride horses at Fourth of July parades.'

This was too much for Louise Reed: 'This talk must stop. And it must not be resumed in my house. My husband is commander of a mixed unit, mixed in all ways, and it must remain harmonious.'

The attention of the two senior women was diverted from the deficiencies of the cavalry to the more exciting behavior of young Nellie Minor, who found time heavy on her hands while her husband was off on an extended scout with his black horsemen. On the first afternoon she arranged an uneasy tea for the other wives. On the second she took the Reed daughter on a canter along the Brazos River. And on the third, following the good example set by Mrs. Wetzel, she went down to Suds Row to encourage the women there, but she was repelled by the conditions in which they worked and could find nothing in common to talk about.

On the fourth day she saddled one of the horses reserved for wives and planned her informal saunter along Bear Creek in such a way that she had a good chance of encountering the Irishman Jim Logan as he returned from a morning canter to the north. They did meet, well apart from the fort, and they rode for several exhilarating miles back toward Jacksborough. They did not dismount, but each was aware of considerable electricity in the air, for as Nellie observed as they rode side by side: 'It's like the quiet before a summer thunderstorm.' Actually, it was well into the winter of 1870, but she was correct in feeling that great events impended, for not only was her attraction to this dashing Irishman becoming known at the fort, but Comanche to the west were about to become active again.

On this afternoon neither she nor Jim Logan was much concerned about Indians, for when they dipped down behind a small hill to the Larkin tank where no one could see them, she rode very close to him, saying as they moved slowly across the grassy plain: 'You ride extremely well.'

'My father taught me, in Ireland.'

'What's Ireland like?'

'Greener than this.'

'Do you miss it?'

'We starved.'

'Were you brave in the war?'

'I knew how to handle horses, I knew how to fight. So they made me a major.'

'I know. Do you mind being a lieutenant now?'

'Wars come and go. I was lucky to have found mine young. But to tell you the truth, Mrs. Minor, I don't feel unlucky to be a lieutenant during the long years.' He turned sideways and smiled, a ravishing, honest smile: 'My level even in war was just about captain. I was never meant to be a major, wasn't entitled. But I'm a damned good lieutenant.'

She leaned over and kissed him: 'You're a captivating man, Major, and in my mind you'll always be a major.'

He grasped at her arm, holding her close to him for a protracted kiss, and each knew at that moment that if either made even the slightest motion toward dismounting, there would be a frenzied scene among the sagebrush, but neither made such a move, and gradually they worked their way back toward Bear Creek, along which they rode with feigned unconcern until the fort became barely visible on the far horizon.

'Shouldn't you ride in alone?' Logan suggested, and she agreed that this might be prudent, but before they parted she moved close again, and kissed him even more passionately: 'I long to be with you, Jim,' but he said simply: 'Johnny's my superior, you know.'

So she rode directly to the fort while he made a far swing to the east, coming in much later on the Jacksborough Road, but such maneuvers fooled no one. Fort Garner quickly knew it had a dangerous love affair on its hands, and Mrs. Reed did not propose to have some young snippet bored with frontier life imperil her husband's already difficult command. As always, she went directly to the source of potential trouble, or rather, she summoned the source to her quarters.

'Nellie, sit down. It's my duty as an older woman and as the wife of the commander to warn you that you are playing a very dangerous game.'

'But—'

'I seek none of your shabby excuses. Nellie, at the fort in Arkansas you behaved the same way, and you came very close to ruining three careers. I shall not allow you to imperil my husband's command. Stay away from Major Logan.'

'I haven't—'

'Not yet. But you intend to.'

'How can you talk like this? I'm not obligated—'

'You're obligated to conduct yourself properly when you're in my husband's command.' She said this with such accumulated force of character that Nellie blanched.

'I will endanger no one,' she said softly.

'Nellie, can't you find happiness with your husband? He's a splendid man. My husband cherishes him.'

'He works with niggers, and he smells of niggers, and he can never amount to anything.'

Very harshly Mrs. Reed said: 'If you believe that, Nellie, you must leave this fort today.' When the sniffling younger woman tried to speak, Mrs. Reed silenced her: 'I said *today*.' Her voice rose: 'Pack your things while I stand over you, and leave his fort, because if you stay, you can bring only tragedy.'

'I can't go. I have nowhere to go.' She began to weep.

Mrs. Reed did not attempt to console her. Instead, she waited for the tears to halt, and then she asked, flatly but also with obvious compassion: 'So what shall we do?'

'We?'

'Yes, this is as much my problem as yours.'

'I can't go. I have nowhere, I tell you.'

'Then I shall tell you what you must do. Love your husband. Help him as Mrs. Wetzel and I help ours. Take pride in his accomplishments, which are many. And stay clear of Jim Logan.'

'Will you tell the others?'

'The others told me.' Now she softened: 'Nellie, I'm always the last woman on the post to know what's happening to the wives in my husband's command. Believe me, I do not look for trouble, I castigate no one. But when trouble is brought to my attention, so blatantly that I cannot . . .' She hesitated, choked, and had to fight back her own tears.

'Nellie, I think we should pray,' and the two officers' wives, there at the remotest outpost of their civilization, knelt and prayed. When they rose Mrs. Reed took Nellie's hand and said: 'Who ever promised you that an army officer's life would be pleasant? Believe me, this storm which assails you now will pass.'

'I am torn apart, Mrs. Reed.'

'Have you ever sat in a lonely fort, with snow about the door, and watched your child die? That's being torn apart, and even that storm passes.'

'I shall try.'

'And I shall . . .' She wanted to say either 'I shall pray for you' or 'I shall watch you,' but she knew that each was inappropriate and inaccurate. So she did not finish her promise, because what she proposed doing was much more practical. She would ask her husband to keep his young Irish cavalryman absent from the fort as often as possible and on missions of maximum duration.

Among the men on the frontier who followed the establishment of Fort Garner with close attention was a small, scrawny fugitive with watery blue eyes and a somewhat withered left arm; he lurked in Santa Fe, waiting for any good chance that would enable him to slip back into his preferred Texas. His name was Amos Peavine, and his ancestors had prowled the Neutral Ground, that bandits' no man's land bordering old Louisiana.

As a young man with a bad arm he had had to be more clever than most and had soon built a reputation throughout East Texas as a holdup man and a ruthless killer. He was so devious, so quick to strike, that men started calling him Rattlesnake, and some, to their quick dismay, tried shooting at him, but he, well aware of his disability, had trained himself so assiduously in the use of guns that it was always he who drew first, fired first, and nodded ceremoniously as his would-be assailant fell.

Frontier gunmen, noticing his affected left arm, assumed that it played no part in his behavior, but they were wrong. Through long practice Rattlesnake Peavine could bring that bad arm up across his belt, providing a rocklike platform on which to rest the gun as it was being fired, and the action was so swift and smooth that even close watchers could not detect exactly what had happened.

In those hectic days he began to carry two Colts, and since his left hand was practically useless, he slung them both on his right hip, the only gunman known to do so. He spent about a year, 1863, perfecting holsters for his two guns, and then another, 1864, in shortening the barrels to make the guns easier to swing loose. This made his draw a fraction of a second quicker than that of a challenger. He also invented a clever way of making the trigger more responsive to his right forefinger: he filed down each sear until even a whisper would release it.

Peavine did not notch his guns to keep track of their effectiveness; he was content to be known as 'that little bastard, about a hundred and thirty pounds, who can shoot faster than a rattlesnake strikes, and more deadly.' At nineteen he was an authentic Texas badman.

During the war he had ranged the northern border, siding now with the Union forces, more often with the Confederate, but proving so unreliable to each that in the end both armies were trying to hang him, and it was then that he felt it advisable to quit Texas: 'I got me a passel of enemies in this state. North or South, they don't realize a man is entitled to make a livin'. No future for me here.' What was more persuasive: 'Hell, come peace they hain't much goods movin', a man hain't got much chance to pick a few bundles off for hisself.'

He had drifted slowly toward Santa Fe on the principle 'A man cain't make it in Texas, he can always succeed in New Mexico,' and after trying vainly to profit from the exposed trade with Mexico, he discovered that the real money was to be made in a trade centuries old and infamously dishonorable. The Plains Indians wanted whiskey and rifles, and generations of disreputable traders had found profitable ways of supplying them. Spaniards had done so in the 1600s, Frenchmen in the 1700s, Mexicans in the first years of the 1800s, and now a wily crew of adventurers from Kentucky, Mississippi and Texas continued the tradition.

Amos Peavine was the most daring of the bunch, for he traded with the most deadly of the tribes. He was a Comanchero, a lawless man who roamed the Comanchería, that vast expanse of wasteland which coincided with the buffalo range. Especially he worked the Texas plains, and when he learned that a new fort was to be established on Bear Creek, he rejoiced, because although it brought more soldiers into the area, which meant a greater chance that he would ultimately be shot, it also brought two developments extremely favorable to him: the Indians under attack would have to have more guns, and the slow military trains crossing the empty plains carrying guns and ammunition would be more open to attack. A really crafty Comanchero stole guns from the army, sold them to the Comanche, then served as tracker for the army when it went out to confront the well-armed Indians. A Comanchero prospered in troubled times, and was adept at devising strategies for keeping them troubled.

While Mrs. Reed was lecturing young Mrs. Minor on proper behavior at a frontier fort, Rattlesnake Peavine was some two hundred miles to the west, astride a winded old horse and leading a Rocky Mountain burro he had obtained from a Mexican family by the persuasive process of shooting the entire clan in one unbroken fusillade.

He was on a mission fraught with a medley of dangers, and any man who was afraid of nature, Indians or the retaliation of the United States Army would have blanched at what faced him as he probed the empty plains, seeking contact with Chief Matark of the Comanche. Scorpions and snakes awaited him if he was careless when he dismounted; death from dehydration got those who missed their water holes, so infrequent and so hot and alkali-ridden when found. Indian tribes at war with the Comanche would surely kill him if they caught him, and he faced equal danger from Comanche to whom he could not identify himself quickly. And there were always new forts with energetic new commanders eager to take up the chase against any despised Comanchero.

Amos Peavine, threading his way through these encroaching disasters, was a brave man, almost a heroic one, for the forces of evil require just as much strength of will as do the angels of goodness; it is only the force of character that is missing. Peavine had enormous will; he had no character at all, not even a consistently bad one, for, as in the old days of 1861–65, he stood willing to trade with anyone, to betray everyone. Now he had a promising scheme which might produce substantial profits if acted upon swiftly, but before action could take place, he had to find Matark.

He had left New Mexico, haven for Comancheros like himself and other bandits who ravaged Texas, and had entered that refuge known throughout the West as the Palo Duro Canyon. It was a formidable depression, more than a hundred miles long, dug through solid rock by millions of years of active water, and so lonely and awesome that white men rarely tried to penetrate or conquer it. Those who did saw sights that were majestic. High walls of colored rock hemmed in valleys of surprising richness, where a man could herd a thousand cattle and be assured that they could feed themselves on the ever-green grasses but not escape from the natural corral which kept them penned.

Cattlemen were not able to try this experiment because the Comanche had reached Palo Duro first and had for more than a hundred years utilized it as their one totally secure hiding place. Within the canyon, at about the center of its east-west reach, rose a pile of reddish rocks known as The Castle, and it was to this traditional meeting spot that Peavine was heading.

He did not ride the well-marked path at the bottom of the canyon, for that would trap him in too dangerously; he kept instead to the less comfortable trail along the south rim, because from here he could look down into the rocky depths and also across to the other side, for the canyon was not extensive in its north-south dimension. And now as he led his complaining burro along the trail from which The Castle should soon be visible, he was satisfied that he had once more negotiated the canyon and brought himself into contact with the Indians he sought. There was, of course, still the possibility that he might encounter some idiot lieutenant from one of the forts, out seeking glory, who had boasted to his troop as he led his cavalry out: 'I shall invade Palo Duro and bring back the scalp of Chief Matark.' Often such a man would utter an extra vow: 'And I'll rescue Emma Larkin,' for she was constantly on the conscience of these soldiers.

Peavine laughed as he thought of the men within the forts: Better they stay home. Come up here, to these walls, they're goin' to get shot. Various expeditions had come to grief at Palo Duro and it seemed likely that more would follow. 'These canyons will be Indian for a long time,' Peavine muttered as he saw the familiar signs which indicated that The Castle was not far off. He was justified in using the plural *canyons* because each small stream that fed the main architecture of this deep cut had gouged out its own smaller canyon, so that at the center, where he now rode, the land became a jumble of lateral cuts, some so deep that they could not be traversed if Peavine kept to the upper plateau.

So, crossing himself as if he were a believing Catholic, he edged his tired horse toward the rim, tugged at the rope guiding his burro, and started down the steep and rocky path to the lower level. He was now at the most dangerous point of his two-hundred-mile expedition, for he rode so close to the wall of the canyon that any rattlesnake, awakening from its winter sleep, could strike him full in the face if it darted forth; also, if either enemy Indians or roving troops were setting a trap, here is where they would spring it. But this time he made his descent peacefully, and when he gained the floor of the canyon he found himself once more in a congenial fairyland which he had known in the past.

Land about The Castle leveled out and produced such a richness of grass, such protection from storms, and had such an equable climate—cool in summer, warm in winter—that it formed a kind of Indian Garden of Eden. Here, within this security, some squaws more adventurous than their sisters even tried growing vegetables from seeds captured on raids against ranches.

Turning a familiar corner, Peavine waved to the scouts he knew would be watching, licked his lips in preparation for the Comanche words he would soon be speaking, and headed his horse toward the Indian encampment. It was an amazing collection of tepees, for in their travels south from their original Rocky Mountain homeland the Comanche had acquired a variety of housing, some with tall cedar poles lifting the buffalo-hide covering high into the air (these were the Cheyenne contribution) and others little more than rounded huts depending not upon long poles but bent branches for their form (a pattern used by the Ute). Most notable were the small, compact tepees built about a minimum of moderately long poles; these were some of the best (a device of the Pawnee). The

Comanche, a wandering tribe that had developed only a limited culture of its own, had borrowed types of tepees from everyone. Their fierce courage and their appalling cruelty to any captive, they themselves invented.

'I seek Great Chief Matark,' Peavine cried loudly as he entered the haphazard arrangement of tepees, and he repeated the announcement until a group of young braves ran over to surround him, leaving behind the half-naked creature they had been tormenting.

'Is that the Larkin girl?' he asked as the young men came up, and they looked back as if bewildered that anyone should care who the child was. They had already burned off her ears, and her nose would disappear before the summer was out; she was thirteen now, a most pitiful thing, but miraculously she retained enough intelligence to know that the arrival of a white man, any white man, meant that her chance of rescue was by that small degree enhanced.

She took a tentative step toward Peavine, praying that he would take notice of her, but he looked the other way, and two of the young men grabbed stones and threw them at her with great force, shouting as they did so: 'Get back!'

Matark and his four wives occupied a large tepee in the Cheyenne style, its cedar poles emitting a pleasing fragrance. It had a low entrance, requiring the visitor to stoop, but inside it was spacious and festively decorated with elkskin hangings on which had been depicted in various colors the history of this portion of the tribe. Matark himself, tall and brooding, was a striking figure whose command over his men was understandable. Obviously he had a superior intelligence, which he began to display immediately.

'What new thing brings you here?' he asked.

'Word from St. Louis.'

'What word?'

'Cavin & Clark, they've been hired to carry guns, many guns and all ammunition, to the new fort at Bear Creek.'

'Oh!' Matark did not try to hide the weight and pleasure he accorded such news. To attack successfully one train of this probable magnitude would supply him with armament for three years. But he was suspicious where white men were involved, and he asked: 'If you know this . . . the guns . . . aren't they already there?'

'The system, Chief. You know the system.' And the plotters had to laugh at the incredible stupidity of the United States Army, which placed men like Captain Reed in remote outposts like Fort Garner, then gave them no authority over or responsibility for their supplies. Desk officers in Washington, inordinately jealous of their prerogatives and aware that their jobs were safe only if constantly enhanced, had prevailed upon Congress, at whose elbows they sat while men like Reed battled Indians, to initiate one of the stupidest plans in military history. Every item shipped to Fort Garner was requested not by the man on the scene but by some desk officer two thousand miles away. And when it was authorized, belatedly, another desk officer in another building in Washington decided when and by whom it would be railroaded from the depot in Massachusetts to the warehouse in St. Louis, and by what frontier carter it would be finally dispatched to the intended recipient.

Because the desk officer in charge of transportation sought a carrier who charged the least or bribed the most, he usually employed some carter with the least reliable drivers and the least expensive horses, and none was more deficient than Cavin & Clark in St. Louis. Cargoes consigned through them sometimes required half a year to cover half a thousand miles, and when they arrived, there would always be shortages due to the C&C drivers' tricky habit of selling off portions to storekeepers en route.

So when Rattlesnake Peavine told Chief Matark that the guns for Fort Garner were being shipped by Cavin & Clark, the Indian knew that anyone who sought to intercept this shipment had plenty of time. There was even the possibility that gunfire from ambush might not be necessary, because it was sometimes possible for a Comanchero to arrange an outright deal with the C&C driver: 'I'll give two hundred dollars for the whole train.'

'Could you buy the guns?' Matark asked.

'They know me too well. I killed two of their drivers.'

'Then we must capture them?'

'I think it's the only way.'

'Will the wagons have an escort?'

'Probably. A new fort. A new commander.'

'And eager young officers,' Matark said. 'Well, I'll send my eager young braves.'

'When I entered the canyon,' Peavine said, 'I saw your young fellows playing with a white girl. Could that be the Larkin girl?'

'Yes.'

'You know, I could earn you a lot of money if you'd let me trade her back to the Texans.'

'I have plans for her,' Matark said. 'And you're right. She'll bring us a lot of money.'

'Then I can't have her?' Before the chief could reply, the wily trader explained: 'Some day I'll have to make peace with the Texans. No more trading. Too old. If I appeared with the Larkin girl, I'd be a hero . . .'

Matark looked at him and thought: Yes, and then you'd turn against us. It would be you, the Rattlesnake, who would lead the blue-coats against us. You'd bring them right into this canyon. For one savage moment he considered calling for his braves and killing Peavine right then, but the canny little trader divined his thinking and quickly said: 'You know you need me. To keep getting guns, you need me.'

'I do,' Matark conceded, and a deal was firmed whereby Peavine would get many Mexican pieces of gold if the guns were captured, but when he left Matark's tent he took great care to seek out Emma Larkin, for if she was ever released, he wanted her to testify to the fact that he had tried to be helpful.

He found her huddled in the shade of a tepee, ignored for the moment by her tormentors, and he was appalled by her appearance. She was thin almost to the point of death, her hair and nails filthy. Only knotted nubs remained to show where her ears had been, and her nose was in fearful condition. Looking at her as she trembled by the tepee, he wondered how the Comanche had fallen into the abominable practices they followed with their prisoners, and he recalled having chided Matark about this: 'Why do you burn the ranchers alive? Why cut them to pieces?' and the chief had replied: 'That's our custom.' Peavine then asked: 'Why not just kill them?' and Matark had said: 'To watch an enemy die is good.' Peavine said: 'But why torture them so?' and Matark had explained: 'If enemy dying is good, long-time dying is better.' Peavine had inquired further: 'Does it mean something? Does it add strength to your braves?' and Matark had said with solemn finality: 'It has always been our custom.'

That explained so much, not only regarding the Comanche but all fighting men, and Peavine, reflecting on the customs of his own profession, could hear his father admonishing him: 'Never shoot a man in the back. Never! It hain't tolerated.' It was also not tolerated to kill women unless in the heat of battle or when they were shooting back. Texans, he noticed, bore no grudge if a man shot another with a rifle, even if from ambush at a safe distance, but they deplored the Mexican who killed with a knife, even at close hand where he ran great risk. The gun was manly, the knife was not.

French, German, Russian armies, he had heard, all had their traditions, as ironclad as the Comanche attitude toward prisoners; he had been told of the Prussian custom of leaving a disgraced officer alone with a loaded revolver, expecting him to blow his brains out— 'Not with me. They got to do the shootin'!' he growled.

But no rationalization could justify the Comanche treatment of their girl prisoners: 'Why do you let them do such horrible things to the little girls?' he had asked Matark, who had again replied: 'It is our custom.' Peavine had not liked being allied with Indians who behaved so barbarously, but with the plains depleted of other tribes, he had few options, and hiding his disgust, he moved closer to the girl, whereupon a transformation took place.

For when she looked up at him she was no longer a terrified object of torture; she was a fighting little tiger with the same determination to survive that animated him. This child was not going to die easily, regardless of what the Comanche did to her, and for a fleeting moment he wanted to embrace her and carry her with him on the raid against the supply train. His life had taught him to revere persistence, and this child was persisting against terrors which would have deranged even strong adults.

'My name is Amos Peavine,' he said. 'I wish I could help.'

These were the first words in English she had heard since the massacre, and she was obviously pleased that she remembered what they meant: 'I am Emma Larkin.'

'I know. I will tell the others you are alive.'

'You!' a surly brave shouted. 'Get back!' And with a well-directed stone he hit her sharply on the leg. Knowing that if she did not obey instantly, the tortures would resume, she scurried away as if she were a frightened dog, but Peavine, catching a glimpse of her eyes, realized that she was not frightened; she was acting so to be rid of the stone-throwing, and he muttered to himself: 'Some night she'll cut that one's throat. Go it, lass!' With that, he turned to the organizing of the raiding party which would ambush the Cavin & Clark shipment.

When Captain Reed received official notice from the young officer in Washington that his supplies, including needed guns and ammunition, would be arriving sometime in May via Cavin & Clark, he shuddered, because he knew that if C&C performed as always, the shipment might arrive in May as scheduled, but it also might arrive in September, or perhaps not at all.

'I cannot understand,' he complained to Wetzel, 'how Washington can ignore our negative reports on Cavin & Clark and still use them.'

'Saving money,' the German suggested.

'But it loses money. We proved that in our last report.'

'Men at the desk never believe men in the field.'

Reed said no more to Wetzel, who, in the great Prussian tradition, respected whatever the higher command ordered, but he did seek out his adjutant, Lieutenant Sanders: 'I'm not easy about this Cavin & Clark shipment. What ought we do?'

'We need those supplies. I'd send a detachment of cavalry to Fort Richardson. Protect the wagons every inch of the way from Jacksborough.'

'We've not been ordered to do so.'

'I'd do it, anyway. Those are our goods, and we need them.'

'Who would you send?'

'Well, the Comanche will probably be reluctant to strike so far behind our lines.'

Reed grew impatient: 'You just said we had to protect the wagons.'

'I'm not afraid of the Comanche. I'm afraid of Cavin & Clark. If we don't watch them, they'll sell the whole consignment.'

The two officers shook their heads in disgust, and Reed spoke first: 'Hell of a situation. We have to fight the Indians. We have to fight Cavin & Clark. And we have to fight Washington. But who to send?'

'With Fort Richardson at the other end, the likelihood of a fight is not great. I'd send young Toomey.' He reflected not on Toomey's ability but on the terrain between the two forts. 'Yes, I'd send Toomey, but I'd also send Sergeant Jaxifer. He knows the lay of the land.'

Sanders, although not a member of the 10th Cavalry, had had ample opportunity to assess the character of Jaxifer, a forty-three-year-old veteran of mounted action. He was a big, very black man, with almost no neck and with forearms that could have wrestled bears. Surprisingly quick on his feet, he leaped into any action that confronted him, and on a horse, was practically unstoppable. He said little, told no one what his antecedents were, and if asked, said New York was his home, even though the roster listed his birthplace accurately as Georgia. He had joined the Union forces in December 1863, after escaping from the Confederacy by swimming the Rio Grande into Mexico, and had attained the impressive rank of first sergeant through a mixture of quick obedience and obvious bravery. When Northern blacks who had never known slavery asked his opinion of the system, he said: 'I had some bad masters, more good. But I run away from both.' The fact that he was now surviving in an army which despised him was proof of his intelligence.

He was harsh with his men: 'This got to be the best unit in the army. You step out of line, I cut your neck off.' Even Wetzel, who had objected to having the black cavalry so close to his white infantry at morning parade and evening retreat, occasionally complimented Jaxifer on the snappy drill his men performed: 'In the Prussian army, a lot more precision, of course, but very good by American standards.' Once Wetzel even placed his hand on Jaxifer's arm as the two stood watching their men drill: 'We have a first-class fort here. We can be proud.'

John Jaxifer was the kind of man one sent to reinforce a junior officer on a scouting expedition, but the importance of the proposed exercise was somewhat diminished when a group of four horsemen arrived from Fort Richardson with headquarters' plans for the movement of Cavin & Clark wagons: 'General Grierson will send some of our troops to protect it halfway. At Three Cairns you'll take over and bring the train safely in.'

'We had stood ready to pick it up at Jacksborough,' Reed said, but the other men assured him that Grierson was more than happy to extend the courtesy: 'We have some young fellows who need the experience.'

'Likewise,' Reed said, and it was arranged that six days after the Fort Richardson men started west, Second Lieutenant Elmer Toomey, supported by First Sergeant John Jaxifer, would ride toward Three Cairns, those informal piles of rock which had been stacked on the treeless plains to mark the way to Fort Garner, to pick up the wagon train and bring it safely home.

Chief Matark and Amos Peavine had been kept informed of both the arrival of the C&C train at Jacksborough and the movement of a four-man escort west from Fort Richardson. 'If they join up with the men from Fort Garner coming east to meet them,' Matark warned, 'they might be too strong for us.' But Peavine reassured him: 'The Fort Richardson men will come only halfway, then ride back to Jacksborough. We'll have to fight only the small escort sent out by Fort Garner.'

'If that, where do we attack?'

'During the last half. Then the stronger force at Fort Richardson would have more difficulty sending help.'

Carefully the two plotters analyzed the situation, with Peavine supplying the relevant details concerning army strength: 'Eight wagons, driver and shotgun each, that's sixteen guns right there, but those C&C drivers don't like to fight. Real cowards. The Buffalo Soldiers, they like to fight and think three of them can lick twenty of us.' Any crusty Comanchero like the Rattlesnake liked to use the pronouns *we* and *us* when talking with his Indians. 'Grierson, he'd send four men at most. Reed, this is his first fort as commander. He'll send maybe a dozen. But whereas Grierson would never send an untried man, not on any mission at all, Reed might.'

'More men in the second half?' Matark asked. 'But weaker?'

Before Peavine could respond, a scout rode up, quivering with excitement but also laughing: 'Come see! You must see!' And he led the two men nearly a mile south to where two other scouts were lying on the ground at the edge of a slight rise, below which nestled a small protected tank near which a soldier whose blue jacket lay beside him was twisting on the ground with a young woman who looked as if she might be very pretty indeed. They were making love, and for a long moment the five watchers looked approvingly.

'Shall we kill them?' one of the scouts asked, and each of the other four men thought how astonished those lovers would be if they were interrupted in their raptures by four Comanche and a white man with a withered left arm.

The three braves were ready to make the charge down the slopes of the little vale when Peavine halted them: 'It would alert the fort.'

'But they're so far away.'

'They would be missed. Their bodies would be found.' He spoke harshly: 'It's the wagons we want,' but as they rode away he had to chuckle: 'Wouldn't they have been surprised?' And he reined in his horse to look again at the lovers sprawled upon the ground in their secluded swale beside the tank.

At the end of May 1870 the eight creaking and complaining wagons left Jacksborough, throwing clouds of dust so high that Comanche scouts well to the north were assured that the convoy was under way. It was attended, the Indians quietly noted, by only seven cavalrymen: four blacks in front, two at the rear, and one white officer riding slowly back and forth to maintain communication. It was not an orderly procession, nor a compact one, because each driver, his own boss and in no way obedient to the army of which he was not a part, chose the track that he thought best, which meant that the line straggled ridiculously.

'I'd keep that line firmed up,' one of the troopers advised the carters, but they snapped: 'You mind your horse, we'll mind our mules.'

'You'll want us soon enough if the Comanche strike.'

'That's what we always hear. If, if . . .'

'Well, damnit, when they do strike, and we've heard rumors out of Santa Fe, I want these wagons in a quick line.'

'They been in line since we left St. Louis.'

Grierson's men brought the wagons safely to Three Cairns, and when the watching Indians saw that an orderly transfer of responsibility was being made, they faced a problem: 'If we attack too soon, the Fort Richardson men may gallop back to help. If we attack too late, men from Fort Garner will hear and come out with support.' They were additionally perplexed when the eastern group, pleased with their work on the plains and loath to ride back to dull garrison duty at Jacksborough, stayed with the Fort Garner men till morning of the second day.

'When will they leave?' Matark grumbled, and Peavine had to reply: 'Who knows? Soldiers, who ever knows about those idiots?'

That morning, however, the Fort Richardson men retired, rode a short distance eastward and fired their guns in the air. Some of the shotgun men riding next to the drivers responded, and now Elmer Toomey, a twenty-one-year-old farm boy from Indiana, fresh from West Point, was in command of his first important detachment. He rode at the front, always attentive to the boundless horizon for indication of storms or Indians; at certain periods only a few trees would be visible, and sometimes he would scan the four points of the compass and see none at all.

At such times Sergeant Jaxifer rode slowly back and forth, checking on his ten horsemen but never speaking to or even looking at the sixteen carters, who were disgusted to think that they were being guarded by niggers. One, a surly fellow from West Virginia who would have sold half his cargo in Jacksborough had not one of the cavalrymen kept close watch, protested to Lieutenant Toomey: 'You keep them niggers well shy of me. You ask me, we fought on the wrong side in the Civil War.'

'They're soldiers of the United States Army,' Toomey said stiffly. 'I'm an officer in their company,' and the carter sneered: 'The more shame for you.'

'Attention, you bastard! One more word like that and I'll have you in the guardhouse when we get there.'

The driver, knowing that he could exercise no control over him, laughed: 'Little boy, don't play soldier with me. Now run along and nurse your niggers.'

An hour after dawn on the next day this driver shrieked in terror: 'Comanche! Where in hell's the army?'

Sixteen unreliable carters and eleven enlisted men led by an untested lieutenant were suddenly responsible for holding off more than a hundred Indian braves on terrain that afforded no protection. But they were not powerless, because the black cavalrymen were toughened professionals and their white lieutenant was about to prove that he more than deserved his rank.

'Wagons form!' he shouted, personally leading the tail wagon toward the head of the line and showing the others how to place themselves.

'Sergeant Jaxifer! Keep your men inside the line of wagons!' When carters were slow to obey, he threatened to shoot them, and before the Indians could strike he had his band in the best defensive position possible, but even so, they were not prepared, not even the black veterans, for the fury with which the Comanche struck.

From his command post Matark ordered: 'Circle them! Set them on fire.'

His entire contingent formed a huge circle around the wagons, his braves wheeling counterclockwise, as they preferred, for this enabled them to fire across their steady left arms as they sped. But as the battle waxed, a cadre of fourteen braves bearing lighted brands detached themselves from the circle and dashed boldly at the wagons, trying to throw their flame so as to ignite the canvas covers. Six fell from their saddles, shot dead, but the other eight delivered their fiery brands, which the carters extinguished.

Inside the ring of wagons no orders were issued, for these embattled men required no exhortation. Each was aware of the terrible tortures he was going to undergo if he lost this fight, and each resolved that there would be no surrender. This was a fight to the death, and several wagoners muttered to their friends: 'If they come at us, at the end I mean, shoot me.'

The eight carters who rode shotgun knew how to use their weapons, and the eight drivers, shaking with fear, also fired with determination, with the early result that the Indians were kept some distance from the wagons; eleven now lay dead before the first member of the convoy had been seriously wounded.

Toomey stayed mostly with the panicky drivers, and he was furious when the mean-spirited men began to blame their plight on the fact that black troops had been sent to protect them: 'Damned niggers, don't know nothin'.' One man growled as he fumbled with his gun, which had suffered a minor jam: 'Niggers is no better than Indians. Curse 'em both.' Toomey said nothing, interpreting the ugly expressions as signs of nervous fear, but he did what he could to reassure the civilians: 'My men know how to hold a line. We'll get out of this.'

'Jesus Christ!' One of the carters pointed to the north, where a line of at least forty shouting warriors came in solid phalanx.

'Hold your fire,' Toomey cried, knowing that Jaxifer would have his own men in readiness. He then called for two of the troopers to help him defend the spot at which the oncoming force seemed likely to hit, and there he stood, heels ground into the sandy soil as if he intended never to be budged.

The Comanche were so determined in what they expected to be their final charge that despite heavy losses to the steady fire of the black troops and the trained shotgun men, they simply rode down the defenders at two points, the victorious braves in the lead galloping right through the circle where mules attached to the wagons lay dead.

But they did not stop. They were not given time in which to rampage inside the circle, because whoever tried was either shot or clubbed down by the troops. They had broken the line, as they were determined to do, but they had not disorganized it, and they had lost many in the attempt. They did, however, succeed in taking with them a good portion of the horses, and had not the mules drawing the wagons been left in harness, they too would surely have been stolen. The men of the 10th Cavalry were now on foot.

Toomey was appalled to see his horses go, but he knew that he must not display either fear or consternation lest the civilians panic: 'Sergeant Jaxifer, your men in good shape?'

'Fine, sir.'

Indeed, the cavalry veterans were handling this battle as if it were a parade-ground exercise; they were not impeded by the loss of their horses, for they had learned that in a dozen typical engagements, they would in at least ten be expected to fight on foot. Said critics: 'They ride comfortably to battle. Dismount and become infantry. Why in hell aren't they infantry in the first place?' Such critics were about to receive the best possible answer, but before it manifested itself, the Comanche organized another frontal assault, and this time they directed it specifically at where the surviving drivers stood, for their clever fighters had detected this to be the weak spot of the circle.

Toomey, seeing them come, stood beside the drivers, and once more twisted his heels to dig them in, but when the Indians struck he was powerless to hold them off, and he was tomahawked twice. His head was split open and his left arm, with which he tried vainly to defend himself, was nearly severed.

Jaxifer was now in control, and he was ruggedly determined to save the remnants of this escort, but when he started to tell the carters how they must arrange themselves to be most effective in the charges that he knew would soon come thundering at them, they refused to obey his commands: 'No nigger tells me what to do.'

He did not respond. Instead he said slowly: 'Two carters, one cavalryman. That way we can cover the space better.'

'Don't you touch me, nigger.'

'You must move to that weak spot.'

'I ain't takin' no orders . . .'

Sergeant Jaxifer stopped, smiled: 'Man, we gonna survive this. They ain't gonna ride us down, never. But we got to do it sensible. You been in this one fight. I been in sixteen. I don't lose fights, and I ain't gonna lose this one. Now fill those gaps.'

After thus disposing of the survivors, he threw a blanket over the corpse of his lieutenant, but even as he did so a terrible pain struck at his heart. He knew that as long as he remained in the service, he would be remembered as the black sergeant who had lost his white commander.

During the fight so far, no member defending the wagons had seen Chief Matark, nor could anyone have been aware that a white man was helping direct the fight, but had the defenders been told that such a man was hidden behind the first small hill, they would have guessed that it was Amos Peavine, for the Rattlesnake's reputation had reached all the forts. He was the Comanchero they despised but also feared, and the men of this train would not have been surprised to learn that he was again trying to steal army guns for sale to his Indians.

At nine-thirty that morning Peavine was counseling Matark: 'Wear them down. Send your men in from a different direction each time.'

'How soon will they surrender?'

Peavine did not want to tell the chief that the behavior of the Comanche toward captives made it unlikely that soldiers would ever surrender, or carters either, so he dissembled: 'By noon we'll have the wagons.'

'The next charge, I lead.'

Peavine did not like this at all, for he had often observed that when a great chief died, the problem of succession could become messy, with the friends of the old chief suddenly the enemies of the new, and he did not like to speculate on what might happen to him if, on this lonely plain, Chief Matark perished in a fruitless attack which he, Peavine, had recommended and helped organize. It was in his interest to see that Matark lived, so he counseled against participation in the charge: 'You are needed here.'

'I am needed there,' Matark growled, and when the charge began, directed at a spot with three fallen horses, he was in the lead. Again his men ripped right into the circle, and again the stubborn black troops with their fiercely effective gunfire drove them out.

But Matark had seen the diminished strength of the defenders, and now he knew for certain that their officer was dead: 'By noon we take the wagons.' And this would have been a safe prediction except for the cautious behavior of two men who were not yet engaged in the battle at Three Cairns.

Hermann Wetzel never slept well if even one of his soldiers, infantry or cavalry, was absent from any fort to which he was attached, and he had been attached to many. His stubborn German conscience and his love of Prussian order hounded him if any man was not safely accounted for. Furthermore, the absence of Toomey made him most uneasy, for the young lieutenant was untested and operated under two severe disadvantages, which led Wetzel to interrupt his breakfast and hurry over to Reed's quarters.

'It's a short ride in from the Cairns, and Toomey's a good man.'

'But he's cavalry and they never know tactics. And his men are niggers, and they don't know anything.'

'None of that, Colonel.'

'I'm still worried, sir. Very.'

Reed had put down his knife and fork, arranging them meticulously beside his plate: 'I'm concerned too. What do you recommend?'

'I'd send troops out to intercept them. The Comanche have been silent for too long.'

Reed, a man who never flinched from hard decisions, looked directly into the eyes of his German adviser: 'I think you may be right, Colonel.' And as soon as these words were uttered, he leaped from the table, rasping out orders for an immediate formation of the remainder of Company R, 10th Cavalry to intercept the incoming train. Of the company's authorized strength of eighty troopers, only sixty-eight had been sent to Fort Garner; of these, one had deserted, seventeen were on guard duty or in the hospital, and twelve, including young Toomey, were already at Three Cairns. Thus, only thirty-eight answered the muster call.

He would lead, of course, for whenever there was a likelihood of action he insisted upon being in the vanguard; Wetzel, who disliked serving with the cavalry, would remain in charge at the fort, which he could be depended upon to defend should the Indians strike when the others had been lured away. Isolated forts were sometimes endangered, but not when Captain Wetzel was in command.

Reed wanted to take Jim Logan as cavalry officer, but the Irishman was absent, on a scout, his men said, and when Reed checked quietly, he learned that Mrs. Minor was absent too, but for the moment he decided to do nothing about this: 'Colonel Minor, you will be second in command.' And then, with that second sight which had made him an able commander, he added: 'Full campaign issue.' Minor deemed it folly to carry full battle gear on such a trivial excursion, considering the abundance of supplies this involved, but he assumed that Reed wished to test his men, so he said nothing, and within eighteen minutes of having made his decision to intercept his young lieutenant, Reed was headed east with Minor and thirty-eight Buffalo Soldiers.

He posted scouts well in advance, of course, but they could find only remnants of Toomey's march in that direction and no signs whatever of Indian activity. However, one of the ragged older men who served the army, a tracker with one-quarter Indian blood, elected to ride well to the north, from where he returned with ominous news: 'General Reed! One hundred, two hundred Comanche headed east, maybe six days ago.' Now it was clear! Chief Matark had made a most daring move.

'Colonel Minor, he's going to attack the wagons between here and Jacksborough.' He was inclined to start immediately at full gallop, but his innate caution directed him to consult his subordinate: 'How could he be trying to trap us, Minor?'

'He could be feinting, then attack the fort.'

'Colonel Wetzel can handle that. How about us?'

'If he tricks us eastward, what gain to him? Moves us closer to the wagons.'

'Bugler!' A muted call, which could be heard only yards away, was sounded and the force of thirty-eight blue-clad troopers spurred their horses into an easy trot. They had gone only a few miles when another scout reported the news which Wetzel had intuitively feared: 'Major battle. Hundreds of Comanche.'

Without halting, Reed shouted his tactics: 'Half left, half right. But the moment we spot where their command is, everyone straight at it. Ignore the wagons.'

When they reached a rise from which they could see the embattled wagons and the Indians assaulting them, Reed ordered his bugler to sound the charge. With Minor and the black cavalrymen at the gallop, they rushed to join the battle.

Reed's men behaved with precision, his group following him in a circle to the north, with Johnny Minor's horsemen riding swiftly to the south, where they picked off several stragglers. At the far end of the circle they joined, then wheeled about to face a main charge of nearly eighty Comanche. It was a mad struggle lasting nearly ten minutes, but in the end the blue-clads were driven back to the wagons, where steady fire from the circle supported them.

It now became a melee, not a battle. Many Indians were killed and five of Reed's men. Minor was badly wounded, taking a bullet through his left hip, but the circle remained intact as the charge of the Indians wavered and then broke. The attack on the Cavin & Clark wagon train at Three Cairns had failed. Thirty-one Indians and nine defenders lay dead, but the fight was over.

When Reed learned that Toomey had died he went to where the body lay, drew aside the blanket, and saluted: 'He died bravely, I'm sure.'

'That he did,' one of the carters said, 'but I'm bringin' charges against them damned niggers. They let us down.'

Reed did not listen, and a few moments later one of the shotgun men came to him: 'That big sergeant, none braver. He held us together.'

'I'd expect him to,' Reed said.

Reed now faced a series of difficult decisions, which he proceeded to make in rapid-fire order, as if he had long contemplated them. First he had to know his exact strength: 'Sergeant Jaxifer, your condition?'

'Started out with Lieutenant Toomey and ten men. Toomey and three dead, three wounded. Five effectives, including myself, sir.'

Reed turned to Corporal Adams, who had ridden with him: 'Started with you, Colonel Minor and thirty-eight men. Five dead. Minor and three men wounded. Thirty-one effectives, sir.'

Reed studied the situation for less than ten seconds: 'Our immediate job, get this valuable train safely to Fort Garner. Our permanent job, catch Matark before he leaves Texas.'

To the horror of the C&C carters, he assigned the six wounded Buffalo Soldiers and Corporal Adams to escort the train on the remainder of its journey. This, of course, brought wild protestation from the carters, who wanted the entire force to lead them to safety.

Reed listened to their protests for about twenty seconds, then drew his revolver and summoned Adams: 'Corporal, if this man gives you any trouble, shoot him.' He rode to the eight drivers, looking each in the eye: 'Men, you've brought your wagons this far. Finish the job.' To the eight men riding shotgun he said: 'My men couldn't have held them off without your fire. Keep it up.' With an icy smile he tapped one of the loaded wagons: 'If you should need more ammunition . . .' He turned on his heel and paid no further attention as the C&C men organized their wagons for the limping journey to Fort Garner.

His job was to pursue Matark, but with Corporal Adams gone, he had only thirty-four men, including himself, to do battle with the much larger Comanche force, but this disparity gave him no trouble, for if he had with him no fellow officer, he did have Sergeant Jaxifer, who was a small army in himself. With such men he could give the retreating Comanche a lot of trouble.

So twenty minutes after the battle at Three Cairns ended, Reed was in fool-hardy pursuit of Chief Matark and his many Comanche, and not one of the black horsemen who followed him was apprehensive about overtaking the Indians or fearful of the outcome if they did: 'They got the men, but we got the guns.'

The chase continued for a day and a half, but when it looked as if the cavalry, with its superior horses and firepower, were about to overtake the Comanche and punish them, another act in the great tragicomedy of the plains unfolded, for when Reed and his men threatened to overtake the Comanche, the latter simply turned north, reached the Red River, swam their horses across, and found sanctuary in Camp Hope, administered by the Pennsylvania Quaker Earnshaw Rusk.

Under the specific terms of General Grant's Peace Policy, the army was free to discipline the Indians as long as they operated in Texas south of the Red River, but the moment they crossed north into Indian Territory the Quakers were in control; specifically, no soldier could touch a Comanche and certainly not fire a gun at him so long as he was north of the river and under the protection of Earnshaw Rusk.

As soon as Reed saw Matark and his men fording the river he knew he was in trouble, but ignoring it and his official directives, he followed them across and with all his men cantered in to Camp Hope, demanding to see the agent. The Indians, now dismounted and almost beatific in their innocence, smiled insolently as he rode past.

'Agent Rusk? I'm Captain Reed from Fort Garner.'

'I've heard the warmest reports of thee, Captain.'

'I've come to arrest Chief Matark of the Comanche.'

'That thee cannot do. Matark and his men are in my charge now, and as the terms—'

'I know the terms, Mr. Rusk, but Chief Matark has just waylaid a supply train and killed ten American citizens, including eight soldiers under my command.'

'I'm sure there's been a mistake in thy reports,' Rusk said.

'And I'm sure there's not, because I personally counted the bodies.'

'It's thy word against his, Captain Reed, and we all know what thy soldiers think about Indians.'

'Will you surrender Chief Matark to me?'

'I will not.'

'Will you allow me to arrest him, then?'

'I forbid thee to do so.'

'What am I allowed to do?'

'Nothing. Thee controls south of the Red. I control north, and it's my duty to bring these Indians to peaceful ways.'

So the two Americans faced each other, the blue-clad soldier representing the old ways of handling Indians, the homespun Pennsylvanian farmer representing the new. Reed was a Baptist who believed that God was a man of battles, a just judge administering harsh punishments; Rusk, a Quaker who knew that Jesus was a man of compassion who intended all men to be brothers. Reed trusted only army policy: 'Harry the Indians and confine them to reservations'; Rusk believed without qualification that he could persuade Indians to move willingly onto reservations, where the braves would learn agriculture, the women how to sew, and the children how to speak English. Reed interpreted his task as clearing the land for occupation by white ranchers and then protecting them and their cattle from Indian raiders; Rusk saw his as helping both the white newcomer to the land and the original Indian owners to find some reasonable way of sharing the plains. In fact, the only thing upon which the two administrators agreed was that the West should be organized in some sensible way that would permit the greatness of the American nation to manifest itself.

They even looked as dissimilar as two men of about the same age could: Reed was not tall, not heavy. He wore his dark hair closely clipped and affected no mustaches. He stood very erect and spoke sharply. His eyes were piercing and his chin jutting. By force of unusual character he had risen in the Union army from being a conscripted teacher from a small town in Vermont to a generalship in command of an entire brigade of troops. He loved the order of army life and expected to obey and to be obeyed, an attitude which manifested itself in all his actions. He looked always as if ready to step forward and volunteer for the most difficult and dangerous task. By the sheerest accident he had stumbled upon the one career for which he was best suited, and he proposed to follow it with honor as long as he lived.

Earnshaw Rusk was a gangling fellow whose unkempt hair matched his ill-fitting clothes. He had such weak eyes that he disliked looking directly at anyone, and his voice sometimes cracked at the most embarrassing moments, as if he were beginning a song. His Quaker parents had trained him never to press an opinion of his own, for Quakers tended to reach decisions by unspoken consensus rather than through exhibitionist voting; but he had also been told that when he felt he was right, 'to forge ahead without let or hindrance.' He had never been sure what those words meant, but he did know from observation that it was fairly difficult to dislodge a believing Quaker from a position morally taken, and he saw no reason why he should be different.

'Agent Rusk,' Reed said as if launching a new problem, 'you and I share a most difficult responsibility.'

'We do.'

'Now you are harboring in your camp—'

'We harbor no one, Captain. We provide a home for Indians on their way to civilization.'

'This time you're harboring a fiendish killer, Chief Matark of the Comanche.'

'I know Matark. I cannot believe—'

'Have you ever heard of the Bear Creek massacre?'

'I've heard the usual ugly rumors people spread.'

'Have you ever heard of the little girl Emma Larkin?'

'I don't know that name.'

'At Bear Creek, Matark massacred fifteen men, women, and children, and he massacred them most horribly. Would you care to hear the details?'

'I am not interested in soldiers' campfire tales.'

Reed did not hesitate: 'When you and I find the little girl, and we will—believe me, Agent Rusk, we will—we'll see that her ears and her nose have been burned off. We'll find that she's been raped incessantly. She'll probably be pregnant, but we'll find her.'

Rusk blanched: 'I find such stories repulsive.'

'They are,' Reed said, 'but in this case they're real. I found the bodies, hacked apart. I reassembled them as best I could. I buried them.'

'That's a terrible charge for thee to make, on a guess.' And there the struggle intensified, for Rusk's continued use of the Biblical *thee* seemed to be parading his virtue, as if to say: 'I am more Christlike than thee. I am of a higher moral order.' This infuriated army men, for they interpreted his pacifism as the behavior of a simple-minded man who could scarcely differentiate dawn from dusk.

Reed, having sworn not to lose his temper with this difficult Quaker, smiled icily: 'I am not guessing, Agent Rusk. I know.'

'Thee is being terribly unfair to Chief Matark.' Impulsively, for he was a good man striving to protect other good men, he sent for Matark, and within a few minutes the three protagonists who would compete for Texas rights so desperately faced one another. Matark appeared as if he had come from a pleasant hunt, his features in repose, his body at ease. It seemed doubtful that he had ever committed an act of warfare, let alone massacre, but Reed noticed that he did stay close to Rusk, as if he realized that this man was now his appointed protector.

'This is my friend Chief Matark,' Rusk began, and he expected the two men to shake hands, but Reed refused to touch the Indian. 'Chief, Captain Reed tells me that thee attacked supply trains.'

'Lies, lies.'

'He has men out there to prove that thee attacked the train, black soldiers whose reports we can trust.'

'Must have been Kiowa. No Comanche. None.'

When the interpreter translated these words, Rusk smiled thinly and held up his hands: 'Thee sees, I was sure it must have been other Indians. We have great trouble with the Kiowa, chiefs like Satanta, Satank.'

'Matark's Comanche were nowhere near Three Cairns?'

'No. Never so far south. We hunting Indians, not fighting. We stay on reservation.'

Reed did not respond to this. Suddenly he asked: 'What have you done with Emma Larkin?'

Matark stiffened, a fact which Rusk noticed, then said: 'Kiowa killed her people. We rescued her. She safe with us.'

Reed bowed his head, visualizing what *safe* meant in such situations. Rusk noticed this too, and asked: 'It is true that thee holds a white child?' and Matark replied: 'For safety. To keep her from the Kiowa.'

Even Rusk could see the cynicism of this response: any white child held captive by Indians should be returned to white protectors, and if the child was a girl, the obligation was doubled. For the first time since he came west, this peace-seeking Quaker experienced a grain of doubt about the goodness of his Comanche, but he raised no questions because he honestly believed that Matark was an innocent man vilified by the rough soldiers at Fort Garner. Rusk still did not comprehend the terrible problems faced by white settlers in Texas, and he refused to admit that his Indians ever raided down in Texas and then found sanctuary a few miles to the north in the Indian Territory.

Reed and Matark understood each other: with them it was a duel to the death, and if Matark had had just a little more time the other day, he would have captured one of Reed's wagon trains and killed every soldier guarding it; on the other hand, if Reed had been able to keep the Indians south of the Red River for one more day, he would have tried to annihilate them. It was brutal, incessant warfare, and each man wondered at the naïveté of Agent Rusk, who did not comprehend this.

Captain Reed accomplished nothing at Camp Hope except his own humiliation, which he accepted silently, but on his return to Fort Garner he felt he must

as a responsible commanding officer broach a subject which threatened to under-
mine the effectiveness of his troops. He summoned Logan and began cautiously:
'Were you able to speak with Colonel Minor when they brought him in? Very bad
knock in the left hip.'

'Two minutes, three minutes. As you would expect, he was smiling.'

'Very good man, Minor. He performed well at the Cairns.'

'You'd expect him to.'

'He'll be a long time mending. Perhaps we should send him home.'

'He wouldn't like that. He asked me to assure you . . .'

Reed had to wonder whether Minor had actually said that, or whether Logan
was merely endeavoring to keep Nellie Minor close at hand, and he judged that
now was the time to be frank: 'Major, Johnny Minor's going to have a rough time
with that hip. He'll need all the support he can muster. From his wife especially.'

'That is sure.'

'I'd take it kindly, Major, and so would Mrs. Reed, if you saw less of Minor's
wife.'

'Yes, sir.'

No more was said, and Reed told his wife: 'I think the matter of Nellie Minor
has been settled,' and Mrs. Reed said: 'Thank God. These things can get so out of
hand in a lonely fort.'

This one was far from settled, however, for even if her lover was willing to
cease the affair, Nellie Minor was not, and one morning, after dressing her husband's suppurating wound, she mounted a horse and rode far out to the tank,
where she had insisted that Jim Logan meet her. They allowed their horses to
wander into that glade where the Indians had observed them before the attack on
the wagon train, and there they renewed their passionate love. When they lay
looking up at the endless blue sky, Logan said: 'The last time. I can't make love to
the wife of a wounded comrade.'

'You damned men! You know he cares nothing for me.'

'He did. And now he needs you.'

'Need! Need! That's all I hear. I need things too.'

Mrs. Reed, who learned quickly of Nellie's brazen escapade, was not disposed
to have this headstrong young woman wreck her husband's command by some act
that would be reported to Washington. Fort Garner had already been marked
unfavorably because of the loss of men in the attack upon the wagons and because
Reed had allowed Matark to reach sanctuary across the river, and one more
unfavorable notice might be decisive. She therefore summoned both Nellie and
her lover to her rooms in the commander's building, the second on the base to be
converted to stone—the hospital invariably being first—and there she presented
them with surprising information.

'I have consulted with the surgeon from Fort Richardson, and he at first warned me that Colonel Minor was too weak to be moved. So I had to bide my time and let you two run wild.'

'We have not—' Nellie tried to break into the speech, but Mrs. Reed ignored her.

'But now your husband is mending, Mrs. Minor, and I am asking that he be taken from here in an ambulance . . . tomorrow. And my husband is recommending that when he is recovered he be assigned to desk duty with Lieutenant General Sheridan in Chicago. You will accompany him when he leaves this fort.'

Logan felt that he must protest: 'There is no cause for such dismissal.'

'Mrs. Minor is not being dismissed. She is merely accompanying her husband, as a good wife should.'

'But—'

'Especially when he has been wounded in a gallant charge against the Comanche.' She was implacable in her opposition to this adulterous pair and had taken the precaution of informing others, before the meeting took place, that the Minors were being shipped out, and had arranged that the ambulance which would carry them away be brought to the rear of the hospital, where its wheels and fittings were being checked.

So when Johnny Minor's lady and her Irish lover left the commander's quarters, everyone on the base, even the black cavalry privates, knew that they were in disgrace, and since her reputation could degenerate no further, Nellie went boldly to the stables, where she asked one of the cavalrymen to saddle her horse, and upon it she rode toward the tank. Moments later Logan, in disregard of the punishment that must surely be visited upon him, rode after her, and the fort buzzed at his arrogant defiance. Even a laundress who worked sometimes in the hospital as a kind of nurse felt obligated to inform wounded Johnny Minor of his wife's intemperate behavior; he ignored the gossip, taking refuge in the fact that very shortly he would be rid of Fort Garner and its complexities, but finding no assurance that when his headstrong wife reached Chicago she would behave any differently.

Before Nellie had reached the tank, Logan had overtaken her, and when he saw the extreme agitation which possessed her, he realized for the first time that their love-making had become considerably more than a mere escapade. It was now something so important in her life that she could not face surrendering it, no matter what cold New England women like Mrs. Reed said or what Reed himself might do to protect the integrity of his command.

'I won't go to Chicago. I won't waste my life with that cripple.'

'You'll have to. Can't stay here.'

'I'll leave the ambulance when we reach Jacksborough. Finish with the army, Jim, and join me there.'

'And do what?' This was a compelling question, for he was an Irishman trained only in the care of horses and their utilization in battle. He had not wanted assignment to a regiment of Negro cavalry, but he had accepted because that was the only pattern of life open to him, and now even that frail opportunity was being threatened. 'I can't leave the regiment.'

She sat on the ground beside the gray water and enticed him to join her, and after they had made love, for the last time he swore to himself, she casually reached across to where his belt lay and took from its holster his heavy Colts, pointing its barrel at her head: 'I think it best if I end this nightmare.'

'Nell! Put that down!' He reached out to retrieve his gun, when he saw to his horror that she was now pointing it at him, and with a skill he had not suspected, she was releasing the safety. The last thing he saw was the steel-gray barrel aimed at his forehead and her finger pressing the trigger.

As soon as he fell, she resolutely and with no regrets placed the barrel deep in her mouth, its end jammed against the roof, and pressed the trigger a second time.

Preoccupation with the tragedy ended when a special courier arrived from head-quarters in St. Louis in response to an urgent appeal from the governor of Texas. Major Comstock, after revealing his purpose to Reed, asked permission to address the officers: 'Gentlemen, as you've probably heard, the Texas Rangers are being reactivated for the first time since the end of the late war. They're needed because that damned bandit Benito Garza has been chewing up American settlements along the Rio Grande. They need our help.'

Wetzel, as a professional soldier, growled: 'If you listen to the Texans, their Rangers can defeat anybody. Why do they need us?'

Comstock had a reply so convoluted that these professionals gasped in wonder at its fatuity: 'Garza holes up on the Mexican side of the river. The U. S. Army can't touch him. From that sanctuary he makes sorties into the United States, robbing and killing. If we catch him over here, of course we can kill him, but we cannot chase him if he escapes to Mexico. Forbidden by international law. Absolutely forbidden by Washington.'

'Then why are we going?' Wetzel asked.

'To support the Rangers. They can cross the river. Not being legally a part of our forces, they can pursue the bandits in what they're calling "hot pursuit," that is, in the heat of battle.'

Reed broke in: 'So our troops are to protect the American side while the Rangers go after them?'

'Precisely. And that's all you're to do. Because if you invade Mexico to get him, you become bandits, just like him.'

For two hours Comstock reviewed this unusual situation, placing before the restless officers so many ramifications that Wetzel snapped: 'Hell, this sounds like our border with Indian Territory. The Comanche sneak in and kill, then dart back across the border and claim immunity.'

'Exactly, but in Garza's case it's even more complex, because a foreign power is involved.'

Now the question became 'whom to send?'—and Reed pointed out that with the deaths of young Toomey at Three Cairns and Logan at the tank, plus the disabling injury to Minor, his staff was pretty well depleted, especially in the cavalry.

'What about this Lieutenant Renfro?'

'Desk duty, Washington. Can't seem to pry him loose.'

'One of those,' Comstock said with disgust, and no more was needed.

Finally, both Reed and Comstock agreed that the ideal man for the assignment was Wetzel, and when this was decided, the courier asked that he meet with Reed and Wetzel alone. As they sat in Reed's stone house the major was blunt: 'Captain Wetzel, I've heard only the highest praise for your military prowess, but this is an assignment fraught with danger. Can you be trusted to take your men right up to the edge of the Rio Grande and keep them there, regardless of provocation, until you catch Garza on our side of the river?'

'Yes, sir.'

'None of this "hot pursuit"?'

'No, sir. Here on this northern border of Texas we learn discipline.'

'Captain Wetzel, on this border you have hundreds of observers to report if you stray. On the southern border you have only yourself to enforce the rules.'

'Sir, I'm an army captain. I'm also a Prussian. I've been trained to obey orders.'

'And you understand those orders?'

'I do. No soldier under my command will step one inch into Mexico.'

'Good. I want it in writing.' And while Reed watched, Comstock took from his papers an order, prepared in St. Louis, stating that the officer who endorsed it would allow no excursions into Mexico. The signing was as solemn an undertaking as Wetzel had ever participated in, and when he finished he saluted.

Comstock resumed: 'Now, as to your mounted scouts. They'll have to be black, of course.'

'We'll send Company R,' Reed said, 'but the only officer we can spare is that chinless wonder Asperson they just sent us from West Point.' When Wetzel groaned, Reed added: 'But this big sergeant, Jaxifer, he'll more than make up.'

Next morning reveille sounded at half an hour before dawn, and when the files were mounted and Reed had delivered a farewell address wishing his men well, Major Comstock, astride a black stallion, motioned Wetzel aside and shared with him certain verbal orders which moved this expedition into its proper military framework. He chose his words carefully, for upon them would hang the reputations of many officers: 'General Sheridan commanded me to tell whoever led the troops to the Rio Grande that he must not, repeat not, cross into Mexico.'

'I endorsed that order.'

'But he told me further that this officer would be responsible for the honor of the United States, and that in extremity the officer must follow the highest traditions of the army . . . as he interprets them . . . on the spot.'

As the sun rose above the buildings of Fort Garner, the two officers saluted.

Wetzel's force consisted of forty-eight infantry plus a truncated company of Buffalo Soldiers, a tough, experienced, well-disciplined group of men. Their path to where Benito Garza was raiding was compass south, then a slight veer toward San Antonio, and another slight jog east toward the small riverfront town of Bravo, where headquarters would be established at Fort Grimm and where contact would be made with the Texas Rangers.

On the trip south only one problem arose: Wetzel still did not like black soldiers and found it impossible to be congenial with them, but he did try to be fair. However, no matter what decision had to be made, the black troops knew that invariably they got the worst location for their tents, the poorest food and the most grudging amenities. The situation was exacerbated by the poor performance of their young officer, Lieutenant Asperson, scion of an old New England family that had prevailed upon their cousin, a senator from Massachusetts, to get the boy into West Point and, upon graduation, an assignment in some post of importance. The authorities, irritated by such pressures, had assured Senator Asperson that his nephew would 'get one of the finest duty stations,' and had then sent him to Fort Garner, one of the most dangerous.

Armstrong Asperson was an awkward, inept, stoop-shouldered fellow who should have worn a frown to reflect his inability to adjust to the normal world. Instead, regardless of what disaster overtook him, and he was prone to disasters, he grinned vacuously and with a startling show of teeth. Did it rain when his men had no ponchos? He grinned. Did Wetzel give him his daily chewing out? He grinned. After he had been at the fort for about a week he went down to Suds Row for his laundry, and one of the toughest washerwomen summarized him in words which ricocheted about the station: 'They hung the clock on the wall but forgot two of the parts.'

So young Asperson, with two parts missing, was heading for his first battle, and both his colonel and his company were aghast to think that soon they might be fighting alongside this grinning scarecrow. Wetzel treated him with contempt and Jaxifer with condescension. 'What we got to do, men,' he said, 'is stay close to him if anything happens so he don't shoot hisse'f in the foot.'

Jaxifer, whose entire life had been spent protecting himself from the peculiarities of white bosses, found little difficulty in adjusting either to Wetzel's injustices or to Asperson's inadequacies. Of Wetzel he said: 'Look, men, he infantry and he just don't know nothin' 'bout cavalry. Keep yore mouf shut.' Of Asperson: 'Remember, even General Grant, he have to start somewhere. But I doubt he start as low as Asperson.'

Thanks to Jaxifer's counsel, the long march ended without incident, and during the second day in their quarters at Bravo they met for the first time a Texas Ranger, and they were not impressed. He wore no uniform; in an almost ludicrous manner he carried strapped to his saddle two rifles and four Colts, and nothing about him was army-clean. A small, wiry man in his late forties, he reported to Wetzel's tent wearing a long white linen duster that came to his ankles.

Without saluting, the small, diffident man said: 'You Wetzel? I'm Macnab.'

'You?' Wetzel said in unmasked surprise. 'I thought you'd be much bigger.'

'I look bigger when I'm on a horse,' Macnab said without smiling. 'I'm sure glad to have your help.' And without further amenities he began to draw maps in the sand outside Wetzel's tent.

'It's tough down here,' Macnab said. 'Maybe even tougher than fighting Comanche.'

'Now that would be pretty tough.'

'Problem is, this Benito Garza, I've known him all my life, he's a lot smarter than me, and if you'll permit the expression, maybe a lot smarter than most of your men.'

'I've heard that,' Wetzel said, displaying a professional interest in a military situation. 'How does he operate?'

'Clever as a possum,' Macnab said, and he let his explanation end as the cook beat upon a ring, signaling supper.

While Wetzel smoked his cigar at sunset, Macnab resumed his map drawing: 'Garza waits till something happens on this side of the border. And things do happen.'

'Like hanging Mexican landowners?'

'Mexicans ask for hanging,' Macnab said. 'But when it happens, Garza feels he must retaliate. And he does.'

'In the same region?'

Macnab looked about for a blade of grass, found one, and chewed on it: 'Now there's the problem. Always he confuses us. Four times in a row he strikes within a mile of where some Mexican was hanged. Next time, fifty miles away.'

'How can you anticipate?'

Macnab chewed on his grass, then confessed: 'We can't.' There was a long silence, then as darkness approached from the east, Macnab said quietly: 'Captain Wetzel, let me tell you what's going on now.'

'Proceed.'

'We have good reason to think that Garza has taken command of a ranch, El Solitario, about ten miles south of here. He has forty, fifty men there, and they fan out to execute their revenge up and down the river.'

No one spoke. More than two minutes passed without a word, for each of the three men attending the meeting knew what Macnab was proposing: that he and his Rangers cross the Rio Grande, make a sudden descent upon the hidden ranch, shoot Garza, and rely upon the United States Army to support them as they beat a frantic retreat with forty or fifty well-mounted Mexican riders striving to overtake them.

Still silent, Macnab drew in the sand the location of Bravo, the river, the distant location of Rancho El Solitario, plus the circuitous route to it and the short, frenzied retreat back to the Rio Grande. When everything was in place he said softly: 'It could be done.'

Bluntly, Wetzel scuffed his foot along the escape route: 'You mean, if someone came along here to hold off your pursuers?'

'Couldn't be done otherwise.'

Wetzel leaned back, folded his arms like an irritated German schoolmaster, and said: 'I have the strictest orders forbidding me to step one inch onto Mexican soil.'

'I'm sure you do,' Macnab said quietly. 'But what if my sixteen Rangers came down that road you just scratched out, with fifty Mexicans sure to overtake us before we reached the river?'

'I would have my men lined up on this side of the river, every gun at the ready. Sergeant Gerton and a Gatling gun would be prepared to rake the river if the Mexicans tried to invade this side. And I would pray for you.'

'Would you allow your men to come to the middle of the river to help?'

'Is that the boundary between the two countries?'

'It is.'

'My best gunners would be there.'

Now came the time for a direct question: 'But you wouldn't come into Mexico to help?'

'Absolutely not.'

That ended the consultation, so without showing his disappointment, Macnab rode back to his own camp upriver, and it was unfortunate that he went in that direction because downriver some recent arrivals from Tennessee slew four Mexicans trying to prevent illegal seizure of their ancestral ranch land.

Next morning, about noon, Otto Macnab was back to consult with Wetzel: 'I'm sure Garza will strike within the next three days. But where?'

'Do you think we should scatter our forces?'

'I really don't know. If he starts out now, within three days he could be almost anywhere. Since spies must have informed him of your arrival, he'll hit somewhere near here, to shame you.'

'So we should stay put?'

'I think so.'

Garza, infuriated by the killing of peasants trying to protect land once owned by his mother, Trinidad de Saldaña, was grimly determined to let the intruders know that this fight was going to be interminable and, as Macnab had predicted, he could do this most effectively by striking close to the new encampment. He allowed five days to lapse, then six, then seven, so that the Rangers and the soldiers would be disoriented. On the night of the eighth day he rode with thirty of his best men across the Rio Grande and devastated two ranches east of Bravo, killing three Texans and escaping to safety before either the Rangers or the soldiers could be alerted.

He took his men on a wide swing back to the safety of El Solitario. This nest of adobe houses was completely surrounded by a high stone-and-adobe wall, which enclosed fruit trees, a well and enough cattle to feed his men for more than a month. It was a frontier ranch, so built as to protect its inhabitants from assaults coming from any direction, but its major asset was that it lay far enough inland from the river to make an attack from Texas unlikely.

Macnab did not think it was impregnable: 'Informers tell us Garza did the job downriver with no more than thirty men, who are now holed up at his ranch with about twenty others. I'm going in there and finish Benito Garza.'

He spoke these words not to Wetzel but to his Rangers, sixteen of them, the youngest only sixteen years old. Then he added: 'I do not order any of you to come with me, but I'm inviting volunteers.' As two men stepped forward he stopped them: 'You know, I've been after Garza for thirty years. I've made it my life's work. I have to go. You don't.'

'I want him too,' a thin, fierce Texan said. 'He killed my brother.'

Every Ranger volunteered, but the boy he turned back: 'No, Sam. It wouldn't be fair.'

'I'm here because he burned our ranch.'

'Well, you stay behind and lead the troops when they come to rescue us.'

'They said they wouldn't do that.'

'That's what they said, but they'll come. Lead them to that fork we saw on our last scout.' When the boy showed his disappointment, Macnab asked: 'You remember where the fork is? We'll be coming there hell-for-leather. Have the soldiers in position to do us some good.'

He took off his duster, folded it neatly, and stowed it. His men placed beside it things they did not care to risk on this adventure, and when everyone was ready, Macnab took out his watch and handed it to the boy, instructing him as to how it should be used. At five that afternoon Captain Macnab and his Rangers forded the Rio Grande, rode north, then cut into heavy mesquite. Through the night they moved cautiously toward Garza's ranch, but at half an hour before sunup they had the bad luck to be spotted by Mexicans living on a smaller ranch. There was some noise and a scattering of chickens, after which a young man shouted: 'Rinches!'

Men started running for their horses, but each was shot before he could mount. There would be no messenger riding forth from this ranch, and to ensure that no woman tried to spread the alarm, all horses in the corral were shot, and Rangers bound the four remaining women and locked them in a room.

It was nearly dawn when Macnab's men reached the high walls of the Garza compound, and now a brief council of war was held, not to devise tactics, for they had been agreed upon days before, but to specify tasks. At a signal, four Rangers crashed through the main gate, paving the way for the rest to follow. There was a blaze of gunfire, and then in the doorway appeared the white-haired figure of Benito Garza, his two pistols drawn, ready for battle.

Macnab, who had anticipated such an appearance, steadied his rifle against a watering trough and for a second recalled that similar moment on the eve of the battle at Buena Vista when through gallantry he had allowed Garza to escape, and he saw also that incredible scene in 1848 when Garza had passed by him within inches during the escape of Santa Anna into exile. 'Not this time, Uncle Benito,' he muttered as Garza started to leave the doorway.

The heavy bullet sped straight to the heart, and the great bandit, protector of his people, lurched forward, expecting to see his ancient enemy in some shadow, but he saw nothing, and toppled to his death.

'Away!' Macnab shouted, and according to plan, three of the Rangers tried to shoot the Mexican horses, but failed. In a wild exit, during which one of the daring Texans was picked off, fifteen Rangers including Macnab made their escape from within the high walls and started their ride of desperation toward the river.

At four o'clock that morning the sixteen-year-old Ranger began looking at Captain Macnab's watch, and at four-thirty he followed instructions. Galloping his horse past the sentries, he pulled up at Captain Wetzel's tent and shouted: 'The Rangers are attacking El Solitario!'

'When?' Wetzel cried as he left his tent with a sheet about his shoulders.

'Right now!'

'Why wasn't I warned?'

'I am warning you. Captain Macnab told me: "Tell him at four-thirty. I don't want him to worry all night." '

'Bugler, sound assembly!' and in the darkness Wetzel mustered his men, ordering them into full battle gear.

'Are we going across to help?' Sergeant Gerton asked, and Wetzel said: 'No.'

At dawn he mounted his black charger and rode about supervising the placement of his troops, putting his best sharpshooters along the American bank of the Rio Grande. He personally directed Gerton and his two men where to place their Gatling gun to command the crossing. He called for volunteers to wade out into the shallow river and point their guns to where the fleeing Rangers would probably appear, and then he rode to where his Buffalo Soldiers were encamped, some distance from the white troops. Almost contemptuously he dismissed Lieutenant Asperson with a curt order: 'Take half your company and guard that other crossing.' Then he rode to where Sergeant Jaxifer waited with ten mounted troopers, and started this crucial conversation:

WETZEL: You know what's happening over there?

JAXIFER: I can guess.

WETZEL: You know my orders?

JAXIFER: Yes, sir.

WETZEL: When those Rangers come galloping to that river, what will you and your men do?

JAXIFER: Wait for orders.

WETZEL: Will you be ready to cross and hold back the Mexicans?

JAXIFER: We ready right now.

WETZEL *(listening for the sound of gunfire to begin):* I've learned respect for you on this trip, Jaxifer. Why do we have so much trouble with our white infantry and so little with your black cavalry?

JAXIFER: Because we black.

WETZEL: What does that mean?

JAXIFER: You white officers never understand.

WETZEL: Tell me.

JAXIFER: In the whole United States ain't nothin' a black man can hope for half as good as bein' in the Buffalo Soldiers. Black mens dream of this, they pray, they do almost anything for white mens, just to get in the Tenth Cavalry. I'm the biggest black man in Texas, because I'm a sergeant in the Tenth. Colonel Wetzel, I will die rather than lose that job.

WETZEL: Why didn't you tell me this before?

JAXIFER: Because it's our secret. We ain't never before had honor, but we got it now, and we will not risk it.

WETZEL: What does that mean to me this morning?

JAXIFER: Without orders from you, we don't move. With orders, we'll ride to Mexico City or die tryin'.

WETZEL: Everything ready?

JAXIFER: When you sent Asperson away, I kept the best men with me. We all want to be on the far side of that river.

WETZEL: If the Mexicans make one wrong move, I'll lead you.

JAXIFER: We hungry to go.

The two men remained astride their horses, immobilized by the great traditions of their army. Jaxifer desperately wanted to lead his men in a charge to rescue the white fighters; that was the whole purpose of his cavalry and the reason for his being in uniform, but he could not move, even though the Rangers died, unless he had an order. And Captain Wetzel, who had followed soldiering since a boy, in both Germany and America, longed for battle. He loved it, loved the excitement of the chase, the fury of the sudden explosion when armies met. But he had unmistakable orders to refrain unless the United States was invaded.

But then the secret words of Major Comstock echoed: 'The officer will be expected to follow the highest traditions of the army.' That had to mean the rescue of fellow Americans in danger, and for such action he was more than prepared. Spurring his horse toward the river, with Jaxifer following, he turned and said: 'I hope those Mexicans make one mistake, fire one bullet into our territory.'

The tangled reflections of the two impatient soldiers were broken by the appearance of the young Ranger. 'Where are you going?' Wetzel asked and the boy replied: 'To lead the niggers to where the trails meet.'

'Who told you to do that?'

'Captain Macnab. He was sure that when you heard gunfire you'd send them, no matter what your orders said.'

Disgusted by this unprofessional behavior on the part of the Rangers and wishing to rid himself of the boy, Wetzel growled: 'They're down there,' indicating the other crossing, where lanky Lieutenant Asperson sat grinning with a smaller group of Buffalo Soldiers.

While Wetzel and Jaxifer were agonizing over their alternatives, Otto Macnab and his Rangers were in full retreat, fighting a rear-guard action of desperation, and they might have escaped without help from the hesitant soldiers had not a daring Mexican bandit, accompanied by six others, known of a shortcut to the river. Pounding down its narrow turns, these determined men reached a point on the escape route just before Macnab, and a furious gun battle raged, forcing the Rangers to move downriver from their planned route.

This threw them onto a trail which would bring them to the lesser crossing of the Rio Grande, guarded by the lesser black cavalry, and as the Rangers and their pursuers approached the river, Asperson could hear the sound of gunfire. Excited by the likelihood of his first battle, he started his Buffalo Soldiers toward the river, then stopped them in obedience to the orders he had memorized. The young Ranger, watching with dismay as the rescue operation halted, pulled a clever trick. Throwing a sharp pebble at Asperson's horse, he made the horse rear, and the nervous lieutenant cried in a high voice: 'My God, we're under attack!'

Consulting no one, waiting for no verification, he waved his revolver in the air as if it were a sword, and shouted: 'To the rescue.' For him there was no anxiety, no nagging moral problem. Americans were under attack by foreigners, and by God he was going to do something about it. With a roar, his black troops followed.

During the disorganized charge, in which black cavalrymen passed and repassed their ungainly leader, he did retain enough control to order the bugler to sound 'Charge' so that the beleaguered Rangers would know of their coming. Because of the uneven terrain, the bugle kept slipping from the bugler's lips, but the broken sounds did reach the battle area, giving the Rangers hope and throwing their pursuers into confusion.

Macnab said later: 'The Buffalo Soldiers came roaring out of the mesquite like six different armies. They were a mob, but they were magnificent.'

The confused battle—more like a riot, really—lasted only a few minutes. Not many Mexicans were killed and no Americans, but when it was over, Macnab and Asperson rode like Roman victors down to the Rio Grande, and as they splashed their horses into that shallow, muddy stream, the regular army on the American side went berserk. The advance guard, standing in the river, fired indiscriminately. Sergeant Gerton and his Gatling gun sprayed the empty Mexican shore, the others cheered, and Wetzel looked on in amazement.

By ten that morning he had a telegram started on its way to headquarters: IN OBEDIENCE HIGHEST TRADITIONS US ARMY 10TH CAVALRY 2ND LT. ASPERSON UNDER ATTACK BY MEXICAN BANDITS RETALIATED WITH GREAT GALLANTRY STOP BENITO GARZA DEAD ONE RANGER CASUALTY, NO ARMY MANY MEXICAN

When Sergeant Jaxifer read his men a copy of this precious verification of their victory, one of his troopers said: 'Cain't understand. They tell me Macnab just kill his best friend, but he act like nothin' happened. Look!' And the cavalrymen watched as Macnab unfolded his white linen duster, threw it about his shoulders, and started that day's routine.

With Captain Wetzel and Lieutenant Asperson absent on detached duty along the Rio Grande, Fort Garner was hurting for officers, and what made the deficiency most painful was that clever Lewis Renfro still malingered in Washington. In some anger Captain Reed dispatched an urgent appeal to St. Louis: 'Fort Garner has acute need services First Lieutenant Lewis Renfro, Brevet Colonel, currently on detached duty Washington.'

In the capital there was a good deal of dickering with Congress before Renfro could be released for active duty, because both he and his wife pulled strings to prevent him from being moved out of his socially pleasing job as liaison with the omnipotent Quartermaster Corps. Mrs. Renfro was especially effective in this campaign, for she knew several senators and representatives on the military committees, and she lobbied to keep her husband in the capital: 'Senator, you served during the late war. You know that speeding supplies to the troops, it wins many a battle.' Since she was pretty as well as clever, her arguments were almost irresistible, but when a gruff colonel who had behaved with distinction at both Gettysburg and the Wilderness presented the Congressional committee with the record of Lieutenant Renfro, they had to pay attention: 'Gentlemen, since that day at Appomattox your Lieutenant Renfro has been constantly assigned to battle stations on the frontier, that's a period of seven years, and during that time he has maneuvered detached desk assignments for all but five weeks. Renfro is another fighting man who never fights.'

One senator, who had been impressed by Mrs. Renfro's defense of her husband, asked: 'But doesn't he make a crucial contribution here? Assuring your men their supplies?'

The colonel refrained from pointing out that anyone with a fifth-grade education could do as well; instead he made a clever observation: 'Senator! I am not for one minute denigrating Renfro's enviable record in the late war. I am thinking only of his career.'

'What do you mean?'

'Unless he can show on his record proof of command in the field, how can he ever be promoted to the high rank which every fighting man aspires to? If he doesn't include active duty in a position of importance, he can never become general.'

Such argument made sense to the congressmen with military records, and shortly thereafter Renfro received orders to report at once to his assigned Company S, 10th Cavalry at Fort Sam Garner on the Texas frontier, to serve under the command of Captain George Reed (Brevet Brigadier General).

When Daisy Renfro heard the doleful news she stormed: 'A nigger regiment! It scars a man for life. Lewis, you will not be in that fort six weeks, I promise. We did it before, we can do it again.' And she started immediately the intense campaign to recall her husband to his preferred job in Washington.

Before the Renfros had time to report, two inspection teams visited Fort Garner, for the army feared that something fundamental might be wrong at this lonely command; newspaper stories had begun asking questions which had to be answered.

The first visit came from regimental headquarters at Fort Sill, and it was led by one of the splendid, tragic figures of the Civil War. Benjamin Grierson, a Pennsylvania farm boy, had been serving as an underpaid music teacher in Illinois when the late war started. Distrustful of horses after having been kicked in the face by one, he protested when assigned to a cavalry unit, of which he became the commander. Soon thereafter, finding no one else eligible, the quiet music teacher was summoned for a most difficult and dangerous mission: 'We must prevent the Confederates from moving reinforcements to the defense of Vicksburg. Take your troops as a raiding party. Move behind enemy lines on the east bank of the Mississippi and disrupt communications as much as possible.'

With no fixed headquarters and no reliable supply, the thirty-seven-year-old music teacher ran wild for sixteen days, always on the verge of capture by superior Confederate forces, always on hand at some surprising moment to wreck a train or burn a stores depot. He fought innumerable small battles, fleeing always to some new position from which to make his next assault. At the conclusion of these incredible raids, his men reported: 'Seventeen hundred of us rode six hundred miles behind enemy lines, losing only three killed, nine missing. We killed about a hundred of the enemy, captured and paroled over five hundred, destroyed more than sixty miles of railroad, captured three thousand stand of arms, and took over a thousand mules and horses.'

Grierson had been a military phenomenon, an untrained layman who intuitively understood the most subtle arts of mounted warfare. His men loved him, for they knew him to be both lucky and brave, an irresistible combination, and he achieved a much greater success in the backwoods of Mississippi and Louisiana than more notable cavalry commanders like Jeb Stuart did in the East. He was one of the foremost cavalry commanders in American history, and as a consequence he had risen to the rank of brevet general.

But when peace came he faced the unalterable opposition of all West Point officers, who leveled four charges against him: he was a civilian; he was a music teacher; on the Texas frontier he tried to treat Indians as if they were honorable opponents like Frenchmen or Englishmen; and he was soiled by being personally responsible for the black troops of the 10th Cavalry, an unacceptable command with which he would be stuck for twenty-two years.

Grierson was a talented man, a true genius, and he suffered the contempt of his fellow officers without complaint. He did believe that if Indians were treated justly, they could be brought into full citizenship, and he did defend the bravery and competency of his Negro troops, for he knew from frontier reports how well the latter performed under fire. It was headquarters that did not believe; most critically, it was the newspapers in Texas that deplored having Negro troops protecting the Texas frontier. Their attacks were savage: 'We need no niggers here. Give us fifty Rangers and we can clear the plains all the way to California.'

When General Grierson, his brevet rank honored along the frontier, arrived at Fort Garner he was forty-six, still lean, still alert. He was stigmatized immediately by the Prussian Wetzel, back from the Rio Grande, as a man deficient in discipline, one of those weaklings who try to rule by the affection of troops rather than by rigorous command, and Wetzel had watched too many times as such officers came to a bad end. Wetzel, like most of the regulars, held the former music teacher in contempt.

The other officers, especially those in the 10th Cavalry, did not. They knew from personal experience that he was a gallant leader who defended the prerogatives of his men and who led them to one quiet success after another; some actually loved him for the legendary heroics he had performed during the war, but most of the infantry officers and men, who could not believe what this quiet man had accomplished, dismissed him as another eccentric leader of colored troops.

In a tremendously concentrated half-day General Grierson satisfied himself on many points, which he stated in the report he wrote that night:

At the Battle of Three Cairns units of the 10th Cavalry deported themselves according to the highest traditions of the service. 2nd Lt. Elmer Toomey directed his men properly and died gallantly at their head. 1st Sgt. John Jaxifer assumed command as expected, and defended an exposed position with valor. I can give no credence to charges made by the Cavin & Clark drivers that Sgt. Jaxifer was in any way deficient. This battle will shine brightly among the laurels gained by this Regiment.

The death of 2nd Lt. Jim Logan, one of our most accomplished horsemen from Ireland, and the scandal attaching thereto, is the kind of tragedy which can overtake any unit of any kind, civilian or military. I treasured Logan as a brave man and I mourn his death.

In all respects I find these units of the 10th Cavalry in good condition, battle-ready and well led. Their desertion rate is 1 in 300. Desertion rate of the white troops at the fort, 48 in 100 over a period of four and a half years. I especially commend these enlisted men who serve so faithfully and with such enthusiasm, and I applaud Capt. Reed's leadership, finding nothing to censure.

On the next day General Grierson reviewed his troops and then asked Sergeant Jaxifer to lead him out to where Jim Logan and Johnny Minor's wife had died. Jaxifer told his men later: 'General, when he see the spot, and the water, and the birds, he dismounts and stands by the spot weepin'. I stayed clear, but he motion me to dismount, and together we placed some stones. "Two good men," he said a couple times, meanin' Logan and Minor. He never mention Miss Nellie.'

That night the Reeds held a gala for the visitors, and one of the Mexicans whom the soldiers employed to work the horses appeared with a violin, one of the laundresses beat a tambourine, and there was dancing, and the best food possible purchased from the post sutler, and much conversation about the old days. Even Wetzel relaxed, telling of his unit's exploits at various battles, and it was 'General This,' and 'Colonel That' as if the old ranks still pertained, as if the old salary scale were still being paid instead of the miserly pay accorded these heroic veterans: once a lieutenant colonel, now a first lieutenant, $1,500 a year; once a general, now a captain, $1,800 a year.

Grierson was at his best, even joking with dour Hermann Wetzel: 'Your boys over in Prussia are going to conquer all Europe one of these days,' to which Wetzel replied: 'They will certainly conquer France.'

That night Reed could not sleep, and when his wife heard his restless turning she asked why, and he said: 'My mother was an educated woman, you know, and she made us memorize poetry. She taught us that the finest single line comes at the end of Milton's sonnet to his dead wife.'

'I don't know that,' Louise said.

'The first thirteen lines tell of how the blind poet dreams that she has come back from the grave to speak with him. "Love, sweetness, goodness in her person shined," that was my mother, too. But then came the fourteenth line, and everything fell apart. Mother said its ten short words were arrows pointed at the heart, showing what blindness meant: "I waked, she fled, and day brought back my night." '

They lay in the darkness for some time, and then the general sighed deeply, making the anguish of his thought echo through the room: 'Tonight I was a general once more. Tomorrow the bugles will sound, dawn will break, and I shall be a captain again . . . and forever.'

The second investigating team was completely different. Lieutenant General Philip Sheridan, a marvelously concentrated Irishman with a bullet head and drooping walrus mustaches—a sort of roundish, ineffectual-looking man until one discovered that every bulge was muscle—rode into the fort with three of his pet colonels, men, he said, of infinite promise. Most powerful was Ranald Mackenzie, a man so intense, said his troops, that 'his eyes could cut rocks'; he was destined to leapfrog his contemporaries and stand at the threshold of commander in chief, until his mind snapped, destroyed by syphilis and by the burdens he had placed upon it.

There was Nelson Miles, not a West Point man but something much better: the nephew-by-marriage of both General William Tecumseh Sherman, head of the Army, and Senator John Sherman, the powerful political leader from Ohio; he was an unproved quantity at the threshold of his career, but with his uncles' help he would gain constant promotion, a vain, arrogant, impossible man with only one credit to his name: he was a phenomenally brave officer when leading men into battle.

Most impressive, to men and women alike, was Lieutenant Colonel George Armstrong Custer, nearly six feet tall, never weighing more than a hundred and seventy, and of such elegant bearing that he commanded attention wherever he went. Like the other two, he was thirty-four, but he was totally unlike them in other respects; they wore ordinary military uniforms, well pressed and tended; he wore custom-tailored trousers and jacket, spats over his General Quimper boots, and a remarkable Russian-type greatcoat cut from a heavy French cloth and with a monstrous cape adorned with Afghanistan caracul fur at the neck, along the front and at the cuffs. His face was cadaverously thin, with romantic hollows under his cheekbones, and he was obviously worried about the gradual retreat of his hair, for like many vain men he twisted and trained it to lie across his forehead and hide the loss. At the neck he wore his hair very long, and since it was naturally wavy, enhanced by his wife's constant attention with hot irons, it added considerably to his appeal. Like most officers of that period, he wore a mustache which he kept so carefully trimmed that it added dignity to a face already as compelling as that of any Roman emperor's.

They were, as both Sherman and Sheridan agreed, three remarkable young colonels, and it was inevitable that one of them would gain supreme command. Mackenzie, perhaps the ablest of the three, would be disqualified because of creeping insanity; Custer would perish because of his inexcusable arrogance at the Little Big Horn; Miles, the political conniver, would prevail. In the military, as in all human endeavor, it can sometimes be the man who merely survives who triumphs, whether his skills warrant it or not.

Sheridan and his three aces needed little time to assess the situation at Fort Garner: 'Second rate in every respect. When a wife misbehaves like Nellie Minor, she should be soldiered out within the day. When an important supply train approaches, it should be protected by more than an untested second lieutenant. And when an Indian marauder like Matark ravages a countryside, he should be caught and hanged. Captain Reed is moderately acceptable, but the only officer present who seems to have an understanding of what a frontier fort should be is Captain Hermann Wetzel, who is hereby commended for his attention to detail.'

No formal rebuke was leveled against Captain Reed, but a kind of sorrow suffused the visit, as if the young colonels regretted that he was not a better man. Colonel Custer went out of his way to applaud Mrs. Reed's handling of the Johnny Minor affair, and he spellbound the other wives with his graciousness and warmth of understanding.

When Sheridan led his team away, the fort continued under the aura of the three colonels and there was much discussion as to which one would triumph in the battle for promotion. Wetzel summarized opinions: 'Miles is political, but very strong in the field, a powerful combination. Custer can achieve anything if he attends to details. Mackenzie's the one I'd like to lead me into battle.' The women did not bother with the credentials of the other two colonels: 'Custer is magnificent.' And he was, for he was considerate, charming, persistent, and suffused with that glamor which can only be called *romantic*. Even their husbands could not denigrate him when their wives applauded, for he was unquestionably the most dramatic leader ever to have visited Fort Garner, and his heavy felt spats and fur-trimmed greatcoat would long be remembered.

The fort received a shock when Lewis Renfro arrived with his alert wife, Daisy, for the traditional desk-hog was apt to be an obese, slovenly fellow with little military bearing. Renfro was quite the opposite, a thirty-six-year-old West Point man from a good family in Ohio, tall, erect, ten pounds underweight from daily horsemanship in the parks of Washington, and a man determined to give a good account of himself on the frontier. He would take Minor's place as head of Company S, 10th Cavalry under the command of Captain Reed, to whom he said unctuously: 'I want you to rely on me as one of the best officers you've ever had. When you give me an order, consider it executed.'

Fawningly eager to create a good impression, he sought out Captain Wetzel and assured him: 'I'll not permit any ridiculous cavalry-infantry unpleasantness while I command the Buffalo Soldiers. They'll be disciplined.' But that same day he implied quite the opposite to Jaxifer, to whom he told an outright lie concerning his experiences in the war: 'I served with Negro troops on three different occasions. None better. If the infantry give you any trouble, you'll find me on your side all the way.' But despite this trickery in fort politics, whenever an expedition against the Indians was organized he wanted to be in the lead, and from that position he gave a good account of himself.

'He knows how to fight,' Sergeant Jaxifer told his troopers. 'We got a good man this time.'

This was a sensible estimation, because when an energetic foray led by Renfro ran into outriders of the main Comanche force, a bitter running battle ensued, forty Indians on mounts of superior speed against nineteen cavalrymen with superior firepower. Neither side could claim a victory, but Renfro pursued the Indians with such vigor that any Comanche whose horse faltered even slightly was overtaken and shot. Renfro was always in the lead, probably the best single horseman on the field that day, and when the chase was over, the black soldiers were satisfied that they had gained a proficient leader.

In a second fray, when Reed was in command, Renfro accepted his subordinate position graciously and moved his contingent instantly when Reed signaled. He was a good officer, and Reed told Wetzel: 'Had he stayed out here with us instead of hiding in Washington, he could have been one of Sherman's Young Colonels,' and the German agreed that Renfro was first class. 'I think his name must be German,' Wetzel said. 'He carries himself so well.'

But Lewis Renfro had no intention of laboring on the frontier to establish his reputation as the fourth of the Young Colonels. He would perform impeccably with the troops, but he would also pull every string to get back to his desk job in Washington. By-passing established channels, he and his wife bombarded everyone in real command with clever petitions, and were assured: 'As soon as anything interesting happens, back you'll come.' What the incident might be the Renfros could not guess, but their hammering at the doors of preferment became so well known that Mrs. Reed felt she had to caution Daisy against her excesses, and in the room where so many had been quietly reprimanded, Daisy now took her place, but she proved to be quite different from her predecessors.

'Do you not see that your actions may be prejudicing your husband's chances?' Louise Reed asked.

'I am improving them. Lewis was born to serve in Washington, and I shall do my best to see that he does so.'

'But he is so capable at the front. He could be one of the great leaders.'

'He's already one of the great leaders, Mrs. Reed. He fights in Washington with a skill that not even Sherman and Sheridan could exhibit.'

'But the real fighting is out here, against the Indians.'

'Half of it is,' Daisy replied. 'And I do believe that the more important half, in peacetime, is back with us, fighting the battles in Congress.'

'But look at this fort, Mrs. Renfro. Does not the building of an establishment like this mean anything to you? When my husband came here . . . not a post erected, not a wall in place. He built a mud fort, and when the dead-house is finished, it will all be stone. A permanent testimony to the brave men who occupied it.'

Mrs. Renfro had to laugh: 'One act of Congress and this fort vanishes. Back to the mesquite. It's in Congress where the peacetime army fights its battles, and Lewis is going back to work with Congress, where he can do some good.'

Mrs. Reed had to be blunt: 'Mrs. Renfro, you certainly must be aware that your husband's report will be written by my husband. Why are you so daring in disregarding my counsel?'

'I do not disregard it, and I'm sure Lewis doesn't disregard your husband's. What can possibly be reported except that Lewis was foremost in battle, striking in his courage and immediately responsive to orders?'

'Yes, yes.'

'We both try to be like that. Haven't you seen that if you even hint at an instruction, I comply?'

'But I am now more than hinting that you should stop these letters.'

Now it was Daisy's turn to be obdurate: 'That's quite a different matter, dealing with the welfare of the entire army, not with a single fort. Lewis can aid immensely in getting our army the funds it needs, the support it requires. Of course I shall continue to help him get the post he deserves.'

The interview ended poorly, with battle lines drawn and animosities flaring, but the impasse did not continue long, because the kind of incident which the Renfro adherents in Washington needed to bring their man back home occurred, with an incandescent explosion that not even the most stalwart Renfro supporter could have anticipated.

During the hottest part of the summer of 1874, Renfro, Jaxifer and all the effectives of Company S, forty-seven in number, set forth on the supposed trail of Chief Matark, whose braves had spent that summer ravaging the ranches along the frontier. The Texas government had warned settlers not to venture too far west, and the United States government had explained that protection even from forts like Richardson and Garner could not ensure safety, but the insatiable hunger for land which would always characterize Texans lured the adventurers farther and farther west. Just as the four Larkin brothers had dared the empty plains, claiming their six thousand acres and holding them nicely until the Comanche struck, so now other daring men and women staked out their claims beyond the forts, and during this summer alone, sixty white men, women and children had been slain, usually in a manner so brutal and horrifying as to shock even those Texans who had become accustomed to the barbarisms.

After the annihilation of four ranch families well to the south and west of Fort Garner, Renfro sought permission to make a major sortie, and with innate clever-ness he did not ride directly south to where the crimes had occurred, but in a contrary direction, far to the west toward the Palo Duro Canyon and the extreme limits of the Indian Territory, for he reasoned that the triumphant Indians would have sped away from the burning ranches, then taken their time to head for sanctuary.

He was right. He and his men attacked the celebrating Comanche from the north, sweeping down on them in a sudden shattering attack, and because news-papers throughout the nation gave much space to what happened next, it is essential that the exact details be understood.

With Renfro in the lead, the 10th Cavalry launched a major attack, and accord-ing to plan, at the height of battle half the troops swung west under Renfro, half to the east under Jaxifer. Renfro and his men performed with signal valor, every-one testified to that, and by tremendous exertion turned the flank of the advancing Comanche, throwing the rest of the Indians into confusion.

When this occurred, Sergeant Jaxifer on the east saw a chance to sweep in and disrupt the Comanche completely, and he did this, but as his men galloped through the Indian ranks he caught sight of what he believed to be a white girl, and the idea flashed through his mind: That must be the Larkin child. Reacting more to instinct than to conscious plan, he wheeled his horse and pursued that group of Indians who held the girl. Alone and threatened by dozens of braves, he plunged on, overtook the fleeing Indians, reached out, and miraculously snatched the girl from her captors, clubbing with his gun the head of the brave who had been holding her.

Turning once more, he broke through the confused Indians to a point where his astonished black troops could give him coverage, and for some moments a violent struggle ensued, but with the girl in his arms, Jaxifer rallied his men until they prevailed. At this moment Renfro galloped up, saw the girl, and perceived at once her magical significance. Taking her gently from the sergeant, he held her close and asked: 'You are Emma Larkin?' and she replied, with full knowledge of what her words meant: 'I am.'

Thus the legend was born. Lewis Renfro, in an attack upon the savage Coman-che when his men were outnumbered a hundred to forty-nine, had recovered the white child Emma Larkin, whose family had been murdered at Bear Creek in 1869 and who had been captive of the savages for five long years. Stories were written in such a way as to indicate that Renfro's feat was the more astonishing in hat he was supported only by Negro troops, whose effectiveness in such warfare was not proved. Apparently it was his heroic persistence that had made the rescue possible.

The story proved wildly popular, with *Harper's* and the New York newspapers sending artists to Texas to depict the battle and the manner of Emma's rescue. Pictures proliferated, but they all faced two difficulties: it was not practical to show black troops at the scene, so faces were blurred, except for Lieutenant Renfro's, and the fact that Emma had no nose or ears meant that she could not be shown either, which meant that Renfro pretty well stole the show. In fact, on two occasions when the press were permitted to see Emma, some of the men vomited, and quite a few of their stories said merely that she had been 'poorly treated by her captors,' and even those two or three reporters who did mention the mutilations did not speak of the rapes. Americans then, as later, wanted their stories heroic but also respectful of the niceties.

More than two dozen detailed interviews spelled out Renfro's heroism and audacity; no one questioned Jaxifer. At one point Emma told a woman reporter the facts, but when this woman searched out Jaxifer, she was frightened by his bigness, his lack of a neck and his thick lips, so his part in the rescue was ignored.

This was the incident that Daisy Renfro needed to get her man back to Washington, and she orchestrated the affair skillfully. She sought a congratulatory telegram from Colonel Custer, and tender stories from other Texas settlers who said they wished that Lieutenant Renfro would rescue their lost children from Matark. Before the month was out, Washington was clamoring for its newest hero to return, and when Daisy and Lewis left Fort Garner they took care to ensure that both Captain and Mrs. Reed received credit for the fine manner in which the fort had been administered. Said Renfro to the press: 'You cannot have brave soldiers at a lonely frontier unless you have a fine commander in charge of them. Than Captain Reed there can be no finer.'

When the train pulled out of the station at New Orleans, he told his wife: 'We'll never see Texas again. What a desolate land.'

Emma Larkin, a twelve-year-old captive of the Comanche, had been a kind of holy grail of the plains, with all decent men striving to rescue her, a challenge that would not dissipate even with the passage of years; but Emma Larkin, a seventeen-year-old young woman aged beyond her years, was an embarrassment, and after the first flush of her victorious recapture, no one knew what to do with her.

The women at the fort, of course, had rejoiced at her return, but quickly they realized that there was no place for her in their lives; nor anywhere else, for that matter. For one thing, she had no family, all of her immediate relatives having been exterminated at Bear Creek and possible ones back east having been lost in the normal experiences of immigration. But more important, she was hideously ugly, a frail, stringy girl with almost no bosom and those terrible scars where her ears and nose should have been. Furthermore, she had formed the habit of speaking in a whisper, so that she often seemed like a ghost wandering in from another world. And after a few days of compassion, no one wanted to have her around.

Mrs. Reed did take it upon herself to represent the girl's interests in the land court at Jacksborough, for it was clear that Emma must have inherited all the lands once owned by her father and her uncles; rapacious men had tried to obtain squatter's rights on the six thousand acres when no surviving Larkins stepped forward to claim them, but it was apparent that if poor Emma had experienced such tortures, the least society could do was return her patrimony. As always when Texas land was involved, the fight became vicious, and Mrs. Reed was advised to withdraw lest she endanger the good community relationship with the fort, and she would have done so had she not obtained unintended support from Earnshaw Rusk, up at Camp Hope.

Rusk now had Matark's fleeing Comanche living peacefully on his grounds, and they had many complaints against Captain Reed and his soldiers: 'This man Renfro, he attacked us when we were hunting buffalo. We were doing nothing but hunting, and his Buffalo Soldiers charged upon us and killed our braves. He also stole one of our women.'

This latter charge, delivered with much excitement and waving of arms, electrified Rusk, for it represented exactly the kind of army behavior that he was determined to stamp out, so on a clear day at the end of summer, 1874, he and two of his Comanche assistants rode the fifty-eight miles south to Fort Garner to lodge an official protest, but before departing he thought it prudent to inform his superiors in the Interior Department of what he was about, lest contrary reports filter in from the fort:

> At last I have a fool-proof case against the Army at Fort Garner, and I intend to pursue it vigorously. In August of this year, when my Comanche under the peaceful guidance of Chief Matark, about whom I have written before, were trailing buffalo, they did, I must admit, stray into Texas territory. But they were behaving like the good citizens I have taught them to be when they were fallen upon by Col. Renfro and a horde of his cavalrymen. Several braves were slain, and an Indian woman was taken from them.
>
> I hold this to be a gross infraction of the rules which govern this area and I shall go personally to Fort Garner to seek redress for my Indians. I am leaving Camp Hope in the hands of Chief Matark during my absence, which ought not be prolonged, but I assure thee that I shall speak harshly to the Army.

When the righteous Quaker appeared at the fort, Wetzel wanted to arrest the two Comanche braves, but Rusk made such a howl that Reed had to promise safe passage, as the Peace Policy required. The discussions continued as before, with Rusk insisting upon the peaceful intentions of his Indians, and Reed enumerating the hideous roster of Texas ranches burned and Texas ranchers slain. None of these charges, which seemed so specific to the army men, would Rusk accept as proof of Comanche guilt; instead, he launched vigorous protest against army brutality, and there the debate hung suspended, with each man accusing the other of duplicity and moral blindness.

'Can't you see, Rusk, that your beloved Indians are a gang of murderers who should be shot?'

'Can't thee see, Captain Reed, that thy men are a gang of undisciplined bullies who love to harass my Indians?'

'What about the murders at the seventeen ranches I've listed?'

'What about your men kidnapping one of my Indian women?'

Reed stopped and gaped at the Quaker: 'You don't know who that woman was?'

'Then thee admits the kidnapping?'

Reed almost laughed: 'Everyone in the world knows who she is, but you live a few miles to the north, and you haven't heard? Rusk, are you truly innocent, or are you stupid?'

'I expect to be abused at your hands, but I also expect—'

'Louise!' Reed shouted. 'Ask Bertha Wetzel to bring the girl here.' As might have been expected, Mrs. Wetzel, the practical frontier woman, had given the unwanted girl a temporary home, and now she grasped Emma's hand and brought her to the commander's office.

Mrs. Wetzel entered the room first, with the girl lagging behind, so that Rusk could not see who was coming, but when the pair were well inside, Mrs. Wetzel stepped aside and Emma Larkin stood revealed. With the ability she had acquired to suffer anything, she kept her chin high and looked right at Earnshaw Rusk, and when he saw her he gasped. Trying to speak, he could not, and for a long moment these two stared at each other—the near-crazed child of torture and the near-godlike believer in the goodness of man. When the moment passed, Rusk stepped boldly to the girl and put his arms about her: 'Jesus Christ has thee in His heart.' He tried to say more, but he could not, and after a moment most embarrassing to Reed, Mrs. Wetzel and even the girl, he bowed his head and quiet tears welled in his eyes.

He was so shaken that he had to sit down, and as he huddled there, his world falling apart, Reed said with less severity than he had intended: 'This is Emma Larkin. Sole survivor of Bear Creek. Prisoner of your Comanche for five years.'

Slowly Rusk regained his feet, staring in anguish first at Reed, then at Mrs. Wetzel: 'Is this truly the Larkin child?'

'It is,' Reed said, 'and I want you to hear her story, every word of it, without my presence or Mrs. Wetzel's. Come, Bertha,' and he led her away.

'Sit down with me,' Rusk said when they were gone, and in the stone-walled office built with such care under the supervision of Mrs. Reed, began the conversation which would change so much along the Red River.

EARNSHAW: Is thee really Emma Larkin?

EMMA *(in her soft whisper):* I am. I remember my family, all fifteen. Do you want me to name them?

EARNSHAW: And thee was present at Bear Creek?

EMMA: This is Bear Creek. This is where it happened. My father and my brothers were killed in our house not far from here.

EARNSHAW: And thee is sure Indians did it?

EMMA: They took me captive, didn't they?

EARNSHAW: But was it Matark?

EMMA: I have lived with Matark for four summers. Matark's sons . . .

EARNSHAW: Thy ears?

EMMA: His sons burned them off, slowly, night after night.

EARNSHAW: That I cannot believe.

EMMA: Look at them.

EARNSHAW: Thy nose?

EMMA: They would take embers from the fire, and dance around me, then jab the embers against my nose. And when the scab formed . . .

EARNSHAW: Please. *(Fearing for a moment that he was going to be sick, he changed the subject.)* Did they beat thee?

EMMA: Especially the women.

EARNSHAW: The men?

EMMA: They came at night. To sleep with me. *(Such a statement embarrassed Rusk so profoundly that once more he stopped the conversation. He had never kissed a woman and deemed their behavior a great mystery.)*

EARNSHAW: Thee mustn't speak of such things. Thee must forget them.

EMMA: I've tried to. It's you who asked the questions.

EARNSHAW: Did no one ever treat thee kindly?

EMMA *(after a prolonged reflection):* No one. But there was a white man with a lame left arm. They called him Little Brother, because he sold them guns. I think his name was Peavine.

EARNSHAW: He was with them?

EMMA: Often. They told him what they needed and he went back and stole it.

EARNSHAW: Did thee ever hear them call him Rattlesnake?

EMMA: No, but things were always better for me when he came, because he brought guns and other things and for a while they forgot me. *(She weighed her next comment carefully.)* He always took me aside and promised that one day I would be set free. I dreamed about that day, but it never happened.

EARNSHAW: This man? Thee is sure he had a weak left arm?

EMMA: They also called him Little Cripple. *(Since both spoke Comanche, she could report precisely what the Indians had called their Comanchero.)* He never beat me or abused me. One time Chief Matark said, and I heard him say it: 'You can sleep with the thing if you wish,' but Peavine said: 'I do not wish,' and that night I was left alone.

EARNSHAW: Did thee ever ride with the Comanche when they came down into Texas?

EMMA: Many times.

EARNSHAW: And did thy Indians burn ranches in Texas?

EMMA: Like here at Bear Creek. Many times.

EARNSHAW: But that was long ago, I'm sure.

EMMA: It was one moon ago, when the black soldiers captured me.

EARNSHAW: Thee was hunting buffalo that time. I know thee was hunting buffalo.

EMMA: We had all the buffalo we needed, north of the river. We came into Texas to burn and kill.

EARNSHAW *(weakly):* Thee means . . . thy Comanche planned it that way? Strike south, then run back north?

EMMA: Why not? Those were the rules. You made them, we obeyed them. *(She spoke these sentences in Comanche, which gave them a lilting, arrogant echo which cut so deeply at Rusk's integrity that he shuddered.)*

EARNSHAW: What will thee do now?

EMMA: I know nothing. *(She said this with such simplicity, such willingness to throw herself upon the mercy of God, that he was awed.)*

EARNSHAW: Surely thee has friends. Thee must have family.

EMMA: I have no one. I am not like others.

EARNSHAW: Thee has the love of Jesus Christ. And thee can be like others. Thee can wear thy hair about thy ears, and no one will see.

EMMA: But this?

EARNSHAW: And thee can make thyself a nose. I'm not sure how right now, but I know it can be done. *(He spoke with great force.)* We will make thee a nose. We will make thee friends.

EMMA: Who would want me as a friend? You know I had a baby?

EARNSHAW: Good God! *(He stalked about the room.)* Good God, thee hasn't told anyone, has thee?

EMMA: Nobody asked.

EARNSHAW: Thee had a child?

EMMA: My moon period came. Like the others, I had a child.

EARNSHAW *(totally disoriented):* Thee must not speak of this, not to anyone. *(Then, overcoming his embarrassment, he regained courage.)* Thee means . . . the Indian men? They?

EMMA: I told you they came to my bed at night. One after another. *(At this appalling news, which he had not fully comprehended before, Rusk drew away from the girl, a fact which she noticed and accepted.)* I'm sorry I told you, Mr. Rusk.

EARNSHAW: Thee knows my name?

EMMA: We all knew your name. The-Man-Who-Lets-Us-Do-Anything they called you.

EARNSHAW: Why did I never see thee at Camp Hope?

EMMA: They never brought us captives . . .

EARNSHAW: There are others?

EMMA: Each tribe has many. They trade us back and forth.

EARNSHAW: Always children? Always little girls?

EMMA: The men they kill, always. Grown women they keep alive for a while, use them, kill them. The boys they train as young braves. They become Indians. The girls they use, like me.

EARNSHAW: Oh, my God. What have I done?

EMMA: My child was a boy. I do not want him.

EARNSHAW: But if he's thy child?

EMMA: I did not want him then. I do not want him now. I want to forget them all.

EARNSHAW: Does thee know what prayer is?

EMMA: We prayed here at Bear Creek. I prayed that I'd be rescued some day.

EARNSHAW: Will thee pray with me now? *(She dropped to her knees, but Rusk caught her by the arm, the first time he had touched her, and brought her upright.)* I am a Quaker, and we do not feel the necessity of kneeling. We speak to God direct.

So the two casualties of the frontier prayed that God would give bewildered Earnshaw Rusk guidance to rectify the errors he had fostered, and that assistance would be provided Emma Larkin in the fearsome decisions she must make. He ended the prayer with the hope that Emma would find in her heart renewed love for her baby boy, but when the prayer ended, she told him bluntly: 'The child is gone. It is all gone.'

When he returned to Camp Hope, Earnshaw Rusk assembled his Comanche and berated them as never before: 'Thee has lied to me. Thee has crossed the Red River not in the chase of buffalo but to burn and kill. And thee keeps hidden from me other children like Emma Larkin. And such behavior must stop.'

Matark said boldly: 'We will go where we wish. And we will give them the children when they offer enough money.'

'Thee hides the man called Rattlesnake Peavine in thy ranks, and he is wanted for many murders.'

'He is our friend. We will always protect him from the army.'

Astonished by the boldness of the Comanche, Rusk pleaded with them to make an honest peace with the army and refrain from any further raids into Texas: 'Noble Chief Matark, I promise thee that even now it is not too late. If thee and I ride to Fort Garner and enter into solemn promises . . .'

'No Indian can trust their promises. They kill our buffalo. They ravage our camps.'

'Up to now, yes. It's been warfare. But warfare always ends, and peace brings consolations.' He was speaking in Comanche, most eloquently, depicting the longed-for solution to the Indian problem, and tears came to his eyes as he pleaded: 'Great Chief Matark, the grandest thing you could give your people, the gift that would make your name sing across the plains . . . peace. A final agreement to stay north of the Red River. An agreement to live a new life here on the vast reservations the Great White Father has promised thee.'

'They are big now,' Matark said with exceptional insight, 'but they will become very small when your people want them back.'

'If we ride south,' Rusk said, imploringly, 'even now we can arrange a peace in which all past raids will be forgiven. Thee will return the stolen children, and thee will live here happily with me.'

'We cannot trust you.'

'Please, please!' the Quaker pleaded. 'Listen to reason. For the love of God and the safety of thy own children, ride with me and let us make peace.'

Matark's response was hideous. Enlisting more than a hundred chanting braves, he led them deep into Texas, where they burned six isolated ranches, killing the men with customary tortures and running off with seven additional children. After they crept back to sanctuary at Camp Hope, he actually boasted in the presence of the agent: 'We taught the Texans a lesson,' and with insulting belligerence he refused to surrender the children, asking Rusk: 'And what are you going to do about it?'

Now a bizarre chain of frontier incidents occurred. To the astonishment of Captain Reed at Fort Garner, Earnshaw Rusk rode south unattended and humiliated himself in the stone-walled headquarters: 'I was deluded. I was lied to. Chief Matark is a dreadful killer who keeps numerous white children in his camps. My way was wrong. I ask thee, Captain Reed, to send thy troops into the Indian Territory and arrest this brutal man.'

'Is this a formal request, Agent Rusk?'

'It is.'

'You know that your superiors at Fort Sill and Washington . . .'

'I know they will be disgusted with me, going against our agreement. But even for a Quaker the time comes when crime must be punished.'

'I will have to have this in writing, Mr. Rusk.'

'And thee shall.' Sitting at the captain's desk, he penned a formal request for United States troops to invade Camp Hope in the Indian Territory, and there to arrest Chief Matark of the Comanche for crimes innumerable. When he signed this document, which negated a lifetime of religious training and abrogated his promises to President Grant, his hands trembled. But it was done, and then he surprised the soldiers by asking if he could see the girl Emma Larkin, for he had brought her something.

More or less in hiding, she was still living with the Wetzels, who were beginning to see in her a sensitive human being with the merits of courage, forthrightness and a surprising sense of humor as she went about the housework which the German family assigned her. When Mrs. Wetzel brought her before Agent Rusk she noticed that the girl actually seemed happy to see him, and he said: 'No, Mrs. Wetzel, thee must stay. I need thy help.'

He took from his pocket a carefully carved wooden nose to which was attached two lengths of braided horsehair, and with Emma standing by a window, he placed the nose in the middle of her face and asked Mrs. Wetzel to hold it firm while he tied the horsehair braids behind the back of Emma's head.

'Oh!' Mrs. Wetzel cried with real joy. 'Now you have a nose!' And she hurried for her mirror, and when the girl saw the transformation that had occurred, she could only look first at Rusk, then at Mrs. Wetzel and then back at the mirror. Finally she put the mirror down and took Mrs. Wetzel's hands, which she kissed. Then she did the same with Rusk, but as soon as she had done this she grabbed the mirror again and studied herself, and as she did so, Rusk reached out and pulled strands of her hair across the stumps of her ears, and when she saw herself whole again she did not burst into tears of gratitude. She jumped straight up in the air and gave a startling Comanche yell: 'I am Emma Larkin. I am Emma Larkin.'

But she was not allowed to keep her nose, because Mrs. Wetzel took it from her and left the room; when she returned she had replaced the horsehair braid with an almost invisible white thread, and now when Emma looked in the mirror that Mrs. Wetzel held for her, neither she nor anyone else could detect that it was the thread which held the wooden nose in place, and seeing this perfection and realizing what it meant—an invitation back into life—she wept.

The men at Fort Garner lost little time in mounting a massive attack on Camp Hope, and although other Quaker commissioners at posts in the Indian Territory tried to halt this breach of the Peace Policy, officers waved Agent Rusk's written request at them and plunged ahead. In a series of daring moves they caught Matark and three of his principal supporters. They also captured nine white

children, whose stories inflamed the frontier so much that the court in Jacksborough sentenced Matark and his men to hanging.

However, the Quakers were not powerless, and they stormed into federal
courts, getting not only injunctions against the hanging but also an agreement
whereby Matark and his men would be assigned temporarily to a low-security
Texas prison. They were there only a few months when another court set them
free, on the theory that they had learned their lesson and would henceforth be
reliable citizens. A month after their return to Camp Hope they broke loose and
raided savagely along the Texas frontier, burning and torturing as before.

The response from Washington was swift. Gentle-hearted Benjamin Grierson
would remain at regimental headquarters in Fort Sill to make way for a real
fighting man, Ranald Mackenzie, who was brought in to lead one of five converg-
ing columns which would bear down on any Indians found outside their reservations. They would come at Matark and his killers from Texas, New Mexico,
Arkansas and the Indian Territory, with Colonel Nelson Miles leading the force
opposite to Mackenzie's. These two fiery colonels would form the jaws of a
nutcracker in which the enemy would be caught.

When grim-lipped Mackenzie set out after Matark, Reed insisted on leading
the three-company detachment from Fort Garner, with Wetzel left behind to
defend the place with one company of infantry. As bad luck would have it, the
Garner contingent found itself facing the most difficult part of the terrain, that
series of smaller canyons which protected Palo Duro on the south, and Jaxifer told
his men: 'Seem like we march one mile down into the canyon, then one mile back
up to make half a mile forward.' Mackenzie, observing the brutal terrain the
Buffalo Soldiers were struggling with, commended them: 'You men are fighting
your battle before the battle begins.' Nevertheless he told Jaxifer: 'Hurry them up.'

The excessive heat was a more serious matter, for this was early September
when the plains of Texas blazed their hottest; many a newcomer to the state
moaned during his first August: 'Well, at least September will soon be here.' But
he was remembering September in New Hampshire or New York; when that
Texas September struck he shuddered.

In 1874, September was exceptionally hot, with the entire surface of the Panhandle becoming a mirage, dancing insultingly along the horizon. Mesquite trees
huddled, scorched by the sun, drawing into their limitless roots what little water
they found deep down, and even jackrabbits hid in their burrows. Rattlesnakes
appeared briefly, then had to seek shade to protect their body temperature, and
those few buffalo that had survived the onslaught of commercial teams wandered
aimless among the bleached skeletons of their brothers.

It was a huge concentration of Indians that gathered in the various canyons of
Palo Duro as a last defense against the approaching army: Kicking Bird and his
thousand Kiowa; White Antelope and his many Cheyenne; Matark and his nine
hundred Comanche. They did not fight as a combined army; Indian custom

would never permit that kind of effective coalition, but they did support one another, and to rout them out of their protective furrows was going to be difficult.

On came the five columns, with Miles and Mackenzie always supplying the pressure, but as they approached Palo Duro the ordeals of a Texas September began to take a heavy toll, and as water supplies diminished, the men learned the agony of thirst.

When Reed's 10th Cavalry ran completely out of anything to drink, Jaxifer, acting on his own, ordered one of his men to kill a horse so that his troops could at least wet their lips with its blood, and after Reed's infantry, lagging far behind, suffered for two days of staggering thirst, he ordered his men to take their knives and open veins in their arms so that their own blood could sustain them. When some demurred, he showed them how by cutting into his own arm, then offering it to two soldiers while he pumped his fist to make the blood spurt. One of the men fainted.

Texas weather, particularly on the plains, could provide wild variations, and in mid-September, at the height of the heat and the drought, a blue norther swept in, and during one daylight period the thermometer dropped from ninety-nine degrees to thirty-nine. For two days the freezing wind blew, threatening the lives of men who had been sweating their health away, and on the third day torrential rains engulfed the entire area. Now the war became a chase through mud, with the sturdier, slower horses of the cavalry having an advantage.

From all sides the blue-clads began to compress the thousands of Indians, and although the latter, under the expert guidance of chiefs like Matark, succeeded in avoiding pitched battles, they could not escape the punishing effect of the swift cavalry raids, the burning of lodges and the destruction of crops. Their most serious defeat came on a day when they lost only four braves: in drenching rain Mackenzie and Reed found a defile on the face of the canyon wall and with great daring led their cavalry down that steep and almost impassable route. When they reached the canyon floor they found a concentration of Chief Mamanti's Kiowa, Ohamatai's stubborn Comanche and Iron Shirt's Cheyenne. Thundering through the Indian camps, they scattered the enemy and burned all their lodges, but with even more devastating effect, they captured their entire herd of horses and mules, 1,424 in number.

With practiced eye, Mackenzie rode through the animals, selecting about 370 of the best, then gave Reed an extraordinary command: 'Kill the rest.' When Reed relayed this to Jaxifer, the big black man who loved horses and who tended his own as if they were his children, objected, but Reed said: 'It's an order!' and the black troops carried it out while from a distance the captured Indian chiefs looked on in horror.

Never did Mackenzie's troops, or any from the other four columns, engage the Indians in a pitched battle, but the despair they spread through the Indian camps, with their incessant burning of villages and routing of camps and slaughter of horses, convinced the enemy that sustained resistance was going to be impossible, and it was a Kiowa chief named Woman's Heart who made the first gesture. Assembling thirty-five of his principal braves he told them: 'We can no longer hold them off. Get your families.' The men supposed that they were about to make a gallant last stand. Instead, when the large group was assembled, he told them: 'We shall ride to Camp Hope.'

'To attack it? There'll be soldiers.'

'No. To surrender to the agent there. This day we start for the reservation that will be our home hereafter,' and while women wept and braves stared at the canyon walls which had for so many decades been their protection, Woman's Heart led his Kiowa away.

Soon Stone Calf and Bull Bear of the Cheyenne, accompanied by 820 of their warriors, straggled in to the reservations, as did White Horse and 200 of his Comanche, and Kicking Bird and Lone Wolf with almost 500 of their Kiowa. What gunfire had been unable to accomplish was achieved by remorseless pressure and destruction. The backbone of Indian resistance had been broken by the irresistible courage of the young colonels, Miles and Mackenzie, and their men.

The last Comanche to operate on Texas soil was Chief Matark, and in those final days at the canyons he had with him an extraordinary ally, the old Comanchero Amos Peavine, for the Rattlesnake, always aware that in troubled times he stood a chance to make a dollar, had slipped through the army forces, moving in from New Mexico with three large wagonloads of guns stolen from the depots of Cavin & Clark. The word *stolen,* when so used, covered a horde of possibilities; after investigations were completed, it seemed likely that C&C personnel had *sold* the illegal weapons to Peavine; or, as another investigator suggested: 'The Rattlesnake stole not only the guns but also two C&C drivers who believed that by working with him, they could earn a good deal more than the company paid them.'

At any rate, Rattlesnake Peavine had come down the rocky trails of Palo Duro some two weeks ahead of the army, but once there, with his guns sold and his Mexican gold pieces safely stowed, he realized that this time the encircling force of blue-clads was so powerful, escape was unlikely. He therefore started to build a close friendship with four white girls, thirteen to sixteen, held by Matark's men, and he became extremely kind to them, giving them most of his food allotment and protecting them from the torments of the young braves.

After the first huge defections, Peavine strongly recommended that Matark and his remnant also surrender and find their home on the reservations north of the Red River, but the Comanche spoke for his men when he replied: 'I live on no reservation.'

But the time came when pressure from the north made it imperative that Matark find temporary refuge by moving south, and he did this with such skill that he evaded Colonel Mackenzie's men pressing north. This placed him south of

Palo Duro, down where the Panhandle joins the rest of Texas, and here he roamed and pillaged.

The great Indian tribes had once covered the land called Texas, from the Gulf of Mexico to the mountains of the Far West, from the Red River in the north to the Rio Grande in the south, and now they were diminished to this handful of Comanche under Matark and a few Apache who would soon be driven into the arid wastes of Arizona. It would fall to Matark to make the last stand.

Scouts quickly informed Mackenzie that Matark was running wild to the south, so he dispatched Reed and the Fort Garner men to capture the raiders, and as winter approached a great chase developed across the northern plains. Matark and Peavine would strike an exposed ranch, and Reed and Jaxifer would pursue them. Matark would make a long swing to the west, and Reed would cannily move northwest to intercept him in that unexpected quarter, but Peavine would warn his Comanche that this might be Reed's strategy, so they would move off in the opposite direction.

But now the Indians were up against a man of both skill and endurance, and he led battle-hardened cavalry units. Slowly but remorselessly, Reed closed in on these raiding Indians, edging them always closer to the southern rim of Palo Duro, where Mackenzie's superior numbers would annihilate them.

The final battle that Reed envisaged did not occur, for a daring move by Jaxifer cut the Indian force in half, with disastrous consequences for the Comanche. Reed, suddenly aware that his portion of the force faced only a segment of Matark's men, made a frenzied attack at four in the morning, encircling Matark's camp, killing many of its inhabitants, and taking the great chief captive.

At the same time, Jaxifer invested the other half, and although many escaped his net, he did capture some three dozen, including Peavine and the four white girls he was protecting. With tears of joy, the Rattlesnake told his captors of how he had been a peaceful rancher in the vicinity of Fort Griffin and of how Matark's men, damn them, had overrun the place and taken his four granddaughters captive, and while the cavalrymen were celebrating and giving the girls attention, he made his quiet escape with three of their best horses.

When Reed learned that Jaxifer had also been successful, he dispatched a scout to inform Mackenzie of his unqualified success, including the rescue of the four white girls, but it was not till after the horsemen had ridden north that he began interrogating his black troops about the details of their splendid victory, and heard about the elderly white man who had delivered the girls.

'You mean,' he asked with a sick feeling, 'that the old man had a withered left arm?'

'Yes, he did.'

Knowing what his next answer would be, he asked the girls: 'Did the old man bring guns for the Indians?' and when they said that he had, but that he had also been extremely protective of them, he asked: 'Did the Indians call him Little Cripple?' and when they nodded, he jumped up and began kicking a saddle.

'Good God! Sergeant Jaxifer, you had Rattlesnake Peavine in your hands and you let him go!' And right there the Fort Garner detachment, all hundred of them, and the four girls entered into a compact: 'We need tell no one about Amos Peavine. Girls, he saved your lives, didn't he? So keep quiet about him. Men, do you want the rest of the army laughing at you? Say nothing.'

He himself did not feel obligated to report more than the bare facts: 'Sergeant Jaxifer and his well-disciplined detachment of Tenth Cavalry routed the other half of Matark's force, and in doing so, gallantly rescued four white girls who had been held prisoner by the Comanche.'

Matark was taken, as the Peace Policy required, to Camp Hope, where he was turned over to new Quakers who had replaced the unfortunate Earnshaw Rusk. He was then moved to a remote reservation in Florida, from which he launched a barrage of appeals. Two Quaker agents new to the frontier lodged a thoughtful appeal for clemency on the grounds that Chief Matark was at heart a well-intentioned man caught up in the tragedy of a war of extermination.

President Grant was touched by this reasoning, and remembering with what high hopes he had launched his Indian policy, told an aide: 'What does that fellow Rusk from Pennsylvania say about Matark?' and when Earnshaw was invited to make a report, he reflected on all he knew about Matark, and then he prayed. After two days of soul-searching he drafted this response:

> I have known Matark for many years. He is a savage striving to find his way in a new civilization governed by new rules which he cannot comprehend. I believe I know every evil thing he has done, and I condemn him for his barbarities. But I assure thee, Mr. President, that except for torture, which can never be forgiven, he has committed no act more reprehensible than what the United States Army committed against him and his people. His tragedy was that he was never given the option of accepting a consistent Peace Policy offered in good faith by the American government, and to punish him now for fighting according to rules established by our side is deplorable.
>
> I have searched my heart to determine what is justice in this affair, and I find I must beg thee to commute his sentence. He is, like thee, an honorable warrior. Allow him to return to his people and to the lands he used to roam.

He was pardoned, with the stern admonition: 'If you ever set foot in Texas, you will be shot on sight,' to which he replied with humility: 'I no want Texas.'

Because the temptation to reinvade Texas might prove irresistible if he was lodged at Camp Hope, from where the traditional hunting grounds would be visible each dawn, he was moved to another section of the Indian Territory, and there a woman reporter for a Texas newspaper found him after peace had been established on the plains:

> Chief Matark can be considered, with much reason, one of the last Indians who warred in Texas. Of all the hundreds of thousands who terrorized our ranches, he was the last, and when I found him sitting peacefully beside an arroyo on his reservation, I asked him what his lasting memories were of our state, and he said: 'Texas, that was the best.'

Two weeks after this interview was published in the Texas papers, Matark quietly disappeared from the reservation, and the Quaker in charge of the area announced: 'He knew he was dying and went, as is the custom of his people, to some lonely spot where he could rejoin the Great Spirit.'

He had actually gone west across the border into New Mexico in response to a smuggled appeal from Amos Peavine, and there he had joined forces with his old comrade, robbing stagecoaches and caravans headed for California. Numerous agitated reports reached Santa Fe and Tucson of this murderous duo who appeared suddenly at the bend of a road: 'There was this old man with a withered left arm, this big Indian who said nothing. They took everything.'

There were also reports, more ominous, of what happened when the travelers had tried to resist: 'The white man was so quick on the trigger, he shot two of our men before anyone knew what was happening.'

The depredations became so offensive that posses were organized both in New Mexico and Arizona, and on a blazingly hot August afternoon in the latter state, a gun battle erupted, and when it ended Chief Matark of the Comanche, not yet fifty years old, lay dead on the burning sand. What happened to Amos Peavine was less certain; said the coroner in reporting his inquest: 'He was last seen headed north, trailing blood. Considering the land into which he disappeared, he must be listed as dead.'

Now came one of the curiosities of Texas history. The Comanche threat having been contained, there was no further use for a frontier post like Fort Sam Garner, and so one day in October 1874, George Reed, who had built it of mud back in 1869 and converted it to stone by 1871, received curt instructions from Lewis Renfro in Washington:

Capt. George Reed, Co. T, 14th Infantry, Commanding Officer Fort Garner, Texas.

You will proceed immediately to the abandonment of Fort Garner on Bear Creek, dismantling such buildings as can be torn down and returning the land to its civilian owners without any obligation on our part to restore its original condition or make compensation.

Obedient to the orders, Reed assembled his men and informed them that the two companies of the 10th Cavalry would be reassigned to Colonel Mackenzie at Fort Sill, while the two companies of the 14th Infantry under Captain Wetzel would remain at Fort Garner to decommission the post.

On a bright morning the two young officers who had replaced Johnny Minor— 'lost his left leg in the battle at Three Cairns'—and Jim Logan—'dead from the shooting at the tank'—flashed hand signals to John Jaxifer, who blew his whistle and headed his Negro cavalry back toward Jacksborough.

As Jaxifer left the parade ground for the last time, Wetzel stopped him to say, with grudging admiration: 'You were first class, Jaxifer. Your men? They're beginning to learn.' Jaxifer looked back to review his men: saddles polished, boots pipeclayed, brass gleaming, faces smiling. He was proud of these dark men, for he knew that rarely had a military unit performed more bravely, more consistently, and with so little recognition.

When they vanished in dust, Wetzel's infantrymen began the task of emptying the buildings, loading the wagons, and demolishing the few wooden structures. The stout stone buildings they did not touch, for these were now the property of an unusual owner who gave every intention of occupying them far into the future.

After careful investigation, Reed had satisfied himself that the legal arrangement which his wife had finally engineered in favor of Emma Larkin still prevailed: 'If I understand you, Judge, the land on which Fort Garner stands reverts to the Larkin girl.'

'It does, and she owns the six thousand other acres we awarded her.'

'Then by Texas law she gets all the buildings we erected?'

'She does. You know that in Texas, the federal government does not own public lands.'

In a quiet ceremony at the fort, which the judge attended, Reed turned the property over to Emma. 'You've been a brave woman. You've earned this land. Occupy it in honor.' He kissed her, as did Wetzel, but the judge whispered to Sanders: 'Small reward. The buildings are worth nothing. The land, maybe ten cents an acre.'

While the men were still dismantling the fort, a general of extraordinary charm sent notice that he intended visiting the fort with the next wagon train, and preparations were made in the diminished quarters to receive him properly. 'What can we do?' Mrs. Reed protested. 'Things half packed. He'll think we're slovens.'

When the general arrived, a big, fleshy man with European manners, he put the wives at ease: 'My wife and I were warned that you were closing down. That's why we hurried.' And from his wagon he produced hampers of food, enough for all the troops.

He was General Yancey Quimper, sixty-two years old, hero not only of San Jacinto but now of Monterrey as well, and as always, a soldier whose first thought was for the welfare of his men: 'Feed the troops, Captain Reed, and while they feast let me explain why we've come so far to pay you honor.'

He personally broke open the hampers of beef and duck, arranging a separate table for the four black cavalrymen left behind as guards, and while they toasted him in beer from the two barrels he provided, he told the Reeds and the Wetzels: 'This gracious lady who stands at my side is none other than the widow of Captain Sam Garner, for whom your fort was named. And those two fine men slicing the beef were Garner's sons. They're mine now, for I adopted them, and they bear the name of Quimper.' He said this grandiloquently, as if by taking away the honorable name of Garner and bestowing upon them the dubious one of Quimper, he had somehow conferred dignity.

'And that stalwart opening the beer keg is my birth-son James, who merits congratulations, for last week he became a father.'

Mrs. Quimper, a gracious lady who said little, leaving explanations to her voluble husband, did slip in a word: 'The general thought it would be proper for us to pay our respects to the fort before it was abandoned,' and her husband broke in: 'I'll wager you've seen a lot of action here.' His lively hands imitated the thrust and parry of cavalry actions.

He made a favorable impression on Wetzel, who said at the conclusion of Quimper's explanation of how his troops had managed the two mountains at Monterrey: 'General, you have a better understanding of uphill attack than anyone I've met in America,' to which Quimper replied: 'It comes from study . . . and experience.' He also explained how the Texas troops had managed to hold the lunette at Vicksburg, 'which was a very ugly show, I can tell you.'

Mrs. Reed, who followed military conversations closely, realized that Quimper never claimed that he had actually been at either Monterrey or Vicksburg, and she was about to query this point when the general delighted everyone by announcing that he had brought a surprise for 'the commanding officer of our Garner fort,' and after a signal to one of his sons, a large package was brought in and delivered to Reed.

'Open it, sir!' Quimper cried. 'Open it so we can see!' And when Reed did, out came a pair of glistening military boots, fawn-colored and decorated with embossed eagles, swords and the word TEXAS in silver.

'They're genuine Quimpers,' Yancey said. 'Fightin' boots for fightin' men, and it's a privilege to deliver them to the commander of our fort.'

'But how did you get my size?'

'Ah-ha! Did you by chance miss a pair of your old army boots?'

Reed looked at his wife, who shrugged her shoulders. 'Don't stare at her,' Yancey bellowed. 'It was him,' and he pointed at Wetzel, who confessed that five months ago he had purloined the boots in order to make this happy occasion possible.

On the next day Quimper disclosed his purpose in coming so far: he asked to see the girl Emma Larkin, and when she was produced he spoke directly: 'I should like to purchase the land which the courts have awarded you.'

'The courts awarded me nothing,' Emma said, staring at him. 'I've always owned it. My parents patented it in 1869.'

'Yes, but since you were a minor and an orphan, the courts . . .'

'They gave me nothing,' she repeated, and it was obvious that Quimper was not going to have an easy time with this young woman.

'You have six thousand acres, más o menos as we say in Old Mexico, more or less.'

'Why would you wish to buy?'

'We have a saying: "If you acquire enough land in Texas, something good will surely happen." With the money I give you, you can live easily, in town somewhere.' He explained that he was prepared to offer ten cents an acre, slightly above the going rate: 'That would mean six hundred dollars, and you could do wonders with six hundred dollars.'

When she said no, he raised his bid to twelve cents, and when she still refused, he said: 'Because of the heroism of your family, twelve and a half cents. That's seven hundred fifty dollars, a princely sum for a young girl like you.' But as the evening closed, she was still refusing.

When she returned to the Wetzel quarters, the others argued with her, telling her that with $750 she could buy a good house in Jacksborough and learn to sew or help in other ways. It never occurred to them or her that she might one day marry, or even have children. She would always be a homeless waif, and they wished for her own good to see her settled: 'We'll be leaving in a few days, you know. You certainly can't live alone in a great empty fort like this, even if you do own it.' But she would not consent.

In the morning the Quimpers, the Wetzels and the Reeds combined to try to make her see the advisability of accepting the general's offer, but she rebuffed them: 'This is the land my father settled. My whole family paid a terrible price for it. I paid a terrible price. And I will not surrender it, not even if I have to live here with coyotes.'

Nothing could be said to dislodge her, and she was dismissed, as if she were seven instead of seventeen.

When she was gone, Reed asked Quimper if he would like to see the fort as it had functioned in its glory years, and when Yancey said with pomp: 'I would appreciate seeing how our fort operated,' off they went, taking the Quimper sons with them.

Mrs. Reed and Mrs. Wetzel were left to entertain Mrs. Quimper, and this was a pleasing arrangement, for it gave the fort women a chance to clarify certain obscurities. Louise Reed started the questions: 'I wasn't aware that your husband had been at Monterrey, your present husband, that is.'

Bertha Wetzel broke in: 'Of course we knew about your first husband, a great hero. We had a pamphlet to educate the troops about the man for whom their fort was named.'

Mrs. Quimper was eager to talk once more with military wives who understood the intricacies of a soldier's life: 'When General Quimper married me, and I was most gratified to find a man so gentle and so helpful . . . You've seen my first two sons. They were on their way to becoming little ruffians when he stepped in to make men of them. I'll be forever grateful.'

'You were saying that when you married . . .' Mrs. Reed rarely allowed a visitor to leave a thought unfinished.

'Looking back, I can now see that he was a big, formless man with no character. But when he married me he found himself with a ready-made character, my husband's. He began to dress like him, speak like him. He stood straighter, learned military talk. He took my sons and gave them his name. And soon he was talking incessantly about Sam Garner's exploits at Monterrey. But soon it was "*our* exploits," and before long, "*my* exploits." One night I heard him explain to a group of generals how *he* had charged the Bishop's Palace atop that Monterrey hill. He had also been very brave at Vicksburg. He adopted me, and my sons, and my dead husband's military career.' She held her palms up and smiled: 'So he is now both my first husband and my second.'

'But he did this from a solid foundation,' Mrs. Reed suggested. 'San Jacinto and all.'

Mrs. Quimper laughed: 'Right after the battle, my first husband told me about Quimper and his capture of Santa Anna. The poor Mexican was hiding in the bushes. His ragged clothing made Yancey think he was a mere peon, but they took him in and only later learned who he was.'

'With such behavior,' Mrs. Wetzel asked, 'how did he become a general?'

'Very simple. One day he announced to the world: "I am a general," and Texas was so hungry for heroes, they allowed him to be a general.'

Mrs. Reed poured Mrs. Quimper a second cup of tea, then said very quietly: 'Have you heard about Lewis Renfro's heroic rescue of that young woman you just saw, the Larkin girl?'

'Everybody's heard. Texas papers were filled with little else.'

'The same.'

Mrs. Quimper looked first at Mrs. Reed, who was smiling, then at Mrs. Wetzel, who was laughing outright, and their humor was so infectious that she had to smile, even though she did not yet understand the reason. 'You mean'—she fumbled for a word that would not be too condemnatory of her husband—'that he was also a gentle fraud?'

Now Mrs. Wetzel could not contain herself: 'This wonderful colored soldier, no neck, could fight anyone. He rescued Emma Larkin from six Comanche.' She collapsed in laughter.

'Yes,' Mrs. Reed said. 'Our very brave cavalry sergeant did just that.'

Mrs. Wetzel told the rest: 'So then our hero, Lewis Renfro, Commander in Chief of Desk Forces, he rides up, recognizes the girl, grabs her, and grabs the glory.'

The three women chuckled at the follies of the self-appointed heroes whose antics they had observed, and when Mrs. Wetzel began to gasp for air, the other two broke into very unladylike guffaws.

When the Quimpers departed, with Yancey pleased at having seen his fort but dismayed by his failure to acquire the land, Mrs. Reed resumed the task of closing down the post, and as she moved from building to building she saw many things to remind her of the good work she had done in transforming this lonely outpost into a haven of civilization. In this stone building she had organized the social teas for each new wife; in a corner of that building she had arranged for everyone to place his extra books so that a library might be started; in this small garden, fertilized with manure from the stables, she had grown flowers for the hospital; and in the dead-house she had made the disfigured corpses acceptable before their friends or families saw them. In the chapel she had persuaded her husband to conduct prayers when there was no regular chaplain; and on Suds Row she had helped when babies had the croup.

Most important, she had been the guiding spirit in converting this mud outpost into a square-cornered fort of limestone. It had lasted, in its complete form, only three years, but she resolved that if her husband was now assigned to a newly established fort, probably some leagues to the west where the settlers were probing, she would encourage him to build of stone from the start: 'We live in any place only briefly, George. They may laugh and ask us as we depart: "Why did you take the trouble to build of stone?" If they don't understand that this was the home of two hundred soldiers, I'll not be able to explain.' She did not weep as they departed, but she did keep looking backward until Bear Creek disappeared, and the Brazos, and the tops of the buildings at the fort, and she kept doing so until only the vast plains and its endless blue sky were visible.

These eventful days had been difficult for Earnshaw Rusk, for the army despised him as a dreamer who refused to look facts in the face, and his own Quakers deplored him as a traitor who in panic had called in the soldiers to settle a temporary difficulty that could have been handled by negotiation.

After his expulsion in disgrace from Camp Hope, he had tried living for a while at Jacksborough, but that robust settlement, where men resolved arguments with guns and fists, provided no place for a man like him. He had also tried the town that had grown up at the edges of Fort Griffin to the south, but that was a true hellhole whose shenanigans terrified him. Then he served as a night nurse in a field hospital at another fort, where his behavior at Camp Hope was not known, and now when he heard that Fort Garner was being disbanded, he came back to the scene of his humiliation.

He went, as he had long planned in his confused imagination, to the house once occupied by Captain Wetzel and his wife, and there he found Emma Larkin working alone as if she were living safely in the heart of some small town. She seemed adjusted to the problem of living without ears or nose, and when, after the first awkward greetings, he asked where she would make her home, she replied in her soft whisper: 'Here at the fort. I like it and it's mine.'

He accepted the tea she offered him in a cup left behind by the Wetzels, and she showed him how she had collected quite a few household items from the other departing officers: 'I'll live.'

Sitting in the chair that was once Wetzel's favorite, he began his awkward speech: 'Emma, I've made a terrible mess of my life.' He did not say it, but she knew he intended to say 'And thee has made a mess of thine. Or, other people made a mess for thee.' Instead he plowed on: 'And I have been wondering . . .'

He stopped. From that first day when he met this pitiful child he had speculated on what might happen to her. How could a human being so abused survive? How could she face the world? It was out of such wonderment that he had been impelled to carve the nose which she now wore. It had not been because of love, for he had no comprehension of that word and little understanding of the complex emotions it represented, but it was out of concern, and caring. And he was caring now.

'I've been wondering what thee would do . . . with thy protectors gone.' By this use of an inappropriate word—for this young woman required no protectors —he betrayed his line of reasoning: 'And I've thought . . .' He could not go on. Nothing in his lonely, bungling life had prepared him to speak the words that should be spoken now.

Emma Larkin, damaged and renewed as few humans would ever be, reached out, touched his hand, and used his first name for the first time: 'Earnshaw, I've been given this land, these buildings. I will need someone to help me.'

'Could I be thy helper?' he managed to stammer.

'Thee could, Earnshaw,' she whispered. 'Thee could indeed.'

. . . TASK FORCE

It was midsummer in Austin, and heat lay over the city like an oppressive blanket which intercepted oxygen and brought blazing discomfort. Day after day the temperature hovered close to a hundred degrees as a cloudless sky glared down like the inside of a superheated bronze bowl. Fish in the lovely lake kept toward the bottom where the sun's incessant beating was lessened if not escaped, and in the countryside torpid cattle sought any vestige of shade. It could be hot in Texas, and all who could afford it fled to New Mexico.

Despite the heat, we were scheduled to hold our July meeting in Beaumont, the famous oil city near the Gulf, where we hoped optimistically there might be breezes. I anticipated a productive meeting, since we were to be addressed by Professor Garvey Jaxifer from Red River State College. My staff assured me that he was not inflammatory, only persistent, and I told them: 'Persistence after truth we can live with,' so the meeting was arranged.

I was therefore disturbed when Rusk and Quimper called me on a conference line to ask that I convene an extraordinary two-day meeting prior to Beaumont. I supposed they were going to protest my invitation to Professor Jaxifer, but they assured me that this was not their concern; Rusk growled: 'I've heard the man twice, here in Fort Worth. If he knew figures, I'd hire him. Solid citizen.'

What the improvised meeting was to discuss I could not guess, but at nine one steamy morning Miss Cobb, Professor Garza and I assembled at Austin's Browning Airport for private planes and watched as two jets landed in swift succession. As they taxied toward us I wondered why two were needed, but when the first opened its doors I saw that Lorenzo Quimper had picked up our three staffers from Dallas, so apparently it was going to be an important session.

The conspirators would not tell us where we were going, but shortly we were flying northwest on a route which would take us, I calculated, over Abilene and Lubbock. 'What's this all about?' I asked Quimper, who rode in my plane, and he winked. I guessed that we were going to hold a preliminary session of some kind in a place like Amarillo, but when we had reached that general area and gave no sign of descending, I knew we must be entering New Mexico.

After Quimper served us a choice of drinks and Danish, we began to descend, and soon one of the young men, a better geographer than I, shouted: 'Hey! Santa Fe!'

Flying low, so that we could see the grandest city of the Southwest, we swung north along the highway to Taos, circled a large ranch, and landed on a private strip, macadamized and six thousand feet long. 'Ransom's hacienda,' Quimper announced, and when we joined the others on the tarmac, Rusk said, almost apologetically: 'Il Magnifico and I, we thought Texas was just too damned hot. I want you to enjoy two days of relaxation . . . anything you'd like to do. The helicopter's here . . . riding horses . . . swimming . . . great mountain trails. Taos up that way, Santa Fe down there.'

It was the kind of gesture the very rich in Texas like to make, but I noticed that everything about the place was low key: Ford pickups with gun racks behind the driver's head, not Mercedes; rough bunkhouses with Hudson's Bay blankets for cold nights; and no Olympic-sized swimming pool, just a small, friendly dipping place in which the girl from SMU was going to look just great, because even if she hadn't brought a swimsuit, Rusk's Mexican housekeeper could offer her a choice of six or seven.

It was a splendid break in the heat, for the Rusk ranch was 6,283 feet high, with magnificent views of mountains higher than 12,000. But the emotional part of our visit, and I use that word with fondest memories, came at dusk on that first day when Quimper signaled his chief pilot to bring before us, as we sat by the pool drinking juleps, four rather long boxes wrapped in gift paper.

'Working with you characters,' Lorenzo said, 'has been both an education and a privilege. Never knew I could get along so amiably with anarchists.' Bowing to Garza, he said: 'On this happy occasion I cannot refrain from sharing my latest Aggie joke. Seems your aviation experts have invented a new type of parachute. Opens on impact.'

'I'm walking home,' Garza said, whereupon Lorenzo grabbed him: 'I thought you might, so I brought you just the thing for hiking.'

Shuffling the four parcels, he selected one and handed it to Rusk, who tore off the paper to disclose a long shoebox, inside which rested a pair of incredibly ornate boots. Products of the workmen at the General Quimper Boot Factory, they had been especially orchestrated, with the front showing a bull of the Texas Longhorn breed Rusk was striving to perpetuate on his Larkin County ranch, the side offering one of his oil derricks, and the back of the boot a fine version of his Learjet in blue and gold. The retail cost of such masterpieces I did not care to guess, but I remembered a catalogue that had offered lesser boots at three thousand dollars.

We were still awed by Rusk's gift when Miss Cobb opened hers to reveal a tall, slim pair ideally suited to her grave demeanor. They were silver and gray, with not a bit of ornamentation to detract from the exquisite patterning of the leather itself; it seemed to have been sculpted in eleven subtle shades of gray.

'What kind of leather?' the young woman from SMU cried, and Quimper replied with obvious pride in his men's workmanship: 'Amazon boa constrictor.' They were once-in-a-lifetime boots, and Miss Cobb was so touched by Lorenzo's gesture that she did not allow herself to speak lest she behave in a sentimental manner ill-befitting her Cobb ancestry.

Now it was my turn, and I could not imagine what Lorenzo had deemed proper for a man with few distinguishing characteristics, but when I opened my box it was apparent that he had gone back to my honored ancestor, Moses Barlow of the Alamo, for across the top rims of my boots, in flaming red letters against a pale-blue background, ran the word *Alamo,* and beneath it, in green-and-white leatherwork, stood a depiction of the famous building. Reaching from the sole of the shoe to the top, along the outer flank of each boot, rested a Kentucky long rifle, in black. My boots were pure Texas, and I was glad to have them, for with my own funds I could never have afforded such perfection.

Because of the incipient animosity between Quimper and Garza, rarely overt but never buried, I had to wonder what Lorenzo would do to catch the professor's personality, but when Efraín opened his box we gasped, because for him Quimper had saved his maximum artistry. In a wild flash of red, green and white, the colors of Mexico's flag, he had provided a peon in a big hat sleeping beside an adobe wall, a depiction of the Shrine of Our Lady of Guadalupe and an intricate enlargement of the central design of the flag, the famous eagle killing a rattle-snake while perched on a cactus.

Referring proudly to the latter, Quimper said: 'I had my best workman do the vulture eating the worm,' and Garza looked up with a mixture of affection and sheer bewilderment. For more than two hundred years his family had had no permanent affiliation with Mexico; he had traveled within that nation only once, and then not pleasantly, and although he spoke its language and followed its religion, he felt no close association with the country. Yet here he was with boots that proclaimed him loudly to be a Mexican.

'Lorenzo,' he said with obvious gratitude, 'I think I can speak for us all. You are magnificent.'

Our three staff members, who had watched the unveiling of our boots, cheered, but now Quimper signaled his other pilot, who came forward with three boxes. When the young people realized that these must be for them, the two young men clapped hands and the girl from SMU squealed, and the highlight of the ceremony was when she opened her box, for Lorenzo had brought her a pair equal to Miss Cobb's in femininity, but precisely the kind a young woman would appreciate. They were tall and slender, with heels well undercut and uppers made of a soft red leather that seemed to shout: 'I'm twenty-three and unmarried!' The simple decoration was in shining black, and the total effect was one of youthfulness, dancing and an invitation to flirtation. Miss Cobb said: 'Every young woman should know what it's like to own a pair of boots like that,' and the recipient began to cry.

The two men received simple cowboy boots made of valuable leather adorned by big hats, lariats and revolvers, and when the seven pairs were set side by side on the floor, we applauded, but Lorenzo rarely did things partially, for now the chief pilot came in with a box for the boss, and as we cheered, Quimper revealed his own fantastic boots. Basically they were a wild purple, but in their lighter leathers they contained a summary of Texan culture: a saucy roadrunner yakking across the desert, a Colts pistol, an oil well, a coiled rattlesnake. 'I like my boots to make a statement,' Quimper said, and Garza responded: 'Those can be heard on the borders of California.' And that night, when we stepped from the front door of the ranch on our way to dinner at a Santa Fe restaurant, we were what Quimper called 'a splendiferous Task Force.'

At dinner, Quimper dominated conversation by expounding in a voice loud enough to be heard at nearby tables his theory that Santa Fe should have been a part of Texas: 'The day will come when Texas patriots will muster an expedition to recapture this town. Then we'll have Texas as it should be, Santa Fe at one end, Houston at the other.'

When we left the restaurant we found our evening somewhat dampened by a sign plastered across our windshield: TEXANS GO HOME, which reminded us that New Mexicans regard the Texans who flood their towns in summer the way Texans regard the visitors from Michigan who invade their state in winter.

Refreshed by this escape from the Texan inferno, we prepared for our forth-coming meeting in Beaumont, where we met Professor Garvey Jaxifer, a sophisti-cated black scholar. The newspapers usually referred to him as Harvey Jaxifer, unaware that he had been named after the incendiary Jamaican black Marcus Garvey, who had lectured American blacks about their destiny and their rights. That first Garvey had been deported, I believe, but had left behind a sterling reputation as a fighter, and our professor was no less an agitator than his name-sake. He presented a short, no-compromise paper, whose highlights follow:

'Throughout their history Anglo Texans have despised Indians, Mexicans and blacks. This tradition started with the Spanish conquistadores, who saw their Indians as slaves and treated them abominably. This attitude was intensified by any Mexicans who were not classified as Indians themselves. We have seen how in 1836, General Santa Anna had no compunction about marching his barefoot, thinly clad Yucatecan Indians into the face of a blizzard, losing more than half through freezing to death.

'The early Texians inherited this contempt for the Indian, strengthened by understandable prejudices engendered in frontier states like Kentucky and Ten-nessee, where warfare with the Indian had been a common experience. But it was fortified in Texas by the fact that many of the Indian tribes encountered by the early settlers were extremely difficult people: the cannibalistic Karankawa, the remorseless Waco and the savage Kiowa. The earliest Americans had to fight such Indians for every foot of ground they occupied, and this blinded them to the positive aspects of the other Indians they encountered, especially the Cherokee.

'Later, of course, the Texians met face-to-face with the fearful Apache and Comanche, and with the most generous intentions in the world it would have been difficult to find any solution to the clash which then occurred. No outsider

ignorant of the bloody history of the 1850 to 1875 frontier, with its endless mas-
sacres and hideous tortures, has a right to condemn the Texas settlers for the
manner in which they responded.

'But Texas lost a great deal when it expelled its Indians, and the debt is only
now being collected. For one thing, the state lost a group of people who could
have contributed to our wonderful diversity had they remained; but much more
important, their expulsion encouraged the Texian to believe that he truly was
supreme, lord of all he surveyed, and that he could order lesser peoples around as
he wished. The Indian was long gone when the real tragedy of his departure
began to be felt, because the Texian diverted his wrath from the Indian to the
Mexican and the black, and the scars of this transferral are with us to this day.

'I am assured that previous scholars have spoken of the heavy burden Texas
bears because of its refusal to adjust to the Mexican problem, so I shall drop that
subject. I shall restrict myself solely to the way in which Texas has handled its
black problem, and because my allotted time is short, I shall address you shortly,
sharply, and without that body of substantiating material I would normally offer.

'The condition of the black in Texas is one of the great secrets of Texas history,
which has been written almost as if the blacks had never existed. Yet in 1860
blacks constituted thirty-one percent of the population and represented a total tax
value of over a hundred and twenty-two million dollars. They vastly outnumbered
either the Mexicans or the Indians, and the economy of the state, dominated by
cotton, depended largely upon them.

'Despite vast evidence to the contrary, two legends grew up around the blacks,
one before the Civil War, one after, and these legends were so persuasive, so
consoling to the Texas whites, that they are not only honored today but also
believed. They continue to affect all relations between the two races.

'The ante-bellum legend is that the slaves were happy in their servitude, that
they did not seek freedom, and that they did not warrant it because they had no
skills other than chopping cotton and could not possibly have existed without
white supervision. The facts were somewhat different. On most plantations slaves
were the master mechanics. They were nurses of extraordinary skill and compassion. They were also custodians of the land, and many saved enough money to buy
their own freedom. Properly encouraged and utilized, they could have earned
Texas far more as mechanics than they did through cotton.

'But the perplexing part of the legend was that while the slaves were supposed
to be happy under the compassionate tutelage of their white masters, Texas newspapers were filled with rumors of slave uprisings, of slaves burning the masters'
barns and of general insurrection. Scores of county histories tell of executions of
slaves to forestall rebellion, and slave flight to Mexico became so common that
from time to time agents were stationed along the border to prevent it. I can speak
of this with some authority, because my great-great-grandfather used that route to
escape from his slavery on the plantation of your ancestors, Miss Cobb, where, I

hasten to add, he told his children that he had been well treated. But once he got the chance—over the Rio Grande into Mexico.'

'What did he do when he got there?' Quimper asked, and Jaxifer replied: 'Made his way to Vera Cruz, caught a ship to New Orleans, where he enlisted in a New York regiment.'

'You mean he fought with the North?' Quimper grumbled, and Jaxifer asked: 'What did you expect?' and Quimper said: 'He could of remained neutral.'

Professor Jaxifer continued: 'The Texians found no difficulty in believing both halves of this ante-bellum legend: that the same slave was deliriously happy, yet thirsting to massacre his master.

'The post-bellum legend was more destructive. The genesis was understandable. The South had been defeated. The North, especially under President Lincoln, wanted to be generous in its treatment, but his assassination opened the way for some radicals in Congress to force upon the South an intolerable Reconstruction. One of the ironies of Texas history is that its newspapers and its people rejoiced when Lincoln was shot, condemning him as one of the supreme tyrants of all time, not realizing that he alone could have enabled their state to avoid the convulsion it was about to suffer. It was 1902 before the first paper was brave enough to print one kind word about Lincoln, and it was abused for having done so.

'The true history of Reconstruction in Texas has not yet been written and probably cannot be in this century; the legend of that tempestuous time is still too virulent. Regarding blacks, it makes three claims: that those blacks elected to office under Northern supervision of the ballot box were incompetent at best, downright thieves at the worst; it claims that blacks who suddenly found themselves with freedom did not know what to do with it; and most important, it claims that the occasional black members of the State Police installed by the carpetbagger government were brutal murderers. Nothing in the history of Texas has damaged the black more than the fact that a few were for a while members of the State Police, that hated and reviled agency.

'Again, the legend is faulty at best, infamous at worst. Black legislators seem to have been no worse than their white contemporaries and successors. Many blacks learned quickly what to do with their freedom, and either established their own homes and small businesses or went back to work on the plantations as sharecroppers. And as for the black policemen, if they did, as charged, kill eight or ten white men without warrant, the Rangers had killed eight or ten hundred Mexicans and Indians, yet the former are reviled and the latter immortalized. It is a disproportion that cannot easily be explained.'

Professor Jaxifer then threw in an obiter dictum which really stunned our Texas landlovers: 'If you suspect I'm overemphasizing the bitterness of Reconstruction, let me cite an incident which you better than most will appreciate. In 1868 a republican-controlled convention, drawing new laws for peacetime Texas, recalled the hardships under which Texans who had fought on the Union side suffered: "These patriots were mercilessly slandered in their good names and property." In recompense they would be issued free land, but it went unclaimed, because in all of land-hungry Texas no man was brave enough to stand before his neighbors as one who "had been false to the Confederacy and no better than a carpetbagger." '

'You mean,' Quimper asked, 'that all this free land was waiting and no one claimed it?' When Jaxifer nodded, Lorenzo added: 'For a Texan to pass up free land is an act of moral heroism.' Jaxifer smiled and continued with these points:

'The hatreds engendered spawned a curious progeny. Many of the gunslingers of the Old West began by shooting blacks who had given no offense, and such bravado gained them the approbation of their fellows. Billy the Kid started by slaughtering a Negro blacksmith who made a pun upon his name, calling him Billy the Goat. He gained much applause for his quick and deadly response. As one hagiographer has said: "A flick of his wrist, a touch of his finger, and Billy silenced forever those thick, black, insolent lips."

'John Wesley Hardin, a cold-eyed, merciless killer who gunned down twenty-nine men before he was twenty-four, was despised prior to the day when he shot two black policemen; then he found himself a Texas hero. But the prototype of the Texas gunman was Cole Yeager, from Xavier County, who announced one day at the age of eighteen: "I cannot abide a freed nigger." He proved it by shooting in the stomach a young black who had argued with an older black. When asked about this, Yeager muttered: "The Bible says 'Ye shall respect thy elders,' " and no charges were lodged.

'Some time later he saddled up at dusk in the small town of Lexington, not far from the capital, galloped through the street, and slaughtered eight unsuspecting blacks. His high spirits were excused on the ground that "this was the kind of incident that was bound to happen . . . sooner or later."

'Pleased with his reputation as a nigger-killer, he was lounging in Jefferson, up in the Cotton Belt, one Sunday morning when he saw two well-dressed blacks, Trajan Cobb and his wife, Pansy, leaving their cottage and heading for the black church. Enraged that former slaves should be "tryin' to be better than they was," Yeager whipped out his guns and killed them.

'They happened to work as freedmen for Senator Cobb, the one-armed hero of the Confederacy, and when he heard in Washington of what had happened, he returned immediately to Texas, determined to bring Yeager to justice, and with his tiny wife, Petty Prue, he roamed the state, looking for the man who had killed his former slaves.

'Federal marshals, afraid of the scandal which might ensue if Yeager gunned down a one-armed United States senator, tried to dissuade Cobb from stalking his prey, but Cobb would not listen: "When a man has affronted the honor of a entire state, he must be taken care of, and if you gentlemen are afraid to go after him, I must."

'The marshals tried to persuade Mrs. Cobb to call off her man, but she snapped: "Trajan Cobb bears our name. He held our plantation together during the war, and if Somerset doesn't shoot the coward who killed him, I will."

'Fortunately, at about this time, Cole Yeager killed a white man, shot him in the back during an argument over fifty cents, and now the law had a viable excuse for arresting him. Under pressure from Senator Cobb, a fearless judge from Victoria County was brought north, and Yeager, who had now killed thirty-seven men, most of them black, was sentenced to be hanged.

'The Cobbs were there when the execution took place, and they groaned as the rope broke, allowing Yeager to fall unscathed. Some in the crowd cited an old English tradition which said that under such circumstances, the condemned man had to be set free, in that God had intervened, and there were murmurs to support this, for many in the audience felt it was unfair to hang a white man primarily because he had killed niggers.

'However, Cobb, with his good right arm, whipped out his revolver and announced: "We are not hanging him according to old English law. We're using new Texas law. String the son-of-a-bitch up"—and it was done.

'One of the more interesting illustrations of how difficult it was for Texans to adjust to the freed Negro came in Robertson County, not far from where we sit. A gifted black, Harriel Geiger, had been elected to the state legislature, and during his tenure in Austin had studied law and become a member of the bar. He excelled in defending black prisoners, but this irritated Judge O. D. Cannon of the Robertson bench, who is described in chronicles as "that hot-tempered segregationist." In any trial involving a black the judge had been in the habit of listening to whatever evidence the white man chose to present—he did not allow any black to testify—then growling, spitting, and sentencing the black to a long term on the prison work force. Naturally, he did not take it kindly when Lawyer Geiger, with the skills he had mastered as a legislator, came into his court arguing points of law.

'One hot afternoon Judge Cannon had suffered enough: "I been warnin' you to watch your step, nigger, but you have insolently ignored my counsel." With that, he whipped out a long revolver, held it three feet from the lawyer's chest, and pulled the trigger five times. The coroner's verdict: Harriel Geiger had been guilty of repeated contempt and had been properly rebuked.

'I agree, there are elements of humor in this incident: the irascible judge, the presumptuous new lawyer, the challenge to old customs, the sullen revenge of the men who had lost a moral crusade in the War Between the States. But I have here in my notes, which you are invited to inspect, a score of other incidents which contain no humor at all, and I shall cite only one more to remind you of the seriousness of the problem we're discussing.

'In 1892 in Paris, Texas, a black man named Henry Smith ravished and killed the three-year-old daughter of one Henry Vance. No doubt of the crime, no doubt of the guilt, no doubt of the sentence of death. But how was he executed? He was driven in a wagon through a crowd of ten thousand, then lashed to a chair perched high upon a cotton sledge, from which Vance, the dead girl's father, asked the horde to be silent while he took his revenge. A small tinner's furnace was brought to Vance, who heated several soldering irons white-hot. Taking one after another, he started at the prisoner's bare feet and slowly worked his way up the body, burning off appendages but keeping the torso alive. When he reached the head he burned out the mouth, then extinguished the eyes and punctured the ears. When he felt sated, he offered the irons to anyone else who wanted to share in the revenge, and his fifteen-year-old son took over. Ten thousand cheered.

'The black man deserved to die, but no man ever deserved to die in such a manner. It was made possible only because legend said that the black was not really human.

'It would serve no useful purpose for us to continue to explore the hideous record, for my point is made. Relations between white and black in Texas have been contaminated by legend. I am not asking that you attack the legend, or even make a great fuss about it. But do not prolong it. Don't give it added vitality. Let it die. Speak of your Texas blacks as human beings, no better, no worse than the Czechs, the Poles and the Irish who have helped build this great state.'

When Professor Jaxifer finished, Lorenzo Quimper said: 'Do you expect us to forget how your colored people behaved during Reconstruction? I remember well hearing my father tell how his grandfather, General Yancey Quimper, was accosted by a colored who wanted a pair of boots, free. This colored, six months from chopping cotton, had been elected to the legislature, and he told my grandfather— I can hear my father's words as he told me. This colored, he said: "General, I'm a legislator now and I'm entitle to free boots." And my grandfather said: "Freemont, you are entitle to a swift kick in the ass." And you know what? That colored had my grandfather arrested.'

'Does this old family legend have any relevance?' the professor asked, and I could see Quimper flush, and he said with roiling bitterness: 'A man in my town, big oilman worth millions, was ridin' home the other day in his Cadillac. He sees this poor old colored in a broken-down Ford, mendin' a tire by the side of the road while three strappin' young blacks is sittin' by the side of the road laughin' at the old man's efforts. My friend stops his Cadillac, gets out in that hot dusty road, and helps the old man change the tire while the three young bucks sit there laughin' at the both of them. Now what do you think of that?'

'Commissioner Quimper, that story's been circulating through Texas ever since we've had automobiles. Do you really believe it happened . . . this year . . . to your friend?'

'Let me tell you . . .'

'Don't you see, Commissioner? It's today's legend—1911 version updated.'

We had the makings of a serious confrontation, for Professor Jaxifer showed no signs of backing down; however, Miss Cobb intervened: 'The story you told, Professor, about my grandfather,' and she accented the *my* heavily, 'is true. He grieved over the loss of Trajan Cobb so painfully that he had a monument erected to him at Lammermoor: TO A TRUSTED FRIEND.'

Ransom Rusk delivered a judicious opinion, which I allowed to stand as the judgment of our group: 'Professor, you've honored us with a thoughtful paper. You must be aware, surely, that we cannot revise all of Texas history and correct all imbalances. The best we can do is project an honest course for the future.'

'You could not have stated the case more eloquently,' Professor Jaxifer conceded. 'All we blacks ask is that the legends not be embellished with new additions. The old ones we can never change .   at least not in this century.'

XI
THE
FRONTIER

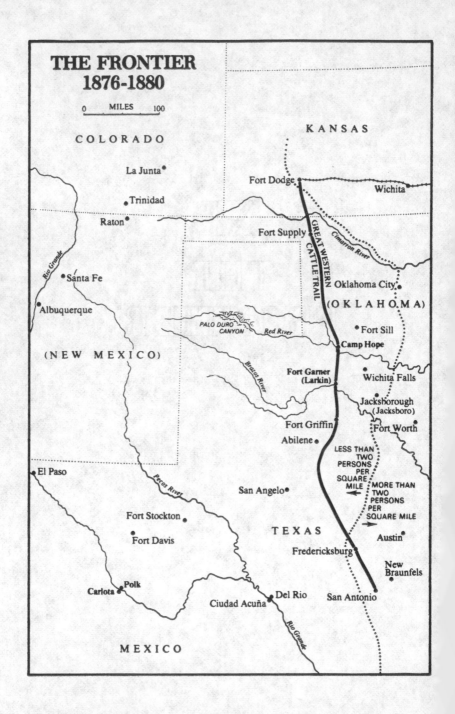

THE FRONTIER
1876-1880

0   MILES   100

KANSAS

COLORADO

La Junta

Trinidad

Raton

Fort Dodge

Wichita

Fort Supply

Cimarron River

Rio Grande

Santa Fe

GREAT WESTERN CATTLE TRAIL

Oklahoma City

(OKLAHOMA)

Albuquerque

PALO DURO CANYON

Red River

Fort Sill

Camp Hope

(NEW MEXICO)

Brazos River

Fort Garner (Larkin)

Wichita Falls

Jacksborough (Jacksboro)

Fort Griffin

Fort Worth

Abilene

LESS THAN TWO PERSONS PER SQUARE MILE ←

El Paso

Pecos River

→ MORE THAN TWO PERSONS PER SQUARE MILE

San Angelo

Fort Stockton

TEXAS

Austin

Fort Davis

Fredericksburg

New Braunfels

Carlota

Polk

Del Rio

Ciudad Acuña

San Antonio

Rio Grande

MEXICO

IT WAS PARADOXICAL. AFTER THE UNITED STATES ARMY ABANDONED FORT GAR-
ner, the real battle for this area began, the contest between the primeval
frontier and the settled town. The struggle had a significance greater even
than the one between white man and Indian. Its adversaries were marvelously
varied: the wild long-horned cattle of the plains versus the ingeniously perfected
beef cattle of England; the lone horseman galloping in from the western horizon
versus the railroad chugging in from the east; the flash of a vengeful pistol versus
the establishment of a courthouse dispensing rational law; the handful of Mexican
coins hidden in a sock versus the fledgling bank with its iron safe; the free-
ranging cattle drover versus the salesman of barbed wire; and in the bosom of Fort
Garner, the nomadic wanderings that Emma Larkin had known with the Comanche versus the steady path toward an ordered life that her husband, Earnshaw
Rusk, strove to establish.

In all parts of the American West this Homeric battle of conflicting values was
fought, but nowhere in more dramatic style than in West Texas. At Fort Garner,
in the quarter of a century between 1875 and 1900, it was conducted with particular intensity, and from the struggle emerged many of the lasting characteristics of
Texas.

The moment Earnshaw Rusk established his home in the abandoned stone
house at Fort Garner, he initiated his fight to bring the civilization he had known
in rural Pennsylvania to this untamed frontier. As a pacifistic Quaker he wanted
to erase memories of the military post and tried to rename the place in honor of
his wife's martyred family; he wanted it to become the village of Larkin. To his
dismay, the United States Post Office Department continued to call it Fort Garner,
but Rusk corrected people in his high-pitched voice: 'It's really Larkin, you know.'

He was equally adamant about longhorn cattle: 'I want none of those fearful
beasts on our land. I'm afraid of them. With those long, savage horns, they seem
to come from the devil. And the human beings they attract are a dissolute,
ungodly lot.' When his wife asked: 'If you don't want cattle on our land, how will
we eat?' he replied: 'I'll think of something,' but it was she who took action. For
with the riding skills she had mastered with the Comanche she sped across the
plains, driving wild mustangs into corrals and then taming them for sale to the
various army posts in Texas and the Indian Territory. She demonstrated exceptional talent in converting them into fine saddle horses, for where others whipped

the mustangs and broke them with punishment, she reasoned with them in a soft plains language they seemed to understand: 'Now, my little roan, we change our life for the better. We'll get to know this rope, perhaps to love it. We'll walk about this post, day after day, until it becomes our home.' During the first two weeks, not with force but through the gentleness of her heart, she spoke invariably to the wild horse as *we,* as if she along with the animal were learning a new way, but when the animal's terror had fled, she addressed it always as *you.* 'Now you have the secret!' she would cry joyously as the animal began to respond spontaneously to her commands, and because of her uncanny ability to think like an animal, she would teach the mustang to work with her until human and animal formed a cooperative pair.

Officers began to come from distant forts to buy a Rusk Roamer, as Emma's trainees were called. The mustangs brought good prices, and were treasured for their curious mixture of gentleness and proud spirit, but it soon became obvious that even with Earnshaw's awkward help she could not, in her advancing pregnancy, catch enough or tame them quickly enough to depend upon this for the limited income they needed.

When Emma raised the question as to how they might earn a living, Earnshaw forestalled her with a problem of his own: 'Emma, we must find people to occupy these houses.'

'I don't want a lot of people . . .'

'It's shameful to own good houses like these and see them stand empty. One of the foot soldiers who used to serve here . . . his wife worked on Suds Row . . . they tell me he's rotting in Jacksborough. They want to come back.'

'How would they earn a living?'

'That's the other thing, Emma,' and with his quiet perception of the years ahead and of how this area along the Brazos must develop, he reasoned with her: 'We'll soon be bringing a baby into our empty home. We must bring people into our empty houses.'

'Who has money for such extravagances?'

'People make money, Emma,' and with the friendly persuasion he had used in trying to bring a vision of peace to the Comanche, he now tried to reveal to his wife the bright future he saw: 'We have thy six thousand acres which no plow could break. We have a wonderful stone village which no storm can attack. And we have ourselves, with only thy savings and no prospects of more. This empty land, these empty houses, we shall use them as our money.'

Emma stayed silent, for she could feel the wonder of her plains slipping away she could feel the press of people invading her lonely acres, her silent houses. She feared change to a different way of life, but she also trusted her husband, who had given such courageous proof of his love. If he had a vision of a new world, she must listen, and when she did she heard the voice of the future: 'Thy empty land Emma, must produce something. Thy empty houses were made to protect fami lies. A man rode by this morning when thee was out with the mustangs and I told him he was welcome to move into one of thy houses.'

When she started to protest this invasion, he said quietly: 'Emma, if the fort is ever to be a town, we must have people.'

In this unstudied way Frank Yeager, his illiterate Alabama wife and their scrawny son Paul, aged three, moved into the house north of the commander's, and from the moment of their arrival Emma knew the Rusks were going to have trouble, for Yeager was a profane man and his wife a committed Baptist who felt it her duty to bring everyone she met under the moral protection of her church. One evening, after she argued loudly that Quakers were headed for hell because of their unorthodox beliefs, Earnshaw asked his wife: 'She's dead set on converting me, showing me the true way, yet she can't even discipline her own husband?'

Frank Yeager was a violent, difficult man, given to drunkenness and poker, when he could find partners. When his new landlord said austerely: 'I don't gamble,' Yeager said: 'You stay around me long enough, you'll learn.'

The Yeagers had been in residence only a short time when Frank captured Emma's full support: 'A woman as gone pregnant as you ought to stop foolin' around with them wild mustangs. Let's round up all the stray longhorns for fifty miles. Build us a real herd and drive it north to them new railheads in Kansas. Let's earn some real money.' Emma, who loved all animals and especially the wild cattle of the plains, replied with real excitement: 'We'll get the first batch this afternoon.' Two days later Earnshaw rode in to Jacksborough to invite the former soldier and his laundress wife to move into another of the houses at the fort, and the newcomers eagerly helped Yeager at the roundups, the woman riding as well as the men, and the Rusk herd grew.

The presence of an extra woman was helpful when Emma had her baby, a chubby boy with a voracious appetite, because Earnshaw was useless both at the birth and during the first difficult days. In fact, he was so much in the way that the former laundress snapped: 'Mr. Rusk, this would be a good time for you to ride in to Jacksborough and register your son with the authorities.'

During this trip Earnshaw learned of two Buffalo Soldiers from the 10th Cavalry who were approaching forced retirement, and when he found that one of them was the well-regarded John Jaxifer, he returned to Jacksborough and offered the two men a free house; so as Emma's herd of cattle increased, so did the population of Earnshaw's village.

Fort Garner now consisted of Emma Rusk and her longhorns, Earnshaw and his vision of a community, their son, Floyd, who grew daily, the Yeagers, who could do almost anything, the white soldier and his rough-and-ready wife, the two Negro cavalrymen, and lots of guns. Rusk hated guns; Emma respected their utility on a frontier. The other six were all practiced in arms; make that seven, because the Yeagers were already teaching their three-year-old how to handle a toy revolver. When Earnshaw protested, Yeager said: 'A Texan who can't handle a gun ain't fit to be a Texan.'

When Emma's longhorns were first rounded up at Fort Garner, Earnshaw was contemptuous of them, but when he awakened to the fact that they might provide the economic base not only for his family but also for the community he hoped to establish, he became more attentive. And when he seriously studied those lean Texas beasts with their excessive horns, his Quaker instincts began to operate and he longed to improve them. Very early he conceded that whereas they were admirably adapted to life on the open range, they were never going to produce much salable meat until they were crossed with the heavier, fatter cattle imported from England. When he proposed to Yeager that they purchase either the Angus or Hereford bulls which agricultural experts were recommending, the lanky herdsman, himself a human longhorn, with all muscle and no fat, protested.

'The longhorn is Texas,' he grumbled. 'Change him, you kill his spirit.'

'Those horns. They're horrible.' When Earnshaw said this he was looking at one of the bulls with horns so wide they were ridiculous, more than six feet tip to tip. 'Look at him. All horns and legs. No meat.'

By ill fortune he was denigrating the longhorn in which Frank Yeager took greatest pride: 'You're speakin' of the best bull we got.'

'Why do you say that?'

'This is Mean Moses. He leads the others to the promised land.' And he explained how this big, ugly creature had nominated himself to be king of this part of the Texas frontier: 'In spring he breeds the cows so they can produce calves big and tough like him. Those horns? He needs 'em to fend off the wolves. Those long legs? He needs 'em to cover the trail north to market without tirin'. Mr. Rusk . . .'

'We Quakers don't like titles. I'm Earnshaw.'

'Mr. Rusk, a longhorn bull is one of God's perfect engineerin' feats. You replace him with one of them fancy English breeds . . .' He spat. 'Mr. Rusk, long ago this frontier was occupied by three powerful things. The Comanche. The buffalo. The longhorn. Only the cattle is left. You replace 'em with fat and blubber, what in hell is Texas goin' to be?'

Earnshaw's desire to build a profitable ranching business received a bad jolt when he tried to sell off a few longhorns: 'I can't find buyers, not even at four dollars a head. That's less than it costs us to tend them.' But Yeager had a solution: 'If we can deliver them to the railhead at Dodge City, I know they'll bring forty dollars a head. Eastern markets are so hungry for beef, they'll take even long-horns.'

'How will we get them there?'

'Me and the boys will drove them.'

To this suggestion Rusk responded instantly: 'We'll not have our people making that trek to Kansas,' and when Yeager protested that it could be done easily, Rusk said firmly: 'I've heard about the Chisholm Trail into Abilene, Kansas, and the debauchery that goes with it. No hands from here will ever drove into Kansas.'

He was so adamant about this that Yeager surrendered: 'Tell you the truth, Mr. Rusk, it would be better to keep the hands here on the ranch, tendin' to things. We'll find us a reliable cattleman headin' north.'

Upon investigation, Rusk learned that the new cattle trail, called the Great Western, started down near the Rio Grande, swung northwest past San Antonio and Fredericksburg, then across empty land to Fort Griffin, passing not far to the west of Fort Garner. From there it lay due north to the Indian settlement at Camp Hope, then to remote Fort Supply in Indian Territory, followed by a relatively short stint into Dodge City, to which the Eastern railroads had recently penetrated. 'What goes on there,' he told his wife, 'I do not choose to know or dwell upon.'

It was Emma who first heard about R. J. Poteet, from a Mexican trail cook: 'The best. First day he told us: "No gambling in my crew. No fighting." And he meant it.'

The more she heard about R. J. Poteet the more she liked him, and when in June the Mexican rode up to her door with the news: 'Mr. Poteet, he's watering at our tank tomorrow,' she saddled up and rode to the northern end of her land to meet him.

She found him in charge of more than two thousand head of longhorns accumulated from various owners during the long trail north. He had with him nine cowboys and a Mexican cook, plus a thirteen-year-old boy to herd the spare horses in the remuda. It was an orderly camp, supervised by an orderly man just turned fifty, tall, thin as a cypress and as dark, with a close-cropped mustache and a wide-brimmed hat. His boots were so pointed at the toe and so elevated at the heel that he walked much like a woman, but he was so rarely away from his horse that this was seldom noticeable. He had a deep, resonant voice, a strong Southern accent, and an elaborate courtesy where women or young boys were concerned. From the manner in which his men went about their duties it was clear that he needed to give few orders, for he respected the men's abilities, including those of two black crew members. He allowed no alcohol in camp except what he himself carried, and that he used only as medicine for others in times of crisis.

'R. J. Poteet, ma'am,' he said when Emma rode up. 'I've heard of your exploits with the Comanche, and I'm deeply respectful of your courage.'

'My husband and I have some two hundred good animals. Well fed.'

'These grasslands should see to that.'

'And the care we give them.'

'Longhorns tend to care for themselves. Look at the condition of mine. Five hundred miles on the trail, some of them.'

'I've been told you give your animals extra care.'

'I try to, ma'am.' He spoke with an appealing directness, which encouraged her to trust him.

'Would you be able . . .' She hesitated. 'I mean, would you be interested? Looks like you're able to do pretty much as you wish.'

'I've been trail-drivin' north for some years, ma'am. And I judge you want me to carry your cattle to Dodge City?'

'Would you?'

'That's my job,' and before she was out of her saddle she was listening to his clearly defined terms: 'This is the tail end of the journey, ma'am, but the crucial part. I've got to get your cattle across the Red River, through the Indian lands, across the Canadian River and the Cimarron, and into Dodge. Find a buyer for them, make the proper deal, and bring you back your money. That's worth a fee, ma'am.'

'I'm sure it is.'

'I like ten percent now, earnest money, the balance when I sell.'

'You seem reluctant to state your fee, Mr. Poteet.'

'I am, ma'am, because some owners, especially the ladies, always think it's too high. But there is much work to do, much responsibility.'

'It's because you're known for reliability that I came.'

'Ma'am, I'd be obliged if you'd get these figures in your head. You owe me one dollar for every animal. I owe you five dollars for every one of your cattle I lose on the way, so I don't intend to lose any. If you want to ride with me to Dodge City to sell your beasts, do so, and I get nothing but my dollar a head. If I act as your agent, and I'm willing, you must rely upon me completely. I'll do my best for you . . .'

'They say so, Mr. Poteet.'

'Reputations aren't earned on one drive.' He coughed, then completed his terms: 'If I arrange for the selling, and sometimes it takes three minutes, sometimes three weeks, I get five percent. Some will do it for less, but frankly, I don't recommend them.'

At the noon hour they joined the cowboys at the chuck wagon, that amazing monument to American ingenuity, that contraption on four wheels from which hung all kinds of utilitarian devices: can openers, bone saws, frying pans, crocks with wire handles for sugar, pie plates with holes in their edges so they could be strung on a nail, clotheslines, folding tables, an awning to protect the Mexican cook from the sun, a bin for charcoal, and two dozen other imaginative additions, including drawers of every dimension.

'I took my first chuck wagon from Jacksborough across the Llano in 18 and 68,' Poteet said. 'Through Horsehead Crossing, all the way to Colorado.'

'The Estacado!' Emma said with awe. 'Even the Comanche stayed clear of that. What did you do for water?'

'We suffered. Next year, all the way to Montana. The chuck wagons in those days were simpler affairs. Everything you see on this wagon is in answer to some strong need. It's an invention of sheer intellectual brilliance, you could say.'

'Will your men run into trouble on the way to Dodge?'

'Now there's a misconception, ma'am. We do our very best to stay out of trouble. If Indians are runnin' wild, we head the other way. If a storm threatens, we try to lay low till it passes. Each of my men is armed, save the boy, but in the last five trips, not a shot fired in anger.'

'Why do you keep trailing, Mr. Poteet?'

Before he could respond, one of his cowboys interrupted: 'You know, ma'am, that some time ago Mr. Poteet started a college in South Texas?'

'I can believe it.'

'He makes so much and he pays us so little he had to do somethin' with his money.' The cowboy grinned.

Poteet made a pistol with his right forefinger and shot the cowboy dead, then turned suddenly to Emma: 'Ma'am, it's bold of me, and maybe it's wrong of me, but these are young men tryin' to learn about Texas. Would you have the courage to show them?' And the forthrightness with which he spoke—indeed, the dignity with which he conducted all his affairs—gave Emma the courage.

Raising her two hands to the sides of her face, she pushed back her hair to reveal the dreadfully scarred ears, and she could hear the cowboys gasp. Then, with her hands still in place, she unloosed the two white strands which controlled her wooden nose, and when it dropped, one of the men cried: 'Oh Jesus!'

'Texas wasn't won easy,' Poteet said.

'I'll have the longhorns gathered and counted this afternoon,' she said, but Poteet interrupted: 'We do the countin' together, ma'am.'

Earnshaw Rusk had always vowed to resist politics, for he had witnessed its lack of principle and its ruthlessness where personal interest was involved. Looking at what politics had done to him in the Indian Territory and to a fine man like General Grierson in Texas, he had concluded: Only a blind man or one whose moral sensibilities were numbed would dabble in it. But when he studied the situation dispassionately, he realized that the goal he sought to attain—the civilization of the West—could be achieved only if Texas had strong representatives in Washington, and as he interrogated various interested persons about whom the Texas legislature might send to the national Senate, the name of Somerset Cobb, the respected gentleman from Jefferson, kept surfacing. And when Cobb felt obligated to run for the U. S. Senate in order to represent the decent parts of the culture of the Old South, Rusk felt obligated to support him, actively.

If any proof was needed to show that this lanky Quaker was a man of principle, this action provided it, because on the surface Cobb represented everything Rusk opposed. Cobb had owned large numbers of slaves in both South Carolina and

Texas; Rusk had risked his life to oppose slavery in North Carolina and Virginia. Cobb was a Democrat; Rusk, like most Philadelphia Quakers, was a Republican. Cobb had served in the Confederate army, rising to high rank; Rusk was a pacifist.

What was worse, Cobb had vigorously opposed Northern interference in Texas affairs, calling Reconstruction 'that bastard child of a vengeful legislature.' It was, he had preached, 'infamous in conception, cruel in execution, and in its final days a thing of scorn'; Rusk had believed that the South, especially Texas, required stern discipline before it could be allowed free exercise of its powers within the Union.

Finally, Rusk knew that Cobb was a Southerner who refused to apologize for his service to the Confederacy, and had committed treason against the United States. Yet here he was, brazenly offering himself to the Texas legislature as a candidate for the U. S. Senate. Rusk had every reason to reject this man, or even work against him, but when it seemed that Cobb's opponent, also a military hero, might win the seat, Earnshaw knew that he must support the one-armed Cobb, so he left his ranch and harangued any members of the legislature he could encounter in the northern areas around Dallas.

Why did he do this quixotic thing? Why did this retiring and painfully bashful man plunge into the center of a political brawl? Because of what his wife had told him about Cobb's opponent, General Yancey Quimper: 'I was helping Mrs. Reed in the big house when General Quimper arrived to inspect what he called his fort. I was in the kitchen, of course . . .' She vaguely indicated her wooden nose. 'But I heard the three women talking.'

'What three?'

'Mrs. Reed. Mrs. Wetzel. Mrs. Quimper.'

'What did they say?'

'That General Quimper had not been a hero at San Jacinto, that he'd been a coward mainly. That he had never dueled Sam Houston or shot wide to spare Houston's life. That he had never been at Monterrey or been anywhere near the Bishop's Palace. That he had not defended the Texas lunette at Vicksburg. And that he was not entitled to the rank of general, because he simply gave himself that title.'

When Earnshaw heard this litany of deceit, he reacted as a Philadelphia Quaker and not as a Texan inured to such colorful imposture; he deemed it his duty to expose the lifelong fraud practiced by Quimper, and to this end he began pestering the Democratic leaders in Dallas. At first they laughed at him: 'You disqualify liars and frauds, you wouldn't have ten men in the United States Senate, nor six in the Texas.'

But he persisted in his crusade, and by chance he encountered one Texas state senator who was eager to listen. He was Ernst Allerkamp, who represented the German districts around Fredericksburg, and when Rusk approached him regarding General Quimper, he listened: 'Are you sure what you say is true?'

'I've made the most careful inquiries.'

'Didn't you hear about the Nueces River affair?' When Rusk said no, the German sat him down on a tavern bench—Earnshaw had lemonade—and recounted the wretched affair in which General Quimper and his roving force had slain the escaping Germans: 'My father, my brother Emil, so many more. Singing in the night as they left for Mexico. Then they were murdered.'

Rusk was horrified by the brutality this onslaught represented, but he was numbed by what Senator Allerkamp revealed about the infamous hangings at the Red River: 'With no evidence or little, with no justification except supposed patriotism run wild . . .' He told of the first hangings, the revulsion, the next surge, the final excesses, and when he was through, Rusk said: 'We must drive this man out of public life.'

Since Rusk had never met Quimper, Allerkamp warned him: 'When you do, you'll like him. Most of the men in the legislature want to send him to the Senate. They say: "He's a real Texan." '

Enraged, Rusk accompanied Allerkamp to Austin, where he continued his politicking among the other state legislators who alone had the right to elect men to serve in the national Senate. He revived so much old rumor detrimental to Quimper that a meeting was arranged with Rusk, Allerkamp, nine of their supporters and General Quimper himself. He appeared in a fine suit, white hair flowing, expensive boots and a big, warm smile that embraced even his enemies. 'Goodness,' Earnshaw whispered to Allerkamp when he first saw the general, 'he looks like a senator!'

He talked like one, too, offering bland reassurances that he understood, and understood fully and generously, why certain men might want to oppose him for this august seat. But Rusk cut him short: 'Quimper, if thee continues to solicit votes for the United States Senate, I shall have to publish this memorandum . . . in Texas . . . then carry it to the United States Senate itself. Sir, if this document is circulated, thy life will be ruined.'

And before General Quimper could defend himself, Earnshaw Rusk, standing tall and thin and rumpled, read off the terrible indictment: a lie here, misrepresentation there, an assumed title, a borrowed military record, a claim that he had served at Vicksburg, where real Texas heroes had died at the lunette, the charge up a Mexican hill he had never seen and, most damaging of all, 'a fraudulent claim that thee had dueled with Sam Houston. Sam Houston? He would have despised thee.'

General Quimper, having insulated himself through the years with a record he had almost convinced himself was his, was not easily goaded into surrendering it and the public accolades to which he felt entitled: 'You blackguard, sir. Publish one word of such blackmail, you die.'

'And what would that accomplish?' Rusk asked. Pointing to Senator Allerkamp, he said: 'Thee must shoot him too, as thee did his father and his brother.'

'What do you mean?'

'At the Nueces River. At dawn. That day of infinite shame.'

As Quimper looked at this circle of unrelenting faces, he had to acknowledge that his charade was over. If he persisted in his pursuit of the Senate seat, his spurious past was going to be assembled and dragged in the mud. He would be excoriated both in Texas and in Washington, and if his anti-Union behavior at the Nueces River, where the pro-Union Germans were slain, and at the Red River, where other Union loyalists were hanged, were dredged up, demagogic Northern senators would bar him from membership in their body, even if the Texas legislature did elect him. How terribly unfair to be destroyed at this late date by a Quaker from Pennsylvania, a man who wasn't even a Texan, and by a German immigrant who had no right being in the state at all.

But in the depths of his tragedy he saw a ray of light: 'If I do withdraw, that paper . . . ?'

'It becomes thy paper,' Rusk said, and the others nodded.

'You won't . . . ?'

'This meeting dies here,' Allerkamp promised. 'All we said, all we wrote.'

'You swear?'

Each man gave his word, and as the vows were uttered Yancey Quimper, hero of San Jacinto, Monterrey and Vicksburg, could feel life returning, could visualize himself climbing out of this dreadful pit which had so suddenly entrapped him. He could still be General Quimper. He would still be remembered for his great feats at San Jacinto. He would retain his profitable boot factory, his wife and sons, the high regard of those other politicians who had supported him in his contest for the Senate. He was only sixty-four, with many good years ahead, and he judged that it would be better to spend them holding on to the reputation he had built for himself than to attempt to be a United States senator and run the risk of losing it.

Rising from the chair in which he had slumped, he braced himself, looked at these pitiful little men who had defeated him, and said: 'It's amazin' what some men will do to win an election.' And with that, he stalked from the room, still a general, still a hero, still one of the most impressive Texans of his age.

When Earnshaw Rusk returned to his ranch at Fort Garner he told Emma: 'As thee knows, I've never seen Somerset Cobb. Let's pray he'll prove worthy of our effort.'

Texans could not be sure whether one-armed Colonel Cobb would prove worthy of the high position to which they promoted him in a special election, but they had no doubt about his spry little wife Petty Prue. When the Cobbs reached

Washington they found resentment, for Somerset was not only an unreconstructed Southerner, he was also a military hero of the Confederacy, and his claim to be sworn in as a member of the Senate was a slap in the face for all loyal Union veterans who had fought against him.

Grudgingly he was seated, President Grant encouraging it as a prudent measure to keep Texas and other Southern states in line for the presidential election that would take place in the fall, but certain unrelenting Northern senators prevented him from obtaining any important committee assignments, so for some time the junior senator from Texas remained in outer darkness, and it looked as if he might stay there for the duration of his term.

It was then that Petty Prue swung into action. Fifty-three years old, five feet one, just over a hundred pounds, she began making her persuasive rounds of Washington, starting with the President himself. When she entered his office she stopped, drew back, and said in her lovely drawl: 'I do declare, General Grant, if you'd been twins, the war would've ended two years sooner.' And with her petite hands she indicated one Union army swooping down the Mississippi while the other attacked Richmond.

She exacted from Grant a promise that he would put in a good word with the Republican leaders of the Senate, after which he reminded her: 'You know, Miz Cobb, I carry little weight in that body,' and she assured him: 'General, you carry the weight of the nation on your broad shoulders. Have no fear.'

She did not hesitate to assault the headquarters of the enemy, barging into the offices of Sherman of Ohio and John A. Logan of Illinois. She told the former: 'Just as your brother, William Tecumseh, did his honorable best for the North, so my husband, Senatuh Cobb, did his honorable best for the South, and it's high time all men of honor be reprieved for whatever they did, either at the burnin' of Atlanta or elsewhere. I'm ready to forgive, and I sincerely trust you are too.'

In the evenings she held small dinner parties, flattering her guests with a flow of Southern charm, never mentioning her past in Georgia. She was now a Texas woman, had been since that November day in 1849 when she pulled up stakes in Social Circle and headed west. She was one of the most attractive and clever women Texas had produced, for this state had a saucy trick of borrowing able women from Tennessee and Alabama and Mississippi and making them just a little better than they would otherwise have been.

At the end of four months, every senator knew Mrs. Cobb; after five months, Cobb found himself on three major committees, in obedience to the principle stated so often by his wife in her arguments with his colleagues: 'You're goin' to have to admit us Southrons sooner or later. Why not give the good ones like my husband a head start?'

On the night before summer recess started, the Cobbs gave a small dinner to which the President and Senators Sherman and Logan were invited. When cigars were passed, Petty Prue excused herself shyly: 'I know you gentlemen have affairs

to discuss which I'd not be able to follow,' and off she traipsed, but not before
smiling at each of the national leaders as she passed his chair. When she was gone,
Grant said: 'The South could not have sent to Washington a better representative
than your wife, Cobb,' and dour Sherman observed: 'Damn shame she didn't
bring a Republican with her.' Grant laughed and took Somerset by the arm and
said: 'He's even better than a Republican. He's an American.' And in this way the
wounds of that fratricidal war between the sections were finally healed.

Sometimes in the early morning when Emma Rusk looked across the plains she
loved, she could not escape feeling that the West she had known was dying: Every
move Earnshaw makes to improve his village condemns my wilderness. She had
been sorely perplexed during these past weeks when a Mr. Simpson, who had
served as sutler to the army when it occupied the fort, came to her husband and
said: 'Mr. Rusk, I'd like to have that company barracks. Can't pay you anything
now, but if the store I plan to open makes money, and I'm sure it will . . .'

Mr. Simpson had taken the building, put in a row of shelves and filled them
with goods purchased in Jacksborough. He proved to be a congenial man who
understood both groceries and housewives, and before that first week was out he
had begun to collect customers from a distance, and by the end of the third week
he was reordering supplies. Fort Garner had its first store.

But an event which moved Emma most deeply began on 21 June 1879, the
longest day, and it caused her abiding grief. At about nine in the morning John
Jaxifer galloped in: 'Comanche attacking from the north!'

Since Jaxifer had served in the 10th Cavalry, Emma and Earnshaw had to think
that he knew what he was saying, and when they ran out to look, they saw that
the warriors were once more on the warpath. In profound consternation Emma
cried: 'Have they come for me?'

Rusk, who hated guns and had never learned to use one, felt that he must
protect his community, so he ran to the kitchen, grabbed an old washbasin, and
started beating it to attract his neighbors. Within a few minutes Frank Yeager
arrived, with his wife appearing a few minutes later laden with three rifles. The
other black cavalryman had been working on foot, and he ran in with his gun. If
the Indians proposed to attack Fort Garner, they were going to face gunfire.

They did not seek war, and when they approached making signs of peace and
calling out words of assurance, the Rusks, who knew their language, shouted: 'No
firing.' In the pause the Fort Garner people saw that this war party consisted of
one old chief attended by fourteen braves, not one of them as much as fourteen
years old. Three could not yet be six. The old chief was Wading Bird, named
seventy years before for an avocet who visited a pond near his mother's tepee, and
when Emma recognized him she whispered his name to instruct her husband.

'Wading Bird!' Earnshaw cried in Comanche. 'What news?'

'To see Great Chief Rusk.' Earnshaw had instructed his Indians not to call him by this title, explaining to them that the true Great Chief was in Washington, but they had persisted in calling him so, because it reassured them that he could grant their petitions.

'What does thee seek?' Rusk asked, repeating the phrase he had used so often in his contacts with them, and as he said the familiar words a kind of joy possessed him: he was again the eager young man in command at Camp Hope and these were the wise chiefs and promising young braves he had been certain he could pacify; it was June again and there was hope both in the camp of that name and in his heart; but when he looked away from the old chief he saw that his wife was trembling, and the day returned to the present.

'What does thee seek?' he asked again, this time as a wary trader, not as a poet.

'A buffalo, Great Chief Rusk.'

'We have no buffalo.'

'Yes. Up where the stream ends,' and the old man pointed north toward the tank.

'Have we any buffalo?' Rusk asked, and Yeager said: 'An old one comes wandering in, now and then.'

'He's up there,' Wading Bird said.

'What does thee want with him?' Rusk asked, and the old man gave an anguished explanation which left both Earnshaw and his wife close to tears:

'Not many days are left, not many buffalo roam the plains. All is forgotten. You and I grow older, Great Chief Rusk, and death creeps ever closer to us.

'The young ones of few summers, they have never known our old ways. The hunt. The chase. The look of the buffalo when you are close upon him. The pounding of the hoofs. The cries. The ecstasy. The hot blood on the hands.

'Great Chief Rusk, you have the buffalo. I have the young men who need to remember. Grant us permission to hunt your buffalo as we used to hunt. At Camp Hope you always tried to understand us. Understand us now.'

Rusk looked at the fourteen boys and asked them in Comanche: 'How many have seen a buffalo?' and less than half indicated that they had. He then consulted with Frank Yeager, who grudgingly conceded that with most of the ranch longhorns in the southern reaches, little trouble could ensue if the Indians hunted a buffalo up by the tank, so permission was granted, and the people in the stone houses watched as Chief Wading Bird arranged his braves for the chase.

He placed his two oldest boys in the lead, and he took position at the rear with the three youngest children, who bestrode their ponies with skill. When the formation was ready, he cried exhortations in Comanche, waved his arms, and pointed north toward the tank. With high-pitched cries the young braves set forth.

The two Rusks, Yeager and Jaxifer followed at a respectable distance, and after about an hour the cavalryman cried: 'They see it!' And there, at a lonely spot where the range tailed off toward the Red River, the Comanche came upon their ancient prey.

With a cry they had learned but had never before used, two boys in the lead urged their companions on, and the chase was joined. Earnshaw, watching this strange performance, had the fleeting thought that perhaps the lone buffalo understood his role in this ancient ritual, understood that this was his last chase, too, for he darted this way and that, over lands which had once contained millions of his fellows, throwing the unskilled riders into gullies from which their old chief had difficulty extricating them.

But at last their persistent nagging at his heels wore him down, and the great head lowered as if he were preparing to fight off the wolves he had resisted in his earlier days, and his feet grew heavy, and his breath came in painful gasps.

In these climactic moments of the last hunt, Emma felt a wild urge to spur her horse forward and drive the Indian boys away from the old monarch of her plains. 'Let him live!' she shouted to the wind, but no one heard, and she watched with pain as the little lads on their little ponies encircled the buffalo while the old man shouted encouragement from his post of guidance, and at midafternoon on that hot June day the young Comanche killed the last buffalo in the vicinity of Fort Garner. They did it ceremoniously, as in the old days when no rations were issued at the Indian post, those old days when the Comanche lived and died with the buffalo, prospering when it prospered, starving when it retreated beyond their grasp.

By no means did that final hunt of 1879 end in solemn ritual, for after the great beast had been slain and his liver cut out for the lads to eat, Chief Wading Bird rode back to the fort, ostensibly to thank his former protector. But when he appeared, Emma suspected that his visit involved not Earnshaw but her, and she was right, because when the boys had tethered their horses he bade them run off, leaving him to talk alone with the Rusks.

'Great Chief, Little Woman who used to live with us, I seek words, important words.'

'Sit with us,' Rusk said, unaware that his wife was trembling.

She had cause, for when the three were seated on the porch of the house which had once been the Wetzels', Wading Bird said: 'I have brought your son.'

At first Earnshaw did not comprehend, but when Wading Bird repeated the words, pointing directly at Emma, he realized that the true purpose of this foray south was not only to hunt buffalo in the old manner, but also to deliver the son of Little Woman to his mother. His impulsive response, the one he could not have stifled had he wished, was one of generous acceptance: 'Wading Bird! He will be welcomed in our home. And he will have a little brother, who now sleeps inside.'

But Emma spoke otherwise: 'I do not want him. Those days are lost. It is all no more.'

The two men stared at her, a mother rejecting her own son. To Wading Bird the experiences which Emma had suffered were an expected part of life, the treatment accorded all prisoners. He could think of a dozen captured women from his warrior days—Mexicans, Apache, many whites—and when, after initial punishments, they had borne children, they had loved them as mothers should and helped them to become honorable braves. It was the Comanche way of life, and now Little Woman was being offered her son, and she was refusing him. It passed comprehension.

Nor could her husband understand. He had seen her joy when she was pregnant with their son and daily witnessed her extraordinary love for young Floyd. Because of her own tormented childhood, she had lavished unusual care on Floyd and would presumably continue to do so. As for her Indian son, Earnshaw had often speculated on where the boy was and what he might be doing. Now he learned that the boy was here, at Fort Garner, on a horse, his lips rich with buffalo liver as in the old days, and he believed that if Emma could see him, she would want to keep him.

'Fetch the lad,' he told Wading Bird, but at this suggestion Emma gave a loud wail: 'No!'

Still believing that sight of the boy would melt her heart, he dispatched the eager chief, who summoned Emma's son. Blue Cloud was eight years old, a fine-looking fellow, somewhat tall for his age, eager, bright-eyed. 'Does he look like his father?' Earnshaw asked with the Quaker simplicity which stunned those around him.

Coldly, staring right at the boy, she said: 'His father could have been one of twenty.' Then she repeated: 'Those days are lost. Take him away.'

'Emma! For the love of God, this child is thy son.'

'It is ended,' she said.

When the two men tried to dissuade her, she pulled the hair away from her ears and ripped off her wooden nose. Thrusting her face close to her son's, she cried: 'Remember me as your people made me.' And she held her face close to his until he turned away.

Wading Bird took the boy by the hand and led him back to his companions. Sadly he mounted his horse, sadly he waved to the Rusks. Earnshaw, standing at the edge of the parade ground, nodded as the Comanche departed, the last he would ever see. With their broken promises they had broken his heart, and brought him to disgrace because of the love he held for them. He had hoped, during the interview with the boy, that this lad might be the agency through which he could regain contact with the Indians, but it was not to be, for when he sought Emma he found her in a corner, as in the days of her captivity, shivering. If there had been sunlit days on the plains which she wished to remember, there were ugly, dark ones she must forget, and when memories of these came surging back, she felt thankful for the refuge her husband's village now provided.

Earnshaw's struggle to establish Fort Garner as a viable community still hinged upon that problem which assailed all the little Western settlements: 'How can we earn enough income to support a thousand people?' Normal farming was impossible; land even fifty yards back from a stream would be so arid that it could not be tilled. Lumbering was not feasible, for the grassland provided no trees. There were no minerals, and the village could not focus upon transportation, for there was none except for the rickety stage that ran spasmodically to Jacksborough. For the time being it seemed that only the ranging longhorns would provide any cash.

With some humility, Earnshaw confessed: 'It may be thy longhorns, Emma, which will save Larkin,' and once he conceded this, he began to take professional interest in the scientific breeding of his wife's ranch stock, even going so far as to purchase from England two good bulls of a different breed.

If numbers alone determined which facts in history would become legendary, the relatively few Texas cowboys who herded their cattle up the Chisholm Trail to Abilene, or up the Great Western to Dodge City, or along the Goodnight-Loving to Colorado, would not qualify. For if you totaled all the cattle these men tended in a decade, you would find that they had accounted for not much more than twenty or twenty-five percent of the cattle produced in America; the vast bulk was bred and marketed east of the Mississippi. But what Texas lacked in quantity it made up for in the dramatic quality of its longhorns and in men like R. J. Poteet who herded them.

Stay-at-homes like Earnshaw Rusk, who never rode a cattle trail, also shared responsibility for the Texas legend, because they saw that if Texas beef was to be competitive with the better beef being produced in the East, a more rewarding breed than the longhorn must be developed. But when these far-seeing men tried to introduce improved bulls onto their ranches, they were greeted with scorn. Even a rational man like Poteet warned: 'The only cattle that can stand those long drives north are Texas cattle, and that will always mean the longhorn.'

Rusk argued: 'If they have railroads in Kansas, won't we have them soon in Texas? Then our cattle won't have to trail hundreds of miles. They'll ride straight through to Chicago.'

Poteet laughed: 'You ever followed the history of railroads in Texas? "Give us five thousand dollars and we'll have a train at your town in seven months." Fifty railroads have been organized that way, and not one of them has seen an engine on its tracks, and most of them haven't seen the tracks.' He studied the bleak land that encompassed Fort Garner and said sardonically: 'You may get trains here about 19 and 81, if then.' And he warned Rusk not to experiment with strange bulls: 'You'll produce an animal that can't trail to market, and I won't try to drove such weaklings north.'

Rusk's own foreman, Frank Yeager, was displeased when Rusk, ignoring all advice, purchased two Hereford bulls from a breeder in Missouri, who told him: 'Great idea, Rusk! Your Longhorn from Texas is an authentic breed, just like my Hereford from England. Your strong cows and my fat bulls will produce a majestic animal,' and when Earnshaw received the bill of sale he noticed that it showed the name of his cattle with a capital L, just as if they had been Black Angus. But when the bulls arrived at Fort Garner, Yeager almost refused to unload them when they arrived by wagon from Jacksborough, but Earnshaw enlisted support from his wife: 'Emma, thy bulls are here and Frank is proving difficult.'

'I didn't order them,' she pointed out, but he pleaded: 'They're thine now. Please help.' So she relented and persuaded Yeager to unload the beasts, but when he saw how fat they were, how listless compared to the rangy Longhorn bull that he preferred, Mean Moses, he refused to deal with them and left that job to the two black cavalrymen and the white infantryman.

But now a problem in ranch management arose, one that was beginning to perplex the entire frontier. Because the imported bulls were so valuable, they had to be grazed in a pasture from which they could not stray. This would have been a simple problem in Missouri, where there were ample oak trees for fence posts and soft soil in which to place them. But in this part of Texas there were almost no trees stout enough to yield wooden posts and split rails, and when they were imported, at prohibitive cost, it was almost impossible to dig post holes in the hard-baked, rocky earth. After many disappointments, Yeager growled: 'If you want to fence in those precious bulls of yours, you've got to buy posts from East Texas.' So a few cartloads were imported at a cost that frightened Earnshaw.

The pastures in which they kept the two bulls were so small that the animals grew fatter and fatter for lack of exercise, and it was Yeager's opinion that if he put half a dozen strong Longhorn cows in with each bull, 'them Longhorn ladies'll chew them dumplin's up.' In this he was wrong; Hereford bull and Longhorn cow mated well, and began to produce stout, reddish-colored calves of great attractiveness and commercial promise, but this merely aggravated the problem, for now more fences were required to keep the more valuable offspring protected. Every time one of the imported bulls produced another calf—and there were now hundreds of such potent sires on the Western ranches—the Texas frontier was threatened a little more, for when a Longhorn worth only five dollars was replaced by an imported beast worth forty, procedures had to change, and Rusk was continually saying: 'We must have more fences.'

In the early 1880s one of the most revolutionary forces in American history appeared in West Texas, a brash young man of such explosive enthusiasm that ten minutes' talk with him was bound to produce visions. He was Alonzo Betz, thirty-two years old, out of a place called Eureka, Illinois. He wore a bizarre mixture of clothing, half dude-Chicago, half rural-Texas, and he chattered like a Gatling gun: 'Folks, I bring a solution to your problems. I come like Aaron leading you to the promised land.' None of his listeners could figure out how Aaron got into the picture, but Alonzo gave them scant time for such reflection.

He talked with his hands, drawing vast imaginary pictures, and as he warmed to his subject, he liked to pull his purple tie loose as if its tightness had impeded his words: 'Folks, right there is the answer to your worries. I bring you the future.'

What he brought was one of those inventions like the cotton gin which modify history, and as soon as he revealed it on the former parade ground at Fort Garner, Earnshaw Rusk appreciated its applications: 'This here we call the barbed-wire fence, because at intervals along it, as you can see, our patented machine twists in a very sharp, pointed barb. We also provide you with a post which even this child could hammer into the sod, and when you've strung three strands of this around your fields, your . . . cattle . . . are . . . penned . . . in.'

Frank Yeager scoffed: 'My Longhorns'll knock that fence down in one minute.'

Alonzo Betz jumped on the threat. He literally jumped two feet forward, grasped Yeager by the arm, and cried loudly: 'You're right to think that. Everybody does at first. From Illinois to Arkansas, I've been told "My bulls would knock that fence down in one minute," just like you said. So let's get your bulls and you and me build a little pasture right here wired in with my barbed wire, and we'll put a load of fresh hay out here . . .'

He engaged the entire population of Fort Garner, eleven families now, in the erection of a corral, and all were amazed at how easily the thin steel posts could be driven into the hard earth and how deftly the wires could be strung. Several men and one woman scratched their hands on the sharp wire, at which Betz chortled: 'If my wire stops you good people, it'll sure stop your stock.'

When the little area was fenced, he shouted for Yeager to bring in some Longhorns, and he shouted—he never just spoke—for the best available hay to be piled out of reach. For nearly an hour the villagers watched as the powerful animals moved up against the unfamiliar fence and backed off when they came into contact with the barbs.

'It works!' Earnshaw cried, and Emma, too, was pleased, but Yeager would not surrender: 'If we'd of had Mean Moses in there, down goes that fence.'

Once more Alonzo Betz jumped at the challenge: 'Let's fetch this Mean Moses and leave him with the others overnight,' and when this was agreed upon he said: 'I'll stand guard, because one thing I've learned. No honest man from Illinois can match a man from Texas when it comes to sheer deviltry. I don't want you goadin' your animals on with no pitchfork.'

So the test was run, with Betz and Yeager enforcing its honesty, and through the long night the two men talked, with Betz proclaiming the glories of the future when every field would be fenced, and Yeager longing for the past when the range from Fort Worth to California remained free. At intervals people from the houses came to watch Mean Moses destroy the fence, but instead they saw the hungry bull start time and again for the succulent hay, only to be turned back by the barbed wire, and when dawn broke over the treeless plains and everyone saw the fence still standing with Moses docile inside, the future of barbed wire in this part of Texas was assured.

But Alonzo Betz was still a showman, one of the best, and when day had well broken he said: 'Now I want to prove to you good people that your Longhorns were really hungry during their vigil. Watch this.' And he produced an instrument they had not seen before, a pair of very long-handled wire cutters. 'The handles have to be long,' he explained, 'so as to apply leverage to these very short, sharp blades. Look what this means, how easy it is to handle barbed wire.'

Going to the fence, he positioned himself halfway between two posts, and with three rapid snips of his cutters, he threw down the fence, and through the opening thus provided, Mean Moses and the hungry Longhorns piled, eager to reach the hay.

'How much will it cost to fence in six thousand acres?' Rusk asked, and Betz replied: 'Show me your configuration,' and when Rusk did, the salesman made a quick calculation: 'Six thousand acres is nine point thirty-eight square miles. If perfectly square, you would need about twelve miles. In your configuration, more like fifteen miles. I can sell you barbed wire and posts for a hundred and fifty dollars a mile, so to do it all, which I would not recommend, would cost you two thousand two hundred and fifty.'

The figure staggered the Rusks. It was quite beyond their reach, but they could see that the future of ranching was going to be determined by valuable cattle enclosed in relatively small pastures protected by barbed-wire fencing. 'What could we do?' Earnshaw asked, and Betz, eager to get a demonstration ranch started in an area which he felt was bound to prosper, said with great enthusiasm: 'My company, D. K. Rampart Wire and Steel of Eureka, Illinois, we want to establish a chain of ranches exhibiting our product. So everyone can see its application. We can fence in about three thousand of your acres for a special price of one thousand and fifty dollars, and we'd be honored at the opportunity to do so.'

It was agreed. Rusk, Yeager and Betz mounted horses, and accompanied by the two black cavalrymen, surveyed the Larkin lands, and all quickly concluded that they should enclose all fields abutting on Bear Creek and place additional fencing around the tank so that access to this steady supply of water could be controlled: 'This way you protect your water. You protect your valuable bulls. You keep everything neat.' At the end of the ride, even Yeager had to acknowledge that a new day had dawned on the Texas plains, and he began to study the pamphlets that would make him an expert on the handling of barbed wire. But before the deal could be concluded there was the question of money, the perennial problem of the frontier.

The growth of any village into a town was a subtle procedure. First came the store, for without it there could be no orderly society, and Fort Garner now had a good one run by the former sutler. Next came the school, and third, there had to be a good saloon to serve as social center for the cowhands and such adventurous young women as might want to try their luck in the settlement. Earnshaw, as a good Christian, did not wish to sell one of his barracks buildings to a soldier who had once been stationed at the fort and who proposed to open such an establish-ment, but he was also a Pennsylvania Quaker, and a cannier lot of businessmen had never been brought across the ocean to America, so a deal was struck, not with Earnshaw, who refused to touch liquor, but with Emma, who said: 'A town needs a little excitement.' The Barracks, as it was named, provided it.

The fourth requisite was a bank, which would lend money, provide stability, and serve as the industrial focus of the surrounding area. Certainly, Fort Garner needed a bank, but it was doubtful that any would regard such a meager economy as a sound basis for taking risks. Where would a bank look for its business? A few stock sales? An exchange of real estate now and then? Money mailed in from stabler societies back east to sons and daughters trying to subdue the plains? It might be decades before a place like Fort Garner could justify a bank, but just as the need became greatest, a man with tremendous vision and steel nerves moved into town, bought one of the better stone houses, imported a big iron safe, and announced himself as the First National Bank of Fort Garner, Texas.

Clyde Weatherby came from Indiana, home of America's shrewdest horse trad-ers, and although he brought with him only limited capital borrowed from his former father-in-law, who wanted to see him, as he said, 'get the hell out of Indiana and stay out,' he did bring a marvelously clear vision of the future, which he confided to no one: Land is the secret. Things have got to happen out here— what, I don't know. Give me some land that touches water, and I'm in business. He had various intricate plans for getting hold of land and using it creatively.

Outstanding because of his well-tailored suits and string ties, he became favor-ably known as Banker Weatherby, generous in lending, severe in collecting, and when Rusk and young Betz appeared before him to seek a loan for payment on the barbed wire, he was enthusiastic.

'It could prove the making of the West,' he pontificated, and the men agreed.

He then asked directly: 'Mr. Rusk, what's the total bill to be?' and when Earnshaw explained, he smiled at Betz and said: 'Not excessive. Your price is lower than your competitors',' and Betz said: 'It better be.'

'Now, Mr. Rusk, how much of the thousand and fifty dollars can you provide?' When Rusk said: 'Emma and I have five hundred and fifty in cash,' he smiled warmly and said: 'Excellent. So what you wish from me is a mere five hundred dollars.' Both Rusk and Betz were surprised that he should refer to this sum as *mere;* to them it was a fortune.

'How could we arrange this?' Rusk asked, and Weatherby said: 'Simplicity itself! You give me a mortgage, extend it for as many years as it will take you to pay off, and pay only three and three-quarters percent interest each year, no mind to the balance.'

'How much would that be?'

'Less than nineteen dollars a year.'

'That would be easy,' Rusk said, whereupon Weatherby added: 'There is the provision, you know, that if conditions change at the bank, we could demand payment in full, but that never happens.'

'And if I couldn't pay . . . in full, I mean?'

'It's known as "calling the loan," but it never happens.'

'But what does it mean?'

Very carefully Mr. Weatherby explained the legal situation: 'Our Texas Constitution of 18 and 76 forbids me from taking your homestead in fulfillment of an ordinary debt. And it forbids me from issuing you a mortgage simply to acquire funds for idle indulgence. But it does allow me to give you a mortgage on your homestead for its improvement, and that's what we're doing here.'

'So my entire ranch is mortgaged?'

'In this case, yes. If you fail to pay us back our money, we take your ranch, and sell it at auction to get our money, and give you what's left over.'

In one respect, this was not an indecent deal, for the original Larkins had acquired their six thousand acres at an average cost of only four cents an acre, so that its base value was not more than $240, less than half the amount of the loan the bank was making; but in a practical sense the conditions being offered were appalling. The Rusks could pay interest for ten years, and reduce the outstanding balance to $100, but if they ever had a bad year in which they could not come up with the interest to keep the mortgage alive—or if the bank at that bad moment chose to demand payment in full—the Rusks could lose not only their land but also the improvements, which might be extremely valuable. It was one of the cruelest systems ever devised for the conduct of business, but it was sanctified by every court; through this device bankers would gain control of vast reaches of Western land, especially in Texas. When Earnshaw Rusk signed his mortgage for $500 he unwittingly placed his future in jeopardy, but as Banker Weatherby assured him: 'We never foreclose.'

So the deal was made: the Rusks gave Alonzo Betz $300 of their $550 as a down payment; the barbed wire was shipped from Eureka, Illinois; Frank Yeager and his men began building fences; and Banker Weatherby had in his big iron safe a mortgage on the entire Larkin Ranch.

Bob wahr they called it throughout Texas, and when Yeager and his men finished driving their posts and stringing their strands they sounded the death knell of the open range, for they had removed the choicest acres and the best water holes once used by the itinerant cattlemen. With timing that was diabolically unfortunate, they had everything in place just as that year's big cattle drives from the south began, and just as one of the most severe droughts in history started to bake the Texas range.

Emma, watching these restrictive procedures, was not surprised when they caused trouble, for as she had warned: 'Earnshaw, you're chopping this great open land into mean little squares, and the people won't tolerate it.' She wanted to add: 'And my Longhorns won't, either.'

The first rumbles of trouble came when school began after Easter vacation, and they were so trivial that neither Rusk nor Yeager could later recall their beginning. Jaxifer had come to Rusk with a curious protest. The two cavalrymen had met an Indian squaw, a Waco from the eastern regions, and had taken her into their stone house, ostensibly as cook-helper. None of the white families could be sure to whom she belonged, but in due time she had produced a pretty little girl baby, half black, half Indian, and because the former cavalrymen had witnessed the advantages children enjoyed if they could read and write—which they themselves could not—they wanted the girl, whosoever daughter she was, to get an education: 'The fence we've put up, Mr. Rusk, it makes the teacher walk the long way round instead of across the field, as before.'

'I am sorry about that.'

'And we wondered if there was some way to cut a hole . . .'

'Where the road runs, we've already put in gates. But cut a fence merely to continue an old footpath? Never. That fence cannot be touched.'

'But the teacher . . .'

When other parents began to protest the inconvenience to their teacher, Rusk and Yeager went out to study the problem, and they saw immediately that this portion of their fence had been unwisely strung, for it did cut off access to the school, but the fence had been so costly and had required so much effort to construct that it had become a virtue in itself, something that had to be protected. 'What we will do,' Yeager promised, 'is give the people lumber so they can build stiles, but cutting our fences except where roads run through, we cain't allow that.'

The next complaint was more serious. A family not connected with either the ranch or the village rode in to complain bitterly about what the fence had done to them: 'For a long time we've used the road which runs south from the tank where the soldier and his girl killed theirselves. Now your fence cuts it off, and we—'

'The fence is on our land,' Yeager interrupted sternly.

'Yes, but it cuts a public road.'

'The only public road is the one that runs east-west from Three Cairns. And we've put in gates to service that.'

'But we've always used this road.'

'Not any longer. We've fenced our land, and that's that.'

'But if the county seat is going to be at Fort Garner, how can we get there?'

'You'll have to go around and catch the Three Cairns road.'

'Go around! Surely you could add one more gate.'

'The fence stands,' Yeager said, terminating that conversation.

Less than a week later, one of the ranch hands rode in with sickening news: 'Come see what they done.' And when Rusk and Yeager rode out to where their new fence blocked the disputed road, they found that someone had cut it and knocked down the posts.

'I'll shoot the son-of-a-bitch who did this!' Yeager threatened, but Rusk restrained him: 'There'll be no shooting.'

But there was. When Jaxifer and another hand rode out to rebuild the fence across the road, someone shot at them, and they quickly retreated. Frank Yeager himself went out, well armed, to repair the fence, and when someone fired at him, he coolly waited, watched, fired back, and killed the man.

Thus began one of the ugliest episodes of Texas history, the Great Range War, in which one group of cattlemen who had been utilizing the open range suddenly found that another group with a little more money had fenced off traditional routes and, much worse, traditional water holes. One of the most severe losses of water occurred at the Larkin Ranch, where the Rusks had fenced in their tank north of town, and not with one line of fence, but three, because the outer ring delineated the perimeter of the ranch, while the double strand, with its guarded gate, protected the water from pressures by either the Rusk cattle or strays that might crowd in.

With the first big drive of the summer it became obvious that there would be conflict, because cattle had to have water prior to the long trail up to the Red River. But for some curious reason, Earnshaw Rusk, this peaceable Quaker, refused to see that his action in closing off the water hole was arbitrary, unjustified, and opposed to the public welfare. His recent years of dealing with Texans had indoctrinated him with their fundamental law: 'Private property is sacrosanct, mine in particular.' So he continued to keep other cattle away from his water; he continued to maintain his fences, even if they did cut people off from their accustomed routes. He was neither irrational nor obdurate; he had become a Texan.

Almost daily, now, one of the hands reported at dawn: 'They cut more fence,' for if Alonzo Betz had been a genius in selling bob wahr, other salesmen had been equally ingenious in selling long-handled cutters that could lay that wire flat within seconds, so daily Rusk and Yeager were forced to ride out and repair the fences.

The war was not an unequal one, for the cutters, those men who loved freedom and the open range, could in one dark night destroy an immense reach of fence; sometimes every strand for two miles would be cut between each pair of posts, at grievous expense to the rancher. The rancher, on the other hand, could post his trigger-happy ranch hands in dark hiding places among the dips and swerves of his land, and then gunfire exploded, with the newfangled wire-cutters left dangling on the fence beside the corpses.

In this warfare the advantage now began to swing to the fence-cutters, for the hardened men trailing their cattle north hired professional gunslingers to ride along, so that when a battle erupted, the firepower was apt to be on the side of the trail drivers. Frank Yeager learned these facts the hard way when one of his new hands was killed while trying to stop a wire-cutting. He retaliated with fiendish cleverness.

Originally opposed to fencing, he was now its primary defender, for in the act of building a fence he identified with it, and any attack upon it was an attack on him. So when his man was killed he announced: 'No more watching at night. We'll find other ways.' He did. Utilizing his imperfect knowledge of explosives, he devised a number of sensitive bombs which would be placed along the wires and activated if the tension on any wire was released by cutting. Each bomb contained so many fragmentations that the cutter did not have to be close when it went off; the shards would fly a long distance to kill or seriously maim.

Now the hands at Fort Garner slept in their beds, rode out at dawn, and counted the corpses. The trail drivers in retaliation began shooting cattle inside the fences and setting fire to pastures, while settled citizens whose modes of travel had been disrupted by the fences began cutting them with hurtful frequency. So more deaths ensued. On all fronts it was now open warfare.

One hateful aspect of the battle at Fort Garner was that Earnshaw Rusk, contrary to every principle of his upbringing, found himself acting as a kind of general defending his fort. Unwilling to handle a gun himself, he directed the strategies of those who did. Even worse, he also served as leader of those other ranchers in the area who had fenced their properties. He became General Rusk, defender of the bob-wahr fence.

The Range War was resolved in a manner peculiar to this state. No police were sent into the area, no state militia, no army units. In August, when the prolonged drought increased the number of killings, a medium-sized man in his early thirties rode quietly into town, Texas Ranger Clyde Rossiter, slit-eyed and with his hands never far from his holsters. His assigned job was to terminate the Larkin County

Range War. He moved soberly, made no arrests, no threats. He was out on the range a good deal, inspecting fences and intercepting herds as they moved north, and wherever he went he made it clear that the fence war was over.

He was successful in halting the carnage, but as the people of the region watched in admiration while he took charge, it became obvious that he always sided with the big ranchers and opposed the little man no matter what the issue, so one night a group of citizens asked if they could meet with him to present what they held to be their just grievances. He refused to listen to their whining, telling them: 'It's my job to establish peace, not to correct old injustices.'

He explained his basic attitude one night when taking supper with the Rusks: 'From what I've seen of Texas, the good things in our society are always done by people with money, the bad things by people without. So I find it practical to work with people who own large ranches, because they know what's best, and against those with nothing, because they never know anything.'

'Do most of the Rangers feel that way?' Earnshaw asked.

'Our experience teaches us.'

'Does thee own a ranch?'

'I do, and I'd not want trespassers cutting my fences.'

'What should I do about the people who protest about our cutting their road?'

'It's your land, isn't it?'

'But how should I respond?'

'I'm not here to pass laws. I'm here to stop the shootin', and I think it's stopped.' But he did, as a careful Ranger, want to inspect all angles of this war, so he left Fort Garner for several days to range the countryside between that town and Jacksborough, and was absent when R. J. Poteet came north with two thousand seven hundred head bound for Dodge City. When Poteet reached the area he found a distressing situation. Not only were the Brazos and Bear Creek bone-dry, but the permanent water hole on the Larkin Ranch had been fenced off. Methodically, but with minimum damage, he proceeded to cut the outer fence that his cattle must penetrate before they could approach the tank, whose double fences would also have to be cut if the cattle were to drink.

Rusk's watchmen were amazed at the boldness with which this determined stranger was cutting their fence, and when they rode back to inform Rusk, they could find only Yeager, who grabbed a rifle and rode breathlessly to the scene, only to discover that it was Poteet who was doing it.

'Hey there! Poteet! What're you up to?'

'Watering my cattle, as always.'

'That's fenced.'

'It shouldn't be. This is open range, time out of mind.'

'No longer. Times have changed.'

'They shouldn't.'

'Poteet, if your men touch that fence, my men will shoot.'

'They'd be damned fools if they did. I've got some powerful gunmen ridin' with me.'

At this point Earnshaw Rusk rode up, and he was preparing to issue orders to his troops when Poteet spoke: 'Friend Earnshaw, I don't want your men to do anything foolish. You see my chuck wagon? Why do you think the sides are up?'

When the Rusk men looked at the ominous wagon, they could see that it had been placed in an advantageous position, with its flexible sides closed. 'Friend Earnshaw, one of my good men in there has his rifle pointed directly at you. Another has you in his sights, Mr. Yeager. Now I propose to water my stock as usual, and I shall have to cut your fences to do it.'

Rusk took a deep breath, then said firmly: 'Poteet, my men will shoot if thee touches that fence.'

For a long time no one spoke, no one moved. R. J. Poteet, born in Virginia fifty-six years ago, had acquired certain characteristics in the cattle-herding business which he was powerless to alter, and one was that his animals must be tended daily, honestly and with maximum care. This included regular watering. Since the close of the War Between the States, he had trailed one large consignment north each year and sometimes two, for a total of twenty-one herds, some of huge dimension, and he had never lost even two percent, not to Indians, or bandits, or drought, or stampede, or shifty buyers, and it was unthinkable that he should vary his procedures now. He was going to water his steers.

Earnshaw Rusk believed profoundly in whatever he dedicated himself to. When he saw that a new day was opening upon the once-free range, he spurred its arrival. And perhaps most subtle of all, he had become infected with the Texas doctrine that a man's land was not only his castle, but also his salvation.

In the long wait no one fired, but all stood ready. Then the two leaders spoke. Rusk, still playing the role of general, said: 'Did thee know, Poteet, that Ranger Rossiter is here to end this fighting? If thee shoots me, he'll hound thee to the ends of the earth,' and Poteet snapped: 'Rangers always side with the rich. I'm surprised a man of your principles would want their help. Friend Earnshaw, what would you do if you had twenty-seven hundred head of cattle within smelling distance of water? And none elsewhere to be found?'

There was silence, when life and the values men fought for hung in the balance; it was prolonged, and in it Earnshaw Rusk dropped his pose of being a general and acknowledged that what he and Frank Yeager had been doing was wrong. It might represent the wave of the future, and perhaps it would prevail before the decade faded, but as things stood now, it was wrong. It was wrong to fence in a water hole which had been used, as Poteet said, 'time out of mind.' It was wrong to cut off public roads as if schoolteachers and children were of no concern. It was wrong to impose arbitrary new rules merely because one was strong enough to get a loan at the bank, and it was terribly wrong to abolish a neighbor's inherited rights simply because thee had bob wahr and he didn't.

'What would *you* do if the cattle were yours?' Poteet repeated, emphasizing the pronoun.

Rusk had been trained to respect the moral implications of any problem, and since he had already conceded that his fencing in the water hole was wrong, he must now correct that error. In a very low voice, as if speaking philosophically on a matter which did not involve him personally, he said: 'If they were my cattle, I'd have to water them.' And with a motion of his right arm he indicated that Yeager and his men should withdraw.

'We'll replace your fences,' Poteet said as his hands started cutting. 'But if I were you, I'd leave them down.'

Rusk could never turn aside from a moral debate: 'For a few years, Poteet, thee wins. But thee must know the old ways are dead. Soon we'll have fences everywhere.'

'More's the pity.'

'Thee will carry my wife's cattle on to Dodge?'

'As always.'

'I'll go count them.'

'I'll do the countin'.'

Like many a politician, Senator Cobb, abetted by Petty Prue, was an outstanding success in Washington but something less when he returned home to explain his behavior to his constituents. On his latest visit to Jefferson he had barely reached his plantation when a group of irate voters drove up, headed by a jut-jawed Mr. Colquitt.

'Senator,' the man demanded, 'why did you let 'em blast our Red River Raft?'

While he fumbled for an explanation, they dragged him from the parlor and down to the Lammermoor wharf, and what he saw came close to bringing tears to his eyes, for the stout wharf which he and Cousin Reuben had built with such care back in 1850 now wasted away some fifty feet removed from the sparse water in which no boat of any size could function.

'You allowed 'em to destroy the value of your land,' Colquitt said. 'And in town it's the same way. Our beautiful harbor where the big boats came from New Orleans. All vanished.'

Another man cried in anguished protest: 'Why didn't you stop 'em?'

Seeing the anger of his constituents, Cobb knew that their questions were vital and that if he wanted to continue as a senator, he must give them a sensible answer, but he was not the man to hide behind platitudes or fatuous promises that could never be kept. He would give them an honest, harsh answer: 'Gentlemen, no one in Jefferson has lost more by the destruction of the Raft than I have. Look at this dry hole. A way of life gone. But on the day that fellow in Sweden made TNT possible, he doomed our Raft. For a hundred years people had been talking about removing the Raft, and they accomplished nothing. TNT comes along and there goes our livelihood.'

'It should of stayed that way,' Colquitt said, and Cobb replied: 'With TNT many valuable things are going to be changed.'

'Well, what are you going to do about it?'

'Do? About the Raft? Nothing. Do you think Louisiana is going to let us rebuild it so that our Jefferson, population eight hundred thirty-one, can have a seaport?'

As soon as he had given this sharp answer he knew he must become conciliatory, so he invited the men back into the parlor, where Petty Prue served tea and molasses cookies: 'Gentlemen, you asked me what I am going to do. Plenty, believe me. First, I'm going to surrender to TNT. It blew our Raft right out of the Red River, and nothing will ever restore it. Second, I will lead the battle to get a railroad into this town, because once we do that, we'll get our cotton to New Orleans faster and better than before. Third, I'm going to make every improvement possible at Lammermoor, because even though we've lost our dock, we'll discover new ways to prosper. In Texas that always happens.'

Mr. Colquitt, jaw still outthrust, growled: 'Cain't you make Washington give us a railroad?'

'I've tried to nudge them, but Washington says: "We have to consider the whole nation, not just little Texas." '

'Senator, I've learned one thing in life,' Colquitt conceded. 'Whenever the United States government meddles in Texas affairs, Texas gets swindled.'

Cobb laughed, as did his wife, who said: 'Our experience has been the same, Mr. Colquitt. Texas is so big, it has imperial problems. Congress is used to handling the little troubles of states like Vermont and Iowa. Texas staggers them. They have no comprehension of our needs.'

'But how do you two people feel about the drop in value of your plantation? Who would buy it now, with no dock?' Colquitt asked.

It was Petty Prue who answered, vigorously: 'Of course the value has dropped. And sharply. But you watch! It'll grow back for some reason we can't even imagine right now. That's the rule in Texas. Change and adjustment and sorrow. But always the value of our land increases.'

'Why don't we just leave the Union?' Mr. Colquitt asked; he had grown up in South Carolina.

'That's been settled.'

'But we can still divide into five separate states, that I'm sure of.' Mr. Colquitt had been in Texas only three years but already it was *we;* two more and he would be a passionate devotee of all things Texan.

'We could divide,' Senator Cobb granted, 'but I doubt we ever would.'

'Why not?'

'Which state would get the Alamo?' he asked with a smile.

If Texas had been powerless to halt the dynamiting of the Red River Raft, it did finally end the Great Range War. A number of bills were proposed and enacted, putting an end to the killing; they worked this way, as a small farmer near Fort Garner, where the fighting had been heaviest, saw it:

> 'Anyone who cuts a fence, anywhere, any time, he's to be arrested, fined, and thrown in jail for a long spell. Anyone found with a pair of cutters —on his person, in his house, in his wagon—he gets similar punishment. Any trail driver like R. J. Poteet who forces his cattle onto land which has been fenced is sent to jail for one to five.
>
> 'But don't you think for one minute that the big owners who have fenced in public land get off scot-free, nosiree. They will be asked politely to unfence land that contains traditional water supplies. They have to provide gates if they've fenced across public roads. And they must not ignore the customary rights of ordinary citizens. But they don't have to do any of these things right away. Government allows them grace periods up to six months, and if they haven't made the alterations by then, they'll be given warnings. When they've ignored such warnings, maybe three years, they'll be severely rebuked . . . in writin'. Fines? Jail? For the big owners? You must be jokin'!'

Inexorably the movements launched by Rusk to turn his village into a proper town continued, often in directions he had not anticipated. With the first four keystones in place—store, school, saloon, bank—he was free to turn his attention to the next three: churches, newspaper, railroad. With these he met both success and failure.

Banker Weatherby, also eager to see his town and his bank grow, was instrumental in solving the problem of the churches. 'Earnshaw,' he said one morning when Rusk came in to pay interest on his loan, 'a town does better if it has a core of strong churches.'

'How do we attract them?'

'We have several informal congregations in town right now. They'd be delighted to have free land. Then we'll ask the Fort Worth newspapers to announce that we'll give any recognized religion a free corner lot of its own choosing.'

Weatherby's advice was resoundingly apt, for when this news circulated through Texas eight different churches investigated and six selected their sites and started building. Baptists chose first and nabbed the best spot in the heart of town; Methodists came second; the Presbyterians chose a quiet spot; and the Epis-

copalians not only selected on the edge of town but also purchased an adjoining
lot because they said they liked lots of space for a generous building. The Church
of Christ would be satisfied for the first dozen years with a small wooden building, and a group that called themselves Saviors of the Bible erected only a tent.

This was one of the best trade-offs Rusk would make, because the churches
brought stability; they encouraged settlers from older towns to move in; and they
deposited their collections in the First National Bank of Fort Garner.

When the bank had been in existence for some time, an official arrived from
Washington to inform Weatherby that the title he had invented for his establishment could not be so loosely applied: 'You can't go around calling just any old
bank a National Bank. Take that sign down.' While the official was in town he
also listened to Rusk's complaint about the name of the place: 'Can thee please
inform the government that we want a better name? Fort Garner existed only a
few years. It's a silly, militaristic name. Much more appropriate would be Larkin.'

Earnshaw made no headway with his plea, but it did serve as further inspiration
for a campaign he would continue for two decades. Whenever he posted a letter
he asked the man in charge: 'When does the name-change take place?' And
always the postmaster replied: 'That's in the lap of the gods.' The gods were either
opposed to the change or forgetful, because the name stayed the same, and this so
irritated Earnshaw that he finally wrote a letter to the President:

> Mr. President:
>
> I have tried constantly to have the name of our post office changed from
> Fort Garner to Larkin, and have not even received the courtesy of a
> sensible reply. The state of Texas has so many post offices bearing the
> word *fort,* it seems more like a military establishment than a civilian
> state. Fort Worth, Fort Davis, Fort Griffin, Fort Stockton and Fort Gar-
> ner to name only a few. We would appreciate if you would instruct your
> Postmaster General to rename our town Larkin.
>
> Earnshaw Rusk

He received no reply, but quickly his attention was diverted to a matter of much
graver significance than the choice of a name. A bright young man from Massachusetts with a Harvard degree, Charles Fordson, had for some time been moving
through the West with two mules, a wagon and a cargo which had since the days
of Gutenberg represented real progress. It was a hand-operated printing press with
ten trays of movable type, and it was seeking a home.

As soon as Rusk learned of the young man's arrival he cornered him, showed
him the five remaining empty buildings, and assured him: 'We need you, and
you'll find no better prospect in all of Texas. Larkin! Sure to become a metropolis.
Join us and grow!' And so this vital link was added to the tenuous chain of

civilization: in 1868, the Larkin brothers had chosen this confluence for the site of their ranch; in 1869, the United States Army confirmed the wisdom of their choice; in 1879, Sutler Simpson thought that if he were to open a grocery here, he could make money, and before long Banker Weatherby thought the same. Now, in 1881, young Charles Fordson with his peripatetic press listens to Earnshaw's blandishments and decides that the newspaper just might succeed, but he names it the *Larkin County Defender,* for he fears that the town alone might not provide enough activity to justify his venture.

During a quiet spell in the winter of 1881, Fordson sought to distract attention from hard times by publishing a series of well-constructed articles combining news and editorial opinion. Random paragraphs indicate the thrust of his argument:

> . . . In Larkin County during the past two years there have been four executions by gunfire on the streets of the county seat and ten in the outlying districts.

> . . . Certainly, at least half the fourteen victims deserved to die, and we applaud the public-spirited citizens who took charge of their punishment. But it would be difficult to claim that the other half died in accordance with any known principles of justice. They were murdered, and they should not have been.

> . . . The only solution to this problem is a stricter code of law enforcement, by our officers, by our juries and by our sentencing judges. This journal calls for an end to the lawlessness in Larkin County and in Texas generally.

The articles evoked a response which Editor Fordson had not anticipated, for although a few citizens, like the Baptist minister and three widows who had lost their husbands to gunfire, applauded the common sense of his arguments, the general consensus was that 'if some popinjay from Massychusetts is afeered of a little gunfire, he should skedaddle back to where he come from.'

The serious consequence of the articles came when the governor directed a fiery blast at the would-be reformer. His defense of Texas was reprinted throughout the state, bringing scorn upon Larkin County:

> Weak-willed, frightened newcomers to our Great State have offered comment in the public press to the effect that Texas is a lawless place. Nothing could be further from the truth. Our lawmen are famed throughout the nation, our judges are models of propriety, and our citizens are noted for their willing obedience to whatever just laws our legislature passes . . .

The governor's theories received a test in the case of the Parmenteer brothers, sons of a law-abiding farmer. The boys, as so often happened in families, followed two radically different courses. The elder son, Daniel, did well in school, read for law in an Austin office, passed his bar examination before the local judge, and became one of the leading lights in Larkin County, where he married the daughter of a clergyman and was in the process of raising four fine children.

His younger brother, Cletus, disliked school, hated teachers, and despised law officials. By the age of eighteen he had been widely known as 'a bad 'un,' a reputation that grew as years passed. At first he merely terrorized people his own age, until boys and girls he had known would have nothing to do with him. Then he started stealing things, which his parents replaced, but finally he launched into the perilous business of stealing horses and cattle, and that put him beyond the pale. As an outlaw he participated in two killings, and following a raid into New Mexico, a price was placed on his head in that territory, but as usual, this was ignored in Texas. He became a shifty, quick-triggered idler who brought considerable ignominy to his otherwise respectable family, and he could find no woman willing to risk marriage with him. He consorted only with other petty outlaws, and it was widely predicted throughout the county that sooner or later young Clete would have to be hanged by one sheriff's posse or another.

Things were in this condition one bright spring day in 1881 when the growing town of Fort Garner heard the familiar sound of gunfire, and then the shout: 'Parmenteer has killed Judge Bates!' People rushed into the streets to find the alarm correct. At high noon, on the main thoroughfare, a respectable judge— well, not too respectable—had been callously shot in the presence of not less than twenty witnesses, all of whom identified Parmenteer as the killer. But it was not Cletus, the outlaw, who had done the killing; it was Daniel, the law-abiding lawyer.

The judge was dead, of that there could not be the slightest doubt, because four quick bullets had ripped his abdomen apart and he lay bleeding in the middle of the street. Lawyer Parmenteer walked steadily and without emotion to the sheriff's office, where he turned in his gun with the words 'A good deed done on a good day,' a verdict in which the town concurred.

Most towns in Texas had known such incidents, but this particular crime posed extraordinary problems for the editor of the *Larkin County Defender*.

'Jackson,' the young man said to his assistant as they discussed how to handle this case, 'we have a problem.'

'I don't think so. Let me talk with the two dozen people who saw the shooting.'

'The facts? We have no problem with them. The question is, how do we deal with them?'

'We just say "Lawyer Daniel Parmenteer—" '

'Did what?'

'Killed Judge Bates.'

'We dare not say boldly "Lawyer Parmenteer killed Judge Bates." Sounds too blunt, too accusatory.'

'The truth is: "Lawyer Parmenteer, brother of the noted outlaw—" '

'Stop. No mention of the brother. We'd have both of them gunning for us.'

'You may be right. So it's "Lawyer Parmenteer murders—" '

'Impossible to say that, Jackson. Murder implies guilt.'

'How about "Lawyer Parmenteer shoots—" '

'I'm afraid of that on two counts. If we stress that he was a lawyer, it might be interpreted as our prejudicing the case. And we cannot use the word shoot. Sounds as if he intended to do it.'

'My God! He walked up to him, if what I hear is true, spoke to him once, and pumped him full of lead. If that isn't shooting . . .'

'You don't understand, Jackson. We must not print a single word that in any way impugns either the motives or the actions of two of our leading citizens.'

So Fordson and Jackson agonized over how to handle the biggest story of the year, and they decided that there was almost nothing they could say which would not infuriate either Lawyer Parmenteer on the one hand, or the relatives of Judge Bates on the other. They could not point out that the lawyer had acted because a court case had gone against him, nor could they state what everybody in two counties knew, that Judge Bates was a drunken reprobate who took bribes on the side, as he had flagrantly done in the case which Parmenteer had lost.

In fact, there was almost nothing that the *Defender* could say about this case except that it had happened, and even that simple statement posed the most delicate problems, and when it came time to draft the headline, young Fordson found himself right back at the beginning. REGRETTABLE KILLING ON MAIN STREET had to be discarded for three reasons: to stress Main Street would imply that the sheriff had been delinquent; to use the word *killing* was simply too harsh, for as the governor himself had argued in his now-famous letter 'Texans do not go around killing people,' and *regrettable* might prove most troublesome of all, because it implied that the killing was unjustified, and to say this could well bring Lawyer Parmenteer storming into the editorial offices bent on another killing that would be justified.

One by one the two newspapermen discarded the traditional headline words: *deplorable, brutal, savage*. They all had to go, until young Jackson wailed: 'What can we say?' and Fordson remembered: 'There was this case in East Texas last year. They got away with calling it a *fuss*.'

'You mean that Copperthwaite case? Three men dead on Main Street, within five feet of one another? They called that a fuss?'

'In Texas you do,' Fordson said, and then in a stroke of genius he dashed off a headline that might work: UNFORTUNATE RENCONTRE IN FORT GARNER.

'What in hell is a rencontre?' Jackson asked, pronouncing the word in three syllables.

'It's a polite French way of saying that someone got shot in the gut. But I'm not too happy about the word *unfortunate*. The Parmenteer people might take unkindly to that. We don't want to launch a feud.' Fordson sighed, then said resignedly: 'No big headlines at all. No talks with any of the witnesses. Just something that happened on Main Street?' And when that week's edition of the *Defender* appeared, readers scanned the front page in vain for any big handling of the story; on page three, buried among notices of meetings and offerings of new goods in the store, appeared the inconspicuous story: RENCONTRE IN FORT GARNER, with no adjectives, no gory details, and certainly no aspersions cast on either side.

The editor was applauded for his good taste and Daniel Parmenteer actually bowed to him as they passed. The lawyer was not apprehended for the killing because no one could be found in Fort Garner who had seen it, and the incoming judge, pleased to have had worthless Judge Bates removed from the bench so he could occupy it, held that because the killing occurred before he assumed jurisdiction, he could ignore it.

Indeed, the Parmenteer-Bates affair would have subsided like a hundred other murders in these frontier areas had not the younger Parmenteer, Cletus the outlaw, suddenly roared back into town, shot the place up, and stolen a horse. The gunfire could be forgiven as an act of high spirits, but the stealing of a horse went so against the grain of Texas morality that a posse had to be organized immediately: 'Men, we can't stand horse theft in this county!' and sixteen amateur lawmen were sworn in prior to setting out to run down the criminal.

By a stroke of poor luck, the leader of the posse—not designated by law but by noisy acclaim—turned out to be the younger brother of dead Judge Bates, and he prosecuted the chase with such a vengeance that by nightfall they had come upon the renegade struggling along with the stolen horse, which had gone lame. It was quite clear from the stories which circulated afterward that Cletus Parmenteer had remained astride his incapable horse and had tried to surrender, thinking no doubt that his brother could somehow defend him against the charge of theft, but Anson Bates as leader of the posse would have none of that.

'What Anson done,' one of the posse members explained to Daniel Parmenteer later, 'was, he rode up to your brother and said "We don't want none of your kind in jail," and he blasted him six times, right through the chest, him standin' no further away than I am from you.'

When Lawyer Parmenteer heard this, he knew there was no possible response but for him to go shoot Anson Bates, which he did as the latter came out of the barbershop. 'Unarmed, without a call so he could defend hisse'f,' a Bates man explained to his clan, 'this proud son-of-a-bitch kilt our second brother,' and with that a general warfare erupted.

The Bates gang killed four Parmenteers, but were never able to get Lawye

Daniel, who moved quietly about the county always armed. His people, fatal phrase, gunned down five Bates partisans, and before long the feud had spread, as such feuds always did, to the surrounding counties. For a while Bateses and Parmenteers fell like leaves, but most of the dead did not bear these names; the typical victim was some unimportant man like an Ashton farming in Jack County or a Lawson in Young who happened for some obscure reason to side with one party or the other. By the close of 1881 seventeen people were dead in the Bates-Parmenteer feud, and the former side vowed that the fighting would never stop 'until that sinful bastard Daniel Parmenteer lies punctured from head to toe eatin' dust.'

In December 1881 word of the Larkin County feud reached the Eastern news-papers, one of which pointed out that more white men had already died than had been lost in most of the Indian attacks in the area during the preceding decade. At that point even the governor conceded that he must do something, and what he did was so alien to what an Eastern governor might do that it, too, attracted considerable national attention.

He summoned to his office in Austin a short, wiry sixty-one-year-old man and told him: 'Otto, this could well be the last assignment I'll ever ask you to take. You've earned retirement, but you're the best lawman we have. Go up there and slow those damned fools down.'

So Ranger Otto Macnab returned to his ranch at Fredericksburg, saddled up his best horse, loaded his mule with a tent, rations of food and one small case of ammunition, and prepared to head north toward Larkin County. His wife, Franziska, now fifty-four years old, had often watched him make such prepara-tions, always with apprehension, for she and Otto had attended many funerals of Rangers who had lost their lives on similar lone-wolf missions, but she did not try to dissuade him. 'Take care, Otto, do take care.' He accepted the white linen duster she handed him, the fifth she had made during his years as a Ranger, then kissed her goodbye: 'Take care of the ranch. Be sure the boys watch things.'

He did not follow main roads, but used back trails through the lonely wastes of Llano, San Saba, Comanche and Palo Pinto counties into Jack County, where he made quiet inquiries as to developments in the Larkin County feud. In an eating house where he was not known, a farmer said at table: 'Gonna get worse over there,' but another contradicted him: 'It'll probably settle down. Friend told me the governor's sendin' in some Ranger to stop the killin',' and the first man replied: 'Well, the Bateses is callin' in some reinforcements of their own.'

'What do you mean?' the optimistic man asked, and the farmer explained: 'I'm told that one of the Bates cousins, Vidal, went to New Mexico to hire Rattlesnake Peavine to come east and get Lawyer Parmenteer.'

This ominous news was greeted with silence, and then the second farmer said, professionally: 'That's gonna produce a flock of new killin's,' to which the first man agreed: 'Sure is.'

They turned to Macnab: 'You ever run across Peavine? Crippled left arm. But
he only needs his right.'

'Haven't heard of him, but if he's a New Mexico gunman . . .'

'He's a Texas gunman. Ran across the border to escape hangin'.'

'Bad?'

'The worst. The Bateses ain't doin' Texas any favor by bringin' him back. And
they ain't doin' Parmenteer any good a-tall.'

In the morning Otto headed due west for Larkin County, knowing that Rattlesnake Peavine was approaching it headed east. Had someone from a superior
vantage point been tracking the movements of Macnab on his western heading
and Peavine on his eastern, he could have predicted that these two must collide
somewhere near the town of Fort Garner, and he would have known that this
would produce considerable wreckage, for Macnab was a man who never turned
back or shied away from a difficult confrontation, while Peavine had acquired
such mastery of guile and unexpected movement that after twenty years of continuous peril he was still known as one of the two or three most dangerous men in
the West.

Otto rode into town late one Thursday afternoon, a small, lone man leading a
carefully laden mule that never looked up. He entered by the dusty road from
Jacksborough, came slowly, quietly down Main Street, and tied up at the rack in
front of the saloon. Watchers noticed that he did not tie the mule, a sign that he
had used this beast many times before. No one guessed that he was a Ranger, for
he bore not a single sign to indicate that.

Inside the saloon he occasioned little comment, and when he asked in a quiet
voice: 'Any place a man could stay?' they willingly told him of a farmer's widow
who took in boarders.

'Food any good?'

'Best in town,' the men assured him, but with a shrug which indicated that
even that wasn't going to be too palatable. He ordered a beer but drank little of it,
then headed out the door, untying his horse, leading it by the bridle, his mule
following behind.

He ensconced himself in the home of Widow Holley, where he said his name
was Jallow, which caused some discussion among his fellow boarders: 'What kind
of name is that?'

'I've often wondered. Mother said it was German, but she was Irish.'

'Where you from?'

'Galveston.'

'Where you headin'?'

'Here.'

'Lookin' for land?' He nodded, and the men offered advice, to which he listened carefully.

He spent the next five days visiting land that might be for sale and listening to

accounts of the region. He was much impressed by the Quaker Rusk, and especially by stories of how he had found his bride, but Rusk said firmly: 'No land of
mine for sale.'

As he went about, returning regularly to Mrs. Holley's for his noon and evening meals so as to catch the gossip, he reached two conclusions: the Bateses were
a mean and ugly lot who had indeed sent to New Mexico to import a notorious
killer, and Lawyer Parmenteer was one of the most unpleasant men he had
encountered in a long time. One night, after a stormy meeting with the man
regarding a farm west of town, he muttered to himself: 'If I ever saw a man who
invites being killed, Daniel Parmenteer's the one.'

The lawyer was sanctimonious, vengeful, hateful in his personal relations, and
mortally afraid of being shot. He apparently felt that his only protection lay in
eliminating the Bateses and those associated with them, and to accomplish this he
had instituted the worst kind of vigilante community, in which men went in fear
of their brothers.

On the sixth day Otto rose as usual, shaved, donned his usual dress, breakfasted
with the boarders, then went to the stables, where he mounted his horse, adjusted
the two pistols at his waist, and rode to where the Bates brothers lived at the
eastern end of town. Dismounting in one quick swing of his leg, he walked
quietly but quickly into the Bates house with pistols drawn, and announced: 'Sam
and Ed, you're under arrest. Otto Macnab, Texas Ranger.'

Before the startled men could respond in any way, even to the lifting of a cup
to throw it, he had shackles about their wrists and a rope uniting them. He
walked them quickly to a stout tree at the edge of town, to which he bound them,
warning that he would shoot them dead if they tried to escape.

He then rode back into town, where he stalked into the law offices of Daniel
Parmenteer, arresting and securing him in the same way. Leading the lawyer into
the street, he banged on the door of the sheriff's office and told him to fetch his
deputy and follow immediately. When the sheriff started to ask questions, he
snapped: 'Otto Macnab, Texas Ranger,' and on foot he led Parmenteer to the east
edge of town, where he lashed him also to the big tree.

When the sheriff arrived, Macnab told the prisoners, and the crowd that had
gathered: 'Bateses, Parmenteers, people of Larkin County. The feud is over. The
killing has ended. My name is Otto Macnab, Texas Ranger, and I am telling you
that this town is at rest.' Some cheers greeted this welcome promise.

He then went to stand before the Bates brothers: 'You've had grievances, I
know. And you've responded to them. But enough's enough. We will stand for no
more.' Taking a long, sharp knife from his belt, he reached out and cut the two
men free.

Moving to Parmenteer, he said: 'Daniel, you felt you had to vindicate your
brother Cletus, and you have. We all understand, but we can tolerate no more.
The feud is over.' And he cut his cords too.

But then Parmenteer asked a sensible question: 'What about Peavine? They've sent to New Mexico to bring him in to kill me and my folks.'

'I've been told that,' Macnab said, never raising his voice, 'and I shall go out now to warn Peavine not to enter this town. He is forbidden.'

With that, he turned to the sheriff: 'Now the job's yours. Watch these men. Keep the peace.' And he walked back to the center of town, where he recovered his horse, packed his mule once again, jammed his felt hat down upon his forehead, and rode out of town to intercept the Rattlesnake.

He rode three days toward the New Mexico border, and toward dusk on the last day, saw figures on the horizon. Neither hurrying nor slowing down, he rode toward them.

They turned out to be three soldiers on patrol from Fort Elliott, and as they camped under the stars, with the soldiers providing much better food than Otto could supply, they told him that they had crossed paths with two men named Bates and Peavine.

'You say Bates and Peavine are still at Fort Elliott?'

'They helped the captain hunt for deer . . . for the mess.'

In the morning the soldiers continued their patrol. Macnab headed for the distant fort, and at about noon he was rewarded by seeing two men coming eastward, each with two horses. Making sure that they must see him, he rode resolutely right at them, and at hailing distance he called out: 'Peavine! Bates! This is Otto Macnab, Texas Ranger.'

With no guns showing, he went directly up to them and said: 'I've been sent to Larkin County to stop the killing. Four days ago I arrested your two nephews, Sam and Ed, and also Lawyer Parmenteer.'

'He's a killer!' Bates growled.

'I know he is, but so were your people, Bates. And now it's ended.'

Neither of the men responded to this, so Macnab said: 'Rattlesnake, you're not to come into Larkin County. You're to turn around and head back for New Mexico. Bates, you can do as you wish.'

'He's comin' with me,' Bates said, and the one-armed man nodded.

'If he steps foot in town, I shall arrest him. And if he resists, I'll shoot him.'

It was a moment of the most intense anxiety. The two men, watching Macnab's hands, realized that if they made an aggressive move, he could whip out his guns and kill one of them, but they also knew that the survivor could surely kill Macnab. Since it was likely that the Ranger would aim at Peavine, Rattlesnake was careful not to make even the slightest false move.

Showing no emotion, Macnab said: 'You can kill me, but you know the entire force of Rangers will be on your neck tomorrow, and they'll never stop. They'll chase you to California, Peavine, but they'll get you.'

There was a very long silence, after which Macnab said gently: 'Now, why don't you two fellows split up? Rattlesnake, go home. Bates, ride back with me to a new kind of town where you can live in peace.'

He edged his horse away, to give the men a chance to talk between themselves, and for nearly half an hour they did while he waited patiently, not dismounting and never taking his hands far from his guns, but moving close to his mule, whose load he kicked once or twice as if adjusting it.

Finally Peavine rode up to Macnab: 'I'm headin' back.'

Otto nodded approvingly as the notorious killer turned and started west, but before the man had gone even a few paces, he called: 'If you try to come back, I'll kill you.' Rattlesnake said nothing.

By the end of December 1883, Ranger Otto Macnab had every reason to believe that he had quelled the feud, as he had been directed to do, but in the back of his mind he still suspected that the Rattlesnake might slither back into Fort Garner to complete the killing for which he had been hired, so Macnab had the prudent thought of reporting in writing to the governor:

> Fort Garner
> Larkin County
> 27 December 1883

> Excellency:

> Obedient to your orders I came to this town, arrested the leaders of both parties to the Larkin County feud and pacified them. They proved to be sensible men and tractable, and I expect no more trouble from them.

> However, there is a possibility that the hired killer Rattlesnake Peavine who is hiding in New Mexico might sneak back to resume the killing, as he was at one time hired by the Bates to do this. I do not know whether to stay here or return to my family and shall await your instructions.

> Otto Macnab

The governor thought it safe to bring the Ranger back, but ten days after Otto rode out of Fort Garner, Peavine rode in. He headed straight for Lawyer Parmenteer's office, where he kicked open a rear door and shot Parmenteer in the back before the latter could reach for his gun.

Macnab was on his way home, well south of Palo Pinto County, riding quietly along his preferred back roads, when he stopped at the growing village of Lampasas and sought lodging with a farmer he had assisted years before when bandits threatened the area. 'They could of used you up north,' the farmer said. 'What happened?'

'Them Larkin County maniacs.'

'What did they do?'

'Rattlesnake Peavine come into town and shot Daniel Parmenteer in the back. All hell broke loose and there must be a dozen dead.'

Macnab said nothing. He ate his evening meal of hard-fried steak and brown gravy, accepted the bed the farmer provided out of gratitude for past favors, and left early next morning. He rode mournfully south, lost in defeat, heading not for home but for Austin, where he told the governor: 'I've got to go get him.' The governor, who had already accepted full blame for ordering Macnab home, said: 'Shoot that son-of-a-bitch if you have to trail him to Alaska,' and Macnab replied: 'You can depend on it.'

Now he rode west to explain things to his wife, and when she expressed her disappointment about his heading back to trouble, and at his age, he said simply: 'The world is a muddy place, and if good men don't try to clean it up, bad men will make it a swamp.'

Emma Rusk often suspected that she was having so much trouble with her white son, Floyd, because she had rejected her Indian son, Blue Cloud, for although she lavished unwavering love upon Floyd, he refused to reciprocate. At the beginning he had been a normal child, robust and lively, but from the age of six, when he began to realize who his parents were and in what ways they differed from other fathers and mothers, he began to draw away from them, and it pained her to watch the bitterness with which he reacted to life. He was not difficult, he was downright objectionable, and she sometimes thought that it would be better if he moved in with the rough-and-ready Yeagers, who might knock some sense into him.

His principal dislike was his mother, for he saw her as unlike other women, and on those painful occasions when he came upon her without her nose, he would blanch and turn away in horror, but it was when he became vaguely aware of how babies were born that he suffered his greatest revulsion, for he had learned from other children in the stone houses about his mother's long captivity with the Indians and of what they had done to her. He was not sure what rape involved, but he had been told by eager informants who knew no more than he that many Indian men had raped his mother, and from the manner in which this was reported, he knew that something bad had happened.

He thus had two reasons for his antipathy, his mother's physical difference and the fact that she had been abused by Indians, and it became impossible for him to accept her love. Whatever she did or attempted to do he interpreted as compensation for some massive wrong in which she had participated, and in time he grew to hate the sight of her, as if she reminded him of some terrible flaw in himself.

He grew equally harsh toward his father, for he had learned from the same cruel children, who, like others their age, were eager to believe the worst and report upon it immediately, that his father was a Quaker, 'not like other people.' They said that he was so cowardly he refused to fight: 'At the tank, which he and Mr. Yeager had fenced in, this man Poteet forced him to back down. He was scared yellow.' In an area where a gun was the mark of the man, the fact that Earnshaw refused to carry one proved this charge.

There had also been an ugly incident in which a wandering badman of no great fame had stumbled into Fort Garner and tried to hold up the place. He had chosen the Rusk residence for his first strike, and finding Earnshaw with no gun, had terrorized the place for some time before Floyd escaped and ran screaming to the Yeagers: 'Pop's being shot at by a robber!'

Within the minute Frank Yeager had dashed across the open space of the parade ground, burst into the Rusk home, and shot the befuddled gunman dead. As they stood over the corpse, Yeager repeated something he had said before: 'Earnshaw, a Texan without a gun is like a Longhorn without horns. It just ain't natural.'

So now, if Floyd saw his mother as stained because of her experiences with the Indians, he saw his father as emasculated because Frank Yeager had been forced to protect the Rusk household. He was therefore a bewildered, unhappy lad as he approached his teens, and it occurred to him that he must do something about the deficiencies in which he was enmeshed. Concerning his mother, he could do nothing except continue to repel the love she tried to bestow upon him, but the glaring faults in his father's character could be corrected. For one thing, he could behave in a manner totally unlike his rather pathetic father, and he began in a calculated way to make this adjustment.

He went to Jaxifer: 'If I can get the money, will you help me?'

'Maybe.'

'How much must I give you for a pistol?'

'Now what do you need a pistol for?'

'Like when that man came to our house.'

'Yep. Man oughta have a pistol, time like that.'

It was agreed that Jaxifer would provide Floyd with a revolver in fairly good working order, and some shells, for six dollars, and now the problem became how to accumulate so much money.

In these troubled days the United States government did not provide enough currency to enable men to conduct their businesses. This did not mean that there wasn't enough to provide charity to feckless idlers who refused to work; it meant there wasn't enough to pay the men and women who did work. The cause of the trouble was avarice; those fortunate few who already had money, or who worked at jobs whose salaries enabled them to acquire some, saw that it was to their advantage to keep the national supply meager, for then those who lacked funds would have to work doubly hard to earn a portion of what the well-to-do already controlled.

On the Texas frontier cash was in such short supply, thanks to policy decisions formulated by the money-masters in New York and Boston, that hard-working cowboys like the two black cavalrymen rarely saw actual cash, and when they did, it was apt to be Mexican, French or English coins dating from the 1700s, with Spanish coins circulating at a premium. It was a great system for the rich, who could command excessive rates for the money they had acquired, a miserable system for people endeavoring to accumulate enough funds to start a business or keep one going.

Earnshaw Rusk, a man of uncommon insight, saw early the great damage being done by the monetary policy of his nation, for although he and Emma had gained their start through the large land grants obtained by her family and from the free horses and cattle that roamed the prairie in those earlier days, he was aware that others who followed were having a desperate time. Out of regard for them, he wrote frequent letters to the *Defender* explaining his interpretation of the money problem. By imperceptible steps, none consciously taken at the time, he progressed from being merely aware of the problem, to a Free Silver man who argued that silver should be cast into coins at a much greater rate and at a higher value than was now being done, to an avowed Greenbacker who pleaded for the printing and circulation of more paper money, to an incipient radical Populist who believed that the government ought to protect and not harass its citizens. Long before a much greater orator and thinker than he took up the subject, Earnshaw was warning the people of Larkin County that 'we are slaves to gold,' and people in the growing town began accusing Rusk of being a radical, a socialist and an atheist, giving his son reason for being an opponent of his father's social beliefs, a loud adherent of religion as practiced by Mrs. Yeager, and a strong advocate of guns. In one of his letters to the editor, Earnshaw had said:

> I do believe the same family income buys less and less each week, even though the total supply of money diminishes. This is self-contradictory, and I cannot explain it.

The cause was simple. Floyd Rusk was systematically stealing as much as he could from both his mother and his father, and after he had paid the cavalryman more than two and a half dollars for the promised gun, his father caught him taking two Mexican coins.

'What in the world is thee doing in that jar, Floyd?'

'I was looking at the different coins.'

'Thee knows thee is not to touch that jar. Nobody is except thy mother. Not even me.'

'She told me I could.'

It was obvious to Earnshaw that his son was lying, because Emma so treasured the few coins she was able to hoard that she allowed no one to approach them. Rusk knew he ought to have a showdown with his son here and now, but he evaded it because to do so would necessitate involving Emma; he knew that she was already in difficult straits with her headstrong boy and he did not want to exacerbate this. So the moment of significant challenge passed, and Earnshaw said weakly: 'Don't touch that jar. Thy mother wouldn't like it.'

He did not report the affair to his wife, nor could he guess that his son had stolen from his savings too. It would have appalled him to know that the combined thefts totaled nearly six dollars, a considerable amount, and he would have been even more distressed had he known that these thefts had been planned and conducted over an extended period of time. His son was in training to be an accomplished thief, and before the year was out he was a thief with a very good army revolver hidden in an unsuspected corner of the Rusk house.

Fort Garner buzzed with rumors when Ranger Macnab rode back into town. He knocked on the Holley door to ask if he could stay there for a few days, during which it became apparent that he had come to deal with Rattlesnake Peavine if he could flush out that murderous fugitive. Floyd Rusk, possessor of his own gun, was at Macnab's side constantly, asking for pointers on how real gunfighters handled their weapons, and Otto told him a secret the boy chose to ignore: 'Only one, son. Know you're right and keep coming.'

When Floyd asked if it was true that he was after Peavine, Otto said: 'Rangers are always after whoever's done wrong,' and then he disappeared, heading south. But Floyd, a student of shootings, told Molly Yeager, a brash child with her own interest in such matters: 'When a Ranger heads south, you can be sure he's really going in some other direction. Macnab is heading west to see if he can track down the Rattlesnake.'

Floyd's guess was correct, for after a long detour to the south Macnab made easy adjustments in his heading, winding up in the general direction of Palo Duro Canyon. As he approached the deep depression he saw signs which tempted him to turn sharply southwest to where a tiny settlement lay across the New Mexico border.

As he rode into town it was like a hundred other episodes on the long frontier: a Ranger comes cautiously into a village, looking this way and that, asking a few questions, nodding and passing on. But this time as Macnab headed toward the western exit, a small, wiry man in his late sixties watched him ride past, waited till he was a few feet down the road, then slipped out, positioned his left arm to serve as a platform, and pumped four quick bullets into the Ranger's back.

With supreme effort Macnab held himself in the saddle, aware that he had been most savagely hit but hoping that the shots might not be fatal. With what strength remained, he turned to face his assailant, who now blasted Otto square in the face and chest. Without a sound, the little Ranger slid from his saddle and fell awkwardly into the New Mexico dust.

Five Texas Rangers set out to kill Amos Peavine, and they tracked him for many weeks, coming upon him one morning at seven in a dirty eating house near Phoenix, Arizona Territory. When the coroner examined the body he found that it had been shot seven times in the back, twice more from the left side and twice more from the right side well to the back. Considering the Rattlesnake's long reign of terror and the relief at his justified death, the coroner saw no reason to publish the fact that the Rangers had killed him with eleven bullets from the rear.

When Floyd Rusk, back in Fort Garner, heard the news, he told Molly Yeager: 'I'll bet he died like a man. I'll bet all five of the Rangers was terrified when they came onto the Rattlesnake.'

Floyd, the would-be gunman, had learned the value of money through stealing enough to purchase a revolver; his father would now learn in an equally perilous game. Although he had scrimped on his family's expenditures and paid his savings into the bank to reduce his loan, 1885 found him with $135 still outstanding, and cautious though he was, he could not seem to get ahead by that amount.

Of course, he paid the interest regularly because he knew that if he didn't, Mr. Weatherby could declare him in default and take his ranch away from him; the terms of the mortgage were quite clear on this, and the possibility so terrified Rusk that he was usually a day or two early in paying the interest.

But now, when money was tightest, he saw that the banker had another stranglehold on him, for on two occasions recently Mr. Weatherby had suddenly and arbitrarily called mortgages on unsuspecting ranchers and farmers; that is, he had demanded full payment at a time when he knew the rancher had no chance of paying it. In each case, according to Texas law, the rancher was judged to have been in default, which meant that if the bank let the man keep his homestead—house and small acreage attached—it could claim title to the rest of the ranch, and thus accumulate valuable land.

'That was so unfair!' Earnshaw cried when he heard of the second foreclosing. 'A man spends two thousand dollars for his land. He spends another two thousand improving it. For seven years he meets every mortgage payment, and then because he can't come up with a hundred and seventy-five dollars, he loses everything.'

Rusk often misunderstood business details, and this time he had the situation only partly right, for in the case cited, when the bank foreclosed, it was merely to obtain its outstanding debt, $175. When the ranch was sold at a sheriff's sale, any income beyond that belonged to the former owner, but now the trick was to rig

the sale so that either the bank or someone associated with it bought the ranch for
a pittance, which meant that there was little or nothing to be returned to the
original owner.

When Rusk found that the courts, the newspapers, the churches and the customs of the countryside all supported such moral thievery, he became so enraged
that he felt compelled to protest in the *Defender*:

> Surely, the Grange and the Farmer's Alliance are right when they argue
> that the laws of a nation ought to support the homeowner, the small
> businessman, the young family trying to get started. No law should
> allow a bank to deprive a man of his residence and his means of earning
> a living. If the United States had arranged its affairs so that money was
> more reasonably available, then the paying off of a mortgage could be
> done, and people who refused to pay should be punished. But the nation
> keeps the money supply so constricted that even a prudent man cannot
> accumulate enough cash to pay his debts, much as he would like to.
> Something in our society is badly wrong when a good rancher like Nils
> Bergstrom loses his ranch because he cannot get his hands on a little
> cash.

No one read Earnshaw's letter with more anger than Banker Weatherby, and
when the economy was at its depth, he informed the Rusks that he must demand
the balance of his loan, $135, payable as the contract stipulated within thirty days.
'But thee promised me thee'd never do this,' Rusk protested, and Weatherby said:
'Conditions have changed. The bank must have its money, now.'

Then began the month of hell, because in all of Fort Garner, or Larkin County
too, there was no one from whom the Rusks could borrow that missing $135.
There were ranches worth $6,000 or $7,000, counting land and cattle, which had
less than $30 in cash, and these meager funds were so necessary to keep the place
operating that to lend them out would have been impossible.

The Rusks themselves, with a ranch now worth nearly $9,000, considering its
fencing and cattle, could assemble less than $50, and Mr. Weatherby would not
consider any partial payment; he was entitled by law to his full amount and he
intended to collect it, or take over the ranch.

In despair, Earnshaw laid the prospects before his family: 'Through no fault of
our own, we stand to lose our ranch. Emma, thy cattle were never better, but we
can't sell them to anyone here. Floyd, we pay only a little for thy schooling, but it
can't be continued. We must all try till the last legal day to find this money, and if
we fail, well, others better than we have failed before us.'

As he said these words the awfulness of his family's position overwhelmed him,
and he wept, an act which sickened his son, who said boldly: 'Someone ought to
shoot that Mr. Weatherby.'

'Floyd!' his mother and father cried simultaneously, and the force of their words so startled him that he caught his breath. Yet it was he who proposed the one solution which had any chance of saving this family: 'Mr. Poteet'll be coming along soon. Why not ride down to meet him?'

As soon as the boy said this, his parents recognized the good sense of his suggestion, and before nightfall Earnshaw Rusk and Frank Yeager were headed south to intercept the cattle drive they knew would be coming north. There were no Comanche now to endanger them, and there was no risk of losing their way, for over the years the thousands of cattle heading north to Dodge City had beaten the plains into a wide, rutted path which a blind man could have followed, and in its dust they spurred their horses.

On the first full day out they came upon one small herd headed for Dodge, and its riders said: 'Poteet can't be far behind. He never is.'

On the third day they saw a huge cloud of dust, like something out of the Old Testament when the Israelites were moving across their desert with the help of God, and they galloped ahead with surging hopes that this might be Poteet. It was, and as soon as he heard of their plight he was interested.

'It's criminal for banks to take over so much land, and for the government to protect them in doing it.' He sat astride his horse with only the left foot in the stirrup, as if he intended to dismount, but first he wanted to talk, and the three men kept moving their horses as he did: 'You got yourself into this trouble, Rusk, through buying that fence. It was against reason and against nature. Now comes the dreadful penalty.'

Rusk did not try to defend himself; he was concerned only with the loan he sought, and at this point he could not detect whether Poteet was going to lend him the money or not, but as the talk proceeded, it became clear that the drover sided with the Rusks and not with the bank: 'Course I'll lend you the money, how could I not?' And before night fell, Earnshaw had the funds with which to save his ranch.

'It's not a loan,' Poteet said when the two men tried to thank him. 'It's an appreciation for the business we've done.' He paused to recall those rewarding years. Then: 'You know, Rusk, you mustn't think too harshly about Weatherby. He's just a part of the system.'

'What does thee mean?' Earnshaw asked.

'Life in Texas is like a giant crap game, a perpetual gamble. To succeed, you need grit, courage to take the big chance. Those who succeed, succeed big. A hundred men tried to drive cattle up this trail. They failed. Some of us, like Sanderson and Peters and me, we took great chances and we succeeded, big.' He seemed to be right about Texas; everything was a colossal gamble: 'Years back, Rusk, when I saw you gambling so heavy on that bob wahr, I disliked you for what you were doing to the range, but I had great admiration for what you were doing in your own interest.'

'Why does thee say a money-grubber like Weatherby is necessary?'

'Because he's the agency that punishes us when our gambles turn sour. He's the right hand of God, administering castigation. You escaped him this time, but don't tempt him again, because if Texas is bountiful in rewarding gamblers, it's remorseless in punishing those who stumble.'

When Rusk and Yeager left Poteet next morning, they rode hurriedly back to Fort Garner, where they reported to Emma and Floyd: 'We are, through the grace of God, saved.' They then went to the bank, where with a certain bitterness they counted out the $135. And now a drama which was being enacted in many small Texas towns unfolded. Banker Weatherby, frustrated in his attempt to steal the Larkin Ranch by legal means, surrendered to the fact that the Rusks were going to be the leading citizens in the town. Knowing that he must in the future do business with them, he now displayed no disappointment or ill feelings. With what seemed unfeigned enthusiasm, he cried: 'I'm so pleased you could scrape up your final payment. It's always good to see a successful rancher make his land prosper.' Then he made an offer which staggered the men: 'Now, you don't have to pay in full. If you wish to extend your mortgage, the bank would be most happy . . .'

'We'll pay,' Rusk said.

'Are you two men partners?'

'Yes, in a manner of speaking. When a man serves me as well as Frank Yeager has, I give him part of my profits. He gets the two hundred acres north of the tank.'

'You should enter that gift at the land office,' Weatherby said. 'It's always best to have things in writing.'

In early 1885, Rusk and all forward-looking people in Fort Garner were electrified by the news: 'The Fort Worth & Denver City Railroad is planning to resume!' And men began to dream: 'Now maybe we can get a spur to drop down into our town!'

In 1881 men of great ambition in Fort Worth and Denver had tried to link their two cities by rail and had started bravely to build west from Fort Worth, but had run out of money during the tight times of 1883. Their line had reached only as far as Wichita Falls, north of Fort Garner, where it came to a painful halt. But now, with more prosperous times looming, workmen were being rehired and iron rails ordered.

When the good news was confirmed, Rusk became a cyclone of energy, his tall, awkward figure moving ceaselessly about the town and to ranches outside to learn whether they might join in offering the nascent railway special cash inducements if its engineers agreed to drop a spur to the south.

In this enterprise he was prescient, because the histories of Texas written a century later would be filled with doleful entries recording the death of similar communities:

> Pitkin, founded in 1866, flourished for a few decades in the later years of the Nineteenth Century as a center for collecting rural products, but during the railroad boom of the Eighties the town fathers refused to grant the railroads any concessions. The tracks bypassed Pitkin and before the turn of the century the town had died, the last resident leaving in 1909.

Rusk, with his keen sense of how the West was developing, realized that the continued existence of the town depended upon attracting some railroad that would speed its growth. Originally he had dreamed of inducing the main line of the F.W.&D.C. to swing slightly south through Fort Garner, but that plum had been lost to Wichita Falls. However, he could now logically aspire to a spur, and he was determined to get one.

To that end he hectored local citizens to contribute funds with which he could approach the railroad barons in Fort Worth in an effort to convince them that a spur south was in their interests. Grocer Simpson contributed enthusiastically to the fund with which Earnshaw would approach the railroad men, and the flourishing proprietor of the Barracks Saloon also chipped in, as did Editor Fordson. Ranchers east of town were shown the advantage of having a railroad for their cattle, and ordinary citizens who wanted to be united to the larger world were invited to join the crusade, but Rusk was astounded at the man who volunteered to do the major work.

The campaign had been under way only a few days when Banker Weatherby came voluntarily to the Rusk home, asked to be invited in, and spoke with a warm sincerity which belied the fact that recently he had tried to steal the Rusk lands: 'I am hurt, Earnshaw, that you did not come to me first with your plan to bring a railroad into our town. It's vital that we get one to come our way.' Having said this, he contributed a thousand dollars to the invitation kitty and then proposed that he and Rusk leave immediately for Fort Worth, where decisions concerning the route were being made.

Rusk had wanted to cry: 'Look here, Weatherby, not long ago thee tried to steal my land. Now thee invites me to travel as thy friend. Why?' But he remained silent because vaguely he understood that Weatherby was merely playing the game of building Texas. In July, Banker A does his best to steal Rancher B's land, but in August, A and B unite to hornswoggle Rancher C. 'Texas poker,' someone called it, because sooner or later, B and C would be certain to gang up on Banker A.

As they rode, Weatherby coached Rusk as to how they must approach the railroad men and how to make them an offer of cash rewards if they could swing the roadway south. By the time they reached the hotel where the F.W.&D.C.

directors were meeting, these two rural connivers were prepared to talk sophisti-
cated details with the big-city bankers and engineers.

Alas, they were one of nineteen such delegations, and by the time they reached
the decision makers the route was set. 'Gentlemen,' the directors apologized,
'we're grateful for your coming to see us, and we appreciate the offer you're
making, for we know that such sums cannot be collected lightly, but we must
allot all our funds to the main line to Denver. There can be no spurs.'

Rusk was crushed, and like a child he showed it, but Clyde Weatherby, an
adroit negotiator, masked his disappointment, wished the Colorado and Texas
financiers well, and concluded: 'Later on, when you do have enough money to run
a spur south, and sooner or later you'll have to, because we're going to amass great
riches down our way, I want you to remember us. Fort Garner, Garden City of the
New West.' They obviously liked this jovial man and assured him that they would
remember, but on the return trip, Weatherby told Rusk in the harshest terms:
'Earnshaw, I like you. But we've got to work in an entirely different way. The
future of our town is at stake, and we either get a railroad to come in or we
perish.'

Before they reached Fort Garner he had a plan: 'Let me have all the money. I'll
spread it around where it'll do the most good. You put up thirty or forty of your
acres and I'll do the same with mine.'

'What will thee do with them?'

'Give them to people who will determine where that first spur to the south
goes.'

'Why?'

'To buy their support. To be sure of their votes when we need them.'

'But isn't that bribery?'

'It is, and so help me God, it's going to buy us a railroad.'

If Rusk had been tireless in his initial work, Clyde Weatherby was remorseless
in his follow-up, yet at the end of six hectic weeks he had to inform Earnshaw:
'I've handed out all the money and accomplished nothing. There's no hope of a
spur south.'

'Are we doomed?' Rusk asked, for already he could see in other aspiring towns
the dreadful effect of having been by-passed by the railroad.

'We are not,' Weatherby snarled, as if he were furiously mad at some unseen
force. 'The people we gave money and land to will remember us. But now I'm
asking for one last contribution. From everyone. We'll see if the folks in Abilene
have vision,' and off he went to the new Texas town that carried the same name as
the famous old railhead in Kansas. Before he left he told Rusk and Simpson: 'If
they won't come south to meet us, by God, we'll go north to meet them.' But
when he came home, with no money left and no promise of anything, he told his
co-conspirators: 'Nothing now, but in this business you plant seeds and pray that
something good will spring out of the ground. I have seeds planted everywhere

and I give you my word on the Bible, something is going to start growing before another five years pass.' So the men of Fort Garner watched hopefully as the years passed and the railroads inched out to other places but not to theirs.

Three weeks after Franziska Macnab had buried her husband in the family cemetery overlooking the Pedernales, she received word from the capitol in Austin that her younger brother, Ernst, had died at his desk in the Senate chamber. It had happened at nine in the evening, when the Senate was not in session; he had been working late.

So within a month she had to conduct two funerals, and this reminded her of how very much alone she now was. Her mother had died some years ago; her beloved father and her youngest brother, Emil, had been killed in the horrid affair at the Nueces River, and now Ernst and Otto were dead. The sense of passing time, of closing episodes, was oppressive.

Her three children, with her encouragement, were preoccupied with their own responsibilities, but this left her in sad loneliness. She experienced a strong desire to reestablish contact with her only surviving brother, Theo, who had gained statewide attention in 1875 by his heroic work in rebuilding the town of Indianola after the destructive hurricane of that year. More than forty places of business had been wiped out by the raging waters of Matagorda Bay, more than three hundred lives lost, and when scores of older men announced that they were abandoning the site, Theo had stated to the Galveston and Victoria newspapers: 'I'm going to rebuild my ships' chandlery bigger than before.'

And he had done so. Encouraging other businessmen, he had been responsible for the rejuvenation of the destroyed town and watched with pride as it returned to prosperity. His own store, which serviced the many ships that sailed into Indianola, doubled in size, and his agency for the Gulf, Western Texas and Pacific Railway Company established him as Indianola's leading merchant. He conducted his affairs from an office which stood at the land end of the pier that reached far into the bay; here he greeted captains of the Morgan Line steamers as they docked with cargoes from New Orleans.

Despite the obliteration of so many businesses in that hurricane, Theo continued to envision Indianola, where he had first set foot on Texas soil, as the state's gateway to the West, and his letters to Fredericksburg displayed this optimism:

> If you walked with me down our main streets you would think you were in Neu Braunfels, because two names out of three would be German: Seeligson, Eichlitz, Dahme, Remschel, Thielepape, Willemin. This is a real German port, with hundreds like me who saw it first from the deck of their immigrant ship and liked it so much they never left.

We have our own ice machine now and are no longer dependent upon the refrigerated ice ships that used to bring us river ice from New England. We have a new courthouse, several hotels, at least six good restaurants, shops with the latest styles from New York and London, our own newspaper and all the appurtenances of a city. You would like it here, and any of you who tire of farming in the hills ought to move here quickly, for this is a glimpse of Old Germany installed in New Texas.

Franziska, welcoming such letters, wondered whether she should move permanently to Indianola to be with her brother for the remaining years of their lives, but after several months of cautious consideration she decided against leaving Fredericksburg, for too many of her cherished memories were rooted there. And Otto had loved the Pedernales, the wild turkeys strutting through the oak groves, the deer coming to the garden, the hurried quail in autumn, the javelinas grubbing for acorns.

However, in the spring of 1886, Theo did send a sensible letter: 'With Otto and Ernst gone, you and I are all that's left. Come spend the summer with me, for I am lately a widower. Besides, it's much cooler here with the sea breezes each afternoon.'

Turning the care of the farm over to Emil's children, all of them married now, she took the stage to San Antonio, where she boarded the new train connecting that city with Houston, and at Victoria she dismounted to catch the famous old train that chugged its way out to Indianola. It left Victoria at nine in the morning and steamed in to Indianola at half past one in the afternoon.

She joined her brother on Friday, 13 August 1886, and shared with him some of the best weeks of her life, for Theo spoke both of his burgeoning hopes for the future, which excited her, and of his memories of the Margravate, which reminded her of how happy she had been as a child. They were old people now, he sixty-four, she fifty-seven, and the bitter memories receded as the good ones prevailed.

'Does your tenor voice . . . can you still sing so beautifully?' she asked, and he tried a few notes.

'We have a singing society here, you know,' he told her, 'but I yield the lead tenor to others.'

On Sunday, when they both attended the German church at his suggestion, he apologized: 'Father wouldn't approve of our going to church, but times are different now.' He then took her for a delightful buggy ride in one of his own carriages. They rode out to the great bayous east of town, where he stopped to explain the winds of a hurricane: 'They come in three parts. A fierce storm blows from west to east. Tremendous noise and rain but not much damage. Then a lull like a summer day as the eye passes over. Then a much wilder storm from east to west, and it's the one that blows everything down.'

'Why does one kill and not the other?'

'Neither kills. Oh, a tree falling or some other freak accident.'

'What does?'

'This does,' and he pointed to the flat, empty lands basking in the sun, so quiet and peaceful that they could not be imagined as threatening anyone. 'You see, Franza, tidal waves throw immense quantities of water onto these flat places, so much you wouldn't believe it. And as the storm abates, it has to go somewhere, and with a great rush it finds its way back to sea.'

He dropped his head, recalling that tremendous surge of trapped water that had destroyed so much of Indianola: 'It took thirty hours to build up . . . high tides, rain, hurricane winds. It ran back in two, an irresistible torrent.'

'How did you survive?' They were speaking in German, and he replied: 'Ein wahres Wunder. And prudence. I guessed that the retreating waters would be dangerous, so I took our family to the upper floor of the strongest building in town, not my own, and tied us all to heavy beds, not lying down, of course, just to the heavy iron pieces.'

'And it worked?'

'When the water swirled past, clutching at everything, we could see it sucking people to their deaths. It tried with us, right through that second floor, but we were tied fast.' He chuckled: 'It tore away my wife's clothes, all of them, and she screamed for the rescue party not to save us.' He laughed again: 'Water can do the strangest things.'

'Will it come again?'

'Records show that once a hurricane hits, it never hits that spot again. That's how I've been able to hold the town together. We know we're safe. Only the cowards fled.'

Indianola, under his driving leadership, had restored itself as the premier port in South Texas and many predicted that it must soon outdistance Galveston. It was clear to Franziska, from the respect in which the citizens held her brother, that this revitalization was due primarily to his optimism, and she saw that he was much like his father: 'Remember, Theo, how during the worst days of our Atlantic crossing, he kept spirits high? You're like him.'

On Tuesday, Franza and her brother entertained at John Mathuly's seafood restaurant, and the guests, most with German names, shared an enjoyable evening 'of fine oysters, rich crabs and other succulent viands which could not be surpassed this side of Baltimore,' the menu boasted, 'and equaled in only a handful of the superior establishments in that German city.' After the meal there was singing, and at ten, ice cream, made possible by the new ice machine, was served; it was accompanied by four kinds of cookies baked that afternoon by Franziska. This was followed by more singing and a speech by Theo—'The Unlimited Progress Possible When Rails Marry Steam'—which alluded to the impending railroad linkage of Indianola, San Antonio and Brownsville.

When they left the restaurant, with some of the men still singing, Franziska became aware of a sharp change in the weather, for while they were dining an excessively humid wind had blown in from the Gulf, and although this disturbed her, it pleased her brother: 'Rain! We've needed it since July.'

But this wind did not bring rain. Instead, when Franziska rose next morning she found Indianola enveloped in billows of dust, and when she accompanied her brother on a visit to Captain Isaac Reed, the United States Signal Service man who now monitored storms in the area, he showed them a telegram he had received from Washington: WEST INDIAN HURRICANE PASSED SOUTH KEY WEST INTO GULF CAUSING HIGH WINDS SOUTHERN FLORIDA STOP WILL PROBABLY CAUSE GALES ON COAST OF EASTERN GULF STATES TONIGHT

When Franziska asked: 'Isn't that serious?' he assured her: 'Government follows these things carefully, and ninety-nine times out of a hundred, such storms collapse and produce no more than a slight rise in our tide.' But later that morning, when the winds became more intense, Theo and Franza returned to the weather office, and Theo, as the elder statesman, asked: 'Shouldn't you hoist the danger signal?' and Reed said: 'Washington would warn us if such a signal was advisable. Rest easy. This storm will die.'

Later Captain Reed did receive a frantic telegram from Washington, warning of the immediate descent of a full hurricane, but now it was too late. Within minutes the hurricane came roaring in, and before Reed could respond, telegraph lines were whipping in the wind.

Reed was a valiant man, and when it looked as if his Signal Service was going to be blown away, he stayed inside to screw down the anemometer so that the maximum velocity of the wind could be recorded. It hit 102 miles an hour before it and the building were simply blown apart. Reed and a medical man, Dr. Rosencranz, were struck by falling timbers as they tried to scramble away, and the incoming waves submerged them. They were seen no more.

When the building fell, a kerosene lamp was thrown to the floor, and its flames were whipped about so violently by the roaring winds, which now gusted to 152 miles an hour, that within an incredible eleven minutes the entire main street was in flames, and residents in panic tried to escape the fire. The Hurricane of 1875, which they said could never be repeated, was now reborn with a fury more terrible than before. Theo Allerkamp, whose ships' chandlery was struck by the first awesome blast of fire, managed to escape the instant conflagration produced when his turpentine and tar exploded into flame, and for one hellish moment he watched as the street he had rebuilt was attacked by flame on its rooftops and flood at its foundations. Buildings spewed sparks hundreds of feet into the storm, then sighed and collapsed as the irresistible flood tore away their walls.

'Mein Gott!' he cried. 'What are You doing to us?'

Mindful of how a hurricane worked, he shouted to those other bewildered men who saw their life's energies destroyed: 'Prepare for the backsurge!' To repeat the precautions which had saved his family before, he struggled through the rising waters to his home, where his sister stood pressed against the wall, protecting herself from the tremendous winds and watching the fiery destruction of her brother's handiwork. 'Oh, Theo!' she cried as he staggered up the three wooden steps which had not yet been washed away by the waters that attacked them. 'How could such punishment come to so good a man?'

He had no time for lamentation, even though flame and flood nearly engulfed him: 'When the calm comes, then's the danger.' And he led her to the highest spot in his house, built to withstand floods such as that of 1875, and fetched ropes with which to bind her to its walls when the waters began to recede.

This time that would not work, for when the tempestuous wind, now gusting occasionally to more than 165 miles, whipped about, it brought with it a summer's sky of flaming meteors. The clouds were filled with embers, thousands of them, and they arched in beauty over the dark space, reaching for the houses not yet aflame.

'We shall burn!' Theo cried, not in desperation or in fear, and he ripped away the ropes that bound his sister to the wall and thrust them into her hands. 'To the trees!'

But before they could escape, a hundred blazing embers fell on the Allerkamp house and a like number on those nearby. In one vast, sighing gasp, heard above the howling of the wind, these houses exploded into leaping flame, and those who had not anticipated this likelihood perished.

Waiting for a lull, Theo and his sister headed for the few trees in Indianola, scrawny things barely meriting the name, and she reached them but he did not. A wave wilder than any before came far inland, caught him by the heels, tumbled him about as if he were a wooden toy, then tossed him with terrible force back against one of the newly burning houses. Nothing could have saved him, and he died in the center of the town he had built beside the sea, and then rebuilt.

Franziska, grief-stricken at seeing him perish, did not panic. With studious care she waited for a pause in the wind, then looked back to check where he had disappeared, lest he mysteriously appear still alive. Seeing nothing, she lashed herself as high into a tree as she could, and when the storm abated into that terrible calm which presaged the arrival of the greater danger, she climbed like a squirrel into the highest branches, but as she did so she saw a young mother with two small children, all so frenzied that none could do anything sensible. So she climbed down, all the way, and found the rope which Theo would have used, and then with her hands and knees scarred from the bark, she goaded the three others into the higher branches of the tree, where she tied them fast.

They were there at dawn on Friday morning, when the cruel part of the hurricane struck, and from their high perch they watched the town continue burning, with more homes blazing from time to time, while the great waters of the flood began to recede.

They came first as a slight movement back toward Matagorda Bay, then as a quickening—about the speed of a rill tumbling over a small rock—then as a surge of tremendous power, and finally as a vast sucking up of all things, a swirling, tempestuous, tumultuous rush and rage of water pulling away from the terrible damage it had caused. Now those houses which had missed the flames and withstood the first part of the flood collapsed as if from sheer weariness; they had fought honorably and had lost.

When the raging floods were gone, and the roaring winds had subsided, and the flames had flickered out, Franziska Macnab untied her ropes and helped the others to untie theirs: 'We can climb down now. The storm is past.'

The two children would not find their father. Franza would not find her brother's body. Some mesmerized survivors would not even be able to identify where their houses had once stood, for when Friday noon arrived, and the sun was back in its full August brilliance, it looked down upon a town that was totally destroyed. Indianola no longer existed, only the charred streets and the vegetable gardens with no houses to claim them showing where commerce and affection and political brawling and Texas optimism had once reigned. The incessant gamble which R. J. Poteet had said was characteristic of Texas had been attempted once more, and Indianola had lost.

By two in the afternoon people were gasping for water as the sun grew hotter and hotter, but there was none to drink, not any in the entire town, and there were no buildings in which the tormented people could take cover. By four in the afternoon children were screaming, and the collecting of dead bodies had to stop as distraught survivors made makeshift plans for the dreadful night that approached.

Franza, conserving even flecks of spittle to keep her mouth alive, comforted the children, putting her finger in her own mouth, then rubbing it about the child's, and in this mournful, moaning way the night passed.

At dawn people from another town, less horribly hurt, appeared with water, and Franziska wept: 'The water destroyed us, and the water saves us.' Those first drops, half a cup to each person, she would never forget.

Emma Rusk, safe in her little town four hundred miles northwest of Indianola, heard of the disaster by telegraph one day after it happened, but she paid scant attention, for she was preoccupied with her son, who each year became more difficult. In addition to his other exhibitions intended to demonstrate that he was in no way associated with the parents he despised, he had taken to eating gargantuan amounts of food. At the age of twelve he weighed more than a hundred and sixty pounds, and when his mother tried to control his gorging, he snarled: 'I don't want to be some thin, scared thing like my father.'

She had wanted to slap him when he said such things, but he said them so frequently now and with such venom that she did not know what to do. Dismayed as she was by his behavior toward her—which worsened as he entered puberty and faced its dislocations, for now he identified his mother with the most specific sexual misbehavior during her time with the Indians—she was even more distraught the next year by his relations with eleven-year-old Molly Yeager, the sprouting daughter of their foreman.

'Earnshaw,' she said delicately to her uncomprehending husband, 'I do fear that Floyd is playing dangerous games with little Molly.'

'What kind of games?'

She had to sit her husband down and explain that if Molly was the little minx she appeared to be, Floyd could fall into deep trouble if he continued to disappear with her from time to time, and when she made no headway with Earnshaw, she went directly to Mrs. Yeager, a thin, stringy woman with a goiter and a passion for singing hymns loudly and off-key: 'Mrs. Yeager, I'm worried about Molly and our Floyd.'

'For why?'

'Because they're alone a good deal. Things can happen, bad things.'

'What happens, happens,' Mrs. Yeager said.

'I mean, your daughter could find herself with a baby.'

'What?' Mrs. Yeager leaped out of her chair and stormed about her kitchen. 'You mean that hussy . . . ?'

Before Emma could halt her, Mrs. Yeager was on the front porch screaming for Molly, and when the girl appeared, a plump, unkempt child with a very winsome face, her mother began hitting her about the head and shouting: 'Don't you go into no haymows behind my back.' There was not a haymow within a hundred miles of Fort Garner, but since this was the phrase her own mother had drummed into her, it was all she could think of at the moment.

Molly, startled by the ineffectual blows, glowered at Emma as the probable cause of her discomfort and tried to run away, but now Mrs. Yeager grabbed her by one arm while the child spun around in a circle like a wobbling top, with both mother and daughter screaming at each other.

It was a lesson in child discipline which Emma could neither understand nor approve, and when she left the Yeager household the two were still at it. Back in her own home, she decided that if her husband would not talk with their son, she must, and when he came straggling in with the snarled inquiry 'When do we eat?' she sat him down and told him that she did not want to see him sneaking off with Molly Yeager any more.

'Why not?' he asked truculently.

'Because it's not proper.'

Her son stared at her, then pointed his pudgy right forefinger: 'Were you proper with the Indians?' And with this, he jumped up and fled from the room, half choking on his own words.

It was this wrenching scene which caused Emma to speak with R. J. Poteet when next he came by on his way to Dodge City: 'R. J., my son is a mess, a sorry mess. Would you please take him to Dodge City with you? Maybe teach him to be a man?'

'I don't like what I've seen of your son, Emma.' At sixty-four, Poteet had lost none of his frankness.

'How have you been able to judge him?'

'I get to know all the boys, all the families we meet on the trail.' He pointed to three of his young cowboys and said: 'A boy unfolds the way a flower unfolds in spring. It's time, and inwardly he knows it. Time to get himself a horse. Time to handle a revolver. Time to court some pretty girl. And in Texas, time to test his manhood on the Chisholm Trail, or on this one to Dodge.'

'What has that to do with Floyd?'

'For the last three years, Emma, I've sort of extended your son an invitation to ride north with me. These other kids, I had only to drop the hint, and they had their horses ready, pestering me. Three years from now they'll all be men.'

'And Floyd did not respond?'

'Your son's a difficult boy, Emma. I don't like him.'

She was tempted to say 'I don't, either,' but instead she pleaded: 'Please take him. It may be his last chance.'

'For you, Emma, I'd do anything.' But when she was about to praise him for his generosity, he halted her: 'I'm gettin' to be an old man. Can feel it in my bones. Last winter I decided I'd go north no more. Had no choice, because Kansas has passed a law forbidding the entrance of Texas Longhorns.'

'For heaven's sake, why?'

'They claim we carry ticks. Texas fever. Fatal to their cattle. They've warned me, no more after this year. I didn't want to watch it all come to an end, too mournful, but a lot of families around San Antone had collected steers they had to sell or go broke. So I agreed to one last trail.' He fell silent, looking across the bleak land he had helped tame: 'Never put together a finer team. Look at those boys, the two good men at point. I wanted this to be the best drive I ever made, and now you force that no-good boy of yours upon me.' He sank down on his haunches and threw pebbles at his horse's left hoof, and apparently this was a signal of some kind, for the animal moved close and nudged him.

'I'll take him,' he said, rising and shaking her hand. 'And I'll bring him back to you, for better or worse.'

was a curious trip. Traveling slowly at fifteen miles a day, it took the herd four days to reach the Red River, and in this trial period Floyd Rusk learned a lot about herding cattle: 'Son, the new man always rides drag, back here in the dust. That's why cowhands wear bandannas, and since you got none, I'm going to give you

mine. Gift from an old cowhand to a new one.' Poteet had smiled when he said
this, but Floyd had not smiled back, nor had he said thank you, but that night
when the hands gathered at the chuck wagon, he asked: 'How long do I ride in
the dust?' and Poteet said: 'All the way to Dodge. Your second trip, you get a
better deal.'

Floyd could not mask his anger, and so livid did he become that his rage
showed beneath the dust that caked his face, so Poteet said: 'Same rules for
everybody. If you don't like 'em, son, you can always drop out. But make up your
mind before we cross the Red River, because gettin' back home from the other
side will not be easy.'

Floyd had gritted his teeth and accepted the challenge, and although he was
almost grotesquely fat, he did know how to handle a horse, so he did not disgrace
himself. In fact, at the fording of the Red he handled himself rather well, remaining on the Texas side and pushing the steers into the water with some skill.

'You know how to ride,' Poteet said with genuine approval, but this did not
soften Floyd's attitude, and during the entire crossing of the former Indian Territory he proved to be the surly, unpleasant fellow that Poteet had expected. He was
by no means useless, for he knew what cattle were, but he was a decided damper
on other young men, and by the time the herd reached the Kansas border, they
had pretty well dismissed him.

Poteet did not. In his long years on the range he had watched boys even less
promising than Floyd Rusk discover themselves, sometimes through being
knocked clear to hell by some fed-up cowboy, sometimes in the thrill of showing
that they could ride as well as any of the old hands, often with the mere passage of
a year and the rousting about with reasonably clean, straightforward men. Poteet
hoped this would happen with Floyd, and he directed his two point men to look
after the boy, but when young Rusk repulsed all their good efforts, they told
Poteet: 'To hell with him. Herd him into Dodge like the rest of the cattle and ship
him home.'

Poteet did not try to argue, for he knew that with three thousand cattle behind
them, more than half Longhorns, they had no time to bother with a surly,
overweight brat, but he himself could not dismiss his responsibility so easily. If
Emma's son could be saved, he would try, and one day when he saw the boy
gorging himself at the chuck wagon as they crossed into Kansas, he took him
aside and said quietly: 'Son, I really wouldn't eat so much. When you want to find
yourself a wife, you know, pretty women don't cotton to young men who are
too—'

'I don't want to look like my stupid father.'

Poteet drew back his right fist and was going to lay the boy flat when he
realized how wrong this would be. Allowing his fist to drop, he said very quietly:
'Son, if you ever again speak of your father or your mother like that in my
presence, so help me God, I will give you a thrashing you'll never forget.'

'You wouldn't dare.'

Poteet stepped forward and said, with no anger: 'Son, you don't know it, and maybe there's no way of telling you, but you are in the midst of a great battle. For your soul. For your immortal soul. I think you're going to lose. I think you're going to be a miserable human being for the rest of your life. But for the remainder of this trip, do your best to act like a man.'

He stalked away, profoundly shaken by this ugly experience, for he was frightened by what he might have done. His fist had been inches from that fat, flabby face. His trigger finger had been twitching when the boy scorned his father, for it was obvious that Floyd rejected his mother, too: Dear God, what a burden. He was not sure whether it was he bearing the burden on this last trip to Dodge City, or the older Rusks, who would have to deal with Floyd back in Larkin County.

So now the entire group had turned away from this pathetic boy; even the Mexican cook was unable to hide his disgust at the way Floyd gorged his food. He rode at the right-rear drag, dust in his face, and grumbled constantly about this experience which could have been so rewarding, this conquering of the range which so many boys his age would have given years of their lives to have shared.

As the herd reached the south bank of the Arkansas River, the men could see on the opposite side the low buildings of Dodge City, and their eyes began to sparkle, for citizens of the town themselves had proclaimed it 'The Wickedest Little City in the West.' Here were the famed dance halls, the sheriff's office once occupied by Bat Masterson and Wyatt Earp, the 'entertainment parlor' once run by Luke Short. What was more important to the stability of the town, well-funded agents like J. L. Mitchener bought the Longhorns and shipped them east.

As the hands prepared to herd their cattle across the toll bridge leading into town, the older men went to Poteet and said: 'Dodge can be a tough town for a young fellow. What'll we do with that miserable skunk Floyd till we head back to Texas?'

'I'll speak to him,' Poteet said, and that evening he assembled the first-timers and talked to them as if he were their father: 'Lads, when you cross the toll bridge tomorrow you enter a new world. The Atchison, Topeka and Santa Fe runs through the town. You can see its water tower. North of the railroad the town fathers have cleaned things up. No more gunfights. No more roaring into saloons on horseback. On that far side of the tracks . . . churches, schools, newspapers.'

'Tell 'em what's south,' a point man interrupted.

'On this side of the tracks, it's like the old days. Saloons, dance halls, gambling. You stay north, the better element will protect you. You move south, you're on your own.' He said this directly to Floyd, then added: 'I suppose you'll head south. If you do, don't get killed. I want to take you young fellows back to your mothers.'

When the meeting ended, Floyd asked one of the point men: 'Will Luke Short be in town? He's from Texas and he's killed a lot of men.'

'They ran Luke out years back. And you act up, they'll run you out too.'

During the approach to Dodge, Floyd had spent hours speculating on what he would do when he reached town. Girls figured in his plans, and the firing of his hidden pistol, and a gallop down Front Street, and a hot bath and good food. A thousand lads coming north from Texas to the railheads had entertained similar dreams, but few had come with such addled visions as those which attended Floyd Rusk, for he envisioned himself as a reincarnation of Wyatt Earp and Luke Short, though what this might entail he could not have explained.

As soon as the Longhorns, the last batch to enter Kansas from Texas, had been led to the Mitchener corrals at the railhead, Floyd collected part of his pay and headed to the ramshackle area south of the tracks, and with unerring instinct, found his way to the toughest of all the saloons, The Lady Gay, once owned by Jim Masterson. He was startled when he saw his first dance-hall girls, for they were enticing beyond his hopes, and when he heard the coarse remarks made about them by the cowhands, he became confused and thought the men were somehow casting public aspersions on his mother. When two rowdy men from another outfit that had started in Del Rio referred to the girls as 'soiled lilies' and 'spattered doves,' he became infuriated and ordered them to shut up.

The men looked at this fat, grotesque boy and unquestionably one of them made a motion as if to push him aside. Anticipating this, Floyd whipped out his gun and shot them dead.

Before the gunsmoke had cleared, Poteet's two point men leaped into action, rushed Floyd out of the saloon, and hid him in a ravine south of the river, for they knew that Poteet, always a man of rectitude, would refuse to cover up for one of his cowboys who had committed murder.

When Floyd was safely hidden, the two men rode north of the tracks to where Poteet had rooms in a respectable hotel, and told him: 'Fat Floyd killed two Del Rio cowboys.'

Poteet tensed his jaw, then asked: 'You turn him in to the sheriff?'

'No, we hid him in a gully. We'll pick him up when we ride south.'

'But why? If he murdered someone?'

'Mr. Poteet, we give you our word, don't we, Charley? It wasn't cut-and-dried. It looked maybe like they might be goin' for their guns.'

'Where did that boy get a gun?'

'He practiced a lot when you weren't around.'

Suddenly all the fire went out of Poteet. He slumped forward with his hands over his face: 'Oh my God, that poor woman. To have borne such a miserable son-of-a-bitch.' Looking up, he asked the point men: 'Must we take him back to Texas?' Without waiting for an answer, he rose as if nothing worried him and snapped: 'We'll dig him out as soon as we sell the herd. Keep him in the ravine till we go south.'

When Floyd was dragged before Poteet, the range boss tried to make him realize the gravity of what had happened: 'Son, on the day a young feller kills his first man, he's in terrible trouble, because it came so easy—a flick of the finger—he may be tempted to do it again. Most gunmen start at your age, killing somebody. Billy the Kid, and he's dead now. John Wesley Hardin killed his first man at fifteen . . .'

His words had the opposite effect to what he intended: 'They'll never hang John Wesley, never.'

'Son, are you listening to me? Hardin is in jail for twenty-five years. Do you realize that if my point men hadn't stepped in to protect you, the people back there would have hanged you?'

'No one will ever hang me.'

Only Poteet's promise to Emma that he would bring her son back home prevented him from thrashing the boy and taking him back to the sheriff in Dodge. Out of respect for Emma, he would tolerate the odious boy, but he would no longer bother with him. The two point men, however, having saved his life, felt a different kind of responsibility, and late one afternoon on the way home they whispered to Poteet: 'We think there'd better be a trial,' and the trail boss agreed.

Just before evening meal, one of the point men rode up to the chuck wagon, where Floyd was first in line, as always: 'Floyd, you're under arrest.'

'What for?' in a whining voice.

'We know you shot them two men in Dodge unjustified.'

'They drew on me.'

'We know what a miserable coward you are, what a skunk, and we're goin' to try you correct, right now.'

Floyd trembled as two other cowhands lashed his wrists and tied his ankles together, and he was terrified when the solemn trial began, with Poteet as judge.

'What charge do you bring against this man?'

'That in Dodge City he willfully gunned down two Texas cowboys.'

'Without provocation?'

'None.'

Floyd tried to raise his hands: 'They were comin' at me.'

'Were they coming at him?' Judge Poteet asked.

'They were not. He done it disgraceful.'

Poteet asked for a vote on Floyd's guilt, and it was unanimous.

'Floyd Rusk,' the judge said solemnly. 'You have been a disgrace on this trail north. You have responded to nothing. You surrendered the respect of your comrades, and in my presence you scorned your father. It is not surprising that in Dodge you murdered two men, and now, by God, you shall hang.'

'Oh, no!' the boy cried, for he had certainly not intended to murder anyone in the saloon, and now he pleaded desperately for his life.

The cowboys were obdurate. Perching him sideways on a big roan, they led him to the branches of an oak tree, from which they had suspended a rope. When it was tied about his neck, Poteet stood near and said: 'Floyd Rusk, on the trail north you proved yourself to be a young man without a single saving grace. As a murderer, you deserve to die. Tom, when I drop my hand, whip the horse.'

In terror, the fat boy watched the fatal hand, felt the man slap the horse, and felt the rope tighten about his neck as the beast galloped off. But he also felt R. J. Poteet catch him as he fell, and then he fainted.

'Emma,' Poteet reported to his friend, 'it was my last trail. Your check is bigger than ever before.'

'And Floyd?'

'He's no good, Emma. If he continues the way he's headed, you'll be attending his hanging.' He stood aside as she wept, and did not try to console her: 'You've got to hear it sooner or later, but in Dodge City your son murdered two men. Shot them dead with a revolver he got somewheres.'

'Oh my God!'

'My point men spirited him out of town. Saved his life. So on the trail south they held a trial, to show your boy what such actions meant.' He told her about the mock hanging and explained how this sometimes knocked sense into would-be gunmen, but when Emma asked: 'How did Floyd take it?' he had to reply: 'When he came to and realized the trick we'd played on him, he spat in my face and shouted: "Go to hell, you stupid son-of-a-bitch." '

Emma covered her face, and when her sobbing ended, Poteet said quietly: 'He's alive, Emma, because I promised you I'd bring him back. If he was my son, he'd already be dead.'

When he handed over the last check he would ever bring to the Larkin Ranch, he said with haunting sadness: 'I'd wanted this last drive to be the best of all. An honorable farewell to the great range that you and I knew so well.' When he tried to look across the plains, his view was cut by fences. 'Sometimes things just peter out, like the dripping of a faucet. No parades. No cannon salutes. Just the closing down of all we cherished.'

He said goodbye to this gallant woman with whom he felt so strong an affinity, then turned his horse toward San Antonio. The open range would see him and his breed no more.

It was known among the neighbors around the square as 'the year Earnshaw and Emma had their battle.' There was no open brawling, of course, and bitter words were certainly avoided, but the differences were profound, and pursued vigorously. When the year ended everyone, including the two participants, understood better what values animated these two diverse frontiersmen.

The Battle of the Bull, as it was called, was a complicated affair. Back in 1880, when Alonzo Betz, the demon barbed-wire salesman, gave his night-long demonstration of how his wire could discipline the biggest Longhorns, Emma had been surprised that her bull Mean Moses had allowed the fragile wires to restrain him. Indeed, it had been mainly his surrender that had established the reputation of Betz's wire as 'master of the range.' Emma could never explain her bull's cowardly behavior, and several times she voiced her disgust.

When Betz's new fences had surrounded a major portion of the Rusk lands, and when the expensive Hereford and Shorthorn bulls imported from England were safe inside to cross with the Longhorn cows, Earnshaw implored his wife to get rid of her Longhorn bulls so that all the Rusk cattle could be improved, but the use of this word irritated Emma: 'What's improvement? Turning strong range cattle into flabby doughnuts?'

Patiently he had explained that the purpose of raising cattle was to produce as much edible beef as possible, in the shortest time and with a minimum consumption of expensive feed: 'The payoff on thy cattle, Emma, is what they sell for at Dodge City.'

She said: 'I thought the important thing about cattle was that they were just that, cattle as God bred them, not man.'

'It seems blasphemous to bring God into this.'

'No, it seems like common sense. When I look at Mean Moses . . .'

'That's a very unfortunate name for an animal.'

'Well, he is mean, and he does lead the others, and in a way I love him.'

'How can thee say that?' and she replied: 'I just said it.' What she did not say was that she prized her big, stubborn bull because he, like her, had survived on the Texas plains. She did not in any sentimental way identify with the bull, nor see him as her surrogate, but she did like him and did not propose to see imported bulls elbow him off her land.

The arguing Rusks had agreed to leave Mean Moses outside the barbed-wire enclosures, free to roam as always, and to range with him, a dozen cows and another bull, breeding in the thickets, their calves going unbranded from year to year, with the herd never increasing fabulously the way the tended cattle did, but with a new bull moving in now and then to give renewed vigor. As a result, the Rusk ranch always had out in its barren wastes a solid residue of Longhorns. In the rest of Texas the breed was dying out, upgraded year after year into the fine cattle so highly prized by the Northern markets, but in Larkin County, Mean Moses and his harem had kept it alive.

A great Longhorn was something to behold, for almost alone among the world's cattle it could produce horns of the most prodigious spread, branching straight out from the corners of the head, then taking a thrilling turn forward and breathtakingly graceful sweep up and out. 'The Texas twist,' this was called, and when it showed in full dignity, men said: 'That one wears a rocking chair on its head.' Men who no longer raised Longhorns were apt to grow maudlin when they encountered on some friend's ranch a beast with really magnificent horns.

The peculiarity of the breed was that only steers and cows produced the great horns, and even then, only occasionally; some unexplained sexual factor caused their horns to grow very large in the first place, and then to take that Texas twist as they matured. A Longhorn bull never showed the twist and only rarely produced horns of maximum size. What horns he did produce were apt to be powerful, straight weapons trained to protect and, if need be, kill, not much different from the horns of a good bull of whatever breed.

So the famed Texas Longhorn of cartoon and poster showing fierce, beautiful-looking horns was always either a castrated male or a cow. Mean Moses, for example, had horns which came out sideways from his head and absolutely parallel to the ground for a distance of about eighteen inches on each side. Then they turned forward, as if controlled by a T-square, ending in very sharp points. Fortunately for the people who had to work him, he had a placid disposition, except when outraged by the misbehavior of some other Longhorn; then he could be ferocious.

In the early years of barbed wire and imported bulls, Mean Moses had stayed off by himself with his Longhorn cows, hiding his yearly calves in forgotten arroyos and testing his saberlike horns on any wolves that tried to attack them. Four or five times he had stood, horns lowered, when wolves attacked, and with deft thrusts had on each occasion impaled some luckless wolf and sent the rest off howling.

Emma sometimes saw her proud bull only three or four times a season, and when she did she was curiously elated to know that he still roamed the range. As she studied the vanishing Longhorns she noticed several things which renewed her determination: The cows never need assistance in giving birth. Sure, Earnshaw's pampered breeds bring in more money, but Earnshaw pays it out for cow doctors at birthing time. And my Longhorns can live on anything. That bad winter when the Herefords died of freezing and starvation, come spring, there my Longhorns were, walking skeletons but alive. Three weeks of good grass, they were ready to breed. And what did they eat during the blizzards? Anything they could chew, just anything they could find in the snow—cactus, wood from old fence posts, sticks. What wonderful animals.

Things might have continued this way had not Earnshaw, always seeking to improve his wife's herd, instructed his Mexican helper González to 'round up that last bunch of cows running wild and bring them within the fence to be properly bred.'

'Okay, boss.' The roundup was not easy, but with the expert help of the two black ranch hands it was accomplished. Mean Moses was deprived of his harem; the cows would be bred to the good bulls; and within three generations even the lesser characteristics of the famed Longhorn would be submerged in the preferred breeds that were developing.

Emma Rusk did not approve of this decision: 'Earnshaw, we don't have to use every cow on the range in your experiments. Let Mean Moses and his cows stay out where they've always been.'

'Emma, thee either breeds cattle properly or thee doesn't breed at all. The utility of the Longhorn is diminishing . . .'

'Those cattle have their own utility, Earnshaw. Play God with your English cattle. Leave mine on the range.'

'Thee will never have first-class cattle . . .'

'I don't want first-class cattle. I want the cattle that grew up here.'

She lost that argument, as did the half-dozen owners in other corners of Texas who struggled to keep the breed alive; like Emma, they were submerged in the sweep of progress. But if Emma was powerless to protect the rights of Mean Moses, the bull was not. During the famous trial of the barbed wire, Moses had been tempted only by a stack of hay, and the pricks of the barbs were sufficiently irritating to fend him off, but now the essence of his being was insulted: his cows had been taken from him, and this he would not tolerate.

Among the two dozen Longhorn cows imprisoned behind barbed wire so that the English bulls could breed them was an extraordinary lady called Bertha, widely known for two virtues: she gave birth to a strong calf each year, and some aberration had allowed her to produce the damnedest pair of horns ever seen in Texas. It must have been a sexual deformity, for her great horns started out flat like a bull's, and when the time came for them to take the Texas twist, they remained flat but turned in a wide sweep right back in huge semicircles till they almost met a few inches in front of her eyes. As John Jaxifer said when he drove her inside the barbed wire: 'You could fit one of them new bathtubs inside her horns.' His description was accurate, for the immense sweep of the horns and their smooth curve back to form an ellipse did take the outline of a gigantic bathtub.

It would be preposterous to claim that Mean Moses was in any way attached to Bathtub Bertha; he bred all cows indiscriminately and in a good year he could handle about two dozen, but it did seem, year after year, that he did his best job with Bathtub, for the speckled cow produced an unbroken chain of excellent calves, often twins, and it seemed likely that when Moses died, one of her young bulls would take his place as king of the herd. At any rate, when Moses lost Bathtub and his other cows it was not in the breeding season, so he felt no impetus to join them, but as the season changed he began to feel mighty urges, and when visceral feelings took charge he was impelled to act.

Sniffing the air for scent of his cows, he lowed softly and started in a straight line toward them. Down steep ravines and up their sides he plowed ahead, across arroyos damp from recent rains, and up to the first line of barbed wire he came.

Pausing not a moment, he walked right through the three tough strands, pushing them ahead of him till his power pulled loose the posts, making them fall useless.

Ignoring the gashes the barbs had inflicted across his chest, he plowed on, and when he reached the second fence, he went through it as easily as the first. Finally he came to where the three concentric fences protected the valuable bulls, and here, close to where his cows were, he simply knocked down the barbed wire, disregarded the wounds that were now pumping blood, and looked for the master bull who had usurped his cows. Head lowered, mighty horns parallel to the earth, he gave a loud bellow and charged.

'Boss! Boss!' González shouted as he cantered in next morning with the rising sun.

'What is it?' Earnshaw asked, slipping into his trousers.

'Something awful!'

The Mexican deemed it best not to explain during the ride out to the tank, and when Earnshaw reached the fences he had so carefully constructed he stopped aghast. Some titanic beast had simply walked through them, laying barbs and posts alike in the dust. It had then apparently turned around and walked back, leaving a trail of blood but taking all the Longhorn cows with it.

'What happened?'

'Mean Moses.'

And then Earnshaw spotted the real tragedy, for in a corner of the corral, his side ripped open in a bloody mess, lay the wounded Hereford for which Earnshaw had paid $180. Trembling, Rusk hurried back to town, where he informed his wife: 'Thy bull has gored my bull.'

Emma, who appreciated the increase in her herd which her husband had supervised, was distraught at the damage to Earnshaw's prize English bull, but when she saw the leveled fences and realized the power which had thrown them down, that primitive power of the open range of which she had once been a part, she exulted.

'Let Mean Moses go, Earnshaw. He was meant to be free.' So, because of her stubborn defense of her stubborn bull, one corner of Texas was able to keep alive the Longhorn strain. When Mean Moses died, she selected his replacement, a fine young bull sired by Moses out of Bathtub Bertha. This Mean Moses II proved to be almost as good a bull as his father, and in time VII, XII and XIX of other bloodlines would be recognized as the premier bulls of their breed. Emma Larkin's love for the integrity of her animals had ensured that.

On a cold, blustery morning in March, Banker Weatherby sent one of his five clerks to fetch Earnshaw Rusk, and when the summons came, the Quaker had a moment of queasiness. For some time now he had suspected that Clyde Weatherby had taken the railroad funds the Fort Garner merchants contributed and the acres which he, Rusk, had thrown into the kitty, and had spent them not on opinion-makers in the Wichita Falls-Abilene area but on himself, and he supposed that Weatherby was now either going to confess his malfeasance or ask for more funds. He'll not get another cent from me, Rusk swore as he crossed the area leading to the bank.

But when he walked into Weatherby's office, Rusk found that Simpson was there, the saloon keeper, Fordson and three others, and when all were seated, the banker threw a map before them and shouted: 'We've done it! I promised you a railroad, and we're getting one.'

The details as he explained them were complicated beyond the comprehension of ordinary men, and both Rusk and Simpson lost the trail early, but it was a standard Texas operation: 'Five different railroads are involved. From the F.W.&D.C. in the north, a spur will come south to be built by a new line, the Wichita Standard. From Abilene north will come a second spur, also built by a new line, the Abilene Major. What will unite them? A third spur built by us, the Fort Garner United Railway. President? Your humble servant. Secretary? Earnshaw Rusk.'

The men cheered, then they danced, then some wept and others sent out for beer and champagne. The five clerks were invited in to hear the good news, and they danced too. Rusk sent for his wife, and others did the same, and soon it seemed that an entire town was dancing and shouting and celebrating the fact that it had been saved.

'The railroad's coming!' men shouted, and some set forth on horseback to inform ranchers whose support had helped achieve this miracle. At the height of the festivities, Weatherby was still trying to explain to the directors of Fort Garner United how the complexities would be resolved: 'When we get our line built, we'll sell out to Abilene Major, which will then join with Wichita Standard. Then they'll both sell to F.W.&D.C., which I'm assured has arranged to sell out completely to a huge new line to be called Colorado and Southern, and I know for a fact that Burlington System will some day buy that. So we'll wind up with baskets full of Burlington stock.'

It was a standard Texas operation, but no one was listening.

Emma had assumed that when her husband finally got his railroad he would relax, but Earnshaw was the kind of Pennsylvania Quaker who had to be engaged in a crusade of some kind or he did not feel alive. Now, in his fifties, with a railroad under his belt, he was determined that Larkin, as the county seat of Larkin County, should have a courthouse of distinction, and he channeled all his considerable efforts to that end.

As secretary of a functioning railroad, he carried a pass which entitled him to ride free across the face of Texas, and he found boyish delight in traipsing from one county to the next inspecting courthouses. On these pilgrimages he began to identify a group of excellent buildings obviously designed by the same daring, poetic architect whose thumbprint was unmistakable, and he wrote to his wife:

> No one can tell me his name, but he builds a courthouse which looks like the embodiment of law. He likes towers and turrets, and so do I. He likes clean, heavy lines, and as a Quaker trained in severity, so do I. And he displays a wonderful sense of color, which is remarkable in that he works in stone. He is the only man in Texas qualified to build our courthouse, which I want to be a memorial to thy heroic family.

At the town of Waxahachie, where the finest courthouse in Texas was under construction, a marvelous medieval poem in stone and vivid colors, he learned that the architect's name was James Riely Gordon, and he found that this genius was then working at Victoria, the distinguished city in the southern part of the state, so he made the long trip there and met the great man. To his surprise, Gordon was only thirty-one, but so masterful in his courtly manner, for he had been born in Virginia and had acquired a stately style in both speech and appearance, that he dominated any situation of which he was a part. He liked Rusk immediately, for he saw in the serious Quaker the kind of man he respected, straightforward and dependable.

Yes, he would be interested in building his next courthouse in Larkin County because he wanted a real showcase in the West. Yes, he believed he could do it on a reasonable budget. Yes, he would try to preserve the existing stone buildings about the old parade ground. But when he saw the cramped dimensions on the plan Rusk showed him, he protested: 'Sir, I could not fit one of my courthouses into that cramped space. My courthouses need room to display their glories.' And with this, he jabbed at the commander's quarters, the flagpole, and the infantry quarters of Company U on the other side: 'Too constricted. To be effective, a courthouse needs space.'

Rusk, not noted for laughing, broke into chuckles of relief: 'Mr. Gordon! This is an old diagram, not a map. Merely to show you where the fort buildings are. The parade ground is very wide. Five times wider than this.'

'You mean . . .' With a quick pencil the architect drew a sketch representing Fort Garner as Rusk was describing it, with the splendid parade ground spaciously fitted among the stone buildings, but before he could react to this new vision, Rusk spread before him six photographs showing the handsome stonework in the houses and the infantry quarters.

Gordon was enchanted: 'You mean, I would have all this space and these fine buildings as a background?'

'That's why I've sought you, sir. We have a noble site awaiting your brilliance.'

'I'll do it!' Gordon cried, and he made immediate plans to follow Rusk west to meet with the officials of Larkin County, but before Earnshaw departed, Gordon warned him: 'I shall design the courthouse. You shall pay for it. Before I reach Fort Garner, I want all the finances arranged and assured. I refuse to work in the dark.'

'How much will you need?'

'I was working on some ideas last night. Not less than eighty thousand dollars.'

'I don't have it now, but by the time you reach us, it'll be there.'

All the way home, Rusk sweated over how he was going to persuade the authorities of Larkin County to finance his latest dream: Goodness, they'll never approve eighty thousand dollars. Bascomb County next door built their courthouse for under nine thousand.

By the time he neared Fort Garner he realized that the only thing to do was to convene the community leaders and confess that in an excess of enthusiasm he had committed them to this large debt, and when he faced them in Editor Fordson's office, he began to tremble, but as soon as he outlined the problem, he received surprising support from Banker Weatherby, who would be expected to find the money: 'The state of Texas, having in mind communities just like ours, has passed a law enabling us to borrow funds for the construction of county courthouses.'

'Oh! I would never want to borrow money again,' Rusk said.

'Not borrow in the old sense. We pass a bond issue. The entire community borrows. The state provides the funds.'

'Would I have to sign any papers?'

'Damnit, man. This is a new system. The public signs. The public gets a fine new courthouse. And we all prosper.'

Weatherby proved to be the staunchest supporter of the bond drive for the new courthouse and the best explicator of the Texas that was coming: 'Let us build good things now so that our children who follow will have a stronger base from which to do their building.' At one public meeting Frank Yeager, now a rancher with his own land, loudly protested that Larkin County could save money by using one of the old fort buildings as its courthouse, and Weatherby astonished Rusk by whispering: 'Ride herd on that horse's ass,' and Earnshaw rose to do so.

'Frank!' he argued. 'That's a little stable suited to a little town lost on the edge of the plains.'

'What are we?' Yeager asked, and Rusk replied: 'Little today, but not tomorrow. I want a noble building symbolizing our potential greatness. I want to fill the imaginations of our people.' After he had silenced Yeager, he addressed the citizens of Larkin County: 'I want something worthy of the new Texas.'

He had ten days before the architect was due to arrive, and he spent them in tireless persuasion, a tall, gaunt figure moving everywhere, talking with everyone, always with a sheaf of figures in his pocket, always with the bursting enthusiasm necessary to launch any civic enterprise of importance. On the ninth day he and

Weatherby had the money guaranteed, and on the tenth day he slept until two in the afternoon.

The visit of James Riely Gordon to the frontier town was almost a disaster, for the austere young architect, one of the most opinionated men in Texas history and its foremost artist, went directly to his room, speaking to no one, not even Rusk. He ate alone and went to bed. In the morning he wished to see no one, and in the afternoon he stalked solemnly about the old parade ground, checking the buildings, satisfying himself that the stone houses were in good repair.

He also ate his evening meal alone, and at seven in the evening he deigned to appear before the local leaders. His appearance created a sensation, for he stepped primly before these hardened frontiersmen dressed in a black frock coat, striped trousers and creamy white vest. He wore a stiff collar three inches high, from which appeared almost magically a fawn-colored cravat adorned by a huge diamond stickpin. The lapels of both his coat and vest were piped with silk grosgrain fabric of a slightly different color.

He had a big, square head, a vanishing hairline which he masked by training his forelocks to cover a huge amount of otherwise bare skin, and he wore pince-nez glasses that accentuated his hauteur. He was the most inappropriate person to address a group of frontier ranchers, and had a vote been taken at that moment, Gordon would have been shipped back to San Antonio, where he kept his offices.

But when he began to speak, the tremendous authority he had acquired through travel, study, contemplation and actual building manifested itself, and his audience sat in rapt attention:

'You have a magnificent site here on the plains. This old fort is a treasure, a memorial of heroic days. Its simple stone buildings form a dignified framework for whatever I do, and I would be proud to be a part of your achievement.

'I have studied every penny, especially the difficulty of bringing materials here from a distance, and I believe I can build what you will want for seventy-nine thousand dollars, but if you insist on making any wild changes, the cost will be much higher. Have you found ways to get the money?'

Satisfied that the funds were available, he astonished the hard-headed county leaders by telling them, not asking them, what the new courthouse was to be:

'It is essential, gentlemen, that we maintain a clear image of what a great courthouse ought to be, and I desire to build none that are not great. It must have four characteristics, and these must be visible to all. To the criminal who is brought here for trial, it must represent the majesty of the law, awesome and unassailable. To the responsible citizen who comes here seeking justice, it must represent stability and fairness and the continuity of life. To the elected officials working here, especially the judges, it must remind them of the heavy responsibility they share for keeping the system honorable and forward-moving; I want every official who enters his office in the morning to think: "I am part of a dignified tradition, reaching back to the time of Hammurabi and Leviticus." And to the town and the county and the state, the courthouse must be a thing of beauty. It must rise high and stand for something. And it must grow better as years and decades and centuries pass.'

And then, as if to prove his point, he asked Earnshaw to fetch the large package from his room, and when an easel was provided, he stunned his audience with a beautifully executed watercolor he had completed earlier. It showed the court-house he would build at the center of the old fort.

First of all, it was beautiful, a work of recognizable art. Second, it was both magisterially heavy and delicately proportioned. Third, it was a kaleidoscope of color, utilizing three types of stone locally available, but stressing a brilliant red sandstone, alternating with layers of a milky-white limestone. Fourth, it had the most fantastic collection of ornamentation an artist could have devised: miniature turrets, balustrades, soaring arches four stories up, Moorish towers at all corners, arched galleries open to the air, fenestrations, clock towers, and perched upon the top, a kind of red-and-white-stone wedding cake, five tiers high and ending in a many-turreted, many-spired tower, from which rose a master spire nineteen feet tall.

Ornate, gaudy, flamboyant, ridiculously overornamented, it was also grand in design and noble in spirit. It was a courthouse ideally suited to the Texas spirit, and it and its fifteen majestic sisters could be built only in Texas. But it was Frank Yeager's comment which best summarized it: 'A building like that, it would show where the seventy-nine thousand dollars were spent. Sort of makes you feel good.'

Each of the officials had changes he wanted made, with Rusk expressing a strong desire for four dominating turrets at the compass points. Gordon listened to each recommendation as if it were coming from Vitruvius, but when the critic stopped speaking and Gordon stopped nodding his head in agreement, the archi-tect patiently explained why the suggestion, excellent though it might be in spirit, could not be accommodated, and as the evening wore on, it became apparent that James Riely Gordon was going to build the courthouse he wanted, for he was convinced that when it was done the citizens would want it, too. At the end of the long evening, with him standing beside his watercolor, his pince-nez still jam-ming his nose, the ranchers were beginning to speak of 'our courthouse' and 'our architect.'

The construction of the Larkin County Courthouse was the wonder of the age,

and one aspect caused nervous comment. To complete the stonework professionally, Gordon had to transfer to the town the team of skilled Italian stonemasons
he had brought to Texas to work on his other civic buildings, and these men did
not exactly fit into the rugged frontier pattern. For one thing, they were Catholics
and insisted upon having a priest visit them regularly. For another, they preferred
their traditional food style and could not adjust to the Larkin County diet of
greasy steaks smothered in rich gravy. But worst of all, as lonely men working
constantly in one small Texas town after another, they clumsily sought female
companionship, and this was resented by the local women and men alike.

There was one stonecarver much appreciated by Gordon, who assigned him the
more difficult ornamental tasks. His name was Luigi Esposito, but he was called
by his Texan co-workers Weegee, and this Weegee, unmarried and twenty-seven,
fell in love with a charming and graceful young woman, Mabel Fister, who
worked for the county judge, who had his temporary offices in one of the old
cavalry barracks. Weegee saw her night and morning, a fine girl, he thought, and
soon his day revolved about her appearances. He could anticipate when she would
come to work, when she would leave the judge's office and on what errands.
Whenever she appeared, he would stop work and stare at her until the last
movement of her ankle carried her away.

At this period he was working on the four important carved figures which
would decorate the corners on the second tier. Gordon had decided they would be
draped female figures representing Justice, Religion, Motherhood and Beauty, and
in a moment of infatuation Weegee started with the last-named, carving a really
splendid portrait of Mabel Fister. When it was finished, he made bold to stop
Mabel one morning as she was going to work; he could speak no English, but he
wanted to explain that this statue was his tribute to her.

She was embarrassed and outraged that he should have intruded into her life in
this manner, and although she could speak no Italian, and certainly did not wish
to learn, she did indicate that she was displeased both with his art and with his
having stopped her.

He next carved Motherhood, again in Mabel's likeness, and again he was
snubbed when he tried to interest her in it. He then turned to Religion, and this
time the beautiful Mabel appeared as a harsh and rather unpleasant type, which
he displayed to her one afternoon as she left her work with the judge. She pushed
his hand away and spurned his tongue-tied efforts to explain his art and his deep
affection for her.

Before he started carving Justice, which he had wanted to be the best of the
series, he asked the interpreter provided by Gordon to arrange some way for him
to meet with Mabel Fister so that he could explain in sensible words his love for
her, so one afternoon Earnshaw Rusk sat with Weegee and listened as the interpreter poured out the sculptor's story. Rusk inspected the three statues and said: 'I

should think that any young woman would be proud to be immortalized so handsomely.'

'Will you speak with her?' Weegee pleaded, and Earnshaw said that he certainly would. Hurrying home, he asked Emma if she would accompany him, and they went together to talk with the attractive secretary: 'Miss Fister, the gifted sculptor Luigi Esposito had asked us if we would—'

'I want nothing to do with him. He's a bother.'

'But, Miss Fister, he's working in an alien land.' Emma was speaking, and when Mabel looked at her wooden nose she wanted very little to do with her, either.

'I would not care to speak with a papist,' she said.

'In Rome they claim that Jesus was the first Catholic,' Rusk said.

'We're not in Rome.'

'Very few young women have themselves depicted in marble by young men who love them.'

'That's a foolish word, Mr. Rusk. I'm surprised you would use it.'

'No one ever need apologize for the word *love.* I would deeply appreciate it if you . . .'

Miss Fister was adamant. She would not meet with Weegee; she hoped that he would soon finish his carvings and go away: 'He has no place in Texas.' When Justice was finished, Weegee did not try to show it to her, but his mates could see that Mabel Fister had been treated harshly in it. Justice was hard, cruel and remorseless, and not at all what James Riely Gordon had intended. Indeed, he asked Luigi if he would consider trying again on that figure, but the Italian told him, through the interpreter: 'You don't change your plans. I don't change mine.'

Emma Rusk, aware that she, too, had been rebuffed by Miss Fister, was experiencing an emotional crisis of her own. Her son Floyd, nearly twenty now and as fat and unruly as ever, had made the acquaintance of one of the Italian workmen who had done some building in Brazil, and from him had obtained a most improbable piece of tropical wood. It was called *balsa,* the Italian said, and while it was lighter than an equal bulk of feathers, it was also structurally strong. He had paid the Italian a dollar for a piece three inches square and had then played with it, testing whether it would float and trying to estimate whether it weighed as much as an ounce, which he doubted.

Satisfied with its characteristics and assured that it would accept varnish, he then retired to his room, and after several abortive experiments on fragments of the balsa, came out in great embarrassment, holding out his hands, offering his mother a beautifully carved nose which weighed practically nothing and to which he had attached a gossamer thread which he himself had plaited.

He insisted that she try it on, explaining that it had been so thoroughly varnished and rubbed that it would resist water. But when she removed her heavy wooden nose, the one carved in oak by her husband, and Floyd saw her again as she was, the experience was so crushing that he fled from the house, weighed down by his haunting images of his mother in the hands of her Comanche captors.

When he returned two days later, neither he nor his mother mentioned the nose. She wore it, with exceeding comfort; it looked better than its predecessor and its feathery weight gave her a freedom she had not enjoyed before. She felt younger and so much more acceptable that she went to the judge's office to speak with Mabel Fister: 'Young woman, not long ago you said some very stupid things. Don't interrupt. If God can accept all children as His own, you can be courteous to this gifted man so far from home.'

'I would never marry an Italian.'

'Who's speaking of marriage? I'm speaking of common decency. Of charity.'

'I do not need you to come here—'

'You shied away from me. I understand why. I might have done the same. But do not shy away from humanity, Miss Fister. We need all of it we can get.'

She accomplished nothing, but with a boldness she did not know she had she sought out Luigi Esposito and, with the aid of the interpreter, said: 'Miss Fister has never traveled. She thinks this little town is the universe. Forgive her.'

When these words were translated, Luigi said nothing, but he did bow ceremoniously to Emma as if to thank her for her solicitude. Then he turned abruptly, strode to his workshop, and without orders from Gordon, toiled with passionate concentration on his secret carving for the fifth and last location. When it was completed he asked three of his fellow workers to help him cement it in place, and when it was fixed on the south façade of the courthouse between Beauty and Motherhood, the other Italians laughed until they were weak to think of the joke Luigi had played on the Americans. Covering it with a tarpaulin, they proposed unveiling it at some propitious moment. Then the three masons went to their quarters and got mildly drunk while Luigi searched for a pistol, with which he blew out his brains.

When the courthouse was completed, a thing of flamboyant beauty, the time came for the unveiling of Luigi Esposito's four symbolic sculptures plus the mystery creation, and since they were presented in the order in which he had done them, it was apparent that his model had grown increasingly harsh and ugly, as if Justice in Texas was always going to be a stern and uncertain affair.

Some commented on this, but most were interested in what the fifth mystery sculpture would show, and when the three Italians who had cemented it into place withdrew the tarpaulin, smiling vengefully, a gasp issued from the crowd, for in amazing and intimate detail, Weegee had carved the private parts of a woman, and before nightfall rumor initiated by the workmen was circulating to the effect that Weegee had carved it from life. They vowed they had watched as Mabel Fister posed.

There it stood on the south façade of this magnificent courthouse, immortalized in stone. Two days later Miss Fister left Larkin for Abilene and did not return.

Earnshaw, of course, wanted the lascivious carving removed, but to his surprise Emma did not: 'It's part of the courthouse experience, let it remain.' And she was supported by Clyde Weatherby, who predicted accurately: 'Ten people will come to see the courthouse, but a thousand to see Mabel Fister's unusual pose.'

Surprising news from Jacksborough diverted attention from the statue. Floyd Rusk had disappeared for several days, and his parents feared that he might have gone to old Fort Griffin, where notorious gamblers clustered, but he had gone to Jacksborough, accompanied by Molly Yeager, whom he had married. She was a flighty girl, almost as round and pudgy as her husband, and Emma could find little reason to hope that she would prove a good wife, but as she told Earnshaw: 'If I criticized Miss Fister for not being gracious toward her Italian, I can't be ungracious to Molly.' What she did not tell her husband was that each day she wore her balsa-wood nose she was reminded that in his grudging way Floyd did love her, and that was enough.

As the century ended, a delightful charade occurred. An official from Washington, eager for a paid vacation, had come to Jacksborough just after Floyd's wedding and had fired the postmaster, stating no reasons for his arbitrary act. He had then announced that henceforth the town was to be Jacksboro, whereupon with elaborate ceremony he reemployed the fired man as the new postmaster.

After the celebration, at which he got roaring drunk, he boarded the coach to Fort Garner, where without explanation he fired that postmaster too. When Earnshaw protested such unfairness, the visitor pointed at him: 'Because of your agitation, this town is now named Larkin,' and the postmaster was reappointed by a letter from President McKinley.

During the festivities celebrating the christening, Emma stood well to one side as she heard Weatherby extolling her husband for the good he had accomplished in this town: 'He brought us the wire fence that made our fortunes, he found a way to get us our railroad, he engineered our noble courthouse, and now he has given us a proper name.' The orator pointed out that this was an example to young people of how . . .

Emma stopped listening, for she was staring toward the plains and calculating how costly this so-called improvement had been. 'The buffalo that used to darken these plains,' she whispered, 'the Indians who chased them, the Longhorns who roamed so freely, the unmarked open spaces . . . where are they? Will our children ever see their like?' She expected no answer, for she knew that the glories which had sustained her through the dark years would be no more.

. . . TASK FORCE

I tried to be polite when the governor intruded upon the planning session for our August meeting in Galveston. I explained that we had intended to invite a meteorologist from Wichita Falls to address us on Texas weather: 'You know, things like hurricanes and tornadoes.'

He said: 'Those are the Texas storms aloft. What I'm worried about are the storms here on the ground.'

When I explained that it would be difficult to disinvite Dr. Clay, he broke in: 'You mean Lewis Clay? He's one of the best.' A governor, it seemed, was supposed to know everyone in his state, and without consulting me he grabbed a phone, dialed his secretary, and said: 'Get me Lewis Clay, that man who supported me in Wichita Falls,' and within a minute he was speaking to our meteorologist: 'Lewis, your old pal, the governor. I hear you're heading for Galveston with these fine people on our Task Force. Now, Lewis, I'm going to have to preempt the morning session.' There was a long pause, after which I heard: 'Lewis, in running a great state, unexpected things sometimes become imperative. And believe me, this is one of those times.' Another pause: 'Lewis, they'll save you the entire afternoon.'

When he hung up I was more irritated than before, because this really was an unwarranted intrusion, but as things worked out, the split meeting was one of the most instructive we would have, for the day dwelt first on those great tempests of the human soul and then on the tempests of the sky which mirror them, and when we were through, our Task Force understood the spiritual and physical settings of Texas much better.

The impromptu morning session was monopolized by three worried Texans who had worked for the governor's election and who now warned him that unless they were given an opportunity to present their opinions about the spiritual base of Texas history, they were going to lead a statewide campaign against our work, against the members of the Task Force, and against the governor himself for his carelessness in selecting the committee members. When we convened that morning in a beautiful room overlooking the peaceful Gulf of Mexico, we were faced by three determined citizens with a tableful of charts, studies and typed recommendations.

Up to that moment they had not known one another personally, although they had been in correspondence regarding the threatened destruction of their state

The first was a tall, cadaverous man from Corpus Christi, an Old Testament prophet accustomed to dire prediction; he was not an ordained clergyman, but was prepared to advise clergymen as to how they should behave and what they should include in their sermons. He had a sharp, angular face, strong eyebrows and a deep premonitory voice. When he spoke, we paid attention.

The second was a stern housewife from Abilene who sat with sheaves of paper which she had trouble keeping organized. About fifty, she had educated her own three children rather rigorously and was now prepared to do the same with the state's. Her forte was to start talking and to keep going regardless of objections or obstructions thrown in her path. She was a verbal bulldozer, extremely effective in leveling opposition with force if not reason.

The third member was a jovial man from San Angelo, conciliatory, nodding agreeably when introduced, and never offensive in what he said or how he said it. But he was often more effective than his companions because he started each presentation with some phrase like 'It would really be hurtful, wouldn't it, if we taught our children that . . .' And he would follow with some established fact which everyone accepted but him, such as the truth that Texas was composed of some twenty radically different ethnic groups. He and the woman objected to any such statement in our conclusions on the ground that 'it would be divisive, stressing differences in our population, when what we need is a constant reminder that Texas was settled primarily by one master group, the good people from states like Kentucky and Georgia with an Anglo-Saxon, Protestant background.'

The rugged session covered four hours, nine to one, and we Task Force members tired of trying to digest the particularist ideas long before the three protesters tired of presenting them. Indeed, our visitors looked as if they could have continued throughout the evening, and next day too.

The thrust of their argument was simple: 'The essential character of Texas was formed by 1844, and our schoolchildren should be taught only the virtues which dominated at that time.' They were much more interested in what should not be taught than what should, and they had a specific list of forbidden subjects that must be avoided. Each of the three had some personal *bête noire* in which he or she was interested, and I shall summarize the main points of their forceful presentations:

The San Angelo man instructed us to downplay the supposed influence of the Spaniards, the Mexicans, the Germans, the Czechs and the Vietnamese: 'As for the colored, there is no real need to mention them at all. They played no significant role in Texas history, and to confuse young minds with the problems of slavery, which rarely existed in Texas and then in a most benevolent form, would be hurtful.' He also advised us to drop excessive coverage of Indians: 'The Texas Indians were cruel murderers, but we don't need to dwell on such unpleasantness. And the fact that we threw them all out of our state proves that they influenced Texas not at all. You needn't be unkind about it. Just ignore it, for they vanished a long time ago.' Most specifically, he warned against adverse comment on the resurgence of the Ku Klux Klan in the 1920s: 'Some people are speaking of this as if it was a blot on our escutcheon, and this has to stop. It really shouldn't be mentioned at all, and if it is, it must be presented as a logical, God-fearing uprising of loyal citizens eager to protect Texas against the radical incursions of coloreds, Catholics, Jews and freethinkers.'

The Abilene woman was gentler in her admonitions: 'The job of the schools is to protect our children from the ugliness of life. We see no reason why you should even mention the Great Depression. It would be a reflection on the American Way. And we're appalled that some textbooks speak of little girls having babies out of wedlock. It's much better not to discuss such things.' She cautioned us against including prominent photographs of Texas women like Barbara Jordan and Oveta Culp Hobby because they made their names in political activity: 'Ma Ferguson is all right, because she was governor and she did stand for old-fashioned virtues, and I suppose you'll have to include Lady Bird Johnson, but feature her as the mother of two daughters. We don't want a lot of mannish-looking women in our books. They're not proper role models for our young girls.' She said she supposed we'd have to include Abraham Lincoln and F.D.R., but she hoped we would not praise them, 'for they were worse enemies to Texas than the boll weevil.'

The Corpus Christi man fulminated against secular humanism and what he called the Four Ds: dancing, deviation, drugs and Democrats: 'And when I say *deviation,* I mean it in its broadest sense. There is a wonderful central tendency in Texas history, and when we deviate from it in any respect, we run into danger.' When I asked for an example, he snapped: 'Labor unions. All Texas will be deeply offended if you discuss labor unions. We've striven to keep such un-American operations out of our state and have campaigned to preserve our right-to-work laws. I have four textbooks here which speak of communists like Samuel Gompers and John L. Lewis as if they were respectable citizens, and this will not be tolerated. Organized labor played no part in Texas history and must not be presented as if it did.' Like the Abilene woman, he wanted the roles of the sexes clearly differentiated: 'Boys should play football and there should be no concession to movements blurring the lines between the sexes.' When he preached against dancing, I think all of us listened with condescending respect, but when he came to drugs, we supported him enthusiastically: 'I simply cannot imagine how this great nation has allowed this curse to threaten its young people. What has gone wrong? What dreadful mistakes have we made?' We nodded when he said in thundering, prophetic tones: 'This plague must be wiped out in Texas.'

At this point Rusk interrupted: 'What positive values are you advocating?' and the man replied: 'Those which made Texas great. Loyalty, religion, patriotism, justice, opportunity, daring.'

As he recited these virtues, most of which I endorsed, I saw these three earnest visitors in a different light. They were striving to hold back the tides of change which threatened to engulf them. They really did long to recover the simpler life of 1844 and find refuge in its rural patterns, its heroic willingness to defend its principles, its dedication to a more disciplined society. I understood their feelings, for all men in all ages have such yearnings.

When we broke for a belated lunch, Miss Cobb, a descendant of Democratic senators, asked the speakers: 'By what route did you become Republicans? Surely, your parents were Democrats.'

The Abilene woman laughed uneasily: 'My father knew only one Republican family. A renegade who joined that party so that the Republican administration in Washington could nominate him postmaster. Father would cross the street to avoid speaking to the scoundrel.' The Corpus Christi man said: 'You mustn't get into that with children. Our families were all Democrats. Nobody thought of being anything else before the 1928 election, when they had to vote Republican to fight Al Smith and his boozing ways.'

Smiling amiably, the San Angelo man said: 'If you do have to explain it, why not use the old joke? Man asked a rancher in the Fort Stockton area: "Caleb, your six boys are all good Democrats, I hope?" and Caleb said: "Yep, all but Elmer. He learned to read." But I agree with the others. Best to omit the whole question.'

I said: 'You seem to be recommending that we omit a good deal of Texas history,' and the dour Corpus Christi man said: 'A good history is characterized by what's left out.'

I said I'd appreciate an example, and he was more than equal to the occasion: 'In the decades after the great storm of 1900 that destroyed Galveston, loyal citizens rebuilt the city, pretty much as you see it here today. But with their enormous losses and few businesses to take up the slack, how could they earn money? They turned the city into a vast amusement area—houses of ill repute, gambling, gaudy saloons. Men from my city . . .'

'And mine, too,' the San Angelo man chimed in. 'They came here to raise hell in Galveston. Wildest city in America, they boasted.'

'Do we need to include that in a book for children?' the Corpus Christi man asked, and I had to reply 'No,' and he smiled icily: 'There is much that can be profitably omitted.'

At our lunch I wanted to make peace with our vigorous critics and said: 'I'm sure I speak for our entire Task Force when I say that while we must disagree with certain of your positions, we support many of them. Like you, we feel that modern children are pressured to grow up too fast. We deplore drugs. We champion private property. We agree that too often the negative aspects of our society are stressed. And we subscribe to Texas patriotism.'

'What don't you agree with?' the Corpus Christi man challenged, and I answered him as forthrightly as I could: 'We think women have played an important role in all aspects of Texas life. We think Mexicans are here to stay. We think

Texas should be proud of its multinational origins. And we are not monolithic. Rusk and Quimper are strong Republicans; Miss Cobb and Garza, equally strong Democrats.'

'What about you?' the San Angelo man asked amiably, and I said: 'I'm like the old judge in Texarkana during a heated local election who was asked which candidate he supported: "They're both fine men. Eminently eligible for the big post, they think. Haven't made up my mind yet, but when I do I'm gonna be damned bitter about it." '

Dr. Clay started his presentation on Texas weather with three astonishing slides: 'Here you see the Clay residence in Wichita Falls at seven-oh-nine in the evening of the tenth of April 1979. That's me looking up in the sky. This second slide, taken by a neighbor across the street, shows what we were staring at.'

It was an awesome photograph, widely reproduced later, for it showed in perfect detail the structure of a great tornado just about to strike: 'Note three things. The enormous black cloud aloft, big enough to cover a county. The clearly defined circular tunnel dropping toward the ground. And the snout of the destroying cloud, trailing along behind like the nozzle of a vacuum cleaner.'

When Clay started to move to the next slide, Rusk stopped him: 'Why does the snout trail?'

'Aerodynamics. It lingers upon the ground it's destroying.'

He then showed us the most remarkable slide of the three: 'This is the Clay residence one minute after the tornado struck.' No upright part of the former house was visible; it was a total destruction, with even the heavy bathtub ripped away and gone.

'How could the man with the camera take such a picture?' Rusk asked, and Miss Cobb wanted to know: 'What happened to you?'

'That's the mystery of a tornado. Its path of destruction is as neatly defined as a line drawn with a pencil. On our side of the street, total wipe-out. Where the photographer was standing . . . merely a big wind.'

'Yes, but where were you?' Miss Cobb persisted.

'Just before it struck, the man with the camera shouted: "Lewis! Over here!" He could see where the pencil line was heading.'

'Remarkable,' Quimper said, but Clay corrected him: 'No, the miracle was that the tornado lifted not only the bathtub from our wreckage but also my mother. Carried her right along with the tub and deposited them both as gently as you please a quarter of a mile away.'

Then, with a series of beautifully drawn meteorological slides, he instructed us on the genesis of the tornadoes which each year struck Texas so violently: 'Four conditions are required before a tornado is spawned. A cold front sweeps in from the Rockies in the west. It hits low-level moist air from the Gulf. Now, this happens maybe ninety times a year and accounts for normal storms of no significance. But sometimes a third factor intrudes. Very dry air rushing north from Mexico. When it hits the front, which is already agitated, severe thunderstorms result, but rarely anything worse. However, if the fourth air mass moves in, a majestic jet stream at thirty thousand feet, it's as if a cap were clamped down over the entire system. Then tornadoes breed and tear loose and do the damage you saw at Wichita Falls.'

'How bad was that damage?' Quimper asked, and Clay said: 'It smashed a path eight miles long, a mile and a half wide. Four hundred million dollars in destruction, forty-two dead, several hundred with major injuries.'

In rapid fire he sped through a series of stunning photographs, throwing statistics at us as he went: 'Most Texas tornadoes strike in May. We get a steady average of a hundred and thirty-two per year, and they produce a yearly average of thirteen deaths. Most tornadoes we ever had in one day, a hundred and fifteen shockers on a September afternoon in 1967. The funnel rotates counterclockwise and can travel over the ground at thirty-five miles an hour, almost always in a southwest-to-northeast direction, and with a funnel wind velocity of up to three hundred miles an hour.'

Numbed by the violent force of the pictures and words, we had no questions, but he added two interesting facts: 'Yes, what you've heard is true. A Texas tornado can have winds powerful enough to drive a straw flying through the air right through a one-inch plank. And there really is such a thing as Tornado Alley. It runs from Abilene northeast through Larkin and Wichita Falls.' Looking directly at Ransom Rusk, who lived in that middle town, he said: 'Statistics are overwhelming. Most dangerous place to be during a tornado is an automobile. The wind picks it up, finds it too heavy, dashes it to the ground. Best place?' He flashed his third slide, the one showing the destruction of his own house: 'Pick your spot. But if you have a tornado cellar, use it.'

The next two hours were compelling, for he gave a similar analysis of the great hurricanes that spawned off the coast of Africa and came whipping across the Atlantic into the Gulf of Mexico, and we sat appalled as he showed us what had happened to Galveston on 8 September 1900: 'Worst natural disaster ever to strike America. Entire city smitten. Whole areas erased by a fearful storm surge that threw twelve feet of water inland. Up to eight thousand lives lost in one night.'

One remarkable series of shots taken by four different photographers on a single March day in 1983 showed Amarillo in a snow-and-sleet storm at 29° Fahrenheit, Abilene in the middle of a huge dust storm at 48°, Austin at the beginning of a blue norther at 91° and Brownsville in the midst of an intolerable heat wave at 103°. 'From northwest to southeast, a range of seventy-four degrees. I wonder how many mainland states can match that kind of wild variation?'

He spoke also of the famous blue norther, which had amazed Texans since the days of Cabeza de Vaca: 'These phenomenal drops in temperature can occur during any month of the year, but of course they're most spectacular during the summer months, when the sudden drop is conspicuous, but the daddy of all blue northers hit the third of February in 1899. Temperature at noon in many parts of the state, a hundred and one. Temperature not long thereafter, minus three, a preposterous drop of a hundred and four degrees.'

But what interested me even more was his statistics on Texas droughts: 'Every decade we get a major jolt, worst ever in those bad years 1953 to 1957. Much worse than the so-called Dust Bowl years. We really suffered, and the law of probability assures us that one of these days we'll suffer again.'

Clay was a man of great common sense. After decades of studying Texas weather, he had come to see the state as a mammoth battleground over which and on which the elements waged incessant war, with powerful effect upon the people who occupied that ground: 'No human being would settle here, with our incredibly hot summers and our violent storms from the heavens and the sea, if he did not relish the struggle and feel that with courage he could survive. What other state has tornadoes and hurricanes that kill more than sixty people year after year? And blue northers and drought and hundred-degree days for two whole months?' He looked at me, and knowing one of my preoccupations, added: 'And a constant drop in its aquifers? This is heroic land and it demands heroic people.'

XII
THE TOWN

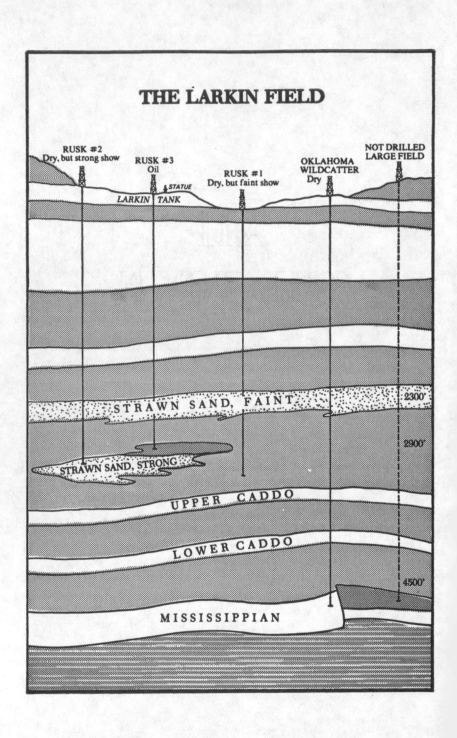

THE LARKIN FIELD

RUSK #2
Dry, but strong show

RUSK #3
Oil

RUSK #1
Dry, but faint show

OKLAHOMA
WILDCATTER
Dry

NOT DRILLED
LARGE FIELD

STATUE

LARKIN TANK

STRAWN SAND, FAINT

2300'

2900'

STRAWN SAND, STRONG

UPPER CADDO

LOWER CADDO

4500'

MISSISSIPPIAN

THE CENSUS OF 1900 ILLUSTRATED A BASIC FACT ABOUT TEXAS: IT WAS STILL A rural state, for out of its population of 3,048,710, only 17.1 percent was classified as urban, and even this was misleading because the scrawniest settlement was rated *urban* if it had more than 2,500.

The biggest city was still San Antonio, with a population of 53,321, much of it German, for the Hispanics who would later give the city its character accounted at this time for not more than 10 percent of the total. Houston was the next largest city, with a population of 44,633, and Dallas was third, with 42,638. Future cities like Amarillo and Lubbock, which would later figure prominently in Texas history, were not cities at all, the former with only 1,442 inhabitants, the latter with a mere 112.

But it was essentially in such small towns that the character of the state was developing, and three were of special interest. The first, of course, was the frontier town of Larkin in the west, with a population of 388. The second was that charming agricultural town with the elfin name, Waxahachie, in the north-central area, just south of Dallas; it had a population of 4,215. And the third was the fascinating little Hispanic town of Bravo, about as far south as one could go in Texas. It stood on the north bank of the Rio Grande in an area where irrigation would turn what had once been unwieldy brushland into one of the most concentrated farming areas in America. Bravo, with a population of 389, guarded the American end of a small bridge over the river; Escandón, a somewhat larger town, marked the Mexican end.

As the nineteenth century drew to a close, the town of Larkin, the seat of Larkin County, found itself embroiled in an intellectual argument which preoccupied a good many other communities: When did the new century begin?

Tradition, accepted modes of expression and popular opinion all agreed that at midnight on 31 December 1899 an old century would die, with a new one beginning a minute later. To any practical mind, even the name of the new year, 1900, indicated that a new system of counting had begun, and to argue otherwise was ridiculous: 'Any man with horse sense can see it's a new century, elsen why would they of given it a new name?'

Yet Earnshaw Rusk, like many thinking men and women across the state, knew that the twentieth century could not possibly begin until 31 December 1900; logic, history and mathematics all proved they were correct, but these zealots had a difficult time persuading their fellow citizens to delay celebrating until the proper date. 'Damn fools like Earnshaw cain't tell their ear from their elbow,' said one zealot. 'Any idiot knows the new century begins like we say, and I'm gonna be ringin' that church bell come New Year's Eve and Jim Bob Loomis is gonna be lightin' the fire.'

Rusk found such plans an insult to intelligence. 'Tell me,' he asked Jim Bob, 'now I want you to just tell me, how many years in a century?' He had stopped using the Quaker *thee* in public.

'A hunnert,' Jim Bob said.

'At the time of Christ, when this all began, was there ever a year zero?'

'Not that I heerd of.'

'So the first century must have begun with the year 1.'

'I think it did.'

'So when we reached the year 99, how many years had the first century had?'

'Sounds like ninety-nine.'

'It was ninety-nine, so the year 100 had nothing special about it. The second century couldn't have begun until the beginning of 101.'

Jim Bob pointed a warning finger at the lanky Quaker: 'You're talkin' atheism, and Reverend Hislop warned us against ideas like yourn.'

For some obscure theological reason that was never spelled out, Reverend Hislop of the Methodist church had taken a strong stand in favor of 1900 as the beginning of the new century, and he had equated opposition to that view as being against the will of God: 'Every man in his right mind knows that the new century begins when it does, and misguided persons who try to argue otherwise are deluded.'

When Rusk asked him: 'All right, how many years were there in the first century?' the clergyman snapped: 'One hundred, like anyone knows.'

'And how could that be?' Rusk pressed. 'How could thy century begin at year 1 and end at year 99 and still have a hundred years?' and the reverend replied: 'Because God willed it that way.' And that became the general opinion of the community; if God had wanted His first century, when Christianity began, to have only ninety-nine years, it was only a small miracle for Him to make it so.

As December 1899 ended, the wood for the bonfire at the south end of the former parade ground grew higher and higher, with most families contributing odd pieces to the pile. Jim Bob supervised the throwing on of additional pieces until a ladder was required to reach the top, and then schoolboys took over the task. Ladies from the two major churches, Baptist and Methodist, prepared a nonalcoholic punch, and a band rehearsed a set of marches.

This irritated Earnshaw, who asked his wife: 'Emma, how can people fly int the face of fact?' and she replied: 'Easy. I sort of like 1900 myself. Obviously the beginning of something new.'

Such reasoning disgusted her husband, who withdrew to the companionship of seven other men—no women engaged in such nonsense—who remained convinced that their century, at least, would start at midnight on 31 December 1900 and not before. They remained aloof from the celebrations, so they did not hear Reverend Hislop intone the prayer which welcomed the new century for everyone else:

'Almighty God, we put to rest an old century, one which brought the Republic of Texas victory in war and membership in the Federal Union. It brought us anguish during the War Between the States and sore tribulation when the Indians attacked us and niggers tried to run things. But we have won free. We have settled the wilderness and conquered distance. We have a glorious town where unobstructed winds used to howl, and the prospects ahead are infinite and glorious.

'We cannot foresee what this twentieth century will bring us, but we have good cause to hope that war will be no more, and it is not idle to think that before the century is far gone we shall have a planing mill providing lumber for the many small houses we shall build. Our town is situated so that it must grow, the Boston of the West, with fine churches and perhaps even a college of distinction. I see great accomplishment for this town. Hand in hand with the new century, we shall march to greatness.'

Either the town or the century was laggard, because the year 1900 was one of drought, dying cattle and frustrated hopes about the planing mill. Banker Weatherby, always eager to advance the commercial prospects of his town and willing to risk his own capital, had put together a consortium of interests that had accumulated a purse of thirteen thousand dollars with which to entice a planing mill to start operations on trees hauled in by the railroad, but in July the venture failed, with the Larkin men losing their shirts. Even Weatherby, a perpetual optimist, was heard to say as he closed the books on this latest failure: 'If God had wanted a planing mill in this town, He'd have given us trees instead of rattlesnakes.'

Rusk lost eight hundred dollars on the deal, which caused him to tell Emma: 'I warned people that 1900 was bound to be a year of ill omen,' at which she snorted: 'You talk as crazy as Reverend Hislop.'

'What do you mean?'

'Well, he says God was in favor of 1900. You argue that nature is against 1900. I don't see much difference.'

Emma Rusk, forty-three now, believed in God and supported the Methodist church in a desultory sort of way, but she avoided theological discussion: 'I think a church is a good thing to have in a town. It civilizes people, especially young people, and it deserves our support. But the mysteries it tries to sell . . . some of the things that Reverend Hislop preaches . . . I can do without them.'

She deplored her husband's gambling on the mill: 'We could have given that money to Floyd to help with our two granddaughters. Don't ever mention a planing mill to me again.'

She now thought more kindly of her son than she had in the past, for at twenty-five he was becoming more like a man. He was still grossly overweight, some two hundred and fifty pounds, and his wife, Molly, was much the same at two-twenty. But they had produced two lively girls: Bertha, aged four, and Linda, eleven months. The children looked as if they were going to have their grandfather's ranging height and their grandmother's lively attitude toward the world about them. They showed no signs of being especially intelligent, but Bertha did seem to have her mother's gift for organizing her little world in the way she wanted.

Emma judged that her son had a fighting chance to make something of himself despite his surly temper and his abhorrence of his father, for Floyd could work; the trouble was, as Emma saw it: 'He never sticks at anything. If I had to leave the handling of our cattle to him, heaven knows what would happen.' Fortunately, she could rely on Paul Yeager, two years older than Floyd and two centuries wiser. The Yeagers now occupied a considerable acreage north of the tank, but as the father pointed out to Emma one morning: 'Earnshaw gave us our first two hundred acres, but he's never entered the deed at the courthouse. Would you remind him that my boy and I are putting a lot of work into those acres? We'd feel safer . . .'

'Of course you would! I'll tell him to get jumpin'.'

In mid-December she told her husband: 'Earnshaw, it isn't right to leave those Yeagers dangling without title to their land. Go to the courthouse and fix that up, please.'

'Thee is right!' There was no argument about the propriety of formalizing the gift, and Earnshaw said that he would attend to it as soon as he and his logician had ushered in the new century properly.

The seven men who had sided with Rusk in his defense of reason were now having a high old time preparing to greet the new century; no church would help them celebrate, for it was already acknowledged that God had ordained 1900 to be the year of change, and troublemakers like Rusk and his gang were seen as disrupters of the peace. Their argument that the first century could not possibly have had ninety-nine years had long since been disposed of, and they were largely ignored as they went about the serious business of greeting their new century.

Denied the use of any public building and supported by only one of their eight wives, these stubborn citizens met at eleven on the night of 31 December 1900, with Rusk uttering this prediction:

> 'Mark my words, and we must get this into the *Defender* as our prediction, in the year 1999 the citizens of this town will relive our debate. Those with no sense of history or responsibility to fact will fire cannon and light bonfires as the last day of that year draws to a close. And I suppose there will be talk of God's preference, too, same as now. But the knowing ones will gather on the last night of the year 2000 to greet the twenty-first century as it really begins on the first day of January 2001.
>
> 'I don't drink, but I do propose a toast to those valiant souls a hundred years from now. It is something, in this world of shifting standards, to respect the great traditions, and tonight I can think of none finer than the one which says: "No century can have ninety-nine years." Gentlemen, with my water and your wine, let us toast common sense.'

It was rumored later, after the tragic events of the evening, that Earnshaw Rusk, the Quaker who personified sobriety, had drunk himself silly with wine at his false New Century, but others like Jim Bob Loomis, who had built the bonfire at the real celebration, argued that God had intervened because of Rusk's blasphemy over the false beginning. At any rate, when Rusk left the celebration and started to cross the old parade ground in the shadow of his beloved courthouse, two young cowboys from the Rusk ranch rode hell for leather into the courthouse square, in about the same way their fathers had invaded Dodge City.

Earnshaw saw the first young fellow and managed to sidestep his rearing horse, but he did not see the second, whose horse panicked, knocked Earnshaw to the ground, and trampled him about the head.

The fifty-nine-year-old Quaker was in such strong condition that his heart and lungs kept functioning even though consciousness was lost, never to be regained. For three anguished days he lingered, a man of great rectitude whose body refused to surrender. Emma stayed by his bed, hoping that he would recognize her, and even Floyd came in to pay his grudging respects; he had never liked his father and deemed it appropriate that Earnshaw should die in this ridiculous manner, defending one more preposterous cause.

On the fourth day a massive cerebral hemorrhage induced a general paralysis, but still he held on; it was as if his mortal clock had been wound decades ago and set upon a known course from which it would not deviate. Indeed, as the doctor said: 'It looks like he refuses to die. He's dead, but his heart won't admit it.'

On the sixth day his damaged brain deteriorated so badly that Death actually came into the room and said softly: 'Come on, old fellow. I've won.' But even this challenge was ignored. Clenching his hands, Earnshaw held on to the sides of the bed, and his legs tried to grasp the bed, too, so that when the end finally came, they had to pry him loose.

On the day of the funeral four Comanche rode into town from the reservation at Camp Hope, and at the graveside they were permitted to chant. Floyd Rusk and his wife were infuriated by this paganism and this hideous reminder of what had happened to Floyd's mother decades ago, and they were further outraged when Emma Rusk, with no ears and a wooden nose, joined the Indians in their chant, using the language with which her ill-starred husband had hoped to tame these avengers of the Texas plains.

The tragedy at Lammermoor, for it could be called nothing less, had begun one morning in 1892 when a field hand ran to the big house, shouting: 'Mastah Cobb, somethin' awful in the cotton bolls.'

Laurel Cobb, the able son of Senator Cobb and Petty Prue and now in charge of the plantation, hurried out to see what minor disaster had struck this time, but he soon found it to be major. 'Half the cotton plants have been invaded by a beetle,' he told his wife, Sue Beth, when he returned.

'Much damage?'

'Total. The heart of the lint has been eaten out.'

'You mean our cotton's gone?'

'Exactly what I mean,' and he took her out to the extensive fields to see the awful damage, this sudden assault upon their way of life.

That was the year when the boll weevil first appeared in the fields of East Texas, and in each succeeding year the scourge became more terrible. Entire plantations were wiped out, and there was no countermeasure to halt this devastation. The weevil laid its eggs in the ripening boll, and as the larvae matured they ate away the choicest part of the lint. When the weevil finished, the plant was worthless.

When times had been good, Cobb was like everyone else in Texas: 'I want no interference from government,' but now when trouble struck he expected immediate help, and he was the first in his district to demand that something be done. A young expert from A&M, a most gloomy man, was sent to share with the local planters what was known:

'Cotton is indigenous to various locations throughout the world. India and Egypt, for example. But our strain comes from Mexico, and a very fine strain it is, one of the best.

'When it jumped north it left behind its major enemies. But now they're beginning to catch up. The boll weevil came across the border into Texas first. Seems to move about two hundred and ten miles a year. Soon it'll be in Mississippi, Alabama. It's sure to move into Georgia and the Carolinas.

'We know of nothing that will halt it, or kill it. All we can do is pray that it will run its course, like a bad cold, or that some other insect will attack it and keep it in bounds. My advice to you? Move to better land, farther west, where it doesn't dominate, because the boll weevil has a built-in compass. It needs moisture and moves always toward the east, seeking it.'

The situation was as bad as he said, and from 1892 to 1900, Cobb watched his once glorious plantation, 'the pride of the bayou' he called it, fall almost into ruin. Fields which had once shipped boatloads and then trainloads of bales to New Orleans could now scarcely put together fifty usable bales.

At the turn of the century, in deep dejection, he went to his wife: 'Sue Beth, we can't fool ourselves any longer. Our fields are doomed.'

'You think Lammermoor is finished?'

'Not if we could find something to kill the weevil. Or some new kind of fertilizer. Or if the government could breed a new strain which could protect itself . . .'

'But you don't expect such miracles?'

He did not answer. Instead, he took from his pocket a report from a cotton growers' advisory committee: 'These men say there's wonderful new land near a place called Waxahachie.'

'What a strange name for a town.'

'I haven't seen it, but from what they say, it could prove our salvation.' He took the train to Waxahachie, and returned bubbling with enthusiasm: 'I can get a thousand acres at thirty-one cents an acre.'

'But hasn't the weevil reached there, too?'

'It has, but the rainfall is so much less, the experts have worked out ways to control it . . . more or less.'

'So you've decided to move?'

'I have.'

'Will we be able to sell this plantation?'

'Who would be so crazy as to buy?'

'Does that mean we lose everything?'

'We lose very little. What we do is transfer it to Devereaux. He claims he can operate it at a small profit.'

Devereaux Cobb was a gentle throwback to the eighteenth century. Forty years old and self-trained in the classics, he was the late-born son of that red-headed Reuben Cobb of Georgia who had died at Vicksburg, but he had inherited none of his father's verve and courage. A big, flabby bachelor afraid of women, he had dedicated himself to tending the white-columned plantation home built by his parents; in lassitude he tried vainly to keep alive the cherished traditions of the Deep South, and although he had no cadre of slaves to tend the lawns as in the old days, he did have hired blacks who deferred to his whims by calling him Marse Devvy while he called them Suetonius and Trajan. He was a kindly soul, a remnant of all that was best in that world which the Texas Southrons had striven to preserve.

Since his widowed mother, Petty Prue, had become the second wife of one-armed Senator Cobb, he had a direct claim to at least half the Jefferson holdings, and now Laurel and his wife were offering him their half: 'You were meant to be the custodian of some grand plantation, Devereaux. We leave this place in good hands.'

'I try,' he said.

On the way home from the lawyer's office where the papers of transmittal were signed, Laurel said to his wife: 'Devereaux's not a citizen of this world. He feels he must hold on to Lammermoor as a gesture, a defense of Southern tradition.' They visualized Devereaux, forty and unmarried, occupying in solemn grandeur the great houses which had once counted their inhabitants in the twenties and thirties. He would combine the libraries and sell off some of the pianos and try to get along with four black servants from the town. Some of the fields he would abandon to weevils and weeds, but others he would farm out on shares in hopes of earning enough to support himself. The afternoons would be long and hot, the summer nights filled with insects. Steamers would no longer call at the wharf, for the Red River now flowed freely to join the Mississippi; 'Jefferson's throat been cut,' as the natives said.

There was still a belief in Northern states that everything in Texas prospered, a carryover from the G.T.T. days, and invariably it did, for some years, but failure was as easy to achieve here as it was in Massachusetts or West Virginia. The woods of East Texas contained as many failed plantations as the plains and prairies of West Texas displayed the charred roots of what had once been farmhouses and ranch headquarters. Some said: 'The armorial crest of Texas should be an abandoned house whose root stumps barely show.'

'Devereaux will survive,' Laurel said as he and Sue Beth packed their last belongings, 'but I do wish he'd take himself a wife before we leave.'

'I've been brooding about that,' his wife said. She was a practical woman, much like her mother-in-law, Petty Prue, and it bothered her to think that a notable catch like Devereaux was inheriting this mansion without a wife to help him run it.

She had therefore scoured the town of Jefferson, striving to find a suitable woman to occupy the place, and she told her husband: 'I'd accept any likely woman from age nineteen to fifty. But I find no one in all of Jefferson fitted to the task.'

'Devereaux's the one to do the judging,' her husband said. 'How do you know he wants a wife?'

'He'll do what I tell him,' she responded, and she was soon off to the major town of Marshall, over the line in the next county, and there she heard of an attractive young widow with a baby daughter. The candidate was from an Alabama family of excellent reputation, which cemented her position with Sue Beth: 'Devereaux would never consider a wife who wasn't from the South, but this one is, and she's a charmer.'

She was that, a twenty-nine-year-old of delicate breeding and considerable poise, with a two-year-old daughter named Belle who had been trained to be a prim little lady. The mother spoke in a low voice, held herself very erect when meeting strangers, and was, said a neighbor, 'the perfect picture of Southern womanhood at its best.'

Sue Beth, eager to safeguard Devereaux's future before leaving Jefferson, wanted to approach the problem frontally, but she knew that this would offend the niceties observed by Southern women, so she said tentatively: 'I do wish you could visit Lammermoor one day.'

As if totally ignorant of what was afoot, the widow said quietly: 'I've heard it's delightful.'

'It is, and alas, we're leaving it.'

'Oh, are you?'

'And when we go, Devereaux . . .' Sue Beth hesitated shyly. 'He'll take over, of course.'

'I've heard of him. People refer to him as the last of the Southern gentlemen.' She knew the names of all the unmarried gentlemen in two counties.

'My husband and I would be so honored if you . . . and your delightful daughter . . .' Both women hesitated, then Sue Beth took the widow's hands: 'You would honor us if you were to assent . . .'

'It is I who would be honored,' and when the widow and her daughter were seated beside the Cobbs on the new train to Jefferson, the purpose of the visit was clearly understood even though it had not yet been mentioned.

At the station, a painfully embarrassed Devereaux waited with a curtained wagon driven by Suetonius, and after awkward introductions were completed, Sue Beth whispered to her guest: 'You'll find him a crotchety bachelor but delightful,' and Laurel added important reassurance: 'He comes from the finest South Carolina and Georgia blood, and the plantation is all his and paid for.'

It was the kind of meeting that had often happened along the Texas frontier, where death was arbitrary and widowhood commonplace. A farm of eighty acres needed a woman to bake the bread, or a plantation of twenty thousand acres needed a mistress to grace the mansion, so friends searched the countryside;

fumbling introductions were completed; a minister who knew neither bride nor groom was summoned; and the life of Texas went on.

At Lammermoor, such a wedding was arranged.

From Lammermoor to Waxahachie was about one hundred and fifty miles, similar to the distance from New York to Baltimore or Berlin to Hamburg, but in Texas this moved the Cobbs across three radically different types of terrain: pine belt, oak forest, and the rich and rolling blacklands of which Waxahachie was the capital. More significant to the welfare of cotton, the Cobbs had escaped the dank bayou country, where the rainfall neared fifty inches a year, and had come to more manageable lands with about thirty-five inches.

The topsoil was eighteen to thirty inches deep, free of large rocks and often invitingly level; since earlier owners had removed the trees, Cobb could start using the land immediately. The boll weevil had of course reached here in its plundering surge out of Mexico, but by the time the Cobbs took over, the once-gloomy expert from A&M was actually smiling with reassuring news:

> 'We're a lot brighter now than when I talked with you during those dark days in Jefferson. We've wrestled with the little devil and come out ahead. First thing you have to do, Cobb, is plant a variety of cotton that bolls early. Earlier the better, because then you have a chance of picking it before the weevil starts. Second, plant a trap-crop of corn between the rows. The weevil really loves corn. Let 'em eat that instead of your cotton bolls. Third, and maybe the most important, you have got to burn your stalks in August, September fifteenth latest, because then the stinkers have no place to breed. Fourth, thank whatever god directs your movements that you've come to Waxahachie, because the rainfall is so much less. Weevils love wet, and out here you'll dust them off. Fifth, we aren't sure whether it will work or not, but we've had some promising results from arsenic. Poison the little bastards.'

By following this military advice, Cobb not only got his new cotton plantation started, but by the close of the first year, found himself with such a rich crop that it was reasonable for him to build his own gin, and this made him one of the major farming figures in the area. To his surprise, he found himself following exactly the advice proffered by the intrusive Northern newspaperman Elmer Carmody when he visited the Jefferson plantations in 1850, and which the original Cobbs had resented so strenuously: 'Sue Beth, I burst out laughing when I realized that I was growing the best cotton in the world without the help of slaves, without even one black man working for me. All whites. All working for wages.

just as Carmody predicted. I owe him an apology,' and he saluted the place in the bookcase where *Texas Good and Bad* stood.

Carefully calculating his profit, he built a modest house for Sue Beth and the children, and with the money left over he associated himself with other cotton people, all of them pooling their funds to underwrite less well-to-do farmers who wanted to get into the business. To his delight he saw the sale price per pound rise from eight cents in 1901 to twelve in 1903. By 1905, when the price remained high, he was the leading agriculturist in the region and a king of the cotton industry, insofar as the boll weevil allowed anyone to gloat.

'I wish there was another crop we could grow,' Cobb complained one night when he realized how totally dependent he was on cotton, but he could devise none which would produce the safe yields and assured profits that cotton did. As early as 1764 the Cobbs of Edisto Island in South Carolina had wanted to diversify their crops, but the presence of slaves to manage the cotton fields and pick the lint from the seed kept them imprisoned in that economy; the Cobbs had made statistical studies which proved that they were penalized by this adherence to one crop and were prepared to branch out when Eli Whitney invented his miraculous gin, which revolutionized the industry, and they fell back, entrapped in lint.

In Texas it had been the same. All the Cobbs who settled there had wanted to diversify—'to break away from our bondage to New Orleans and England,' Senator Cobb had cried in several of his speeches—but none had done so, and now in their new home, on land which would have welcomed different forms of agriculture, Laurel Cobb and his wife persisted with their cotton.

'We're prisoners of that damned fiber,' Laurel cried one night. 'It binds us to it like the threads of a spider binding its victims.' Then he laughed: 'But it's a glorious bondage. No farmer in the world enjoys a better life than the man who owns a cotton plantation and his own gin.'

Such thinking was making Texas the world's most important cotton-producing area. Strangers thought of the Carolinas and Georgia as the capitals of the Cotton Kingdom, but inexorably the centers were moving west and coming to rest in Texas, and on some mornings in the autumn when Laurel and Sue Beth rode into Waxahachie they were dazzled by the splendor of the scene which greeted them and of which they were a leading part.

'God, this is a fine sight!' Laurel cried one day when bright October sunlight filled the central square, and he was justified in his assessment.

Waxahachie had a town square of most pleasing dimensions, for it was compact and lined on four sides with fine low buildings, some of real distinction, yet it was spacious enough to accommodate the red-and-gray masterpiece of that inspired courthouse builder James Riely Gordon. Here, with a budget more than twice what the less affluent men of Larkin County had been able to put together, Gordon had built a fairy-tale palace ten stories high, replete with battlements and turrets and spires and soaring clock towers and miniature castles high in the air. It was a bejeweled treasure, yet it was also a sturdy, massive court of judgments, one of the finest buildings in Texas.

But it was not the noble courthouse which captivated Laurel Cobb this morning; it was what crowded in upon the building, cramming the copious square that surrounded it, for here the cotton growers of the region had brought cartloads of the best cotton, more than two thousand bales, their brown burlap sacking barely hiding the rich white cotton crop.

Here was the wealth of Texas, these mountains of cotton bales, these pyramids, these piles strewn before the courthouse where buyers would come to make their choices; trains would carry the bales to all parts of the nation and to Europe, and even to Asia or wherever else cloth was needed.

'Look at it!' Laurel shouted to his wife as he reined in their horses. 'This will go on forever.'

When he compared this vital, robust scene to the tentative, cautious way they had been living previously on their plantation in the dark woods at Jefferson, he impulsively kissed his wife and exclaimed: 'My God, am I glad we came to Waxahachie!'

In the chain of Spanish-speaking counties which lined the Texas side of the Rio Grande, three types of elections were held, each with its highly distinctive character. There were, of course, the general statewide elections in November in which Democrats contested with Republicans for the governorship of Texas or the presidency of the United States, but because of the lingering animosities growing out of the Reconstruction years, when Black Republicans tormented the state, no Republican would be elected to major office in Texas for nearly a century. So these November elections were a formality.

The statewide election which counted came in the summer, when Democrats, often of the most lethal persuasion, fought for victory in their primary, for then tempers rose so high that sometimes gunfire resulted. Prior to 1906, the Democrats had nominated their contenders in convention, which encouraged chicanery, but in that year a reform act was passed requiring nomination by public election, with a lot of frills thrown in so that the professionals could still dominate. Now statewide brawls took place, and nowhere were these new primaries more corrupt than along the Rio Grande, where some county would have a precinct with a total population of 356, counting women, who were not eligible to vote, and their babies, and report late on election night that its favorite Democrat had won by a vote of 343 to 14. Quite often two Texas Democrats of great probity, one a judge from along the Red River in the north, the other a distinguished state senator from the Dallas area, would conduct high-level campaigns across the state, only to see their fate determined in the so-called Mexican Counties of the Rio Grande, where elections were conducted with the grossest fraud.

But it was the third type of Rio Grande election which displayed Texas politics at its rawest. This was the strictly local election, town or county, in which Republicans and Democrats vied evenly, victory going first to one, then the other. A local election in these counties could be horrendous.

How, if Texas never voted Republican statewide, could that party expect to win local elections along the river? The answer was threefold: legal citizens of Texas who could not speak English could be manipulated by bosses; citizens of Mexico could be handed fake poll-tax certificates and enrolled as Republicans or Democrats; and the presence of the international bridges that gave employment to political henchmen. These bridges were sorry affairs, often wooden and sometimes one-lane, but they were staffed by customs officials appointed in Washington, and since these were years when Republican Presidents like McKinley, Roosevelt and Taft ran the country, it was their Republican appointees who ran the bridges. Republicans hired local toll collectors and customs inspectors. Republicans controlled the flow of federal funds, and Republican functionaries, often newcomers from Republican states in the North, were told by Washington: 'Forget the statewide offices but vote your county Republican, or else.'

Sixty miles upstream from where the Rio Grande debouches into the Gulf of Mexico, a rickety wooden bridge connected Mexico and the United States, and on each bank of the river a small town of little consequence had grown up; the bridge was more important than either of the towns.

As was to be the rule along the entire reach of the Rio Grande, and along the land border as well in New Mexico, Arizona and California, whenever two such towns faced each other in the two countries, it was invariably the Mexican one which came to be the larger. Thus, Matamoros with its advantageous Zona Libre (free customs zone) was larger than Brownsville; Reynosa, much larger than Hidalgo; Nuevo Laredo, substantially bigger than the Texas Laredo; and, to the surprise of many, Ciudad Juárez, bigger than El Paso.

The reasons for this were clear. No Texan town bordering Mexico constituted any irresistible magnet drawing Texas citizens wishing to settle there permanently; Dallas was always a much more promising town than Laredo. But the contrary was not true; Mexican citizens caught in the poverty-stricken parts of northern Mexico were lured to the border towns, where jobs across the river might become available and where American stores stocked with bargains were a temptation. There were a hundred reasons why Mexicans sought to crowd the Rio Grande, and they did.

At this particular bridge the rule prevailed. At the Mexican end the town of Escandón, named after the excellent man who had explored this region, contained about two thousand citizens; on the Texan end the little town of Bravo had less than half that number. The bridge was important, and sometimes it seemed as if the history of the county was identical with that of the bridge.

In these early years of the century the Bravo Customs Office was occupied by a ruthless gentleman of great ability and considerable charm. He was a big, brawling, red-headed Irishman named Tim Coke, imported from New York, forty years old and a graduate of that corrupt school of Republicanism which existed only to fight the worse corruption of Tammany Democrats. With the brazen assistance of three others like him from Eastern cities and nine tough local men, Tim Coke had long ago declared war on the Saldana Democrats, and saw this year of 1908 as a real chance for victory: 'Time has come to turn this county Republican, once and for all. Last two local elections we won one, lost one. This year we nail it down.'

In Saldana County, as elsewhere along the Rio Grande, it was the custom to smuggle across the river large numbers of Mexican nationals, pay each one a small fee, vote him illegally, and send him back to the jacales south of the river. Since the legal population of the county tended to be Democratic, the Republicans were required to sneak in a good many more transient voters than the Democrats, and no one was more adept at this than tough-minded, inventive Tim Coke. A newspaperman from Austin, summarizing Texas politics, wrote: 'When loyal Democrats along the Rio Grande see red-headed Tim Coke manipulating the patronage at his bridge, they tremble.'

'The sumbitch has one big advantage over us,' the Democrats whined. 'He controls the bridge. He can march his voters across bold as you please. Ours we have to swim.'

When Coke heard such complaint he cursed: 'We may have the bridge, but they have that damned Precinct 37.' It was a legitimate protest, because the wily Democrats kept sequestered deep in the heartland of Saldana County a rural precinct which had the habit of waiting till four or five in the morning to report its tally. By then the leaders of the party in Bravo would know how many Precinct 37 votes they needed to win the election, and the call would go forth: 'Elizondo, you've got to turn in figures which give us a three hundred and three majority,' and half an hour later Elizondo would report: 'Democrats, three forty-three; Republicans, fourteen.' There was always a howl, charges of fraud, and threats of federal action, but always Elizondo explained: 'We were a little late, but up here everyone votes Blue.'

It was the rule along the Rio Grande, where vast numbers of voters could not read English, to identify the two major parties by color, which varied from county to county. In Saldana the Republicans had always been the Reds, Democrats the Blues, so that when a vote was held, each party devised some trick to help its imported constituents know how to cast the votes for which they had been paid. The color scheme was also helpful to those Hispanics who lived in Texas and were legally entitled to vote but had not yet mastered English: 'Pablo, when they hand you your ballot, you'll find a little red mark at the right place. You scratch your big X there and you get your dollar.' Before the ballot was deposited, Republican workers would erase the telltale red mark, aware that Democratic workers would be doing something similar with their blue marks.

Any election in Saldana County was apt to be a lively affair, and for two good reasons. First, after the voting booths closed and the counting began, both the Reds and the Blues threw parties for their imported voters, with tequila, hot Mexican dishes and whiskey, and if the Reds won, their partisans were apt to grow rambunctious, with the losing Blues growing resentful. Gunfire was so customary at Saldana elections that some thoughtful anglo residents said: 'It would be better if one side was clearly superior. Let them celebrate and leave the rest of us alone.'

The second reason for unrest was that Democrats, denied the patronage associated with the Customs Office, had to work extra hard, and for some years they had placed their fortunes in the hands of one of the most competent political leaders Texas had so far produced. Horace Vigil was an anglo, of that there could be no doubt, for he was somewhat taller than an ordinary Mexican, more robust, whiter of skin and more confident in manner, yet the pronunciation of his name, Vee-*heel*, indicated that at some time long past he must have had Mexican or Spanish ancestors. Much of his genial manner seemed to have stemmed from them, for he was a markedly courteous man, and when he used his fluent Spanish he sounded like a born hidalgo.

When people first saw Vigil standing beside Tim Coke they were apt to think: What an unfair competition!—for the big Irishman, with his forthright and engaging ways, was in the full force of his vigorous manhood and seemed to dominate all about him; at the bridge he was unquestionably in charge, while Vigil, twelve years older and slightly stooped, was obviously a retiring man seeking to avoid notice. He accomplished this in two ways: by twisting his torso slightly to the left, creating the impression that through diffidence or even cowardice he was going to avoid any impending unpleasantness; and by speaking in public in a voice so soft that it seemed a whisper. Women especially thought of him as 'that dear Señor Vigil.'

But if in public he gave the appearance of a somewhat bumbling and well-intentioned grandfather, in private, when surrounded only by his Spanish-speaking subordinates, he could rasp out orders in a voice that was completely domineering. In protecting his personal interests and in furthering those of the Democratic party he could be ruthless, and observers of the system warned: 'Don't touch his beer business or the way he buys his Democratic majorities.'

He had for many years operated a lumber and ice establishment, and in developing the latter he had eased over into the lucrative trade of distributing beer, so that now he controlled how men built their houses, how they stayed cool in summer, and how they relaxed when the brutally hot Rio Grande days turned into those very hot Rio Grande nights. He was not a scholarly man and he lacked formal instruction in politics, but he understood the two essentials required for governing his county: he hated customs officials—'They prey off the public, they contribute nothing to the community, they're all Northerners, and damnit, they're

Republicans'—and he loved Mexicans, holding them to be 'God's children, warm-hearted, kind to their parents, and loyal up to a point.'

He was an American patrón, one of those fiercely independent rural leaders so common in Mexico. They were self-appointed dictators who paid lip service to the central authority but continued to rule their regions according to their own vision. Horace Vigil decided who would be judge and what decisions that judge would hand down when he reached the bench; he did not collect taxes but he certainly spent them, rarely on himself but with joyous liberality among his Mexican supporters; it was he who determined which daughters of which friends got jobs in the school system; it was he to whom the people came when they needed money for a wedding or a funeral.

In return, Vigil demanded only two things: 'Vote Blue and buy my beer.' Any who voted Red found themselves ostracized; those who tried to buy their beer direct from the breweries in San Antonio awakened some morning to find their establishment afire or their beer spouts running wide open, with no thirsty patrons to catch the flowing brew.

In the 1908 local election the great showdown between Coke and Vigil occurred. Prior to the balloting, Customs Officer Coke had so many Mexican nationals in compounds just north of the river that Vigil had to become alarmed. Twice at the end of the last century Coke had stolen elections in this manner, and with rambunctious Teddy Roosevelt still in the White House, he could depend upon vigorous support from the federal courts. Indeed, word had come down from the Justice Department in Washington: 'You must break Vigil's stranglehold,' and Coke was determined to do so.

On the Friday morning prior to the election, Vigil received disturbing news: 'Señor Vigil, Señor Coke he is bringing a hundred and fifty more Reds from Mexico.' The report was true; about half these men had voted in previous elections, each receiving his dollar plus a couple of good meals for doing so, but the other half had never before stepped foot in Texas. Like the Mexicans imported earlier by Democrats, they were herded into adobe-walled compounds, and there they whiled away the time until the customs people arrived with instructions as to how they must vote.

'Héctor!' a worried Vigil called to his principal assistant, a smiling young man of eighteen, 'you've got to cross into Mexico and round up at least a hundred more votes.'

'Yes, sir!' He had spent his last three years doing little but saying 'Yes, sir' to Señor Vigil, so as soon as the orders were given he knew what to do. Reporting to the campaign treasurer, he asked for twenty dollars to entertain his voters while they were still on the Mexican side, knowing that if he could swim them across and slip them into the Blue compound, additional payoff money would be awaiting him there. With the coins secured in his belt he entered Mexico, but not via the bridge, because there the Republicans would be on watch, and if they spotted him entering Mexico they would deduce that he was going there to import more Blues, and he could hear Coke bellowing: 'Hilario, bring us a hundred more Reds.' So Héctor rode his horse west about two miles, swam it across the river, and doubled back to Escandón, where he picked up a group of congenial men who could use a dollar.

This enterprising young fellow was Héctor Garza, descendant of those Garzas who had immigrated to these parts from San Antonio in the 1790s and grandson of the outlaw Benito Garza, who had caused such consternation among the Texans in the 1850s. Héctor and his immediate forebears had been good United States citizens; he loved Texas and wanted to see it enjoy good government, which was why he associated himself with Horace Vigil.

Like the vast majority of Hispanics, he had received only spasmodic education, partly because Texas did not consider it necessary to educate Hispanic peasants and partly because he was, like Benito Garza, a free wandering spirit who could not be trapped in any schoolroom. His real education had come from watching Vigil, and he was confident that if he continued to work for the beer distributor, he would learn all that was necessary about Saldana County.

Had the election of 1908 gone according to schedule, the Democrats, with Garza's last-minute voters, would have won by a comfortable margin, but a Mexican storekeeper who acted as spy for the Customs Office alerted Tim Coke to the hidden influx of Blue voters, and Coke summoned his aides: 'Round up every Mexican in Escandón who can walk,' and this was done.

On Saturday, Vigil, having learned of this, called a meeting of his war cabinet and told them: 'We face a major crisis. Coke and his Yankees are tryin' to steal this election. If we can win it, we can hold this county for the next fifty years. Teddy Roosevelt will be out of the White House and the pressure from Washington will end. So whatever can be done must be done. If Precinct 37 has to give us five hundred to seven, it must.'

'But the precinct only has a hundred and seventy-nine registered voters.'

'Come voting day, it'll have more.'

But even so, Vigil knew that he needed some additional miracle to win, and next morning it arrived, for at about noon a man came shouting: 'Dead girl! In the bushes by the river!' And when the town officials, Republicans and Democrats alike, ran to verify the report, most of Bravo forgot the election, but Horace Vigil did not. Assembling his precinct workers, he asked them: 'How can we use this sad affair to our advantage?' and much thought was given. When the meeting ended, Héctor Garza performed his part of the strategy which had been agreed upon; he moved through the town whispering to citizens: 'The Rangers have uncovered mysterious facts, but they won't say what.'

The morning before election the voters of Saldana County read the startling details: TIM COKE, REPUBLICAN LEADER, ARRESTED FOR HIDEOUS MURDER.

Under the lash of Horace Vigil's demand that justice be done, detectives under his control had uncovered clues, not very substantial, which led to Tim Coke, so the police, also in Vigil's pay, had arrested the Republican leader. The local judge, a reliable Vigil man, had refused to issue a writ of habeas corpus, so that when the voting started, Coke was still in jail.

The Republicans did their best to preserve their slight lead; they voted their Mexicans, stole ballots when they could, and put into practice the tricks Tom Coke had mastered while fighting Tammany Hall in New York. But the awful charge that their leader had committed a murder, and of a girl, sickened the voters, and many who had intended voting Republican found themselves unable to do so.

Vigil and Garza, meanwhile, were whipping up enormous enthusiasm for the unsullied Blue cause, and even before Precinct 37 reported its traditional count— 343 to 14 in favor of the Democrats—it was known that the Blues had won.

On Wednesday, when Coke was released from jail, Vigil personally apologized: 'Deplorable mistake. The Mexican informant couldn't speak English, and the Rangers misinterpreted his information.' He also drafted a statement for the press: 'Every right-thinking citizen feels how wrong it is when a respected member of our community is subjected to unwarranted indignities. All Saldana County sends Tim Coke, custodian of our Bravo-Escandón Bridge, an apology and a solemn promise that nothing like this will ever happen again.'

With crusading Teddy Roosevelt about to leave the White House and with Precinct 37 sticking to its habit of not reporting its count till dawn, the Democrats of Saldana County appeared to be safe for the coming decades.

Laurel Cobb had never considered running for the seat in the United States Senate once held by his father, but in 1919 a surprising chain of events forced him to change his mind. To begin with, a revival tent was pitched on his farm, and as a consequence he began to teach a Sunday School class, which led to the excommunication proceedings within the Jordan Baptist congregation.

The little towns of North Texas never seemed more exciting and attractive than in those hot summers when some wandering evangelist pitched his tent in a country grove and conducted a revival. If the man was noted for either his piety or his eloquence, people streamed in from forty or fifty miles, pitching their tents or boarding with strangers. Family reunions were held; courtships were launched; choirs came from distant churches; food abounded; and for fifteen joyous days the celebration continued. But the basic attraction was the fiery religious oratory, allowing people whose lives were otherwise drab a glimpse of a more promising existence.

The revival was an important aspect of Texas culture, some thought it the major aspect, for it determined that Texas would become largely a dry state, it reinforced the power of local churches, it kept stores closed on Sundays, and it defined in fundamentalist terms what religion was. But it was also a social celebration, and the family that did not participate found itself in limbo.

Some of the wandering evangelists ranted, some threatened, while others were little more than vaudeville performers with an overlay of Old Testament religiosity. All had their loyal patrons, but there was one who excelled in all aspects of the calling. He was Elder Fry, not associated with any specific Protestant denomination but equally at home with all—Methodist, Baptist, Presbyterian, Campbellite—and a servant to all. He did not, like some others, come into a community to denigrate the local clergymen, claiming that only he had the truth while they were straying; he came to help, to ignite the fires of faith so that when he left, the resident pastors could do a better job. It was said of Fry: 'He sometimes roars but he never rants. He warns of punishment in afterlife but he does not terrify. And he never tears down, he builds up.' If the phrase 'a man of God' had any meaning, Elder Fry tried to be such a man.

In the summer of 1919 he drove his buggy south from Waxahachie to the Cobb plantation, as they called their acreage, where he met with Laurel and his wife: 'I know that a revival tent causes problems to the landowner, but if you let me use that far field, I'll keep our visitors to only one road and we'll do little damage.'

'Elder Fry,' Sue Beth interrupted, 'we think of the good life we enjoy as a gift from God, and the least we can do in return is to thank Him. Will it be for fifteen days, as usual?'

'The older I get the more I think that I ought to cut back to one week. Half as much work for everyone, but to tell you the truth, Mrs. Cobb, I need a week to instruct, a week to inspire, and that final glorious day for rejoicing and salvation. I'll need the fifteen days.'

His manner was deceptive, for he was sixty-six years old, white-haired, almost childlike, with only a modest voice incapable of filling a tent, and during the first week of a revival some had difficulty hearing him, but in the second, as he became inspired, he seemed to change: he was taller, more fiercely dedicated, and possessed of a voice which thundered its impassioned message that Jesus Christ had come down to earth to rescue human beings otherwise condemned to darkness. He never tried to force conversion, nor did he promise cures; he simply offered the testimony of a man who had lived a long life in the service of God and who believed without question that heaven awaited such faithfulness.

Laurel instructed his servants to help the old man pitch his tent and personally worked at arranging the chairs. Sue Beth helped organize the picnic tables that would be so important a part of the two-week festival, and workmen from the farm repaired the road that would give access. As a consequence, the Waxahachie revival of 1919 was one of the best; the weather was clement and the crowds tremendous. Although the recent world war had barely touched daily life in the state, it had claimed many sons of Texas, and now people wanted to celebrate the coming of peace and were ready to accept Fry's thesis that God Himself had been responsible for the victory. Cobb, listening to the long sermons, gained the impression that Fry thought that God watched over the United States with special attention and the state of Texas with a deep personal concern: 'He loves Texas, and it grieves Him when a community degrades itself with liquor. Do not cause Him remorse! Halt any evil behavior which might offend Him!'

During the second week Fry lodged with the Cobbs, at their insistence, and they enjoyed several long talks: 'Dear friends, I find in North Texas a degree of spiritual concern unmatched anywhere else. God has chosen your territory for some special commission. He holds Texas close to the bosom, for here He sees the working-out of His Holy Bible.'

On Wednesday of the final week he launched into that steady ascendancy of voice and manner which brought his revivals to such triumphant conclusions, and on Friday he preached so compellingly, Cobb got the feeling that the words were directed specifically at him. Laurel was not an overly religious person—his wife was—but he did believe that society improved when it stayed close to the Bible, so on the last Saturday night he was spiritually prepared to be touched by Fry's farewell sermon; it dealt with the Faithful Servant, and as Cobb listened to the majestic voice of this good and kindly man, he felt that he, Cobb, was undergoing what could only be termed a rebirth.

Certainly it was a rededication, for when his local Baptist minister came out to the plantation on Monday to ask a favor, Cobb greeted him warmly: 'Come in, Reverend Teeder. Wasn't that a splendid two weeks?' Teeder, a much different man from Fry, admitted grudgingly that it had been: 'But Elder Fry seems to lack the fire that marks a true man of God.' Cobb, not wishing to argue at a time when his heart was filled with new understandings, said merely: 'But he wins a lot of souls,' and Teeder said: 'For the moment, yes, but permanently, no. I believe a sterner message is required than the one he delivers.'

Teeder and the Cobbs belonged to the Jordan Baptist Church, situated in a pretty village just south of Waxahachie, and because it dominated a large rural population, it enjoyed a membership rather greater than one might have expected and a minister of more than ordinary fervor. In 1919, Simon Teeder stood at the midpoint of his religious career; he had started in a devout community in Mississippi, had been promoted to this good job in Texas, and would soon be moving on to a really important church in the new state of Oklahoma. He was an intense man, convinced that he understood God's will and driven by a determination to see it prevail.

He had been surprisingly effective in making the members of his Texas congregation feel that he, Teeder, had a personal interest in each one's welfare, and as soon as he had settled in he established two groups to help him with the work of the church. After studying carefully the character of his parishioners, he nominated seven devout men for election to the church Council; they would advise on doctrine. He then selected a quite different group of men, respected for their business acumen, to serve as his Board of Deacons; they would look after the financial and household affairs of the congregation.

When he had his structure completed—seven devout councillors, nineteen prosperous deacons—he pretty well controlled his area of rural Texas, and he exercised his control sternly:

> 'Jordan Baptist is founded on sturdy principles, and if all live up to them and glorify them in our hearts, we shall never have a rumble of trouble in this church, nor a confusion of scandal among its membership.

> 'First, we believe in the Bible as the revealed Word of God, and we accept every single passage in that Holy Book. We admit no popular modern questioning, no cheapening of that Sublime Word. If you cannot accept the Bible as written, this church cannot accept you.

> 'Second, we believe that every man who aspires to membership in our church must take it upon himself to live a Christian life, in the fullest sense of that commitment.

> 'Third, we condemn all those forms of loose and licentious living which have crept upon us since the end of the Great War, and anyone who aspires to the fellowship of this church must take a solemn oath to avoid drinking, gambling, horse racing, prize fighting, licentiousness with women, and other immoral behaviors. Particularly, young and old must reject dancing, which is the principal agency by which the devil seduces us.'

When these stricter rules had been circulated and understood, Reverend Teeder began visiting various members of his congregation, pleading with them to assume additional responsibilities for the success of Jordan Baptist, and it was largely due to his imagination and drive that his church improved yearly.

Up to now he had not visited the Cobbs, for he had good reason to suspect that Laurel did not accept the stern fundamentalism that he preached, and he wanted no dissidents or infected liberals in his congregation, but word of Cobb's strong support for Elder Fry's revival had caused Teeder to change his mind, and when he discussed the matter with the members of his Council, they agreed that Laurel was a man worth keeping within the body of the church; it was in pursuit of this decision that he drove out to see the Cobbs.

'Brother Laurel,' he said when discussion of the Fry revival ended, 'God has an important mission for you, and I pray you will accept.'

'I already tithe. Have for years.'

'It's not money, although God notices and appreciates your generosity. It's you he wants.'

'I have no calling to the ministry,' Laurel said.

'No, that comes to few, and it's as much a burden as it is a glory. I'm speaking of something much simpler.'

'What?'

'I want you to teach Sunday School. Every Sunday. To a group of young boys that I shall assemble.'

'I'd be no good at that.'

'Ah, but you would. Boys fear their minister. They see him only on the pulpit. But if you, a man like themselves, only older, a plantation owner who wrestles with his fields the way their fathers wrestle with theirs . . . That could make a great deal of difference.'

The two men talked for more than an hour, with Cobb reminding himself of how lucky their congregation had been to find this devoted minister. He had been on the search committee back in 1918 and had traveled to Mississippi to hear Teeder preach: 'He's a little too intense for my taste, but in the pulpit he glows like a burning ember. I'll vote for him.'

At the end of the hour Cobb found himself ensnared by Teeder's persuasiveness, but the manner of Cobb's submission startled the minister: 'Reverend, if you have a weakness, it's that you always speak of our church as if it were composed only of men. You ignore women.'

'I follow Jesus and St. Paul. They placed their church in the hands of men. There were no women disciples, no women preachers, no women in command of the manifold churches of Asia. A woman's responsibility is to find herself a Christian man, to support him, and to rear children who will follow Christian ways.'

'Well, I won't teach a class of boys. If you want me to help, you must arrange for a class of girls, because I want them to be a part of our church, too.'

'That's quite impossible.'

'Then my participation becomes impossible.' At this point Laurel called for his wife to join the discussion, and when Sue Beth understood what her husband was saying, she approved: 'Reverend Teeder, it's really time women were brought more closely into your church.'

'They could not serve on the Council or the Board of Deacons. That's man's work.'

'But—'

'Our church provides joyous opportunities for women. You women are too delicate to make decisions. Yet there's still much important work to be done. Ou little church seems twice as holy since you good women have been decorating with flowers.'

'We're entitled to do much more,' Sue Beth argued, but Reverend Teeder put stop to such complaint: 'Jesus and St. Paul have decided the character of th church, and you must find your spiritual happiness within the rules they established.'

So the first meeting ended in a stalemate, but as he was leaving, Teeder did make one concession: 'About that girls' Sunday School class, you could be right. Let's both ponder it,' and Cobb knew that what Teeder really meant was: I must discuss this with my councillors and my deacons.

Laurel belonged to neither group, for he was not stern enough to serve on the Council, nor had he the spare time to tend the household chores of a deacon. He was merely another silent member of one of the two major religions in North Texas: Methodist, the majority; Baptists, the more vigorous. But Cobb did take his religion seriously, as he had recently demonstrated during the revival, and he believed that God was a reality who governed the significant parts of his life.

There was nothing spurious in this Texan preoccupation with religion. Citizens like the Cobbs believed in the Bible; they tithed; and they strove to lead lives of Christian observance, if they were allowed to define what that meant. Specifically, they sought a society founded on a universal brotherhood in Christ, so long as the brotherhood did not have to include Indians, blacks or Mexicans.

On Saturday, Cobb told his wife: 'I have a feeling the men are going to approve the class for girls. They must know it's long overdue.' And on Sunday, at the conclusion of the worship services, Reverend Teeder, accompanied by Willis Wilbarger, the dour head of the Council, stopped him at the exit from the church: 'Cobb, the men have approved your idea of a class for girls, and from their group alone they've enrolled eleven young ladies for next Sunday.'

The class became a great success—eleven at the first session, then nineteen, then more than thirty. Cobb was a stern taskmaster, requiring his pupils to memorize crucial verses and to study entire chapters for later discussion. Always he drew the moral of the assignment back to life in Waxahachie, and especially to the region contiguous to Jordan Baptist. This caused Jane Ellen Wilbarger to complain to her father that 'Mr. Cobb always talks about Waxahachie and never about heaven,' a complaint which the sour-visaged man reported to the other members of the Council.

A deputation led by Reverend Teeder and Councillor Wilbarger visited Cobb, advising him that the Baptist religion concerned itself principally with spiritual matters, not temporal, and Laurel became aware that young Miss Jane Ellen Wilbarger was taking careful note of every word he said.

The real trouble arose that spring when the Waxahachie newspaper, goaded by Councillor Wilbarger, who used reports provided by his daughter, printed a list of forty-two boys and girls from Jordan Baptist who had brazenly attended a dance at the country club, where they were seen by many reliable witnesses to be doing the 'bunny hug, the fox trot, the grizzly bear, the tango and other immoral

African extravaganzas.' Of the nineteen girls listed, fifteen were members of
Laurel Cobb's Sunday School class, a fact that was noted in the report.

The newspaper appeared on Wednesday afternoon, and long before prayer
meeting convened that night, outraged members of the church were telephoning
one another and scurrying about the countryside in their new Fords and old
buggies. During the service, attended by almost every member of Jordan Baptist,
no allusion was made to the scandal, but during the long prayer Reverend
Teeder's voice broke several times when he sought guidance for the perilous tasks
which lay ahead, and at the conclusion of the prayer meeting he asked both the
deacons and the councillors to remain behind to face the infamy which had
stained their community and which threatened the foundations of their church.

Cobb, of course, was not allowed to attend this somber meeting, but by Thursday noon he was aware of what had transpired: 'Laurel, they're going to throw all
your girls who attended that dance out of the church, and they're going to censure
you as the cause of their sin.'

'That's downright preposterous. Those girls . . .'

On Friday a general meeting was held, and he was powerless to prevent it from
passing a resolution ousting the girls from the church, but before a confirming
vote could be taken, he demanded the floor. This was denied, but he ignored the
rebuke, rose to his feet, and in quiet, forceful words defended his girls:

> 'They danced! Did not the guests attending at Cana dance? Do little
> children not dance with joy when they receive a goody? Does your heart
> not dance at the coming of spring?
>
> 'To throw these Christian girls out of their church for such a trivial
> offense would be an error of enormous magnitude. Do not make either
> the church or the men who command it appear ridiculous by inflicting
> such a harsh penalty.
>
> 'I oppose your verdict for three reasons. Dancing is not a mortal sin.
> Young children of high spirit must not be denied the rights of their
> church because of an infraction of a man-made rule. And as their
> teacher, I know the goodness in their hearts. You must not do this wrong
> thing.'

Reverend Teeder did not want a public debate over what was essentially a matter
of church discipline, but he could not allow a layman to question his authority.
'Dancing is forbidden by church law,' he thundered, whereupon Cobb thundered
back: 'It shouldn't be.' From his place in the congregation Councillor Wilbarger
shouted: 'That's apostasy! Repent! Repent!' What had begun as a sedate meeting
ended in wild recrimination.

On Sunday, Reverend Teeder preached for ninety minutes, a passionate, well-reasoned defense of church discipline. Never raising his voice, never condemning any individual, but always defending the right of the church to set its own rules, he took as his text that powerful proclamation of St. Paul as delivered in Second Thessalonians, Chapter 3, Verse 6:

> 'Now we command you, brethren, in the name of our Lord Jesus Christ, that ye withdraw yourselves from every brother that walketh disorderly, and not after the tradition which he received of us.'

At the eighty-fifth minute of his exhortation he entered upon a most remarkable display, for without warning he stepped aside from the pulpit and extended his left leg toward the audience, and holding his extremity in this position, he concluded his sermon:

> 'Nine years ago when my church in Mississippi faced a scandal far less severe than the one we face here in Texas, I preached for ninety minutes with my leg upraised like this, where none could see it, because it was so inflamed by an abscess that I almost fainted with pain. But I carried on because it was my duty to explain to my congregation why we must expel one of our deacons who had transgressed our law. And tonight I charge this congregation with the task of expelling one of its members. Let God's will be done.'

After the elders met in secret on Monday night, it became common knowledge that Laurel Cobb was to be haled before a public meeting, where he would be tried for 'destroying the morals of the young women of this congregation in that he encouraged them in the lewd and lascivious exhibition of dancing, and that he further defended them against the due strictures of this church.'

The trial would be Thursday night, which meant that Cobb had only two days for preparation, and this distressed him, for as he told his wife: 'I love the church, but I cannot stand silent if it makes a horrendous mistake. Have you seen the law they propose passing the minute I've been expelled?' He showed her the startling document which Councillor Wilbarger and his fellows, in their Monday night meeting, had concocted as the basis for Baptist faith:

> We, as Christians and brethren in full fellowship with one another, pledge ourselves not to drink, play cards, gamble, dance or look at others dancing, or attend card parties, theaters, music halls, moving picture shows or any other worldly and debasing amusement. And we shall expel from church membership any who do participate in the behavior we have forbidden.

The Cobbs agreed that this was extremism of the worst sort; they had seen certain theater performances, especially by Walter Hampden and Fritz Leiber, which were ennobling, and they could not agree that all moving picture shows entailed damnation, although some might, but when they tried to enlist support for Laurel's defense and for a more sensible church discipline, they were met with silence, and by Tuesday night it looked as if Cobb would be expelled at the huge public assembly.

However, early Wednesday they were awakened by an extraordinary member of their church, a man to whom they had never spoken. He was five feet two, about a hundred and fifteen pounds, with a lower jaw that protruded inches as if its owner were constantly seeking a fight. His snow-white hair was cropped close, and his beady blue eyes challenged anyone to whom he spoke to refute even one comma on pain of getting his head bashed. He was Adolf Lakarz, son of Czech emigrés, and he made his living caning chairs and doing odd jobs of carpentry. He was not an easy man to do business with, for when a job was proposed, he studied it, made calculations on a note pad, and quoted a price, with his jaw so far forward that the customer was terrified to comment.

This was deceiving, for one day when he told a church member, an elderly lady, that it would cost her three dollars and twenty-five cents for him to rebuild her favorite rocker, she snapped: 'Far too much,' so he recalculated and said: 'You're right. Two dollars and seventy-five cents,' and she said: 'That's more like it.' She said later: 'Mr. Lakarz always looks at you as if you were evil and about to do him in, and I suppose that in politics he's right.'

His visit to the Cobb plantation had a clear purpose: 'Cobb, what they're doing to you is wrong. My parents came to Texas to escape that kind of tyranny. We've got to stop them.'

'How?'

The two men, with the sun coming up behind them, stood by an old pump and discussed strategies, and the more Lakarz talked the more Cobb realized that he now had a supporter who was going to fight this battle through, even though the end might be bloody: 'You know, Lakarz, if you do this, it could hurt your business.'

'This is why we came to America.'

When nine struck in the kitchen, they had still decided upon nothing, but then Sue Beth happened to show the carpenter the proposals for the new discipline, and as he read its prohibitions against theater and motion pictures and entertainment generally, he became furious, but in his rage he kept a cool head, and Mrs. Cobb saw his eyes flash when he studied more carefully the other details of the new regime.

'By God, Cobb, we've got them!' And without explaining his intentions, he dashed to his third-hand car and sped toward the county courthouse in Waxahachie.

At two o'clock that afternoon the community was staggered by a scandal much worse than the dancing of Laurel Cobb's girl students. Two policemen strode into the office of Councillor Willis Wilbarger and arrested him for playing high-stakes poker in a shebang north of town.

Adolf Lakarz had never played in the games which met regularly in a hidden spot, but he had heard several times from men who had, and for some arcane reason of his own—'I'll throw it at them in some election'—he had kept a diary of dates, participants and amounts wagered. When the local judge saw his evidence, and listened to the testimony of four or five of the players summoned to his chambers, a bench warrant was issued; the players had never liked Wilbarger, who pouted when he lost and gloated when he won. 'Besides,' as one man told the judge, 'he was so damned sanctimonious. Never allowed us to drink while we were playin'. Claimed it was against the law of God.'

Now the whole crusade fell apart. Reverend Teeder, outraged that the criminal element should have attacked a member of his Council, was more determined than ever to expel Cobb, but he further insisted that Adolf Lakarz be thrown out too, so on a hot August day in a large tent usually reserved for revivals, the good farmers from the area south of Waxahachie convened to try the two men in the same spirit that had animated such trials in southern France in 1188, Spain in 1488, England in 1688.

Three members of the Council recited the charges against Cobb, and two others outlined the misdeeds of Lakarz; Wilbarger himself was unable to lead the attack, for he was still in jail. Cobb refused to speak in his own defense, for he judged accurately that the affair had become so ridiculous that he would be acquitted, but Lakarz, having joined a defense of moral freedom, could not remain silent. Great issues were at stake, and he knew it; in Central Europe his forefathers had fought these battles for centuries:

> 'Dear Brothers in God of Jordan Baptist. The dearest thing in my life is my wife, brought here under vast difficulties from Moravia. Second dearest is my membership in this church, which I love as a bastion of freedom and God's love.
>
> 'It is wrong to condemn young girls for dancing. Our greatest musicians have composed gigues and gavottes and waltzes so that the younger ones can dance.
>
> 'It is equally wrong to condemn Laurel Cobb for teaching his girls the joy of life, the joy of Christ's message. I am not wise enough to tell you how to live, and you are not wise enough to pass this kind of foolishness . . .'

Here he waved the proposed new laws, and with biting scorn read out the in-
terdictions against Shakespeare and Mendelssohn and Sarah Bernhardt. When he
was through, no one spoke.

But now came the vote, and white with anger, Reverend Teeder called for those
who loved God and righteousness and an orderly church to stand up and show
that they wanted Cobb and Lakarz expelled. The voting process was somewhat
demoralized, because only twenty-six out of that entire multitude stood up, and
when they saw how few they were, they tried to sit down. But at this moment of
victory, Adolf Lakarz shouted in a powerful voice: 'Keep 'em standin'. I want the
name and look of every man who voted against me.'

And with pencil and note pad he moved through the crowd, chin thrust out,
blue eyes flashing as he stood before each man, taking his name and address. For
the remainder of his life in Waxahachie he would never again speak to one of
those twenty-six.

The scandal in Waxahachie over the dancing Sunday School girls was an amusing
diversion which might have happened in any Texas town of this period and which
could be forgiven as misguided religiosity. But the much more serious madness
that gripped Larkin at about the same time was an aberration which could not be
laughed away, for it came closer to threatening the stability of the entire state.

Precisely when it started no one could recall. One man said: 'It was patriotism,
nothing more. I saw them boys come marchin' home from the war and I asked
myself: "What can I do to preserve our freedoms?" That's how it started, best
motives in the world.'

Others argued that it had been triggered by that rip-roaring revival staged in
Larkin by the ranting Fort Worth evangelist J. Frank Norris, a type much different
from the spiritual Elder Fry. Norris was an aggressive man who thundered sul-
phurous diatribes against saloon keepers, race-track addicts, liberal professors, and
women who wore bobbed hair or skirts above the ankle. He was especially opposed to dancing, which, he claimed, 'scarlet women use to tempt men.'

His anathema, however, was the Roman Catholic church, which he lambasted
in wild and colorful accusation: 'It's the darkest, bloodiest ecclesiastical machine
that has ever been known in the annals of time. It's the enemy of home, of
marriage and of every decent human emotion. The Pope has a plan for capturing
Texas, and I have a plan for defeating him.'

He was most effective when he moved nervously from one side of the pulpit to
the other, extending his hands and crying: 'I speak for all you humble, God-
fearing folks from the forks of the creek. You know what's right and wrong
better than any professors at Baylor or SMU. It's on you that God relies for the
salvation of our state.'

One man, not especially religious, testified: 'When J. Frank Norris shouted " need the help of you little folks from the forks of the creek," I knowed he was speakin' direct to me, and that's when I got all fired up. I saw myself as the right arm of God holdin' a sword ready to strike.'

A University of Texas historian later published documents proving that in Larkin, at least, it had originated not with Norris but with the arrival of three quite different outsiders who had not known one another but who did later act in concert. The earliest newcomer was a man from Georgia who told exciting yarns of what his group had accomplished. The next was a man from Mississippi who assured the Larkin people that his state was taking things in hand. But the greatest influence seemed to have been the third man, a salesman of farm machinery who drifted in from Indiana with startling news: 'Up there our boys are pretty well takin' over the state.'

From such evidence it would be difficult to assess the role played by religion, for while very few ministers actually participated, almost every man who did become involved was a devout member of one Protestant church or another, and the movement strenuously supported religion, with the popular symbols of Christianity featured in the group's rituals.

Whatever the cause, by early December 1919 men began appearing throughout Larkin County dressed in long white robes, masks and, sometimes, tall conical hats. The Ku Klux Klan, born after the Civil War, had begun its tempestuous resurrection.

In Larkin it was not a general reign of terror, and nobody ever claimed it was. The local Klan conducted no hangings, no burnings at the stake and only a few necessary floggings. It was best understood as a group of unquestioned patriots, all of them believing Christians, who yearned to see the historic virtues of 1836 and 1861 restored. It was a movement of men who resented industrial change, shifting moral values and disturbed allegiances; they were determined to preserve and restore what they identified as the best features of American life, and in their meetings and their publications they reassured one another that these were their only aims.

Nor was the Larkin Klan simply a rebellion against blacks, for after the first few days there were no blacks left in town. At the beginning there had been two families, offspring of those black cavalrymen who had stayed behind when the 10th Cavalry rode out of Fort Garner for the last time. At first these two men had kept an Indian woman between them, but later on they had acquired a wandering white woman, so that the present generation was pretty well mixed.

They were one of the first problems addressed by the Ku Kluxers after the organization was securely launched. A committee of four, in full regalia, moved through the town one December night and met with the black families. There was no violence, simply the statement: 'We don't cotton to havin' your type in this town.' It was suggested that the blacks move on to Fort Griffin, where anybody was accepted, and a purse of twenty-six dollars was given them to help with the expense of moving.

One family left town the next morning; the other, named Jaxifer, decided to stay, but when a midnight cross blazed at the front door, the Jaxifers lit out for Fort Griffin, and there was no more of that kind of trouble in Larkin. The Klan did, however, commission four big well-lettered signs, which were posted at the entrances to the town:

NIGGER!

DO NOT LET THE SETTING SUN

FIND YOU IN THIS TOWN.

WARNING!

Thereafter it was the boast of Larkin that 'no goddamned nigger ever slept overnight in this town.'

Nor did the Klan stress its opposition to Jews. Banker Weatherby, an old man now who had been among the first to join the Klan, simply informed three Jewish storekeepers in town that 'our loan committee no longer wishes to finance your business, and we all think it would be better if you moved along.' They did.

The strong opposition to Catholicism presented more complex problems, because the county did contain a rather substantial scattering of this proscribed sect, and whereas some of the more vocal Klansmen wanted to 'throw ever' goddamned mackerel snatcher out of Texas,' others pointed out that even in as well-organized a town as Larkin, more had drifted in than they thought. They had not been welcomed and their mysterious behavior was carefully watched, but at least they weren't black, or Indian, or Jewish, so they were partially acceptable.

The Larkin Klan never made a public announcement that Catholics would be allowed to stay, and at even the slightest infraction of the Klan's self-formulated rules, anyone with an Irish-sounding name was visited, and warned he would be beaten up if he persisted in any un-Christian deportment.

When the town was finally cleaned up and inhabited by only white members of the major Protestant religions, plus the well-behaved Catholics, it was conceded that Larkin was one of the finest towns in Texas. Its men had a commitment to economic prosperity. Its women attended church faithfully. And its crime rate was so low that it barely merited mention. There was some truth to the next signs the Klansmen erected in 1920:

LARKIN

BEST LITTLE TOWN IN TEXAS

WATCH US GROW

If the Klan avoided violence against blacks or Jews or Catholics, who were its targets? An event in the spring of 1921 best illustrates its preoccupations, for then it confronted a rather worthless man of fifty who had been working in the town's livery stable when Larkin still had horses. He now served as janitor and polishing man at the Chevrolet garage, but he had also been living for many years with a shiftless woman named Nora as his housekeeper; few titles in town were less deserved than hers, for she was totally incapable of keeping even a dog kennel, let alone a house. Jake and Nora lived in chaos and in sin, and the upright men of the Klan felt it was high time this ungodly conduct be stopped.

In orderly fashion, which marked all their actions, they appeared at Jake's cabin one Tuesday night carrying a lighted torch, which all could see, and in their clean white robes, their faces hidden by masks, they handed down the law: 'All this immoral sort of thing is gonna stop in Larkin. Marry this woman by Friday sundown or suffer the consequences.'

Jake and Nora had no need of marriage or any understanding of how to participate in one had they wanted to. By hit-and-miss they had worked out a pattern of living which suited them and which produced far fewer family brawls than some of the more traditional arrangements in town. The Klansmen were right that no one would want a lot of such establishments in a community, but Jake felt there ought to be leeway for the accommodation of one or two, especially if they worked well and produced neither scandal nor a horde of unruly children.

On Wednesday the Klansmen who had handed Jake and Nora their ultimatum watched to see what corrective steps the couple proposed taking, and when nothing seemed to have been done, two of the more responsible Klansmen decided to visit the couple again on Thursday night, and this they did in friendly fashion: 'Jake, you don't seem to understand. If you don't marry this woman . . .'

'Who are y'all? Behind them masks? What right . . . ?'

'We're the conscience of this community. We're determined to wipe out immoral behavior.'

'Leave us alone. What about Mr. Henderson and his secretary?'

The boldness of this question stunned the two Klansmen, each of whom knew about Mr. Henderson and his secretary. But it was not people like Henderson whom the Klan policed, and for someone like Jake to bring such a name into discussion was abhorrent. Now the tenor of the conversation grew more ominous: 'Jake, Nora, you get married by tomorrow night or suffer the consequences.'

Jake was prepared to brazen the thing out, but Nora asked in real confusion: 'How could we get married?' and the two hooded visitors turned their attention to her: 'We'll take you to the justice of the peace tomorrow morning, or if you prefer a church wedding, Reverend Hislop has said he'd do it for us.'

'Get out of here!' Jake shouted, and the two men withdrew.

The next day passed, with Jake sweeping at the Chevrolet garage and showing no sign of remorse for his immoral persistence. Those Klansmen in the know watched his house—or was it Nora's house?—and saw that nothing was happening there, either, so at eight that Friday evening seven Ku Kluxers met with the salesman from Indiana, and after praying that they might act with justice, charity and restraint, marched with a burning cross to Jake's place. Planting the cross before the front door, they summoned the two miscreants.

As soon as Jake appeared he was grabbed, not hurtfully, and stripped of his shirt. Tar was applied liberally across his back, and then a Klansman with a bag of feathers slapped handfuls onto the tar. He was then hoisted onto a stout beam, which four other Klansmen carried, and there he was held, feet tied together beneath the beam, while the moral custodians tended to the slut Nora.

Around the world, in all times and in all places, whenever men go on an ethical rampage they feel that they must discipline women: 'Your dresses are too short.' 'You tempt men.' 'Your behavior is salacious.' 'You must be put in your proper place.' This stems, of course, from the inherent mystery of women, their capacity to survive, their ability to bear children, the universal suspicion that they possess some arcane knowledge not available to men. Women are dangerous, and men pass laws to keep them under restraint. All religions, which also deal in mysteries, know this, and that is why the Muslim, the Jewish, the Catholic and the Mormon faiths proscribed women so severely and why other churches ran into trouble when they tried belatedly to ordain women as ministers.

The men of the Ku Klux Klan were as bewildered by sex as any of their reforming predecessors, and on this dark night they had to look upon Nora-with-three-teeth-missing-in-front as a temptress who had seduced Jake into his immoral life. But what to do with her? There was no inclination at all to strip her, but there was a burning desire to punish her, so two men dragged her out beside the flaming cross and tarred her whole dress, fore and aft, scattering feathers liberally upon her.

She then was lifted onto the rail, behind her man, whereupon two additional men supported it, and in this formation the hooded Klansmen paraded through the streets of Larkin behind a sign which proclaimed:

EMORALITY IN LARKIN
WILL STOP

Jake and Nora did not respond as the Klansmen had hoped. They did not marry, and when the long parade was over they returned home, scraped off the tar, and said 'nothin' to nobody.' Early Saturday morning Jake was at the garage sweeping as usual and saying hello to any who passed. He had no idea who had disciplined him, and at noon he walked home as usual for his lunch. Nora went to the store late Saturday for her weekend supplies, and on Sunday, Jake fished as always, up at the tank, which contained some good-sized bass, while Nora sat on her front lawn where scars from the burned cross still showed.

Such behavior infuriated the Klansmen, who convened after church on Sunday a special meeting at which it was discussed with some heat as to whether the two should be flogged. The Indiana man was all for a public whipping in the court house square, but the Georgia man argued against it: 'We found it does no good. Creates sympathy. And it scares the womenfolk.'

Instead, the men found an old wagon and a worthless horse, and these they drove to Jake's place on Monday evening. Throwing the two adulterers into the back, they piled the wagon with as many of their household goods as possible, then drove west of town till they were beyond sight of the beautiful courthouse tower which bespoke order and justice for this part of Texas. There the Klansmen plopped Jake onto the driver's bench and gave him the reins: 'Straight down this road is Fort Griffin. They'll accept anybody.'

The hooded posse returned to Larkin after sunset, and two hours later Jake and Nora, driving the old horse that Jake had often tended in the livery stable, came back to town. With no fanfare they rode down familiar streets to their home, unpacked their belongings, and went to bed.

That was Monday. On Wednesday night Jake was found behind the garage, shot to death.

No charges were ever filed against the Klansmen, and for the very good reason that no one knew for sure who they were, or even if they had done it. At least, that was the legal contention. Of course, everyone knew that Floyd Rusk—who could not hide his size even under a bedsheet—was one of the leaders, perhaps *the* leader, because he was obvious at all the marches and the cross burnings, but no one could be found who could swear that yes, he had seen Floyd Rusk tarring Jake.

It was also known that Clyde Weatherby was an active member, as were the hardware merchant, the doctor, the schoolteacher and the druggist. Some four dozen other men, the best in the community, joined later. With an equal mix of patriotism and religion, these men of good intention began to inspect all aspects of life in Larkin, for they were determined to keep their little town in the mainstream of American life as they perceived it.

They forced six men to marry their housekeepers. They lectured, in an almost fatherly manner, two teen-aged girls who seemed likely to become promiscuous, and they positively shut down a grocer against whom several housewives had complained. They did not tar-and-feather him, nor did they horsewhip him; those punishments were reserved for sexual infractions, but they did ride him out of town, telling him to transfer his shop to Fort Griffin, where honesty of trade was not so severely supervised.

By the beginning of 1922 these men had Larkin in the shape they wanted; even some of the Catholics, fearing that reprisals would next be directed at them, had moved away, making the town about as homogeneous as one could have found in all of Texas. It was a community of Protestant Christians in which the rules were understood and in which infractions were severely punished. Almost none of the excesses connected with the Klan in other parts of the nation were condoned here, and after two years of intense effort the Klansmen, when they met at night, could justifiably claim that they had cleaned up Larkin. With this victory under their belt, they intended moving against Texas as a whole, and then, all of the United States.

In 1922 they got well started by electing their man, Earle B. Mayfield, a Tyler grocer, to the United States Senate, but this triumph had a bitter aftermath, because for two years that august body refused to seat a man accused of Klan membership, and when it did finally accept him, he was denied reelection. The Larkin members assuaged their disappointment by achieving a notorious victory in the local high school, where the principal, an enthusiastic Klansman, inserted in the school yearbook a well-drawn full-page depiction of a nightrider in his regalia of bedsheet, mask and pointed hat astride a white stallion under a halo composed of the words GOD, COUNTRY, PROTESTANTISM, SUPREMACY. At the bottom of the page, in a neatly lettered panel, stood the exhortation LIKE THE KLAN, LARKIN HIGH WILL TRIUMPH IN FOOTBALL.

In the growing town, however, the Klan suffered other frustrations. The editor of the *Defender,* an effeminate young man from Arkansas, had the temerity to editorialize against them, and in a series of articles he explained why he opposed what he called 'midnight terrorism.' This unlucky phrase infuriated the Klansmen: 'We have to guard the morals of Larkin at night because during the day we have to run our businesses. Terrorism is shooting innocent people, and no man can claim we ever done that, and live.'

They handled the newspaper with restraint. First they approached the editor, in masks, and explained their lofty motives, pointing out the many good things they had done for Larkin, like eliminating vice and increasing church membership, but they made little impression on the young man.

Next they threatened him. Three Klansmen, including one of enormous bulk, visited him at his home at two in the morning, warning him that he must halt all comment on the Klan 'or our next visit is gonna be more serious.'

The young editor, despite his appearance, was apparently cut from a robust Arkansas stock, because he ignored the threats, whereupon the governing committee of the Klan met to discuss what next to try. The meeting was held in the bank, after hours and without masks. Nine men, clean-shaven, well-dressed, giving every evidence of prosperity and right living, met solemnly to discuss their options: 'We can tar-and-feather him. We can whip him publicly. Or we can shoot him. But one way or another, we are going to silence that bastard.'

There was support for each of these choices, but after additional discussion, the majority seemed to settle upon a good horsewhipping on the courthouse steps, but then Floyd Rusk, huffing and puffing, introduced a note of reason: 'Men, in this country you learn never to bust the nose of the press. If you flog that editor publicly, or even privately, the entire press of Texas and the United States is goin' to descend upon this town. And if you shoot him, the federal government will have the marshals in here.'

'What can we do?' the banker asked.

'You have the solution,' Rusk said.

'Which is what?'

'Buy the paper. Throw him out.' When this evoked discussion, Rusk listened, judged the weight of various opinions, and said: 'It's quick, it's effective, and it's legal.'

So without even donning their hooded costumes, the leading members of the Klan accumulated a fund and bought the paper, then, avoiding scandal, quietly drove the young editor out of town. That source of criticism was silenced, because before hiring a new editor, also a young man but this time from Dallas, the leading Klansmen satisfied themselves that he was a supporter of their movement and had been a member in the larger city.

The second problem was not so easily handled. Reverend Hislop was no irritating liberal like the editor from Arkansas, for he was against everything the Klan was against—immorality, adultery, drunkenness, shady business practice, the excesses of youth, such as blatant dancing—but he taught that these evils could best be opposed through an orderly church; he suspected that Jesus would not have approved of nightriders or flaming crosses, for the latter symbol was too precious to be so abused. Hislop was not a social hero; he kept his suspicions to himself, but as in all such situations wherein a man of good intention tries to hide, the facts had a tendency to uncover him, and that is what happened.

The Klansmen, eager to adopt a procedure which had proved effective in many small towns across the state, initiated the policy of having a committee of six members dress in full regalia each Sunday morning and march as a unit to either the Baptist or Methodist church, timing their arrival to coincide with the collection. Silently, and with impressive dignity, they entered at the rear, strode up the middle aisle in formation, and placed upon the altar an envelope containing a substantial cash contribution. 'For God's work,' the leader would cry in a loud voice, whereupon the six would turn on their heels and march out.

Such pageantry impressed the citizens, gaining the Klan much popular support, especially when the amount of the contribution was magnified in the telling: 'They give two hunnerd big ones for the poor and needy of this community.' Many believed that God had selected them as His right arm, and the moral intention of most of their public acts supported this view. Some thoughtful men came to believe that soon the Klan would assume responsibility for all of Texas, and that when that happened, a new day of justice and honest living would result.

Reverend Hislop did not see it this way. As a devout Southerner and a strong defender of the Confederacy, he understood the emotions which had called forth the original Klan back in the dark days after 1865, and supposed that had he lived then, he would have been a Klansman, because, as he said, 'some kind of corrective action was needed.' But he was not so sure about the motives of this revived Klan of the 1920s: 'They stand for all that's good, that I must confess. And they also support the programs of the church. They're against sin, and that puts them on my side. But decisions of punishment should be made by courts of law. In the long range of human history, there is no alternative to that. When the church dispensed justice in Spain and New England, it did a bad job. When these good men dispense their midnight justice at the country crossroads, they do an equally imperfect job. Martha, I cannot accept their Sunday contributions any longer.'

The decision had been reached painfully, but it was set in rock. However, Hislop was not the kind of man to create a public scandal; that would have been most repugnant. So on Sunday, when the six hooded Klansmen marched into his church, their polished boots clicking, he accepted their offering, but that very afternoon he summoned Floyd Rusk and the Indiana salesman to his parsonage, where he told them: 'It is improper for you to invade the House of the Lord. It's improper for you to assume the duties of the church.'

'Why do you tell me this?' Rusk asked, and Reverend Hislop pointed a finger at the rancher's enormous belly: 'Do you think you can hide that behind a costume?'

'But why do you oppose the Klan?' Rusk asked. 'Surely it supports God's will.'

'I am sometimes confused as to what God's will really is.'

'Are you talkin' atheism?' Rusk demanded.

'I'm saying that I'm not sure what is accomplished by tarring a silly woman like Nora.'

'Surely she was an evil influence.'

'They thought that in Salem, when old women muttered. They hanged them. What are you going to do to Nora now?'

'Nora has nothing to do with this. We're turning Larkin into a Christian town.'

'In some things, yes. Mr. Rusk, don't you realize that for every wayward person you correct, there are six others in our town who cheat their customers, who misappropriate funds . . . Life goes on here much as it does in Chicago or Atlanta, but you focus only on the little sinners.'

'You do talk atheism, Reverend Hislop. You better be careful.'

'I am being careful, Mr. Rusk, and I'm asking you politely, as a fellow Christian who approves of much that you do, not to enter my church any more with your offerings. The money I need, and it can be delivered in the plate like the other offerings, but the display I do not need.'

On Sunday the six Klansmen in full regalia entered the church as usual. Led by a portly figure, they marched to the altar, where the large one said in a loud voice: 'For God's work.'

Before they could click their heels and retreat, Reverend Hislop said quietly: 'Gentlemen, God thanks you for your offering. His work needs all the support it can get. But you must not enter His church in disguise. You must not associate

God with your endeavors, worthy though they sometimes are. Please take your offering out with you.'

No Klansman spoke. At the big man's signal they tramped down the aisle and out the door, leaving their money where they had placed it.

On previous Sundays the deacons who passed the collection plates and then marched to the altar, where the offerings were blessed, had rather grandiloquently lifted the Klan donation and placed it atop the lesser offerings, but on this day Reverend Hislop asked them not to do this. To his astonishment, one of the deacons who was a member of the Klan ostentatiously took the envelope from where Rusk had left it and placed it once more atop all the offerings, as if it took precedence because of the Klan's power in that town and in that church.

The battle lines were drawn, with a good eighty percent of the church members siding with the Klan rather than with their pastor. On the next Sunday the same three characters played the same charade. Floyd Rusk in his bedsheet made the donation; Reverend Hislop rejected it; and the deacon accepted it.

On the following Tuesday the church elders met with Reverend Hislop, a quiet-mannered man who deplored controversy, and informed him that his services were no longer required in Larkin. 'You've lost the confidence of your people,' the banker explained. 'And when that happens, the minister has to go.'

'You're the elders,' Hislop said.

'But we want to make it easy for you,' the man from Indiana said. 'There's a Methodist church in Waynesboro, Pennsylvania, lovely town among the hills. It needs a pastor, and the bishop in those parts has indicated that he would look kindly upon your removal there.'

Like the purchase of the newspaper and elimination of its editor, the Larkin Methodist Church was purified without public scandal. Reverend Hislop preached on Sunday; he rejected the Klan offering; the deacons accepted it; and on Thursday he quietly disappeared.

The Klan now ruled the little town. All blacks were gone; all Jews were gone; no Mexicans were allowed within the town limits; and the lower class of Catholics had been eased out. It was a town of order, limited prosperity, and Christian decency. All voices of protest had been effectively silenced. Of course, as Reverend Hislop had pointed out, the same amount of acceptable crime prevailed as in any American town: some lawyers diverted public moneys into their own pockets; some doctors performed abortions; some politicians contrived election results to suit their purposes; and a good many deacons from all the churches drank moderately and played an occasional game of poker. There was a fair amount of adultery and not a little juggling of account books, but the conspicuous social crimes which offended the middle-class morality of the district, like open cohabitation or lascivious dancing, had been brought under control.

Then, just as the Ku Kluxers were congratulating themselves, a small, dirty, sharp-eyed man named Dewey Kimbro slipped into town, bringing an irresistible alternative to the Klan, and everything blew apart.

He first appeared as a man of mystery, under thirty, with sandy red hair and a slight stoop even though he was short. He would often ride his horse far into the countryside and tell nobody anything about it. He spoke little, in fact, and when he did his words fell into two sharply defined patterns, for sometimes he sounded like a college professor, at other times like the roughest cowboy, and what his inherited vocabulary had been, no one could guess.

He attracted the attention of the Klansmen, who were not happy with strangers moving about their domain, and several extended discussions were held concerning him, with Floyd Rusk leading the attack: 'I don't want him prowling my ranchland.' To Rusk's surprise, the banker said: 'When he transferred his funds to us, he asked about you, Floyd.'

'He did? He better lay off.'

Things remained in this uncertain state, with Kimbro attracting increased attention by his excursions, now here, now there, until the day when Rusk demanded that his Klansmen take action: 'I say we run him out of town. No place here for a man like him.' But the others pointed out that he had transferred into the Larkin bank nearly a thousand dollars, and that amount of money commanded respect.

'What do we know about him?' Rusk asked with that canny rural capacity for identifying trouble.

'He boards with Nora.'

'The woman we tarred-and-feathered?'

'The same.'

'Well,' announced a third man, 'he sure as hell ain't havin' sex with someone like her.'

'But it don't look good,' Rusk said. 'We got to keep watchin'.'

Then Kimbro made his big mistake. From Jacksboro he imported on the Reo bus, which ran between the two towns, a twenty-year-old beauty named Esther, with painted cheeks and a flowery outfit she could not have paid for with her clerk's wages. Kimbro moved her right into Nora's place, and on her third night of residence the couple was visited by the hooded Klan.

'Are you two married?'

'Whose business?' Kimbro asked the question, but it could just as well have come from Esther.

'It's our business. We don't allow your kind in this town.'

'I'm here. And so is she.'

'And do you think you'll be allowed to stay here?'

'I sure intend to. Till I get my work done.'

'And what is your work?' a masked figure asked.

'That's my business.'

'Enough of this,' a very fat Klansman broke in. 'Kimbro, if that's your real name, you got till Thursday night to get out of town. And, miss, you by God better be goin' with him.'

On Tuesday and Wednesday, Dewey Kimbro, named after the Hero of Manila and just as taciturn, rode out of town on his speckled horse. Spies followed him for a while, but could only report that he rode awhile, stopped awhile, dismounted occasionally, then rode on. He met no one, did nothing conspicuous, and toward dusk rode back into town, where Esther and Nora had supper waiting.

The three had gone to bed—Kimbro and the girl in one room—when four hooded figures bearing whips appeared, banging on the door and calling for Kimbro to come out. Under the hoods were Lew and Les Tumlinson, twin brothers who ran the coal and lumber business, Ed Boatright, who had the Chevrolet agency where the dead Jake had worked, and Floyd Rusk, the big rancher.

When Kimbro refused to appear, the Tumlinson twins kicked in the door, stormed into Nora's small house, and rampaged through the rooms till they found Kimbro and his whore in bed. Pulling him from under the covers, they dragged his small body along the hallway and through the front door. On the lawn, in about the same position as when Jake and Nora were tarred, Rusk and Boatright had erected a cross, and were in the process of igniting it when the twins shouted: 'We got him!' When the cross lit up the sky, a horde of onlookers ran up, and there was so much calling back and forth among the hooded figures that the crowd knew who the four avengers were: 'That's Lew Tumlinson for sure, and if he's here, so's his brother. The fat one we know, and I think the other has got to be Ed Boatright.'

Dewey Kimbro, who never missed anything, even when he was about to be thrashed, heard the names. He also heard the fat man say: 'Strip him!' and when the nightshirt was torn away and he stood naked, he heard the same man shout: 'Lay it on. Good.'

He refused to faint. He refused to cry out. In the glare of the flaming cross, he bore the first twenty-odd slashes of the three whips, but then he lost count, and finally he did faint.

At nine o'clock next morning he barged into Floyd Rusk's kitchen, and the fat man, who was an expert with revolvers from an early age, anticipated trouble and whipped out one of his big six-shooters, but before he could get it into position, he glared into the barrel of a small yet deadly German pistol pointed straight at a spot between his eyes.

For a long, tense moment the two men retained their positions, Rusk almost ready to fire his huge revolver, Kimbro prepared to fire first with his smaller gun.

Finally Rusk dropped his, at which Kimbro said: 'Place it right here where I can watch it,' and Floyd did, sweating heavily.

'Now let's sit down here, Mr. Rusk, and talk sense.' When the big man took his place at the kitchen table, with his gun in reach not of himself but of Kimbro, a conversation began which modified the history of Larkin County.

'Mr. Rusk, you whipped me last night—'

'Now wait!'

'You're right. You never laid a rawhide on me. But you ordered the Tumlinson twins and Ed Boatright . . .' Rusk's glistening of sweat became a small torrent. 'I ought to kill you for that, and maybe later on I will. But right now you and I need each other, and you're far more valuable to me alive than dead.'

'Why?'

'I have a secret, Mr. Rusk. I've had it since I was eleven years old. Do you remember Mrs. Jackson who ran the little store?'

'Yes, I believe I do.'

'You wouldn't remember a boy from East Texas who spent one summer with her?'

'Are you that boy?'

'I am.'

'And what secret did you discover?'

'On your land . . . out by the tank . . .'

'That's not my land. My father gave it to the Yeagers.'

'I know. Your father promised it in the 1870s. You formalized it in 1909.'

'So it's not my land.'

Kimbro shifted in his chair, for the pain from his whipping was intense. He had a most important statement to make, and he wanted to be in complete control when he made it, but just as he was prepared to disclose the purpose of his visit, Molly Rusk came into the kitchen, a big blowzy woman who, against all the rules of nature, was pregnant. She had a round, happy face made even more placid by the miracle of her condition, and with the simplicity that marked most of her actions, she took one look at Kimbro and asked: 'Aren't you the man they whipped last night?' and he said: 'I am.'

She was about to ask why he was sitting in her kitchen this morning, when Rusk said respectfully: 'You better leave us alone, Molly,' and she retired with apologies, but she had barely closed the door when she returned: 'There's coffee on the stove.' Then she added: 'Floyd, don't do anything brutal with that gun.'

'True, the land is no longer yours, Mr. Rusk,' Kimbro said quietly. 'Your daddy promised it to Yeager, but when you transferred it legally, you were clever enough to retain the mineral rights.'

Rusk leaned far back in his chair. Then he placed his pudgy hands on the edge of the table, and from this position he sat staring at the little stranger. Finally, in an awed voice he asked: 'You mean . . .'

Kimbro nodded, and after readjusting his painful back, he said: 'When I stayed here that summer I did a lot of tramping about. Always have.'

'And what did you find at the tank?'

'A small rise that everyone else had overlooked. When I kicked rocks aside, I came upon . . . guess what?'

'Gold?'

'Much better. Coal.'

'Coal?'

'Yep. Sneaked some home and it burned a glowing red. Kept on burning. So I kept on exploring . . .'

'And you located a coal mine?'

'Nope. The strain was trivial, played out fast. But I covered the spot, piled rocks over it, and if you and I go out there this morning, we'll find a slight trace of coal hiding where it's always been.'

'And what does this mean?'

'You don't know? I knew when I was ten. Read it in a book.' He shifted again. 'I read a lot, Mr. Rusk.'

'And what did you read, at ten?'

Kimbro hesitated, then changed the subject entirely: 'Mr. Rusk, I want you to enter into a deal with me, right now. Word of a gentleman. We're partners, seventy-five to you, twenty-five to me.'

'What the hell kind of offer is that? I don't even know what we're talkin' about.'

'You will. In two minutes, if you make the deal.'

'You'd trust me, after last night?'

'I have to.' Kimbro banged the table. 'And by God, you have to trust me, too.'

'Is it worth my while? I have a lot of cattle, you know.'

'And you're losing your ass on them, aren't you?'

'Well, the market . . .'

'Seventy-five, twenty-five for my secret and the know-how to develop it.'

Again Rusk leaned back: 'What do you know about me, personally I mean?'

'That you're a bastard, through and through. But once you give your word, you stick to it.'

'I do. You know, Kimbro, when I was fourteen or thereabouts I rode to Dodge City with a—'

'You went to Dodge City?'

'I did, with the greatest trail driver Texas ever produced, R. J. Poteet. He tried to make a man of me, but I wouldn't allow it. At Dodge, I killed two men, yep, age fifteen I think I was. Poteet's two point men spirited me out of town. Just ahead of the sheriff. But on the ride back to Texas he and his men held a kangaroo court because they knew damned well I hadn't shot in self-defense. Found me guilty and strung me up. I thought sure as hell . . .' He was sweating so profusely that he asked: 'Can I get that towel?'

'Stay away from the gun.'

'They slapped the horse I was sitting on, I fell, I felt the rope bite into my neck. And then Poteet caught me. He lectured me about my wrong ways, and I spat in his face.' He laughed nervously. 'I was scared to death, really petrified, but I wouldn't show it. Poteet went for his gun, then brushed me aside.'

He rocked back and forth on the kitchen chair, an immensely fat man of forty-seven. Replacing his hands on the table, he said: 'That hanging was the making of me, Kimbro. Taught me two things. You've uncovered one of them. I am a man of my word, hell or high water. And I have never since then been afraid to use my gun when it had to be used. If you're partners with me, be damned careful.'

'That's why I brought this,' Kimbro said, indicating the gun which he had kept trained on the fat man during their discussion.

'So what did you learn?' Rusk asked.

'Partners?' Kimbro asked, and the two shook hands, after which the little fellow delivered his momentous information: 'At ten I knew that coal and petroleum are the same substance, in different form.'

Rusk gasped: 'You mean oil?' The word echoed through the quiet kitchen as if a bomb had exploded, for the wild discoveries in East Texas had alerted the entire state to the possibilities of this fantastic substance which made farmers multimillionaires.

'At fourteen,' Kimbro continued, 'I studied all the chemistry and physics our little school allowed, and at seventeen I enrolled at Texas A&M.'

'You a college graduate?'

'Three years only. By that time I knew more about petroleum than the professors. Got a job with Humble, then Gulf. Field man. Sort of an informal geologist. Worked the rigs too, so I know what drilling is. Mr. Rusk, I'm a complete oilman, but what I really am is maybe the world's greatest creekologist.'

'What's that?'

'A contemptuous name the professors give practical men like me. We study the way creeks run, the rise and fall of land forms, and we guess like hell.' He slammed the table. 'But by God, we find oil. It's downright infuriating to the college people how we find oil.'

'And you think you've found some on my land?'

'From the run of the creeks and the rise in your field, I'm satisfied that we're sitting near the middle of a substantial field.'

'You mean real oil?'

'I do. Not a bunch of spectacular gushers like Spindletop. But good, dependable oil trapped in the rocks below us.'

'If you're right, could we make some real money?'

'A fortune, if we handle it right.'

'And what would right be?'

'How much of this land around here do you own?'

'I'm sure you've checked at the courthouse. Well over seven thousand acres.'

'Where does it lie, relation to the tank?'

'South and some across Bear Creek to the west.'

'I'm glad you can tell the truth. But if I'm right, the field runs north and east of the tank. Could you buy any of that land?'

'Look, I don't have much ready cash.'

'Could you lease the mineral rights? I mean right now. Not tomorrow, now.'

'Is speed so necessary?'

'The minute anyone suspects what we're up to . . . if they even guess that I'm a creekologist . . . Then it's too late.'

'How does an oil lease work?'

Kimbro had to rise, adjust his scarred back, and sit gingerly on the edge of the chair: 'There can be three conditions of ownership. First, you own your seven thousand acres and all mineral rights under them. Second, Yeager owns the good land we want, the surface, that is, but he owns nothing underneath. Tough on him, good for us.'

'Yes, but do we have the right to invade his property in order to sink our well?'

'We do, if we don't ruin his surface. And if we do ruin it, we pay him damages, and he can't do a damned thing about it.'

'He won't like it.'

'They never do, but that's the law. Now, the third situation is the one that operates mostly. Farmer Kline owns a big chunk of land, say three thousand acres. He also owns the mineral rights. So we go to him and say: "Mr. Kline, we want to lease the mineral rights to your land. For ten years. And we'll give you fifty cents an acre year after year for ten years. A lot of money." '

'What rights do we get?'

'The right to drill, any place on the farm, as many holes as we want, for ten years.'

'And what does he get?'

'Fifteen hundred dollars a year, hard cash, year after year, even if we do nothing.'

'And if we strike oil?'

'He gets a solid one-eighth of everything we make, for as long as that well produces. To eternity, if he and it last that long.'

'Who gets the other seven-eighths?'

'We do.'

'Is it a good deal . . . for all of us, I mean?'

'For Farmer Kline, it's a very fair deal. He gets an oil well without taking any risk. For you and me, the deal with Kline is about the best we can do, fair to both sides. It's his oil but we take all the risks.'

'And between you and me—seventy-five, twenty-five?'

'Tell you the truth, Rusk, with some men like me you could get an eighty, twenty deal, but nine out of ten such men would never find a bucket of oil. I know where the oil is. For you, it's a very good deal. As for me, if I had the land or the money, I wouldn't say hello to you. But I don't have either.'

'So what should we do?' Rusk asked permission to pour some coffee, whereupon Kimbro pushed the big revolver across the table to him.

'I trust you, Rusk. I have to. We're partners.'

When reports of the notorious Sunday School trial at Waxahachie circulated through Texas, accompanied by sardonic laughter, the voters began to realize that in Laurel Cobb, son of the famous post-Reconstruction senator, they had a man of common sense and uncommon courage, and a movement was launched to send him to Washington to assume the seat once held by his father. Said one editorial, recalling the older man's dignified performance in the chaotic 1870s: 'He restored honor to the fair name of Texas.'

Prior to 1913, Laurel would have had little chance to win the seat, for in those years United States senators were elected by their respective state legislatures and he would have enlisted only minor support, for he was more liberal than the Democratic leadership. In fact, his father had been acceptable in 1874 only because Texas wanted to show the rest of the nation that it was not ashamed of how it had conducted itself during the War Between the States: 'Damnit, we want a man who held high rank in the army of the Confederacy, and if the rest of the nation don't like it, the rest of the nation can go to hell.' However, the men who sent him to Congress on those terms were often embarrassed by how he acted when he got there, and it would have been impossible for their sons to accept Laurel.

But with adoption of the Seventeenth Amendment, senators were elected by popular ballot, and the general public wanted Cobb, so a serious campaign was launched in his behalf. It was Adolf Lakarz, the fighting little fellow who had defended him in the Sunday School trial, who persuaded Cobb to run, using this argument: 'If you fight for justice in a church, you can do the same in a nation.' As soon as Cobb accepted this challenge, he began contesting the Democratic primary in earnest, and this took him to Saldana County and the machinations of Horace Vigil and his dexterous assistant Héctor Garza.

Cobb, aware of Vigil's unsavory reputation, had balked at paying court to the old patrón, but Lakarz had quickly put an end to such revolt: 'Laurel, you're one of four good Democrats who want this Senate seat, and the other three will do anything short of murder to grab it from you. The competition will be especially tough for those easy votes that Vigil keeps in his pocket. We need them, and if you have to kiss ass to get them, start bending down.'

'How does one man control so much?'

'Because he still has that good old Precinct 37.'

'I should think the government would take it away.'

Lakarz laughed: 'Texas tried to, many times. Federals try to every time there's a Republican administration, but old Horace holds on.'

'Sounds illegal,' Cobb said, but Lakarz corrected him: 'Sounds Texan.'

So Cobb and Lakarz drove from Waxahachie along what might be called the spine of settled Texas: Waco on the Brazos, with its rich agricultural land; Temple, with its proud high school football team; Austin, with its handsome buildings and growing university; Luling and Beeville, in the sun; Falfurrias, with its multitude of flowers; and then that shocking emptiness which had been the stalking ground of Ranger Macnab and the bandit Benito Garza.

'It can be hot down here,' Cobb groaned as the temperature rose to a hundred and stayed there.

"Oooooh, Mr. Candidate, never say that! Down here they call a day like this bracing, and if you want their votes, you better call it bracing, too."

'I imagine it could be glorious in winter.'

'Say that to everyone you meet, and you'll win.'

When Cobb thought he could begin to smell the river, Lakarz told him: 'This land up here used to be attached to Saldana County, but about 1911 huge chunks were lopped off the old counties to form new ones. But what's left is still big enough to carry a lot of weight.'

'What advice on handling Horace Vigil?'

'Easy. Let him know you're a loyal Democrat. If you're thinking of opening a saloon, buy your beer from him. And always speak well of his Mexicans. For without their support, you will never go to Washington.'

As they approached the outskirts of Bravo, Cobb saw an astonishing sight: 'Are those palm trees?' For mile after mile the tall swaying trees baked in the sun, as if standing on the banks of the Nile, and sometimes in their shade would rest acres of experimental orange or grapefruit trees. In the blazing heat a new industry was quietly expanding into Texas, and some of the farmers who had pioneered it were becoming richer than their neighbors in other parts of the state who had oil wells.

'Vigil doesn't need to bother with votes. He has a paradise here,' Cobb said, but Lakarz warned: 'Horace always bothers with votes.'

They found Vigil in the adobe-walled building from which he ran his beer distributorship. He was an old man now, white-haired and in his late sixties. He was markedly stooped, but no one could doubt that he was still the shrewd dictator of his county; as always when meeting strangers he spoke in near-whispers: 'Never met your daddy, but they tell me he was first rate. I heard about him trackin' down that gunman who shot his two niggers. In those days that took courage.'

He sat surrounded by his usual cadre of young men, sons of the functionaries who had served him in the past; they fetched his cigarettes, instructed the judge as to the cases in which Mr. Vigil had a special interest, supervised the counting of ballots, and distributed alms to the needy. Little had changed politically. Vigil was still the patrón, dispensing his rude justice, and to the citizens of Saldana County he was still Señor Vee-heel.

The old man coughed: 'Mr. Cobb, of the four Democrats runnin' for the Senate, I prefer you. Now tell me, what can I do to help you win?'

Cobb liked this old dictator; he felt the man's warmth and respected his authority: 'No, you tell me.'

'That's reasonable, because I know this territory. Not as big as it once was, but more voters, more leverage.' He turned away from Cobb and called to his principal assistant: 'Héctor, I want you to meet the man we're sendin' to Washington to take his daddy's place.' And the four laid plans for nailing down the primary.

But as Cobb toured other sections of the state he became aware that one of his opponents was taking his own bold steps to steal the election, and this embittered Adolf Lakarz, who reminded Cobb: 'We've got to get a huge majority in Saldana County, because, as the papers keep saying, "in Texas winning the Democratic primary is tantamount to election." '

'You ever think about that word, Adolf? It's one of those curious cases in which a perfectly good word has been restricted to only one use. You never hear "A hot dog is tantamount to a sausage." ' Lakarz, irritated that his candidate was wasting his time on such nonpolitical reflection, warned: 'You better hope this primary is tantamount to your election.'

The campaign in Saldana had only begun when one of those political events which perplexed outsiders took place. Horace Vigil, who had fought the Republican customs officer Tim Coke for decades, learned that his old nemesis was leaving the Bravo-Escandón Bridge for a better job in New York, so he organized a gala farewell to which he contributed a new Chevrolet in which the Cokes could drive to their new post. In his speech of thanks, Coke said: 'I hate to leave Saldana just as the Democrats are preparing to tear themselves apart in their primary. I'd like to see my old friend Horace get his nose busted. But I say this here and now. I want all my Republicans to cross party lines and get into the polling booths one way or another. And you're to vote for Vigil's man, Laurel Cobb, and vote three or four times, like you always did for me. Because in thirty years of fighting that sumbitch Vigil, I always had respect for him. I never knew what infamous or criminal thing he was going to hit me with next, but the battles were fun. I look forward with relief to fighting those Democratic hoodlums in Tammany Hall. They're the worst snakes ever got thrown out of Ireland. But these damn Democrats in Texas, they're rattlesnakes.'

Three days before the election Lakarz slipped back into Bravo for a strategy meeting, and what he learned was ominous. Vigil himself outlined the sorry details: 'Reformers in Washington, bunch of Republicans, they're comin' down to take control of Precinct 37.'

'We've got to have those votes.'

'We'll be allowed to count them and report whatever totals we need. Texas law demands that, but as soon as the countin' ends, we have to deliver the ballot boxes to the federals.'

'What do you think they'll do?'

'Send me to jail, if they can prove anything.' Lakarz could see that this possibility frightened the old man, who said quietly: 'Jail I do not seek, but if it's the only way we can win this election, jail it will have to be.'

'Our friends will never let that happen.'

The old warrior was not so confident, but he did not lament his problems; he had one more election to win, and he would speak only of it: 'When the boxes reach Bravo, they'll recount the votes in the presence of a federal judge. We could be in a lot of trouble.'

'Have you a plan for getting out of this?'

'Normally we'd bribe the judge, but this time he's a federal. I'll think of somethin'.'

A council of war occupied Saturday afternoon, and it was Héctor Garza, a little taller, a little bolder than his predecessors, who devised the winning strategy: 'We must have absolute secrecy. So that when the federals come after us, we can honestly swear: "We don't know." '

'You think they will come?' Vigil asked in a whisper, and Garza said: 'For sure. The Republicans will see to that. But I know a way to hold them off.'

Sharing his intricate plan with no one, not even Vigil, he orchestrated a strategy in which no one except he and the person performing one small part of the job knew what anyone else was doing. On the eve of the election he said to Vigil and Lakarz with confidence: 'As soon as the votes have been counted across the state, tell me how many votes we'll need to win.'

Late on election night Vigil telephoned Garza, standing watch at Precinct 37: 'We've got to have more than four hundred and ten,' and an hour later the three officials at the precinct certified the vote to have been 422 to 7.

When the men from Washington, waiting in Bravo, heard this, they exulted: 'Now we have them! Impossible for a vote to be so lopsided.' And almost hungrily they waited to get their hands on the incriminating box: 'This time Vigil goes behind bars, and not in some half-baked county jail. The federal pen.'

But now a singular thing happened. The ballot box disappeared. Yes, on its way down FM-117 it disappeared, and since the elections officials had legally reported their results, those results had to stand. The preposterous 422 to 7 stood, enabling Laurel Cobb to win the election by a twenty-seven-vote margin.

How could an object as big as a ballot box disappear? It was never fully explained. It had been handed by the judges to a Mr. Hernández, who passed it along to a Mr. Robles, who gave a receipt for it, and he gave it to a Mr. Solórzano, and that was where it disappeared, because Mr. Solórzano could prove that he had been in San Antonio when all this happened.

Texas newspapers, which had supported one or another of Cobb's opponents, screamed for an investigation, while the more impartial journals in New York and Washington editorialized that the time had come to cleanse American politics of the stigma of Saldana County. However, the case became somewhat more complicated when it was revealed that the mysterious Mr. Solórzano had been in the employ of the Washington men.

Héctor Garza revealed to no one his role in this legerdemain, but Horace Vigil, in a show of righteous morality, did issue a pious statement deploring the carelessness of the men, whose ineptness had allowed aspersions to be cast upon the fine officials of Precinct 37: 'I personally regret the loss of that box because had its contents been counted by the federal judge, the results would have proved what I have always claimed. The election officials of Precinct 37 are honest. They're just a mite slow.'

This time their tardiness enabled a good man to go to Washington.

On a gray morning in October 1922, schoolboys sitting near the window cried: 'Look at what's comin'!' and their classmates ran to see three large trucks moving down the Jacksboro road. They carried long lengths of timber, piles of pipe, and ten of the toughest-looking men Larkin County had seen in a long time. Two lads who had been reading science magazines shouted: 'Oil rig!' and in that joyous, frenzied cry the Larkin boom was born.

The trucks rolled into Courthouse Square, pulled up before the sheriff's office, and asked where Larkin Tank was. Then, consulting the maps they had been given, they headed north toward the land whose surface was owned by the Yeagers but whose mineral rights were still controlled by Floyd Rusk.

No sooner had the three trucks left town than Rusk appeared in his pickup, accompanied by Dewey Kimbro, and when the new newspaper editor shouted: 'What's up?' Rusk cried back: 'We're spudding in an oil well.'

Much of the town followed the trucks out to a marked depression east of the tank where Rusk #1 was to be dug, and what they saw became the topic of conversation for many days, because when Paul Yeager, forty-nine years old and soft-spoken, saw the three men on the lead truck preparing to open his gate and drive onto his land, he ran forward to protest: 'This is Yeager land. Keep off.'

'We know it's Yeager land. We've been lookin' for it,' and the truck started to roll toward the opened gate.

'I warned you to stop!' Yeager cried, his voice rising.

'Mister, it ain't for you to say.' And in the next frantic moments, with Yeager trying to halt the trucks, the people of Larkin learned a lot about Texas law.

'Mr. Yeager,' the man in charge of the drilling rig explained, 'the mineral rights to this here land reside with Mr. Floyd Rusk, and he's asked us . . .'

'Here's Rusk now. Floyd, what in hell . . . ?'

'Drillin' rig, Paul. We think there may be oil under this land.'

'You can't come in here.'

'Yes, we can. The law says so.'

'I don't believe it.'

'You better check, because we're comin' in.'

'You can't bring those big trucks through my crops.'

'Yes we can, Paul, so long as we compensate you for any damage. The law says so.' And with that, huge Floyd Rusk gently pushed his brother-in-law aside, so that the three trucks could drive in, make a rocky path through the field, and come to a halt at the site decided upon intuitively by the creekologist Dewey Kimbro.

A lawyer hired by Yeager did come out to contest Rusk's right to invade another man's property and destroy some of its crop, but reference to Texas law quickly satisfied him that Rusk had every right to do just what he was doing: 'He's protected, Paul. Law's clear on that.'

So the town watched as Rusk #1 was started in the hollow, and the efficiency of the crew dazzled the watchers, for the men, using an old-style system popular in the 1910s, set to work like a colony of purposeful ants, digging the foundations for the rig, lining the tanks into which the spill would be conserved for analysis, and erecting the pyramidal wooden derrick which would rise seventy feet in the air, that consoling feature of the Texas landscape which proclaimed: 'There may be oil here.'

When the pulley sheaves were fixed atop the derrick and the cables rove through them, the men were ready to affix one end of the cable to the huge drum that raised and lowered it, the other end to the cutting bit that would be dropped downward with considerable force to dig the hole. The rig, when set, would not drill into the earth in any rotary fashion; by the sheer force of falling weight the bit would pulverize its way through rock.

And how was this repetitive fall of the two-ton bit assembly controlled? 'See that heavy wooden beam that's fixed at one end, free at the end over the hole? We call it the *walking beam,* and every time it lifts up, it raises all the heavy tools in the hole. When it releases— Bam! Down they crash, smashing the rock to bits.'

The townspeople could not visualize the force exerted at the end of that drop, nor the effectiveness of the tools used to crush the rock, but after the walking beam had operated for about two hours, the man in charge of the rig signaled for the cutting bit to be withdrawn from the hole, and now the ponderous process was reversed, with the cables pulling the heavy tools up out of the hole, so that the worn bit at the end which had done the smashing could be removed to be resharpened while a replacement, keen as a heavy knife, was sent down to resume the smashing.

'What do they do with the old one?' a garage mechanic asked, and he was shown a kind of blacksmith's shed in which two strong men with eighteen-pound sledges heated the worn bit and hammered it back into cutting shape.

And that was the basic process which the people of Larkin studied with such awe: sharpen the bit, attach it to the string of tools, raise it high on the cable, lower it into the hole, then work the walking beam and allow the sharp edge to smash down on the rock until something gave; then undo the whole package, fit on a new bit, resharpen the old, and hammer away again.

To the newspaper editor who wanted to share with his readers the complexity of the process, the rig boss said: 'One bit can drill thirty feet, more if it encounters shale. But when it hits really hard sandstone or compacted limestone . . . three feet, we have to take it out and resharpen.'

'Where does the water come from that I see going into the tank?'

'If we're lucky, the hole lubricates itself. If not, we pump water in. The bottom has to be kept wet so that the bit can bite in. Besides, we have to bring up samples.' And he showed the newsman how a clever tool called the *bailer* was let down into the hole from which the drilling bit had been removed: 'It has this trick at the bottom. Push it against the bottom, and water swirls inside. Let it rise, it closes off the tube. Then pull it up on the cable and dump it into the slush pit.' When the newsman looked at the big square hole the crew had prepared, thirty feet on a side, ten inches deep, he thought that the waste water was being discarded.

"Oh, no! Look at that fellow. One of the most important men we have. He samples every load of water. What kind of rock? What consistency? What kind of sand?'

'Why?'

'It's his job to paint a picture of the inside of our well. Every different layer, if he can do it. Because only then do we know what we have.'

The operation of the rig, twenty-four hours a day, was so compelling—with men delving into the secrets of earth, lining the hole with casing to keep it open, cementing sections of the hole, fishing like schoolboys for parts which had broken and lodged at the bottom, calculating the tilt of the rocks and their composition—that it became a fascinating game which preoccupied all of Larkin and much of Texas, for it was known throughout the oil industry that 'Rusk #1 west of Jacksboro is down to eighteen hundred feet, stone-dry.' Spectators learned new words, which they bandied deftly: 'They're underreaming at two thousand.' 'They've cemented-in at two thousand two.' And always there was the hope that on this bright morning the word would flash: 'Rusk #1 has come in!'

But the town was also involved in something equally colorful, for the ten roughnecks who had come with the rig were proving themselves to be of a special breed, the likes of which Larkin had never before seen. Rugged, powerful of arm, incredibly dirty from the slop of the rig, impatient with anyone who was not connected with the drilling business, they were among the ablest professionals in the country. The three top experts had come down from the oil fields of Pennsylvania, where their forebears had been drilling for oil since 1859, when Colonel Drake brought in that first American well at Titusville; he had struck his bonanza at a mere sixty-nine feet. The next echelon were Texas men who had worked in Arkansas and Louisiana in years when activity focused there. But the men who gave the crew character were Texans who had worked only in this state. They were violent, catlike men who knew they could lose a finger or an arm if the dallied with the flashing cable or did not jump quickly enough if something went wrong with the walking beam.

On the job they were self-disciplined, for if even one man failed to perform, the safety of all might be imperiled, but off the job they wanted things their way, and what they wanted most was booze, women and a good poker game. This brought them into conflict with the Ku Klux Klan, which had disciplined Larkin along somewhat divergent lines, and the trouble started when three of the men imported high-flying ladies from Fort Griffin and set them up at Nora's place, where the creekologist Dewey Kimbro and his girl Esther still maintained quarters.

Within two nights the Klansmen learned of the goings-on, and in their hoods three of them marched out to Nora's to put a stop to this frivolity, but they were met by the three roughnecks, who said: 'What is this shit? Take off your night-shirts.'

'We're warning you, get those girls out of town by Thursday night or face the consequences.'

'You come out here again in those nightshirts, you're gonna get your ass blown off. Now get the hell out of here.'

The Klansmen returned on Thursday night, as promised, but the three sponsors of the girls were on the night shift, so the protectors of morality satisfied them-selves by having the three girls arrested and hauling them off to jail. When the oilmen reached Nora's after a hard night on the rig, they expected a little com-panionship, but instead found Nora weeping: 'They warned me that if the girls ever came back, and that included Esther, they was gonna burn the place down.'

The oilmen, collecting the other two from their shift, marched boldly to the jail and informed the custodian there, not the sheriff, that if he didn't deliver those girls in three minutes, they were going to blow the place apart. He turned them loose, and with considerable squealing and running, the eight rioters—three girls, five oilmen—roared back to Nora's, where they organized a morning party with Esther.

The Klan met that night to decide what to do about the invaders, and many of the men looked to Floyd Rusk for guidance: 'What I say is, let's get the well dug. If we find oil like Kimbro assures me we will, we'll all have enough money to settle other questions later.' When there was grumbling at such temporizing, he said: 'You know me. I'm a law-and-order man.'

'There ain't much law and order when a gang of roughnecks can raid our jail and turn loose our prisoners.'

'Oilmen are different,' Rusk said, and there the matter rested, for in Texas, when morality was confronted by the possibility of oil, it was the former which had to give . . . for a while.

Dewey Kimbro had guessed wrong on Rusk #1. It went to three thousand feet, and was still stone-dry. So the great Larkin oil boom went bust, but it was not a wasted effort, for at two thousand three hundred feet Dewey had spotted in the slush pond indications of the Strawn Sand formation, which excited him enormously. Sharing the information only with Rusk, he said: 'Let them think we missed. Then buy up as many leases as we can west of our dry Number One, because Strawn is promising.'

So, wearing his poor mouth, Rusk went to one landowner after another, saying: 'Well, looks like the signs deceived us. But maybe over the long haul . . .' He offered to take their mineral leases off their hands at twenty-five cents an acre, and when he had vast areas locked up, he asked Kimbro: 'Now what?'

'I'm dead certain we have a major concentration down there. I see evidences of it wherever I look. It's got to be there, Mr. Rusk.'

'But where?'

'That's the problem. East of Number One or west? I can't be sure which.'

'Your famous gut feeling? What's it say?'

Kimbro drove Rusk out to the area and showed him how Rusk #1 had lain at the bottom of a dip: 'It's the land formations west of here that set my bells ringing. Damn, I do believe our field is hiding down there, below the first concentration of Strawn Sand, like maybe three thousand feet.'

'We have money for only one more try. Where should it be?'

'I am much inclined toward the tank,' and he indicated a spot close to the statue which sentimentalists had erected to mark the spot where the lovers Nellie Minor and Jim Logan had committed suicide by drowning—that was the legend now—but Rusk objected to digging there: 'The women in town would raise hell if we touched that place.' So they moved farther west, and finally, on a slight rise, Dewey scraped his heel in the dust: 'Rusk Number Two. And I know it'll be good.' When he said this, Rusk asked: 'If you know so much, why don't the big boys? They have their spies here, you know.'

'The big companies depend on little men like me to find oil for them. Then they move in, fast. We get our small profit. They get their big haul.'

'I want the big haul, Kimbro.'

'So do I. So let's drill over here where I've marked Rusk Number Two.'

'That's on Yeager's land.'

'But it's in your mineral rights.'

'We'll have trouble if we go back again.'

'Law's on our side.'

So Rusk #2 was started, with the same drilling team and the same girls staying at Nora's; when there was still a good chance for oil, even the Klan had to adjust

With scouts from nine large companies watching every move Dewey Kimbro made, Floyd Rusk drilled a second dry hole at three thousand one hundred feet, and now his money began to run out. He had invested most of his ready cash in hiring the drilling crew, and a good portion of his savings in buying up leases.

But when the crunch came, Dewey Kimbro, like a true wildcatter, wanted to risk more money: 'Mr. Rusk, so help me God, what we must do is acquire more leases. If you have to pawn your wife's wedding ring, do it and get those lease

They'll be dirt cheap now. People are laughing at us. But they don't know what we know.'

'And what's that?'

'More signs of oil, I saw them myself when I took the samples at twenty-nine hundred feet.'

'Was that significant?'

'Significant? My God, don't you realize what I'm saying? On Rusk Number One we found indications at twenty-three hundred feet. Now, over here, at Rusk Number Two, we find it at both twenty-three hundred and twenty-nine hundred. Means that oil is down there somewhere. My judgment is our next well has got to hit. I know the field must lie between Number One and Number Two, and we've got to get those leases.'

'You find the money. I don't have any more.'

So Dewey Kimbro set out to con the entire state of Texas into supporting his wild dream of an oil field north of Larkin, in an area which had never produced a cup of oil. He hectored his friends from his student days at A&M, and young men who specialized in the practical courses offered there often did well, so they had money, but they refused to risk it. He badgered his oil acquaintances from the eastern fields, but they knew from their own studies that Larkin held no promise. And he buttonholed any gambler who had ever taken a chance on Texas oil, traveling as far as Nevada and Alabama to trace them.

He was, of course, only one of several hundred visionaries who were flogging the Texas dream that year. Some crazies were trying to convince their friends that there had to be oil in unlikely places like Longview, Borger and Mentone. Others claimed that the area north of Fort Stockton had to have oil, and a hundred others lobbied for places of their choice, where oil would never be found. It was a time of oil fever, and no one had the malady more virulently than Dewey Kimbro.

Except, perhaps, Floyd Rusk, for when the fat man realized that all his savings and even his ranch were committed to this adventure, he became monomaniacal about bringing in the field that Dewey kept assuring him existed under the leases which he already controlled. He was determined to see this exploration through, for he had convinced himself that he could recognize the formations when Kimbro pointed them out. Millions upon millions of years ago a lake of oil had been trapped down there among the sandstone and the limestone tilts, and he wanted it.

But he had no money. Digging the two dry holes had exhausted his funds, and with Kimbro finding little success in borrowing replacements, he did not know where to turn, but one morning when the drillers said they wanted to haul their rig back east to more promising sites, and would do so unless paid promptly, he went to the one person in whom he did not wish to confide.

Emma Larkin Rusk, the onetime prisoner of the Comanche, was sixty-six that year, a frail shadow weighing not much over a hundred pounds. The stubs of her ears showed beneath the wisps of hair that no longer masked her deformity, and her balsa-wood nose seemed to fit less properly, now that she had lost so much weight. But she was alert and already knew that her difficult son was in trouble.

'My first two wells were dry,' he said.

'I know.'

'But we're sure the next one will hit.'

'Why don't you drill it?'

'No money.'

'None?'

'Not a dime.'

'And you want me to lend you some?'

'Yes.'

She sat with her hands folded, staring at her unlovely son, this glutton who had never done anything right. When she had hoped to make a man of him, through R. J. Poteet, he had fumbled the opportunity, and when in 1901 after her husband's death she had turned over the operation of the ranch to him, he had bungled it so badly that she had to step back in and save it. Now he wanted to borrow her life savings, the funds which allowed her to live in her own house rather than impose on him and Molly.

There was no sensible reason why she should lend this grotesque man the money he wanted, but there was an overpowering sentimental one. He had carved the nose she wore and which had made such a difference in her life, and although their relationship had been a miserable one, she loved him for that one gesture. She had known great terror in her life, and little love apart from that which her daydreaming husband had given so freely, so she cherished every manifestation made in her behalf. Floyd was her son, and at one accidental point in his miserable life he had loved her. She would lend him the money.

But life had made her a wily woman, so before she relinquished her funds she drove a bargain. When he asked her 'What interest?' she said 'None,' and he thanked her. Then she added: 'But I do want five thousand more acres for my Longhorns,' and since he was in the perilous position of having to accept any terms in order to get his gambling money, he said: 'Promised,' and she asked: 'Fenced in?' and he had to reply: 'Yes.'

However, when they went out to inspect the land she had thus acquired for her chosen animals, she saw that the proposed rig was going to stand very close to the statue commemorating the two lovers, and Floyd expected her to raise the devil. Instead she stood quietly and looked at the unassembled derrick. 'How appropriate,' she said. 'They lived in turbulence. Better than most, they'll adjust to an oil boom . . . if we get one. I'm sure they hope you hit, Floyd. I do.'

And so with his mother's money Rusk kept his gamble alive.

Then began the days of anxiety. Even with Emma's contribution the partnership lacked enough funds to start drilling its third well, the one that seemed likely to produce, and this meant that the ill-assorted team—gross, surly Floyd and tenacious, ratlike Dewey—faced double disasters. The leases on the very promising land, which they had taken for only one year, were about to run out, and the drilling crew was eager to move east. The partners knew they had less than two months to resolve these problems.

The nature of a Texas oil lease was this: if a lease expired on 30 June 1923, as these did, the holder had a right to start drilling at his choice of time up to one minute before midnight on the thirtieth. If he did not or could not start, the lease lapsed and could be resold to some other wildcatter. But if the holder did start his drilling within his time allowance, the full provisions of the lease came into effect and prevailed for centuries to come. So each of the partners, in his own way, began to scrounge around for additional funds.

Rusk stayed in Larkin, badgering everyone, begging them to lend him money, and he was embittered when his Ku Klux Klan compatriots turned him down. Some did so out of conviction, because they felt it was his greed that had brought the ten oil-field roughnecks, with their devil-driven ways, into Larkin. But most rejected him because they saw him to be a burly, aggressive, overbearing man who deserved to get his comeuppance.

Kimbro, on the other hand, traveled widely, still hoping to find the speculator who would grubstake him for the big attack on the hidden field. He would go anywhere, consult with anyone, and offer almost any kind of inducement: 'Let me have the money, less than a year, ten-percent interest, and I'll give you one-thirty-second of my participation.' He offered one-sixteenth, even one-eighth, but found no takers.

When he returned to Larkin in April 1923, he was almost a defeated man, but because he was a born wildcatter he could not let anyone see his despair. Each morning when he was in town he repaired to the greasy café where the oilmen who had begun to infiltrate the area assembled to make their big boasts, and he knew it was essential that they see him at the height of his confidence: 'We expect to start Number Three any day now. Big investors from Tulsa, you know.' But each day that passed brought the partnership closer to collapse.

Now the serious gambling started, the reckless dealing away of percentages. One morning Floyd rushed to the café, took Dewey into the men's room, and almost wept: 'The drilling crew is hauling their rig back to Jacksboro.'

'We can't let them do that. Once they get off our land, we'll never get them back,' so the partners, smiling broadly as if they had concluded some big deal in the toilet, walked casually through the café, nodding to the oilmen, then dashed out to the rig.

Rusk had been right, the men were starting to dismantle it prior to mounting it on trucks, but when Dewey cried: 'Wait! We'll give you one-sixteenth of our seven-eighths,' they agreed to take the chance, for they, too, had seen the Strawn signs.

Later Rusk asked: 'Could we afford to give so much?' and Dewey explained the wildcatter's philosophy: 'If the well proves dry, who gives a damn what percentage they have? And if it comes in big, like I know it will, who cares if they have their share?'

A week before the termination of the leases the partners still had insufficient funds to drill their well, but now Kimbro heard from two of his A&M gamblers who wanted to get in on the action, but to get their money he had to give away one-eighth of his share to the first friend, one-sixteenth to the other—and the final ownership of the well became so fractionized that the partners could scarcely untangle the proportions.

Three days before the leases expired, scandal struck the operation, for the two A&M men, always a canny lot, heard the rumor that their old buddy Dewey Kimbro had pulled an oil-field sting on them, and they rode into town ready to tear him apart: 'He sold two hundred percent of his well. Peddled it all over East Texas.'

'What's that mean?' the Larkin men asked.

'Don't you see? If he drills dry, and he's already done so twice, he owes us nothing. He's collected twice, spends about one-quarter of the total, and goes off laughing with our dough.'

They drove out to the proposed drilling site at the tank to challenge Kimbro, but when they found him hiking back and forth over the rolling terrain, trying to settle upon the exact spot for his final well, they found him honestly engaged in trying to find oil. He had not sold two hundred percent of what he knew was going to be a dry well; he was gambling his entire resources upon one lucky strike, and as Texas gamblers, they were satisfied to be sharing in his risk.

Two days before the lapse of their leases, Rusk and Kimbro finally got a break. An Oklahoma wildcatting outfit had figured that if Dewey Kimbro, once of Humble and Gulf, thought there was oil in the Larkin area, it was a good location in which to take a flier. They had drilled a well just to the east of Rusk #1, gambling that the suspected oil lay in that direction and not toward the tank. These men, of course, could not know that Dewey had struck indications to the west, so down they went to five thousand feet, missing the field entirely and producing nothing but a very dry well, whose failure they announced on June 28.

This helped Kimbro in two ways: it verified his hunch that the field did not lie to the east of Rusk #1, and it so disheartened the Larkin landowners—three test holes, three buckets of dust—that they became determined to offload their worthless leases throughout the entire area. In a paroxysm of energy, Dewey shouted at Rusk and his two A&M buddies: 'Now's the time to pick up every damned lease in the district. My God, won't somebody lend me ten thousand dollars?' Faced by total disaster if his Rusk #3 did not come in, he spent two days committing his last penny to his belief that he would strike it rich this time. By dint of telegram, telephone calls and the most ardent personal appeals to speculators in the Larkin-Jacksboro-Fort Griffin area, he put together a substantial kitty, which he spent on leases that encapsulated the field.

At six in the morning of 30 June 1923, Dewey Kimbro appeared at the oilmen's café with a smile so confident and casual that a stranger might think he was about to start a well with the full weight of Gulf Oil behind him, and when Floyd Rusk came in, sweating like a pig, Dewey caught him by the wrist and whispered: 'Dry your face,' for he, Dewey, had been in such perilous situations before; Rusk had not.

When they rode out to the field, with Dewey commenting on the brightness of this summer's day, Rusk was vaguely aware that if Rusk #3 did strike oil, profits would be divided in this typically Texan way, the intricate details of which had been worked out by lawyers and filed in long legal documents:

PARTICIPANTS		LEGAL DIVISION	ACTUAL SPLIT OF ALL INCOME
Owner of mineral rights, standard lease	1/8	.125000	.125000
Rusk and Kimbro for their enterprise	7/8	.875000	
		1.000000	
But Rusk and Kimbro split their 7/8 :			
Drilling team for staying on job	1/16	.054688	.054688
Rusk and Kimbro will share	15/16	.820313	
		.875001	
Rusk and Kimbro split their .820313:			
Rusk 3/4		.615235	
Kimbro 1/4		.205078	
		.820313	
But Rusk must split his .615235:			
Emma Rusk 1/4		.153809	.153809
Floyd Rusk 3/4		.461426	.461426
		.615235	
And Kimbro must split his .205078:			
A&M first investor 1/8		.025635	.025635
A&M second investor 1/16		.012817	.012817
Kimbro 13/16		.166626	.166626
		.205078	1.000001

Thus, the second A&M investor was entitled to $7/8 \times 15/16 \times 1/4 \times 1/16$ of the whole, or $105/8192$ (.012817), which meant that every time the well produced $100,000, he received $1281.74 for as long as the well operated.

On an August afternoon in 1923 a hanger-on who had watched the drilling of Rusk #3 as he would a baseball game, came riding back to Larkin in his Ford, screaming: 'They got oil!'

The citizens, hoping to see a great gusher sprouting from the plains, sped out to the tank, where, on its flank, hardened men were dancing and crying and slapping each other with oil-splattered hands. They did not have a gusher; the famous field at Larkin did not contain either the magnitude or the subterranean pressure to provide that kind of spectacular exhibition, but Dewey Kimbro, seeing the oil appear and making such guesses as he could on fragmentary evidence, said: 'Could be a hundred and ten barrels a day, for years to come.'

He was right. The Larkin Field, as it came to be known, was going to be a slow, steady producer. Spacious in extent but not very deep, it was the kind of field that would allow wells to be dug almost anywhere inside its limits with the sober assurance that at around three thousand feet in the Strawn Sand a modest amount of oil would be forthcoming, year after year after year.

'And the glory of it is,' Kimbro told Rusk when they were back home at midnight, 'we know pretty well the definition of the field. Our first dry well to the east plus the dry Oklahoma wildcatter showed us where it ends in that direction. Our dry Number Two proved where it ends in the west. What we don't know is how far north and south.'

'Forever,' Rusk said, 'and by God, we control it all.' For one glorious moment these two men who had once wanted to kill each other danced in the darkened kitchen.

In the early fall of 1923, Larkin became the hottest boom town in Texas, with oilmen from all parts of America streaming in to try their luck at the far perimeters of the undefined field. To a stranger, the Larkin Field did not look like a typical oil site, because as soon as a well was dug, the towering pyramidal structure that meant oil to the layman was quickly moved to some other location for more drilling. The actual pumping of oil from deep below the surface was turned over to an unromantic donkey engine, a small low-slung affair which could barely be seen from a distance. The donkey, powered by gasoline, worked its relatively short arm up and down incessantly, and from it poured the oil which was turning Larkin gamblers into millionaires.

Companies big and little rushed in their landmen to acquire leases, and wherever they turned they found themselves confronted by Floyd Rusk, who either owned the land, controlled the leases, or had power of attorney for handling the leases owned by his partner, Dewey Kimbro.

It was now that Rusk demonstrated both his devious managerial skill and his untamed voraciousness, for he saw quickly that he and Kimbro controlled far more land than they could ever drill. And if they didn't act quickly, they would lose certain of their short-term leases outright and then watch as other men's wells sucked out the oil from under their long-term ones. As if he had been in the business for generations, Rusk dealt out his leases to the major companies, scattering them so they would do his own holdings the most good, and using the money he obtained from them for the drilling of his own additional wells.

'A man could make a good livin',' he told Kimbro, 'just buyin' and sellin' leases and never drillin' an inch into the ground. Let some other dumb bastard do the hard work.'

Now a fundamental difference between the two partners surfaced. Kimbro loved oil itself, the endless search, even the heartbreaking failures, the lucky hit, the bringing of oil to the surface, while Rusk's interest blossomed only when the bubbling oil came into his actual possession. He reveled in the tricky deals, the exploitation, the pyramiding of the wealth that oil provided.

If left alone, Kimbro would have ranged over all of Texas, identifying new fields, bringing them to fruition, and then turning them over to the managerial care of Floyd Rusk; his only interest in the money which his wells produced was that it enabled him to search for others. However, under Rusk's canny leadership, Kimbro was kept close to the Larkin Field, which the partners manipulated as if it were some giant poker game, and more than one major company entered into its files a recommendation that Floyd Rusk be either shot or placed on the board of directors: 'That son-of-a-bitch knows oil.'

They were only partly right, for if Rusk quickly mastered the intricacies of dealing in leases, he never could visualize the lake of oil which lay hidden under his ranch and under the leases he controlled. Kimbro was powerless to explain that an oil field was one of the most delicately balanced marvels of nature: 'Floyd, goddamnit, our field has a limited life. The pressure which delivers the oil to us must be maintained.'

Kimbro drew maps of the underground reservoir, showing Floyd how the entrapment by rocks kept the lake of oil in position, and how water and gas provided the pressure which enabled the drillers to bring it to the surface: 'Destroy that pressure, or dissipate it, and you can lose your field.'

He astounded Rusk by predicting that if wells continued to be dug so promiscuously at Larkin, the pressure would be drawn off at so many random sites that only about ten percent of the oil locked underground would ever be recovered, and when Rusk did finally understand this, it had exactly the opposite result from what Kimbro had intended.

'By God, if it's limited, let's get ours now.'

So he dug numerous wells on his own property, producing vastly more raw petroleum than could be marketed, and on his better leases he encouraged everyone else to do the same, until Larkin fairly groaned with oil. When all the fuel lines were jammed and the open earthen pits were rotting with the dark stuff, whose volatile oils were thus dissipated, he watched as the price dropped from a dollar a barrel to the appalling figure of ten cents, and even then he could not comprehend the need for more disciplined measures. Like a true Texan he bellowed: 'We don't want no government interference. We found this field. We developed it, and by God, we'll work it our way.'

His wasteful procedure was not preposterous, so far as he was concerned, because he had varied ways to multiply his wealth. He owned thirty-three wells outright; he shared a seventy-five-percent interest in nineteen others; and he received huge yearly rentals for leases which the big companies held on the acreage he could not himself develop. By the close of that first year he was a millionaire four times over, with every prospect of doubling and then redoubling and then quadrupling.

His tremendous good luck had little effect upon him personally, for he rarely spent money on himself beyond the sheerest necessities. He still moved his huge bulk about the oil fields in a Ford truck; he wore the same rancher's outfit, the same battered Stetson, the same cheapest-line General Quimper boots. At the morning breakfasts in the café, which now had thirty tables filled with oilmen, he never picked up the checks at his corner unless he had specifically invited someone to eat with him, which he did infrequently. He gave no money to the Baptist church, none to the school, none to the hospital. In fact, he attended only spasmodically to his income and would have been unable to tell anyone how much he had accumulated.

He did buy three good bulls, for in Texas, oil and ranching enjoyed a symbiotic relationship which no Northern oilman ever understood. If you took a thousand Texas oil wells, you could be sure that nine hundred were drilled so that some dreaming man without a dime could buy himself a ranch, for it was said in the business: 'Ain't nothin' makes a steer grow better than good pasturage, a pinch of phosphorus in the soil, and freedom to scratch hisself on an oil derrick.'

With his first big check from Gulf for his leases, he purchased an additional five thousand acres for his ranch, and with his second check, he drove north to meet with Paul Yeager: 'I think my father made a mistake promisin' you this land, and I made a bigger mistake transferrin' it to you legal. Paul, I want to buy it back. Name your price.'

'I'm not selling.'

'Paul, you got no mineral rights. You got no leasin' rights. To you this is just so much rock and grama grass. You'll never do anything with it. I need it.'

'I told you, it's not for sale.'

'You know, we're goin' to put six, seven more wells on your place.'

'I don't think you are.'

'Now, Paul! Law's the law. Name your price—sixty dollars an acre? Eighty dollars?'

Rusk was unable to swing a deal, and some days after he had sent his men up to the tank to start a new well on the Yeager land, they came roaring back with a horrendous story: 'Like you ordered, we was headed for the north end of the Yeager lease, but he met us at the gate with a shotgun. We said "We got legal right" and he said "No more laws. You come on my land, I shoot." So we drove right in, as you said to do, and by God, he shot.'

'Kill anybody?'

'Elmer's hurt bad. Doctor's tendin' him.'

In gargantuan fury Floyd Rusk rampaged around town looking for the sheriff, and after he found him, a posse drove north to handle Paul Yeager. They found him standing at the gate to his ranch, shotgun still in hand.

'Don't come in here!' he warned.

'Paul, the law says—'

'Stand back, Fat Belly. No more of your trucks on my land.'

'Yeager!' the sheriff shouted. 'Put down that gun and—'

Yeager fired, not at the sheriff but at Rusk, who with extraordinary nimbleness dropped to the ground, whipped out his Colts, and drilled his brother-in-law through the head.

There were seventeen witnesses, of course, to testify that Paul Yeager had aimed a shotgun at the sheriff and had nearly killed Floyd Rusk, who had fired back in self-defense. No trial was ever held, and after the burial Rusk asked the sheriff to ride out to the Yeager ranch and offer Mrs. Yeager a good price for her lands without saying who the bidder was. Before the month was out, Rusk had regained the land his father should never have given away, and the Rusk rigs were free to move about it as they wished.

If Floyd Rusk was little moved by his sudden wealth, this was not the case with Molly, for when that first check from Gulf Oil proved that prosperity was real, she went to Ed Boatright at the Chevy garage, rented a car and a driver, and posted in to Neiman-Marcus in Dallas. There she went to the most expensive salon in the store and announced, in a loud voice, that she wanted the head saleslady and a very large wastebasket.

When she was shown into a discreet area where only the best clothing was sold —fabrics from England, styling from France—she started undressing, throwing each of her old and long-worn garments into the wastebasket, and when it was filled with every item except her panties, she announced: 'I want them burned.'

'We'll take them to the basement.'

'I want them burned here. I never want to see those damned rags again.'

'But, madam—'

'Don't madam me, burn them.'

The manager was called, but since Molly was nearly naked, he could not speak with her directly; he did, however, give strict orders that there would be no burning of anything on that floor, but Molly was so vociferous that he asked: 'Who is this crazy dame?' and Molly heard the saleswoman explain: 'She's the wife of that fellow who hit the big oil field at Larkin,' and the manager said: 'Burn them.'

Firemen were alerted, but before they could appear, Molly was covered with an expensive lounging robe, of which she said: 'I'll take it.' And so draped, she watched as men with fire extinguishers supervised the burning of her old wardrobe. When the fire went out, and her applause died down, she proceeded to spend $5,600 on replacements and left an order for $3,800 worth of other items to be sent to Larkin as soon as they arrived from New York and London.

She sent Ed Boatright's driver home alone, carrying in the back of his Chevy many of her purchases. For herself she bought a large new Packard from a Dallas dealer recommended by Neiman-Marcus and hired one of the firm's drivers to chauffeur her back to Larkin.

In four months the population of Larkin jumped from 2,329 to more than 19,700, and this resulted in revolutionary change. Take housing, for example. The little town obviously could not accommodate such a tremendous influx in existing structures, so extraordinary solutions had to be sought, and old-time residents gaped when they saw a convoy of sixty mules on the road from Jacksboro, each four hauling on a farm flatbed a house lifted from its foundations farther east. Tents were at a premium, and any householder with a spare room could rent it at three dollars a day to each of four occupants. Many beds were used three times a day, in eight-hour shifts, and food was grabbed wherever it was provided and in whatever condition.

Every businessman saw his turnover quadrupled within the month, and by the end of the year, men who sold what the oil crews needed found themselves enormously wealthy. The Tumlinson twins maintained six trucks to haul in the long lengths of lumber required for building derricks and the associated small buildings at a site. They also imported huge supplies of coal for the winter months and almost any hardware they could find in places like Fort Worth and Dallas. One twin said: 'All we are, really, is a turnover point. We rarely keep anything past the weekend.'

And Ed Boatright sold absolutely any car he could get his hands on and employed six new mechanics to keep the cars he had sold running: 'The roads to an oil field are murder on cars, but my men are geniuses.'

The sudden inflow of money altered many things, because it was the very type of man who had played a major role in the reactionary Ku Klux Klan who found himself in position to make the most profit from the exploding trade, and onetime leaders like the Tumlinson twins and Boatright became so preoccupied with their expanding business that they no longer had time to monitor community morals. An older man who had taken the Klan quite seriously tried to summon his cohorts back to the continuing task of policing, but some of the younger men told

him: 'Let's get this oil thing settled . . . the buildings we need and everything
. . . and then we'll take care of the riffraff that's wandered in.' The Klan did not
intend closing shop; its impulses were too deep and strong for that, but it did
propose to make a dollar while the chance existed.

Some activities of the boom did eventually occasion real soul-searching on the
part of Larkin citizens, whether they were members of the Klan or not. The
woman Nora, whom the Klan had once punished, now ran a house which contained eleven young women who had flocked in from as far away as Denver, and
no one could ignore what business the young ladies were conducting. The
founder of the town's good fortune, Dewey Kimbro, still lived in the house with
his girl Esther, but he had to be indulged because he was now well on his way to
becoming a millionaire, and that excused a lot.

As a matter of fact, the former puritans would have been happy if the seamier
side of their town had been as quietly run as Nora's place, but Larkin received a
black eye when a reporter for the *New York Times* came to town to verify the
rumor that 'Larkin is the most sinful little town in America.' He probed about for
nine or ten days, picking up the usual colorful stories about 'a saloon called The
Bucket of Blood, and a gambling hall named The Missionary's Downfall,' but
such accounts could have applied to almost any oil-boom town or any temporary
railhead in the West. What made this man's story provocative was his detailed
account of how the town fathers were profiting from the boom:

> Each Sunday morning, just after dawn, the sheriff and his enthusiastic
> men prowl the dives and the haunts, arresting any ladies of the night
> found therein and carting them off to jail in the Ford paddy wagon
> belonging to the police. This happens in any frontier town and is not
> remarkable.
>
> What is remarkable is that on Monday morning these ladies, some of
> them extremely beautiful, are lined up on a public balcony of the fine
> red-and-white courthouse in the public square, and while the oilmen
> and the young fellows of town gather enthusiastically below, a judge of
> some kind steps onto the balcony, lifts the left arm of one of the young
> women, and announces the amount of her fine.
>
> The men below then bid vigorously for the right to pay her fine, but the
> first bid must be the fine itself. Thus, if Mary Belle has been fined three
> dollars, the bidding must start there, but it can rise as high as the young
> woman's charms justify, and calls from all parts make the bidding quite
> exciting.
>
> When a winner has been determined, he pays the amount bid and then
> receives all rights to the young lady for the next twenty-four hours. On

Tuesday through Saturday, of course, she works at her regular stand, but on Sunday she will be arrested and on Monday the auction will resume.

When this reporter asked a Larkin official how such behavior could be justified, he explained: 'We have to pay for the extra police somehow.'

When this story reached New York, the editors of the *Times* felt, with some justice, that here was a case where the legend of the paper ought to be respected— 'All the News That's Fit to Print'—and they decided that such a yarn, with its many implications, would have to be excluded if the legend were to be honored. They killed the story, which so angered the young reporter that he gave it lock, stock, and barrel to a reporter from Chicago, whose paper not only refrained from censoring it, but telegraphed for pictures. A professional photographer took a series of graphic shots and provided a caption explaining that the rowdy young ladies had on this Monday morning fetched an average price of $9.80, which figured to be $6.80 above their basic fines.

Such affairs were amusing, but another aspect of the boom was more ominous. Any town which found itself the center of an oil strike, and especially one which expanded horizons with each new well that struck oil, was bound to attract the really criminal elements of society, and as the winter of 1924 started, Larkin had a plethora of gamblers, holdup men, con artists, thieves, escaped murderers, and every other kind of human refuse imaginable.

'This town is becoming ungovernable,' Floyd Rusk cried one January morning when two corpses were found in an alley near the courthouse, but when he spoke he did not yet know who one of the dead men was.

'My God, Floyd! It's Lew Tumlinson!'

It was. There was no record of his having been involved with any of the hoodlums, and he was not robbed. True, he was some distance from his coal and lumber business, but he was in a respectable part of town and no one recalled his having been mixed up with any of the imported girls. His death was a mystery, but was soon forgotten.

The shootings in Larkin produced an average of one murder every two and a half weeks, by no means a record for an oil town. Usually the deaths occurred as a result of gambling or fighting over women; there was almost no murder for profit, as in the old days when Rattlesnake Peavine prowled these parts. Opined the editor of the *Defender:* 'It is understandable that men who have been too long restrained in less adventurous occupations will find release for their spirits in an oil town.'

But then Ed Boatright was found shot dead, and people began to ask: 'Is the lawlessness going to attack all of us? Have things gotten out of hand?' Some of the old Ku Kluxers felt that maybe they would have to reconstitute the vigilantes and bring the town back under control. Affairs drifted along in this way, with gambler or a roughneck being shot now and then, until one day in early March when the town echoed with gunfire and the other Tumlinson twin was found dead.

Now terror gripped the area, and men working in oil began employing armed guards. Chief among those frightened by the spate of killings was Floyd Rusk, who, because of his preeminence and his new fortune, would seem to be an attractive target, and when associates suggested that he hire himself a bodyguard, he listened. But one night as he sat alone in his kitchen—he did not yet have an office—contemplating the dismal condition into which his oil town had fallen, a terrible thought attacked him: My God! Boatright! The Tumlinsons! They were with me when we whipped Dewey Kimbro.

He began to sweat. Desperately he tried to recall anything that Dewey had said either during the flogging or next day when they made their pact about the oil field: I'm sure he didn't speak during the flogging. Nothing. He deserved it and he knew it. But then Floyd's assurance left him, for he could remember bits of conversation in the kitchen that next remarkable morning: He knew I hadn't touched him. He said so. Yes, he did say that, I remember clearly. Taking hope from the fact that he had not actually whipped his future partner, he was beginning to breathe more easily, when an appalling recollection gagged him: My God, I'm sure he mentioned the names of the other three. I can hear him now: 'But you ordered the Tumlinson twins and Ed Boatright . . .'

Jesus! He discovered all our names and he's killed three of us. As soon as he thought this, he corrected himself, eagerly, nervously: Not *us*. I had no part in that affair. I never touched him. He's killed the three who did. Then he rose and padded about the kitchen, a huge, sweating man: He's my partner. We bought leases together, surely . . .

He fell back onto his chair and stared bleakly at the wall. Three dead and one to go. Deceiving himself no longer, he reflected on the cleverness of this wiry little man with the sandy red hair: He waited till the town was filled with drifters. He waits till there's action in the streets. Remember the little pistol he had that morning when we talked? God, the man's a determined killer.

Taking a pen from the fruit jar in which he and Molly had always kept one, he drafted a letter to the governor, whose campaign he had supported:

> The town of Larkin, in Larkin County, is no longer governable. Please send militia.
>
> Floyd Rusk

He came into town on a horse, as his grandfather had done in 1883. Like him, he announced himself to no one, sharing a bed with the oilmen and quietly patronizing the saloons and the gambling halls. He visited the cribs in which the prostitutes lived their rowdy lives and studied the bank which had already been held up once. He walked out to the cemetery and checked the rude tombstones for any names which tallied with his printed list of desperadoes to be apprehended on sight, and at the end of five careful days, during which he alerted no one as to his identity, he gained a clear impression of how the town of Larkin functioned.

He was twenty-five years old, about five-seven, not much over a hundred and fifty pounds, and he had the blue eyes so common among both the lawless and the lawmen on the frontier. He was quick with a gun and more prone to use it than his grandfather had been, and like him, he was fearless. He did not consider it unusual to be dispatched alone to clean up a rioting boom town, for that was his business, and on the sixth day he began.

Presenting himself unostentatiously at the café where the oilmen met with town leaders at six each morning, he banged a glass with a spoon to attract attention, and announced: 'I'm Oscar Macnab, Texas Ranger, sent by the governor to bring order to this town.' Before anyone could respond, he moved like a cat, gun drawn, and arrested three men well known to be dealing in stolen oil gear. Rounding them up in a corner, he turned them over to the frightened sheriff, with the warning: 'When I get to your place I want to see these men in jail.'

Deputizing three well-regarded citizens, which he had no legal right to do, he asked: 'Are you armed?' and when one said no, an extraordinary admission in Larkin, he asked for the loan of a gun, and with his aides he left the café and started through the town.

Fortunately, most of the desperate characters, the worst troublemakers, were in bed at that hour, so he had little trouble finding them, and in nightshirts or trousers hastily climbed into, the gamblers, the thieves and the pimps were moved to the courthouse, in whose basement he crowded some three dozen malefactors. This was not a jail, but it was reasonably secure, and he posted at the door two men with shotguns, giving them orders that chilled the captives: 'If anybody tries to escape, don't hesitate. Fire into the mob.'

He then went to the sheriff's office and demanded that he summon the town's policemen, and when representatives of these two agencies stood before him and his new deputies, he asked scornfully: 'Why have you let this town run so wild?' and they said truthfully: 'Because everybody wanted it that way.'

Oscar Macnab, despite his youth and his bravado, was no fool, and after pumping some self-respect into the local officers he went to the telegraph station and wired Ranger headquarters, asking for a famous lawman who had faced similar situations in the boom towns back east: I NEED HELP SEND LONE WOLF. Then he quietly proceeded to consolidate his position before the rabble discovered that he was alone.

He went to the home of Floyd Rusk and sat with him in the kitchen, no gun visible, no scowl on his face: 'I understand it was you who wrote the governor. Tell me about it.'

Rusk was more than eager to; in fact, he blurted out such a lava-flow of information and complaint that Macnab had frequently to direct it: 'But you *were* among the men who flogged Dewey Kimbro that night?'

Later he asked: 'Let me be sure I understand. Dewey Kimbro is now your partner? And as a partner you like him just fine?'

Finally he bore in: 'Have you any possible clue, any proof at all that Kimbro shot your three companions?'

'They were never companions of mine, Ranger Macnab. They just happened to be assigned that job by the Klan.'

'You were, I'm told, the leader of the Klan?' He did not accuse Rusk of this; he merely asked the question, which Floyd rebutted vehemently: 'I was never the Kleagle. We didn't have one, really.'

'But you made the decisions?' Again it was a question, not an accusation, and again Rusk denied that he had held any position of leadership: 'I was just another member.'

'I believe you. Speaking as just another member, why did your group decide to horsewhip Dewey Kimbro?'

'Well now, he was behavin' immorally. He was livin' with this woman. You've met her, Esther, and we told him he had to quit that or get out of town.'

'You didn't tell him. You flogged him.'

'But we had warned him. We warned everybody. We would not tolerate immoral livin'.'

Macnab smiled as much as he ever smiled: 'You seem to tolerate a good deal of it right now. All those women, those cribs.'

'Times have changed, Ranger Macnab.'

Just how much they had changed, Macnab was still to learn, because he had not yet been in Larkin on a Monday morning to see the auction of the whores, and when the legal officials who had not yet adjusted to his presence proceeded with the Monday bidding, Macnab did not interrupt. He stood in the background, appalled by what he saw, and decided to take no further steps until help arrived.

It came in the presence of a legendary member of the Texas Rangers, Lone Wolf Gonzaullas, an extremely handsome man in his thirties noted for his meticulous dress and Deep South courtesy. His greater fame, however, derived from his ever-ready willingness to use the pearl-handled revolvers given him by citizens who had profited from the law and order he had brought to their ravaged towns, and from the fact that he would be the only Ranger captain of partly Spanish descent.

Like Oscar, he came into Larkin on a horse, and like Otto, he did not announce himself to anyone but his fellow Ranger. When he had studied the situation, checking the jail and the cellar of the courthouse, he told Oscar: 'You've handled this right so far, but now we need something that will attract their attention.'

'What did you have in mind?' Macnab asked, and he said: 'I've had good luck in spots like this with a snortin' pole.'

'What's that?'

'Find me two shovels,' and when he had them, he and Oscar rode to the edge of town, where they dug a deep hole, lining it with rocks. Then the two Rangers mounted their horses and dragged in a twelve-foot telephone pole, which they placed in the hole, tamping it with more rocks.

Then, in a series of lightning-swift moves, the two Rangers stormed into one saloon after another and into all the gambling areas, grabbing unlovely characters at random, dragging them out to the edge of town and handcuffing them to chains circling the pole. 'Now snort,' Gonzaullas said, 'while the decent people of this town laugh at you.'

While he stood guard, Macnab hurried to the basement of the courthouse, where he brought forth his original three dozen prisoners. Marching them with his revolvers drawn, he drove them to the snortin' pole, where Gonzaullas bound them to the chains.

When the pole was surrounded by milling outlaws, he issued his orders: 'Think things over till four this afternoon. Then we'll reach decisions.'

As they sweated in the blazing sun, one of the men who had been drinking beer whimpered: 'I have to go to the toilet,' and Lone Wolf said: 'No one's stopping you,' and it was this humiliation which broke the spirit of these culprits.

At four, Gonzaullas revealed his plan: 'If you men are out of town by sunset, no further trouble. If you're in town after dark, beware. Ranger Macnab, start releasing them.' And as the handcuffs were unlocked and the ropes loosened, the prisoners started making plans to flee.

When the field was fairly well cleared, Lone Wolf addressed the citizens: 'People of Larkin, it's all over.' Turning on his heel, pearl-handled revolvers riding on his hips, he went to his horse, signaled Macnab, and rode back to town, where he wanted to meet with Floyd Rusk.

When the two Rangers sat in Floyd's kitchen with him, reviewing the case against Dewey Kimbro, Gonzaullas did the questioning: 'In the period when the Tumlinson twins and Boatright were murdered, how many other men were shot in this town?'

'About nine.'

'What makes you think their case was something special?'

'The others were drifters . . . no-goods.'

This impressed Gonzaullas, and he spent two days interrogating townspeople, especially Nora and Esther, whom he met together: 'You say, Nora, that you and Jake were tarred and feathered and later he was shot?'

'Yes.'

'Do you know who did it?'

'I can guess.'

'And you, Miss Esther, you saw your man Kimbro horsewhipped? Did you know who did it?'

'I heard names.'

'What names?'

'Lew Tumlinson.'

'Who else?'

'His brother Les.'

'Anybody else?'

'Ed Boatright.'

'And all three are dead?'

'They deserved to be.'

'Did Kimbro know those names?'

'He told me to remember them. After they let him go.' She hesitated, suspecting that she was doing her man no good by these admissions: 'He was all cut up, you know. His back . . .'

'Do you think he shot those three men? Getting even?'

'I'm glad somebody did. They came back, you know, and threatened to whip me, too, if I stayed around.'

'Why did you stay?'

'Dewey made a deal with Mr. Rusk. Me stayin' was part of the deal, Dewey said.'

'But if Dewey, as you call him, if he's Mr. Rusk's partner, he must've made a lot of money. Why does he still live in a house like this? Why do you live here?'

'We live simple.'

It was clear to Gonzaullas and Macnab that Dewey Kimbro had probably shot his three assailants, but there could never be any proof, so one morning when the town was pretty well subdued, and permanently, Lone Wolf suggested to Macnab: 'I think we better deal with the principals,' and they summoned Kimbro to Rusk's kitchen.

In ice-cold terms they spelled out the situation, with Macnab doing the talking, since although Gonzaullus was eight years senior, he was the man officially in charge: 'Rusk, you led the posse that night on your partner Kimbro. Kimbro, we know that you learned the names of the men who flogged you, and we have very solid reasons to suspect that you shot those men, one by one, in revenge. But we can't prove it.

'We know something else. If you, Kimbro, have killed three men, so have you, Mr. Rusk, two in Dodge City and Paul Yeager at his ranch gate. And Ranger Gonzaullus and I have had to kill men in our day, in line of duty. So all of us in his room are equal, in a manner of speaking. Ranger Gonzaullus, will you tell 'em what we recommend?'

'It's simple. The flogging happened a long time ago. If you forget it, we'll forget it. You've been partners for some time now, good partners we're told, reliable. Now, Mr. Rusk, you told us that you were afraid you were going to be shot, by Mr. Kimbro, of course, although you didn't say so in your letter to the governor. I have a surprise for you, Mr. Rusk. Did you know that Mr. Kimbro told us he was afraid *you* were going to shoot *him?* To get his share of the partnership, the way you got Yeager's land? And we think he had good reason to be afraid.'

Rusk looked at his partner in dismay: 'Dewey, my God, I'd never shoot you.'

'So here it is,' Lone Wolf said, hands on the table. 'You two are partners, for better or worse, like they say at the wedding. Make the best of it, because when we leave, if we hear that either of you has been shot, we're comin' back to swear out a warrant for the survivor.'

'No court in the land—' Rusk began, but Gonzaullus cut him short: 'Tell him, Macnab.'

'It won't go to court. Because you will be shot, by him or me, resisting arrest.'

In this rough-and-ready way the oil town of Larkin, after eighteen months of flaming hell, was cleaned up. It was a Texas solution to a Texas problem, and it worked.

The little town of Larkin, population reduced to a sane 3,673, now boasted seven millionaires: the richest was Floyd Rusk, whose fortune from his main wells and leases was becoming immense; he was followed by his partner, Dewey Kimbro, who shared in some of Rusk's wells and owned others outright. The Larkin Field was proving out as shrewd Kimbro had predicted, a large, shallow field with an apparently unlimited supply of oil that seemed to dribble out of the ground, not gush. No single well was now producing much over a hundred barrels a day, but 100 barrels × 365 days × 40 wells meant a lot of oil.

Some of the new millionaires spent their money conspicuously, and Dewey often spoke of one who had never fully appreciated the intricacies of the oil game: 'When I went to talk him into leasing us his land, I offered him the standard one-eighth royalty, but he said: "I know you city slickers. I want one-tenth," so after considerable pressure I surrendered. Sometime later he came to me, all infuriated "You dirty scoundrel, you cheated me." I said: "Hold on a minute. You set the royalty, not me," and he said: "I know that. But Gulf offered me one-twelfth."'

Rusk and Kimbro built no big houses and bought no extra cars, but they did almost desperately long for some way to express their wealth, and it was in thi uneasy mood that they discovered football; not Texas A&M football or Universit of Texas football, but Larkin High School football, and in those years, once a oilman or a well-to-do rancher became alerted to the grandeur of Texas hig school football, he was lost, for he developed a mania which lasted foreve growing each year more virulent.

It started because such men worked hard all week—Dewey Kimbro nev ceased looking for oil—and longed for some vigorous relaxation on the weekends. There was hunting, and fishing, and breeding cattle and breaking horses, but in time these palled, and it was then that these men plunged into the Friday afternoon madness.

In those days Texas had no worthy professional football teams, or basketball, either, and good baseball teams played far to the north in St. Louis. Even the universities were far to the east, but there was always the local high school football team, and in time its partisans became as madly concerned with its fortunes as men elsewhere became involved emotionally with the New York Yankees or the Detroit Tigers. Competing area teams, like Wichita Falls, Jacksboro, Abilene and Breckenridge, became monsters who had to be subdued, fair means or foul, and the glorious days of autumn in Texas became heroic.

The mania started casually, with Rusk and Kimbro attending a Friday game in which Larkin's small high school was playing Jacksboro, which had a slightly larger student body. It was a good game, nothing special, with scattered scoring in the first half and Larkin holding on to a 19–14 lead as the game drew to a close. Jacksboro had the ball and it looked as if they might score, for they had mounted a determined drive down the field, but as the seconds ticked away, both Rusk and Kimbro started shouting: 'Hold that line! Get them!' and the roar of the little hometown crowd must have taken effect, for the Larkin men—average age sixteen—did muster courage from somewhere and they did hold.

It was fourth down and nine, twenty seconds to go, with the crowd roaring encouragement, when the Jacksboro coach signaled his captain to call for time-out. Always alert in such situations, Rusk noticed that the coach was wigwagging frantically from the lines, and he whispered to Kimbro: 'I don't like this. Something's up.'

It was a play which would be discussed for years on the oil fields, because just before the whistle blew to resume, Jacksboro made a last-second substitution. A tall end was taken out of the game, and a much shorter boy was inserted, a fact which caused Rusk to tell Kimbro: 'Now that's crazy. They have to pass. You'd think they'd keep the tall fellow in there.'

However, the tall end did not quite come off the field. With the attention of the Larkin team and most of the spectators focused on the kneeling linemen as they prepared for the last play, Rusk saw to his horror that the tall end had not left the field. He had run purposefully to the sidelines but had stopped one foot from the chalk, remaining legally in bounds. At that moment, on the far side, another player calmly stepped off the field, leaving the required eleven players eligible for the final play.

Rusk was one of few who saw the evil thing the Jacksboro coach was doing, and he began punching his seatmate in the arm and screaming 'Pick him up,' and Dewey bellowed 'Hey, he's eligible!' But no one could hear the two oilmen, and when the ball was snapped, the Jacksboro quarterback coolly dropped back and lofted the ball easily across the field to his tall end, who caught it and ran untouched into the end zone: final score, Jacksboro 20, Larkin 19.

Rusk and Kimbro went berserk. Roaring out of the stands, they shouted that someone ought to shoot any sumbitch who would pull such a trick. They wanted the referee banned for life. And they shouted loudly that never again should a team from Jacksboro be allowed on that field. When Kimbro finally cooled Rusk down they sought some other oil-field men, with the proposition: 'Let's waylay their bus before it gets out of town and give that coach a thrashing,' and they went in search of it, but the Jacksboro team, fearing just such action, had scuttled out before sunset.

In the angered days that followed, Rusk gave orders that no employee of his should ever purchase anything, no matter how small, from any outfit in Jacksboro, and when he was forced to go there on business, he spat on the sidewalks when no one was looking.

Of course, when Wichita Falls came down and administered a 31–7 drubbing, he gave the same orders about that infamous town, charging it with having brought in ringers who had never set foot in a Wichita Falls classroom, and Kimbro joined him in condemnation. In their new-found hatred for Jacksboro and Wichita Falls, the two former adversaries buried their suspicions of each other.

It was Dewey who had the bright idea: 'Floyd, if Wichita Falls hires outsiders, why can't we?' Assembling the Larkin millionaires, they proposed that 'we do something to restore the honor of this town,' and Rusk threw himself into this project with all the energy he had once given to the Ku Klux Klan. He and his men gave the coach, a mild-mannered fellow, a hundred dollars a month in cash to spend as he deemed best. Rusk himself built a dressing room at the edge of the field so that, as he was fond of saying, 'Larkin can go first class.' The oilmen scouted the region for big, tough boys and moved their families into Larkin so that the lads could play on the local team, and when the next autumn came around, it was obvious that Larkin High had a fighting chance to become a football power.

One morning, when Rusk delivered his mother's royalty check to her—more money than she and Earnshaw had spent in a dozen years—he found her playing with his son Ransom, a big-boned child, and he cried impulsively: 'Damn, I wish he was old enough to play for Larkin!' Catching the boy and throwing him high in the air, he caught him and started running through the room like a halfback. Dropping the child back in his crib, he shook his finger at him: 'Son, you're gonna see real greatness in this town. And maybe you'll even be on the team yourself, some day.'

He then turned his attention to the serious problem of finding an appropriate name for what he now called 'my team,' and he found that the desirable names had been preempted: Lions, Tigers, Bears, Bearcats, Panthers, Pirates, Rebels,

Gunslingers, Hawks. Any animal whose behavior was terrifying had been used, any role requiring violent or even murderous deportment had been adopted by some small school in the area. One town famous for its hunting called its team the Turkeys, an unfortunate name, but Larkin did little better. By a process of painful elimination it came up with the name of a beast once common in those parts, the antelope, and when this was reluctantly adopted, a more difficult problem arose, because every Texas team had to be the Fighting This or That: the Fighting Tigers, the Fighting Buffalo, the Fighting Wildcats. So it had to be the Fighting Antelopes, even though, as Rusk said: 'There's no man in Texas ever saw an antelope fight anything.'

Under their new leadership, and with a level of support from the oilmen that they had never known before, Larkin's Fighting Antelopes had an autumn of glory, up to a point. The team played nine regular games, and won them all. As Rusk boasted at the morning breakfasts in the café: 'We really crucified Jacksboro, thirty-seven to six.' They manhandled Breckenridge, too, 41–3, and they even took much bigger Wichita Falls to the cleaners, 24–7. When they won the regional championship in a tight game against Abilene, 9–7, it became clear to Rusk and his associates that 'our team can go all the way,' and the heady prospect of a state championship began to be discussed seriously.

'By God, if we can win our next game,' Rusk bellowed in the café, 'we'll get a crack at Waco,' but his enthusiasm for such a game distressed the coach of the Fighting Antelopes, for he knew the facts, which he tried to explain to Rusk and Kimbro: 'We've played some good teams, yes. But Waco, they're much different.'

'Are you chicken?' Rusk demanded, and the coach surprised him by saying: 'Yes. Our little team would have no chance against Waco.'

'You oughta be fired!' Rusk bellowed. 'What kind of talk is this, welshing on your own team?'

'Mr. Rusk, Waco is coached by Paul Tyson. Does that mean anything?'

'He puts his pants on one leg at a time, don't he?'

'Yes, but when he gets them on, he's something special.' Almost in awe the coach recited the fearsome accomplishments of that Waco powerhouse: 'One year the Waco Tigers scored a total of seven hundred eighty-four points; opponents had thirty-three.'

'Who did they play?' Rusk asked. 'The Sisters of Mercy?'

'The best. Of course, there was one game with the Corsicana Orphans Home, one hundred nineteen to nothing.'

'Did the Orphans have eleven men?'

'Only thirteen, but they were a real team.'

'No real team loses by a hundred points.'

'Against Waco they do,' the worried coach said, and he continued: 'They brought down a team from Cleveland, Ohio. National championship. Waco, forty-four, Cleveland, twelve. And in their best year, Waco, five hundred sixty-seven, opponents, zero, with no opposing team ever moving the ball inside the Waco thirty-five-yard line. And you ask me if I'm scared.'

But Rusk and his optimistic oilmen were not, and when the Fighting Antelopes won their thirteenth straight game—for high schools played barbarous schedules —the big showdown with Waco for the state championship became inevitable. Most of Larkin and all of Waco found ways to get to Panther Park in Fort Worth that memorable Saturday afternoon. For a mere high school game, more than twenty thousand showed up; the newspapers had skillfully promulgated the myth that in this age of miracles, Antelopes had an outside chance of defeating Tigers.

It was a day Floyd Rusk would never forget; it eclipsed in significance even that wonderful morning when Rusk #3 came in with its verification of the Larkin Field, because this game would be remembered as one of the extraordinary events in the annals of Texas sporting history, but not in a way that Rusk would have wished: Waco Tigers 83, Larkin Antelopes 0.

Before the excursion train left Fort Worth, copies of a Dallas newspaper with mocking headlines were available: IT REALLY WAS TIGERS EATING ANTELOPES, and during the train ride home, Rusk took an oath. Brandishing the offensive paper in the faces of his friends, he swore: 'This will never happen again. If we have to chew mountains into sand, it will never happen again.'

Assembling any oilmen who had gone to the game, he extracted promises that Larkin would regain its honor, regardless of cost, and Dewey Kimbro supported him: 'Whatever you need, Floyd. The dignity of our town must be restored.'

Prowling the train to locate the unfortunate coach whose prophecy of Waco invincibility had proved correct, the fat man snarled: 'You're fired. No team of mine loses by more than eighty points. Tomorrow we start searching for a real coach.'

Revenge for the dreadful humiliation in Panther Park became Rusk's obsession, and as he roamed the state looking for what he called 'my kind of coach,' he kept hearing of a man in a small school near Austin, and men who knew football assured him: 'This here Cotton Hamey, he's a no-nonsense coach, knocks a kid on his ass if he don't perform,' so Rusk telegraphed three of his oilmen to come down from Larkin to look the young genius over.

As soon as the committee met Hamey they knew they had their man. He had gone to A&M to learn animal husbandry, but had been so good at football that he switched to coaching, with the not unreasonable hope that one day he might return to his alma mater in some capacity or other, line coach perhaps, or even head coach, for he had the intelligence to handle either job.

They met a man who stood only five feet eight but who was still a crop-headed bundle of muscle and aggression. In college he had been such a relentless opponent that sportswriters had started a legend, which still clung to him: 'At the training table they feed him only raw meat, two pounds with lots of gristle at each sitting.' Nicknamed Tiger, he told one sportswriter: 'I like to play in the other team's backfield,' and this imaginative reporter produced a great line: 'Tiger Hamey invades the opposition backfield, grabs three running backs, and sorts them out till he finds who has the ball.'

The oilmen got right down to cases: 'Did you see the state championship?' and Hamey said: 'That's my job,' and Rusk asked: 'What did you think?' and Hamey said: 'Your team had no right being on that field.'

'If you had unlimited power, and I mean unlimited, could you build us a championship team for next December?'

Hamey rose and walked about the meeting room, flexing his muscles. He was an attractive young man, quick in his movements, intelligent in his responses to questions, and compact both physically and mentally. He wasted little time on nonessentials: 'I can get you into the play-offs, and Waco is losing many of its best players. But I don't think I could beat Paul Tyson next year.'

'Could you beat him year after next?' Rusk asked, and Hamey said: 'You get me the horses, I'll get you the championship.'

'You're hired,' Rusk said. He had no authority to hire or fire anyone, for that was the prerogative of the school board, but when a Texas town set its heart on a state football championship, everything else had to give, and when the oilmen returned to Larkin, the board quickly confirmed the appointment of Cotton Hamey as teacher of Texas history. On the side he would also do some coaching.

Now it became the responsibility of the wealthy oilmen to provide the horses, and as soon as Hamey was relieved of his duties at the small school near Austin, he moved to Larkin. On his first day in town he gave Rusk a list of nine boys living in various parts of Texas whom he would like to see in Antelopes uniforms when the season opened in September. When Rusk visited these boys he found they all had certain characteristics: 'They seem to have no neck. Their legs aren't all that big, but their shoulders . . . carved in granite. And they all look about twenty-two years old.' Rusk said on one return to Larkin: 'Coach Hamey, I don't think any of those boys can run,' and Hamey explained a fact of life: 'To produce a really good team, you have to have linemen. That's where the battles are determined, in the trenches.'

'But you will get some runners?'

'I have a second list, almost as important.' And when the oilmen went to scout these boys, they found quite a different set of characteristics: 'None of them much over a hundred and sixty. But they are quick. And only half of them seem to be in their twenties.'

When they reported back to Hamey, Rusk asked: 'Aren't some of these boys a trifle old?' and he said: 'You move them in here. I'll worry about their ages.'

So now the oilmen began prowling the country, visiting with the parents of these young fellows and offering the fathers good jobs in the oil field, the mothers employment in the local hospital or in stores. One widowed mother said she gave piano lessons, and Rusk said: 'You get two pianos. One for you, one for your students.'

In some twenty visits the question of grades was never raised, for it was supposed that if a boy was good enough to play for Cotton Hamey, some way would be found to keep him eligible, and as July came, Rusk could boast: 'Not one player on that pitiful team last year will even make the squad this time.' He was wrong. Part of the greatness of Hamey as a coach was that he could take whatever material was available and forge it into something good, so he found a place for more than a dozen of last year's Antelopes; but he also knew that if he wanted a championship team, he had better have an equal number of real horses, and when August practice started, he had them, brawny young men from various parts of Texas, practiced hands of twenty and twenty-one who had already played full terms at other schools, and two massive linemen who must have been at least twenty-two, with college experience. In this frontier period the rules governing eligibility in Texas high school football were somewhat flexible.

On the eve of the first game, Coach Hamey convened a meeting of his backers: 'We have a unique problem. We must not win any of these early games by too big a score. I don't want to alert teams like Abilene or Amarillo. And I certainly don't want to let Waco know we're gunning for them.'

'What are we goin' to do?' Rusk asked.

'Fumble a lot. When we get the ball, we'll run three, four powerhouse plays to see what our men can do.' He never used the word *boys*. 'And when we're satisfied that we can run the ball pretty much as we wish, we'll fumble and start over. I don't want any Waco-type scores, eighty-three to nothing.'

'I want to win,' Rusk said, and Hamey snapped: 'So do I. But in an orderly way. When we go into Fort Worth this year to face Waco, I want them to spend the entire first half catching their breath and asking: "What hit us?" '

So in the first seven games against the smaller teams of the area, Coach Hamey kept his Fighting Antelopes under wraps; 19–6 was a typical score, but as the Jacksboro game approached, at Jacksboro, Rusk begged for his team to be unshackled: 'Erase them. Leave grease spots on the field. I believe we could hammer them something like seventy to seven and I'd like to see it.'

Hamey would not permit this, and the game ended 21–7, enough to keep the record unblemished but not enough to alert the public that Cotton Hamey had a powerhouse. However, in the Wichita Falls game, everything clicked magically and at the end of nine minutes the Antelopes led 27–0, and the first team was yanked. 'It could of been a hundred and seven to nothing,' Rusk said.

The Antelopes won their division, undefeated, and then swept the regionals which placed them once more in the big finals against the supermen from Waco.

The big newspapers ridiculed the match-up, pointing out that something was wrong with a system which allowed, in two successive years, a team as poorly qualified as Larkin to reach the finals against a superteam like Waco, and a papers had long articles about the disaster of the previous year, with speculation as to whether or not the Antelopes could keep Waco from once again scoring over eighty.

There were a few cautions: 'We must remember that Cotton Hamey does not bring any team into a stadium expecting to lose. This game is not going to be any eighty-three-to-nothing runaway. I predict Waco by forty.'

Because the Larkin Antelopes appeared to be so weak, the crowd in Fort Worth was not so large as the previous year, but those who stayed home missed one of the epic games of Texas football, because when Waco received the opening kickoff and started confidently down the field, they were suddenly struck by a front line which tore their orderly plays apart, and before the startled champions could punt, a huge Antelope with no neck had tackled a running back so hard that he fumbled. Larkin recovered, and in four plays had its first touchdown.

On the next kickoff almost the same thing happened. Larkin linemen simply devoured the Waco backfield, again there was a fumble on third down, and once more the rampaging Antelopes carried the ball into the end zone: Larkin 13, Waco 0.

But Paul Tyson, considered by many to be the best high school coach ever, was not one to accept such a verdict, and before the next kickoff he made several adjustments, the principal one being that against that awesome Antelope line, his men would pass more, depending upon the speed of their backs to outwit the slower Larkin men.

Now the game developed into a mighty test of contrasting skills, and for the remainder of this half the Waco men predominated, so that when the whistle blew to end the second quarter, the score was Larkin 13, Waco 7.

But the power of the new Larkin team was obvious to everyone in the stands, and people who had tired of Waco's domination during the Tyson years began to cheer in the third period for the Antelopes to score again, and this they did: Larkin 19, Waco 7.

That was the last of the Antelope scoring, for now the superb coaching of the Waco Tigers began to tell: pound at the line and get nowhere; a quick pass for nineteen yards, deceptive hand-off, a deft run for seventeen yards. Three times in that third quarter the Tigers approached the Larkin goal line, and three times the Fighting Antelopes turned them back in last-inch stands, but at the start of the fourth quarter the Waco quarterback pulled a daring play. Faking passes to his ends and hand-offs to his running backs, he spun around twice and literally walked into the end zone: Larkin 19, Waco 13.

The fourth quarter would often be referred to as 'the greatest last quarter in high school history,' because the Waco team, smelling a chance for victory, came down the field four glorious times, bedazzling the Antelopes with fancy running and lightning passes, but always near the goal, the Antelope line would stiffen and the drive fail. After a few futile rushes, the Larkin kicker would send long punts zooming down the field, and the inexorable Waco drive would restart. Four times Coach Tyson's men came close to scoring, four times they were denied, and from the stands a leather-lunged spectator cried: 'They sure are Fightin' Antelopes.' But on the fifth try, with only minutes on the clock, the Waco team could not be stopped, and the score became Larkin 19, Waco 19.

Then one of those beautiful-tragic episodes unfolded which make football such a marvelous sport, beautiful to the victors, tragic to the losers. With little more than a minute to play, Waco fielded a punt deep in its own territory, and instead of playing out the clock, unleashed three swift plays that carried the ball to the Larkin eleven. Time-out was called, with only seconds left, and Waco prepared for a field-goal attempt. 'Dear God, let it fail!' Rusk prayed and he could see around him other oilmen voicing the same supplication: 'Just this once, God, let it fail.'

The stadium was hushed. The teams lined up. The ball was snapped. The kicker dropped the ball perfectly, swung his foot, and sent the pigskin on its way. With never a waver, the ball sped through the middle of the uprights: Waco 22, Larkin 19.

On the train trip home, Floyd Rusk surprised himself, for he could feel no bitterness over the loss; passing back and forth through the train, he embraced everyone, spectators, team members, his fellow oilmen, and to all he said: 'This is the proudest day in my life.' Then he would begin to blubber: 'Who said our Antelopes couldn't fight.'

But when he reached Coach Hamey, who also had tears in his eyes, he said: 'I want the names of fifteen more men we could use next autumn. I want to crush Waco. I want to tear 'em apart, shred by shred.'

'So do I,' Hamey said grimly, and within a week of their return home he had given Rusk eighteen names of high school players whose presence in Larkin would reinforce the already good team. Before the first of January, Rusk and his oilmen had more than a dozen of these fellows transferred into the Larkin district, where their parents were given jobs in the local businesses. Score that following year: Larkin 26, Waco 6.

These were the years when the Fighting Antelopes met in Homeric struggle with teams from much larger towns like Abilene, Amarillo, Lubbock and Fort Worth. With one winning streak of thirty-one regular games and two additional state championships, the team attracted national attention, and when a Chicago sportswriter asked Cotton how he accounted for that record, the coach replied: 'Two things. Attention to detail. And character building.'

While Floyd Rusk was enjoying his victories with the imaginary Antelopes, and they were his victories because he had purchased most of the players, his mother was having her own victories with her real Longhorns.

In 1927 the federal government became aware that on its Western plains the

Longhorn breed was about to become extinct, like the passenger pigeon and the buffalo. When agitation by lovers of nature awakened national attention, a bill sponsored by Wyoming Senator John B. Kendrick was passed, allocating $3,000 to be used in an attempt to save the breed.

A large buffalo refuge in the Wichita Mountains of Oklahoma, not far from the Texas border, was set aside for such pure stock as could be found, but then it was discovered that in all the United States there seemed to be less than three dozen verified Longhorn cows and no good bull. Even when these were located, most were found to be of a degenerative quality, untended for generations and bred only by chance. Loss of horn was especially noted, for the famous rocking chairs were being produced no more.

Often the federal research team would hear of 'them real Longhorns down to the Tucker place,' only to find six miserable beasts not qualified to serve as breeding stock. Better luck was found in the rural ranches of Old Mexico, where unspoiled cattle that retained the characteristics of the Texas Longhorn could occasionally be found. Some ranchers objected to basing the revived strain of what was essentially a Texas breed on imports from Mexico, but the U.S. experts stifled that complaint with two sharp observations: 'Mexico is where they came from in the first place' and 'When you Texas people did have them, you didn't take care of them.' So the famous Texas cattle were saved in Oklahoma by a senator from Wyoming importing cattle from Mexico.

However, late in their search the federal men heard of a magical enclave near the town of Larkin, Texas, where a feisty old woman with no nose had been rearing Longhorns for as long as anyone could remember. In great excitement they hurried down from the Wichita Refuge to see what Emma Larkin had stashed away in her own little refuge, and when they first saw Mean Moses VI grazing peacefully among his cows, his horns big and heavy and with never a twist, they actually shouted with joy: 'We've found a real Longhorn!' And what made this bull additionally attractive were the cows and steers sired by him, their horns showing the Texas twist, some to such an exaggerated degree that they were museum pieces.

'Can we buy your entire herd?' the federal men asked ten minutes after they saw Emma Rusk's Longhorns.

'You cannot,' she snapped.

'Can we have that great bull you call Mean Moses VI?'

'Not if you came at me with guns.'

'What can we have? For a national project? To save the breed?'

When she sat with them and heard the admirable thing they were trying to do, and when she saw the photographs of the terrain at the Wildlife Refuge, she became interested, but when they showed her the scrawny animals they had been able to collect so far, she became disgusted: 'You can't restore a breed with that stock.'

'We know,' the men said, allowing the logical conclusion to formulate in her mind.

She said nothing, just sat rocking back and forth, a little old woman whose mind was filled with visions of the vast plains she had loved. She saw her father and his brothers probing into the Larkin area and deciding to establish their homestead on the Brazos. She saw scenes from her life with the Comanche, when she and they galloped over terrain from Kansas to Chihuahua. But most of all she saw R. J. Poteet droving his immense herds of Longhorns to market at Dodge City, and from that herd of swirling animals emerged the creatures she had identified as worth saving. Lovingly she recalled the morning when Earnshaw cried: 'Thy bull has gored my bull!' And then she visualized that first Mean Moses striding through strands of barbed wire. The wire had kept him away from the hay when he wasn't really hungry, but when he knew his cows needed him, he had pushed it aside as if it were cobwebs on a frosty morning.

She knew what she must do: 'I'll let you have Mean Moses VI and any four of his bull calves you prefer. But of greater importance, I suspect, will be the cows in direct line from Bathtub Bertha. I've always thought that the tremendous horns we find in our Longhorns can be traced to Bathtub. Have you ever seen a photograph of her?'

From her mementos she produced two photographs of the extraordinary cow, and when the visitors saw those incredible horns, the tips almost touching before the cow's eyes, they realized that they had found something spectacular, something Texan. At Wichita the Larkin strain would become known as MM/BB, and wherever in the United States men attentive to history sought to reinstitute the Longhorn breed, they would start first with a good MM/BB bull from the Wichita surplus and a score of cows descended from Bathtub.

Emma was not content to have the federal people load her animals into trucks and haul them into Oklahoma; she wanted to deliver them personally, and when she saw Moses fight his way down the ramp and make a series of lunges at everything around him, she felt assured that in the dozen good years he still had ahead of him, he would get his line firmly established. As she watched her animals disperse into the grasslands of their new home, one of the federal men asked: 'Are you sorry to lose your great bull?' and she snapped: 'What you didn't see at Larkin was his son, the one I hid aside to be Mean Moses VII. That one's going to be twice the bull his father was.'

She was not allowed to see this prediction come true, for on the trip home she began to feel a heavy constriction across her chest. 'Would you drive a little faster?' she asked, and each time the pain became greater she called for greater speed.

The car was now near the Texas border. Ahead lay the Red River, that shallow wandering stream which had always protected Texas on the north, and she was eager to cross it. 'Could you please drive a little faster?' she pleaded in her customary whisper, and only later did the occupants of the car realize that she had been determined to get back to Texas before she died.

. . . TASK FORCE

Because our members were always striving to identify which special agencies produced the uniqueness of Texas, we invited the dean of writers on high school football to address us at our October meeting in Waco, and although he said he had no time to prepare a formal paper, since this was the height of the football season, he would be honored to join us on any Monday or Tuesday when the high schools were not holding important practices. We informed him that we would adjust our schedule to his and that he had things backward: we were the ones who would be honored.

He was Pepper Hatfield of the *Larkin Defender,* and when Miss Cobb and I met him at the airport we saw a man of seventy-three who retained the same lively joy in things he'd had at forty: 'They gave me the best job in the world. Still love it. Still amazed by what young boys can accomplish.' His eyes sparkled; his Marine haircut was a clean iron-gray; and his voice had a lively crackle.

He launched our three-hour discussion on a high philosophical note: 'The essential character of Texas, at least in this century, has been formed by three experiences, but before I say what they are, let me remind you of this essential truth about things Texan. The significant ones have never been determined by the big cities. Houston, Dallas, San Antone, they've never defined what a Texan is. That insight comes only from the small towns. Always has and I'm convinced always will. The good ol' boy with his pickup, his six-pack and his rifle slung in the rack behind his head, he's a small-town creation. Limited to places of under eight thousand, I'd say.'

Miss Cobb would not accept this: 'Do you mean to say the pickup and the six-pack define Texans?'

'I do not. What I intended to point out was that *even* these modern characteristics are predominantly small-town.'

'What are the essentials?' she asked.

'I was about to say,' Hatfield said, with just the slightest irritation at having been interrupted on the subject of football by a woman, 'that my significant characteristics derived from the small town, and I think you'll agree that they account for most of the Texas legend as it exists today: the ranch, the oil well, Friday night football.

'Now, it's curious and I think particularly Texan that books and plays and movies and television shows galore have idealized the first two. How many cowboy films have we had? How many television shows about Texas oil people? You ever see that great Clark Gable, Spencer Tracy, Claudette Colbert picture *Boom Town?* Or the best Texas picture made so far, *Red River,* or the second best, *Giant?* All oil and ranching, and I could name a dozen other goodies.

'That's because outsiders made the pictures. That's because outsiders were defining how we should look at ourselves. But there's never been a really first-rate book or play or dramatic presentation of Friday night football. And why not? Because people outside of Texas don't appreciate the total grandeur of that tradition.

'I never met a single stranger to Texas who had any appreciation of what high school football means to a Texan. Closest were those clowns in the Pennsylvania coal regions. They started boasting that they were the hotbed of high school football, and I do admit they sent a lot of their graduates to colleges all over America, like Joe Namath to Alabama, but I started a movement to send an All-Texas high school team north to play the All-Pennsylvanians. You know what happened. A slaughter. Texas won every game.' He rattled off the scores as if the games had occurred yesterday—26–10, 34–2, 45–14—and he could do this with all the statistics of his chosen field. He needed no notes.

'So after we'd clobbered Pennsylvania three times, they called off the game. Too humiliating. And if we'd played any other state on the same basis, our scores would have been higher. Texas high school football is unbelievable. We have about a thousand schools playing each weekend. Five hundred fascinating games. In a year, maybe half a million spectators will see the eight Dallas Cowboys' home games. Eight million will see their favorite high school teams.'

He now dropped his voice to that whispered, seriotragic level which clergymen use when conducting funeral services for people they had never known while living: 'As you know, an All-Oklahoma high school team beat an All-Texas the last two years. We didn't send our best players, but you just can't explain it,' and he sighed.

'But let's get back to fundamentals of the Texas character. The ranch gives us the cowboy, and now that there are hardly any of them left, what's more important, the cowboy clothes. You ever see that great picture of Bum Phillips walking across the football field in his Stetson hat and his General Quimper boots? That's Texas. Or the Marlboro man herding his steers in a Panhandle blizzard? That's Texas.'

'I thought the Marlboro man was from Wyoming,' Garza said, and Peppe dismissed him: 'They shoot all the photos out on the 6666 Ranch in Guthrie, King County. Keep the Marlboro store right on the ranch.

'And the same goes for the oilman. He may no longer be the dominant economic factor, what with OPEC misbehavior and the rise of Silicon Valley over in Dallas, but emotionally he is still emperor of the Texas plains. Best thing ever happened to oil, it moved from being a monopoly of East Texas out to Central

Texas, where I grew up, and then on to the Permian Basin, real out west. Made it universal Texan the way cattle never were, and gave us some powerful imagery, not only in the production of the oil well itself, that wonderful gusher blackening the sky, but in the oilman, too. Best cartoon on Texas I ever saw showed a typical West Texas wildcatter, living in this shack with his bedraggled wife. Behind them you see a gusher coming in on their pasture, and the old woman is yelling to her husband "Call Neiman-Marcus and see how late they stay open on Thursdays!" '

'You seem to incline always toward the cheapest view of our state, Mr. Hatfield,' Miss Cobb protested, and Pepper replied, with never a pause: 'I don't do the choosing, ma'am, the people do, and one of the best things I ever heard about any state came from Hawaii. Group of local politicians there, about 1960, awoke to the fact that their new state was no longer a bunch of hoolie-hoolie girls waving their hips. It was a modern state, with a sugar industry and pineapple and a good university. So they started advertising such things in mainland magazines, and tourism dropped forty percent. Right quick they went back to the hoolie-hoolies, and there they stay, with tourism way up. Texas, ma'am, is ranches and oil and Friday night football, and you people in command better not try to sell anything else.'

Pepper was at his best when reminiscing about the great high school teams and players he had known: 'I started as a boy, watching Coach Cotton Hamey's immortal teams at Larkin: they won three state championships. As some of you may remember, I got my big break as a sportswriter by a romantic piece I submitted to a Dallas newspaper about the five awesome linemen Coach Hamey brought with him to Larkin. I called them the Five Oil Derricks, and the name caught on.'

He smiled, recalling that lucky shot: 'Three papers spoke to me about jobs, so I prepared a second article about my Five Derricks, because they awed me. They all seemed older than my pop, because eligibility rules were a little looser then. Well, my second article proved that when those five men enrolled as freshmen at Larkin, they'd already played a total of twenty-three years in high school or beyond.

'Do you know what that means? Four years of high school in some place far distant for each man, with three of them having one year beyond that. The oldest man was married, had two children and had played for an Oklahoma college. Now he had four more years with us. Ten years in all and still in high school.'

'I never read that story,' Rusk said, 'and as you know, my father was crazy about Larkin football.'

'There was good reason you didn't read it. Someone warned your father about my story before I finished it, and he came to me one night: "Son, you're not going to print that pack of lies, are you?" I showed him my documentation, and he brushed it aside: "Son, would you pee on your mother's grave? To befoul Texas football is the same thing." He grabbed my story and tore it up, my notes too. And next day the editor of the *Larkin Defender* called and said: "Mr. Rusk has recommended you highly for a job on our paper." I've never left.'

He smiled at Ransom Rusk, then said: 'Other sportswriters didn't have the same high regard for the welfare of the game. During the year of our second championship, maybe the best high school team Texas ever produced, a cynical writer on a Dallas newspaper did a famous column in which he wrote: "My All-Texas high school team for this year is the Larkin Fighting Antelopes, because each player on that team comes from a different town in Texas and is the state's best in his position." I never stooped to cheap shots like that.

'But certain fundamental facts must be remembered if you're searching for the true Texas character. The population of Larkin in those days after the oil boom had retreated to its natural level, leaving just a little boost, thirty-six hundred. But when the Antelopes played at home in the golden years, forty-two hundred attended each game, and when they played at some nearby bitter rival like Ranger, Cisco, Breckenridge or Jacksboro, nineteen hundred of our thirty-six hundred would travel to the other town.

'It was mass mania. Nothing in life was bigger than Friday football, and when lights made it possible to play at night, even more people could attend and the field became a kind of cathedral under the stars. Now it was Friday Night Football, as grand an invention as man has made, with the entire community meeting for spiritual warmth.

'A storekeeper who wasn't a hundred percent behind the team, his business would go bust. A bank would have to close shop if its manager wasn't at every game, and putting up money on the side to pay for uniforms, and paying for training tables and other goodies. Every man in town had to root for the Antelopes, or else. And that still applies throughout this state.'

'It sounds to me,' said Miss Cobb, 'like the birth of the macho image. A lot of grown men playing like boys and no women allowed.'

'Ah, now there's where you make your great mistake, ma'am! Because the genius of Texas football was that early on, it realized it must also involve the girls. So in Larkin we started the cheerleader tradition, and the drill team, and the rifle exhibition, and the baton twirlers, and the marchers in their fluffy uniforms. On a good Friday night now a big high school may have two hundred boys doing something, what with the squad and the band, but it'll have three hundred pretty girls in one guise or another. So girls play almost as important a role as the boys. Otherwise, the spectacle might have lost its grip on the public.'

Like all Texas football coaches and sportswriters, Pepper aspired to be the perfect gentleman, and now he smiled at Miss Cobb: 'You were right on one thing, though, ma'am. Football does carry a strong macho image. One of the reasons why Texans distrust Mexicans, or even despise them at times, they can't play football. Quite pitiful, really. Put them on a horse, they can swagger. But the one game that matters, they can't play.'

'Aren't you stressing the values rather strongly, Mr. Hatfield?'

'Not at all! Texans identify honest values quickly. They can't be fooled, not for long. That's why seventy-eight percent of our high school administrators are ex-football coaches.'

'That may account for the sad condition of Texas education,' Miss Cobb said.

'Wait a minute! Back up! School boards hire football coaches to be their administrators because they know that anyone connected with football has his head screwed on right. He understands the important priorities, and he isn't going to be befuddled by poetry and algebra and all that. He knows that if he can get his students involved in a good football program, girls and boys alike, the other things will take care of themselves.'

Miss Cobb had a penetrating question: 'I read that last year Texas colleges graduated five hundred football coaches and only two people qualified to teach calculus. Is that the balance you recommend?'

'For many Texas boys high school football will be the biggest, noblest thing they'll ever experience. Calculus teachers you can hire from those colleges in Massachusetts.'

He was especially ingenious in outlining the symbiotic relationship between oil and football: 'Never underestimate the importance of oil. That's where the extra money came from. Great teams like Breckenridge and Larkin and Ranger were fanatically supported by oilmen. Odessa Permian, too, in a way. You see, each stresses the big gamble. If you're in oil, you wildcat and lose everything. If you're that first Larkin team, you go up against Waco and lose eighty-three to nothing. You don't give a damn. You come back with another try. Oilmen and football heroes were made for each other.

'But there was another aspect, equally strong. An oil millionaire in a place like Larkin had damned little to spend his money on. No opera, no theater, no museums, no interest in books, and when you've had one Cadillac you've had them all. What was left? The high school football team. You cannot imagine how possessive the oilmen of Ranger and Breckenridge and Larkin became over their football teams. Most of them hadn't gone to college, so they didn't become agitated over SMU or A&M. The high school team was all they had. And they supported it—boy, did they support it! I know high school teams right now that have a head coach and ten assistants. Yes, a coach for tight ends, one for wide ends. Two coaches for interior linemen, offensive and defensive. Quarterback, running backs, linebacker, defensive backs, a coach for each. Special-teams coach, kicking coach. The four top Texas high school teams could lick the bottom fifty percent of college teams up north.'

The highlight of his comments came toward the end of the afternoon, when he said, with his eyes half closed: 'I can see them now, those legions of immortal boys who got their lives started on the right track through Friday night football. They were enabled to go on to college, and some to big money in the pros, and there wasn't a hophead or a drunk or a bum among them: Sammy Baugh, Davey O'Brien, Big John Kimbrough, Doak Walker, Don Meredith, Kyle Rote, Earl

Campbell. And add the two who were famed only in high school, they may have been the best of the bunch—Boody Johnson of Waco, and Kenny Hall, the Sugar Land Express.'

His eyes misted over. He was an old man now, but he could recall each critical game he had attended, each golden boy whose exploits he had described as if they had been fighting not on the football fields of Texas but at the gates of Troy or on the plains of Megiddo.

'Thank you, Mr. Hatfield,' Miss Cobb said in closing. 'We needed to be reminded of the values you represent. You see, I was sent north to school.'

'Ma'am, you missed the heart of Texas.'

XIII
THE
INVADERS

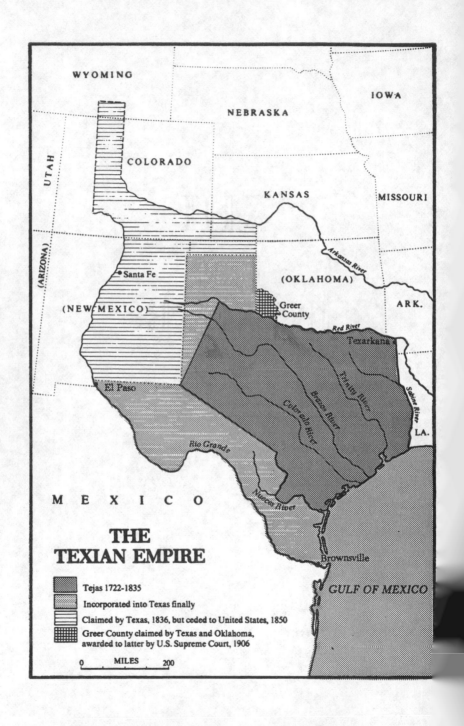

WYOMING

IOWA

NEBRASKA

UTAH

COLORADO

KANSAS

MISSOURI

(ARIZONA.)

• Santa Fe

(OKLAHOMA)

Arkansas River

(NEW MEXICO)

Greer
County

ARK.

Red River

Texarkana

El Paso

Colorado River

Brazos River

Trinity River

Sabine River

Rio Grande

LA.

M E X I C O

Nueces River

THE
TEXIAN EMPIRE

Brownsville

GULF OF MEXICO

Tejas 1722-1835

Incorporated into Texas finally

Claimed by Texas, 1836, but ceded to United States, 1850

Greer County claimed by Texas and Oklahoma,
awarded to latter by U.S. Supreme Court, 1906

0   MILES   200

IN THE FOUR DECADES FOLLOWING THE LARKIN ANTELOPES' LAST FOOTBALL championship, 1928–1968, that little oil town witnessed many changes, as did the state. In World War II, Texas fighting men performed with customary valor: one native son, Dwight D. Eisenhower, was leading the Allied armies to victory in Europe while another, Chester W. Nimitz, was doing the same with the fleet in the Pacific; and still another, Ira Eaker, was sending his Eighth Air Force planes to devastate Nazi military production. One tough little Texas G.I., Audie Murphy, was so eager to get into combat that he lied about his age, and won so many medals that he leaned forward when he walked.

Equally important was the emergence of Texas politicians as powers in Washington, because previous Texans with leadership possibilities had usually seen Texas politics as more important than national. For example, John Reagan, Postmaster General of the Confederacy and one of the very greatest Texans, had served in the national Congress for many years and was a United States senator when an appointment to the Texas Railroad Commission opened in 1891. Without hesitation he surrendered his Senate seat to help regulate this important aspect of Texas life, apparently in the belief that what happened in Texas was what really mattered. Under the principles laid down by his prudent leadership, this commission became the arbiter not only of railroads so essential to the state's development, but eventually, also of trucks, utilities and particularly the oil business, including the transport in pipe lines of petroleum products to the rest of the country. Insofar as his career was concerned, Texas was more important than the nation.

This provincialism denied Texas the voice in national affairs to which it was entitled. But now a trio of ornery, capable, arm-twisting Democratic politicians came on the scene, to become three of the most capable public servants our nation has had. In 1931, Cactus Jack Garner became Speaker of the House of Representatives in Washington, and soon after, a powerful Vice-President. In 1940, Sam Rayburn became one of the most effective Speakers of the House, a job he held, with two short breaks, till his death in 1961. And tall, gregarious and able Lyndon Johnson became a congressman, later, majority leader of the Senate, then Vice-President and, finally, on 22 November 1963, in an airplane standing on Love Field in Dallas, the thirty-sixth President of the United States.

Coincident with these accomplishments in war and politics, Texas surged to the fore in another aspect of American life, which sometimes seemed to have equal importance. Motion pictures of striking originality and power began to depict life in Texas in such a compelling way that the grandeur and the power of the state had to be recognized. Audiences by the millions swarmed to see movies like *Giant, The Alamo,* and the various John Wayne cowboy epics, especially the excellent *Red River.* Other good westerns involved Texas in no specific way but did help keep alive the legend: *Cimarron* (1931), *Stagecoach* (1939), *The Ox-Bow Incident* (1943), *High Noon* (1952), *Shane* (1953), and the film of his which Wayne preferred above all others, *The Searchers* (1956). Even in faraway Italy, the 'spaghetti western' created an alluring vision of the West, and Texas reaped the benefit. The state was seen as heroic, colorful and authentic. Its men were tall, its women beautiful, its Longhorns compelling. Even its Mexican villains displayed uniqueness, if not charm, and each year the legend grew.

Of course, there were disadvantages. Many thoughtful people in other parts of the nation began to resent this emphasis on Texas and saw the state as a haven for broken-down cowboys, rustlers and prairie misfits, men who treated Indians, Mexicans and women with contempt. Jokes about Texas braggadocio became popular, one of the most imaginative concerning the Connecticut river expert who was hired by Dallas to determine whether the Trinity River could be deepened so as to give the city shipping access to the sea. 'Very simple,' the engineer said. 'Dig a canal from Dallas to the Gulf, and if you characters can suck half as hard as you blow, you'll have a river here in no time.'

Thousands of Americans developed a love-hate relationship with the state, with the love predominating, and starting in the mid-sixties, citizens in what Texans called 'the less favored parts of our nation' began to drift toward Texas, attracted by the myth, the availability of good jobs, the pleasant winter climate and the relaxed pattern of life. Men wrote to friends back in Minnesota: 'Down here I can wear the same outfit winter and summer.'

To appreciate the various ways in which the magnetic attraction of Texas could be exerted, it is necessary to understand the related cases of Ben Talbot and Eloy Múzquiz. Neither was born in Texas, yet each came to treasure it as a home he did not wish to leave.

Talbot was tall and thin, a reticent man born in northern Vermont close to the Canadian border, and since his father had served for many years as a U. S. Border Patrol officer checking the movement of Canadians south from Montreal, he, too, decided to apply to the service after graduating from the University of Vermont in 1944. Instead, the son was tapped by Selective Service for the army and sent to the South Pacific, where on steaming Bougainville up the Slot from Guadalcanal he vowed that if he got out alive, he would never again live in a hot climate— 'Vermont for me!'—and on sweltering nights, lying beneath his mosquito net bathed in sweat, he thought of his father's cold assignment along the Canadian border.

When he returned to the States he found that his military duty in a hardship post had given him so many credits that the Immigration and Naturalization Service was almost forced to accept him, but after he had been sworn in, with his father watching in approval, Talbot Senior told his son: 'Ben, work hard in the Spanish school, master the language, and serve your obligatory stretch along the Mexican border. We all had to learn Spanish and do our tour down there. But do everything you can, pull every trick in the book to get assigned back here for your permanent duty.'

'I intend to.'

The Spanish teacher in the academy despaired of ever teaching Talbot a word of that mellifluous language, for his flat Vermont drawl caused him to pronounce every word in a high, nasal wail, with equal emphasis on each syllable; *mañana* came out *mah-nah-nah*—no tilde—as if each group of letters was personally repugnant, and he pronounced longer words like *fortaleza* as if the syllables were a chain of connected boxcars bumping slowly down a track.

'Candidate Talbot,' the instructor pleaded, 'don't you ever sing words, when your heart is joyous?' and he replied: 'I sing hymns. Words I speak.' But because of his studious mastery of vocabulary and his skill in putting those words together in proper sentences, his teacher had to concede: 'Talbot, you speak Spanish perfectly, but it isn't Spanish.'

'They'll understand,' Ben countered, and when he reached his indoctrination assignment at El Paso and began apprehending illegal Mexican aliens trying to sneak into the country, the wetbacks did understand when he interrogated them, for he spoke very slowly, like a machine running down, and enunciated each of his Vermont-style syllables clearly. Older officers would listen in amazement to the sounds which came from his lips and watch with sly grins as the Mexican listening to them gazed in wonder. But slowly, after about his third question, a light would suffuse the Mexican face as the alien realized that the tall man with the severe frown was speaking Spanish. Often the captive would gush out answers in relief at having solved the mystery, so that Talbot proved quite effective. At the end of his training his superior reported: 'Ben looks so stiff and forbidding and speaks such horrible Spanish that he starts by terrifying the men he interrogates. But when they see the sympathy in his eyes and listen to the slow, careful way he pronounces each syllable, I think they feel sorry for him. At any rate, he gets better results than most.'

His avowed plan of doing well along the border so that he might return to the more pleasant duty along the Canadian frontier received its first slight tremor when he was assigned to the duty station at Las Cruces, up the line in New Mexico. He had been there only a few weeks when he realized that he wanted rather strongly to be back in El Paso: That's where the real work goes on. He was not homesick for the place, and certainly not for the food or the heat, but he did miss the teeming vitality of that bilingual town, with Ciudad Juárez across the river, and he must have conveyed his feelings to his superiors, because after six months of chasing illegals through the brush of New Mexico he was reassigned to El Paso, and there began the long years of his service.

His childhood days in the Vermont woods had enabled him to master the tricks of tracking, and to him the traces of all animals, including man, told a clear story. He could look at a dry riverbank around El Paso and determine how many Mexicans had made it across during the night, their approximate ages by the patterns of their shoes, whether he was seeing the signs of a group or merely an accumulation of many singles, and where they were probably heading. He was uncanny in predicting, or as he said, 'making a wishbone guess' as to where these fugitives would intersect some main road, and often when they appeared he would be there awaiting them.

He never abused a Mexican he captured. Calling them all *Juan*, which he pronounced as if it were *Jew-wahn*, he talked with them patiently, offered them coffee or a drink of cold water and shared his sandwiches, explaining in his oxlike Spanish that they would not be mistreated but that they must be sent back home. Of course, once they were back across the Rio Grande, they would probably turn around and come north again. That was understood by all.

Nothing deterred them, not the clever detective work of Border Patrol Officer Talbot, nor the formal checkpoints along the highways, nor the surveillance airplanes that flew overhead, nor the dangers involved in running across a rocky yard and jumping onto a moving Southern Pacific freight train headed east. They came alone, in pairs, in well-organized groups of eighteen or twenty and in casual hundreds. They were part of that endless chain of Mexican peasants who left their homeland in search of employment in a more affluent country. How many crossed the river illegally? Thousands upon thousands. How many were caught? Perhaps only ten or fifteen percent. But if dedicated men like Ben Talbot had not been working diligently since the Border Patrol was first established in 1924, the flood northward would have been three times as great.

In early 1960, Talbot sent a well-reasoned report to his superiors stating that in his opinion more than two million illegal Mexican aliens had crept into the United States in the preceding decade and that there appeared to be no diminution of the flood: 'The pressures which send them north—poverty, the cruel indifference of their government, the mal-distribution of wealth in a wealthy country, and the awful pressures of population growth which both church and government encourage—show no signs of being brought under control, so we must expect an unending continuation of the present inflow and must begin to study what it will mean when the southern part of Texas becomes a de facto Hispanic enclave.' He ended his report with two revealing paragraphs:

The gravity of the situation is exemplified by the case of one Eloy Múzquiz, citizen of Zacatecas, 850 miles to the south. Thirty-one year old, perpetually smiling, and apparently a good citizen whether in Mex ico or the United States, he leaves his home in Zacatecas every winter about the tenth of February, travels by bus to Ciudad Juárez, crosses the Rio Grande illegally, either evades me or is captured by me. If I catch him, I send him back to Mexico, and that afternoon he recrosses the river and eludes me. He hops a freight, heads east to where I do not know, works in Texas till the fifteenth of December, when he reappears in El Paso heading south. Since he is then leaving the States, we let him go. He returns by bus to his home in Zacatecas, plays with his sons, gets his wife pregnant once more, and on the twelfth of February is back in Ciudad Juárez trying to break through our lines. He always succeeds, and just before Christmas we see him with that perpetual smile, walking briskly along and wishing us a Merry Christmas as he heads home. Eloy Múzquiz is our perpetual problem.

One other thing. I should like to withdraw my application for reassignment to the Vermont-Canada border. I have now learned colloquial Spanish and feel a growing affection for El Paso and its problems. I would like to continue my duty on the Texas-Mexico border.

He was accurate in every statement he made about Múzquiz, but there were a few crucial facts which the persistent Mexican worker had succeeded in keeping hidden. He did smile all the time, even when captured at the railway yards, and he was a good citizen in both his countries. He did go home each Christmas to be with his family, and he judged his visit successful if he left his wife pregnant; his daughter and two sons were each born in September. He did invariably move east by hopping a Southern Pacific freight, and he did reappear in El Paso about the fifteenth of December, each year with a somewhat larger roll of American fifty-dollar bills, which he would deliver to his wife in Zacatecas. It was the long period from 12 February to 15 December that remained a blank in Ben Talbot's records.

In 1961, for example, Múzquiz came north to Ciudad Juárez on schedule, and as always he went to a Mexican grocery, where he filled his small canvas backpack with the staples required for the trip northeast: two small cans of sardines, six limes, four cans of apricots with lots of juice, two very important cans of refried beans, and a large bag of the one essential for an excursion into the United States, pinole, a mixture of parched corn, roasted peanuts and brown sugar, all ground to the finest possible texture. When mixed with water it produced a life-sustaining beverage, but it could also be eaten dry, and then it was more tasty than candy. As Eloy told the woman shopkeeper: 'Four pinches of pinole keeps you moving for a whole day. A bag like this? It could carry me to Canada.'

With all items packed according to what he had learned on seven previous trips, he left the store casually at about one in the afternoon, walked down to the dry riverbed, watched for an appropriate time when the immigration officers were occupied with three Mexicans they had caught, and slipped into the United States. Working his way cautiously eastward, he came upon the familiar freight yards of the Southern Pacific, where he hid beside a line of stationary boxcars, peeking out to watch the freight engines shunt long lines of laden boxcars before they started on the cross-Texas trip to San Antonio and on to Houston.

That was the train he would be catching within a few hours, and during the waiting period he reminded himself of safety precautions he had accumulated on various trips: Remember, if it should rain in the next hour, don't try. Let the train ride off without you. That was how Elizondo lost his legs, slipping on mud. Remember, if it should be rocky where you make your jump, let the train go. That's how Gutiérrez died, tripping and falling under the wheels. Remember, keep your hands clear of the coupling. That's how Cortinas lost his left hand, when the engines stopped suddenly. And remember, if the car you land in has cargo that can shift, get out, even if you have to jump. When the marble blocks shifted sideways they crushed Alarcón, didn't they? And when that cargo of grain broke loose it smothered Salcedo, didn't it?

On the freight trains east, death was a constant companion, and it was prudent to wedge a block in the sliding doors to keep them from slamming irrevocably shut; once forty were trapped in a freight car which had to lay over in a blinding Texas blizzard; all froze to death. In another instance, thirty-seven died from the stifling heat, which reached one hundred and forty degrees.

At two-ten on this February day, Eloy Múzquiz watched the freight forming with the greatest concentration, calculating his line of approach and trying to identify some car in which it would be relatively safe to ride. At two-twenty he adjusted his bundle, grasping the strings at the bottom and securing them about his waist so that his groceries would not bounce about as he ran. At two-twenty-five the engineer sounded his whistle, and the first straining of the heavy wheels occurred.

As long as the train remained stationary, the wetbacks dared not board, since the Border Patrol would pick them off, but once the boxcars started forward, there would be a general rush in which so many Mexicans dashed for the train, the guards had no chance to intercept everyone. Now as the train lurched forward in sudden jolts, Eloy and some seventy other men—looking like a horde of ant rushing toward some fallen morsel—made a wild dash for the boxcars and th metal framework under them. Múzquiz, easily in the lead, was about to reach th cars when the tall, thin figure of Ben Talbot stepped out from behind his ow hiding place to intercept him and two others.

There were two rules in the El Paso game: it was widely known that America officers would not treat their captives brutally, and it was understood that n Mexican fugitive would strike or fire at an immigration officer. It was a relentle struggle, carried on through all the hours of a day, but it was honorable, and no when Talbot grabbed the three Mexicans, it was as if they had been playing a friendly game of touch football. They stopped trying to run, Talbot said 'Okay, compadres,' and Eloy looked up at him, smiled as if they were brothers, and walked calmly into captivity.

He was led to a clearing station, documented for the eighth time, and returned once more to Ciudad Juárez, where without even changing stride he walked to the river, crept across when no one was patrolling, made his way to the railroad yards, and headed for the next freight, which hauled more than a hundred and fifty boxcars. With customary skill, his bundle tied close to his back, he sped across the yard, calculated his leap, and made his way into a boxcar filled with freight that was safely lashed down.

The Border Patrol in El Paso always assumed that Múzquiz remained aboard the train to San Antonio, losing himself in that growing metropolis where Spanish-speaking citizens were commonplace, and Officer Talbot had sent inquiries to that city, asking immigration people there to be on the lookout for Eloy, but Múzquiz was too clever to act in so predictable a manner.

When the freight train stopped for water in Fort Stockton, 245 miles to the east, he remained hidden for twenty minutes, knowing that La Migra—the immigration people—would be chasing the men who jumped off right away. When this did happen, with him watching the frantic game from a peephole, he casually dropped down from the boxcar and sauntered across the yard to a rusted Ford station wagon that had stood beside a deserted road for years. Opening the creaking door carefully lest it fall off, he crept inside, pulled the door shut behind him, and went to sleep, the fourth time in four years he had done this.

At dusk, with the train long gone for its destination in Houston, Eloy started walking up the familiar road to Monahans, Odessa, Midland and Lubbock. He covered many of the two hundred and twenty-three miles on foot, caught a few hitches, turned down job offers from two different ranchers, and paid American dollars for the bus ticket which carried him from Midland to Lubbock; at the station in the former city a well-dressed woman asked if he needed work and was obviously disappointed when he said no.

As he neared Lubbock on its unbelievably flat plain his heart expanded, for now he was on land he knew and loved. Nodding to several acquaintances in the bus station, he assured them that when summer came he would again tend their lawns, but then he started walking west on Highway 114, and before long a rancher who recognized him carried him on to Levelland, where, with his usual broad smile, he bade the man goodbye and headed for the customary cotton gin, where he reported to the foreman of the idle plant: 'I'm back.'

'Where you working till we start our run?'

'Mr. Hockaday, he asked.'

'Good man. But come August first, we want you here.'

'I'll be here.'

That year he had fourteen different jobs. Everyone he met sought his help, for he was known throughout the community as reliable, congenial and the father of three children down in Zacatecas to whom he sent nine-tenths of his wages. He did yard work; one woman of considerable wealth arranged for him to get a driver's license, strictly illegal, so that he could chauffeur her about; he worked at stores cleaning up after midnight; and he did occasional baby-sitting for young couples.

By 1968, Múzquiz had become a fixture at a local cotton gin, supervising the machinery, and as December approached he went to see the owner of the installation. Before he had spoken six words he broke into tears. When the owner asked in Spanish what the matter was, Eloy handed him a letter from his oldest boy: Señora Múzquiz, Eloy's stalwart wife who had run their family without a man, had died, leaving the three children motherless.

'Dear trusted friend, this is a tragedy. My heart goes out to you.'

'Señor, if I bring my children north with me, could you find them work?'

'How would you get them here?'

'I get here, don't I? Señor, I love Lubbock. I love Texas. This is my home now.'

'Any rancher in Texas would want a man like you. If they're good children . . .'

'They are. Their mother saw to that.'

Suddenly it was the owner who was sniffling: 'We'll find a place. Here's some money for your trip.'

As Eloy stepped off the bus in El Paso he found Ben Talbot waiting for him and he supposed that he was going to be arrested, and the tall officer who spoke the peculiar Spanish took him by the arm, led him to a bar, and said, over Dr. Peppers: 'Eloy, the big man has given me hell. Says I let you come in and out of the country as if you owned it. He wants you arrested.'

'General Talbot'—Múzquiz called every officer General, in either Mexico or Texas, for he had learned that such an error produced few reprisals—'you must not arrest me! My wife has died.'

After Talbot studied the sweat-stained letter, he blew his nose and delivered his warning: 'Eloy, go back to Zacatecas. Take care of your children. And don't come up this way again. Because next time I catch you, the big boss insists, you go to jail.'

'But I must come back, General Talbot. And I must bring my children.'

'Damnit, Eloy. There is no way you can sneak past us with three kids. You'll be caught, and into the calaboose you go. Then what will happen to your children?'

'General Talbot, we must come back. We are needed.'

That was the haunting phrase which put this border problem into perspective. The Mexicans who were streaming across in such uncounted numbers were mostly illiterate and they showed no inclination toward becoming Americanized, as immigrants from Europe had done in the early 1900s; instead, they clung to their Spanish language and their Mexican ways, and there were fifty other things wrong with them, but they were needed. They were needed by ranchers who could not otherwise find cowboys and by young mothers who could not find helpers. They were needed in restaurants and hotels and shops and in almost every service activity engaged in by the people of Texas. They were desperately needed, and as long as this was true, they would be enticed over the border by the millions.

As 12 February 1969 approached, Border Patrol Officer Talbot, who now wore cowboy boots, a large hat and a bolo tie when off duty, and could scarcely remember when he had been a Vermonter, realized that his old friend and nemesis Eloy Múzquiz was due to make his appearance in Ciudad Juárez in preparation for his dash to paradise, this time with three children in tow, so he telephoned a Mexican officer in Juárez with whom he had established good relations, and asked: 'You see a man about forty years old with three kids buying groceries for a dash across?'

'No, but I'll keep watch,' and after a while the Mexican called back: 'Yep. Buying sardines, canned refried beans, canned fruit juices and a big bag of pinole.'

'Let me know when he crosses.'

As if obedient to some inner schedule, one which had worked in the past, at about one in the afternoon Eloy led his three children across the dry river and eastward toward the freight yards. From a distance Talbot, marking their progress through field glasses, saw the father instruct his children as to how they must run to leap aboard the moving freight. He saw the engine getting up steam, the surreptitious movement of illegals edging toward the still-motionless boxcars, and he could feel the tension. Then, to his dismay—almost his horror—he saw that his fellow officer Dan Carlisle had spotted Eloy and his children and was placing himself in position to nab them within the next few minutes. Without hesitation he activated his walkie-talkie: 'Three-oh-three! Two-oh-two calling. I'm on to a crowd that might prove difficult.'

'Three-oh-three speaking. Cannot help. Following my own crowd.'

'Could be I'll need help.'

'You want me to come over?'

'You'd better.' With relief he saw Carlisle stop his tracking of the Múzquiz family and start west: When he reaches here I'll think of some explanation.

With his glasses he watched the engineer climb aboard the diesel, saw the trainmen wigwag their signals, and studied carefully the long line of boxcars as it strained to get started. Wheels spun; the engines coughed; the cars started to inch forward. Another spin, then all the wheels seemed to catch at the same instant, and the long train began to pick up speed.

Almost trembling, he watched as Múzquiz started his three children for the boxcars, urging them forward. Christ in heaven, Talbot prayed, don't let them slip. And he watched with strange satisfaction as the two boys leaped for the train, grasping the proper handholds.

Now the little girl, twelve years old, had to make the flying leap, and Talbot watched, teeth clenched, as her father spurred her on, her long dress flapping in the February sunlight. 'Faster, kid!' Talbot cried under his breath, and he sighed with relief when he saw Eloy lift her and almost throw her toward the train, where her brothers dragged her to safety. 'Okay, Múzquiz!'

He gasped, for at this moment one of the many scrambling wetbacks slipped and fell toward the implacable wheels, which had destroyed so many in such situations. Was it Múzquiz? Talbot saw the sliding man frantically clutch at rocks, until with bleeding fingers he caught one that saved him, and there he lay as the train moved past, its wheels turning always faster.

Eloy, leaping over the fallen man, grabbed the handholds, swung himself into the boxcar, and disappeared.

At the Fort Stockton stop Múzquiz explained to his children why they must wait till the first frenzied action dissipated, then quietly he led them to the rusted Ford station wagon that still stood beside the road. In it they slept for some hours, side by side, waking when it was time to head cautiously for Midland, where they caught the bus to Lubbock.

When they reached Levelland they were greeted with warmth and even embraces, for many families needed their help. When they were safe in the two-room shack which the plantation owner provided, Múzquiz told his children: 'This is our home now. We will never leave.'

If Ben Talbot developed a feeling of brotherhood toward Eloy Múzquiz because of the latter's decency and courage, he knew another Mexican for whom he felt only loathing, and this slimy operator preoccupied his attention, both when Talbot was on the job or resting beside the swimming pool at the house he and his wife, María Luz, had built at the edge of El Paso. His notes on this infamous man explained why he despised him:

> El Lobo, real name unknown. Birthplace unknown. Frequents the cantina El Azteca. About thirty-two, slight, neatly trimmed mustache, toothpick in corner of mouth. Always present when some deal is being engineered. Never present when trouble starts. Stays in Ciudad Juárez mostly, but is willing to come boldly into El Paso when business requires it. Occupation: coyote. Smuggles groups of wetbacks to rendezvous in the desert. Collects his fee and often deserts them.

> 1. Locked 63 wetbacks into a closed truck with space for 16 at most. Drove across desert to Van Horn in blazing heat. More than 20 died.

2. Dropped 17 wetbacks into the small opening of a tank car that had been carrying gasoline, closed the hatch at El Paso yards. All dead when hatch opened at Fort Stockton.

3. Packed 22 into a Chevrolet, plus two locked in the trunk. In order to protect springs on car, wedged wooden posts between them and body. Friction from driving set wood on fire. He ran from car, but did not stop to open trunk. Two men incinerated.

4. On at least two occasions led groups of girls who wanted to be waitresses across the desert and sold them to the men from Oklahoma City.

Talbot vowed that he would catch this evil man during some foray north of the river, but El Lobo was so clever and self-protective that he could not be trapped, and often Talbot had to watch with disgust as the slim, tricky fellow came boldly into El Paso on the maternity gambit, leading some pregnant peasant girl to Thomason General Hospital, and charging her a fee for the service. Since El Lobo broke no law during such missions, and since the deaths listed on his dossier could not be proved against him, he moved with impunity, but events were about to unfold in a dusty little town well south of the border which would place him in real jeopardy.

On the bleak and sandy plains of northern Mexico, midway between the cities of Chihuahua and Ciudad Juárez, stood the adobe village of Moctezuma, seven small huts, one of which served as a roadside shop dispensing allegedly cold drinks to American motorists. The place was called by the grandiloquent name La Tienda del Norte and was operated by the Guzmáns, a widowed woman with two daughters and a son.

The older girl was married to the man who ran the nearby Pemex station, and it was her responsibility to wash the windshields of any cars that stopped, and to send orders to the national gasoline monopoly for such additional supplies as her husband thought he might sell to motorists who found themselves short of gas on his rather frightening road. If one did not fill up at Moctezuma, one could well be stranded before reaching Chihuahua.

It was this constant flow of big cars passing south that caused discontent in the little village, for when one stopped for either gas or a cold drink, the Mexicans could see the wealth the owners possessed: 'They are all richer than the archbishop. It must be fun to live in los Estados Unidos where money is so easy!'

The young wife, Eufemia, had often thought of this as she tended the rich travelers, but more so now that she was pregnant. Her condition occasioned great discussion among the residents of Moctezuma, for what a young woman did when she was pregnant made a universe of difference, as two of the older women reminded the mother, Encarnación: 'It is important. It is life and death, really, that you get her to El Paso.'

'True, but neither her husband nor any of his friends have done this thing, and they have no way of instructing her.'

'What you must do,' one of the women said, 'is get her to Juárez and put her in touch with my cousin. El Lobo, that's his name, and his job is to slip people into the States.'

The other woman had a simpler plan: 'To get into El Paso is nothing, you just walk across the bridge. But to leave El Paso for the rest of the States, that's when you need El Lobo.'

'You think that Eufemia can just go to Juárez, cross over and reach Thomason General without getting caught?'

'Others have done it, haven't they?'

And that was the nagging fact: other pregnant women from villages far off the main road had somehow reached Juárez, got across the river and entered the hospital, had their babies and come home with that precious piece of paper, more valuable than gold, which certified that this child, male or female and of such-and-such a name, had been born within the United States.

Such a paper meant that for as long as he or she lived, that child could enter the States, assume his citizenship, get a free education, and build a good life. Without such a certificate, life would almost certainly be one of unending poverty in northern Mexico; therefore, women like Eufemia were willing to undergo any hardships to ensure that their unborn children received a fair start in life, and that was why even the poorest, even the least-educated, headed for El Paso in their ninth month.

But these benefits did not fully explain why so many citizens of Moctezuma yearned to live in the States. Nothing differentiated their land from that of New Mexico or Arizona, and it was actually better than many parts of West Texas; the strain of people was no different from that of people who prospered in those American states; and the climate was the same. But the sad fact was that in Mexico no way had been devised whereby the unquestioned wealth of the land, almost unequaled in the Americas, could be justly distributed. The wealthy grew immensely wealthy; the Guzmáns could see the great cars sweeping north to the shops across the Rio Grande and then come roaring back loaded with goods purchased in American stores. But in the Mexican system none of that wealth filtered down to the peasants who did most of the work. Indeed, it would be difficult to find a more cynical system than that which trapped Encarnación Guzmán and her three children, for the national leaders had been preaching since the 1920s the triumph of La Revolución, and each succeeding administration had cried at election time: 'Let us march forward with La Revolución!' but the same reactionary cadre had remained in power, cynically stealing the nation's wealth and allowing the great masses of the people to plod along, sometimes at the starvation level.

Any young person living in Moctezuma would try to get to the States, and if a pregnant woman wanted to ensure that her baby was born with rights to that superior economic system, she was entitled to try every known device to accomplish it. The flood of people streaming north never seemed to diminish.

The plan that the Guzmáns worked out was this: brother Cándido, a clever seventeen-year-old, would take his sister Eufemia to Juárez, where he would make contact with El Lobo, and for a small fee, which Cándido would carry in his shoe, Eufemia would be taken across the bridge two or three days before her labor was supposed to begin. She would be kept in a house run by El Lobo's friends, and on the morning when birth seemed imminent, she would be taken to a place close to the hospital. At the proper time, and this would be crucial, but women in the area could help determine it, she would be rushed as an emergency patient to the hospital, where she would give birth, she hoped, to a son. Then her friends would show her how to acquire a birth certificate and purchase three or four photographed copies. She would then recross the bridge, rejoin her brother, and return to Moctezuma—and eighteen years later she would bid her son goodbye when he left to take up residence in the States.

The awful price exacted by this system was the inevitable breakup of the family, for the time would come when this child with his precious documents would leave Mexico forever; but the good part was that when as a young man he established his American citizenship, he could send down to Moctezuma and bring in his entire family under 'the compassion rule.' So once Eufemia gained entrance to Thomason General, she was guaranteeing future American citizenship for herself and, perhaps, as many as a dozen family members. 'Make no mistake,' warned an older man who had worked as an illegal in Texas, 'many things happen up there that no one in his right mind would wish, but it's better than here. It's worth the risk.'

Cándido and his sister caught a ride north with one of the Pemex trucks, and as they neared Juárez the driver said: 'You understand, it's easy to cross over into El Paso. Anyone can do that. But it's hell to slip out of the city and move north. Guards and stops everywhere.'

'I don't intend to stay,' Cándido said, and the driver said: 'They all say that. When you see it, you'll want to.'

Although Juárez was a large city, they had no difficulty in finding El Lobo: 'I'll get your sister to the hospital at the right time. I can also take you to fine cities in Texas, Cándido. Lots of work.'

'I'm not staying.'

'For fifteen dollars, all the way to Fort Stockton and a good job.'

'Just my sister.'

It was agreed that Cándido would accompany her to the first stopping house and would at the appropriate time move her close to the hospital, and he did this effectively, so that Eufemia had a minimum of worry. At the stopping place six other pregnant women counseled with her, and she watched as they moved on to the American hospital; she saw two of them when they returned with their babies, both girls, and displayed the precious birth certificates. 'You are so lucky,' she said, and they replied: 'We know you'll be lucky, too.'

She was. With the skill of an expert, Cándido moved her nearer the hospital, and when her labor pains became intense, he led her to the emergency entrance, where a young intern with a mustache cried: 'Here's another Aztec princess!' and before Cándido could ask even one question, his sister was whisked away.

It cost the city of El Paso about twelve hundred dollars to deliver a Mexican baby and care for the mother prior to release, but the most Thomason General could extract from the constant stream of pregnant women was seventy-five dollars each, and most, like Eufemia, could pay nothing. Why did Texas allow this preposterous system? 'I'll tell you,' Officer Talbot explained to a newspaperman from Chicago. 'We're a compassionate people down here. We do not turn away pregnant women. But we also like the cheap labor the Mexicans provide. Mercy and profit, one of the most rewarding combinations in world history.'

The Pemex driver had been right. Once Cándido saw the riches of El Paso and the good life available to even poor Mexicans, he wanted to stay, not in that crowded city but in the hinterland, where he heard that jobs were plentiful, and this desire tempted him to come back across the international bridge as soon as he placed his sister and her baby on the Pemex truck heading south.

Since he did not purchase the services of El Lobo, he was able to penetrate only a few miles past the immigration blockades when a tall Border Patrol officer named Talbot detected him on the road and sent him back to Mexico.

On his next try he did use El Lobo, who put him well inland, but again he had the bad luck of running into Officer Talbot, a misfortune that was repeated on his third attempt. 'Haven't I seen you before?' Talbot asked, and this time when he shoved the boy across the border he warned: 'Next time, jail.'

So Cándido, with his burning memories of riches in the United States, returned to Moctezuma, but in June of the following year, when he was eighteen and working at his brother-in-law's garage, his younger sister, Manuela, informed her family that she wanted to try to get into the States, and again the women of Moctezuma decided that Cándido should take her to Juárez, where, for fifteen dollars, El Lobo would lead her not into El Paso, where she would be apprehended if she tried to sneak past Officer Talbot, but to a safe crossing he had developed some seventy miles to the east. Said a man who had used that route under El Lobo's guidance: 'It's not easy. You cross the Rio Grande, walk inland about a mile, and a truck picks you up. Costs another fifteen dollars, but you can't make it alone. Cándido, warn your sister that she cannot make it alone.'

For Cándido the next days were agonizing, because the old longing to get into the United States revived, but he knew that if he went, he would leave his mother alone: Eufemia married. Manuela gone. If I go, who's left to help? But then he began to think of his sister: I can't leave her in a truck at the edge of the desert. By the time he and his sister were ready to board the Pemex truck he had not made up his mind, but as he said farewell to his mother he embraced her with unusual ardor and burst into tears. She must have known what tormented him, for she said: 'Do whatever's right.'

When they reached Ciudad Juárez and Cándido actually saw El Lobo again, he knew he must not leave Manuela in that man's corrupt hands. So without having made a major decision himself, he eased into the Lobo operation, reserving the right to back out at the last moment.

The truck carrying the would-be emigrants left Juárez at five in the afternoon with seventeen passengers, eleven men and six women at fifteen dollars a head, and drove southeast along a bumpy road traveled by other trucks returning empty from the trip to the crossing. At dusk the emigrants pulled up at a lonely spot east of Banderas, and there Cándido had to make up his mind: 'Well, are you joining them or not? Fifteen dollars if you do.' And on the spot the boy said: 'I'll stay with my sister.'

At this place the Rio Grande was so shallow that the Mexicans could walk almost completely across, needing to swim only the last few yards to the American side, and there the American guides had stationed two Mexican men, who helped the women. When all were safely ashore, El Lobo blinked his lights and was gone.

They had come to some of the loneliest land in Texas, that stretch along the river which not even the hardiest settlers had attempted to tame. Rocky in parts, steeply graded, bereft of trees, with only dirt trails leading inland, it was a terrain so forbidding that Cándido was glad he had stayed with his sister: 'This is dangerous. Stay close to me.'

The eighteen wetbacks were led to a miserable truck, which had bounced over these roads many times, but before they were allowed to climb in, a man named Hanson growled: 'Fifteen bucks, and I put you on a back road to Fort Stockton.' He stood in the shaded glare of the headlights, verifying the payments, and when all were accounted for, he piled the Mexicans in and started north, but as he drove, a cohort rode atop the cab of the truck, keeping a shotgun aimed at the passengers.

'Don't no one try to jump off,' he warned. 'We don't want to show La Migra how we move about.'

There was a moon, rising at about nine and throwing only modified light, but it was enough to permit the Mexicans to see the wild terrain they were traversing.

'Oh, this can't be Estados Unidos!' a woman cried, and the gunman replied in Spanish: 'It sure is. Three hundred miles of it.'

At four in the morning, when they were far from the river, the driver, seeing a chance to earn a lot of money with no responsibility, made the engine cough and then conk out. 'Damnit,' he cried, 'we've got to fix this,' and he ordered the Mexicans to leave the truck and stand well back while he worked on it. To their delight the engine began to sputter, caught, and then purred nicely. At these welcome sounds the Mexicans started toward the truck, when, to their horror, the two anglos revved the motor and took off across the desert, leaving the wetbacks stranded, with no guide, no food and, worst of all, no water.

It was a trip into hell. At ten in the morning of the second day, when the sun was blazing high, the first Mexican died, a man in his forties whose swollen tongue filled his mouth. An hour later, six others were dead, but the two Guzmáns still survived. 'Manuela,' Cándido whispered, 'we must look for plants, anything.'

They found nothing, none of the big cacti which often saved lives in such circumstances, and by noon, three more were dead. Overhead, the sky was an arch of blue; not a blemish obscured the sun, which beat mercilessly on the hapless Mexicans. Two o'clock passed, with more than half the wetbacks, ironic name, dead, and in the late afternoon, in that dreadful heat, Manuela gasped one last plea for water, stared madly at her brother, and died.

Three men made it to U.S. 80, a hundred and forty miles west of Fort Stockton. In despair they tried to flag down motorists; none stopped. Cándido finally threw himself in front of an approaching car while his companions waved frantically, but they did not need to do this, for the man driving the car was Officer Talbot, who had been searching for them.

'Poor sons-a-bitches,' he said to his partner, 'let's get them something to drink.' They drove eastward to Van Horn, where Talbot tossed the three in jail, but not before providing them with all the liquid they could drink.

They were returned to Mexico, of course, and since Cándido was too ashamed to go back to Moctezuma to inform his family of Manuela's death and of how it had occurred, he slipped back into El Paso, found a job, saved his money, bought a gun, grew a mustache so as to alter his appearance, and went back to El Lobo as if he had never seen him before: 'Is it true, you take people into los Estados Unidos?'

'Fifteen dollars to me, fifteen to the men on the other side.'

'I'll go.'

'I'll take you through the barriers in north El Paso.'

'I was told there was a better crossing at Banderas.'

'You want to go that way, all right.'

This time a party of nineteen illegals drove beside the Rio Grande to the little town, where the emigrants paid their fee and swam the river. On the far side

Hanson was waiting with his same rickety truck, the same shotgun assistant. They left the river at dusk, rode through the night, and at about three in the morning, the truck broke down again.

'Move over here while we fix it,' Hanson said, but as he spoke, Cándido and two other wetbacks whom he had recruited en route shot him and the assistant dead. Commandeering the truck, they sped toward where U.S. 80 would have to be, and long before dawn they were at the outskirts of Fort Stockton. Disposing of the truck in a gully, they shook hands and made their way variously into the town and into the fabric of American life.

Cándido, moving alone along the highway, started back west, to give the impression, if questioned by police regarding the desert murders, that he had been in the States for some time. But he had walked only a few miles when he was met by a pickup roaring eastward from El Paso. As soon as the driver spotted Cándido, whom he easily identified as a wetback, he screeched to a halt: 'What you lookin' for, son?'

The driver was a big, florid man in his late thirties, dressed like a sheriff, and he terrified Cándido, who whispered: 'Solamente español, señor,' whereupon the man surprised him by saying in easy Spanish: 'Amigo, if you seek work, you've met the right man.'

He invited Cándido to sit beside him, and together they rode to Fort Stockton and a short distance to the north, where they came upon a frontier ranch with an ornate stone gate and a sign which said:

EL RANCHO ESTUPENDO
LORENZO QUIMPER
PROPRIETOR

'Come in and grab yourself some grub,' the rancher said, and in this way Cándido Guzmán became a permanent resident of the United States and a life-long employee of Lorenzo Quimper, who owned some nine ranches for which he needed reliable workmen. Few immigrants had ever dared so much to find haven in Texas, few would serve it more faithfully.

In the city of Detroit things were not going well for the Morrisons. Todd, the father, could see that within a few more months his branch of the Chrysler Corporation might have to shut down. The ax had already fallen on his wife, Maggie, for one Friday morning three weeks earlier the principal of her school had handed her the gray-toned sheet of paper teachers dreaded:

The Cascade Public Schools District Board of Education, meeting in regular session, voted last night to take certain actions necessary for its survival. It is my duty to inform you that your teaching contract will not be renewed upon its expiration at the close of the 1968 spring term, and both your job and your salary will end at that time.

The Morrisons were aware that even with the loss of Maggie's income, they could survive if Todd kept his job, but there was an additional aggravation: their two children—Beth, an extremely bright thirteen, and Lonnie, aged eleven—had already stated that under no circumstances did they want to leave the Cascade schools, which they had grown to love and which enrolled all their friends.

The Morrisons had long practiced the art of family democracy, with ample discussion of most problems, and they did not back off from this unpleasant one: 'Kids, if things get worse at Chrysler, I'm going to get laid off. What then?'

'That would be horribly unfair,' Beth cried.

'They fired your mother, didn't they?'

'Yes, but the school board's a bunch of cruds.'

'We must consider the possibilities if I do lose my job,' Todd said.

'You could become a policeman,' Lonnie suggested. 'The *News* had an article about needing more cops.'

'Not my age, and not my salary,' his father replied. He was thirty-seven, his wife thirty-three, at the exact time in their lives when they needed every penny to enjoy the amenities they treasured—a good movie now and then, books—and to afford careful attention to health, orthodontics, a sensible diet, durable clothes. And these cost money. Their house carried only a six-thousand-dollar mortgage, and they had never been extravagant with cars or socializing; they drove one new Plymouth and one very old Ford.

Normally they should have been at the cresting point in their careers, with Todd looking forward to rapid promotion and Maggie being considered for a principalship. Now the bottom was falling out of their world, and they could not even guess where the terrifying drop would end.

'Well, what shall we do if I'm fired?' Todd asked again, and his three advisers sat silent, so he explored the subject: 'Ford and GM won't take me on, that's for sure. Stated frankly, my type of work is ended unless I can find a job in Japan.'

The Morrisons laughed at this suggestion, but then Beth asked: 'Transfer? What's a practical possibility?'

'I don't really know. For your mother, no school jobs in these parts, nor in places like New York, but I hear there are openings in California and boom towns like Atlanta.'

'I'm attracted to neither,' Beth said bluntly in her surprisingly adult manner, whereupon her mother said: 'You'll like whatever we have to do, Miss Beth, and remember that,' and the girl said: 'I know. I don't want to leave Cascade, but if we have to, we have to.'

'I vote for California,' Lonnie said. 'Surfing.'

Todd ignored this suggestion: 'I really think I'll have to start looking for a new job.'

'What could you do?' Beth asked.

'I'm good at what I do . . .'

'Yes, you are, dear,' Maggie said quickly.

'I can keep an organization on its toes. Maybe labor relations. Maybe selling something.'

'*Death of a Salesman!*' Beth cried. 'Willie Loman of the auto trade.'

'You'd be awfully good at labor relations,' Maggie said as she cleared the table. 'But where?'

The next three weeks passed in growing apprehension as Maggie Morrison applied to one school district after another; the results were not depressing, they were terrifying. At night she told her family: 'Enrollments dropping everywhere in the city. Everyone suggests we move to some new area. We may have to.'

In the month that followed, the spate of news from Chrysler was so depressing that Todd could barely discuss it with his family, and it was at one of these doleful meetings that the word *Texas* was first voiced. Todd said: 'I hear that electronics is real big in the Dallas area. If they're expanding . . .' Beth said she did not want to go to Texas, too big, too noisy, but Lonnie could hardly wait to get started: 'Cowboys! Wow!'

On the next Friday night Todd was fired.

In their despair, the Morrisons organized as a team: Todd studied the want ads; Maggie continued to seek work as a teacher, or even as a teacher's helper; Beth, with remarkable maturity, took charge of the housework; and Lonnie volunteered for extra chores. But each week the family savings declined, and the children knew it.

Todd applied for three dozen different jobs, and was rejected each time: 'I'm too old for this, too young for that. I know both the assembly line and sales, but can't land a job in either. This is one hell of a time to be out of work.'

It was Maggie who found him a job, and she did it in a most peculiar way. She was in the industrial section of the city interviewing at a school for children with special problems, when she met a woman whose husband worked for a firm that had developed a new line of business: 'What they do, Todd, they overhaul automobile engines. They have new diagnostic machines to spot weaknesses, other machines to fix them. They've had real success in Detroit and Cleveland, and they want to franchise widely. This woman said there were real opportunities.'

Early next morning Todd was at the new company's office, and he learned that what his wife had reported was true. Engine Experts had hit upon a system for adding years to the life of the average automobile engine and its subordinate parts; intricate new machines diagnosed trouble spots and instructed the workmen how to repair them. The initial cost of the system was rather high, but the cash return of the four installations that Todd was allowed to inspect was reassuring, and he entered into serious discussion with the owners.

'What we want to do,' the energetic men said, 'is break into the Dallas, Houston market. Go where the cars are, that's our motto.'

'I don't have the funds to buy in,' Todd said truthfully, but the men said: 'We don't want you to. You know cars. You have common sense. We want you to go to Texas, scout out the good locations, what we call the inevitables, and buy us an option on the corner where the most cars pass, but where an industrial shop would be allowed. Would you be interested?'

'What are the chances I'd fall on my ass?'

'We'd carry you for one year, sink or swim. But we think you'd swim, especially in Texas, where they have poor public transportation and people are nuts about their cars.'

They offered Todd a year's assignment in Texas—Dallas or Houston, as he wished—during which he was to identify eight locations and arrange for the purchase of real estate and the issuance of licenses to open Engine Experts shops. That night he handed his wife and children pencils and paper and asked them to take notes as he lined out their situation: 'Six months ago this family had income as follows. Father, twenty-six thousand dollars; mother, eight thousand dollars. Total how much, Lonnie?'

'Thirty-four thousand dollars.'

'Well, we both lost our jobs. Salary right now, zero. We can get something for the house. Our savings go steadily down, but still nineteen thousand dollars. Should have been a lot more, but we didn't anticipate.'

'We can cut back,' Beth said. 'I don't need special lessons.'

'We can all cut back, or starve. I've been offered a job in Texas . . .'

'Hooray!' Lonnie cried. 'Can I have a horse?'

'The salary will be eighteen thousand dollars, with promise of a bonus if I do well.'

'You'll do well,' Maggie said.

It was agreed. The Todd Morrisons of Michigan, a family deeply imbedded in that state, would move to Houston, Texas. On a morning in July 1968, with tears marking all their faces, they left Michigan forever and headed south. They did not paint on their truck the ancient sign G.T.T., but they could have, for the social disruptions which were forcing them south were almost identical with those which had spurred the migrations to Texas in 1820 and 1850. They, too, were in search of a better life.

In that summer of 1968 a different family of immigrants—mother, father, four daughters—moved quietly into the oil town of Larkin, and within three weeks had the owners of better-class homes in a rage. They were such a rowdy lot, especially the mother, that an observer might have thought: The rip-roaring boom days of 1922 are back!

They were night people, always a bad sign, who seemed to do most of their hell-raising after dark, with mother and daughters off on a toot marked by noise, vandalism and other furtive acts. They operated as a gang, with their weak and ineffective father along at times, and what infuriated the townsfolk particularly was that they seemed to take positive joy in their depredations.

Despite their unfavorable reputation—and many sins were charged against them which they did not commit—they really did more good than harm; they were an asset to the community, and they had about them elements of extraordinary beauty, which their enemies refused to admit.

They were armadillos, never known in this area before, a group of invaders who had moved up from Mexico, bringing irritation and joy wherever they appeared. Opponents of the fascinating little creatures, which were no bigger than small dogs, accused them of eating quail eggs, a rotten lie; of raiding chicken coops, false as could be; and of tearing up fine lawns, a just charge and a serious one. Ranchers also said: 'They dig so many holes that my cattle stumble into them and break their legs. There goes four hundred bucks.'

The indictment involving the digging up of lawns and the making of other deep holes was justified, for no animal could dig faster than an armadillo, and when this mother and her four daughters turned themselves loose on a neat lawn or a nicely tilled vegetable garden, their destruction could be awesome. The armadillo had a long, probing snout, backed up by two forefeet, each with four three-inch claws, and two hind feet with five shovel-like claws, and the speed with which it could work those excavators was unbelievable.

'Straight down,' Mr. Kramer said, 'they can dig faster than I can with a shovel. The nose feels out the soft spots and those forelegs drive like pistons, but it's the back legs that amaze, because they catch the loose earth and throw it four, five feet backwards.'

Mr. Kramer was one of those odd men, found in all communities, who measured rainfall on a regular basis—phoning the information to the Weather Service —and who recorded the depth of snowfall, the time of the first frost, the strength and direction of the wind during storms, and the fact that in the last blue norther 'the temperature on a fine March day dropped, in the space of three hours, from 26.9 to 9.7 degrees Celsius.' He was the type who always gave the temperature in Celsius, which he expected his friends to translate into Fahrenheit, if they wished. He was, in short, a sixty-two-year-old former member of an oil crew who had always loved nature and who had poked his bullet-cropped sandy-haired head into all sorts of corners.

The first armadillos to reach Larkin were identified on a Tuesday, and by Friday, Mr. Kramer had written away for three research studies on the creatures.

The more he read, the more he grew to like them, and before long he was defending them against their detractors, especially to those whose lawns had been excavated: 'A little damage here and there, I grant you. But did you hear about what they did for my rose bushes? Laden down with beetles, they were. Couldn't produce one good flower even with toxic sprays. Then one night I look out to check the moon, three-quarters full, and I see these pairs of beady eyes shining in the gloom, and across my lawn come these five armadillos, and I say to myself: "Oh, oh! There goes the lawn!" but that wasn't the case at all. Those armadillos were after those beetles, and when I woke up in the morning to check the rain gauge, what do you suppose? Not one beetle to be found.'

Mr. Kramer defended the little creatures to anyone who would listen, but not many cared: 'You ever see his tongue? Darts out about six inches, long, very sticky. Zoom! There goes another ant, another beetle. He was made to police the garden and knock off the pests.'

Once when a Mrs. Cole was complaining with a bleeding heart about what the armadillos had done to her lawn, he stopped her with a rather revolting question: 'Mrs. Cole, have you ever inspected an armadillo's stomach? Well, I have, many times. Dissected bodies I've found along the highway. And what does the stomach contain? Bugs, beetles, delicate roots, flies, ants, all the crawling things you don't like. And you can tell Mr. Cole that in seventeen autopsies, I've never found even the trace of a bird's egg, and certainly no quail eggs.' By the time he was through with his report on the belly of an armadillo, Mrs. Cole was more than ever opposed to the destructive little beasts.

But it was when he extolled the beauty of the armadillo that he lost the support of even the most sympathetic Larkin citizens, for they saw the little animal as an awkward, low-slung relic of some past geologic age that had mysteriously survived into the present; one look at the creature convinced them that it should have died out with the dinosaurs, and its survival into the twentieth century somehow offended them. To Mr. Kramer, this heroic persistence was one of the armadillo's great assets, but he was even more impressed by the beauty of its design.

'Armadillo? What does it mean? "The little armored one." And if you look at him dispassionately, what you see is a beautifully designed animal much like one of the armored horses they used to have in the Middle Ages. The back, the body, the legs are all protected by this amazing armor, beautifully fashioned to flow across the body of the beast. And look at the engineering!' When he said this he liked to display one of the three armadillos he had tamed when their parents were killed by hunters and point to the miracle of which he was speaking: 'This is real armor, fore and aft. Punch it. Harder than your fingernail and made of the same substance. Protects the shoulders and the hips. But here in the middle, nine flexible bands of armor, much like an accordion. Always nine, never seven or ten, and without these inserts, the beast couldn't move about as he does. Quite wonderful, really. Nothing like it in the rest of the animal kingdom. Real relic of the dinosaur age.'

But he would never let it end at that, and it was what he said next that did win some converts to the armadillo's defense: 'What awes me is not the armor, nor the nine flexible plates. They're just good engineering. But the beauty of the design goes beyond engineering. It's art, and only a designer who took infinite care could have devised these patterns. Leonardo da Vinci, maybe, or Michelangelo, or even God.' And then he would show how fore and aft the armor was composed of the most beautiful hexagons and pentagons arranged like golden coins upon a field of exquisite gray cloth, while the nine bands were entirely different: 'Look at the curious structures! Elongated capital A's. Go ahead, tell me what they look like. A field of endless oil derricks, aren't they? Can't you see, he's the good-luck symbol of the whole oil industry. His coming to Larkin was no mistake. He was sent here to serve as our mascot.'

How beautiful, how mysterious the armadillos were when one took the trouble to inspect them seriously, as Mr. Kramer did. They bespoke past ages, the death of great systems, the miracle of creation and survival; they were walking reminders of a time when volcanoes peppered the earth and vast lakes covered continents. They were hallowed creatures, for they had seen the earth before man arrived, and they had survived to remind him of how things once had been. They should have died out with Tyrannosaurus Rex and Diplodocus, but they had stubbornly persisted so that they could bear testimony, and for the value of that testimony, they were precious and worthy of defense. 'They must continue into the future,' Mr. Kramer said, 'so that future generations can see how things once were.'

'What amazes,' Mr. Kramer told the women he tried to persuade, 'is their system of giving birth. Invariably four pups, and invariably all four identicals of the same sex. There is no case of a mother armadillo giving birth to boys and girls at the same time. Impossible. And do you know why? Because one fertilized egg is split into four parts, rarely more, rarely less. Therefore, the resulting babies have to be of the same sex.

'But would you believe this? The mother can hold that fertilized four-part egg in her womb for the normal eight weeks, or, if things don't seem propitious, for as long as twenty-two months, same as the elephant. She gives birth in response to some perceived need, and what that is, no one can say.'

As he brooded about this mystery of birth, wondering how the armadillo community ensured that enough males and females would be provided to keep the race going, he visualized what he called 'The Great Computer in the Sky,' which kept track of how many four-girl births were building up in a given community: and some morning it clicks out a message—'Hey, we need a couple of four-boy births in the Larkin area.' So the next females to become pregnant have four male babies, and the grand balance is maintained.

Mr. Kramer could find no one who wished to share his speculation on this mystery, but as he pursued it he began to think about human beings, too: What grand computer ensures that we have a balance between male and female babies? And how does it make the adjustments it does? Like after a war, when a lot of men have died in battle. Normal births in peacetime, a thousand and four males to a thousand females, because males are more delicate in the early years and have to be protected numerically. But after a war, when The Great Computer knows that there's a deficiency in males, the balance swings as high as one thousand and nine to one thousand.

So when he looked at an armadillo on its way to dig in his lawn, he saw not a destructive little tank with incredibly powerful digging devices, but a symbol of the grandeur of creation, the passing of time, the mystery of birth, the great beauty that exists in the world in so many different manifestations: An armadillo is not one whit more beautiful or mysterious than a butterfly or a pine cone, but it's more fun. And what gave him the warmest satisfaction: All the other sizable animals of the world seem to be having their living areas reduced. Only the armadillo is stubbornly enlarging his. Sometimes when he watched this mother and her four daughters heading forth for some new devastation, he chuckled with delight: There they go! The Five Horsewomen of the Apocalypse!

Another Larkin man had a much different name for the little excavators. Ransom Rusk, principal heir and sole operator of the Rusk holdings in the Larkin Field, had a fierce desire to obliterate memories of his unfortunate ancestry: the grand fool Earnshaw Rusk; the wife with the wooden nose; his own obscenely obese father; his fat, foolish mother. He wanted to forget them all. He was a tall, lean man, quite handsome, totally unlike his father, and at forty-five he was at the height of his powers. He had married a Wellesley graduate from New England, and it was amusing that her mother, wishing to dissociate herself from her cotton-mill ancestry, had named her daughter Fleurette, trusting that something of French gentility would brush off.

Fleurette and Ransom Rusk, fed up with the modest house in whose kitchen Floyd had maintained his oil office till he died, had employed an architect from Boston to build them a mansion, and he had suggested an innovation which would distinguish their place from others in the region: 'It is very fashionable, in the better estates of England, to have a bowling green. It could also be used for croquet, should you prefer,' and Fleurette had applauded the idea.

It was now her pleasure to entertain at what she called 'a pleasant afternoon of bowls,' and she did indeed make it pleasant. Not many of the local millionaires— and there were now some two dozen in the Larkin district, thanks to those reliable wells which never produced much more than a hundred barrels a day, rarely less—knew how to play bowls, but they had fun at the variations they devised.

Ransom Rusk, as the man who dominated the Larkin Field, was not spectacularly rich by Texas standards, whose categories were popularly defined: one to twenty million, comfortable; twenty to fifty million, well-to-do; fifty to five hundred million, rich; five hundred million to one billion, big rich; one to five billion, Texas rich. By virtue of his other oil holdings in various parts of the state, and his prudent investments in Fort Worth ventures, he was now rich, but in the lowest ranks of that middle division. His attitudes toward wealth were contradictory, for obviously he had a driving ambition to acquire and exercise power in its various manifestations, and in pursuit of this, he strove to multiply his wealth. But he remained indifferent to its mathematical level, often spending an entire year without knowing his balances or even an approximation of them. Impelled by an urge to control billions, he did not care to count them. On the other hand, he had inherited his father's shrewd judgment regarding oil and had extended it to the field of general financing, and he always sought new opportunities and knew how to apply leverage when he found them.

He was brooding about his Fort Worth adventures one morning when he heard Fleurette scream: 'Oh my God!' Thinking that she had fallen, he rushed into the bedroom to find her standing by the window, pointing wordlessly at the havoc which had been wreaked upon her bowling green.

'Looks like an atomic bomb!' Ransom said. 'It's those damned armadillos,' but Fleurette did not hear his explanation, for she was wailing as if she had lost three children.

'Shut up!' Ransom cried. 'I'll take care of those little bastards.'

He slammed out of the house, inspected the chopped-up bowling lawn, and summoned the gardeners: 'Can this be fixed?'

'We can resod it like new, Mr. Rusk,' they assured him, 'but you'll have to keep them armadillos out.'

'I'll take care of them. I'll shoot them.' In pursuit of this plan, he went to the hardware store to buy a stack of ammo for his .22 rifle, but while there, he happened to stand beside Mr. Kramer at the check-out counter, and the retired oilman, who had worked for Rusk, asked: 'What are the bullets for?' and unfortunately, Ransom said: 'Armadillos.'

'Oh, you mustn't do that! Those are precious creatures. You should be protecting them, not killing them.'

'They tore up my wife's lawn last night.'

'Her bowling green? I've heard it's beautiful.'

'Cost God knows how much, and it's in shreds.'

'A minor difficulty,' Kramer said lightly, since he did not have to pay for the repairs. And before Ransom could get away, the enthusiastic nature lover had drawn him to the drugstore, where they shared Dr. Peppers.

'Did you know, Ransom, that we have highly accurate maps showing the progress north of the armadillo? Maybe the only record of its kind?'

'I wish they'd stayed where they came from.'

'They came from Mexico.'

'One hell of a lot comes from Mexico—wetbacks, boll weevils . . .'

'A follower of the great Audubon first recorded them in Texas, down along the Rio Grande, in 1854. They had reached San Antonio by 1880, Austin by 1914, Jefferson in the east by 1945. They were slower reaching our dryer area. They were reported in Dallas in 1953, but they didn't reach us till this year. Remarkable march.'

'Should have kept them in Mexico,' Rusk said, fingering his box of shells.

'They're in Florida too. Three pairs escaped from a zoo in 1922. And people transported them as pets. They liked Florida, so now they move east from Texas and west from Florida. They'll occupy the entire Gulf area before this century is out.'

'They aren't going to occupy my place much longer,' Ransom said, and that was the beginning of the hilarious adventure, because Mr. Kramer persuaded him, almost tearfully, not to shoot the armadillos but to keep them away from the bowling green by building protection around it: 'These are unique creatures, relics of the past, and they do an infinite amount of good.'

The first thing Rusk did was to enclose his wife's resodded bowling green within a stout tennis-court-type fence, but two nights after it was in place, at considerable expense, the bowling green was chewed up again, and when Mr. Kramer was consulted he showed the Rusks how the world's foremost excavators had simply burrowed under the fence to get at the succulent roots.

'What you have to do is dig a footing around your green, six feet deep, and fill it with concrete. Sink your fence poles in that.'

'Do you know how much that would cost?'

'They tell me you have the money,' Kramer said easily, and so the fence was taken down, backhoes were brought in, and the deep trench was dug, enclosing the green. Then trucks dumped a huge amount of cement into the gaping holes, and the fence was reerected. Eight feet into the air, six feet underground, and the armadillos were boxed off.

But four days after the job was finished, Fleurette Rusk let out another wail, and when Ransom ran to her room he bellowed: 'Is it those damned armadillos again?' It was, and when he and Mr. Kramer studied the new disaster the situation became clear, as the enthusiastic naturalist explained: 'Look at that hole! Ransom, they dug right under the concrete barrier and up the other side. Probably took them half an hour, no more.'

The scientific manner in which Kramer diagnosed the case, and the obvious pleasure he took in the engineering skill of his armadillos, infuriated Rusk, and once more he threatened to shoot his tormentors, but Kramer prevailed upon him to try one more experiment: 'What we must do, Ransom, is drive a palisade below the concrete footing.'

'And how do we do that?'

'Simple, you get a hydraulic ram and it drives down metal stakes. Twenty feet deep. But they'll have to be close together.'

When this job was completed, Rusk calculated that he had $218,000 invested in that bowling green, but to his grim satisfaction, the sunken palisade did stop the predators he had named 'Lady Macbeth and Her Four Witches.' The spikes of the palisade went too deep for her to risk a hole so far below the surface.

But she was not stopped for long, because one morning Ransom was summoned by a new scream: 'Ransom, look at those scoundrels!' and when he looked, he saw that the mother, frustrated by the palisade but still hungry for the tender grass roots, had succeeded in climbing her side of the fence, straight up, and then descending straight down, and she was in the process of teaching her daughters to do the same.

For some minutes Rusk stood at the window, watching the odd procession of armadillos climbing up his expensive fence, and when one daughter repeatedly fell back, unable to learn, he broke into laughter.

'I don't see what's so funny,' his wife cried, and he explained: 'Look at the dumb little creature. She can't use her front claws to hold on to the cross wires,' and his wife exploded: 'You seem to be cheering her on,' and it suddenly became clear to Rusk that he was doing just that. He was responding to his wife's constant nagging: 'Don't wear that big cowboy hat in winter, makes you look like a real hick.' 'Don't wear those boots to a dance, makes you look real Texan.' She had a score of other don'ts, and now Ransom realized that in this fight of Fleurette versus the lady armadillos, he was cheering for the animals.

But as a good sport he did telephone Mr. Kramer and ask: 'Those crazy armadillos can climb the fence. What do we do?' Mr. Kramer noted the significant difference; always before it had been 'those damned armadillos,' or worse. When a man started calling them crazy, he was beginning to fall in love with them.

'Tell you what, Ransom. We call in the fence people and have them add a projection around the upper edge, so that when the armadillos reach the top of the fence, they'll run into this screen curving back at them and fall off.'

'Will it hurt them?'

'Six weeks ago you wanted to shoot them. Now you ask if it'll hurt them. Ransom, you're learning.'

'You know, Kramer, everything you advise me to do costs money.'

'You have it to spend.'

So the fence builders were brought in, and yes, they could bring a flange out parallel to the ground that no armadillo could negotiate, and when this was done Rusk would sit on his porch at night with a powerful beam flashlight and watch as the mother tried to climb the fence, with her daughters trailing, and he would break into audible laughter as the determined little creatures clawed their way to the top, encountered the barrier, and tumbled back to earth. Again and again they tried, and always they fell back. Ransom Rusk had defeated the armadillos, at a cost of $238,000 total.

'What are you guffawing at in the dark?' Fleurette demanded, and he said, 'At the armadillos trying to get into your bowling green.'

'You should have shot them months ago,' she snapped, and he replied, 'They're trying so hard, I was thinking about going down and letting them in.'

'You do,' she said, 'and I'm walking out.'

That was the beginning of the sensational Rusk divorce case, though of course many problems more serious than armadillos were involved, and most of them centered upon the husband. He had wanted the social cachet of an Eastern bride, but he had also wanted to remain a Texan. He had wanted to forget his noseless grandmother, his strange Quaker grandfather and especially his obese and ridiculous parents, but Fleurette often dragged them into conversation, especially when strangers were present. And although he had wanted a wife and had courted Fleurette arduously, he also wanted to be left alone with his multitude of projects. Had he married a woman of divine patience and sublime understanding, he might have made a success of his marriage, but Fleurette had proved increasingly giddy and insubstantial. A wiser woman would never have inflated armadillos into a cause célèbre, but once it reached that status, there was no turning back.

She charged him with numerous cruelties and more insensitivities. She swore, in her affidavit, that life with such a brute had become quite impossible, and when the case was well launched, she did the one thing that was calculated to ensure her victory: she hired Fleabait Moomer from Dallas to press her claim for a financial settlement in the Larkin County court.

Ransom's lawyer almost shuddered when he learned that Fleabait was coming into the case: 'Ransom, we're in deep trouble.'

'Why?'

'Fleabait tears a case apart. When he's in the courtroom anything can happen. Do you really want to go ahead with this?' And when Rusk replied: 'I sure as hell do, I want to get rid of that millstone,' the lawyer felt he had better explain Fleabait Moomer:

> 'He's a country genius. Very bright, no morals at all. He'll do anything to win, and I warn you right now that with a case like this, he'll probably win.
>
> 'He gets his name from his habit of scratching himself like a yokel while he's pleading. Scratch here. Scratch there. But twice in each case he stops, looks at the jury, crosses his arms, and scratches with both hands. The jury expects this, and they lean forward with special attention because they know he's going to make an important point. And

God help you when he scratches with both hands, because that's when you're going to be crucified.

'He'll charge you with sodomy, with theft of public funds, with the corruption of juveniles, with murder, with surreptitious dealing with the enemy, anything to make you the hideous focus of the case and not your poor, wronged wife. Are you strong enough to go up against Fleabait?'

Ransom said he thought he was, and the notorious trial began. It was held in that majestic room designed seventy years earlier by James Riely Gordon, and when the disputants began their inflamed accusations, an observer might have wished that the dignified hall of justice had been reserved for worthier cases.

The judge was a serious jurist, aware of the sensational nature of the trial he was conducting, but he was powerless against the antics of Fleabait Moomer, who told the jury: 'My client, that beautiful and distressed woman you see over there, all she claims in this divorce proceeding is twenty-two million dollars. Now, that might seem a lot to you, especially if you have to work as hard for your money as I do.' And here he wiped his brow, his wrists and his fingers. 'But it will be my duty to prove that the defendant, that slinkin' man over there—'

'I object, your Honor!'

'Objection sustained. Mr. Moomer, do not cast aspersions on the defendant.'

'That unfeeling, ungentlemanly, ungenerous and—'

'I object, your Honor!'

'Objection sustained. You must not attack the defendant, Counselor Moomer.'

'It will be my task to show you good people of the jury that Ransom Rusk, who inherited all his money from his father and never did a day's lick of work in his life—'

'I object, your Honor!'

'Objection sustained. The jury will disregard everything Counselor Moomer has said regarding the defendant.'

Fleabait, who wore a string tie, suspenders, a belt, and his hair combed forward in the Julius Caesar style, scratched and mumbled and fumbled his way along, playing the role of the poor country boy doing his best to defend the interests of a wronged wife, but on the third day he stopped abruptly, crossed his arms, and scratched himself vigorously while the jury, having expected him to do this, smiled knowingly. When he finished scratching, he asked ominously: 'Have you members of the jury considered the possibility that Ransom Rusk might have been involved with a gentleman in the neighborhood, whose name I refuse to divulge because of my innate sense of decency?' There was a flurry of objections, stampedes to the telephones and general noise, after which the trial continued.

The second time Fleabait scratched with both hands, the jury leaned forward with almost visible delight to hear what scandalous thing was about to be revealed, and this time the lawyer said: 'You might well ask "How did Ransom Rusk acquire his wealth?" Did he do it by ignoring every decency in the book, every law of orderly business relations between men of honor?'

The judge properly ordered this to be stricken, but the jury were as powerless to forget what had been said as they were to ensure Rusk the impartial justice to which he was entitled. Their recommendation was for the full $22,000,000, which the judge would later scale down to $15,000,000. Fleabait had told Fleurette: 'We'll go for twenty-two and be happy if we get twelve.' Of the award, he would take forty percent, or $6,000,000.

On the evening of the adverse verdict, and while it still stood at twenty-two million, Ransom returned to his big house overlooking Bear Creek and watched with satisfaction as the sun went down. In the darkness, Mr. Kramer stopped by to check on the new fence, and Ransom told him: 'I'm happier tonight than I have been in years. Free of that terrible millstone.'

'How did you happen to marry her?' The men of Larkin had long known her to be quite impossible.

'Worst reasons in the world. Reasons I'm ashamed of, believe me. Like a lot of Texas boys, I went north to Lawrenceville School, in New Jersey. One of the best. Strong teachers and all that. Well, they had this Father's Day or something, and my parents came up. Filthy rich. My father weighing three hundred, my mother the cartoon version of a Texas oilman's wife. He a slob, she ridiculous in her jewels and oil-field flamboyance. The worst three days of my life, because all the boys knew they were super-Texas, but out of decency no one said anything unkind. They just looked and laughed behind my back. When, by the grace of God, my parents finally left, I overheard one of the boys on my hall say: "She was a walking oil derrick, with the dollar bills dripping off. Poor Ransom." '

In the darkness he shuddered at that searing memory: 'Right then I decided that I would never be oil Texas. I dated the most refined girls from Vassar and Wellesley. I talked art, philosophy, anything to be unlike my father and mother. That's how I met Fleurette. I think the French name had a lot to do with it. And her determination to be so refined . . . so Eastern.'

'To tell you the truth, Ransom, you picked one hell of a lemon. You're well off especially if you can afford the settlement.'

'Kramer, do you have a pair of wire cutters?'

'In the back of my truck.' When he returned with the long-handled instrument which had once been outlawed in these parts, he was surprised when Rusk grabbed it and marched to the wire fence protecting his former wife's bowling green. With powerful clicks he cut a vertical path from ground to bending tip, then moved to a spot three feet away and cut another. When this was done he called for Mr. Kramer to help him knock the panel flat, trampling it on the ground.

Moving farther along to where he thought the armadillos nested, he cut down two more panels, and then the fence-busters, who would have been shot for such action eighty years earlier, returned to the porch, where they sat with flashlights, and when the moon was up, Ransom cried with sheer delight: 'Here they come!'

By morning the armored destroyers would have that green looking as if it had been run over by careless bulldozers, and Ransom Rusk, $22,000,000 poorer, plus $238,000 for the fence, was happier than he had been in a long time.

As soon as Todd Morrison started digging into Houston he liked what he found. 'This town has room for a stepper,' he told his wife, 'and I think I can step.' With the funds provided by the men in Detroit, he began looking around for likely spots at which to locate his franchises, and he became excited about the possibilities.

'This place is incredible!' he told the family one night. 'A population this large and absolutely no zoning. A man can build anything he pleases, and no one can say him nay.' He pointed out that this remarkable freedom did not result in a hodgepodge: 'Some kind of rational good sense seems to prevail. Builders don't go wild. They just do what they damned well please, but they sort of hold things together.'

As with many operations in a democracy, cost seemed to enforce common sense, for no builder would erect his monumental new set of condominiums next to some hovel. What he did was buy up four hundred shacks, level them, and on this cleared land erect his Taj Mahal. Some other builder would do the same half a mile away, erect his Taj Mahal. Some other builder would place his huge Shangri-La half a mile away, and then, out of self-respect, all the property in between would be subtly cleaned up. Houston was not a city; it was an agglomeration of stunningly beautiful spots connected by strips that would be beautiful later on. 'Zoning on the measles principle,' Todd called it. 'A red splotch here, one over there, and finally, all bound together in interrelated patterns.' Houston was the last bastion of free, private enterprise, laissez faire at its best, and Todd relished it.

As he worked he found that a good many of the locations he preferred were controlled by a hard-working real estate agent named Gabe Klinowitz, sixty-three years old and hardened in the Houston way of doing things. He was a small, round man, smoked a cigar and wore conservative business suits when the rest of Houston preferred less formal dress. And he was bright, as the success of his firm proved.

During his first meeting with Todd he revealed one of his guiding principles: 'I look for the bright young man just entering the field. Help him get started right. Then expect to do profitable business with him for the next thirty years.'

When Todd said he'd appreciate guidance, Gabe suggested: 'What you must do is master the wraparound.'

'Which is what?'

Taking a piece of paper, Klinowitz showed Todd the secret of buying real estate for a large corporation like a gasoline company: 'You find a good spot, on the corner of two busy roads. The owner has two acres, won't break it up into smaller lots. The company, say Mobil or Humble in the old days, they can use a quarter of an acre, only. That leaves you with an acre and three-quarters wrapping around the corner in a kind of capital L. Your job as buyer is to buy the entire piece, but not before you've found someone like me who'll take the wraparound off your hands. Do you see the economics?'

When Todd said that he did not, Klinowitz asked him to write down the figures: 'You personally buy the whole two acres from the farmer for sixty thousand dollars. You've already arranged to sell the choice corner to Mobil for seventy-five thousand. And you sell me the wraparound, all that good land next to the corner, for fifty thousand. Your profit on the deal, a cool sixty-five thousand dollars.'

Morrison studied this for a while, then pointed to the flaw: 'But I'm buying this for the company, not for myself,' and Klinowitz said: 'Before long, I suspect you'll be buying it for yourself.'

The more Todd worked with Klinowitz, the more he liked him. The man was forthright, quick and impeccably honest. He was constantly making sharp deals, but he insisted that all participants understand the intricacies, and he would go to great lengths to explain to a farmer whose land he was trying to buy what the good and bad points of the proposed deal were. Often Todd heard him say: 'You wait eight, ten years, undoubtedly you'll get a better buy. But why wait? I promise you, you'll not get a better deal right now than I'm offering.'

From watching many sales, Morrison learned one secret of Gabe's remarkable success in Houston real estate: 'Todd, you must go to bed each night reassuring yourself: "This is going to go on forever." I think it is. Houston is going to grow and grow and grow. You told me the other day that compared to Detroit prices, these are outrageous. Todd, I give you my solemn word, the two acres you buy today for sixty thousand, you'll live to see them resell for six hundred thousand. You must tell yourself that every night, and you must believe. This can go on forever.'

Once when he gave this sermon he grabbed Todd by the arm: 'So you warn me: "Gabe, the bottom can fall out of this dream," and I'm the first to confess: "Yes, it can. But only temporary. Two, three bad years, then we come zooming back." Todd, this really can go on forever.'

Having confessed that the bottom might drop out, temporarily, he gave Todd his first piece of long-range advice: 'Always keep yourself in position to weather a few bad years. Fire three-fourths of your staff. Put your wife and kids on a severe allowance. Draw in your horns. Bring the wagons into a circle. But never lose faith. Houston real estate will always bounce back.'

And then he reached the operative part of his counsel: 'Do you see the logical consequences of this situation? If real estate is bound to zoom, it does not really matter how much you pay for a good site today. If you think the corner is worth no more than forty thousand and the farmer wants sixty thousand, give him the sixty, but he must allow you to write the terms.'

'What terms?'

'Smallest possible down payment, longest possible payout, lowest possible interest.' And he shared with Todd the details of one of his latest deals: 'This big corner, prime shopping area in the future, worth, I'd say, a hundred thousand dollars. Farmer thought he'd make a killing and ask a hundred and twenty-five thousand. Without blinking an eye I agreed, but then I insisted on an eleven-year payout, and a six-and-a-half-percent interest. He was glad to sign.'

'What's the point?'

'Don't you see? Suppose I was able to buy it at my price, but had to pay eight-percent interest for eleven years. Total interest, eighty-eight thousand dollars. If I pay his price with interest at six and a half percent, my interest bill for eleven years is eighty-nine thousand three hundred and seventy-five, only about a thousand dollars higher. Add that to the extra twenty-five thousand he chiseled me out of, I spent only twenty-six thousand extra dollars to make him very, very happy. He can boast to all his friends: "I certainly handled that sharp Jew real estate fellow." '

'But it still cost you twenty-six thousand extra bucks.'

'Todd, you miss the whole point! If Houston real estate is going to climb like I think, eleven years from now that corner will bring me not the hundred and twenty-five thousand I paid, but more than a million. You give a little today, you make a million tomorrow.'

And when Todd still deemed it imprudent to pay more now than one had to, Gabe revealed his last principle: 'Always leave a little something on the table for the other guy. Six years from now, when the rest of that man's property is for sale, he'll come to me because he'll remember that I treated him square in 1969. I left a little on the table.'

It was strange, but perhaps inevitable, that of all the advice Gabe Klinowitz shared with his new friend, the one thing that Todd remembered longest was a chance remark: 'You may be buying for the company now, but before long you'll be buying for yourself.' And the more he contemplated this prediction the more sensible it became. One night he told his wife: 'With a little cash and a lot of gumption, a man could make a killing in this market.'

He began riding tirelessly about the highways and country roads, looking not for franchise sites, because he had that end of his business rather well in hand, thanks to leads provided by Klinowitz, but for any stray properties which he might one day purchase for himself, and as he rode he found himself drawn northward, almost as if by magnet, to a peculiarity of the Texas scene: FM-1960.

Up to about 1950, Texas had been predominantly an agricultural state, with its laws, banking procedures and business habits attuned to the rancher and the farmer. Not even oil had exceeded in general and financial interest the importance of the land, and a generation of Texas politicians had invented and supported a creative idea of high quality, the farm-to-market road, which ignored the through highways in favor of the small rural roads that wound here and there, enabling the farmer to bring the produce of his fields to the marketplace in the big towns. Forget the fact that if the quiet farm-to-market road was not well planned, it quite promptly became a jammed thoroughfare; the end result of this commendable system was a network of rural roads equaled in few states.

So far to the north of central Houston that it seemed construction could never reach it, a modest farm-to-market had been established in the 1950s, called FM-1960. It was a narrow, bumpy road, well suited to a farmer's slow-moving trucks, but Morrison could see that with a little impetus from a growing population, it had a strong chance of becoming a major thoroughfare. He was so enthusiastic about its possibilities that he took options on two corners, well separated, believing that automobiles must soon be careening past, but when one of the owners of Engine Experts flew down from Detroit, the man decided instantly that these two corners were too far out to be of any use to his company, and Todd was ordered to unload.

'We have eight thousand dollars tied up in option money,' he protested, and the man said: 'That's why you pay out option money, so you gain time to correct mistakes.' In no way did he rebuke Todd, for he appreciated what a good job the latter had done in Houston, but long after he had flown back to Detroit, his decision rankled, and it was what happened as a consequence that launched Morrison on his unexpected career.

Without telling Klinowitz that he had been forced to unload the options, he went to him and said: 'I think I'd better stay closer to town. The kind of market I'm in. I have eight thousand tied up in these two options on FM-1960. Must I lose the down payments, or is there some way I could unload?'

When Klinowitz saw the excellent sites he said immediately: 'I'll give you twelve thousand for your options right now. They're choice.'

'Why give twelve when you know I'd be glad to get back my eight?' Todd asked, and Gabe said: 'Always leave a little something on the table.'

Now Morrison faced a grave moral problem: Should he inform the Detroit men of the $4,000 profit he had made on the deal, or should he pocket the windfall? He consulted with no one, not Gabe, not his wife, and certainly not the big men in Detroit, but he did argue with himself: First, I was acting as their agent. Second, they laughed at the deal. Third, what are the chances they'll find out? In the end he decided to keep the money, and that, along with the $3,000 bonus he received at Christmas, plus the money his wife was earning as receptionist in another big real estate firm, enabled him to enter the new year with a nest egg of more than $11,000 and some tantalizing ideas.

In January, as he was exploring further possibilities along FM-1960, he came upon a wedge of farmland owned by an elderly Mr. Hooker, and while Todd was more or less jousting with him over the possibility of buying a corner lot, a white Ford pickup screeched onto the gravel and came to a dusty stop. Apparently the driver was in the oil business, for big letters along the side proclaimed ROY BUB HOOKER, DRILLING. From the cab, which had a two-gun rack behind the driver's head, stepped a big, jovial twenty-four-year-old wearing overalls, cheap cowboy boots and a checkered bandanna. He was your typical Texas redneck, of that there could be no doubt, but when he spoke, it was obvious that he had received a good education. It came not from his teachers, for he had despised school, but from his mother, who had taught him both a proper vocabulary and acceptable manners, neither of which he felt much inclination to use.

As soon as he stepped up to Morrison and stuck out his hand, grunting: 'Hi, I'm Roy Bub Hooker, his son,' it was obvious that details of any sale would be in Roy Bub's hands, and during one of the early meetings he explained: 'My older sister couldn't say *brother,* so she stuck me with *Bubba,* and it became Roy Bub.'

He was so shrewd a bargainer, quoting what prices corner lots had brought along FM-1960, that Todd had to warn him: 'Hey, look, Roy Bub, two things. I'm not a millionaire and I'm not even sure I want to buy,' and Roy Bub snapped back: 'Who said my old man wanted to sell?'

Since he was almost offensive in the brusque manner in which he dismissed Morrison, Todd felt he must strike back to maintain balance in the bargaining: 'They warned me I could never do business with a redneck.'

'Hey, wait!' Roy Bub cried as if he were sorely wounded. 'I'm no redneck. I'm a good ol' boy.'

'What's the difference?'

'Hey! A redneck drives a Ford pickup. He has a gun rack behind his ears. He has funny little signs painted on his tailgate. He drives down the highway drinking Lone Star out of a can, which he tosses into the middle of the road.'

'I don't see the difference. You have a Ford. You have that gun rack. Look at the signs on your tailgate.' And there they were, revealing the emotional confusions that activated Roy Bub and his compadres:

HONK IF YOU LOVE JESUS

THE WEST WASN'T WON WITH A REGISTERED GUN

NATIVE BORN TEXAN AND PROUD OF IT

SECESSION NOW

SURE I'M DRUNK—
YOU THINK I DRIVE THIS WAY ALL THE TIME?

And off to one side, a little dustier than the others:

IMPEACH EARL WARREN

'And,' Todd added, 'I see you have one of those holders for your Lone Star. So what's the difference?'

'Old buddy!' Roy Bub cried. 'A redneck throws his empties in the middle of the road. A good ol' boy tosses his'n in the ditch.'

No sale could be agreed upon at this time, and the uncertainty gave Morrison sleepless nights in the darkness as he lay beside Maggie, exhausted after her long hours of work and housekeeping; he could never discern whether she liked Houston or not, but she certainly worked at making a good home from whatever Houston provided, and this he appreciated.

His nervousness sprang from real causes. The Hooker corner could be bought, he felt sure, for $71,000, two and three-quarter acres at a location any expert would classify as superb. He would have to make the deal on his own, because he already knew that Engine Experts would not be interested, but if he could locate a big gasoline company that wanted a prime spot for a filling station, one that would dominate the market, he might sell off the corner for $60,000, leaving him with two and a half acres for a cost of only $11,000, which would exhaust his savings.

However, if he could sell off even a small portion of his wraparound, he could discharge his debt and have two acres or even more scot-free. Then, if he was energetic, he could sell off more segments of the wraparound and come out a big winner. Also, if he could interest Gabe in some of the land he acquired in this way, he could have his profit in hand before July. And then he could take that profit . . .

During the entire month of January he slept only fitfully, for the temptations of the deal were so alluring that he spent the first half of each night calculating his possible winnings and the second half staring in the darkness at the possible catastrophes. In early February he took his wife, but not his children, into his confidence: 'Maggie, I face the chance of a lifetime. This young fellow Roy Bub Hooker has power of attorney to sell a corner lot on FM-1960. We could swing it if, and I repeat if, we could find an oil company to take the corner bit off our hands. We'd wind up with two and a half choice acres practically free, and then if, and again I repeat if . . .'

'Are you trying to convince me, or yourself?' she asked.

'You know what Houston real estate is doing. I don't have to prove anything.'

'I know what it's doing for others. Who have the land or the money. I'm not so sure what it could do for us.'

'Would you be willing for us to take the risk? All our savings?'

She said a curious thing: 'You'd have to tell Detroit, of course.'

'Why?'

'Dealing in property on the side. The temptation would always be to give them the poor deal, keep the good one for yourself.'

'I don't see why they'd have to know anything.'

'I do. Business ethics. The sanctity of the arm's-length deal.'

'Now what do you mean by that?'

'It's something they drummed into me when I got my license. An honest deal involves two people who shake hands across a carefully protected distance. No internal hanky-panky. No secret brother-in-law shakedown.' Something in the recent behavior of her fast-moving husband caused her to warn: 'Todd, any deal you engage in must be at arm's length.'

On Sunday she rode out to FM-1960, and as soon as she saw the corner, she wanted to buy it, and after they had supper with Roy Bub, she liked him even more than she had his land: 'You're an original, Roy Bub, don't ever change.'

'Minute we sell that land, I'm gettin' me a Cadillac.'

'That'll be the day,' she said, and he confided: 'I'll tell you this, your husband buys that corner, I'm gettin' me a first-class stereo for my truck.'

She shuddered: 'The new Texas. Roy Bub roaring down the highway at ninety with his stereo full blast. Won't even hear the siren when the cops chase him,' and he said: 'Ma'am, that's exactly what I have in mind.'

So on the fourth of February she gave permission for the deal, if Todd thought he could swing it, and on the fifth, adhering to Gabe's strategy, he agreed to Roy Bub's price if he could dictate the terms: 'Nine thousand cash on signing, so's you can get that stereo. Eleven-year payout. Six-percent interest.' Roy Bub, who had studied so hard to determine the fair price for his land, had paid no attention to the going rates of interest and did not realize that he might have got seven and a half percent on the unpaid balance.

But now the sweating in the rented house in Quitman Street really began, for when Todd inquired casually among the men who bought land for the big oil companies, he found they were not eager to locate their filling stations so far north of the city, and although he praised FM-1960 rather fulsomely, they tended to say: 'Sure it's good, but we can wait till traffic picks up, if it does.'

He went through March, April and May without a nibble, and one night as he tossed sleeplessly he faced the fact that come next January, only seven months away, he would be required to pay Roy Bub the first installment of interest plus a reduction of the balance, and he could not imagine where he could find that kind of money. Nor had he located anyone interested in his remainder of the wrap-around. The future seemed extremely bleak, and he joined that endless procession of Texan gamblers who had risked mightily on the chance of winning big. Mattie Quimper had tried to claim both banks of the river in the 1820s, and Floyd Rusk had pulled his own tricks a hundred years later when trying to sew up the Larkin Field. It was the Texas game, and all who played it to the hilt sweated in the dark night hours, but like Todd Morrison in 1969, they gritted their teeth: 'Something will turn up.'

His savior, as he might have anticipated, was Gabe Klinowitz: 'Todd, I believe you're on the pointy end of a long stick.'

'I am. But I put myself there.'

'Have you told the people in Detroit what you're doing?'

'No.'

'You should. Fiduciary responsibility. When lawyers forget about this, they go to jail. You forget, you could be fired.' He spoke from the widest possible experience in oil, insurance, real estate and the legal profession; men who cut too many corners ran the risk of jail.

'I'll tell them when I get it sorted out.'

'I hope that won't be too late.' He changed his tone: 'I've heard that an independent is looking for a choice site on FM-1960.'

'Independents pay bottom dollar, don't they?'

'But they pay.' When Todd said nothing, Gabe said: 'Always remember the advice J. P. Morgan gave a young assistant. Young fellow said: "Mr. Morgan, how much should a man my age buy on margin?" and Morgan said: "That depends." And the young fellow said: "I've borrowed so much I can hardly sleep at night," and Morgan said: "Simple. Sell to the sleeping point." '

'Meaning?'

'Your prime responsibility, Todd, is to get some cash back in your hand. If I offered you forty thousand dollars today, grab it. Pay off your obligations. Make a little less on the deal, but remain in condition to hold on to the rest of your wraparound.'

'Could you get me forty thousand?'

'I'm sure I can do better. Fifty-one thousand, maybe as much as fifty-three.'

'My God! That would get me off the hook.' He grasped Gabe's hand, then asked: 'But why would you do this for me? You know you could take it off my hands at whatever price you set, and make yourself a bundle.'

'Todd, I have sixteen deals cooking. I think you're going to be in this business for the rest of my life. In years to come we'll arrange a hundred deals. I can wait for my big profits. You need your fragile profits right now.' They shook hands formally, and Todd said: 'A man like you is worth a million.'

And then, just as Todd was about to sign the papers Gabe had sent him, Gulf Oil decided that after all, it would experiment with an FM-1960 location, and they heard that Todd had the inside track on a fine corner. With his knees shaking, Todd told them: 'I think I could put you on the inside track for seventy-one thousand dollars.' The Gulf representative, eager to close a deal once the decision had been made by his head office, agreed, and the sale was closed, with Todd and the Gulf man shaking hands.

Elated but nervous, Todd now had to inform Klinowitz that the deal with the independent had to be canceled, even though a gentlemen's agreement had been reached: 'Nothing was signed, you know, Gabe, and Gulf was so hungry to get that land, they demanded an answer right away. I tried to call you, but you were out.' And although each man knew that a handshake had sanctified the sale to the independent, Gabe merely said: 'I'll find them something, but, Todd, I hope you inform Detroit that you've been dealing on your own. There are rules to this game, you know,' and Todd said: 'Absolutely!' but the letter he had drafted in his head, aware that it ought to be sent, was never written.

The Morrisons as a family ran into their first serious Texas decision when daughter Beth entered Miss Barlow's junior-high class in Texas history. Each child in the Texas system studied state history at two different levels, first as legend when young, then as simplified glorification at Beth's age. The scholarly could also take it as an elective in high school and as an optional course in college. The goal of this intense concentration was, as one curriculum stated, 'to make children aware of their glorious heritage and to ensure that they become loyal Texas citizens.'

Few teachers, at any of the four levels, taught with the single-minded ferocity exhibited daily by Flora Barlow. She was in her sixties, a cultured, quiet woman whose ancestors had played major roles in the periods she talked about, and while she was not family-proud, as some teachers of her subject tended to be, she was inwardly gratified that her family had helped to shape what she was convinced was the finest single political entity in the world, the semi-nation of Texas.

Standing before a massive map of Texas that showed all the counties in outline only, she said softly: 'Your Texas has two hundred and fifty-four counties, many times more than less fortunate states, and one day when I was just starting to teach, a young fellow teacher, educated in the North, looked at our map with its scatter of counties and said, rather boldly I thought: "Looks as if Texas had freckles."'

When her children laughed, she said: 'It would be quite silly of me, wouldn't it, if I required you to memorize the names of all the counties?' When the children groaned, she said solemnly: 'But I can name them. With their county seats.'

She called to the front of the room one of her pupils, and it chanced to be Beth Morrison: 'Here is the pointer, Beth. Point as you will at any county on that map, and I shall give you its name and the name of its county seat.'

Stabbing blindly at the center of the map, Beth's pointer struck a large, oddly shaped county: 'That's Comanche County, named after our raiding Indians; county seat, Comanche.'

When Beth tried the northeast corner, Miss Barlow said promptly: 'You've chosen Upshur County, named after a United States Secretary of State, Abel P. Upshur; county seat, Gilmer.'

Now Beth indicated one of the many squared-off western counties, a score of them almost identical in size and shape, but without hesitation Miss Barlow said: 'You're on Hale County, named for our great hero Lieutenant J. C. Hale, who died gallantly defeating General Santa Anna at San Jacinto; county seat, the important city of Plainview. If you're going to live and prosper in Texas, it's prudent to know where things are.'

When Beth reported this amazing performance to her parents, they at first laughed, for they had undergone an amusing embarrassment over one of the Texas counties, Bexar, which contained the attractive city of San Antonio. 'It's spelled B-e-x-a-r,' Mrs. Morrison said, 'and for the longest time your father and I pronounced it Bex-ar, the way any sensible person would. But then we kept hearing on the radio when we drove to work "Bare County this and Bare County that," and one day we asked: "Where is this Bare County?" and the old-timers laughed: "That's how we say Bexar." So now your father and I know where Bare County is.'

But as the family studied this matter—Beth in school, her parents in their daily life—they discovered that Miss Barlow was not being arbitrary in insisting that her pupils know something about the multiple counties of Texas, because unlike any other state, Texas wrote its history in relationship to its counties. This was partly because the state was so enormous that it had to be broken down into manageable regions, but more because the towns within the regions were often so small and relatively unimportant that few people could locate them. A man or a family did not come from some trivial county seat containing only sixty persons; that man or family came from an entire county, and once the name of that county was voiced, every knowing listener knew what kind of man he was.

The statement 'We moved from Tyler County to Polk' told the entire story of a farmer who had sought better land to the west. 'My grandfather raised cotton in Cherokee County, but when the crop failed three times running, he tried cattle in Palo Pinto.' That summarized three decades of Texas agricultural history.

One either knew the basic counties or remained ignorant of Texas history, and Miss Barlow did not intend that any of her students should have such a handicap. To help them master the outlines, she had devised an imaginative exercise, and it was in the execution of this that Beth, and indeed the entire Morrison family, fell afoul of the Deaf Smith school system: 'My former students have found it helpful to identify five counties. Choose any five you wish, but they must be in five widely separated parts of the state. After you select your counties, memorize them and their county seats. Then you will always have a kind of framework onto which you can attach the other counties in that district.'

Most of the students, eager to escape extra work, chose easy picks whose important county seat bore the same name as the county, such as Dallas in the north, El Paso in the far west, Lubbock in the west, and Galveston on the Gulf of Mexico. Boys usually picked popular names like Deaf Smith along the New

Mexico border, Maverick on the Rio Grande, or Red River on the boundary stream of that name. And of course, there were always some smart alecks who chose 'Floyd County; county seat, Floydada' or 'Bee County; county seat, Beeville.' Miss Barlow indulged such choices because she had learned that any student who nailed down his five counties, wherever they were, could build upon them the relationships required in Texas history.

'I'll start with Kenedy,' Beth told her mother that night, 'because even though it's a different spelling, it's practically your maiden name.' This took care of the southeast corner of the state, and she was about to move on to four other regions when she happened to jot down in her notebook the salient facts about Kenedy County, and as soon as she had done so, a naughty idea flashed into her mind, and for about an hour she pored over the data in an old copy of the *Texas Almanac,* checking this county and that. Somewhat irritated by Miss Barlow's constant hammering on the size of Texas, she was seeking the five most insignificant counties, and in the end she came up with a startling collection, as the extremely neat page in her notebook proved:

THE FIVE LEADING COUNTIES OF TEXAS

NAME	POP.	DERIVATION OF NAME	COUNTY SEAT	POP.
Kenedy	678	Cattle baron, helped start King Ranch	Armstrong	20
King	464	Great hero, member Gonzales Immortal 32	Guthrie	140
Loving	163	Cattle driver, corpse hauled in lead box	Mentone	41
McMullen	998	Famous Irish immigrant, found murdered	Tilden	420
Roberts	967	Chief Justics and Governor of Texas	Miami	746
	3,271			1,367

As soon as Beth's parents saw the cynical heading, they realized that if she submitted it in that form, she was going to get into trouble not only with her teacher but with her xenophobic classmates as well, and her mother asked tentatively: 'Don't you think, Beth, that your heading is . . . well . . . couldn't it be considered inflammatory?'

'I'm sick and tired of being teased because I wasn't born in Texas.'

'But don't you think this is rather arrogant? I mean . . . aren't you rubbing their noses in it?'

Beth considered this carefully, and although she refused to alter her choice of counties on the grounds that Miss Barlow had said she could choose any she wished, so long as they were well scattered, she did have to agree that her title was combative, so she changed it to MY FIVE FAVORITE COUNTIES OF TEXAS. And without complaining she redid her chart, making it even more attractive than before.

Unfortunately, on Saturday night several of Beth's classmates dropped by the

Morrisons' for an after-the-movies snack, and the matter of county choices came up. Todd, overhearing a discussion in which minor counties were accorded the deference usually reserved for continents, cried: 'Hey! Don't you kids have things slightly out of proportion?' When they asked what he meant, he questioned them: 'Where is Korea? Can you identify Belgium on the map? Where do you think Rumania is? Where's Thailand?'

He learned to his astonishment that whereas Beth's friends could identify Borden County—population 907; named after the man who invented condensed milk; county seat, Gail, population 178—few of them could accurately place Argentina—population 22,000,000; name derived from the Latin word for silver; capital city, Buenos Aires, population 3,768,000—and none of them had heard of places like Mongolia, Albania or Paraguay.

In school on Monday these students would remember that Mr. Morrison had laughed at the counties of Texas, remarking that he considered Malaysia, with a population of more than eleven million and occupying a strategic point on the world's trade routes, was at least as important as his daughter's King County, Texas, with its population of 464 and its roads leading nowhere.

Even this ungenerous comparison would have led to nothing had not Miss Barlow, hoping to get this important lesson properly launched, called on Beth to recite her five, and with the sureness of a trained cartographer, Beth rattled off name, population and county seat, jabbing accurately with her pointer at Kenedy to the southeast, King hidden among the central squares, Loving far out west, McMullen, the Irish county due south of San Antonio, and Roberts up in the northwest.

It was, as Miss Barlow had anticipated, a sterling performance, but then the teacher spoiled it by asking: 'What was your principle of selection, Beth?' and the latter replied honestly: 'I looked for the five with the smallest population.' At this the class began to giggle, and one of the boys who had been present Saturday night reported: 'Mr. Morrison said that Malaysia, or somewhere, with eleven million people was a damned sight more important than King County, Texas, with four hundred and sixty-four.'

'What word did you use?' Miss Barlow said sternly.

'I didn't use it. He did.'

At this, Miss Barlow held out her hand for Beth's notebook and looked at the mocking table. Her face flushed, and after school she telephoned the senior Morrisons, informing them that she must see them.

When she sat, prim and defiant, in their living room, she launched her complaint against a girl who should by every indication have been her prize pupil. 'Your daughter is talented, to be sure, but she lacks a proper respect for subject matter.'

'Where is she deficient?' Mrs. Morrison asked.

'She laughs at Texas history,' Miss Barlow said stiffly.

'I believe she studies very hard,' Mrs. Morrison said defensively.

'Studies, yes. But she does like to make fun of things.'

'Whatever do you mean?'

'Wait a minute,' Mr. Morrison interrupted. 'Was it her list of counties, Miss Barlow?'

'Indeed it was, Mr. Morrison. But that's only part of my complaint.'

'Look, Beth is a bright child, an imaginative one. If you ask me, her choice showed industry, wit, a sense of . . .'

'Mr. Morrison, no child will get far living in Texas if she makes fun of Texas history.'

'Well, you must admit that a county like What's-its-name, with a population of a hundred and sixty plus or minus and a county seat of forty people, by normal standards . . .'

'Texas is not judged by normal standards. Did you know, Mr. Morrison, that when nine-tenths of our counties were first authorized by the legislature, each contained less than fifty white people? We were subduing a wild, empty land, and we did it very cleverly, I believe, by first establishing the counties and hoping that people would come along to fill them. The county you refer to so inaccurately is Loving, I believe. It hasn't received its people yet, but it will be waiting there, and in good order, when the people finally arrive.'

'I'm sure Beth meant no disrespect,' Mrs. Morrison said.

'Well, she showed it.'

'Miss Barlow, Beth identified five counties with a total population, if I remember correctly, of less than three thousand three hundred persons. Crossroads villages in Michigan have more than . . .'

What an unfortunate comparison! Miss Barlow stiffened and said: 'Texas is not to be judged by the standards you would use for Vermont or Indiana,' and the scorn she poured into those two names indicated her opinion of the backward states referred to. 'Texas was its own sovereign nation, and it still forms an empire off to itself. Neither you nor your daughter will be happy here if you fail to acknowledge that.'

Mrs. Morrison said mildly: 'I'm sure that if Beth has offended either you or your class, she will apologize.'

'Your daughter has not misbehaved in any overt way, but her attitude has been almost frivolous. One must take Texas history seriously, and sometimes children unlucky enough to have been born in other . . .' She dropped that sentence, for although she used it often inside her classroom, she realized that outside, it did sound rather chauvinistic. She was emotionally and morally sorry for those children who had not been born in Texas, but she realized that blazoning her condescension was not always fruitful.

'Beth is a bright child,' she conceded. 'And if she acquires the right attitudes she can go far . . . perhaps even the university at Austin.'

'We're thinking of Michigan,' Mr. Morrison said coldly.

'I'm sure it's respectable,' she said, and then, with that honest warmth which made her a successful teacher, she added: 'No one in our grade writes more beautifully than your Beth. In her mature use of words she's exceptional. Don't encourage her to waste such marked talent by being what the children call "a smart ass." '

No more was said about the counties, either in class or out, until one blustery day at the end of February, when Miss Barlow said quietly: 'Beth, in your list of counties, if I remember, you had King County. Could you locate it now if I hand you the ruler?' And it was remarkable, but almost every child in that class could now go to the big outline map and point unerringly to his or her five counties; Miss Barlow's exercise had imprinted these locations forever, and as she predicted, her students were now beginning to relate the other two hundred and forty-nine counties to those already learned.

Without hesitation Beth pointed to four-square King, almost identical in shape to another twenty clustered about it. 'Now, Beth, do you remember whom that county was named after?'

'William P. King of the Immortal Thirty-two from Gonzales.'

'And do you know who the Immortal Thirty-two were?'

Frantically Beth scoured her mind, and only the vaguest data came forth, so that finally she was forced to confess: 'I don't know, Miss Barlow, but somehow I think they had to do with the Alamo.'

'You are right, and you may sit down.'

Then, in a low voice which none of the children who heard it that day would ever forget, Miss Barlow began a quiet recitation of the facts surrounding one of the overwhelming incidents of Texas history, and as she spoke, time shifted backward and her listeners were in the small town of Gonzales, east of San Antonio:

'It was on this very day, one hundred and thirty-three years ago, that a messenger galloped into Gonzales with the dreadful news that the Alamo was surrounded by General Santa Anna's troops and that the brave defenders inside were doomed to death, all of them, unless they received help. "They must have reinforcements" was all the messenger said. As he uttered these words the men of Gonzales knew that even if they did march to the rescue, the Alamo was doomed. There was no way that so few Texans, however brave, could hold off so many Mexicans, however cowardly. Whoever entered the Alamo was certain to die.

'So what did they do? Thirty-two of the bravest men Texas would ever produce shouldered their muskets, kissed their women goodbye, and marched resolutely into the sunset. And I want you to remember this, young people. The men of Gonzales didn't just go up to the gates of the

Alamo and cry "Let us in!" No, they had to fight their way in, cutting a path through the Mexican army. At any point they'd have been justified in turning back, but none did. They fought to enter, and in doing so, found death and immortality.

'As sure as the sun rises, every one of you in this classroom, boys and girls alike, will some day find yourself in the town of Gonzales, listening to your messenger cry "Help us or we perish!" It may happen to you in El Paso or Lubbock or Galveston.' (Miss Barlow was incapable of visualizing her graduates as living outside Texas.) 'And each of you will be called upon to make a decision of the most vital importance: right or wrong . . . life or death. And the manner in which you respond will determine whether you will be known as immortal or craven.

'If I tell you about the glories of Texas history with pride and deep feelings it's because one of the thirty-two Immortals was my great-grandfather Moses Barlow, and the woman he kissed goodbye as he marched off to the Alamo was my grandmother Rachel, who was four years old at the time but who remembered that day until she died in 1930 in Milam County at the age of ninety-eight. So I heard of Gonzales personally from a woman who was there that day, and when you are an old person in San Antonio or Fort Worth, you can tell your grandchildren in the year 2036 that you yourself heard me speak of a woman who was present when the heroes of Gonzales marched voluntarily to death and immortality.'

On no student did the impact of that lesson fall more heavily than on Beth Morrison. For two days she went directly to her room after supper, preferring to speak to no one and refusing even to answer her telephone when it rang. On the third day she asked wanly: 'What parts of Texas did we like best when we saw those slides?' and she joined her family in analyzing the virtues of the forested northeast, the blazing sands of the Rio Grande and the mountains of the west. Her brother said he liked best the sign in the park which said BEWARE RATTLE-SNAKES. She ignored this, and on the fourth morning she appeared at breakfast with a single sheet of paper, which she hesitantly showed her mother, who cried: 'Beth, this is really good. This is much better than I could have done.' When her father asked to see it, Beth grabbed it nervously and said: 'Later.'

She went to school early, slipped into her classroom and deposited on Miss Barlow's desk a brown envelope that showed no indication of its source, and when class began Miss Barlow coughed and said: 'Today we have a most wonderful

surprise. One of our members has written a beautiful poem, which I want to share
with you. It's called "A Song of Texas."

> 'Bluebonnets, paintbrush on trails through the pine,
> Sweep of the meadow that climbs to the hill,
> My hungry heart makes this loveliness mine.
> Sleep or awake I shall cherish you still—
>   O Texas, your beauty enchants me forever.
>
> Cactus and mesquite, the bold Rio Grande
> Cuts a deep swath through your perilous waste,
> Marks me a path through the treacherous sand,
> Leads me to wonders that I have embraced—
>   O Texas, your harshness invites me forever.
>
> Blue mountains, brush on wild plains of the west,
> Challenging eagles to soar to new heights,
> Offering refuge to only the best,
> You dazzle us all with your wondrous delights—
>   O Texas, your greatness rewards me forever.'

The room was very quiet as Miss Barlow folded the paper and returned it to its
brown envelope: 'I think we can guess who wrote this lovely poem, can't we?' and
with no exception, all in the class turned to look at Beth, for only she ever used
such words or framed them into such images.

That evening Miss Barlow telephoned the Morrisons to reassure them: 'I think
your little Beth is coming around. She's developing a proper attitude toward
things that matter.' And next morning at breakfast Beth startled her parents,
almost to the point of making them choke on their coffee, by saying with great
fervor: 'Gosh, wouldn't it be awful to marry a man who wasn't from Texas?'

In the Rio Grande Valley things were not going well for Héctor Garza. Seventy-
eight years old and far less agile than he had been in the days when he helped
Horace Vigil run the Valley, he had been forced to watch his Mexican community
fall into sad disarray, for the dictatorship had been taken over by Horace's
nephew, an austere, grasping man named Norman Vigil, who considered the area
to be his fiefdom but did not accord peasants like Héctor the courtesies due them.

'He derives his power from us,' Héctor complained to younger men, 'but he
shows us no thanks. Worst of all, he shows us no respect.'

Héctor could have made his protest much stronger, for Norman Vigil, displaying none of that classic grandeur of the typical Mexican patrón who robbed and
ruled with style, was a mean-spirited man who grabbed everything and shared

nothing. 'He sends his beer trucks over three counties but never gives the Little League a dime.' He also never gave hospitals or schools a dime, either, and Héctor sometimes thought that the slim strand of inheritance that had once kept Horace Vigil so strong a member of the Hispanic community had vanished in the case of Norman.

'He's not Mexican at all,' Héctor said. 'He's pure gringo, and in this Valley that's a bad thing to be.'

To explain how Vigil managed to keep his power was rather difficult, for the anglos with whom he associated exclusively represented only twelve percent of the population, while the Hispanics made up eighty-eight. Yet Vigil saw to it that the anglos controlled the school board, the police department, all the banks and most of the retail establishments. He did this by dominating the politics and determining who should run for what office; obviously, he could not himself cast all the ballots for his candidates, but because of his economic power he could terrorize the local Mexicans, forcing them to vote for his men, and he did still control that vital Precinct 37, and from it, late on election night, he extracted whatever number of votes he required to keep his preferred Democrat in power. He was also protected by state officials, who appreciated his votes, and in the wild Senate primary of 1948, when the upstart Democrat Lyndon Johnson defeated the established Democrat, ex-Governor Coke Stevenson, by eighty-seven votes out of nearly a million cast, Norman Vigil had provided from Precinct 37 a vote of Stevenson 13, Johnson 344, and such a reliable man was not going to be treated roughly by state investigators so long as the Democratic party stayed in power.

But the principal reason why Vigil continued his dictatorship was one which would have applied in no other state, even though its police could be as rough as those in Texas: for several decades the captain of the Texas Rangers along the border had been Oscar Macnab, now sixty-nine years old and retired from active duty, but still a dominant figure in Saldana County politics and one of Norman Vigil's chief supporters.

Macnab had made his reputation as a young Ranger in the oil fields of Larkin County when he tamed its boom-town frenzy almost single-handedly. Cool in temperament, determined when he got started, and severely just according to his own definitions, he had transferred about 1940 to the Rio Grande, where, during the years of World War II, he ran the territory pretty much as he wished. Since he had acquired the Ranger's traditional distrust of Indians, blacks and what he called 'Meskins,' and the traditional respect for anyone who had acquired an unusual amount of money, he had found it easy to fit into Rio Grande life; white American men of importance, like Norman Vigil, were to be protected; brown Hispanics, like Héctor Garza, were to be kept in their place; and outright Mexians, like those who swam across the river to vote for Norman Vigil in elections, were to be eliminated if they stepped out of line.

In his nearly thirty years of control in Saldana County, Macnab had served as the right arm of Norman Vigil, arresting those Vigil wanted arrested, frightening those Vigil wanted to chase out of his county. At election time he policed the polls, keeping away troublemakers and suspected liberals. After the votes were counted, he saw to it that any complaints were muffled, and if the protester pursued his objections, Macnab helped muscle him out of the area.

The captain never thought of himself as the colleague and protector of the local dictator, but that's what he was. Nor would he admit that he was prejudiced against Mexicans or Hispanics: 'I don't like Meskins. Don't trust them. And I expect to give them an order only once. But I am certainly not prejudiced against them. I have solved many murders involving only Meskins and will do so again if called upon. But you cannot force me to like them.'

He had had in his company from time to time Rangers who had blazed away at Mexicans with almost no provocation, and there were, he would admit privately, 'a few scoundrels on my team that could have been tried for murder, but this is a frontier area and I must insist that by and large, justice was done. I saw to that.'

Justice for Macnab consisted of identifying the interests of those in command, Norman Vigil, for example, or the big landowners, and then seeing that those interests were protected and if necessary furthered; in an orderly society that was the only thing to do. For example, when field workers on the big citrus plantations, now the principal source of wealth in the Valley, sought to form a labor union, an un-Texas thing to do, Captain Macnab found every excuse for hampering their efforts, including arresting them, threatening them, and keeping them from holding public meetings. He never opposed them as union agitators, which they were, but only as people threatening the peace of an otherwise quiet and pleasant valley: 'If their hearts are set on a union, let them move to New Jersey, where anything goes.' He was equally stern when teachers agitated for higher wages in the Saldana school system: 'To strike or even talk about striking is un-American and will not be tolerated in my district.'

It was still customary, in the Spanish-speaking communities, to refer to Rangers as Rinches, and Captain Macnab was the premier Rinche of his district. It was he who enforced the laws on the Hispanics, who kept their children in line the way the anglos preferred, and who dictated the terms of general behavior. If a Hispanic behaved himself and made no move to strike the citrus growers for higher wages, he encountered no trouble from Captain Macnab.

During his first twenty years of duty along the Rio Grande he arrested two white men. One had holed himself up in a shack with his estranged wife, threatening to kill her if anyone moved toward the place. Macnab never hesitated. Gun at the ready, he walked in and saved the distraught woman, who then refused to bring charges against her man. The other was a persistent drunk who tried to deliver the Sunday sermon at the Baptist church; he was easily removed.

But he found it necessary to arrest hundreds of Mexicans who seemed not to fit into Texas life. They either stole things, or beat their wives, or refused to send their children to school, or ran off with cars belonging to white men. If one had talked with Macnab during these years, he would never have heard of the count- less law-abiding Hispanics. Like the Swedes of Minnesota or the Czechs of Iowa, the Hispanics of Texas were good and bad. Macnab dealt only with the bad, and in this group he placed anyone of Mexican heritage who endeavored, by even the slightest move, to alter any aspect of Valley life from the way he believed it had always been, and should remain. He was therefore alerted when Norman Vigil, who now lived in a spacious house far removed from the beer-distribution office, summoned him to an unscheduled meeting.

'Captain, I can see trouble, real trouble, coming at us down the road.'

'Like what?'

'This Héctor Garza, used to work for my uncle, reliable sort normally, he wants to run a damned Meskin for mayor.'

'You already have a mayor, don't you?'

'Good man. Selected him myself. Used to work on one of the big citrus planta- tions.'

'Then why should Héctor . . . ?'

'He says it's time the Meskins had their own mayor.'

'Hell, how old is he?'

'You won't believe it, but he must be past seventy-five.'

'Why don't he roll over and quit makin' trouble?'

'How old are you, Captain?'

'I'm sixty-nine, but I'm not tryin' to run the Ranger office. Tell him to knock it off.'

'He won't do it. I think he sees this as his last battle.'

'It *will* be his last if he tries to mess up this county. Things are in good shape here. Let's keep them as they are.'

'I don't think he sees it that way. One of my men heard him speak to a group. He told them: "The time has come to exert our numbers," or some damned nonsense like that.'

'He certainly doesn't want the office himself, does he? At his age?'

'No! He's been coaching his grandson.'

'Simón? The one who went to college up in Kansas?'

'Yep. You give one of those Meskins a book, he thinks he's Charlemagne.'

'We should of slowed Simón down years ago.'

'Once they go to college, they should never be allowed back.'

And that was how the Bravo Incident, which commanded the national press for several months, began. Héctor Garza, in the waning years of his life, thought that if his Hispanics constituted over eighty-five percent of the Valley population, they should have some say in how the Valley was run, but once he publicly voiced this belief, he put himself athwart the political power of Norman Vigil and the police power of Oscar Macnab.

The confrontation started on a low key, with Macnab utilizing every political trick to keep the Hispanics off balance. Wearing his fawn-gray whipcord suit, his big hat and his boots, he appeared suddenly wherever they were proposing to hold a rally, and quietly but forcefully informed them that this was illegal without permission from the local judge. He would also dominate hearings convened by the judge and guide the decisions handed down. He was tough in breaking up political meetings, citing possible subversion or endangerment to the community, and whenever the two Garzas devised some way to neutralize his quiet tyranny, he would come up with a new trick to harass them.

He refrained from ever touching either the elder Garza or his grandson, but he did have them arrested twice, for blocking the highway, and he did see to it that they spent three nights in jail. But with the lesser Hispanics he could be extremely rough, knocking them about and threatening them with greater harm if they persisted in their attempt to elect a Mexican mayor in opposition to the perfectly good man who had been running the town, with Norman Vigil's help, for the past dozen years.

One morning, in frustration, Macnab marched in to the Hispanic political headquarters and demanded to see Héctor Garza: 'What in hell are you Meskins tryin' to do?'

'We're trying to govern this town, as our numbers entitle us to do.'

'Your numbers, as you call them, have no right to trespass on the rights of those good folks who have given us good government for all the years of this century.'

'That's not good enough any more, Captain.'

'It'll be good enough if I say so. You stop this nonsense, Héctor, and get back to your patio. These are things that don't concern you.'

'They concern us very much. Mr. Vigil can't run this town any longer the way he wants to.'

The meeting ended in an impasse, with Ranger Macnab, a little heavier now, handing out the orders as in decades past, and Héctor Garza, a little thinner, resisting them. As Macnab left the headquarters, frustrated by this sudden emergence of a power he could not suppress, he warned: 'Héctor, if you go ahead with this, you're goin' to get hurt, bad hurt.' To him, Bravo and its resurgent Mexicans were exactly like Larkin and its rioting roughnecks: you subdued each by the application of steady force, and he was prepared to import all the force required to put down this insurgency.

But then Héctor Garza sent a telegram to Washington, and a Mr. Henderson appeared in town, a tall man in a blue-serge suit. Summoning Norman Vigil and Oscar Macnab to his hotel room, he informed them: 'Thomas Henderson, Justice Department. I'm here to see that the civil rights of your Hispanic citizens are protected in the coming election. I'm bringing in two deputies, so you men keep your noses clean.'

The Vigils of Saldana County had been fending off Washington since 1880, and never had they allowed its representatives to penetrate the power structure of the Rio Grande. Norman assumed that he could resist them again, but Mr. Henderson sought his injunctions not in Bravo but in the federal court in Corpus Christi, and he opposed every connivance put forward by Vigil and the Rangers. Finally, in irritation because these men continued acting as if the twentieth century had never dawned, he went to see Oscar Macnab, for whom he had considerable respect: 'Captain, why does a man of your apparent good sense always side with a man like Norman Vigil?'

'Because he represents the law.'

'You ever hear of justice?'

'I've noticed, sir, that whenever somebody starts talkin' about justice, everybody else runs into a lot of trouble. Law I can understand, it's specific. Norman Vigil has represented the law in this community since I can remember. Justice is something people make parades about.'

'Why do you always side with the few whites against the many Mexicans?'

'This is a white man's country, Mr. Henderson, and when you fellows in Washington forget that, you're headin' into deep trouble. We don't want that trouble down here. We seek to avoid it as long as possible.'

'You seem to classify all Mexicans as crooks and rioters?'

'In my experience, that's what most of them are.'

'Captain Macnab, it's two weeks before election. If you don't change your attitude, right now, when the election is over I'm going to hale you into federal court with a list of charges this long.'

In a dozen similar situations Mr. Henderson had been able to strike fear into the hearts of local tyrants, but he had never before tried to interfere in a Texas county filled with many Hispanics and a few determined whites. He was startled by the brazen defiance Vigil and Macnab threw at him, and when election day arrived he was unprepared for the open violence with which these two men threw back the Hispanics who wanted to vote, the repressions, the animosities, and he was shocked to find that Vigil had imported from south of the Rio Grande more than a hundred peons who had been paid two dollars each to vote against the interests of their Hispanic cousins north of the river.

The Garza challenge lost, for Precinct 37, with more than ninety percent Hispanic voters, reported an overwhelming majority for the Vigil slate, which meant that Norman would remain patrón for four more years.

Héctor and his grandson vowed to resume the fight in the next election, but this was not to be, for shortly after the failed election Héctor fell ill, passed into a coma, and died without regaining consciousness. From the time of his youth in the early 1900s, and during the violent years of Horace Vigil, ending with the old man's death in the 1920s, he had been a loyal foot soldier for the dictator. He had then served Norman Vigil faithfully, but in his seventies he had begun to see what a fearfully heavy price the Hispanics paid for this allegiance. He had tried to break it and had failed, but he had inspired his grandson Simón to launch an effort, and he died trusting that Simón would carry on this crusade.

In the meantime, law and order, Rio Grande style, remained in effect.

With a little money in their pockets, the Morrisons of Detroit were having an exciting time in Texas. When the big bosses in the home office discovered that Todd had been buying and selling real estate on his own without informing them, they summarily fired him. Loss of the salaried job meant that Todd had to work more diligently at his deals, but with continued advice from Gabe Klinowitz he accumulated commissions and outright deals in his own name. Also, Maggie, having obtained her own real estate license, was now selling rather effectively for a large central-city firm. She wrote to her friends in Detroit:

> Each week we like it more. Todd is doing amazingly well as what the Texans call a wheeler-dealer, and with my own license I am becoming Madam Real Estate.
>
> What has been most difficult to adjust to? You'd never guess! The size of the cockroaches. I mean, as big as sparrows and terribly aggressive. The other evening I heard Lonnie screaming in the kitchen, and there he stood with a broom. 'Mummy!' he cried. 'Two of them were trying to drag me outside.' I gave him a real swipe.
>
> You would be unprepared for the noise and bustle of Houston. Where Detroit was dying, this place springs to a more abundant life each morning. Whew! Life in the fast lane! Dips and darts on the roller-coaster! And you'd also never guess the little things that we like so much.
>
> Beth and Lonnie both excel in school, claiming that Texas schools are about two years behind the ones they attended in Detroit. I doubt this. Just a different approach.
>
> The city is a joy, and half you kids ought to pack up right now and move down here, for this is tomorrow. I'm sure I wouldn't have advised this fifteen years ago, because the temperature in summer can be ugh! But air conditioning has remade the city, and they should erect a monument to Westinghouse or whoever invented it. A step forward in civilization.
>
> The barbecue, about which we heard so much, has been a disappointment. Not that delicious stuff we bought on Woodward Avenue, bits of beef with that tangy sauce. Here it's great slabs of beef, well roasted I'll grant, but no sauce, no taste unless you like the smell of charred mesquite, which I don't.

What do I miss most? You'd never guess. The *New York Times* cross-word puzzles. Remember how we used to wait for the one o'clock arrival of the Sunday *Times,* and then we'd call one another about five in the afternoon: 'Did you get 43 across? Sweet idea, eh?' It sort of made the week legitimate, a test of whether the old cranium was still functioning. Well, I doubt there's a person in Houston does that puzzle, and we're all the worse for it.

Todd was entering the most rewarding span of his life, for in Roy Bub Hooker he had discovered a man who loved the outdoors as much as he did, and after the sale of the Hooker corner was completed and Roy Bub did buy the expensive stereo for his truck, they drove about the suburbs of Houston, talking real estate, listening to country and western music, and sharing their attitudes on wildlife.

'Todd, they ain't nothin' on this earth more fun than stalkin' a brood of wild turkey. Man, them birds has radar, they can outsmart you ever' time. Only thing saves the hunter is that they are also some of the dumbest birds God ever made. They escape you, run in a circle, then double right back to where you're waitin'.'

'Best I ever experienced,' Todd said, 'was hunting whitetail deer in northern Michigan when snow was on the ground. Icicles in the trees. Brown grass crackling. And all of a sudden, whoosh, out of a hollow darts this buck. Temptation is to shoot him in the rear, but that always loses you your buck. You cannot kill him from the rear. So you wait. He turns. Wham, in that instant you got to let fly.'

They continued to differ on turkey, which Todd had never hunted, and whitetail, which Roy Bub scorned, but they did agree on quail, and that was how their long and intense friendship began: 'Todd, I got me these two partners, sort of. A young oilman who may be goin' places, and this dentist who loves dogs. We've been rentin' a place, week by week, and if you cared to come along . . .'

It startled Todd to learn that in Texas one leased a place to hunt, for he was familiar with Michigan and Pennsylvania: 'A man wants to hunt, say he lives in Detroit or Philadelphia, he just buys himself a gun and a license, and he can go out in the country almost anywhere and shoot his heart out. Millions of acres, thousands of deer just waiting for him.'

'That ain't the way in Texas. Someone owns ever' inch of our land, and if you trespass without payin' a prior fee, the owner'll shoot your ass off.'

'Prehistoric,' Todd said. 'Where is your place?'

'Close to Falfurrias.'

'Never heard of it. How far—fifty miles?'

'Two hundred and forty.'

'I wouldn't drive two-forty to shoot a polar bear.'

'This is Texas, son. You drive two-forty to go to a good football game . . . and some not so good.'

When Todd met the oilman and the dentist, both in their early thirties, he liked them, for they were true outdoorsmen, and like most men of that type, each had his strong preferences. 'I like to hunt on foot, without dogs,' the oilman said. 'I got me this fabulous A.Y.A. copy of a Purdy with a Beasley action . . .'

'What's that?' Todd asked.

'A Purdy is the best shotgun made. English. Sells for about eleven thousand dollars. Who can afford that?'

'You can,' Roy Bub said.

'Maybe later. But there's this amazing outfit in a little town in Spain. They make fabulous copies. Aguirre y Arranzabel. They made me a Purdy, special order, my name engraved on it and all—forty-six hundred bucks.'

'You paid that for a gun?' Todd asked, and the oilman said: 'Not just for a gun. For an A.Y.A.'

The dentist did not take any gun with him to the hunts; he loved dogs and had rigged up the back of his Chevrolet hunting wagon with six separate wire pens, three atop the others, in which he kept six prize dogs: two English pointers, two English setters, and the two he liked best, a pair of Brittany spaniels. He had trained them to a fine point, each a champion in some special attribute, and when they reached the fields he liked to carry the men and dogs in his wagon, with Roy Bub driving, till Todd, keeping watch from an armchair bolted to the metal top of the wagon, spotted quail and gave the cry 'Left, left,' or wherever the covey nestled.

Then as the car stopped, the dentist would dash out, release the dog chosen for this chase, and dispatch him in the direction Todd had indicated. In the meantime, the three men with their guns would have descended, Todd scrambling down from his perch and Roy Bub from behind the wheel, and all would leave the car and proceed on foot after the dog, who would flush the quail and follow them deftly as they ran along the ground.

It was not light exercise to follow the birds and the dog, heavy gun at the ready, but at some unexpected moment the covey of ten or fifteen quail would explode into the air and fly off in all directions, seeking escape by the speed and wild variety of their flight. Then the guns would bang, each hunter firing as many shots in rapid succession as his gun allowed. Fifteen birds in fifteen heights and directions, maybe a dozen shots, maybe three birds downed.

Then came the excitement of trying to locate the fallen quail, and now the dog became a major partner, for he scoured the terrain this way and that, in what seemed like frantic circles but with the knowing purpose of vectoring the land until he smelled the blood of the dead bird.

'It could be the best sport in the world,' Todd said one day after the team of three guns and six dogs had knocked down forty-seven quail, each a delicious morsel relished by the families of the three married hunters—Maggie Morrison roasted hers with a special marinade made of tarragon vinegar and three or four tangy spices. Roy Bub had no wife yet, but did have four likely prospects whom he took out at various times and to various honky-tonks.

In September one year the oilman presented a stunning offer to his three buddies: 'I've located forty-eight hundred acres of the best quail land in Texas. Just north of Falfurrias. Owner wants four dollars and twenty cents an acre just for quail; five dollars for quail and deer and one turkey each; six for twelve months, including javelina and all the deer and turkey we can take legally.'

On Tuesday the four men took off from their obligations in Houston, thundered south to Victoria, then down U. S. 77 to Kingsville and across to the proposed land. They covered the two hundred and forty miles in just under three hours, thanks to an electronic fuzz-buster that Roy Bub had installed in the dentist's car; it alerted him to the presence of lurking Highway Patrol radars. The four arrived at the acreage about an hour before dusk and spent those sixty minutes in a dream world, because this land was obviously superior. 'Look at that huisache and mesquite,' Roy Bub cried, for he was the expert. 'No tall trees, but those gorgeous low shrubs providing plenty of cover. And the mesquite aren't too close together, so the quail will have to strike open ground.' He pointed out that the fence rows had not been cut, which meant there would be plenty of protection for the quail during nesting seasons, and he was especially struck by the richness of the weed cover.

'Look at that seed supply. All the right weeds, all properly spaced. This place, to tell you the truth, is worth double what they're asking.'

The owner, eager to get top dollar but not hurting for the money, was a rancher who said frankly: 'I'd like to rent it for the full six dollars, but you're working men. If you want it during a trial period just for quail in the autumn, I'll be more than happy to rent it for the four-twenty I said. Feel it out. See if it seems like home. If so, we might have ourselves a longtime deal.'

'Have you other prospects?' the oilman asked, for the $20,160 involved was a little steep and the $28,800 for twelve months, all rights, was forbidding.

'I do, but people tell me you're four responsible men. They say you'll help keep the hunting good. For the long haul, I'd prefer someone like you.'

That night the four Houstonians held a planning session, and it was clear that the oilman and the dentist could afford rather more of the total fee than could Roy Bub and Morrison, so a deal was arranged whereby Roy Bub would continue to drive the dentist's wagon while Todd would occupy the armchair topside and also care for the land. This meant that in the off season he would lay out roadways through the mesquite, drag the earth so that weeds would prosper, and look after the quail and turkeys in general.

'We promise you this,' Roy Bub told the owner, 'when we leave, your land will be in better shape than when we came.'

'One important thing,' the oilman said, for he was an expert in leases. 'We have the right to shoot October to January?' The owner agreed. 'But we have the right to visit all year long. Picnics, families?' The owner said of course. 'And we have the right, as of now, to build ourselves a little shack?'

'You certainly do,' the man said. 'But you understand, anything you erect on my land remains my property.'

'Now wait!' the oilman said. 'If we affix it to your land, dig cellars and all that, it's yours. But if it remains movable, we can take it with us if you close us out.'

'Of course!' There was a moment of hesitation, after which he said impulsively: 'I like your approach to the land. Twenty thousand even.'

So the four young men obtained the right to hunt this magnificent land—flat as a table, few trees, no lake, no river—during the legal quail season, and permission to roam it during the other months. The elaborate division of labor they had worked out to protect the oilman and dentist who were paying more than their share of cost was unnecessary, because those two worked as hard as anyone. They built the lean-to; they planted seeds along the trails so that weeds would grow; they tended the hedgerows where the quail would nest; and they cared for the dogs.

The team's first autumn on their lease was gratifying. With the dentist running his dogs and Todd spotting from his perch atop the wagon, they uncovered quail almost every day, and with the practice they were getting, the three gunners became experts. From time to time the oilman allowed one of the other two to use his A.Y.A., and one day toward Christmas, when they were huddling in the lean-to after dark, he asked quietly: 'Either of you two want to buy that Spanish gun? Real bargain.'

'What about you?' Roy Bub asked.

The oilman went almost shyly to the wagon, and as if he were a young girl showing off her first prom dress, produced an item he had sequestered when they packed in Houston. Unwrapping it, he revealed one of those perfect English guns, a Purdy with a Beasley action which he had purchased for $24,000. When it stood revealed in the lantern light, it was not handsome, nor garishly decorated, nor laden with insets of any kind. It was merely a cold, sleek, marvelously tooled gun which fitted in the shoulder like a perfectly tailored suit. 'There it is,' he said proudly.

'How much for the Spanish job?' Todd asked.

'It cost me forty-six hundred, like I said. I'd like to keep it in the crowd, maybe use it now and then for old times' sake. I'll let you have it for twenty-six.'

'Time payment?'

'Why not?'

So at the end of the season, and a very fine season it had been, the quartet had both a genuine Purdy and an A.Y.A. copy, and Roy Bub also had a very good gun, because Morrison sold him the good weapon he'd been using at a comparable discount.

They were a congenial crowd that winter, for at least twice a month, when no hunting was allowed at their lease, they left Houston at dusk on Friday, roared down to Falfurrias, and worked on their place. They turned the lean-to into a real house, with eight bunks, two temporary privies and a portable shower, and they improved the roadways through the far edges of the fields. In March everyone but Roy Bub brought wife and children down for a festival, kids in sleeping bags, older ones in blankets under the cold stars, and Maggie said to one of the other wives: 'I wouldn't want to cook like this four Saturdays a month, but it's worth every cent the men spend on it.'

In June, after a serious meeting in the bunkhouse, Roy Bub drove to the owner's house and invited him to join them. When he appeared, the oilman said: 'Mr. Cossiter, you know we like your place. We'd like to take it all year, at six dollars an acre, unrestricted. That would be twenty-eight thousand eight hundred. And we were wondering if you could shade that a little?'

'Men, you care for this place better than I do. Twenty-six thousand for as many years as you care to hold it.'

'A deal,' the oilman said, but Roy Bub cried: 'Hell, we could of got him down to twenty,' and the owner said: 'Blacktop me a four-lane road north and south through the middle so I can subdivide later on, and you can have it for twenty.'

Maggie Morrison analyzed it this way: 'I'm sure Roy Bub felt totally left out during our family stay at the hunting lease. Everyone else with a wife and kids.' At any rate, shortly after their return home, Roy Bub informed his team that they and their wives were invited to his wedding, which was to be solemnized at midnight Tuesday in Davy Crockett's, a famous Houston honky-tonk on the road to the oil fields near Beaumont.

'Do we really want to attend such a rowdy affair?' Maggie asked, but Todd said: 'Not only are we going, so are the kids.'

Maggie did not like this, not at all, and went to speak with Roy Bub: 'It's not proper to hold a wedding at Crockett's, you being in oil and all that.'

He looked at her in a funny way and said: 'I'm not in oil,' and she said: 'But I remember your white truck that first day. Roy Bub Hooker, Drilling.'

'That was my truck. But I don't drill for oil. I put that on so that people would *think* I did.'

'What do you drill?'

'Septic tanks. When your toilet clogs up, you call me. I wouldn't feel happy bein' married anywhere but Crockett's.'

So at ten in the evening the six adults and seven children drove out to the huge unpaved parking lot that was already crowded with pickups whose owners were hacking it up inside.

The oilman, who had been here once before, assembled his crowd outside the door and warned: 'Nobody is to hit anybody, no matter what happens,' and he led the way into the massive one-story honky-tonk.

Wide-eyed, they found Davy Crockett's, the workingman's Copacabana, a riotous affair, with more than a thousand would-be cowboys in boots and Stetsons, neither of which they ever took off, dancing the Cotton-Eyed Joe and the two-step with an abandon that would have horrified any choreographer. The place had numerous bars, dance bands which came and went, and an atmosphere of riotous joy.

It was a gala place, and the Morrisons had not been inside ten minutes before a cowboy approached Beth, bowed politely, and asked her to dance. Maggie tried to object, but the girl was gone, and once on the floor, she did not wish to return to her family, because one attractive young fellow after another whisked her away.

Roy Bub, rosily drunk, welcomed everyone enthusiastically. The bride appeared at about eleven-fifteen, twenty-two years old, peroxide-blond hair, very high heels, low-cut silk blouse, extremely tight double-knit jeans, and a smile that could melt icebergs. When Roy Bub saw her, he rushed over, took her hand, and announced in a bellow: 'Karleen Wyspianski, but don't let the name scare you. She's changin' it tonight.' She was, he explained, a waitress in a high-class diner: 'Honcho of the place, and I grabbed her before the boss did.'

She had grown up in one of those little foreign enclaves so numerous in Texas and so little known outside the state. In her case it was Panna Maria, a Polish settlement dating back to the 1850s whose inhabitants still spoke the native language. She had quit school after the eleventh grade and come immediately to Houston, where she had progressed from one job to another, always improving her take-home pay. Her present employment, because of the large tips she promoted, paid more than a hundred and fifty a week, and had she married the boss, as he wished, she would have shared in a prosperous business.

But she had fallen in love with Roy Bub and his white pickup, and the fact that he went hunting almost every weekend did not distress her, for those were her busiest days, and she was content to join him on Tuesdays, Wednesdays and Thursdays as a Crocketteer. They were good dancers, liberal spenders, and never loath to join in any moderate fracas that was developing.

Karleen had for some time been aware that Roy Bub intended sooner or later proposing marriage, but she was not overly eager for this to happen, for she had an enjoyable life and did not expect marriage to improve it substantially. But she did love the energetic driller, and when he returned from the family outing at the Falfurrias ranch with the blunt statement 'Karleen, I think we better get married,' she said 'Sure.'

Neither partner considered, even briefly, getting married anywhere but Crockett's. Karleen was Catholic and intended staying so, but she cared little about church affairs. Roy Bub was Baptist, but he was willing to let others worship as they pleased, so long as he was not required to attend his own church. But each was resolved to rear their children, when they came along, as devout Christians in some faith or other.

At quarter to twelve the minister who would conduct the marriage arrived, Reverend Fassbender, an immensely fat fellow of over three hundred pounds who served no specific church but who did much good work as a kind of floating clergyman. One of his specialties was weddings at Crockett's, where the cowboys revered him. Dressed in black, with a cleric's collar size twenty-two, he exuded both sanctity and sweat as he passed through the crowd bestowing grace: 'Blessings on you, sister. Glad to see you, brother, may Christ go with you.'

The wedding was an emotional affair, for when a space was cleared beneath one of the bandstands, Reverend Fassbender put an end to the frivolity and began to act as if he were in a cathedral, which in a sense he was, for this honky-tonk was where the young working people of Houston's refineries worshipped, and when two bands struck up Mendelssohn's 'Wedding March' Maggie Morrison and other women in the audience began to sniffle.

Karleen, in her tight jeans, and Roy Bub, in his tight collar, the only one he had worn in a year, formed a pair of authentic Crocketteers, and cheers broke out as they took their place before the minister, who quickly halted that nonsense: 'Dearly Beloved, we are gathered here in the presence of God . . .' Maggie whispered to Beth: 'Jesus attended a wedding like this at that big honky-tonk in Cana.'

When the ceremony ended, and an honor guard of cowboys fired salutes in the parking lot, Roy Bub's hunting partners watched with approval as the white pickup was delivered at the door to serve as the honeymoon car. While the wedding was under way it had been decorated with leagues of streaming toilet paper, Mexican decorations, and a broom lashed to the cab. But what Maggie liked best, as the pickup drove off, was the new sign Roy Bub had added to his tailgate, for its emotion and the design of the heart seemed appropriate to this night:

IF YOU ♥ NEW YORK
GO TO HELL HOME

When the *Rusk v. Rusk* divorce proceedings revealed just how much money Ransom Rusk had, a score of beautiful women, and Texas had far more than its share, began plotting as to how each might become the next Mrs. Rusk, but the austere man directed most of his attention to multiplying by big factors the wealth he already had. He did not become a recluse, but his divorce did make him gun-shy, so he focused on the main problem, never voicing it publicly or even to himself. Intuitively he realized that if he retained, after paying off Fleurette, nearly $50,000,000, there was no reason why he could not run that figure up to 500,000,000, which would move him into the big-rich category.

His first decision in pursuit of this goal was to shift his operations from the pleasant little town of Larkin, population 3,934, and into the heart of Fort Worth, population 393,476. He chose Fort Worth rather than Dallas because the former city was a Western town, with its focus on ranching, oil and fearless speculation in both, while Dallas was more a Texas version of New York or Boston, with huge financial and real estate operations but little touch with the older traditions that had made Texas great. In brief, an oil wildcatter and a Longhorn man like Ransom Rusk felt at home in Fort Worth; he did not in Dallas: 'Those barracuda are too sharp for me. I feel safer paddling around with the minnows.'

In Fort Worth he associated himself with many others who were risking ventures in oil, and especially the servicing of the oil industry. With his strong basic knowledge of how petroleum was found and delivered to the market, he was an asset to the men who financed those operations, and before long he was in the middle of that exciting game. The joy his father had found in Texas high school football he found in Texas big-time finance.

He was major partner in a company which built and sold drilling rigs; the wooden one that had spudded in Rusk #3 back in 1923 had cost $19,000; the ones he now built were well over a million each. He had also bought into a mud concern, that clever process whereby a viscous liquid, whose properties were modified according to the depth and character of the hole, was pumped into a hole while it was being drilled to correct faults and ensure production if oil was present. But mostly he toured Texas, like a hound dog chasing possums, looking for promising land that could be leased, and this took him to the Austin Chalk, the petroliferous formation around Victoria, where he made a killing, and to the Spraberry Field, where he bought up seventy leases which produced dust and seven which were bonanzas.

At the end of one of the most aggressive campaigns in recent oil history, the value of Rusk's holdings had tripled, and he felt with some justification that 'I'm really just at the beginning. What I need now is to find that big new field.'

He was in this pattern of thought when into his modest Fort Worth office came an old man whose vision had never faded but whose capacity to capitalize upon it had. The years since 1923 had not been kind to Dewey Kimbro, now a seedy seventy-one with no front teeth and very little of the millions he had made on the Larkin Field. When he stood before the son of his former partner, he was a small, wizened man who had been married three times, each with increasing disaster: 'Mr. Rusk, my job is to find oil. I've found three of the good fields, you know that. I want you to grubstake me, because I have my eye on a real possibility north of Fort Stockton.'

'Wouldn't that put you in the Permian Basin?'

'On the edge, yes.'

'But everyone knows the good fields in the Permian have been developed.'

The men were speaking of one of the major oil fields in the world, a late discovery that had occurred in the middle of a vast, arid flatland of which it was once said: 'Any living thing in this godforsaken land has thorns, or fangs, or stingers, or claws, and that includes the human beings.' It was a land of cactus, scorpions, mesquite and rattlesnakes. Some intrepid heroes had tried running cattle on it; in a cynical deal the University of Texas had been given vast amounts of the barren land instead of real money, and an occasional oil well had been tried, with more dust at two thousand feet than at the surface.

Then, on 28 May 1923, when the latest dry well had sunk beyond three thousand feet, workers were eating breakfast when they heard a monstrous rumble and felt the ground shake. Down in the depths of the earth, an accumulation of oil under intense pressure broke through the thin rock which had kept it imprisoned for 230,000,000 years and roared up through the well casing, exploding hundreds of feet into the air. Santa Rita #1 had come in, signaling a vast subterranean lake of oil in the Permian Basin. The first wells were on university lands, and hundreds of the subsequent wells would be too, providing that school with a potential revenue exceeding that of any other university in the world.

Later, when the Yates Field came in with its Permian oil, one well produced nearly three thousand barrels an hour from a depth of only eleven hundred and fifty feet: 'Drilling in the Yates, you just stick a pole in the ground and jump back.'

With its incredible millions from the Permian, the university would leverage itself into becoming a first-class school, and a thousand dry-soil farmers would find themselves to be millionaires, with a ranch in the country—the old homestead dotted with oil rigs—and a bright new home in Midland, identified by the Census Bureau as 'the wealthiest town per capita in the States,' with more Rolls-Royces than in New York.

But by 1969 those days of explosive wealth were over; the Permian had died down to a respectable field that still produced more oil than most, but did not throw up those soaring gushers whose free-flowing oil had once darkened the sky. Midland now served as husbandman to wells already in operation and was no longer in the exciting business of drilling new ones. As Ransom Rusk told his father's favorite wildcatter: 'Dewey, the Permian Basin is a discovered field.'

'Don't you believe it, Mr. Rusk. Petroleum products come in at a dozen different levels. Maybe the easy oil is finished, but how about the deep gas?'

'Dewey, stands to reason, if there was oil or gas out there, the big boys would have found it.'

'No, Mr. Rusk,' Dewey pleaded, still standing, for Ransom had not invited him to sit and he knew he must not appear presumptuous. 'Big boys only find what little boys like me take them to. I know where there's oil, but I need your money to buy the leases and sink a well. This time it'll be a deep well.'

'Dewey, you've been peddling that story across Texas. What I will do, because you were a good partner to my father, here's four hundred dollars. Get yourself some teeth.'

'I was going to do that, Mr. Rusk, but what I really need is your support on this new prospect.'

He was given no money beyond the four hundred dollars, which he did not use for teeth; he spent it traveling to other oil centers in search of funds which would enable him to pursue his latest dream, and in the meantime Ransom was visited by someone who wanted a contribution for a much different enterprise. It was Mr. Kramer, the old-time oilman who was now interested only in wind velocities and armadillos.

'Mr. Rusk, to put it bluntly, I'm asking you for four thousand dollars to trap armadillos and deliver them to this leprosy institute in Louisiana.'

'What are you talking about?'

'You may not know it, few people do, but the armadillo seems to be the only living thing besides man that can contract leprosy. Their low body temperature, twenty-nine point seven to thirty-five degrees Celsius, encourages the bacillus.'

'You mean those critters in my front lawn . . .'

'Don't get excited. It's not transferrable to humans, the kind they develop. But it is the only way that our scientists and medical people can experiment on what causes and cures this dreaded disease.'

'Of course you can have the money, but you mean that our little bulldozers have some utility in the world?'

'That's just what I mean. You see, with nature, you can never tell. The armadillo has been preserved through these millions of years, so we must suppose that it can host a particular disease which has also existed for millions of years.'

'Now wait a minute, I don't want you trapping Lady Macbeth and her Four Witches.'

'Make that eight witches. She just had four more pups, all female again.'

'Where do the males come from?'

'It balances out. Don't ask me how.'

It was a hundred miles from Fort Worth to Larkin, but with Rusk driving, it would require only an hour and twenty minutes, so the men decided to dash out to inspect the armadillo problem, and as they sped along the broad and well-engineered roads Ransom asked Mr. Kramer what he thought of Dewey Kimbro, who had haunted the oil fields during the period that Kramer had worked them.

'Standard Texan. Always going to hit it big. Wastes his money on women. You'll have to bury him some day, two hundred dollars for the funeral, because he'll wind up without a cent.'

'He brought in a lot of wells.'

'You're not thinking of bankrolling him, are you?'

'Most of the big finds in Texas, even the real gushers, have been found by crazy geologists like Dewey. He says he knows something . . .'

'I'll admit this, Mr. Rusk. Men like me, we work the fields, it's a living. We get paid well, we save our money, we retire to a decent life. A man like Dewey, he never retires. Four days before he dies, not a cent to his name, he'll be promoting the next well. I was an oil worker. He's an oil dreamer.'

In Larkin, after Rusk noticed with some satisfaction that Lady Macbeth and her eight helpers had by now pretty well chopped the onetime bowling lawn to shreds, he asked: 'Now, where do you propose to trap these armadillos for the hospital in Louisiana?' Kramer took him a few hundred yards to the banks of Bear Creek where a family of about fifty of the armored animals centered and to a spot farther along the creek where another settlement of about forty maintained its headquarters: 'They like moist ground. Two things that can kill the armadillo, very cold winters and a prolonged drought.'

'Do they need so much water?'

'Like camels, they can exist on practically none, but when the sun bakes the earth during a drought, they can't dig easily. And that means they can't eat.'

The part of any visit to Mr. Kramer's place that Rusk liked best came when he was allowed to play with the three tame creatures that Kramer still kept in his kitchen and out in the yard, and it was difficult for Ransom to explain why he found so much pleasure in them: 'They aren't cuddly, and they aren't very responsive, but they are endlessly fascinating.'

'I think you like them because of the oil derricks on their back.'

'Now that makes sense.' But what really pleased him was the way they rousted about like oil-field workers, bruising and brawling, knocking one another over, then scampering like a team to the latest noise or the newest adventure. They were social animals, accustomed to working together, and when holes were to be dug, they were formidable.

'It just occurred to me, Kramer. If we could train those little devils, we could dig oil wells in half the time.' The armadillos seemed to sense that Rusk was their friend, for when he sat in a chair they enjoyed romping with his feet, or sitting in his lap. They had no teeth that could bite a person, and when at ease, kept their eighteen formidable, lancelike toes under control.

But in the long run, it was the extraordinary beauty of their armor and the ever-present sense that these were creatures from a most distant past that allured. Sometimes Rusk would sit with one in his hands, staring at its preposterous face— all nose, beady eyes that could barely see—and he would ask Kramer: 'In what bog did this one hide for twenty million years?'

He provided the funds for leprosy research, but was pleased when his gardener informed him that more than twenty armadillos now resided in the Rusk fields. None of them were tame, but they made a noble procession when they set out at dusk to excavate some neighbor's lawn.

When he returned to Fort Worth he found Dewey Kimbro, still with no teeth, perched outside his office, talking excitedly with his secretary. As soon as the old wildcatter spotted him, he jumped up, took his arm, and accompanied him into the inner office: 'Mr. Rusk, I don't want to talk if or how or even how much. Just when.'

'What do you mean?'

'I've spotted a field you have to put under lease. And then you have to pay for the exploration well.'

'Now look, Kimbro . . .'

'No, you look. Where do you suppose you got the money you now have? They say in the papers more than a hundred and fifty million. Because I found a field for your daddy. I'm an oilman, Mr. Rusk. You owe me one last shot, because I know where oil can be found.'

The plea was irresistible. In an average year Rusk had been spending three million dollars on the hunches of men with far dimmer track records than Dewey Kimbro and with far less dedication to the oil business. He did owe the old man one last shot: 'I'll do it.'

'No tricks. I'm too old for tricks.'

'My father warned me that you were completely honest, Dewey, but if anyone crossed you, you bided your time, then shot him in the back . . . dead of night.'

'Your father ever tell you how we got the Yeager land back under our control? He had me goad the poor devil till he lifted his shotgun, then your father drilled him.'

'It's a deal. Now where is this precious land that's going to make us both rich?'

'You richer, me rich.' And he drove Rusk to a big ranch, El Estupendo, tucked away among the mesas north of Fort Stockton.

'This land couldn't produce goats,' Rusk complained, but Dewey's enthusiasm could not be quenched, and in their secret explorations he showed the financier faults whose edges protruded and domes half hidden by mesquite.

'There could be oil down there,' Rusk conceded, and Dewey cried: 'There has to be!'

The ranch was one of the nine accumulated by Lorenzo Quimper in obedience to the principle laid down by his famous ancestor Yancey: 'If you grab enough Texas land, somethin' good is bound to happen.' Quimper was not in residence, and in his absence the place was run by a young Mexican in whom he apparently placed much confidence. 'I am Cándido Guzmán,' the manager said in carefully enunciated English. 'Mr. Quimper's the man in charge.'

'Where is he?'

'Who knows? Maybe at the Polk ranch, down on the Rio Grande.'

They made a series of phone calls and located Quimper, not at any of his western ranches but in his newly built ranch on the shores of Lake Travis near Austin, and as soon as he heard the name Rusk he told Guzmán: 'Keep him there. I'll fly right out.' Climbing into his Beechcraft, he directed his pilot to drop him off at the improvised runway at El Estupendo, where Cándido was waiting, as always, with his pickup. 'What's the focus?' he asked, using a phrase he liked, and Guzmán replied: 'Oil, I think. I went in to Fort Stockton to ask about Kimbro and they told me "Oil." '

'Well, if a man has nine Texas ranches, one of them ought to have oil,' Quimper said, and Cándido replied: 'Mr. Quimper, the papers say you already have two with oil,' and Quimper said: 'You can never have too many.'

When Rusk and Quimper met in a tin-roofed shack on the ranch, they formed a powerful pair, Rusk older and more cautious in Texas gambling, Quimper more eager to leap at a promising chance. In personal appearance, too, they were contrasting, Rusk leaner and more sharklike, Quimper fleshier and more prosperous-looking. Ransom said little, and Quimper could hardly be stopped, indulging in such Texas phrases as 'Wiser'n a tree full of owls' and 'We'll dig the damned well and nail the coonskin to the barn door.' He also uttered a great truth about oil in Texas: 'My pappy told me: "Lorenzo, in an oil deal always be satisfied with the overriding royalty of one-eighth. Let the other dumb bastards do the drillin' and grab their seven-eighths. You'll always come out ahead." And time has proved him right. Gentlemen, you can have your lease, but in some ways I'm a lot wiser than my pappy. Not ten years, like the early ones. Two years. Not fifty cents an acre, like he did. Three dollars, because this is prime land. And not one-eighth, three-sixteenths.'

'They told me you were a miserable bastard, Quimper,' Rusk said, 'but you have the land, you've been to law school, even though you flunked out, and they say they're putting you on the Board of Regents at the university, so you must know something. It's a deal.' They shook hands, and that's how the exploration of those barren wastes north of Fort Stockton began.

They left the positioning of the first well to Kimbro, but from a distance they hovered, watching him. 'Vultures waiting for the old man to die,' Dewey said of them one day as his drilling probed deeper and deeper, with no results. 'They'll wait in vain.'

This enforced waiting had one productive consequence; it became an opportunity for Rusk to renew acquaintance with a gifted gentleman who worked the oil fields. He was Pierre Soult, collateral descendant of one of Napoleon's better marshals, and another of the engineering geniuses France was producing in these years.

Pierre Soult, latest of this enterprising breed, had worked with Rusk before; it was his genius that prodded development of the procedure of digging a deep hole in the earth, filling it with dynamite, and then placing a dozen sensitive detectors at varied distances and exploding the charge. His detectors recorded how long it took for the reverberation to penetrate the earth below, strike a granite base, and come bouncing back. Exquisite timing and even more exquisite analysis revealed secrets of the substructure, and from these Soult could advise his clients as to what lay beneath the ground and where best to dig to find it.

'Seismographic exploration,' Soult called his process. 'We are like the scientists who detect and record earthquakes thousands of miles away. With our dynamite we make the little earthquake and record it half a mile away.'

Of course, his procedures were now much advanced over those primitive ones Rusk had employed in his early days of oil exploration, and when Rusk complimented him on this, Soult said: 'I've about run my course with seismography. I'm thinking seriously about a new device to solve mathematical problems, useful in all fields, very daring. A hand-held computer.'

'What?'

'Given the proper technical advances, and I think I know a way to ensure them, you can carry in your hand, Mr. Rusk, more mathematics than Newton and Einstein together ever mastered.'

'Come see me when this is over. That is, if we strike oil.'

'If there is any around here, you'll find it. My little earthquakes ensure that.'

One very hot afternoon, temperature 104 degrees, humidity seven percent, when the log at 22,000 feet had shown not a sign of carbon, a mighty roar from below signaled an upsurge of oil and gas so powerful that it tore away the superstructure as it struck the air, ignited from a spark thrown by crashing steel girders, and flamed into a beacon visible for seventy miles across the flat and arid land.

Five crew members were incinerated. A hundred thousand dollars' worth of petroleum products burned for days, then a million dollars' worth. Dewey Kimbro's men tried every trick to control the wild flames of Estupendo #1; they poured in tons of mud to seal off the flow of oil, they tried dynamiting the hole to exhaust its oxygen, but nothing worked. The flames roared into the midnight sky and helped the sun illuminate the day.

Red Adair, the Texan who specialized in the dangerous task of subduing oil-well fires, was summoned, and after three weeks he brought this tremendous conflagration under control. Rusk, bleary-eyed from watching the flames, told his new partner: 'Quimper, it hurts to see so much wealth vanishing in smoke. But when you know that a million times as much is still down there . . .'

With his royalty from the Estupendo field, Quimper more than doubled his wealth and was promoted into the rich category. Dewey Kimbro's share was more than two million, with which he purchased some new teeth, but within two years he was back prowling marginal fields, listening for leads at the morning breakfasts, searching for some new source of exploration capital; his wealth had vanished in divorce settlements, the acquisition of a fourth wife, and extensive lawyers' fees for getting rid of her after seven months.

The knowledge that his assets now totaled just under $400,000,000 altered Ransom Rusk very little. He retained four Mexican servants at his Larkin home but because he still tried to avoid entanglement with women, the mansion saw little social life. He spent most of his time in Fort Worth, where his frugal offic had to be enlarged, for he now required a full-time accountant to keep track of his intricate participations in the various wells he supervised.

But he was never satiated; always he looked for that next big field, that lucky wildcatter who was going to lead him to the next gusher, and it was in pursuit of what he called 'the significant multiplier,' that he sought out Pierre Soult: 'Is what you told me that day while we were waiting for Estupendo Number One true?'

'You mean about the radical new system for calculators?'

'Yes. How much would you need?'

'We must invent a new way to form silicon chips, and I believe I have it.'

'How much?'

'I'll have to hire real brains, you know. The best the Sorbonne and Cambridge and MIT produce.'

'How much, damnit?'

'Real brains cost real money. Maybe twenty million.'

'If we're going to do it, let's do it Texas style. You can count on fifty.' They shook hands, and because of the way the world was developing, this investment would turn out to be the wisest he would make.

Spending so much time in Midland, a city ninety-eight-percent Republican, produced a significant change in Ransom Rusk. Already conservative, like most oilmen who took great risks but did not want others to do so, he moved steadily right to become a reactionary, dedicated to the principle that all government was bad and that enterprising men should be allowed to write their own rules. But at the same time he defended the depletion allowance, which enabled him to retain a huge percentage of the income he gathered, and he sought to drive from public life any political leader who spoke or acted against this preferential treatment enjoyed by oilmen. Government was all bad except that which furthered his interests.

He was partly justified in this stand: 'I gamble fantastic sums trying to find oil. Fifty, sixty million, and three-fourths of it can go down the drain. I deserve protection.'

Of course, on the one-fourth of his venture capital which was not lost he made gigantic profits, and these he spent freely in trying to defeat candidates who were not supportive of the oil industry: 'A basic rule of self-defense. The man who attacks my interests is my enemy.' It so happened that only Republicans could be seen as protecting his interests, so he was forced to oppose most Democrats, which he did with huge sums of money.

He had never liked Lyndon Johnson personally, but Johnson had been one of the staunchest defenders of big oil, so with his left hand Rusk slipped him generous contributions while with his right he continued to pull the straight Republican lever. He was quietly pleased when Johnson decided not to run in 1968, but when Hubert Humphrey was nominated to succeed him, he sprang into furious action: 'The man's an ass, a bumbling ass. The Republic will fall if he's elected.' And in his sour, sharply focused way, Rusk spent millions to defeat him, all the Democratic senators running that year, and sixteen selected Democratic congressmen whose votes had offended him.

He was delighted when the Republicans nominated Richard Nixon, for here was a man who had proved over a long period in public service that he knew what was good for the nation. Ransom invited Nixon to Texas, spent lavishly to influence his fellow oilmen, and literally bit his fingernails on election night when it looked as if Humphrey and George Wallace might, because of the inane electoral college, succeed in throwing the election into the House of Representatives. He did not go to bed all that night, and when morning came, with Nixon the victor by a precarious margin, he cried to the empty rooms at Larkin: 'The Republic has been saved!'

While these developments were taking place, another aspect of Texas life was undergoing a radical change, which might, in the long run, prove more important to the state than either oil or financing. Sherwood Cobb, grandson of the late United States senator from Waxahachie, had decided regretfully that the splendid plantation his family owned just south of that engaging town was so beset by the boll weevil, the declining bale-per-acre ratio and the inflated value of land that the only sensible thing to do was to leapfrog his entire cotton operation out to the far western part of the state, where land was still cheap, flat and so high in altitude that the boll weevil could not survive the winters.

Nancy Nell Cobb, raised on a farm, asked about the extreme dryness of the region in which her husband proposed to grow his cotton, a crop which needed a lot of water, and he assured her: 'Aridity makes it impossible for boll weevils to breed.' But she countered: 'If weevils can't grow, neither can cotton. Jefferson had forty-six inches of rain a year, and cotton thrived. Waxahachie has thirty-six inches, and cotton did well till the weevils took over. But Lubbock had only sixteen inches last year, and I can't see how your plants can prosper.'

It was then that he revealed to her one of the miracles of the United States, and of how Texas profited from it. Spreading before her a map which the Department of Agriculture had provided cotton growers in the Waxahachie area in a commendable effort to make them quit trying to grow cotton there and move out to the high plains, where production was booming, he indicated the eight Western states—South Dakota to Texas—under which lay hidden the nation's greatest water resource, barring the Mississippi: 'Think of it as a vast underground lake. Bigger than most European countries. Dig deep and you invariably find water. It's called the Ogallala Aquifer, after this little town in Nebraska where it was discovered. Fingers probe out everywhere to collect immense runoffs, and the aquifer delivers it right to our farm.'

'How can you know all this? If it's hidden, like you say?'

'They've been studying it, in all the states. Seems to be an interrelated unit. And it's inexhaustible.'

'You mean it's down there and anyone can use it?'

'That's how we're going to grow cotton in Lubbock. You pay for your well once, and you have water for the rest of your life.'

Nancy Nell had trouble believing that an area which gathered only sixteen inches of rainfall a year could grow a crop which required thirty-six or more, and she told Sherwood: 'Seems like an enormous risk to me. I really think we ought to stay where we are and fight the weevil with field-dusting, like the Andersons are doing.'

'Nancy Nell,' he said, singing her name as if it were one unbroken syllable, 'hundreds of farmers out in that dryland are getting the best cotton crop in Texas, and with the know-how they're accumulating, it's bound to be the best in the world within a decade. We're going to make the try.'

To show her the land where her home was to be, he roused his family one morning at four, packed them into the big Buick, and headed west at sunrise, displaying the same excitement that his grandfather had shown in the early 1900s when shepherding his family from the closed-in Old South atmosphere of Jefferson to the black earth and open spaces of Waxahachie.

They angled across to Fort Worth, avoiding the breakfast traffic about Dallas, and as they drove west, Sherwood became sensitive to one of the miracles of Texas, operative for the past five thousand years. With each fifteen miles of travel, east to west, the yearly rainfall dropped by one inch, and through one of the coincidences of nature, the ninety-eighth parallel of longitude coincided roughly with the line that demarcated thirty inches of rainfall. East of that line the standard agriculture of planting and harvesting crops was possible; to the west it was not. There settlers had to rely not upon farming but upon ranching and perhaps mining.

'It's as if a mighty wall had been erected along this line,' Cobb told his family as they approached the imaginary ninety-eighth, 'to warn farmers "halt here!" Each mile we go from here on, not enough rain to grow a crop.' After his passengers had digested this unpleasant fact, he laughed: 'What saves us is hiding down below. Because it's also true that each mile we travel, we get closer to the Ogallala. And that means cotton.'

Once past the ninety-eighth, they were into the real West: Jacksboro, past Three Cairns, where the state had erected a monument recalling the 10th Cavalry stand against the Comanche, and on to Larkin, where they stopped to see the famous courthouse with the portraits of Mabel Fister; they did not allow their children to find the notorious fifth sculpture.

West of Larkin the rolling plains began, sometimes not even a tree visible in any direction, but with softly dipping hills, and far beyond that they entered upon the high plains, as flat as earth could be and twice as empty. Awed by the immensity of the land they proposed to occupy, they drove past Lubbock and west to locate their six thousand acres which, in their pristine state without irrigation, could feed only one cow and calf to every sixty acres.

They had come three hundred and forty-nine miles in one day, touching neither the eastern border of the state nor the western, and had traversed four different terrains as distinct from one another as Italy and Portugal: the Black Prairies of Waxahachie, the Cross Timbers of Larkin, the Lower Plains marked only by little towns, and the High Plains of Lubbock. As they pulled into the little town of Levelland, where they would spend the night, population 10,445, Sherwood said: 'Our farm will lie north of here. Properly handled, it's going to be a gold mine. All the land we'll ever need, and all the water.' That night, ravenously hungry after their long ride, they had some of the best chicken-fried steak and grits they'd had in a long time, while the restaurant jukebox ground out a song which had gained recent popularity: 'It takes a lot of squares to make the world go round.'

When they inspected their land next morning, Nancy Nell and the children gasped, for it was flatter by far than any seen on the previous day and it contained not one tree or shrub of noticeable size. The horizon was so endless that Nancy Nell asked: 'How many other farms can we see from here?' and her husband quipped: 'Sixteen in Montana and seven in Canada.'

He showed the children where the house would stand and assured them that it was going to be first class: 'With the money we get for the old place, we can build a little paradise here.'

'Will you plant a windbreak to the northwest?' Nancy Nell asked, and he said: 'That goes in tomorrow.' But like his ancestors when they occupied their new lands in Texas, the first thing he erected was a cotton gin, because like them he expected to be the leading cotton grower in his region.

Even before the house was started he entered into a contract with the Erickson brothers, the deep-well people, and they took pleasure in teaching him about the water situation: 'Two hundred feet below us as we stand, a thick, impermeable rock formation, the Red Bed. The Ogallala rests on it. Water level rises to within thirty feet of the surface, but to play it safe, so that not even the severest drought can affect you, we're going to drill your wells down to one hundred feet.'

'How many?'

'We calculate that to work the good center areas of your land, you'll need six wells.'

'I thought five would handle the job,' Cobb said, and they agreed: 'Sure, you can do it with five, but you might be puttin' a mite of strain on them. Take our advice, go with six.'

'How much?'

'We give you the best well ever drilled, thirty-five hundred dollars a well, and that includes a converted Chevy 1952 engine set in a concrete box three feet down to protect it from rain and dust.'

'What's it run on?'

'We provide a butane tank, two hundred gallons, they fill it for you from town.'

The Ericksons also showed him how to rent a tractor before he bought his own, throw a fourteen-inch ridge around his entire cotton area, and box it in: 'That way, you trap every drop of water that falls on your land.'

'We get sixteen inches a year,' the second man said, 'steady as God's patience with a sinful man, and you ought to be here the afternoon it falls.'

After Cobb had consulted with the experts at Texas Tech in Lubbock to learn which strains of cotton were appropriate for his new land, and when his first fields were planted by tractor, broad and open and requiring no stoop work by imported Mexicans, he heard from the college expert the best news of all: 'This year Lubbock cotton is bringing top dollar.'

'Sounds like we're home safe,' Cobb said as he studied his fields with the banked-up ridges hemming them in.

'There's one small cloud on the horizon,' the expert warned. 'Each year, from South Dakota to Lubbock, the Ogallala seems to drop an inch or two.'

'You mean the level could go down, permanently?'

'Unless we use it properly,' the man said.

Maggie Morrison's life in Houston was made more pleasant when she located a drugstore that received an airplane shipment of the *New York Times* each Sunday afternoon at two. Since her husband was usually down at the quail camp with his three buddies—grown men playing at games—she put on her bathrobe and slippers, made herself comfortable in a big chair, and wrestled with the crossword puzzle, her chief intellectual enticement of the week.

As in Michigan, she had found several other wives who enjoyed the puzzle, men apparently not having adequate intellect for this teaser, and when she had completed filling in her little white squares, she delighted in calling these other women to compare notes and gloat if she had found all the answers and they had not. She recalled with keen pleasure one Sunday evening when she had unraveled one of the more tantalizing puzzles. At the start, the clues for the five long lines were of little help:

17 across.	Precious metal things.
33 across.	Cheap metal things.
54 across.	Alloy metal things.
79 across.	Soft metal things.
89 across.	Valuable metal things.

Not until she had solved many of the difficult *down* words could she assemble enough letters to provide clues, but even when she had a goodly selection she could not fathom the secret of the word fragments thus revealed. Finally, on the 'Alloy metal things' line she had the letters *kn* and this encouraged her to decipher the word *knuckles,* and like the sudden flashing of a light in a darkened room, she perceived that the alloy had to be brass, and the precious metal, gold:

Precious metal.	B U G D U S T F O I L L E A F A N D S T A N D A R D
Cheap metal.	E A R G O D T Y P E P A N H A T H O R N A N D C A N
Alloy metal.	B A N D K N U C K L E S A N D C A N D L E S T I C K
Soft metal.	P E N C I L P I P E S H O T A N D P O I S O N I N G
Valuable metal.	C H L O R I D E F I S H F O X W A R E A N D S T A R

When she made her nightly calls that Sunday she found that only one of her team had solved the five lines, and the two congratulated themselves on having superior intellects, but some weeks later both were rebuffed by what all the players agreed was one of the most ingenious of the puzzles.

As before, the four *across* lines gave only bewildering clues; they were not intelligible at first, nor even after some serious speculation, and she surrendered: 'I'm ignorant about the military. I give up.' She failed to solve it, but that night one of her friends gloated: 'Maggie! I got it quicker than usual,' and Maggie said: 'Yes, but your husband was an officer. You know about battles and stuff.' And then her friend cried: 'Maggie! It's not about war. It's about automobiles.' And with that simple clue Maggie was able to fill in the squares, chuckling at her stupidity in not having discovered that the lines referred to a car at a stoplight:

19 across.	March!	B A C K B E R E T S W A R D G A G E H O U S E H O R N
41 across.	Halt!	H A N D E D L E T T E R I N K S H I R T H E R R I N G
63 across.	Mark time!	G R I S J A C K I F E R O U S B E A D S F O R E V E R
89 across.	Retreat!	B E N C H E R G A M M O N L A S H S L I D E W A T E R

With her husband prospering in his business, her children adjusting to their schools, and her small circle of friends sharing crossword-puzzle results on Sunday evenings, Maggie, without being aware of the change in her life, was becoming a Texan. She revealed this in a letter to a friend in Detroit:

> Tonight I feel joy about being in Texas. It's so big, so alive, so filled with a sense of the future. In fact, I'm so kindly disposed that I even want to apologize for the unkind things I said about our Texas cockroaches. I told you they were as big as sparrows. Well, I had one this morning as big as a robin. But an oilman who bought some land from me told me that roaches may be the oldest continuing form of life on earth, and he

showed me a fossil his geologists dredged up from the Pennsylvanian Level. That's 330,000,000 million years ago, he said, and anything that can survive this Texas heat for that long has earned my respect.

She was congratulating herself on defending the cultural life in Houston—'We're candles blowing in the wind,' she had once said to one of her friends—when she received a stupefying counterblow which stunned. Daughter Beth, a willowy fifteen now, came shyly into the room where her mother was tangled in her big chair, and said: 'Mummy, I'm going to be a cheerleader.'

'You're what?'

'All the girls, it's the very best thing you can be, they vote for you.'

'What are you saying?'

'That I'm reporting for cheerleader practice tomorrow. I have to be at school an hour early.'

'Beth, are you out of your mind?'

'No, Mummy. It's what I want most.'

'Well, you can't have it. A cheerleader! Beth, cheerleaders are pretty little fluffs who can't do anything else. You can do math. You can write poetry. You can do anything you put your mind to, but not cheerleading, for heaven's sake!'

'But all the girls . . .'

'Sit down, Beth. You must understand one thing and keep it always in mind. You are not "all the girls." You have an extraordinary mind, inherited it from your grandmother, I think. God knows it skipped me. Beth, you're special. You could win top honors at Michigan. You're not a cheerleader . . .'

'I don't want to go to Michigan.'

'Where do you want to go?'

'Texas, where all the good kids go. Or A&M, it's real neat.'

'For God's sake, stop saying "real neat." A&M is not real neat and neither is cheerleading.'

Beth was so persistent in her desire to have what every Texas high school girl was supposed to want that Maggie finally said: 'We'll talk to your father about this when he gets back from Falfurrias,' and when Roy Bub Hooker pulled the hunting wagon up to the Morrison residence at eleven-thirty that night, Maggie called upstairs: 'Beth, come down and let's talk about this.'

To her joy, her father sided with her: 'I don't see anything wrong with a little cheerleading, if that's what her school features.'

'But, Todd, it's a step backward. It surrenders all the gains women are beginning to make. Next you'll be entering her in a beauty contest, bathing suits yet.'

'Nothing wrong with bathing suits, properly filled out.'

Beth allowed her parents to fight the thing out and was gratified when her father won, but next morning she found that it had only appeared that way, because her mother blocked the door at seven-thirty when Beth prepared to run out and join the kids in the car for first-day practice of the cheerleading squad. 'Hey, Killer!' they called. 'Time's wastin'.'

'Beth cannot join you,' Mrs. Morrison informed them. 'I'm so sorry.'

Inside the door, Beth stood white and trembling. 'Mom!' she cried, dropping the customary *Mummy*. 'If I can't be a cheerleader, I'll die.'

'If you can't be a contributor, a brain at whatever level you're capable of, you'll really die. Now eat your cereal and be off to school like a proper scholar, which you are.'

For three unhappy days the sparring continued—Mr. Morrison siding with his daughter, and Mrs. Morrison standing like Horatius at the bridge table, as he said, refusing to allow her daughter to take what she called 'this first step down to mediocrity.' It then looked as if Beth was going to solve the problem by refusing to eat until she starved; poetry, math, her designs for a new fabric, all were forgotten in her determination to be one of the gang and to gain the plaudits of her fellow students.

The impasse was resolved in a manner which Maggie Morrison, trained in Michigan and with Michigan values, could never have anticipated, but on the Friday of that first awful week she was summoned from her real estate desk to the office of Mr. Sanderson, principal of Deaf Smith High in north Houston: 'Mrs. Morrison, I'm sure you know you have a most superior daughter.'

'I want to keep her that way.'

'But you cannot do it by opposing her natural desire to be one of our cheerleaders.'

'I doubt that cheerleading is natural.'

'At any serious Texas high school it is.'

'It oughtn't to be.' She was startled by her willingness to fight but was convinced that she was fighting for the preservation of her daughter's integrity and intelligence.

'Mrs. Morrison, I think we'd better have a serious talk. Please sit down.' When she was seated, her legs fiercely crossed, her jaw forward, he charmed her by saying: 'I wish we had more mothers concerned about the welfare of their daughters. Feel free to come here and visit with me about these things at any time.'

'I'm visiting now, and I don't like what you're doing to Beth.'

'Mrs. Morrison, she is no longer in Michigan. She's in Texas, and there's a world of difference. No girl in Houston can achieve a higher accolade than to be chosen for our cheerleading team, unless maybe it's to be the baton twirler. To have the approval of the whole student body. To stand before her peers, the prettiest, the most popular. Mrs. Morrison, that is something.'

'Is it true, Mr. Sanderson, that your high school has eleven football coaches?'

'We need them. In this state, competition is tough.'

'And is it true that four out of five of Beth's teachers this year are not prepared in their academic subjects, because their first responsibility is coaching?'

'Our coaches are the finest young men the state of Texas produces. Your daughter is lucky to share them in the classroom.'

'But can a coach of tight ends teach a girl poetry?'

'At Deaf Smith we don't hit poetry very heavy.'

'What do you hit?'

'Mrs. Morrison, I run one of the best high schools in Texas, everybody says so. Beth will tell you the same. These aren't easy years, drugs and all that, new social pressures, Negroes and Hispanics knocking at the door. Holding a big school like this together is a full-time job, and one of the strongest binders we have is football. I want every child in this school to be involved in our team, one way or another.'

'Even the girls?'

'Especially the girls. Football at Deaf Smith is not a boy's empire.' He pointed to the stunning photographs that decorated his office: 'The girls' marching squad, best in the state. The cheerleaders, runners-up last year. The rifle-drill squad, have you ever seen a nattier bunch of kids? And look at the number of girl musicians we have in our band, and their spiffy uniforms.'

There were also girl baton twirlers, three of them, the pompon squad and the marshals. Maggie was startled by the overflowing abundance of girls, smiling, stepping, preening, twirling their wooden rifles, tossing their batons in the air.

'And I've saved the good news till last, Mrs. Morrison. Here's a report I received from Mrs. Crane the week before you startled us by your refusal to let Beth take her logical place in the system,' and he handed her a typed report from the woman who directed the girls' activities and who taught world history on the side:

> I have been watching Beth Morrison closely, and she gives every indication of having the hands, the necessary skills and the innate sense of balance which are required to make a great baton twirler.

> Let's keep her on the cheerleading squad for the time being, but let's also watch her very closely, because I think she has the ability to become a twirler of university class.

Mr. Sanderson rocked back and forth on his heels as Maggie read the heartwarming report, and he reflected on how many mothers in his district would be overjoyed to learn that their daughter might one day be chief twirler at a major college. He waited till she had digested the report, then smiled and lifted his hands, as if to indicate that this had resolved all problems.

'Mrs. Morrison, your daughter has a chance to achieve what every girl dreams of.'

Maggie felt beaten, but she still wanted to protect her daughter: 'I don't think

Beth would find much happiness being a baton twirler,' to which Mr. Sanderson said, with some asperity: 'If she's going to make her life in Texas, she will.' Quickly he modified that harsh statement: 'You and your husband are happy here, aren't you? I've heard he's doing famously. Syndications and all.'

'We're increasingly happy.'

'Then look to the future, Mrs. Morrison, that's all I'm asking of you.'

So Beth Morrison appeared one day with pompons and what she called 'a really cool uniform,' and apparently Mrs. Crane liked what she saw of Beth's coordination because two weeks later Beth came home with a silver baton and the exciting news that 'Mrs. Holliday, who's trained all the real cool kids, is willing to give me special lessons, Saturday and Sunday. Fifty dollars for the first course.'

She did not immediately drop her interest in words and colorful images, for she had become addicted to a silly game called 'The White House.' It consisted of asking a partner: 'What do you call the White House?' and when the other person said: 'I don't know. What do you call the White House?' you said: 'The President's residence.'

For several weeks she pestered her parents and her brother with her questions, and one night she crushed them with what she called 'a four-alarm sizzler': 'What do you call a Canadian Mountie who works undercover?' and the answer was: 'A super-duper trooper-snooper.'

About this time Maggie came upon that remarkable study of child genius and music in which it was pointed out that from a society much like America's between 1750–1830, Europe produced hundreds of gifted musicians because that was the thrust of the society; that was what counted in Germany and Austria and Italy. 'Today in America,' reasoned the study, 'we have the same amount of innate talent, we must have because the genetic pool assures that, but we concentrate on games, not music or the arts. So we produce a plethora of great athletes and no musicians, because parents and schools do not want Mozarts or Haydns. They want Babe Ruths and Red Granges, and so that's what they get.'

She was about to discuss this with Beth when her daughter appeared one evening after school dressed in one of the sauciest, sexiest costumes the older Morrisons had ever seen—certainly they had not expected to see their daughter in anything like it—the uniform of a baton twirler, with padded bosom, padded rump and tightly drawn waist. She was totally fetching as she pirouetted before her family: 'What would you call me tonight?' When each had guessed wrong, she said: 'A sassy lassie with a classy chassis.'

Beth Morrison, once headed for English honors at the University of Michigan, had changed her plans.

In these exciting days her father was playing a game much more daring than twirling or football. He had learned from his mentor, Gabe Klinowitz, how to put together a real estate syndicate, and he had already launched three, with outstanding success. 'What you do,' he explained to his wife, 'is find a group of people with money to invest, doctors and dentists primarily, because they often have ready cash, and oilmen if you can get to them. You have to keep it less than thirty-six, because beyond that level Internal Revenue says: "Hey, look, that's not a syndicate, that's an ordinary stock offering," and you fall under much stiffer rules. But suppose you find seven partners, twenty thousand dollars each. There's a lot of people around Houston who have twenty thousand dollars they'd like to play with.'

As he said this he stopped: 'God, Maggie, doesn't Detroit seem a far distance? Nobody up there had even two thousand dollars.'

He went on: 'Now, everybody knows that seven people cannot run a business, so they agree that you, who have the time, will be the general partner in charge, and they will be the limited partners. Very careful legal papers spell this out. You are to make the decisions. So with the hundred and forty thousand from the seven of them . . . you put in no money of your own, you're the manager. So with their dough as down payment, you buy this great piece of property worth three million dollars. Immense future. You get ten percent of the action as your fee, plus another five percent as broker if and when you arrange a deal to sell it.

'With your hundred and forty thousand dollars you've sewed up a hundred acres of choice land, worth millions later on, but you've paid only a down payment, long-term payout, everybody happy. Now, here comes the tricky part, and you have to have nerves of steel. The day comes when you sell that gorgeous piece of land so that your investors can get their money out plus a reasonable profit. And who do you sell it to? To yourself. You wave around a little money of your own as if you were putting it up, a new set of investors who pay for everything, and under the legal document determining what you can do as general partner, you sell it to the new group, not informing your earlier partners of your participation in the new syndicate.

'You already own ten percent of the sale price, and there's that five percent for acting as broker, and here's the clever part. You leave on the table—'

'What do you mean *leave on the table?*'

'Gabe taught me. Always leave on the table a reasonable profit for the other man. You see to it that your original partners each make a nice profit. Not spectacular, respectable. Everybody's happy, presto-changeo a lot of action, and you wind up with forty percent of the new syndicate, which now owns one hundred extremely valuable acres, and you started without a cent in the kitty.' He chuckled: 'And of course, you pay yourself a nice brokerage fee, which gives you even more ready cash.'

'Sounds illegal to me.'

'As legal as the Bank of England. All you have to do is keep your group of investors so happy that they won't try to oust you as general partner.'

It was legal, but it was not honorable, and after a second syndicate had been sold by its original owners to another consortium controlled by Morrison, at a price far below real value, Gabe Klinowitz, one of his partners, came to see him: 'Todd, this is an unhappy day. I'm pulling out of your deals.'

'You've made money on them.'

'You've seen to that. But nowhere near what I should have made. I'm like your other partners. You trickle down just enough to keep us from suing you. I can't afford scandals, neither can they. But we know what you've been doing.'

'But wait a minute, Gabe. You and I . . .'

'That's the sad part, Todd. If you would do this to me . . . Do you realize how much you owe to me?'

'It's on my mind constantly. I told Maggie just the other day . . .'

'If you would do this to a friend, Todd, some day you'll do it to a stranger, and he'll throw you in jail . . . or into a coffin.'

'Now wait . . .'

'We play hard in Texas. In Houston we play very hard and very rough. But we play honest. A handshake is a handshake, and by God, you better not forget it. Twice with me you've abused a handshake, Todd, that Gulf Oil deal and now this. Sooner or later when you do that around here, somebody blows a very loud whistle, and either the sheriff or the undertaker comes running. Goodbye, Todd. Keep your nose clean. Right now it's very dirty.'

As if he were intuitively aware that what he was doing was immoral if not illegal, Todd would not permit his quail-hunting friends to participate in his first syndicates, but when they heard of the considerable profits being made in such deals, they wanted in. Now, when he had a firm grasp of the intricacies, he told them on a ride south to their lease: 'All right, you clowns, you wanted to share in the action. I have a lead on a swell chunk of property north of FM-1960 but well south of Route 2920, place near Tomball, two hundred choice acres, about ten thousand an acre.'

'Hey,' the oilman said, 'that's two million bucks.'

'But we don't put it up. Most we have to contribute, maybe ten thousand each. The rest, a mortgage, long payout, whatever interest the seller demands, because the rate of growth on this property is going to be sensational. Let time take care of the mortgage and the interest.'

They were approaching Victoria when he made this proposal, and Roy Bub who was driving as usual, slowed down and stared at him: 'You sneaky sumbitch When you bought my place you didn't have a nickel to your name, did you? Al hokey-pokey and fancy dance steps.'

'Did you lose a penny on the deal, cowboy?'

'No, and I've been tryin' to figure out who did.'

'Nobody, that's who. We were playing the Texas game, all of us, and that tim it worked. It can work this time too.' His final talk with Gabe Klinowitz ha scared him, and he had vowed that on this deal with his three friends, he would play it completely honest; they would share totally in any growth this land achieved, and if there was a sale, it would be at arm's length to some complete stranger, with all the papers visible to the partners.

He was so determined to avoid the traps that Gabe had warned about that he even called on Gabe in the latter's grubby office: 'You scared me, Gabe. I can see what you were warning me about, been brooding over it. Three of my close friends and I are organizing this syndicate for some choice land up by Tomball. I want you to come in, open books and a final sale to some third party. Clean.' But Gabe said: 'I never double back.' And when the time came to liquidate the Quail Hunters' Syndicate, as they termed it, Todd could not resist putting together a secret syndicate in which he had an unannounced share and of which he would be the sub rosa general partner, and he sold the Tomball acreage to this syndicate for about half its real value.

In addition to his share of the Quail Hunters' profit, he took a ten-percent brokerage fee for handling the sale, and a huge percentage of the new syndicate. Todd Morrison was now a multimillionaire.

When Maggie Morrison made out the family's income tax she discovered that in liquidating the Quail Hunters' Syndicate, her husband had inadvertently failed to distribute to his three hunting partners profits to which they were legally entitled, and she drew his attention to this oversight. Todd, not wishing to reveal that his retention of those profits had been far from accidental, said with ill-feigned astonishment: 'Maggie, you're right. There's forty-eight thousand dollars they should split among them,' and she replied: 'At least.'

So on the next drive down to Falfurrias he told the men, as if bringing good news which he had uncovered: 'Hey, you junior J. P. Morgans! Final figures on our syndicate show that we have an unexpected forty-eight thousand to split up,' but when the cheering stopped and time came to tell them it would be split three ways, for it was their money, he found himself saying: 'So that means an extra twelve thousand dollars for each of us. Come Monday, we can all buy new Cadillacs.'

When the Cobbs settled into their home north of Levelland, Sherwood started immediately to make his gin the premier one in the area, and he began in the traditional way: He became a vociferous supporter of the Levelland Lobos, who consistently seemed to wind up their seasons three and seven, if they got the breaks. The countryside appreciated his enthusiasm and entered the judgment that 'this here Cobb is dependable.' From this solid foundation he could build.

At the end of the third year, Sherwood gathered Nancy and their children in the kitchen and spread the figures before them: At Lammermoor, 119 pounds of lint to the acre, bringing 9¢ a pound. In Waxahachie, 239 pounds at 28¢ a pound.

Here in Levelland, 391 pounds at 42¢ a pound. Year's profit from cotton, gin and other operations—$149,000.

In view of these figures he advised his family not to complain about the disadvantages of living atop the Cap Rock: 'This is the cotton capital of the world, and no gin in the United States processed more of it last year than we did. I'm putting every cent we earned into more land and more wells. This can go on forever.'

It was a sultry afternoon in May when Ransom Rusk and Mr. Kramer were on Rusk's patio discussing the latter's work in providing armadillos for the leprosy research in Louisiana. It was going well, Kramer said, and new discoveries were being made every month, it seemed, toward an ultimate cure for Hansen's Disease: 'They don't like to call it leprosy any more. The Bible gave what's an ordinary disease a bad name.'

To the surprise of the two experts, Lady Macbeth and her eight witches were moving about, long before sunset, and this was so unusual that Rusk commented on it, and Kramer said: 'Something's afoot,' and they watched the little insect-eaters for some minutes as they darted here and there, their armor reflecting in the sun.

Then, suddenly, the mother began rounding up the four youngest pups and nudging them toward their burrow in the middle of the former bowling lawn, and as she herself headed for the hole, the four older pups galloped across the lawn and beat her to the entrance.

'They must know something,' Kramer said, and before he could begin to speculate on what it was, a maid came onto the patio: 'Radio says tornado watch!' and Kramer dashed inside. Telephoning a friend who helped him maintain a close guard on the weather, he spoke only a few words, then ran back to Rusk: 'Not a watch. A real warning. Tornado touched down at the southern end of Tornado Alley.' The words were ominous.

'I must get to my anemometers,' Kramer cried, running toward his car.

'Stay here!' Rusk bellowed, and so imperative was his voice that the expert on weather obeyed.

From a vantage point on the second floor of the mansion, they studied the southwestern sky, supposing that the tornado, if it sustained its forward motion, would move north along its customary corridor, and they had been in position only briefly when they saw a sight that meant horror to anyone who had ever experienced a tornado. As if some giant scene shifter were rearranging the sky, the desultory clouds which had been filtering the heat were moved aside, their place taken by a massive black formation.

'It's a real one,' Kramer said quietly. He started below, seeking some sturdy archway under which to hide, but Rusk grabbed his arm: 'We have a cellar.' So for some minutes the two stayed aloft to watch the frightening cloud.

It came directly at Larkin on its way to Wichita Falls, and Kramer spotted the twister first, a terrible, brutal finger reaching down, a black funnel twisting and turning and tearing apart anything unlucky enough to lie within its path. It was going to hit, and hard.

'One of the big ones,' Kramer said.

But still Rusk held fast, mesmerized by the awesome power of that churning finger as it uprooted trees, tossed automobiles in the air and disintegrated houses. His final view, before Kramer dragged him to the first floor, was of the upper cloud moving much faster than the lower spout, with the latter trailing behind and trying to catch up, destroying everything in its way as it did so.

Rusk showed remarkable control, checking rooms as he ran: 'Everybody to the cellar!' On the ground floor he led the way to the heavy door that opened upon a flight of steel stairs, at the bottom of which waited a small, dark room lined with bottles of water, dehydrated foods, medical supplies and blankets. With that door closed, the household members were as safe as anyone could be with the needle of a tornado passing overhead.

Walls shook, windows shattered as suction pulled them outward from their frames. A roar like that of a train passing echoed through the heavy door, and even this strongly built house trembled as if made of the frailest adobe. For one sickening moment it seemed as if the rooms above were being torn apart, and a Mexican maid began to sob quietly, but Rusk reassured her in an effective way: 'Magdalena, when the storm ends, the people out there will need your help,' and he issued directions: 'As soon as I open the door, fan out and collect the wounded. If you find any dead bodies, put them on the lawn out front.'

When Rusk gingerly opened the door, the servants scrambled up the steel stairway to view the desolation. No windows were left along the south and west faces of the mansion. Large chunks of the roof had been torn away. In the garden, trees had been uprooted, and to demonstrate the grotesque power of the storm, a small bungalow had been carried two hundred feet through the air and deposited upside down in the middle of the bowling lawn, its structure intact.

After a brief survey, the servants began to search the streets and alleys, and the tragic task of finding bodies in the rubble began. Some were miraculously pulled free minutes before they would have suffocated; others would not be found for two days. Mr. Kramer saved four men by piping oxygen to them through metal tubes which he forced through debris that could not at the moment be moved. One woman was distraught, for her five-year-old son had been torn from her arms and sucked high into the air, to be thrown down she could not guess where. Frantically she searched for him through the mass of damaged buildings, and she was trying to tear boards away to look for him when a neighbor found him four hundred yards away, unscathed.

Fourteen people died in Larkin, ten of them in automobiles, a heavy toll for such a small town. 'Remember, damnit,' Mr. Kramer muttered as men helped him pull a body out of one of the crushed cars, 'worst place to hide in a tornado, your car. Wind must have lifted this one three hundred feet in the air and smashed it down. We'll need torches to get him out.'

The dead man inside was Dewey Kimbro. For seventy years he had roamed Texas, looking for carboniferous signals. Four times his discoveries had made him a millionaire; four times he had allowed the money to slip away. His will distributing his final fortune displayed his customary gallantry, for it awarded two hundred thousand dollars each to the five women with whom he had been entangled, and that included the girl Esther, whom he had brought to Larkin with him that first time but had never married. When the citizens heard of his generosity to the women who had given him so much trouble, they forgot how they had censured him, and said at his funeral: 'Good old Dewey, he was a character.'

Of course, when his will was probated the court found that it had less than three thousand dollars to distribute; all the wealth Dewey had accumulated in those last wonderful years in the Permian Basin had been dissipated. The tombstone, which Ransom Rusk erected, said: A REAL TEXAS WILDCATTER.

. . . TASK FORCE

For the past twenty-eight years Lorenzo Quimper had participated in the Texas Olympics, that is, Man *versus* Mesquite, and the score stood Mesquite 126, Quimper 5, which was better than many Texans did.

Whenever Lorenzo had acquired a new ranch he started the same way, as if following the score of a ritual ballet: 'Cándido, we've got to clear these fields of mesquite!' In 1969 he had tackled his first field: 'Cándido, we'll chop it down.'

He and his Mexican work force did just that, using power saws instead of axes, and they did a respectable job: 'Meadow's completely clean.' But since the pesky mesquite had one very deep taproot plus innumerable laterals for every branch that showed above, this laborious cutting was nothing more than a helpful pruning. Nearly two years later: 'Good God, Cándido! There's more out there than when we started!'

So in 1970 he and his workers burned off the mesquite, but this was a dreadful mistake, because the ashes served as a perfect fertilizer for the roots; a year later the fields were positively luxuriant, not with grass but with new mesquite.

In 1972, following the advice of experts at A&M, he once more cut down the trees and then used acid on the visible roots, and this did kill them, definitely. But his acid reached only some six percent of the roots, whereupon the survivors leaped into action to take up the slack. 'You'd think there were devils down there, proddin' them to spring up through the soil,' he groaned one day, and Cándido said: 'You may have something there, boss.'

In 1974 a new group of experts, including men from the great King Ranch in South Texas who had fought mesquite for half a century, visited the Quimper ranches to demonstrate a new technique: 'What we do, Lorenzo, is cut the tree off at the base of the trunk, then use these two huge tractors to drag a chain which cuts deep beneath the soil. We don't just pull up the main roots, we root prune the entire plant, get all the little trailers.'

For three years the Quimper ranches looked fairly good, with a minimum of mesquite, but by 1977 the savage trees were back in redoubled force: 'They been sleepin', Mr. Quimper, jes conservin' their strength.' They had a lot of it when they reappeared, so that in 1978, Lorenzo said: 'To hell with it,' and his costly fields grew a little grass for his cattle, a lot of mesquite in which his quail, his deer and his wild turkeys could hide.

Of course, Il Magnifico did not lose completely; as the score indicated, he did win five times, but only because he poured into selected fields a modest fortune in dynamite, tractors, chains, acid and muscle. He calculated that for a mere $6,000 an acre any man could effectively drive mesquite off land which had cost $320 an acre to begin with. His victories were Pyrrhic, but he did have a limited revenge.

Since our June meeting was to be held in the nearby German community of Fredericksburg, Quimper invited us to spend the preceding evening at what he called 'my home ranch,' on Lake Travis, west of Austin. When we entered his living room we saw that he had finally triumphed over his mesquite. He had directed Cándido to cut down two hundred of their biggest mesquites—most of them not over ten feet tall or eight inches across—and from the cores of these trunks his men had cut a wealth of squares, three inches on the side, half an inch thick. Using them as parquetry, he had fitted them into a heavy cement base and then burnished the surface with heavy buffers usually reserved for marble.

When the floor was leveled and smoothed, and after a thin silicone paste had been applied and polished to a gleaming finish, the result was a most handsome floor. The jagged patterns of the mesquite thus laid bare formed an intricate work of art: predominantly purple but with red, green, yellow and brown flecks or scars. 'It's a floor of jewels!' said one delighted visitor. And it was, the neat squares of wood showing a thousand different patterns, a hundred variations in color.

Lorenzo had triumphed, but it had not been easy: 'Come out here to the workshed. Look at that pile of burned-out saw blades. Cutting that floor was hell.' He looked at the stack of blades, nearly three feet high, and said: 'Of course, doin' the library was even worse. The blocks were smaller.'

Our session the next day was memorable, for it consisted of three unique stages.

When we convened for breakfast in Fredericksburg, one of the finest small towns of Texas, with an immensely wide main street, good German restaurants, European music and citizens eager to make visitors welcome, we were met by representatives of six of the state's minorities: Germans, Czechs, Italians, Poles, Scots and Wends, and we could have talked with twenty other such groups had we had the time, for Texas is truly a state built from minorities.

When the speaking ended, the groups brought in dance teams in native costume and regional orchestras playing unfamiliar instruments, and as we applauded, older people served ethnic dishes of wondrous complexity. This was a Texas which not many outsiders imagined, and among the scores who entertained us, there was not an oilman or a cowboy.

After lunch we drove fourteen miles east to adjacent rural parks, one national, one state, honoring Lyndon Baines Johnson. At the heart of the parks, overlooking the Pedernales, stood an unpretentious one-room house which had been converted into a recreation center. Here we held our afternoon session, at which three scholars from New York and Boston addressed us on the significance of Johnson's occupancy of the White House. As we met there in a meeting to which the public had been invited, we could see the hill country that L.B.J. had loved, we could feel his tall, gangling presence, a sensation that was enhanced when Lady Bird herself came unannounced to invite us to refreshments at her ranch across the river. Texas history seemed very real that day.

When we ended our meeting at six-thirty, we were handed another surprise by Il Magnifico: 'The missus and me are throwin' a little do back at our ranch in favor of our daughter, Sue Dene, her sixteenth birthday, and we want y'all to come. Spend the night.' So we piled into the limousines which Rusk and Miss Cobb provided for the occasion and drove the forty-odd miles back to the Quimper ranch. As we saw that splendid rolling country of scattered oak, mesquite and huisache, Efraín said to Miss Cobb: 'I imagine a newcomer from the wooded hills of New Hampshire or from the real mountains of Montana would find this rather ordinary. But when you've worked all day in steaming Houston and fly up here in your own plane on Friday night, this must seem like heaven.'

'It is,' she said.

As we approached Lake Travis, which came into being in 1934 when the Colorado River was dammed, I commented on the incredible good luck that seemed to crown any Quimper real estate venture: 'Do you have a crystal ball?' and he replied apologetically in country style: 'I swear to you on a stack of Bibles, my pappy was just ridin' along here one sunny day in 1930 and said to hisself: "Some day they'll build a dam here and make theirselves a lake." So he bought seven thousand acres at sixty-three dollars each, and now it's worth six thousand an acre, five times that much if it fronts the lake.'

'How was he clever enough to foresee that?' I asked, and Lorenzo said: 'He had no privileged warnin'. Just believed that whenever you grab onto Texas land, somethin' good is likely to happen.'

At the entrance to his ranch a massive stone gateway had been erected in a style borrowed from ancient Assyria, monstrous blocks of granite piled helter-skelter but with dramatic effect; as we passed through these stones uniformed police hired for the evening directed us to an assembly area—ten or fifteen acres kept cleared by a flock of sheep—where several hundred people awaited instructions.

After our cars were unloaded, a whistle blew, policemen waved, and a make-believe train of nine cars dragged by a tractor-locomotive pulled up to carry us to wherever the girl's birthday party was to be held. The train took us along a country lane, through a stand of oak trees and onto another empty field. Traversing this at slow speed, it brought us into an area which caused us to gasp.

To prove to his daughter that he loved her, Quimper had hired a complete circus: there stood the Ferris wheel, the two merry-go-rounds, the Bump-a-Car enclosure, the Krazy Kwilt Palace of Delights with its distorting mirrors, the barkers luring people into the free sideshows, and the line of cages with lions, tigers and bears. Six clowns did impossible things and the high-wire act was enthralling.

At the height of the show the lead clown came roaring across the field in a Mercedes 450SL, vanity license plates Q-SUE, which he presented to the Quimper girl as her birthday present. Miss Cobb whispered: 'Doesn't every lassie get a Mercedes?' But my attention was diverted to a scene that was taking place between Quimper and his wife. I heard him tell her: 'Honey, we're in trouble! We're runnin' out of food.'

'Impossible,' she said. 'I baked the cookies myself. Thousands of them. And we have more than enough barbecue.'

'That's not the problem. About a hundred of our neighbors have seen the lights and they've come over to join in the fun.'

It was a warm-hearted party, and by Texas-rich standards, not preposterous or even ostentatious. The Quimpers had the ranch, they had the money, and they enjoyed entertaining their neighbors. Above all, they wanted to be sure their daughter and her friends met the right kind of young people against the day when they must choose their marriage partners, for, as Mrs. Quimper said, 'if they don't meet people from the right schools and the right families, they might marry just anybody.'

We were sitting in Quimper's living room and congratulating ourselves on one of the best days our Task Force had spent when the whole façade collapsed, for Mrs. Quimper brought into the room one of the men who had addressed us that afternoon, a Professor Steer from Harvard, forty-eight years old, suave and sure of himself in his gray-touched hair, bow tie and London tailoring. 'What a coincidence,' he said as he reached for a drink, and settled down. 'My son, who's doing graduate work at SMU, is one of the young men out there dancing with the young ladies, especially a Miss Grady, and he dragged me along. I never dreamed you were the people I'd been addressing this afternoon.'

'We're mighty glad to have you,' Quimper said, bringing him a plate of barbecue.

The conversation started well, with Steer asking our two older men: 'In Texas, are you considered oilmen or ranchers?' to which Quimper replied: 'In this state a man can have thirty oil wells and a little ol' nothin' ranch with a thousand acres and six steers, but he calls hisself a rancher.'

Rusk, trying to be amiable, said: 'I have many friends who never wear a cowboy Stetson in Texas but always when they go to New York or Boston.'

Miss Cobb said: 'You'll find, Professor Steer, that Texas ranchers like to brag about their prize bull, the pilot of their airplane and their unmarried daughter, in that order.'

Tricked by the apparent warmth of this greeting, Steer said: 'I'm so glad to find you here. I sort of held back on certain fundamentals this afternoon. Too many of the public listening.'

'Like what?' Quimper asked, and the professor startled me by the frankness with which he responded.

'I should have pointed out that Lyndon Johnson suffered bad luck in ascending to the presidency in the way he did.'

'How so?' Quimper probed.

'Well, John Kennedy, for whom I worked, was a charismatic type, handsome, well groomed, educated, able in leadership, and gifted with a beautiful, sophisticated wife.'

As this was said I happened to be looking at Rusk, a Republican leader who had contributed to Johnson's campaigns but voted against him. He was studying his knuckles, not looking up, so I could not ascertain how he might be receiving this attack upon a fellow Texan.

Steer continued: 'A regrettable aspect of Johnson's ascendancy was that he came, in our interpretation . . .' Here I noticed that Steer had subtly changed from referring, as he had in his speech, to the Eastern Establishment as *them*, and was now including himself in the ruling group.

'We saw Vice-President Johnson as a prototypical citizen of Dallas, the city which had killed the real President.'

Miss Cobb interrupted: 'Dallas didn't kill anybody. A crazy drifter from New Orleans and Moscow did.'

'But the nation perceived it as a Dallas crime, and I must admit, so did I.'

'Why?' Miss Cobb asked.

'I was working for President Kennedy in those delicate days . . . twenty-one years ago this week. I'd accompanied Adlai Stevenson to Dallas when the women leaders of your society spat upon him.'

'It was not my society,' Miss Cobb protested. 'They were right-wing extremists. You find them everywhere.'

'But especially in Dallas.'

Since no one could reasonably contest this, Steer plunged ahead: 'I was in the advance party that bleak November day in 1963 when Kennedy made his fatal visit. I was not near him . . . far off to the side when the motorcade came swinging into Dealey Plaza. But at breakfast I had presented him with the *Dallas Morning News* and its dreadful, irrational attack. You know what the last words he said to me were? "We're heading into Nut Country today." And a short time later he was dead. In my interpretation, and it remains very firm this November, Dallas killed him.'

There was with Texans like the five of us a residual shame for what had happened back in 1963, and we were sophisticated enough to realize that some of what Professor Steer was so arrogantly reconstructing was true. The climate of Texas at that time, especially in Dallas, had been antithetical to much of what Kennedy as President stood for, even though the state had voted for him in 1960, and even though our own son, L.B.J., had been instrumental in squeaking him into the White House by the slimmest margin ever. We were not disposed to argue vehemently in defense of Dallas.

But now Steer, obviously pleased with the progress he was making in hacking Texas down to size, continued his impetuous drive: 'What happened was that Johnson came to impersonate the worst of Texas as opposed to the best of New England. Texas was anti-labor, we were pro. Texas was fundamentalist in religion, we were enlightened. Texas was deficient in education, we stressed it. Texas was uncouth, the voice of the barbarian, New England was gently trained, the voice of academe. Texas was cowboys and oil, the North was libraries and theater and symphony orchestras. Texas was the raw frontier, Boston was the long-established bulwark of inherited values. And what was especially difficult for us to accept, Texas was flamboyant nouveau riche, and the Northeast had long since disciplined such ostentation.'

I saw that Quimper was about to explode, but what Steer said next delayed the fuse: 'I grant you that in those days Texas had energy and wealth and sometimes valuable imagination. But it was not a likable place, and few in the Establishment liked it.'

For the first time Rusk spoke, deep in his chest: 'How exactly do you define the Establishment?'

This was the kind of question Steer liked, for it provided an excuse to parade his skill at summarization: 'I suppose I mean the opinion makers. The agencies that give us our mind-sets. Two newspapers, *New York Times* and *Washington Post.* Three magazines, *Time, Newsweek,* the London *Economist,* the three networks, and one special publication, the *Wall Street Journal,* plus the faculties of the better universities and colleges.'

'And what are those better schools?' Rusk asked as if he were ignorant, and Steer obliged: 'Yale, Harvard, Princeton and maybe Chicago. Brown, yes, and maybe Dartmouth. A few of the smaller colleges like Amherst and Williams. A smattering of the old girls' schools, Vassar, Smith, perhaps Bryn Mawr.'

'They're the ones who passed judgment on Lyndon Johnson?' Rusk asked.

'We found him quite unacceptable.'

Again I watched Rusk carefully, and he said no more, just kept studying his knuckles, which were now white. He was not under pressure, but he was listening intently.

Steer, unaware of how close he was to a live volcano, proceeded with what was for him a fascinating bit of social phenomena: 'I think Texas is destined to play Rome to our Greece.'

'What do you mean?' Quimper asked, and Steer responded: 'When Greece lost world leadership to Rome, she fell back to the perfectly honorable role of providing Rome with intellectual leadership—art, history, philosophy, logic, world view. Rome had none of these, could create none from her own resources. But she could borrow from Greece . . . import Greek tutors, Greek managers. And the symbiosis proved a fruitful one.'

'What's *symbiosis* mean?' Quimper asked naïvely, even though I'd heard him use the word at our last meeting.

'Interlocking relationship, each part depends on the other.'

'Could the Texas-Massachusetts symbiosis be fruitful?' Quimper asked, and Steer said he thought that perhaps it could: 'You'll continue to inherit our representation in Congress, and you'll provide the money, the energy and, yes, the vitality I suppose, all very necessary if an organism is to survive.'

'What will you give us in return?' Lorenzo asked sweetly, and Steer said: 'The intellectual analysis, the philosophical guidance, the historical memory. Believe me, a raw state like Texas will not be able to go it alone. Rome couldn't.'

'Will Texas ever be accepted? By your Eastern Establishment, I mean?' Quimper asked.

'Oh, when time softens your raw edges. When the television show *Dallas* slinks off the tube, if it ever does. When your petroleum reserves deplete and you can no longer terrorize us with your oil money.' Up to this point neither Rusk nor Quimper showed any inclination to dispute our visitor's analysis, but Steer stumbled ahead and triggered a bear trap: 'The real test will be whether any of your colleges or universities can become first class. If they do, maybe the rest of America will be able to tolerate your extravagances.'

Now came an ominous pause, during which I looked at Professor Garza, who was smiling quietly and shrugging his shoulders as if to ask me: 'Why should we two sane people get mixed up in this?'

So I was not watching when Rusk rose from his chair and straightened his drooping shoulders to their full height, but I did turn quickly when I heard him say in his deep, rumbling voice: 'Get out of here!'

When Steer mumbled 'What? What?' Rusk lost control and fairly bellowed 'Get the hell out of here!' and I saw with horror that he was trying to grab our visitor by the neck.

'You can't do this!' I cried, interposing myself between the two men, but then Quimper lunged forward, as if he too wanted to throw the Harvard man out, and I looked to Miss Cobb for help, but to my dismay, she was encouraging the men.

Before either Rusk or Quimper could reach Steer, I engineered our tactless visitor out the door and put him on the path to where his son would be. When I returned, I looked in dismay at my associates, but they showed no remorse. They had been mortally offended by the Establishment's renewal of its assault on the dignity of Texas and had absorbed all the abuse they could tolerate. They were pleased at having ejected him.

'Why did you become so enraged?' I asked, and Rusk said: 'When a Yankee denigrates L.B.J., he denigrates Texas. And when he insults Texas, he insults me.'

'You never supported Johnson,' I said, and he agreed: 'Voted against him every time he ran. But he was a Texan, and I cannot abide—'

I broke in to ask Quimper if he'd ever voted for Johnson, and he said: 'I've voted in various ways at various times.'

At this point Mrs. Quimper appeared with a plate of fresh barbecue, and I was privileged to witness Quimper's face-saving victory in his war with mesquite. When Garza asked: 'How do you make your barbecue so delicious?' Lorenzo took him by the arm: 'I'll show you!' and he led us to a huge woodpile back of the house where rows of mesquite logs, twenty-one inches long, lay stacked.

'On each of my ranches I have crews doin' nothin' but harvestin' mesquite. We grow it now as a cash crop.'

'What for?' Garza asked, and Quimper said: 'We ship it to topflight restaurants all over America. 'Twenty-One' in New York, the Plaza, that type. Everyone with money to spare orders Texas-style beef.' He kicked at the pile affectionately: 'I'm known as The Mesquite King of Texas. I'm makin' more on mesquite than I am on my boots. Like I always said, don't ever think Texas is licked till the fat lady sings.' Then he stared at us and snapped his fingers: 'Tomorrow mornin' I'm stoppin' all shipments to Boston. Those Ivy Leaguers don't deserve mesquite.'

XIV
POWER AND
CHANGE

WYOMING

Cheyenn•

Denver•

COLORADO

SOUTH DAKOTA

NEBRASKA

IOWA

Lincoln•

KANSAS

MO.

Santa Fe•

OKLAHOMA

20"

98°

Amarillo

WEST OF 98°
DEFICIENT RAINFALL
FOR AGRICULTURE

EAST OF 98°
ADEQUATE RAINFALL
FOR AGRICULTURE

NEW
MEXICO

ARK.

25"

Lubbock
DENVER

Wichita Falls•
Minneapolis

30" 35"

40"
Red River

45"

Jefferson•
Memphis

10"

15" 20"

15"

Abilene•
Sioux Falls

Athens•
St Louis

LA.

El Paso•
Phoenix

50"

Waco•
Detroit

Fort Stockton•
Los Angeles

TEXAS

Beaumont•
Charleston

20" 15"

Houston•
New York City

50"

15"

MEXICO

Rio Grande

40" 45"

35"

30"

TEXAS RAINFALL

Figures show yearly average precipitation in inches
with comparison cities

0   MILES   200

20"

25"

98°

GULF OF MEXICO

D URING MOST OF ITS HISTORY THE CITIZENS OF TEXAS WERE POOR.
When the Garzas trekked north from Zacatecas in 1724 they were
virtual slaves, with pitiful housing, inadequate food and never a second set
of clothing. The early Quimpers lived in an earthen cave without knowing bread
for almost a year. The Macnabs did through a ruse get land, but they were always
land-poor, and when young Otto finally became a Texas Ranger he served for
miserable pay, if any, and was expected to provide his own horse, gun and clothing. Because the supply of money was so rigidly controlled, he rarely had any.

The Allerkamps labored like lackeys, all of them, and it was a long time before
they had enough to live with any sense of ease. The two Cobb families from
Carolina and Georgia had real slaves, a thriving gin and a lumber mill, but their
Jefferson neighbors did not. Of a hundred Cobb slaves, the ninety field hands lived
in poverty; they had enough food but not a decent house or proper clothes. And
during the Civil War and the Reconstruction, even the white folks in the plantation mansions knew real deprivation.

When Fort Garner folded, Emma Larkin and her husband, Earnshaw Rusk,
owned a fine set of stone buildings and thousands of acres, but they had no money
with which to operate; they spent carefully, but because they could not save up
even a few dollars in ready cash, they almost lost their holdings.

That was the condition of Texas: plenty of land, a niggardly existence, a dream
of better days. However, with the 1901 discovery of limitless petroleum deposits at
Spindletop near Beaumont, some Texans began to accumulate tremendous riches,
and by the 1920s even families as far west as the Rusks in Larkin County shared in
the bonanza. In Texas one could leap from land-poor to oil-rich in one generation
. . or one weekend.

Now the perpetual poverty of Texas was obscured by the conspicuous display of
wealth, and the history of the state began to be told in dollar signs followed by big
numbers, and some could be very big, because here and there certain lucky Texans
became billionaires. To the rest of the nation it sometimes looked as if the dollar
sign governed the state.

For example, as the decade of the 1980s opened, the whole state seemed to be
in what gamblers called a roll, with each throw of the dice producing a winning
even or eleven. Everything looked so promising that enthusiasts started voicing
the old boast: 'This can go on forever.'

There was solid reason for believing that Texas was certain to achieve national leadership, for the census then under way would show that the state had gained so much population—3,009,728 in ten years—it would gain three new seats in Congress, while the less fortunate states in the cold Northeast would lose twice that number.

As always, oil was the harbinger of good fortune and when, with help from the Arab states, it soared to thirty-six dollars a barrel, Ransom Rusk's bank in Midland told its depositors: 'Oil has got to go to sixty, expand now,' and funds were provided for this next round of extraordinary gambling.

Airlines with a strong Texas base, like Braniff and Continental, freed at last from the petty regulations of the Civil Aeronautics Board, were flying into scores of new cities and picking up astronomical profits, while TexTek, the computer sensation based in Dallas, was, as its shareholders boasted, 'soaring right off the top of that Big Board they run in Wall Street.' More than two dozen millionaires had been created through ownership of this stock, with three or four early investors, like Rusk, garnering nearly five hundred million each.

The sensation of the Texas scene, however, was Houston real estate, for it had no discernible upward limit. Farmers who owned land to the north and west of the city could demand almost any price an acre—$50,000, $100,000—and there were many takers who knew that with just a little break, they could peddle it off at a million an acre. Investors from West Germany and Saudi Arabia were hungry for Houston real estate, but the major profits came from those Mexican politicians who had stolen their country blind and were now stashing their fortunes in the security provided by Houston hotels and condominiums. Anyone who could build anything in Houston could sell it: office space, hotels, condominiums, private homes. And if real estate ever did lag, the city could rely upon its oil industry. 'Houston is the hottest ticket in the world,' its boosters said.

The aspect of Texas life which seemed to give its noisier citizens the greatest boost was the Dallas Cowboys football team. Dubbed by an enthusiastic publicist 'America's Team,' it caught the nation's fancy, and year after year its stalwarts appeared in the play-offs and Bowl games. At the same time, in obedience to the sage precepts established by Friday night high school football, young women were enrolled in the madness, the Dallas Cowboy Cheerleaders becoming famous for the skimpiest costumes and the sexiest routines. A Cowboys' home game became ritual at which devout Texans worshipped, for the players on the field were heroic and the cheerleaders along the sidelines irresistible. Boasted one partisan: 'Our football girls make those in New York and Denver look like dogs.' Just as the Larkin Fighting Antelopes had consolidated public enthusiasm in that small Texas town, so the Dallas Cowboys solidified enthusiasm and loyalty across Texas and in many other parts of the nation.

Nowhere was Texas optimism more obvious than in Larkin, where Ransom Rusk judged the week beginning 2 November 1980 to be the finest he had ever known. He was fifty-seven years old and resigned to the fact that the rest of his days would be spent in convenient bachelorhood; his mansion in Larkin was now staffed exclusively by illegal Mexican immigrants who performed well and taught him Spanish; the bowling lawn, which had dominated his life during his married years, was now a pleasant grassland, kept reasonably neat by a gang mower that shaved it twice a month.

One could say that he spent Sunday of this week with his beasts, for as his relations with other human beings, starting with his divorce from Fleurette, diminished, his reliance upon animal friends increased. Early morning was dedicated to his armadillos, a mother, father and four males this time; they had dug themselves into both his garden and his heart and had learned to come for vegetable roots when he whistled, their golden bodies shimmering in the dawn.

At about ten in the morning he rode out to his ranch, also run exclusively by Mexicans, none legal residents, and a more pleasant day he could not recall. Some seven years back he had gotten rid of his white-face Herefords, the breed introduced by his grandfather Earnshaw, and had started raising Texas Longhorns, whose strain had been kept alive by his grandmother, Emma Larkin Rusk. He had purified his herd until it contained only the MM/BB strain, animals descended from Mean Moses and Bathtub Bertha.

On Sunday mornings he liked to observe a ritual that re-created the grandeur of the vanishing Texas frontier: throwing a heavy paper sack in his Jeep, he would drive down the lane leading away from his ranch house and into a large fenced-in field at whose far end stood a beautifully scattered grove of trees. There, on a rise, he would halt the Jeep, blow the horn three times, and stand in the open, rustling his stiff paper bag.

On this Sunday, he did so for at least ten minutes, accomplishing nothing, and then slowly from distant trees shadowy forms began to emerge, hesitant, cautious, for they were wily animals. But as the sound of possible feed reached them they became more daring, and big Longhorn steers, handsomely mottled in gray and brown and white, began walking tentatively toward Rusk.

Another appeared and then another, until more than thirty had left the trees, and when they were in the open, reassured that no danger awaited them, they broke into a quiet lope that soon turned into a run. On they came, these wonderful animals out of the past whose survival had been made possible only because some Texans loved them, and as they drew closer, Rusk could see once more the tremendous horns these selected steers carried, great rocking chairs set on their heads. When they were nearly upon him, hungry for the food he promised, he studied them as if they were his children, and jumbled thoughts raced through his head:

No plotting man framed your character. Nature built you, alone on the prairies. Storm killed off your weaklings. Drought slaughtered those that had no will to survive. In years of hunger, you learned to eat almost anything, to forage off the moss of rocks. Through merciless selection, you learned to produce very small calves with a fantastic determination to grow into big adults. I don't waste money on veterinarians when I raise you Longhorns. You animals raise yourselves, just like us Texans.

When the first steers were eating all about him, so close that he could reach out and touch them, a huge old animal emerged from the woods and started walking in stately steps toward the feast, and when he approached, the others moved aside. He was Montezuma, self-appointed lord of the herd, and he maintained his noble advance until he stood nose-to-nose with Rusk, demanding to be fed by hand. For a moment these two survivors, gamblers of the plain, stood together, the great horns of Montezuma practically encircling Rusk.

Of all the cattle in the world, only you Longhorns produce a steer worth saving. Steers of all other strains are sent off to the butcher at age two, but you live on because men prize you, and want to see you sharing their land, for you remind them of the cleaner days. It's good to see you, Montezuma.

As he stood there surrounded by these incredible beasts, he could not escape, as a businessman, making a calculation: After the War Between the States, when Texas hadn't a nickel, our grandfathers herded ten million Longhorns to cowtowns like Dodge. At forty dollars a head, that meant four hundred million dollars pumped into the Texas economy when scarcely a dime was reaching it from other sources . . . Montezuma, you Longhorns rebuilt this state.

Saluting his treasures, he drove back to a remarkable new building adjoining his mansion, and there, as his Mexican butler served cold drinks, he watched his favorites, the Dallas Cowboys, play at St. Louis. Had the game been in Dallas, he would have occupied his private box, entertaining, as usual, twelve or fourteen business acquaintances. He cheered when Wolfgang Macnab, a linebacker he had sent to the University of Texas on a football scholarship, mowed down St. Louis like an avenging scythe: 'Tear 'em apart, Wolfman. I knew back then you were headed for greatness.'

The building in which he sat was named the African Hall, for it resembled a stone lodge he had seen in South Africa's famed Kruger Park. He had built the place in his loneliness after his divorce when he had associated himself with a group of bachelors in similar circumstances who took safaris to Kenya, where in the splendor of its animal parks they shot kudu and giraffe and lion, bringing the heads home to be displayed on Texas walls. Rusk's hall was one of the best, and to sit surrounded by his handsome trophies while his Cowboys rampaged on the TV screen was a delight.

On Monday, when he drove to his office in Fort Worth, his two accountants asked if they might see him, and he expected trouble, for they rarely approached with good news, but this time was different: 'Mr. Rusk, a singular development in Mid-Continent Gas has produced a situation in which you may be interested.'

At the mention of this name, Rusk had to smile, one of his thin, sardonic smiles, because he was thinking of the time when the Carpenter Field roared in with an almost unlimited supply of natural gas: 'Remember how my stupidity made me miss that bonanza completely?'

But the field had been operating only briefly when he saw an opportunity for a gamble of staggering dimension: 'The owners had no way of getting their gas to market. So I organized Mid-Continent and guaranteed them thirty-two cents a thousand cubic feet for all they could produce for the next forty years. They jumped, thinking they'd stuck me with gas I wouldn't be able to market, either.'

'I worked on that pipeline you bulldogged through the hills,' the chief accountant recalled. 'Nobody believed you could do it, including me. That was one hell of a job, Mr. Rusk.'

Against professional advice, against prodigious odds, Rusk had driven his pipeline across sixty-seven miles of rolling hell, and when he was through he found an insatiable market for his gas: 'I bought it at thirty-two cents, sold it for a dollar ten and thought I was making a fortune. But when it went to three dollars and twenty-two cents, I did make a fortune. A thousand-percent profit. And for the past two years, we've sold it for nine dollars and eighteen cents. That's a nearly three-thousand-percent profit, and all because we took those insurmountable chances.'

'That's what we wanted to show you,' the accountants said, and on a pristine sheet as neat as a tennis court they presented him with two figures:

New estimated value Mid-Continent Gas at present prices	$448,000,000
New estimated value your total holdings	$1,060,000,000

When Rusk looked briefly at the figures, he realized that he was now officially Texas rich. It was in large part due to the antics of the Organization of Petroleum Exporting Countries, which had so increased the value of his oil holdings that he had accumulated some ninety million dollars which he had not known about.

Rusk had never been heard to say a bad word about OPEC, his standard comment among his friends being: 'Maybe those Arabs are extortionists, but they do our work for us.' If oil still brought ten dollars a barrel, he would not be a billionaire, but when the price soared to nearly forty, he became one.

'It will go to sixty,' he predicted, and based on this hope, he doubled his stable of rigs and drilling crews. He also believed that the northeast section of the United States must accustom itself to much higher prices for Texas gas, of which he was now a major supplier: 'For too long they've had a free ride at our expense. I don't want to gouge them, but I do want them to pay their share of the freight.'

To arguments, advanced by some, that such talk represented an economic holdup and a conscious drive to steal the leadership of the United States away from New York and Boston and into the so-called Sun Belt, he replied: 'The leadership of this nation rests with those of us who see its future clearly and who use creatively whatever leverage God has given us. The future must lie with those parts of the nation which have our remarkable mix. Oil, brains and courage.'

He was never arrogant about his beliefs, advancing them quietly but with irresistible force. When truckdrivers employed by his companies to move oil pasted insulting bumper stickers on their vehicles—LET THOSE BASTARDS UP THERE FREEZE—he made them scrape them off, but he did allow them to keep others that came close to representing his thoughts—YANKEES OUT OF GOD'S COUNTRY—and he positively chuckled over the brilliance of the beer advertising which proclaimed that Lone Star was THE NATIONAL BEER OF TEXAS.

'We are our own nation,' he told his friends, 'and it's our duty to see that our ideas prevail throughout the friendly nation which lies to the north.' He was not speaking of Canada.

It would be a mistake to visualize Rusk as some wizened gnome, evil in purpose, huddling in his vault at night, counting his wealth. He was tall, straight, beetle-browed, good-looking, and easily able to smile when not furiously pursuing some special interest. But more than a year could pass without his being more than vaguely aware of the value of his holdings; he certainly never brooded about it. He knew it was tremendous and he intended keeping it that way, as his daring support of Pierre Soult's Texas Technologies proved. TexTek had not merely been a good idea; it had been stupendous, and under the inspired leadership of the Frenchman, had often swept the field before competitors even guessed what the company had in its long-range plans. Office-sized computers, word processors, software, superb merchandising, TexTek had pioneered them all, and in doing so, had multiplied Rusk's impulsive investment many times.

This enabled him to operate rather boldly in fields which concerned him, such as the disciplining of labor and the expulsion from public life of woolly-headed liberals like many of the Northern senators, but he never thought of himself as reactionary: 'I represent the Texas experience. The land, always the land. My grandmother had no nose, no ears, but she did have this glorious land we sit on. My grandfather, that crazy Quaker, was a dreamer who stocked their land with those great bulls from England. My father probed the land for oil. And because I was working the land with seismology, I stumbled into TexTek. We never had any nefarious designs, no special tricks. We stayed close to the land and accumulated power, which I am obligated to use sagaciously.'

But it was not the placid Sunday in the country or the startling financial news on Monday which made this week so memorable. Tuesday was Election Day, the culmination of Rusk's effort to bring this nation back to its senses, and he rose early in his frugal Fort Worth apartment and drove out to Larkin to cast his vote. He rarely used one of his Mexicans as a chauffeur, because he loved the feel of a big car eating up the superb Texas highways, and on this exciting day, when he had lots of time, he opted for a road that was only slightly longer than the direct route through Jacksboro. He preferred this more southerly road, for it took him through Mineral Wells, where he liked to stop at the edge of town and contemplate an enormous building that dominated the skyline: Fifty years ago it was one of the supreme hotels in America. Hollywood stars, New York bankers, everybody came here to take the waters. How many rooms? How much glory? And now a rotting shell. On three different occasions excited investors had come to him with plans for revitalizing the great spa, and always he had told them: 'It was a fine idea in its day. Well, that day has gone. Look at it standing there empty, a ghost of Texas grandeur. And look at the little motel at its feet, filled all the time. You change with the times, or the times steamroller you.'

From Mineral Wells he headed for Graham, where he controlled a dozen wells, and then on to Larkin, where the ten o'clock crowd of women voters filled the polling places. He cast his ballot in the basement of the handsome courthouse, then went to his home to make and receive telephone calls.

Six years earlier he and a handful of other Texas oilmen had quietly assembled to discuss the future of their state and their nation, in that order, and he had warned them: 'God and the American way have allowed us to accumulate tremendous power in this Republic and we would be craven if we did not apply it intelligently. That means that we must defeat communists in office, regardless of what state they operate from, and replace them with decent Americans.'

'Have we the right to interfere in other states?' a timid man from Dallas asked, and he snapped: 'When McGovern casts his South Dakota vote in the Senate against our interests, he becomes a Texas senator, and I say: "Kick him the hell out of South Dakota." We've got to protect South Dakota from its own errors.'

'You're saying that we'll enter campaigns in all the states?'

'Wherever there's a man who votes against the interests of Texas. To accomplish this cleansing of public life we must spend money . . . and I mean a great deal. We're fighting for the future of this great nation.'

In the present election he had, by various intricate devices, poured contributions into different campaigns across the country. The bulk of it went to support Ronald Reagan, a most attractive man who had often lectured to Texas business groups on the dangers of communism, the need to muzzle our central bureaucracy and the absolute necessity of eliminating the national debt, but Rusk had also pinpointed various Democratic senators, real crazy liberals, who had to be defeated, plus a variety of notorious congressmen who had spoken against what he called Big Oil.

All of them were to be expunged, and as the long day wore on, he spoke with various allies around the nation: 'Rance! Looks like we might oust them all. Glorious day for the Republic!'

Before the sun had set in Texas he was assured, as he sat alone in his Larkin mansion before the two television sets, that Reagan had won, but he was startled by the ineptness of Jimmy Carter in handling the situation: My God! He's conceding while the Western polls are still open! That must damage his people in tight races out there. He threw down the newspaper whose tabulations he was checking off: That poor peanut grower never had a clue. How did we ever allow him to be President?

Still the resplendent night rolled on, and during an exulting phone call to friends in Houston, he shouted: 'By damn, we showed them how to win an election. We cleaned house on the whole damned bunch.'

He did not go to bed, for he wanted to hear the final Alaska returns, and when he learned that candidates he had backed so heavily retained a slight lead, with prospects of a much larger one when the rural districts came in, he leaned back, stared at the ceiling, and reflected: A man works diligently for what he believes in, and when the fight grows hot, he'd better throw in all his reserves. What did we contribute, one way and another? Eleven million dollars, more or less. Small price to pay for the defeat of known enemies of the people. Small price to ensure good government.

Toward morning he learned that the Democrats had held on to their seat in Hawaii, but he dismissed this with a growl: 'They're all Japs, anyway. They'd bear some looking into. Maybe next time we can fix that.' Of nine Democratic incumbents that his team had targeted, seven had been defeated, and as the sun rose on Wednesday morning he told his fellow conspirators on the conference call: 'We're going to rebuild this nation to make it more like Texas.' When an oilman in Midland asked what that meant, he said: 'Religion, patriotism, the old-fashioned virtues, and willingness to stand up and fight anybody. The things that make any nation great.' His father, Fat Floyd, had voiced exactly those sentiments sixty years earlier.

But then, when Texas seemed impregnable, changes began to take place in all aspects of Texas life, subtly at first, like a wisp of harmless smoke at the edge of a prairie, then turning into a firestorm which threatened all the assumed values.

The Sherwood Cobbs, at their cotton farm west of Lubbock, were one of the first families to detect the shift. One afternoon an event occurred which seemed a replay of that day in 1892, when a former slave ran to the plantation house at Jefferson with the startling news that boll weevils had eaten away the heart of the cotton crop. That information had altered life in Texas, and now another virtual slave, brown this time instead of black, Eloy Múzquiz, the illegal Mexican field hand, came running to the Cobb kitchen with news of equal import: 'Mister Cobb! Deep Well Number Nine, no water!'

'Electricity fail?' The 1952 Chevy engines were no longer used.

'No, we tested. Plenty spark.'

'Maybe the pump's gone.' Cobb said this with a sick feeling, because for some months he had been aware that the water table upon which the Lubbock area depended had dropped toward the danger point. Could the failure of #9, a strong well, be a warning that the mighty Ogallala Aquifer was failing? He did not hazard a guess.

During the first ten years on their cotton farm in Levelland, the Sherwood Cobbs realized that they had, by some fortunate chance, stumbled upon a paradise. Of course, it had required a special aptitude for anyone to appreciate that it was a paradise, for their land was so flat that even when the slightest haze intervened, no horizon could be identified; it started level and went on forever. Also, it contained not a tree, and what locally passed for a hedgerow was apt to be six inches high and covered with dust. Distances to stores and towns were forbidding, and when the sun went seriously to work in June, the average temperature stayed above ninety, day and night, for nearly four months. In 1980 there had been twenty days, almost in succession, when it soared above one hundred.

But with air conditioning it was bearable, and during the winter months there were about a dozen inches of snow; 'white gold,' the farmers called it, because it lingered and seeped into the ground. Of course, extreme cold sometimes accompanied the snow, with the thermometer dropping to minus seventeen on one historic occasion.

Only rarely did the year's total rainfall exceed sixteen inches, but with deep pumps working, water from the aquifer was poured out in a stream so reliable that the cotton really seemed to jump out of the ground. 'The part I appreciate,' Cobb said, 'is that you can lay the water exactly where you want it, when you want it.' He also mixed fertilizer and needed minerals in the flow, so that while he irrigated he also nourished.

'You might call it farming by computer,' he told his sons. 'We calculate what we've taken from the soil and then put it back. Same amounts. Properly handled, fields like ours could go on forever.'

The results were more than gratifying. Back east, a bale of lint to an acre; here, two bales, and of a superior quality. This area around Lubbock was the dominant producer in America and one of the best in the world. A gin like Cobb's on the road from Levelland to Shallowater produced five-hundred-pound bales of pure silver, so consistent was the quality and so assured the value. Brokers in Lubbock often dominated the world's markets, for what they supplied and in what quantity determined standards and prices.

'Imagine!' Cobb exulted one night after finishing a long run with his gin. 'Finding land where there's always enough water and a boll weevil can't live.' It was a cotton grower's dream, which explained why so many of the plantation owners in East Texas had made the long leap west.

But now, as he jumped in his pickup to inspect #9, he had a suspicion that the great years might be ending, and he inspected the silent well only a few minutes before telling Múzquiz: 'Go get the Ericksons.'

When the brothers drove up to the well, Cobb clenched his teeth as they delivered the fatal news: 'Same everywhere. The Ogallala has dropped so fast . . . these dry spells . . . the extra wells you fellows have put in.'

'What can I do?'

'For the present, we can chase the water.'

'Meaning?'

'Deepen all your wells.'

'How much deeper?'

'The Red Bed, on which our part of the Ogallala rests, is two hundred feet down. The wells we dug for you back in 1968 go down only one hundred feet.'

'What did they cost?'

'Thirty-five hundred dollars per well.'

'How many must I deepen?'

'Twenty,' and the estimates they placed before him showed that the cost of merely deepening an existing well was going to be more than twice the cost of one of the original five: 'To do the digging, fifteen hundred dollars. To install the submersible pump, five thousand. To wire for electricity and protect the system, one thousand. Total per well, seventy-five hundred. Total cost per twenty wells, a hundred and fifty thousand dollars.'

'Have I any alternative?' Cobb asked, and the brothers agreed: 'None.' Then the younger added: 'Each year the aquifer drops only slightly. But the rate of fall is steady, and soon it'll fall below your present pumps. But if we go down to Red Bed, you ought to be safe for the rest of this century.'

The older brother summed it up: 'Stands to reason, Cobb, you wouldn't want to call us back to redig your wells two or three times, just to keep pace with the drop. Dig 'em once. Dig 'em right. Dig 'em deep.' So Cobb chased the aquifer downward.

Even those farms which used windmills to work their pumps, and many did, had to deepen their wells, but when the pipes were safely down, these farms had assured water, because the winds on the plains could be relied upon: 'And sometimes they can be trusted to blow the whole mill flat as a freshly plowed field.'

Weather in the Lubbock area was rugged, no doubt about it, with the blazing summers, the frigid winters and now and then a tornado to keep people attentive, but the challenges could be rewarding, and the warm social life of the area diverted attention from the hardships. The Cobbs were especially appreciative of the local university. Texas Technological College it had been called when they arrived, but with the hard practicality which governed so much of Texas life the legislature had listened to the complaint of a West Texas representative: 'Hell, ever'body calls it Texas Tech, and that's how those who love it name it. I propose that the name be officially changed to Texas Tech, and while we're about it, let's make it a full university.'

So there it was, Texas Tech University, with a curriculum of agricultural, mechanical and modest liberal arts programs. Its students were sought after in the oil fields and in Silicon Valley, but what residents like the Cobbs especially appreciated were the cultural programs it sponsored: a string quartet now and then, a choral presentation of an opera—no sets, no costumes—or a series of three Shakespearean plays. Challenging lectures were available, with notable conservatives like William Buckley applauded, and farmers like the Cobbs could easily arrange casual meetings with the professors.

But what gratified Nancy Cobb, and attracted her most often to the university, was the unequaled ranch museum it had put together: a collection of houses and buildings assembled from all over the state, showing how ranchers had lived in the various periods. Thirty minutes among these simple structures, with their rifle ports for holding off the Comanche, taught more of Texas history than a dozen books.

One hot afternoon in 1981 when Nancy had taken a group of visitors from the North to see the open-air museum—it covered many acres—she was standing before one of the box-and-strip houses built by the 1910 pioneers and explaining how the settlers, deprived of any local timber, had imported it precariously from hundreds of miles to the east, and had then used it like strips of gold to shore up their mud-walled huts, and as she talked she began to choke: 'It must have been so hellish for the women.'

One symposium series gave the Cobbs a lot of trouble, for a lecturer predicted that the day would come, and possibly within this century, when the rising cost of electricity and the constant lowering of the water table would make agriculture on the Western plains uneconomic:

> 'And I do not mean marginally uneconomic. I mean that you will have to close down your wells, abandon your cotton fields, and sell off your gins to California, where their farmers, because of sensible planning, will have water. We would then see towns like Levelland and Shallowater revert to the way they were when the Indians roamed, except that here and there the traveler would find the roots of houses which had once existed and the remnants of towns and villages.
>
> 'We could avoid this catastrophe if all the states dependent upon the Ogallala Aquifer united in some vast plan to protect that resource, but all would have to obey the decisions, because any one state, following its own selfish rules and depleting the aquifer, could defeat the strategy.'

Cobb, extremely sensitive to the problem of which he was a vital part, and interested in possible solutions, raised enough donations from local farmers and ranchers to offer Texas Tech funds for conducting a symposium on 'Ogallala and the West,' which attracted serious students from across Texas and representatives of the governments of all the Ogallala states.

It was a gala affair, with Governor Clements giving the keynote address and with two lectures each morning and afternoon on the crises confronting the Western states. As the talks progressed, especially those informal ones late at night, several harsh and inescapable conclusions began to emerge:

. . . The Ogallala was not inexhaustible, and at its present rate of depletion, might cease to function effectively sometime after the year 2010.

. . . Diversion of rivers and especially the snow-melt from the eastern face of the Rockies could be let into it to revitalize it, but such water was already spoken for.

. . . Strict apportionment at levels far below today's usage would prolong its life.

. . . State departments of agriculture were prepared to recommend more than a dozen ways in which farmers and ranchers could use less water.

. . . Texas would soon see the day when it would be profitable to purchase from surrounding states like Oklahoma, Arkansas and Louisiana, and perhaps from those as far away as Colorado, entire rivers and streams whose water would be piped onto its thirsty fields. (Delegates from the named states hooted this proposal.)

. . . Commercial desalinization of Gulf waters plus great pipelines west might well be the answer, if nuclear energy were to become available at low rates.

. . . Every state, right now, must organize itself on a statewide basis to ensure the most prudent use of every drop of water that fell thereon.

It was in the working out of this last recommendation, which the conference adopted unanimously, that Cobb learned how divisive a subject this was insofar as Texas water users were concerned, because when the Texas delegation met, these points were stressed by the more active participants:

Ransom Rusk, Longhorn breeder: 'Every word said makes sense. But what we must take steps to ensure is that cattle raisers be allowed to retain the water rights on which they've built their herds, often at great expense.'

Lorenzo Quimper, operator of nine large ranches, some with serious water deficiencies: 'Regulation and apportionment are inescapable, but we must protect the backbone industries of the state, and in them I include ranchin'. Cattle cannot live without water, and from time immemorial their rights have been predominant and must remain so, if Texas is to continue the traditions which made it great, and I must say, unique.'

Charles Rampart, cotton grower, north of Lubbock: 'You need only look at the level of the aquifer year by year to know that something must be done, but the prior rights of our wells in this agricultural area, and I drilled mine in the 1950s, they've got to be respected. All the wells in this region will have to be grandfathered. If they're in, they stay in.'

Sam Quiller, farmer, Xavier County: 'The irrigation ditches that lead off the Brazos River to water my fields date back to 1818. Any court of law would support my claim that those rights, and in the amounts stated, are irreversible. Read *Mottl v. Boyd* and you'll find you cannot impede the flow of the Brazos.'

Tom and Fred Bartleson, fishermen, mouth of the Brazos: 'Water must be regulated, we all know that. But I would ask you to keep in mind that Texas courts have said repeatedly and confirmed repeatedly that a constant flow from rivers like the Brazos must be maintained so that a proper salinity in the waters just offshore be protected. That's where we catch our fish. Those are the waters our restaurants and supermarkets depend upon.'

At the end of the conference it was pathetically clear that Nebraska, Colorado and all the other aquifer states would repel even the slightest attack upon their sovereignty, and that every user in Texas appreciated the need for others to conserve water so long as his inherited rights were not infringed. Almost every drop of water inland from the Gulf Coast had been spoken for, usually in the nineteenth century, and to reapportion it or even control it was going to be impossible. Since the Ogallala Aquifer was a resource which could not be seen, the general public had no incentive to protect it; the Brazos and the Colorado and the Trinity were already allocated and could not be touched. Arkansas and Louisiana needed the water they had, and would repel with bayonets anyone who attempted to lead away even a trickle. So all that could be done was to continue exactly as things were, and then sometime in the decade starting in 2010, when disaster struck, take emergency measures.

'No!' Cobb cried when the insanity of this solution hit him. 'What we should do right now is build a huge channel from the Mississippi into Wichita Falls, and pipelines from there to the various Texas regions.' The idea was not fatuous, for millions of acre-feet of wasted water ran off each year past New Orleans, but when he seriously proposed such a ditch as a solution, experts pointed out: 'Such a channel would have to run through Arkansas and Oklahoma, and that would not be permitted.'

When Cobb checked the water level at the new pumps the Erickson brothers had installed, he found that it had fallen by an inch and a quarter, and it was then that he decided to seek nomination as a member of the Water Commission.

A second Texan to become personally aware of the big shifts under way lived at the opposite end of the state. Gabe Klinowitz, the real estate operator who had sponsored Todd Morrison when the latter drifted down from Detroit, was immensely informed concerning land values. His last big venture had been with a group of seven Mexican political figures to invest the massive funds they controlled.

They had stunned him with the magnitude of what they wanted to do, but in obedience to their orders, he had quietly assembled the costly land and then watched as they spent $170,000,000 on The Ramparts, an interlocking series of the finest condominiums in Houston. Irritated by this brazen display of wealth by citizens of a nation which sent a constant stream of near-starving peasants into Texas for food and jobs, Gabe consulted with a University of Houston professor who specialized in Latin-American finances: 'Tell me, Dr. Shagrin, how do these people get hold of so much money?'

'Quite simple. They've learned how to outsmart our New York bankers.'

'You lose me.'

'Don't apologize. Took me two years to unravel the intricacies.' And with that, he spread upon his desk a series of figures so improbable that they perplexed even Klinowitz, who was accustomed to the chicaneries of mankind: 'From impeccable United States government sources I find that our big banks have loaned the Latin countries to the south three hundred billion dollars. And from equally reliable sources in the recipient countries, I find that clever politicians and business magicians have diverted one hundred billion dollars into either secret Swiss accounts or business ventures here in the U.S.'

'Would you care to give me a synonym for that word *diverted?*'

'How about *legally embezzled* or *cleverly sequestered* or good old-fashioned *stole?*' He laughed: 'Whichever you elect, the result's the same. The money we loaned them is no longer in the country where we hoped it would serve a constructive purpose.'

'The original loans, will they ever be repaid?'

'I don't see how they can be, with the money vanished from the countries. I see no way that the Mexican government can recover the money your group has wasted here in Houston.'

'Have you the figures for Mexico?'

'I haven't assembled the accurate figure for the total loans, but I can prove that in 1980 they borrowed sixteen billion from us and allowed their manipulators to siphon off more than seven billion of our dollars into their private accounts.'

'As an American taxpayer,' Gabe said, 'I'd like to know what happens if the original loans go sour.'

'You guessed it. One way or another, you'll pay.'

Gabe frowned: 'If the American money had been kept in Mexico, could it have forestalled the poverty we see?'

'Now you touch a very sore point, Mr. Klinowitz. From the very beginning, Mexico was always much richer than Texas. Anything we did for our people, they could have done for theirs.'

'What went wrong?'

'I use the word *diverted*. It avoids moral judgment.'

So Klinowitz was not surprised when the peso, its backup funds having been so callously diverted, began to stagger: 36 to the dollar one day, 93 the next, 147 later, then 193, with a threat of further plunging. He was prepared and almost gleeful when the Mexican politicians flashed the distress signal: 'For the time being, halt all construction.'

But he was a professional real estate man and was actually relieved when the Mexicans rounded up some additional capital and resumed building, for as he told Maggie Morrison: 'I have pains in my stomach when a client of mine runs into trouble.' However, he was shrewd enough to add: 'If I were you, Maggie, I'd keep my eye on those three towers of The Ramparts.'

'I'm no rental agency,' she protested. 'That's a heartache business.'

'I don't mean rentals. I've learned that if a building falls into trouble once, it'll do so again.'

'What could I do for the Ramparts people?'

'Maggie! How I wish I was thirty years old, with a small nest egg. In a fluctuating market like this, a daring trader can perform miracles.'

'I don't depend on miracles,' she said cautiously.

'Real money is made in a falling market. Look at the unrented space in this city.'

And when she did she perceived two startling facts. The sharp decline in oil values had caused the bankruptcy of many smaller firms servicing that industry, and this meant that space which should have been rented for offices stood idle. When she totted up the appalling figures she found that 32,000,000 square feet of the finest office space in America stood vacant in Houston.

But what alarmed her more, with the rich Mexicans unable to visit the United States because of the disastrous devaluation of their peso, some twelve or thirteen major Houston hotels were suffering from lack of business. Fine establishments accustomed to seventy- and eighty-percent occupancy were getting no more than twenty or thirty, so that those which had depended on the Mexican trade were shutting down for the time being while others were going onto a five-day week to stanch the hemorrhaging.

Every intuition she had acquired in Michigan warned Maggie to retrench; every lesson she had learned from wise old Texans like Gabe Klinowitz urged her to make bold moves. In this impasse she would have liked to consult with her husband, but he was preoccupied with other ventures, so taking counsel only with herself, she monitored the chaos that seemed to have struck Houston business, but always at the end of day she drove past The Ramparts to check on what the seven Mexican politicians were doing with their beautiful chain of buildings, and every sign she saw whispered confidentially: 'Gabe was right, these Mexicans are in deep trouble.'

The precipitous fall in the peso endangered more than the Mexican politicians, because all along the border, from Brownsville to El Paso, the Rio Grande bridges that once had brought thousands of brown-skinned people into American shops, where cameras, fine clothes, stereos and perfume were sold at bargain prices unattainable in Mexico itself, were strangely empty. The devalued peso bought nothing. For three painful days the Bravo-Escandón bridge, so long the scene of Mexican inflow, had no visitors from the south, and then the activity resumed, but in an ugly way that brought shame to the United States.

American citizens streamed into Mexico to buy at bargain prices all the gasoline, baby food, vegetables and beef the Mexican markets provided, for if the peso was down, the dollar had to be up. The drain of essentials continued. 'The norteamericanos are stealing us into starvation!' came the justified cry from south of the border, and it was in this crisis period that feisty Simón Garza, now the mayor of Bravo as a result of the revolution in voting patterns following the disturbances in the 1960s, projected himself into prominence. By the simple, illegal device of stationing his policemen at the Bravo end of the international bridge and forbidding its citizens from going into Mexico to buy what were bargains for them but subsistence for the Mexicans, he attracted statewide approval.

'We do not profit from the despair of others,' he announced repeatedly, and he said this with such force that even those who had been depriving Mexico of its foodstuffs and means of movement applauded. Belatedly, the Mexican government placed an embargo on its dwindling supplies of food, and the situation righted itself, with the peso at the shocking black-market rate of 193 to the dollar.

But now Mayor Garza was confronted by his own problems, for with the absolute cessation of Mexican traffic into the town, the Bravo stores began to close down, as they were doing all along the Rio Grande. Seeking guidance as to what he must do to halt the strangulation of his community, he attended a meeting of the Valley mayors in Laredo, and in that city he saw real panic, because fully forty percent of the luxurious emporiums were boarded up. Their business had not declined, it had vanished; there was no escape but the immediate firing of all employees and the barring of doors.

If one had ever needed proof of the symbiotic relationship between northern Mexico and southern Texas, it was provided now, because each side of the river, deprived in its own way, staggered toward economic breakdown. Unemployment on the American side rose to twenty, then to forty, percent, and a movement was started to have the region declared a disaster area.

Among all the leaders on both sides of the river, one man stood out for the coolness with which he handled the catastrophe and the steps he took to alleviate it. Simón Garza had been reared in a rugged school, fighting the remnants of the Horace Vigil dynasty, combatting the Texas Rangers who had been determined to keep that dynasty in operation, and insisting that his fellow Hispanics go to college and learn the tricks of American life. 'Eat tortillas at home. Speak Spanish in your games. But learn who Adam Smith and Milton Friedman are.' In this drive toward educating his constituents he was assisted by his brother Efraín, the professor at A&M, who uncovered scholarships at all the Texas universities to which bright girls and boys from Bravo could apply. 'The revolution of the mind,' the Garza brothers cried repeatedly, 'that's what we must engineer.'

It was Simón who persuaded President Reagan, by means of a hard, nonhysterical telegram to the White House, to come down to the Valley to see for himself the devastation wrought by the drop in the peso, and as he led the well-intentioned President past the empty bridge and the boarded-up stores he was photographed with Reagan time and again, so that when the summary meeting was held in Laredo, the Northern reporters, to whom conditions along the Rio Grande were a mystery, suddenly discovered that in Simón Garza, Texas had a Hispanic politician who made sense and who used most cleverly the perquisites of his office. Considerable attention was paid to the grateful statement of the Escandón mayor, who told the reporters in Spanish: 'Garza, he knew what to do. He closed the bridge to keep us from starving.' People would remember this.

In his modest offices in Fort Worth, Ransom Rusk was facing such an assault from all sides that he groaned: 'God must be mad at Texas!' And while he was trying to sort things out, he received a preemptive call from his bank in Midland: 'Better come down here and give us help.' So in his private plane he flew to the Midland-Odessa airport, linchpin in the Texas oil complex, where he was met by the three managers of his service companies, who reported unanimous ruination for anything connected with oil.

'Mr. Rusk, Activated Mud can find no customers at all. I think we'll have to fire everybody.' Electronic Logging was little better, for it showed a ninety-two-percent decline. But it was when he drove to the vast parking area between the two oil towns that he found visual proof of what had happened to the bonanza region, for there, stacked neatly in rows like dinosaurs whose time had passed, stood rusting in the bright sunlight nineteen of the twenty-three giant drilling rigs that would normally have been standing proudly erect in fields scattered across the landscape from the Gulf to New Mexico. Now their towers lay prostrate, their drilling engines silent and gathering dust.

'What did we pay for that last batch?' Rusk asked, and when his drilling manager said: 'Special electronics, special everything, thirteen million each.' Instantly calculating thirteen times nineteen, Rusk said quietly: 'That's two hundred forty-seven million dollars down the drain.' He had multiplied thirteen by twenty and subtracted thirteen.

'Not completely lost,' the manager assured him. 'If oil comes back, which it will have to . . .'

'What could you get for this, right now?' Rusk asked, kicking one of the rigs.

'Maybe a hundred and fifty thousand . . . if we could find a buyer.'

'That's one percent of its value. I call that loss.'

And in that sickening moment by the fallen rigs, there among the dinosaurs whose days of rampaging were gone, Rusk had to make his decision. A powerfully organized man just entering his sixties, he should have been free to enjoy his favorable position in the world, his power and his billion dollars; instead, he found himself attacked on all sides, with foundations crumbling. But he did not propose to go down whimpering. He would fight back with all the energy he had been acquiring through past decades. He would ride out this storm, husband his resources, and prepare to fight back when conditions were more favorable.

'Close down Activated Mud. Just close it down. We'll find something for the top people to do till oil recovers. Electronic Logging, it's got to be of permanent value. What do you suggest?'

It was agreed that logging services would always be required, so long as one man wildcatted anywhere in Texas: 'Mr. Rusk, I think we should retain a core of the real experts, no matter . . .'

'I think so, too. Cut to the bone and hunker down. And these?' Almost lovingly he touched with the toe of his cowboy boot the nearest prostrate rig. 'What in the world do we do with these?'

The question was almost academic, for it had no sensible solution. There lay the mighty rigs, their towering superstructures humbled, and unless prospecting for oil resumed, they would not rise again. They would be valueless.

When none of his advisers offered a sensible solution, Rusk cut the Gordian knot: 'Fan out across Texas. Find young men who are willing to take a risk. Sell off these nineteen idle rigs for whatever they'll bring. But get rid of them. We'll keep the four that are working. For when things start up again.'

'You mean, sell them regardless of what we can get?'

'Exactly what I mean. The gamble for oil passes into younger hands.'

'Mr. Rusk, I want your firm order on this. You're willing to sell this thirteen-million-dollar rig for a hundred and fifty thousand dollars?'

'For a hundred thousand, if that's what it brings.'

With that harsh decision behind him he drove into Midland, where the managers of the bank in which he was heavily invested were in quiet panic: 'Ransom, the bottom is dropping out. It's all quicksand.'

'Just how bad?' And they explained what he had already suspected: 'If you drove in from the airport, you saw the service fields lying idle, your own among them. Did you notice the string of motels? Two years ago they had to limit guests to three nights in a row. Everybody wanted to come to Odessa to get in on the action.'

'I noticed the few cars parked outside.'

'Paul here owns three of them. Eight-percent occupancy. Foreclosures every where.'

Rusk looked at Paul Mesmer, the distressed motel owner, and swore that under no circumstances would he, Rusk, allow himself to look like that. Firmly he asked: 'What's the worst aspect of our situation?' and he listened in a shock he did not betray as these good men, who had expected oil to go to sixty dollars a barrel, explained what they faced when it dropped to twenty-seven.

'Bluntly . . .'

'That's the way I want it, bluntly.'

'We may have to close our doors.'

'How much?'

'A billion and a quarter dollars.'

'That's a manly sum. Depositors protected?'

'In part.'

'Us investors?'

'A complete wipe-out.'

Rusk heard this doleful news without wincing. He had $16,000,000 in bank shares, and to lose it on top of his heavy losses in the oil business would be inconvenient but not disabling. Still, he hated to admit that his business judgment had been faulty, so he asked: 'Any way we can prevent the Feds from moving in?'

'If we all chipped in more of our own money . . .'

'How much you want from me?'

'If you could see your way clear . . . five million.'

'Done.'

'Before you sign anything, Ransom, you realize that whatever you give will be in jeopardy?'

He did not answer the question. Instead, he looked at the embattled directors, these sturdy men of the plains who had gambled fantastically, making it big when things went their way, now willing to put up small fortunes when things turned sour. They were Texas gamblers and they did not whimper.

'I like the way you're handling things,' and he flew back to Fort Worth.

But on the way east he had a vision, you could term it nothing else: The action has got to swing to Dallas. With Houston in trouble on its real estate, and Midland in shock over oil, and the Rio Grande with up to forty-five percent unemployed, leadership passes to Dallas. That's where the big fight for the soul of Texas is going to be conducted. That's where I want to be.

So he directed his pilot to land not at Meacham Field, the city airport for Fort Worth, but at Love Field in Dallas. Radioing ahead for his driver to meet him at the new destination, he sped, immediately upon landing, toward that imposing complex of new construction in North Dallas, some fourteen miles out from the traditional center of the city, and in one of the many rental offices peddling space in the bright new buildings, he rented what would become a major center of Dallas power: Ransom Rusk Enterprises.

He had been in position only a few weeks when the wisdom of this move was proved, because as a major stockholder in TexTek, he was summoned to their board room when that huge conglomerate stumbled into trouble. Pierre Soult, founding genius of the electronics end of the business, had died, throwing his pioneering but fragile company into such temporary disarray that the new management had to inform Rusk: 'Due to increased competition from Japan and an unforeseen collapse in electronic games and home computers, we've experienced a loss in the first quarter of a hundred million dollars and can expect a repeat or worse next quarter.'

'When do we inform the public?' Rusk asked as he calculated the effect on his huge holdings.

'Tomorrow.'

So Rusk was on hand when the devastating losses were announced to Wall Street, and he sat grim-lipped as the ticker reported the sensational drop in TexTek. Within one trading day in New York, the paper value of TexTek stock dropped by one billion dollars.

He was also on the scene, as a major investor, when Braniff Airlines, once the pride of Dallas, stumbled and fumbled, striving vainly to stay alive but missing every tenuous opportunity. In the panic meetings, he gave Braniff management counsel he had given his oil-field managers in Odessa: 'Cut back. Decide ruthlessly what must be done. And do it now.'

He supervised the cutting away of the once-profitable South American routes. He tried to halt the tremendous losses on the new routes the company had unwisely pioneered in recent months, and he did his best to find new funds, but in the end he had to admit: 'We gave it a good try. It's bankrupt.' And Texas travelers through the massive new Dallas-Fort Worth Airport looked shamefacedly at the varicolored Braniff planes stowed aimlessly on the parking lots and tried to calculate the loss in money and pride which their clipped wings represented.

One New York banking expert, dispatched to Dallas to investigate the mood in Texas, reported confidentially to his superiors:

> People outside Texas, especially those in less-favored states like Michigan, Ohio and Pennsylvania, had begun to look upon Dallas and Houston as places where the figures could only go up. Now they are learning with the rest of us that they can also come down. Houston, Midland, Abilene, El Paso, Laredo and the so-called Golden Triangle are disaster areas, and in certain hard-struck industries unemployment reaches past fifty percent.

> Friends in the know advise me that Ransom Rusk, heavily involved in all the fields which have been hit, has suffered staggering losses. I have verified the following: his commanding position in TexTek, loss $125,000,000; sharp drop in the value of his oil holdings, loss $85,000,000; bankruptcy of his mud company and idleness of his nineteen drilling rigs, loss $35,000,000 now, with more to come later; his position in Braniff Airlines, loss $45,000,000; Houston real estate reversal due to peso, loss $14,000,000. Collapse of the Midland Bank, loss maybe $21,000,000. Total Rusk loss in one calendar year: $325,000,000 minimum.

How did Rusk react to these losses, which were much greater than the visitor had estimated? He sat in his new office, surveyed the Dallas skyline with its multitude of soaring new construction, and said only to himself: Now is when I dig in. I have more work to do than ever before. His shoulders did not slump, nor did he try to avoid inquisitors who wanted to ferret out the effect of these stupendous reversals. Instead, he showed his icy smile, stuck out his lower jaw, and predicted: 'Every item in Texas will revive. The Mexican peso will stabilize. Oil will come back. We'll see the rigs operating again. Braniff will fly, we'll see to that. TexTek has a dozen new inventions ready to astound the market. And the Dallas Cowboys will win the Super Bowl.'

'Then you're not pessimistic?'

'I don't know that word.'

When the bad years ended and his accountants showed him the final figures on his losses, he laughed and asked: 'How many of your friends can say they lost nearly half a billion dollars in one year?' and they said: 'Not many.'

But even his aplomb was shaken by a series of those family tragedies which so often enmeshed the very rich in Texas. His famous father, Fat Floyd, had produced two daughters, Bertha and Linda, born almost a full generation before Ransom. Each had had four children, so that Ransom had eight nieces and nephews for whose fiscal welfare he was responsible.

Just as his father had seen ownership of his first well split into minute fragments, so Ransom and the courts supervised the various allocations of ownership of the Rusk Estate. Insofar as the offspring of Bertha and Linda were concerned, the pattern was this:

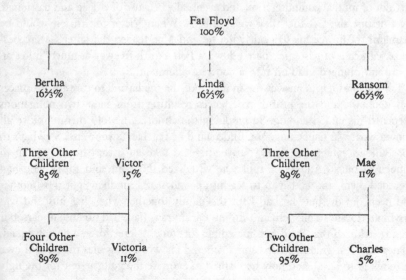

To take only the case of the two fourth-generation children, Victoria and Charles, if one multiplied out the percentages, one found that Victoria owned 0.002750 of the Rusk Estate and Charles 0.000917. Since the Estate, which participated only in the oil portion of Ransom's total holding, was now worth some $700,000,000, this meant that Victoria's share, at an early age, was worth $1,925,000 and Charles' $641,900. And since Ransom's adroit handling of the oil reserves produced a yearly income of about sixteen percent on investments, young Victoria received some $308,000 each year, and Charles $102,700. Various young Texans had comparable holdings.

But these two, and their six siblings, were not enjoying their money these days because their parents had become involved in shattering tragedies. Mae, of the third generation, had married a worthless young man who had angled for her shamefully, caught her, and then found himself unable to maintain pace with her lively interest in Texas life. He had escaped his deficiency by committing suicide.

Victor, Mae's cousin and a most likable fellow, had fared little better. His wife, a beautiful girl but lacking in both character and will, had taken to the bottle early and with great vigor, deteriorating so totally that she had to be placed in an institution. It was one of the finest drying-out establishments in Texas, but it had an inadequate fire-alarm system, and when an inebriated gentleman on the ground floor fell asleep while smoking a cigarette, the entire wing burst into flame, and only the heroic efforts of two Mexican caretakers saved Mrs. Rusk. She was horribly burned, but did survive; however, any chance of escaping her addiction to alcohol vanished, and both she and her family could look ahead only to her lifelong hospitalization.

In this dual impasse, the cousins Victor and Mae started seeing each other, at first out of mutual commiseration and eventually because of a deep and passionate love, despite the fact that they were cousins. When Victor felt that it would be shameful to divorce his stricken wife, he and Mae loaded the latter's Mercedes-Benz with cans of gasoline, roared down a Fort Worth freeway at ninety miles an hour, and plunged head-on into a concrete abutment.

Ransom was left to answer the inquiries of the media and to care for his niece and nephews, and the pitiful experiences resulting from these two obligations deepened his understanding. Summoning the children, he told them: 'You've all known what was happening. You understand better than anyone else. So what's to do? Pull up your socks. Grit your teeth. And take an oath: "It's not going to happen to me." ' And as he spoke he visualized those intrepid Rusks who had preceded them, and he began to see his ancestors in a kindlier light. His mother had been dowdy, but she had kept the family together when her husband was striving to locate an oil well, and Emma Larkin may have had no nose or ears, but he now realized that she'd had incredible fortitude. 'Never forget,' he continued, 'that your great-grandmother Emma suffered far worse tragedies than you'll ever be required to face.' And now he wanted to exorcise the guilt he felt for the ugly manner in which he had once dismissed his parents: 'Don't forget that your ancestor, the one they called Fat Floyd, was willing to gamble his last penny on the oil well that got our family started. He had courage, and so must you.' As he watched the effect of his words upon these young people, he thought: This generation isn't going to be defeated. But then he realized that something more fundamental than fighting spirit was required to build a satisfactory life, so with much embarrassment he stood before them and said softly: 'I love you very much. I will be here to help no matter what happens. Let's stick together.'

Back in his new office, after the accountants had his family's affairs straightened out, he said: 'Well, we can be sure of one thing—1984 has to be better.' And then his old fire returned: 'Reagan'll be reelected, best President we've had in more than sixty years, but a mite long in the tooth. We'll eliminate more of those communists in the Senate. And we'll see oil bounce back. Maybe even Braniff will fly again.' On the phone to Houston he said cheerfully: 'Good and bad, I'd rather be working in Texas than anywhere else in the world.' Then, supremely confident that he would recover his lost dollars within two years, he flew to Kenya for a safari with his friends.

If Ransom Rusk was finding new challenges in North Dallas, a small, sparkling, dark-eyed young woman of twenty-five named Enriqueta Múzquiz was having an even more exciting adventure in South Dallas.

Dallas consisted of three separate cities, really, and it was possible to live in any one and scarcely be aware of the other two. There was downtown Dallas, the historic city on the Trinity River which had boasted two log cabins in 1844 and not much more by 1860. An unpublished diary tells what happened in that year:

> On Sunday, 8 July 1860, the citizens of this town awoke to find every store and rooming house ablaze. When the terrible conflagration was finally brought under control a jury of 52 leading citizens was impaneled and upon their finding that the fire must surely have been part of a slave plot, three Negroes were promptly hanged.

Despite its slow start, downtown Dallas had prospered, and now contained the business heart of a metropolis with more than a million inhabitants and of a metropolitan area with more than three million.

North Dallas, where Rusk had his new office, was a golden ghetto of palatial homes, resplendent new skyscrapers, luxurious shopping centers and a way of life that was, said one critic, 'both appealing and appalling.' It was appealing because it provided what its inhabitants wanted; it was appalling because of its brazen flaunting of wealth. But the true secret of North Dallas was that it was a world to itself; residents could live there quite happily and rarely bother about venturing into the clutter of Central Dallas. Boasted the average North Dallas housewife: 'I go into that maelstrom only when there's a meeting of the Art Museum board.'

And almost no one from North Dallas ever crossed the Trinity River to enter South Dallas, where blacks and Hispanics lived, and rarely did anyone from Central Dallas go there. It was a city to itself, impoverished, poorly cared for, and constantly embattled with its wealthier neighbors to the north. Those residents of Northern states who had imbibed from television and newspapers the illusion that Texas, and Dallas in particular, was populated only by millionaires received a shock if they ventured into South Dallas.

There were many reasons for the impoverishment of this area. Texas, perhaps the wealthiest of the states, was among the most niggardly in its services for the poor, and in certain criteria like unemployment benefits, it stood at the bottom of the fifty states. It was not good to be a poor person in Texas, and downright miserable to be one in South Dallas.

But this was where Enriqueta Múzquiz was having her exhilarating experience. Following that February afternoon in 1969 when she leaped aboard the Southern Pacific freight train in El Paso, she spent her first years in Texas in Lubbock, where she had suffered the full force of West Texas discrimination, which in many ways was worse than anything known along the Rio Grande, since the northern region held so few Hispanics and disregarded them with such insolence.

'When I was young,' she told her fourth-grade pupils, 'no Hispanic was allowed in the better restaurants, and we were not welcomed in the movie theaters. We were expected to quit school at the eighth grade. Boys could not get haircuts in the regular barbershops. And we were held in contempt.' When she gave such lectures, which she did repeatedly and to all her classes, she invariably ended with a refrain which summarized the major triumph of her life:

> 'In 1974 the Supreme Court of the United States handed down a decision called *Lau v. Nichols,* which you must remember, because it is your Declaration of Independence. It did not deal directly with us but with a Chinese boy named Lau, and it said: "Even if he is Chinese, and even if he cannot speak a word of English, the United States of America must provide him with an education, and since he cannot speak English, this education must be in Chinese." Don't you see? The Supreme Court is saying the same to you children. If you cannot speak English, you must be educated in Spanish, and that's why I'm here.'

Señorita Múzquiz, as she wanted her students to call her, even though she, along with her father and two brothers, had attained United States citizenship, spoke to her thirty children in Grade Four and her thirty-three in Grade Three only in Spanish, and in this language, which she was supposed to use only temporarily as a bridge to English, she spent about half her time haranguing them about the injustices of American life, with special emphasis on the inequities they suffered in Dallas.

She did this because she visualized herself as an agency of revenge for all the suffering she and her people had undergone in West Texas, and as she labored to create in her students a burning appreciation of their Spanish heritage and the glories of Mexican culture, she foresaw the day when the Spanish-speaking people along the Rio Grande, south and north, would form a kind of ipso facto republic, half Mexican, half American, in which pesos and dollars would both be used. A common currency and a common outlook on life would prevail, and a common language, Spanish, would be spoken: 'Of course, it will be an advantage if you have English as a second language—to work in stores and such—but the effective language will be Spanish. And the mode of life will be Mexican, with large families closely bound together and with priests who give their sermons in Spanish.'

'What citizenship will we have?' her older children sometimes asked, and she said: 'It really won't matter, because Mexico will not rule the area, nor will the United States. It will be a union of the two, with free passage across the river.'

'How big will it be?' the children asked, and on the map of Mexico that she kept in her room—a map in Spanish, so cut across at the top that it included Texas as far north as Lubbock—she used her pointer to indicate a swath which encompassed San Antonio, San Angelo and El Paso on the north, and Monterrey, Saltillo and Chihuahua on the south: 'The new nation of our dreams already exists. Spanish is spoken up here, and English is understood down there. Trade between the two halves is already flowing and will grow as years pass. Brownsville and Matamoros at the eastern end of the river, who can tell which is which?'

'Will the nation reach all the way to California?' a child asked one day, and she said: 'It already does,' but another child said: 'Señorita Múzquiz, I grew up in San Angelo and they don't speak much Spanish there,' and she said: 'They will, when enough of us come north and fill the places.'

Her dream was not an idle one. There were many living along that protracted border who were already effecting the change which she promulgated with her students during the day and with her adult friends at night. Experts, and even those with only a casual interest, could see that the unstoppable flow of Mexican nationals into the United States must inevitably create a new society with new attitudes and, perhaps, new political affiliations.

Señorita Múzquiz's early appreciation of this fact was intensified when in the summer of 1982 she enrolled in a special seminar in Los Angeles, and when she returned she carried exciting news to her Texas friends:

'Los Angeles is already the second largest Spanish-speaking city in the world, larger even than Madrid, smaller only than Mexico City. The food, the culture, the manner of thought are totally Mexican, and our newspaper, *La Opinión,* prints sixty thousand copies a day. More than ten theaters show movies only in Spanish, and the schools are filled with dedicated teachers like me, keeping our beautiful language alive and reminding our children of their Mexican heritage.

'What is happening is simple in process, glorious in effect. We are quietly reclaiming the land which Santa Anna lost through his insane vanity. Vast areas which are rightfully Mexican are coming back to us. No battles . . . no gunfire . . . no animosities, simply the inexorable movement of people north. The anglos still control the banks, the newspapers, the courts, but we have the power which always triumphs in the end, the power of people.'

Proof of her contention came dramatically when Immigration agents raided a big ranch south of Dallas and arrested some twenty illegal immigrants who had evaded the Border Patrol. From Dallas came a general cry of approval, but when officials looked more deeply into the matter, they found that Lorenzo Quimper, owner of the ranch, had arranged for his traveling factotum, Cándido Guzmán, to obtain citizenship, and Cándido, in turn, had imported from his small hometown of Moctezuma six young nephews who, he claimed, had proof of having been born in that hospital in El Paso. So instead of having nearly two dozen wetbacks to deport, the agents had fewer than fifteen, and the affair caused much amusement in Dallas.

Señorita Múzquiz jumped on this unfortunate affair as a major topic for her two classes to analyze, and with her careful guidance, the young Hispanics learned of the government's brutality and of the heroism of the Mexicans, legal or otherwise, who had worked their way so far north without having been detected: 'They are the heroes of our conquest. And like my father, they will stay.' Studiously she avoided uttering the word *revolución,* and even when she voiced it silently to herself she always followed it with *pacífico;* she did not visualize gunfire or rebellion, because there was no need. Everything she desired was attainable through slow but persistent penetration. For the present she did not include Texas cities as far north as Dallas in her looming confederacy: 'At least not for the remainder of this century. The anglos are too strong. But I can see it happening sometime after 2030.' When she assured personal friends that it must happen, she called it: 'The inevitable triumph of the marriage bed. Mexican women have many children. Anglos don't.'

In her general activity Señorita Múzquiz conducted herself with strict legality, but without advising her superiors, she operated against the rules as they were intended. The Supreme Court decision *Lau v. Nichols,* and the subsequent orders which implemented it, known as Lau Relief, had as their purpose the education of very young children in America, whether citizens or not, in their native tongue so that an easier transition into English could be made. Thus, certain large cities throughout the nation—and many with no Spanish-speaking minority at all—were required to teach elementary-school classes in many different tongues, and to accomplish this, they had to find qualified young persons who could teach arithmetic, geography, music and science in Chinese, Portuguese, French, Russian, Polish and some fifty other languages.

As a consequence, the teaching of Chinese flourished, but that of science and arithmetic did not, for there were few of the hastily enlisted teachers who had the solid competence in their subject areas that Señorita Músquiz had in hers. 'She's one of the best teachers in Dallas,' her supervisor said. 'Her only fault is that she is slow in getting her pupils to switch over into English.'

This tardiness was not accidental, for after these new teachers of Spanish had been on the job only a little while, they promoted the theory called *maintenance,* which meant that even after their pupils had reached a stage at which they could switch over to English, instruction in Spanish continued on the principle that the mastery of a second language was so valuable to the United States that proficiency in that language became a goal in itself.

Thus, Señorita Múzquiz's students came to school at age six knowing almost no English, and at seven or eight they were supposed to swing over to the English-speaking classes, but under the new theory of maintenance, they were kept in Spanish right through elementary school, until learning in Spanish, with inadequate mastery of subject matter, became the rule. And in Spanish they learned from certain teachers like the Señorita that they were an oppressed group, discriminated against and obligated to lead the great social changes which would transform their portion of America into a reclaimed Mexican homeland.

Señorita Múzquiz did not have clear sailing in her program, for SMU had a charismatic professor of history who had worked for five years in the Peace Corps in various South American countries, and he had come home with a few hard-won conclusions about life in that world. His name was Roy Aspen—University of Texas, Stanford, University of Hawaii—thirty-seven years old and iron-tough. He first attracted Señorita Múzquiz's attention in 1983, when he gave a widely discussed lecture, 'The Error of Bilingualism,' in which he pointed out with scholarly precision the dangers inherent in establishing even accidentally a two-language nation.

Had he kept to the main point his lecture might have gone unnoticed, but at the end he added two unfortunate paragraphs, which aroused unnecessary antagonism:

> 'A major corollary to this problem can be expressed in a question which we consistently avoid: "Why did those parts of the Western Hemisphere which fell under Spanish control fail to develop rational systems of self-government? And why did those regions falling under English control

succeed? The facts are overwhelming. No American nation deriving from a Spanish heritage, except possibly Costa Rica, has learned to govern itself in an orderly and just manner. Those with a different heritage have.

'Now, you may not want to admit that the non-Spanish nations have achieved responsible government and a just distribution of wealth, while the Spanish-speaking nations never have, but those are the facts. So to encourage a bilingualism which might bring into Texas the corrupt governmental systems of our neighbors to the south would be folly, if not suicide.'

When she left the lecture hall, Señorita Múzquiz was trembling, and to the fellow Hispanics she met that night, she said: 'We must declare war on this racist pig. He's reviving the Black Legend that was discredited a century ago.' And she drafted a letter to the editor, which surprised readers with its daring argument:

I am sick and tired of hearing that Spanish-speaking nations cannot govern themselves. Since Lázaro Cárdenas was elected President of Mexico in 1934, our well-governed nation to the south has had an unbroken sequence of brilliant leaders, each of whom has served his full six years without incident. In that same period the United States has had Roosevelt die in office, Truman, Ford and Reagan attacked by would-be assassins, Kennedy murdered, Nixon expelled, and Johnson, Ford and Carter denied reelection.

Mexico is the stable, well-governed nation. The United States terrifies its neighbors by its reactionary irresponsibility.

And as for the vaunted American system of distributing income fairly, we who live in South Dallas see precious little of either generosity or reward.

Her assault was so bold and her data so relevant that she was encouraged by her Hispanic friends to keep fighting, and when Dr. Aspen ended the session with the acerbic comment that Señorita Múzquiz should remember that a return passage to Mexico was always easier than an infiltration of our border, her infuriated sympathizers urged her to initiate what developed into the notorious Múzquiz-Aspen Debates of 1984. They focused on bilingual education—and generated intense partisanship.

The protagonists were evenly matched: this dedicated, attractive young woman of Mexican derivation opposing an able professor of Swedish heritage who knew the Latin countries better than she. Each spoke from the most sincere conviction, and neither was reluctant to lunge for the jugular.

She made two points which gave thoughtful Texans something to chew on, and she did so with enough insolence to command attention and enough validity to command respect:

> 'Let's look at this anglo charge of cultural impoverishment in Mexico. Where in the United States is there a museum one-tenth as glorious as the new archaeological one in Mexico City? It celebrates with explosive joy the glories of Mexico. And where can I go in the United States to see the grandeur of your Indian heritage? Are you ashamed of your history?

> 'Don't tell me about the Metropolitan Museum in New York or the Mellon in Washington. They're fine buildings, but they're filled with the work of Europeans, not Americans. Impoverished intellectually? Who is impoverished?'

Her second bit of evidence received wide circulation and verification from various social agencies:

> 'If you check with social services here in Dallas, you will find that they carry on their books three hundred and sixteen otherwise responsible anglo men who ignore court orders directing them to help support children whom they have abandoned, while your post office reports that Mexican workers in this metropolitan area, poorest of the poor and under no compulsion other than human decency, send home to their families south of the border more than four hundred thousand dollars monthly. Which society is more civilized?'

Dr. Aspen, realizing that he could not best Señorita Múzquiz in the disorderly brawling at which she excelled, sought to bring the debate to a higher level by convincing SMU to organize a powerfully staffed symposium entitled 'Bicultural Education, Fiction and Fact.' From the moment the brochures were printed, everyone could see that this was going to be an explosive affair, and experts from many states crowded into SMU, filling the university dormitories and occasionally standing at the rear of conference halls in which every seat was taken.

The United States as a whole had a profound interest in this subject, and national newspapers carried summaries of the opening address, in which a United States senator said:

> 'I voted for the legislation which spurred the initiation of bilingual education, and of course I applauded the Supreme Court decision of *Lau*

v. Nichols. I did so because I believed that all young people in this country, whether citizens or not, deserved the best education possible, the soundest introduction to our system of values.

'I now realize that I made a dreadful mistake and that the Supreme Court decision, *Lau v. Nichols,* is one of the worst it has made in a hundred years. Together we have invited our beloved nation to stagger down a road which will ultimately lead to separatism, animosity and the deprivation of the very children we sought to help. I hereby call for the revocation of the system we so erroneously installed and the abolishment of the legislation sponsoring it.'

There was an outcry from the floor, and a man from Arizona who supported Señorita Múzquiz's theories demanded the podium for an immediate rebuttal, but with a calm which infuriated, Professor Aspen ignored the clamor and called for the second speaker, an elderly Jewish professor from Oregon, who gave a most thoughtful analysis of past American experience:

'I will be forgiven, I hope, if I draw upon my family's experience, but my grandfather came to New York in 1903 from the Galician region of what was then Austria but which had through most of history been Poland. He landed knowing not a word of English, and when in 1906 he was able to send to Galicia for the rest of his family, his wife and three children, including my father, landed at Ellis Island, again with no English.

'My grandfather spoke abominable English, my grandmother never learned. But the three children were thrown into the American school system and within four months were jabbering away. Both my father and my aunt Elzbieta were writing their homework in English by the end of that first year, and both graduated from grade school with honors.

'That was the grand tradition which produced a melting pot from which poured an unending stream of Italian, German, Polish, Slavic and Jewish young people prepared to grapple on equal terms with the best that Harvard, Yale and Chicago were producing. In fact, my father went to Yale, and others from the various ghettos went to Stanford and Michigan and North Carolina.

'To change a system which has worked so well and with such honorable results is a grave error and one which, having been made, requires immediate reversal.'

Again there was an outcry from those whose careers had been enhanced by the introduction of bilingualism, but once again Professor Aspen ignored the hullaba-loo, taking the podium himself to speak of his experiences:

'If one looks at the linguistic tragedy that impends in Canada, where French speakers want to fracture the nation in defense of their language, or in Belgium, where French speakers fight with Walloons who speak Flemish, or in the Isle of Cyprus, where Turk and Greek quarrel over languages, or in South Africa, where a nation is rent by language differ-ences, or in India, where thousands are slain in language riots, or any-where else where language is a divisive force, one can only weep for the antagonisms thus inherited.

'These countries bear a terrible burden, the lack of a common tongue, and more-fortunate nations ought to sympathize with them and give them assistance in seeking solutions to what appear to be insoluble problems. Charity is obligatory.

'But for a nation like the United States, which has a workable central tongue used by many countries around the world, consciously to intro-duce a linguistic separatism and to encourage it by the expenditure of public funds is to create and encourage a danger which could in time destroy this nation, as the others I spoke of may one day be destroyed.

'India inherited its linguistic jungle; it did not create it willfully. History gave South Africa its divisive bilingualism; it did not seek it. Such na-tions are stuck with what accident and history gave them, and they cannot justly be accused of having made foolish error, but if the United States consciously invents a linguistic dualism, it deserves the castigation of history.

'Let us focus on the main problem. If we continue to educate our Spanish-speaking immigrants and native-born in Spanish for the first six years of their education, and if we teach the vital subjects of literature and history in that language, we will see before the end of this century exactly the kind of separatism which now plagues Canada, but our example will be much worse than theirs, because our sample of the disaffected will be larger and will have on its southern border a nation, a Central America and an entire continent speaking that language and sponsoring that separatism. Let us face these ominous facts and see what we can do to counteract and forestall them.'

At the close of his address, reporters immediately crowded about Aspen: 'Do you oppose Miss Músquiz personally?' and he replied amiably: 'Not at all. She serves a most useful purpose in providing Mexican immigrants with leadership. Texas profits from its Mexican workers, and they're entitled to her guidance. But when her ideas are so erroneous that they might lead our entire nation into irreversible error, they must be corrected.'

'What did you think of her statement that if history had been just, Los Angeles and Houston would now be Mexican cities?'

He considered this for a moment: 'Interesting speculation. The cities might be Mexican but they would not be Los Angeles and Houston. Under traditional Mexican mismanagement, they'd be more like Guaymas and Tampico.'

When Señorita Músquiz gained the floor to counteract the strong points made by Professor Aspen, she controlled her seething fury and gave one of the better presentations of the symposium. She denied that teachers like her kept their students imprisoned in Spanish when they must lead their adult lives in English; she denied that she ever taught Mexican imperialism; she denied that the Supreme Court case infringed in any way on American rights. Since she really believed that she acted only in the best interests of her pupils, she had no hesitancy in denying that she or teachers like her kept their students from learning English.

Then, in sober terms, she reminded her audience of the grave disadvantages Mexican immigrants had suffered in Texas, the cruel way in which their culture had been abused, the remorseless way they had been handled by Rangers along the border, and the thoughtless contempt with which they were so often treated:

> 'We have lived side by side with the North Americans since 1810, and we have made every concession to their superior power. They had the votes, the guns, the law courts and the banks on their side, and we bowed low in the gutters and allowed them to usurp the sidewalks. But when they now demand that we surrender our language and our patterns of life, we say "No." '

She gave a stirring defense of bicultural life, which she refrained from equating with bilingual education paid for by the host state, and in the end, in a peroration that brought tears to some, she shared her vision of a de facto state along the border, from Brownsville to San Diego, in which the two cultures, the two economic systems and the two languages would exist in a mixed harmony.

As the symposium wound to a close, argument over the Simpson-Mazzoli Bill erupted, shattering her carefully nurtured impression of reasonableness. Simpson-Mazzoli was an effort by a Republican senator and a Democratic representative to stanch the hemorrhaging along the Mexican border and to bring order among the estimated ten million illegal immigrants who had drifted north and who existed in a kind of judicial no man's land. The bill offered three solutions: halt further illegal entry, grant generous amnesty to those well-intentioned and well-behaved Mexicans already here, and penalize American employers who hired illegals. It was a good bill, basically, but Hispanic leaders like Señorita Múzquiz opposed it vehemently on the dubious grounds that it would require immigrants like her who had later obtained legal status to carry identification cards. 'Am I to wear a yellow star, like Hitler's Jews?' she shouted. 'Must I carry proof that I'm a legal resident? What anglo employer will run the risk of hiring me when he can hire a fellow anglo with no danger of breaking the law?'

Professor Aspen dismissed such reasoning with one compelling question: 'Can a sovereign democracy control its borders or can't it?' Without waiting for an answer, he added: 'The incessant flow of illegals from Mexico and Central America must be halted, or the United States will be engulfed by hordes of uneducated persons who will try to convert it into just another Hispanic dictatorship.'

Señorita Múzquiz opposed the bill for defensible reasons, but there were other Hispanic leaders who fought it for personal gain: they wanted either an assured supply of cheap labor or a constant inflow of potential voters to bolster Hispanic claims. To all opponents of the bill, Dr. Aspen asked: 'Are you recommending a completely open border across which anyone in Mexico can come as he or she wishes?' and the Señorita replied: 'You'd better keep the border open, because Texas and California prosper only because of the profit they make on this guaranteed supply of cheap labor. Stop the flow, and Texas will collapse in depression.'

A television newsman, overhearing the argument, asked her: 'But if the Mexicans and Central Americans keep pressing in, won't this mean that eventually most of Texas will become Mexican?' and she said, looking defiantly into the camera: 'If Hispanic mothers in Central America have many babies and anglo mothers in Texas have few, I suppose there will have to be an irresistible sweep of immigrants to the north. Yes, Texas will become Spanish.'

And even as she spoke, the American Congress, debating in Washington, refused to pass the reasonable Simpson-Mazzoli Bill, thus destroying any attempt by the United States to control the influx of illegals across its borders. For the most venal reasons the citizens of Texas were in the forefront of this cynical rejection of common sense; they were willing to accept immediate profits while ignoring future consequences. As a result, the Immigration authorities along the Rio Grande stopped trying to stem the unceasing inflow of illegals, turning their attention rather to keeping them out of the larger cities like Dallas and Amarillo; the creation of the ipso facto Mexican-American nation along the Rio Grande was under way. So the embittered Múzquiz-Aspen Debates ended with a rousing victory for the Señorita. And the well-intentioned peasants from Mexico, Guatemala, Nicaragua and El Salvador, yearning for freedom and a decent life, continued to stream across the Rio Grande.

When Señorita Múzquiz heard on the evening news that Simpson-Mazzoli was dead, she cried in Spanish to those who were listening with her: 'Hooray! We'll win back every bit of land Santa Anna gave away. And we won't have to fire one shot.'

Professor Aspen, when he heard the same news, told his students: 'Before the end of this century Texas will start contemplating her privilege of breaking into smaller states. There'll be a movement to create along the Rio Grande a Hispanic state.'

'Are you serious?' they asked.

'Doesn't matter whether I am or not. The unquenchable flood of immigration will determine it.'

Sociologists called them 'rites of passage,' and this theory enabled them to predict certain inevitables which had to occur in any society, no matter how primitive or advanced. At age two, babies would begin to assert their own personalities, often with reverberations that altered family relationships; at fifteen, young males would begin to concentrate on girls, who had been concentrating on boys since thirteen; and at about twenty-seven, men would begin thinking about challenging the older leaders of the tribe, with similar inevitables trailing a man to his grave.

In Houston comparable rules dictated behavior. Among society's more fortunate few, men in their early thirties, like Roy Bub Hooker, Todd Morrison and their two friends, the oilman and the dentist, would want to find themselves a quail lease somewhere to the south along the borders of the great King Ranch; in their late thirties they'd want an airplane to fly them quickly to their preserve; in their early forties they'd begin to do what all sensible Texans did, aspire to take their vacations, summer or winter, in Colorado; and in their late forties, sure as thunder after a lightning stab, they'd want to find themselves a ranch in that glorious hill country west of Austin; and when this happy day occurred they would almost certainly switch to the Republican party.

On schedule, these urges hit the four members of Roy Bub's hunting team, with results that could have been anticipated: in their occupations the men had prospered unevenly, with the oilman finding headline success, and Todd Morrison, once of Detroit, approaching the well-to-do category of a real estate millionaire with close to twenty million. But the dentist was mired in the lower levels with only one or two million, and Roy Bub still dug sewers with no millions at all.

So Morrison and the oilman bought the plane, a four-seater Beechcraft, but it was Roy Bub who learned to fly it, and for three memorable years they flew almost each weekend during hunting season and at least twice a month thereafter down to Falfurrias to their lease, which was now a minor Shangri-La, but they had not been doing this for long when the greatest of the Houston urges trapped them, and they began to think about purchasing a ranch west of Austin.

In Houston a young man of ambition and talent was allowed so much elbowroom that he could progress pretty much at his own speed, but if he passe into his forties without owning a ranch, he betrayed himself as one who had left the fast track to find refuge in mediocre success along the more relaxed detours.

Although Morrison and the oilman had the money, they still looked to Roy Bub as the outdoor expert, so that when they started searching seriously for their ranch, they placed in his hands the responsibility for finding it. Often in the late 1970s Roy Bub and one or two of the others would fly out for scouting trips through the lovely hills and valleys beyond the Balcones Fault.

Few visitors from the North ever saw this wonderland of Central Texas, this marvelously rich congregation of small streams winding down valleys, of sudden meadowlands encompassed by hills, of a hundred acres of bluebonnets in the spring, and of the probing fingers of the man-made lakes, creeping deep into the rolling corners of the land. To see it from the highways that wandered through was delectable, but to see it as the four hunters now did, from low altitude in their plane, was a privilege of which they never tired. This was the golden heart of Texas, and a man was entitled to a share after he had brought in his third oil well or built his fourth skyscraper.

It was Roy Bub who first spotted their dreamland. He had flown west from Austin and was keeping to the south shore of the huge lake which had appeared one day among the hills, when he saw a small feeder river winding here and there, aimlessly and with many bends, as if reluctant to lose its identity in the larger body of water. He told Morrison, who had accompanied him this time: 'That's got to be the Pedernales,' and he pronounced the name as Texans did: Per-dnal-iss.

As he followed the little stream westward he suddenly twisted the Beechcraft about, doubled back, and shouted: 'There it is!' They were over the magnificent ranch put together by Lyndon Johnson, and for some minutes they circled this Texas monument to a prototypical Texas man. Morrison, looking down at the airstrip built with federal taxes, the roadways paved by the state, the fences built by friends, and the pastures stocked by other friends, thought: Who really cares if he was a wheeler-dealer? He was a damned good President and one day this will all seep back to public ownership. I'd like to be President . . . for just one term.

And then, after they passed the Johnson ranch, Roy Bub saw it, a stretch of handsome land on the north bank of the Pedernales. It contained everything the four hunters sought: a long stretch fronting the river, good ground cover for grouse and turkey, ample trees for deer to browse, plus a kind of park along the river and bleak empty spaces for wildlife to roam. It was the original Allerkamp ranch of five thousand acres, to which had been added the Macnab holdings of equal size, and when Roy Bub landed his plane at Fredericksburg, he and Morrison discovered to their delight that it was for sale. Once they satisfied themselves that it suited their purposes, neither man ever turned back, Roy Bub assuring his partners that it was the best available ranch in Texas, and Morrison convincing the oilman that it was a bargain, regardless of what the German owners wanted, and a deal was struck, with Todd and the oilman putting up most of the money and Roy Bub and the dentist doing most of the work.

On a sad November Friday in 1980 they flew down to Falfurrias to inform the owner of their present lease that they would be terminating it on March first, and he was genuinely unhappy to see them go: 'You lived up to every promise you ever made. I'll miss you.' The oilman said: 'Now, if this causes you to lose any money —' but he interrupted: 'I'll be able to arrange a new lease by tomorrow noon. Must be two hundred young tigers in Houston panting for a lease like this.'

On one point the old contract was clear: any building which they had erected belonged to him . . . if it was fastened to the ground; any that remained movable belonged to them, and Roy Bub surprised the owner by saying: 'We'll want to take all the buildings with us.'

'They're yours, but I was hopin' you'd want to sell them . . . at an attractive price . . . save you a lot of trouble,' but Roy Bub said: 'No, we can use them at the new place,' and the owner looked in amazement as the oilman moved in three of his crews, who sawed the six small houses apart, mounted them on great trucks, and headed them two hundred and forty-one miles northwest to their new home, where they would be reassembled to form an attractive hunting lodge in a far corner of the Allerkamp land.

The four hunters and their families had occupied the new ranch only two years when once more the inevitable pressures exerted by the rites of passage attacked them. The dentist discovered that he was now strong enough financially to abandon his practice and devote himself full time to the propagation and sale of his hunting dogs; he withdrew from the consortium and opened a master kennel on the outskirts of Houston. At the same time, the oilman was struck by an insidious disease which affected many Texas oilmen: 'All my life I've dreamed of shooting in England and Scotland. The moors. The hunt breakfasts with kippers under the silver covers. The faithful gillies. The long weekends. Gentlemen, I've leased a stretch of good salmon river near Inverness and you're invited to come over in season.'

His Scottish adventure so absorbed him, what with the purchase of another Purdy gun and the making of arrangements for his Highland headquarters, that one night he informed Morrison and Roy Bub that he wanted to sell off his portion of the Allerkamp ranch, but when Todd said, almost eagerly: 'I think I could swing it,' he surprised both men by saying: 'I'd want to cut Roy Bub in. Let him get a grubstake.' And he persisted in this decision, arranging for Hooker a long-term payment with no interest: 'I owe it to you, Roy Bub. You taught me what the outdoors was.'

Six months later the Houston social pages displayed photographs of the oilman at his lodge in the Scottish Highlands, where he had been entertaining a British executive of Shell Oil, a Lord Duncraven, and a financier involved with the big oil operation in the North Sea, a Sir Hilary Cobham. It was an engaging shot, with the Houston man looking more like a Scottish laird than the locals.

So now Todd Morrison and Roy Bub Hooker owned a ranch on the Pedernales and half a Beechcraft airplane, but the latter awkwardness was resolved when the oilman, totally preoccupied with his holdings in Scotland, offered to sell his part of the plane at a tremendous bargain, which Todd and Roy Bub gladly accepted. When the deal was closed with this remarkably generous old friend, they saw him no more. He had leaped five steps up the social ladder.

But Morrison was generating enough income from his manifold real estate deals to permit him to absorb most of the cost of the ranch, and after an airstrip had been installed well away from the river, the private planes of many Houston real estate managers appeared at Allerkamp, and the place became known as a site where developers and their wives could enjoy a good time.

Despite this concentration on business, and Morrison was never far removed from a deal of some kind, his love for the land never diminished, and he was therefore in a receptive mood when Roy Bub came to him one weekend with a challenging proposition: 'Ol' buddy, I think we got ourself a gold mine here. My recommendation, we fence it in . . .'

'It's already fenced in.'

'I mean gameproof fence.'

These were startling words, and Todd remained silent for some time, simply staring at the driller of septic tanks. Finally he asked, very slowly: 'You mean those fences eight and a half feet high?' And before Roy Bub could respond, he asked: 'You thinking of exotics?' Then Roy Bub said: 'I sure am. Todd, with your money and my management and my feel for animals, we could have us a ball on this ranch.'

'Do you know what gameproof fencing costs?'

'I do,' and from his wallet he produced a study of costs: 'Very best, guaranteed to hold ever'thin' but an armadillo, around nine thousand dollars a mile.'

Rapidly Todd analyzed their situation: 'Ten thousand acres, divide by six hundred forty acres to the mile, that's about sixteen square miles. If it was a perfect square, which it isn't, that would be a perimeter of twelve miles we'd have to fence. But we'd need cross fencing to break it into pastures, so add eight miles. Twenty miles of fencing at nine thousand a mile. Jesus, Roy Bub! That's a hundred and eighty thousand, just for the fences, without the stock, which doesn't come cheap.'

'Todd, I got me a lead on some of the best exotics in the United States. Everybody wants to deal with me. The basic stock I can pick up for a hundred and thirty thousand, believe me.'

They sat in the evening darkness reviewing these notes, and when Karleen and Maggie came in to see if they wanted drinks, the men asked their wives to stay.

'The land isn't square,' Todd explained, 'so the fencing might be even more than we've calculated.'

'But I'll bet I can get us a lot better bargain than nine thousand a mile,' Roy Bub said.

'What do you ladies think?' Todd asked, and Maggie responded quickly: 'I believe we could swing it. So long as real estate stays up,' and Karleen said: 'Roy Bub's always liked animals. I suppose we'd want to move up here to get things organized,' and Roy Bub said: 'We sure would.'

He did manipulate a much better price than $9,000 a mile, and when the fences were erected, nearly eighteen miles of the best, he fulfilled the rest of his promise, for he knew where to locate real bargains in aoudad sheep, sika deer, mouflon rams and eight American elk. He astonished Morrison by also acquiring nine ostriches and six giraffes: 'We won't allow anyone to shoot them, but they do add color to the place.'

When the animals began to arrive, often by air, Roy Bub greeted each one as if it were a member of his family, showing it personally to the large, almost free fields in which it would roam: 'Madam Eland, you never had it better in Africa than you're gonna have it right here.'

From the start it had been intended that when the exotics were well established, and this would come soon, for the Allerkamp ranch was much like the more interesting parts of South Africa from which the elands and other antelopes came, big-game hunters would be invited to come and test their skill against animals in the wild. 'Year after next,' Roy Bub said, 'when we have the lodge fixed up and my wife has hired some cooks and I've got guides, we're in business.'

They would charge substantially for the privilege of killing one of their exotics, but as the pamphlet which Roy Bub composed pointed out: 'It's a danged sight cheaper coming to Allerkamp for your eland than going to Nairobi.' Extremely practical where his own money was concerned, he established a rather high rate for the Texas hunters:

ANIMAL	SOURCE	OUR COST PAIR YEARLINGS	OUR COST MATURE MALE	HUNTER PAYS TROPHY SIZE
Axis deer	India	$ 500	$ 850	$1,800
Sika deer	China	500	850	1,200
Blackbuck	India	250	850	1,100
Fallow deer	Germany	250	450	1,000
Whitetail	USA	450	800	2,500
Red stag	Scotland	2,400	3,800	6,650
Elk	USA	3,500	4,500	7,000
Aoudad ram	Africa	360	850	1,500
Corsican ram	Corsica	75	100	250
Mouflon ram	Sardinia	380	500	1,000

Eland	Africa	1,750	1,500	3,000
Ibex	Africa	3,500	2,400	4,500
Horned oryx	Africa	3,500	2,000	4,000
Gemsbok	Africa	5,000	2,750	3,750
Zebra, Grant's	Africa	4,500	2,800	4,000
Turkey, wild	USA	100	150	250

But when they were in place, with Morrison paying one bill after another for their purchase and their transportation, Roy Bub introduced a stunning addition, which he paid for out of his own pocket. One morning he called Houston with exciting news: 'Todd, Maggie! Fly right up. It's unique.'

When they reached the ranch they found that a large trailer had moved in with animals of some kind. 'You'll never guess,' Roy Bub cried.

The van was maneuvered to one of the smaller fields where hunting was forbidden, and when the gate was opened and men stationed so that the animals, when released, could not scamper back toward the trailer, ramps were placed, the door swung out—and down came a quiet, noble procession. The watchers gasped, for Roy Bub had acquired from an overstocked zoo four of nature's loveliest creations: sable antelope, big creatures as large as a horse, but a soft purplish brown, a majestic way of walking and the finest horns in the animal kingdom.

When they felt themselves to be free, they sniffed the unfamiliar air, pawed at the rocky soil so like their own in South Africa, then raised their stately heads and began moving away. When they did this, the observers could see the full sweep of their horns, those tremendous lyrelike curves that started at the forehead and turned backward in an imperial arch till the tips nearly touched their flanks. Almost as if they appreciated how grand and eloquent they were, they posed at the edge of a tree cluster, then leaped in different directions and lost themselves in the woodlands of their new home.

Sometimes a whole month would pass without anyone seeing one of the sables; then a visitor would be driving aimlessly along the ranch roads and suddenly before him would appear that stately animal, purplish gold in the afternoon sun, with sweeping horns unlike any the traveler would have seen before, and he would come scrambling back to the lodge, shouting: 'What was that extraordinary creature I saw?' and Roy Bub would ask: 'Sort of purple? Huge horns?' and when the man nodded, he would say proudly: 'That was one of our sables, glory of the Allerkamp.'

'What would it cost me to shoot one?'

'They ain't for shootin'.'

During the early years of the Houston crises, no real estate people escaped the adverse effects, but since Maggie Morrison had always avoided the rental business, she did not suffer immediately from the collapse of petroleum prices. Associated with one of the solid firms, she continued to specialize in finding a few inexpensive homes for Northern executives whose corporations had moved them into the Houston area: 'I sometimes wonder who's running the store up there. All the bright vice-presidents seem to be moving down here.'

She did not yet have the courage to do what her husband did so easily: put together a really big operation with outside financing from Canada or Saudi Arabia, but she was doing well and could have supported herself had she been required to do so. She had fallen into a Texas pattern of thought in which any gamble, if it had even a forty-percent chance of success, was worth the taking: 'And anyway, Todd, if it all did collapse, we could start over as clerks in somebody's office and within six months own the place.'

That she was now a complete Texan manifested itself in two ways. In her letters home to her friends in Detroit she no longer even spoke of returning:

> Something in Houston catches the imagination and sets it aflame. Last week I found a home for one of the most famous of the astronauts out at NASA east of here. For years he'd been saying: 'One of these days I'll go back to Nebraska.' Last week he bit the bullet and will be staying here, even after retirement from the program. He has a little business going on the side.
>
> The thing that catches you, I think, is the dynamism of the place. It's like watching some great flywheel whirring about. In the first moments you marvel at its speed, and then suddenly you find yourself wanting to be a part of it, and you're sorely tempted to jump in. Well, I've jumped. Would you believe it, Pearl, I've put together a deal for three Arabs involving some of the finer houses, $14,000,000, of which I hold on to a small part. Until I close, I'll be so nervous I won't sleep.

That turned out to be a frightening one-week nightmare, which, when disposed of, she swore never to repeat. She took this oath because she had become aware that her husband frequently found himself in rather delicate positions from which he extricated himself by moves which she supposed she would not have approved had she known the details. For example, when the oilman who had been their partner shifted from the ranch on the Pedernales to the hunting lodge in Scotland, he confided: 'Maggie, I don't like to say this, but I'm very fond of you, and so is Rachel. Protect yourself. I've been in four financial deals with your husband, and damn it all, in every case he pulled some swifty. The Lambert Development, the ranch at Falfurrias, the airplane, out at Allerkamp. He cuts corners. He gigs his friends. He's always looking for that little extra edge. And that's one of the reasons why I'm switching my hunting to Scotland.'

'Have his actions . . . I mean . . . have they been . . . ?'

'Illegal?' He intertwined his fingers until they formed a little cathedral. 'The line is tenuous . . . shady. When you deal with big numbers you face big problems. But you must never gig your own associates.'

'Certainly he's treated Roy Bub fairly?' The fact that she asked this as a question indicated that doubt had been sown.

'Roy Bub's the best man in Texas. Everybody treats him fair. But even Roy Bub had better watch out, because some day he's going to find he owns no part of that ranch. "So long, Roy Bub, nice to have known you." '

'I can't believe that.'

'And you better watch out, Lady Meg, or you're going to be out on your keester with the rest of us.'

He did not see her again, and to her surprise, the dentist with the big kennel ignored her too, so one day while she was surveying corner lots that might be converted into modest wraparounds, she stopped by the kennels and asked bluntly: 'Did my husband have anything to do with your pulling out of the Allerkamp deal?' and he said frankly: 'After a while, Maggie, men get fed up with dealing with your husband. Watch out.'

The second way in which Maggie indicated that Texas had captured her was the manner in which she adjusted to her daughter's strange behavior. Beth, a spectacular beauty in her late teens, had refused to attend the University of Michigan: 'The only place I want to go is UT.'

'Stop using that nonsensical phrase! If you mean Texas, say so.'

'That's certainly what I mean,' and at UT she had become chief baton twirler.

In disgust, Maggie had refused to attend any games, but one Saturday afternoon when Texas was playing SMU she chanced to see on the half-time television show a most remarkable young woman from the other university, a real genius at twirling. The SMU girl wore a skimpy costume that revealed her lovely grace and she threw the baton much higher than Maggie would have believed possible, catching it deftly, now in front, now behind.

'Extraordinary,' Maggie said. As a girl she had seen circus performers who were no better than this young artist, so she stayed by the television as her own daughter appeared for Texas, and what she saw made her catch her breath.

When the SMU band and performers left the field, the mighty Texas band swung into action, more than three hundred strong, dressed in burnt-orange. In front came the six-foot-seven drum master, followed by sixteen cheerleaders, men and women. After them came the three baton twirlers, with Beth Morrison in the middle. Behind her came the endless files of the musicians, all stepping alike, all inclining their cowboy hats in rhythm.

At the rear came a couple of dozen drummers, cymbalists, glockenspiel players and whatnots, followed by the sensation of the Texas campus: a drum so huge that three men were needed to keep it secured to its carriage and moving forward. It was taller than two men and was clubbed by a player whose arm muscles were huge; its deep, booming sound filled the stadium.

And then Beth stood forth alone, this poet manqué, and with a skill that staggered Maggie, she sent first one, then two batons into the air, catching them unfailingly and creating a kind of mystic spell for this important autumn afternoon.

'Who in his right mind,' Maggie asked aloud as she switched off the television, 'would invent something like that spectacle and call it education?' But later, when she was forced to reconsider all aspects of the situation, she conceded that Mr. Sutherland, principal at Deaf Smith High, had been right when he predicted that Beth would find her life within the Texas syndrome and be very happy in it. Beth had been pledged by one of the premier sororities, the Kappas, whose senior members arranged for her to meet one of the more attractive BMOCs. Wolfgang Macnab, descendant of two famous Texas Rangers, was indeed a Big Man on Campus, for he stood well over six feet, weighed about two hundred and twenty lean pounds, and played linebacker on the Longhorn football team.

He was five years older than Beth and should have graduated before she entered the university, but in the Texas tradition he had been red-shirted in both junior high school and college—that is, held back arbitrarily so that he would be bigger and stronger when he did play. He was a bright young fellow, conspicuous among the other football giants in that he took substantial classes in which he did well. After their meeting in the Kappa lounge, he and Beth studied together for an art-appreciation seminar, in which he excelled, and before long they were being referred to as 'that ideal Texas couple.' What happened next was explained by Beth's mother in one of her periodic letters to Detroit:

> What you Northerners never appreciate, Pearl, is that Texas is so big that you can live your life within its limits and never give a damn about what anybody in Boston or San Francisco thinks. A girl like our daughter Beth can enjoy a stunning life at the university here without giving a hoot what the social leaders at Vassar or Stanford think. Matrons here do not have to consider Philadelphia or Richmond. They're their own bosses. All that matters is how they're perceived in Dallas and Houston.

> A writer can build a perfectly satisfactory reputation in Texas and he doesn't give a damn what critics in Kalamazoo think. His universe is big enough to gratify any ambition. Same with businessmen. Same with newspapers. Same with everything.

> I share these reflections because I've been thinking of Beth. She could have had a noble career at Michigan or Vassar, of that I'm sure. The kid's a near-genius, and was a wonderful poet at fourteen, when the real poets start. But at her local high school she was brainwashed into be-

coming a baton twirler . . . pompons . . . the bit, and when I challenged this, she said: 'Let's face it, Mom, how could Texas produce a poet when its favorite food is chicken-fried steak smothered in white library paste?' She went her way, and damned if she didn't become the best baton twirler of the lot. Also a puffy-pretty sorority girl without a brain in her head, you know the type.

So what happens to my adorable little nitwit? She marries one of the handsomest football players God ever made, and at their wedding his brother Cletus appears, six feet six, a full-fledged Texas Ranger with big hat and hidden gun holster. When the three of them stood before the minister, Baptist naturally, with little Beth in the middle and those two gorgeous hunks on either side, all I could do was hide my tears and recall the Biblical quotation 'Male and female created He them.'

And then I got two real surprises. What do you suppose they did with the wedding purse her sorority and his fraternity contributed? They bought a Picasso print. Yep, those redneck hillbillies bought a Picasso. And this evening's news announces that Wolfgang has been drafted by the Dallas Cowboys, said to be the best football team in America. Surely it's better than Detroit. So I'm not to be the mother of a poetess but the mother-in-law of a football hero, and I find myself shouting with the rest of Texas: 'So who gives a damn about Vassar? The real world is down here.'

Of course, when the recession grew acute in 1982, and oil dropped to twenty-nine dollars a barrel, and the fall of the Mexican peso prostrated Houston real estate, threatening many of the big hotels with bankruptcy because those spectacular ten-room suites were no longer being rented to Mexican millionaires, even fortunately situated couples like the Morrisons began to feel pinches. Todd had only a vague awareness of the economic slump until he saw at the commuter airport the number of private planes that were suddenly for sale. This struck home, and he quickly convened a strategy session with his wife: 'Now, now's the time to make our big moves.'

'You must be crazy! The bottom's falling out.'

'That's exactly when opportunities appear. A good real estate agent, and you're one of the best, Maggie, can make a bundle when the market is going up. But he can make even more when it's going down. Because people have to sell, and there's damned few buyers around.'

'How can we buy?'

'Credit. We hock everything we have. We look for distress bargains, and we buy it to the hilt.'

When they had done this, and exhausted their own funds, Todd said: 'The luscious plums, the real big ones, are beginning to ripen. Go up to Dallas and line up some real money.'

It was in this manner that Maggie Morrison, a onetime schoolteacher in a suburb of Detroit, fired during retrenchment, walked into the office of Ransom Rusk in Dallas, trying to interest him in a Houston real estate speculation requiring $143,000,000. In the first eight minutes of their meeting she learned much about Texas financing: 'I apologize, Mr. Rusk, for coming at you like this when the papers say you've suffered reverses,' and he laughed: 'My dear Mrs. Morrison, it's precisely at such times that a man like me is looking for new ventures. Some of the old ones have worn thin.'

'Then you'll consider the deal?' and he said: 'I've always been willing to consider any deal . . . if there's enough leverage. That's how I landed with TexTek.'

She next asked: 'How much would you expect my husband and me to throw in?' and he said: 'Every nickel you have. I want you to be as concerned about this as I would be.'

Finally he said: 'You want a hundred and forty-three million dollars. I'll put up twenty-five million if you put up four,' and she said: 'But that leaves us more than a hundred million short. Where do we get it?' and he said: 'The banks. You'll be amazed at how eager they are to lend money to anyone with a hot idea, and yours is hot.'

She asked: 'Why are you doing this?' and he said: 'Winning, losing, I care little about either. But I do like to be in the game.'

If one kept focusing attention on big ranchers like Lorenzo Quimper, or big oilmen like Ransom Rusk, or big cotton growers like Sherwood Cobb, or real estate honchos like Todd Morrison, one might conclude that power in Texas was exerted only by those who controlled large sums of money, but this would be wrong. In many aspects of Texas life it was 'the little folks from the fork in the creek' who cast the deciding ballots. They kept race-track gambling out of Texas. They allowed no state lotteries. And with refreshing frequency they bullheadedly voted in a way that surprised the big cities. An excellent example of this strong-mindedness came in Larkin in 1980 when some misguided liberals reminded the town that one of its first occupants had been a respectable saloon keeper and that alcohol had been outlawed only by the ill-conceived Prohibition movement: 'It's high time our town had stores that sold liquor and saloons in which law-abiding citizens could enjoy a sociable drink.' Eager to put their money where their mouth was, these energetic people collected a huge war chest, hired Kraft and Killeen, the public relations firm from Dallas, and petitioned for a referendum. The war was on.

Under Texas law a county had the right to vote itself dry if a majority so desired, and out of 254 counties, 74 did, but there were so many ramifications that newcomers rarely understood what was happening. One county would outlaw everything—wine, beer, whiskey—another would allow beer but not wine or whiskey; and a third, fourth and fifth would create their own mixes. As a result, only 36 counties were totally wet.

After the wild years of the oil boom, Larkin had voted itself dry, and in both the sixties and seventies, had repulsed efforts to rescind that law. 'This town,' boasted Reverend Craig, pastor of the First Baptist Church of Larkin, 'is a haven of decency and sobriety in a state which has too many examples of the opposite character.' Craig was a good clergyman, especially revered for his fatherly interest in orphans and his loving attention to elderly people without families. Much of the good that occurred in Larkin could be attributed to his acts, and wealthy oilmen like Ransom Rusk kept him in funds sufficient to cover the numerous little charities he performed. He preached well, did not rant, was ecumenical toward the lesser churches that had crowded into Larkin, and had goaded his congregation into welcoming even Mexicans and blacks into the church, if they were passing through.

'Craig adds a touch of humanity and decency to our town,' one of the oilmen said when making his annual contribution, and this was the general opinion. Young people appreciated him because in a willing effort to keep up with the times, he had encouraged his elders to allow dancing at church socials, a radical move when one recalled the old days.

Craig was not a fanatic where morals were concerned, and he had several times helped prostitutes stranded by their pimps, for he suspected that Jesus would have done the same, and he served as a surrogate father for children who fell into trouble; but he could be remarkably forceful when discharging two of his Baptist obligations: he believed in a literal interpretation of the Bible, and he abhorred demon rum: 'I have been forced to witness so much human tragedy resulting from alcohol that I stand in wonderment that any man would willingly allow this evil substance to pass his lips, and as for women who do so, they are anathema.'

He was, in many respects, the most powerful force in Larkin, and when one particularly offensive oil tycoon flouted all the implicit laws of North Texas, Craig preached such a powerful pair of sermons against him that he was in effect excommunicated, not only from the Baptist church but from the community as well. The miscreant moved to Dallas, where he was quite happy.

It was largely due to Craig that Larkin remained dry, for it had been his vigorous leadership which had repelled the last two attempts to turn it wet, and he was now girding his loins to fight again. He chose to ignore the fact that a large majority of his flock enjoyed a short snifter now and then, but he did frequently praise his congregation for hiding no outright drunks in its membership. He was contemptuous of those Rio Grande counties which, because of their heavily Hispanic population, refused to outlaw alcohol, and in his more inflammatory prohibition sermons he sometimes referred to them as 'our southern cousins to whom drunkenness is a way of life,' refusing to acknowledge that their orderly use of beverages produced less actual drunkenness than did Larkin's severe code.

Of course, under the complex Texas system anyone who wanted a drink could find one, and each dry county contained its quota of enthusiastic topers, because the law contained a built-in weakness which drinkers were quick to take advantage of. A respectable county like Larkin could vote itself dry while its more disreputable neighbor remained stubbornly wet, and since most counties, especially in the west, were small and square—something like thirty miles to a side, with the county seat dead center—it was possible for a town at the heart of a dry county to be only fifteen miles from a flowing source of liquor. In Larkin's case, the distance from bone-dry to sopping-wet was twelve miles down Highway 23 to Bascomb County, 'that notorious and nauseous sink of sin,' as Reverend Craig liked to describe it in his sermons.

When officials at the Larkin County Courthouse announced that a referendum had been authorized for the spring of 1980, Craig looked with awe at the forces arrayed against him, and told his deacons: 'Brethren, this is the fight that will determine the character of our county for the rest of this century. Look at those who assault us! All the distilleries of America. All the breweries of Texas. All the saloon keepers of those wet Red River counties. Kraft and Killeen of Dallas. Brother Carnwath, please tell the gentlemen the size of the war chest we face.'

A tall, thin man, with deep-set eyes and a lock of hair that fell across his brow, rose: 'We have good reason to believe that they have amassed more than seven hundred thousand dollars to crush us, for they know that if they can bring their whiskey in here, they can lug their barrels into any county.'

'Gentlemen,' Craig said, 'the battle lines are drawn. Once more it is David against Goliath, and once more God will favor the pure in heart, puny though we may seem at the start.'

It really was little David against the forces of darkness, but the shepherd boy was by no means powerless, for Craig organized groups on three levels: The Sages of the Community, Children for a Decent Texas, and in the middle, a large and forceful group, The Watchdogs of the Fort. With all the skills remembered from former battles he brought pressure to bear on the editor of the *Larkin Defender*, who if left alone might have sided with the liquor people on three solid grounds, which he espoused privately to his friends: 'Orderly sale would be good for trade. Keeping our kids at home would stop those car crashes when they go seeking booze. And I hate the hypocrisy of drinking wet and voting dry.' But when he found that his larger advertisers ardently supported Reverend Craig, even though they were themselves heavy drinkers, he found himself compelled to write a series of hard-hitting editorials favoring retention of the ban.

To one outsider, the situation in Larkin seemed paradoxical: 'Everyone in this crazy town drinks but wants to stop anyone else from doing so.' An explanation of this curious Texas trait was spelled out in a letter written by a Baptist woman to a friend in New Mexico:

> It is true that Albert takes a small drink now and then, but only socially when we are in the homes of those who favor alcohol. Even I am not above a congenial nip on holidays, and I'm told that boys in school, and especially the older ones who work in town, drink somewhat. Yet all of us who have the vote prefer to keep alcohol out of the stores, and saloons off our quiet streets.
>
> We do this, I think, because we know that to restrain evil in even the smallest degree is good, in that it sends a signal through the community that we shall not allow it to run rampant. On the three nights prior to the vote Reverend Craig will hold prayer meetings in which we will commit ourselves to fighting the devil, for we are convinced that unrestricted use of alcohol is a principal agency through which he attacks individuals and their communities.

The crusade against alcohol, which had to be fought repeatedly in what Reverend Craig called 'our Christian counties of the north,' produced one grave weakness, which the people of Larkin did not like to discuss. Highway 23 leading to Bascomb became a well-traveled route, and when young men and women roared south to get liquored up, often drinking out of their bottles as they weaved their way back, there were apt to be accidents, more coming north than going south, and there were many involving some solitary drunk heading north who smashed head-on into some innocent car coming south with its four sober passengers. TRAGEDY IN SUICIDE GULCH became the headline, and often it was the four sober travelers who were killed, while the solitary drunk survived because he had sped into the accident completely relaxed.

Rarely did a year pass without some horrendous accident along Highway 23, and occasional protests appeared in the press about this nasty habit of young people driving down to Bascomb to buy their liquor and then guzzling it on their way home, but no one seemed to blame the carnage in Suicide Gulch on Larkin's lack of orderly places in which to buy a drink.

So as the critical vote approached, the lines were drawn in typical North Texas fashion: outside forces pouring in huge sums in hopes of being allowed to peddle their product, the Baptists fighting valiantly to maintain the status quo they had inherited from their God-fearing parents. Partisans on each side were sensible, and patriotic, and driven by respectable motives, but there was such enmity between them that no meeting ground could ever be established.

Watchers of the campaign refused to predict how this one was going to result: 'Can't never tell the effect of all that money on their side or prayers on ours.'

A peculiarity of the Texas system was that any plebiscite on booze was effective for only a few years, after which the other side could try again; ordinarily, the losers licked their wounds for about six years before storming back, but regardless of the outcome, it was never final. As Reverend Craig said five days before the vote: 'In this world of sin the forces of evil never rest.'

This year it looked as if evil would triumph, for its Dallas managers, Kraft and Killeen, had run a masterful campaign focused not on alcohol but on human rights and the advantages of a free society, but at almost the last moment the drys received help from an unexpected quarter. In the oil town of San Angelo, a hundred and seventy miles to the southwest, a Catholic priest named Father Uecker awoke to the fact that during the past twelve months he had been required to conduct burial services for five impetuous young men of his congregation who had been shot and killed during five different drunken brawls on church property. In anguish over such mayhem he had, with considerable publicity, announced that he would no longer rent his parish hall for any dance or entertainment at which liquor was consumed.

He said that this would cost his church more than three thousand dollars in lost fees, but he felt that this would be a small price to pay if it would halt or even slow down the carnage. Father Uecker ended his announcement with a paragraph which somewhat dampened its effect among the Larkin Baptists, but even so, they clutched at the support his action provided:

> We are fairly certain that Jesus himself enjoyed the wedding feast at Cana, which certainly included wine and dancing. We believe that wine is also a part of God's creation and, therefore, it is good. We believe that dancing can be very wholesome recreation. We categorically deny that drinking and dancing are evil of themselves, but it seems to be impossible at this time and in this place to conduct public dances with the abuse that alcohol brings.

This tragic news from San Angelo, that five young men in one small parish had died of gunshot wounds, plus Reverend Craig's imaginative use of the report, neatly ignoring the priest's reminder that he was not a prohibitionist, swung just enough votes to the drys to ensure that once again Larkin County had obeyed the voice of its religious leader. When the vote was announced church bells rang and some members of the various congregations, including the pastor's sixteen-year-old son, rode through the county seat, tooting their horns in celebration of the victory.

The other three youngsters in the car containing young Craig were so jubilant that when the informal parade in town ended, they rode joyously down Suicide Gulch to the grogshops of Bascomb County, drank immoderately, and then came zigzagging homeward with two bottles of Old Alamo, one for the front seat, one for the back.

As they approached the intersection of Highway 23 and FM-578 the driver became confused by the lights coming at him from dead ahead and by those angling in from 578. In a moment of supreme confidence he decided to thread his way right through the middle; instead, he smashed broadside into the car coming from the right. The driver, young Craig, the other two passengers and the husband and wife in the other car were killed, not instantly but in the flames which engulfed them.

The changes which assaulted Texas affected everyone. On the day before the regents' meeting the new governor called the Quimper ranch: 'Lorenzo, the new regent I appointed is flying up from the Valley. You've been a regent for two terms. Would you please meet him at the airport and more or less explain how things work?'

The new man was Simón Garza, the thoughtful mayor of Bravo and the first Hispanic to be appointed to the university's Board of Regents. Quimper, who had always employed Mexican wetbacks on his nine ranches and who had promoted one of them, Cándido Guzmán, to general foreman, found no difficulty in talking with Mayor Garza, brother of the A&M member of the Task Force with whom he had argued so congenially.

It was a thoughtful conversation because Garza immediately showed his desire to learn, and faced with that sincerity, Il Magnifico realized that he must not clown around with his redneck humor: 'You do us honor joining the regents, Mayor Garza. You've built a fine reputation throughout Texas.' When Garza looked down at his hands to avoid having to respond to this formal flattery, Quimper said: 'Being a regent is a privilege. One of the most important assignments in Texas.'

'And I'm honored to be the first Mexican-American. Although I do think it's about time, seeing how many of our people attend the place.'

'I'm glad to have you aboard,' Quimper said, and when Garza asked: 'Wasn't your father the famous regent?' Lorenzo was encouraged to speak with him as a serious equal.

'He had the job for years, and people either exalted or despised him, depending on whether or not they could read.' When Garza smiled at the joke, Lorenzo grew more specific.

'My father did everything practical to promote the university football team, and everything possible to annihilate any influences he felt were not in harmony with the spirit of the gridiron. On the positive side, he created generous scholarships for football players, initiated the plan of having wealthy ranchers contribute steers to feed his athletes at their training table, and organized a fleet of private planes, some of them jets, which the dozen coaches could use when recruiting in the fall and winter months. He also provided, out of his own oil money, two different sets of uniforms for the 334 members of the university's show band of the Southwest, "biggest and best in the nation and twice as big as anything in Europe or Asia," he said. On crisp October days when the Texas football team ran onto the field in the enlarged stadium he had helped provide, and the band marched out to greet them, he could sit back in his special box and think: I'm responsible for a hell of a lot of that, and when boys he had recruited swept to national championships, he could say truthfully: "I brought most of that backfield to Texas. What a bargain." '

'Why is your father's name so familiar?' Garza asked, and Quimper said frankly: 'Bad publicity,' and he explained.

'There was a negative side. My father practically destroyed the faculty, disciplining anyone he disliked and firing those he distrusted. At the height of his reign of terror he told me: "Runnin' a university is like runnin' a ranch. The man with money owns it, and he hires a manager and assistants. He gives them wide latitude in day-to-day operations, but he never lets them forget who's really in charge." He had an interesting theory about professors: "I like to have colorful men on my staff. Fellows who wear old-fashioned clothes, or who go to northern Sweden in their summers, or who wear string ties. Makes the campus distinctive, but I do not want them meddling in the running of the place or speaking out on politics." Teachers who ignored his rules or openly contested them did not last long on my father's academic ranch.'

'What was that famous fracas about Frank Dobie?'

Quimper seemed to ignore the question, for he launched instead into a philosophical discussion about the arts in Texas: 'Compared to the other Southern states, Texas has not produced its quota of artists, musicians, novelists or philosophers, and my old man was one of the reasons. If we did not have world-class intellectuals, we did have, in my early days, two men who were building a foundation, and my father scorned them. Walter Prescott Webb had a fine, clear vision of the West and wrote about it with skill and passion, but he favored liberal causes, and for my father that was forbidden. Frank Dobie! What a man! Traipsed about the campfires gathering cowboy yarns and tall stories about coyotes, Longhorns and rattlesnakes. I knew him and loved him. He could be as gentle as a hummingbird, as mean as a scorpion. He defined our state in terms of its rural heritage and made us proud of what we had accomplished.'

'Did Dobie ever write anything of national importance?' Garza asked, and Quimper snapped: 'He did a damned sight better. Carried the culture of Texas overseas to Cambridge University, where he was a star. But he also had strong feelings about the long-term welfare of the state. And that infuriated my father. I remember him roaring one night: "Until we get rid of that communist sumbitch Frank Dobie we'll never have a safe university." As a fellow regent, let me advise you on one thing. The phrase *a safe university*'s a contradiction, because a real university must question everything, but with my old man ridin' herd, few professors dared.'

He laughed and suggested that perhaps Garza might like a fire, so big mesquite logs were dragged in by two Mexican workers, and soon the unique aroma that made mesquite barbecue so flavorful permeated the room, and talk grew more casual: 'The things my old man said! At the height of his battle with Dobie he told me: "The faculty should accept the buildings we give them and keep their mouths shut." And how about the time he told the reporters: "The University of Texas has one overriding obligation. To turn out football teams of which the state can be proud." '

'Your father fire Dobie?'

'Yep. And muzzled Webb, two of the most original performers our university ever produced.' He leaned far back in his chair, studied the mesquite flames, and reflected on a problem which had agitated him of late: 'If our Southern sisters to the east have produced this outpouring of fine writers—Eudora Welty, William Faulkner, Robert Penn Warren, Truman Capote, Tennessee Williams, Thomas Wolfe, Flannery O'Connor, I can never remember whether she's a woman or he's a man—why have we produced only one? Katherine Anne Porter?'

He knew part of the answer: 'Texas was a true frontier, right down to 1920. We were far removed from east-west routes of travel, and we offered damn little to the north-south travelers. When a man in 1840 or a woman in 1860 crossed the plains up north, what did they find? Thriving places like California and Oregon. You cross Texas and what do you face? The deserts of New Mexico and Arizona. The empty cactus lands of northern Mexico. Also, the railroads reached us pathetically late. In those years when European artists were crossing Wyoming as a matter of course on powerful continental trains, Texas had a couple of rural stations.'

Pouring Garza a drink, he asked: 'You know much about Austin? You'll love it. Marvelous town. But it's failed to produce the artists and thinkers it should have. Somehow we were cheated.' He thought about this for some moments, then growled: 'But damnit, with your help we can catch up.'

Mayor Garza took from his pocket a confidential report supplied him by the university, and as he studied it by the light of the mesquite fire, he thought: How strange that Lorenzo Quimper should be telling me about the devastation his father had wrought!

And it was strange, because the secret report told how Lorenzo, this redneck who played the loudmouth buffoon, had, when he became a regent in 1978, initiated at his own expense a study comparing salaries at Texas with those at first-class state universities like North Carolina, Wisconsin and California, and what he learned disgusted him: 'We pay twenty thousand dollars, thirty thousand less than they pay their top chairs. What in hell is wrong with Texas?'

With guidance from a thoughtful administration, he had visited many graduates of the university who had profited from the education it had provided them: 'Herman, the great power that the state of Texas is accumulatin', and the wealth our university commands means nothin' if we don't use that power constructively.' All agreed with this, for the clever application of power was a Texas tradition. 'So what I'm recommendin', and I'll need your help, fellows like you who've struck it rich. Give us five hundred thousand dollars to endow a chair in your name. The Herman Kallheimer Chair in Jurisprudence. And if you have an associate who can't handle that amount, he can give us a hundred thousand to provide extra funds for some good professor at the lower levels.' All across the state he had moved, appealing to what he called 'The National Pride of Loyal Texans,' and he succeeded in amassing funds for seventy-six full endowments and for five hundred and twenty lesser supports.

Garza looked across the top of his paper at the inscrutable man staring into the fire: the big hat beside the chair, the expensive whipcord suit, the wide leather belt with brass buckle in front showing the state of Texas and the bold engraving Garza had seen on the back: IL MAGNIFICO. The man conformed in no way to the data on the paper, and Garza raised the question: 'This report says that in a relatively short period you provided the administration with an unexpected forty-two million dollars for upgrading teachers' salaries. With that kind of money, we can have one of the best faculties in America.'

Quimper downplayed his contribution: 'In my principal mission I've failed.'

'I don't call a sum like that failure.'

'It's those damned clowns out on the prairie. They'll give unlimited endowments for the Law School. Same for the School of Business and Science. Or the geology of oil. But not a thin dime for poetry, or drama, or fine arts, or English, or philosophy, or history. That young professor who came to see me after our last meetin' was right. We've established a university for the trainin' of technicians. The work of the spirit, to hell with that.'

And as soon as he said these words he realized that he was condemning himself and, especially, his father: 'It was us Quimpers who set the style. Frank Dobie asked questions about ultimate values, so kick him to hell out. Walter Webb asked about the sources of Texas power, so move him gently to one side. I bear a heavy burden.'

As they talked an ember fell from the fire, and since Quimper was at the portable bar pouring a drink, Garza grabbed the poker to push back the flaming mesquite, but as he did so he noticed the curious shape of the poker. It was, to his surprise, a branding iron such as cattlemen used to mark their cattle, and when he brought the business end forward to study it, he found that it consisted of a four-inch letter U, inside of which rested a smaller, neatly forged T.

He was about to ask what this meant when Quimper reached for the brand, waved it about in his left hand, and said, with impressive emotion: 'This represents one of the highlights of my life.'

'Your first cattle brand? What do the letters signify?'

'Mayor Garza! That's the University of Texas.' And he proceeded to unfold a story so improbable that Garza sat riveted: 'When my father enrolled at the university, there was a kind of secret society—all the important men on campus, those judged to be winners. There were arcane rites, secret handgrips . . . all that stuff. Father was a member, of course. One of the proudest achievements of his life.'

'What did the society do?'

'Defended the honor of the university. And they had a unique initiation rite, which the university made them abandon in 1944 when a student's life was endangered. By the time I entered in 1949 that special deal was long gone.'

'What was it?'

Quimper ignored the question, laid aside the brand, and gazed intently at Garza: 'I was a sophomore when they took me in. Paddling . . . a little drinking . . . you know, the usual. And I'll confess I was very proud. But when I'd been a member about six months my father and three big wheels here in Austin, judges, bankers, you know, all graduates of the university, they invited me to a posh dinner, then drove me out to a lonely spot on the shores of Lake Travis, a rather wild spot, where they built quite a large fire.'

He stopped talking, took a swallow of his drink, and stared once more at Garza: 'When the fire was extremely hot, they placed this brand, this one here, in it. Then they spread-eagled me on the ground, tied my arms and legs to stakes they'd driven in the earth, ripped off my shirt, and branded me on the chest with that brand over there.'

Garza gasped: 'You're kidding.'

Slowly, as if he were a priest conducting a ritual, Quimper opened his shirt, revealing a powerful chest on which was a deeply imbedded ⨄.

'Is that a tattoo?' Garza asked, to which Quimper replied forcefully: 'No! It's a brand, like you brand cattle. And when it was burned in, my father rubbed it with salt so as to make a real scar, like they do after those duels in Heidelberg, and he told me in awed tones: "Now you're really one of us. Each of us carries the same brand." ' He reached for the brand, placed it against his chest, and allowed Garza to satisfy himself that the conformance was perfect.

Rebuttoning his shirt, he said: 'As you move about Texas you'll come upon many men in their sixties who carry this secret brand under their vested suits. Leaders of the state. We never speak of it. Never reveal who else carries it. But I will tell you this. At the regents' meeting tomorrow, I won't be the only one hiding it.' He paused: 'My father told me that night by the lake as he rubbed in the salt: "I'd not want to have a son who didn't carry over his heart the badge of the university." He loved the place you're about to help govern. And so do I.'

The night grew late, and he told Mayor Garza: 'We've needed you on our board for some years. Talk sense to us. Support the good proposals.' He sounded like a philosopher.

But next morning, when he drove Garza onto the campus and saw the poster announcing that next week the university baseball team would play A&M, he reverted to type. Once more he became the florid, beefy, extroverted Texas rancher whom the undergraduates would noisily toast as the fifth inning came to a close: 'Il Magnifico . . . the Bottom of the Fifth,' with the leader finishing off a bottle of whiskey. He hoped they would smother A&M.

Chuckling, he asked Garza: 'You ever hear about the time some years back when the state decided to make A&M a full-fledged university? Dreadful mistake. Ambitious A&M alumni wanted to upgrade the name of their town, College Station, to something more exalted. So I offered a hundred-dollar prize for the most appropriate suggestion. The winner? Malfunction Junction. A&M officials were not amused.'

Then he confided: 'Actually, I think it's a fine school. I help it whenever I can. But our board expects me to turn up at every meeting with a new Aggie joke, and this time I have a zinger.'

So after Mayor Garza had been introduced to warm applause, for the regents were relieved to have the Hispanic barrier broken, Quimper said:

> 'This Aggie was infuriated by the way people in Texas downgraded him and he consulted a counselor, who advised: "Best way in the world to demonstrate intellectual superiority is to salt and pepper your conversation with French phrases." So off he goes to Paris to a tutoring school, and on the day of his return he marches boldly into the best store in Austin and says: "Garçon, I would like some pâté de fois gras avec poivre, four croissants, a coq-au-vin, and a bottle of champagne très, très sec."
>
> 'The clerk looks up and asks: "When did you go to A&M?" and the former Aggie sobs: "How did you know?" and the clerk says: "Son, this is a hardware store." '

He had barely stopped receiving congratulations on his latest masterpiece when a folded note was passed along the table to him:

> I don't think Aggie jokes are funny. My brother teaches there and says it's a fine school. Next you'll be telling Mexican jokes, and I won't like that, either.
>
> Your new friend,
> Simón Garza

Quimper flushed, recognized the propriety of this complaint, and concluded that the new regent was not going to be anybody's pushover. Bringing his palms together under his chin in the Buddhist gesture of deference, he nodded to his friend of the previous evening, then, using his right thumb in a gesture of cutting his throat, he indicated that there would be no more Aggie jokes.

Then he submitted his report as chairman of the finance committee, informing his colleagues that with the unexpected increase in oil prices, Texas now had a much higher return on its endowment than places like Harvard and Stanford: 'This has enabled us to bring onto our faculty winners of the Nobel Prize, outstanding figures in science like John Wheeler of Princeton, and a whole bevy of notable experts in law and business. We're headin' for the very top ranks of academia and will not be denied.'

As for the other financial aspects, he said: 'Like the comedian, I have good news and bad news. The good news is that the program we launched to under- write our professors has enjoyed amazin' success. As of today we have no room to accept any more five-hundred-thousand-dollar endowments in law, business or science, because all the chairs have been funded.' This brought applause from the board, some of whose members had funded endowments.

'The bad news is that we have not received one endowment in the liberal arts such as English, poetry and philosophy.' Allowing time for this striking news to percolate, he added: 'I've argued fruitlessly with successful lawyers and business- men, till my tongue has cleaved to the roof of my mouth, remindin' them that they are able to succeed in life not because of the technical trainin' they received at our university but because of the solid instruction they had in the meanin' of life . . . in their basic courses in the liberal arts. They haven't understood a word I said.

'Gentlemen and ladies, if this continues, the great universities of Texas are goin' to become trade schools, places to train mechanics, centers for the crunchin' of numbers in computers. The ideas which will govern our society will be delivered to us from Harvard and Oxford and the Sorbonne.'

He became eloquent, Texas-ranch style, in defending those values which his father had outlawed, and after prolonged discussion he said: 'I'll tell you what I'm goin' to do. I'm goin' to accept ever' one of the proposed contributions for additional endowments in law and business and divert 'em to the humanities.'

'But, Lorenzo,' a cautious regent asked, 'what will you tell the donors?' and without hesitation he snapped: 'I'll lie.'

'I think we'd better consider this,' a lawyer said, and the others laughed, but Quimper silenced them: 'I feel so strong about this that I am herewith establishin' full endowments, half a million each, for two chairs, one in philosophy, one in poetry.'

It was in this spirit that Regent Quimper, Il Magnifico, started to reverse the damage done by his father, that inspired builder of the university campus.

When Maggie Morrison, forty-seven years old, discovered how easy it was to borrow large sums of money in Texas, especially from big oilmen, she studied the real estate market in Houston with special care and learned that after the savage devaluation of the Mexican peso many fine buildings were near bankruptcy, so that remarkable bargains were available, but only if one had faith that the market would rebound. She had that faith.

Her fourteen years in what Houstonians liked to call 'our go-go town' had almost obliterated memories of Detroit. She no longer made comparisons between Michigan and Texas, being content to accept her new home as *sui generis,* obedient only to its own rules. She had grown to like Western dress, the informality of social life, the Texas brag, and she positively adored Mexican food, especially the tang of a fresh chile relleno or a really well-made enchilada. And her affection for Houston itself had grown solidly, so that when the figures for the 1980 census were extrapolated to 1981, she found positive joy in learning that Houston was now the fourth largest city in the United States, having displaced Philadelphia, with every prospect of surpassing Chicago before the century ended.

But now Houston's unoccupied office space had grown to 43,000,000 square feet: The builders have built too much, too fast and with funds that carried too high a rate of interest. With mortgages at seventeen percent, somebody must go broke.

Wherever she looked she found telltale signs of the city's perilous position. The big oil companies were cutting back on personnel; the little ones were solving that problem more simply: they were in bankruptcy. And this sent echoes throughout the business community, as leasing experts closed shop, drilling rigs were sold for ten cents on the dollar, and banks foreclosed loans. Registration at local colleges dropped because parents could not scrape together the tuition, and retail stores began to lay off salespeople.

But the crunch that interested Maggie was the one in real estate, and in the late afternoons when she sat in the fifteenth-floor condominium overlooking Buffalo Bayou, her attention focused on that splendid set of tall buildings erected by Gabe Klinowitz's Mexican politicians—The Ramparts. Their wraparound glass facings shone in the sunset, but they were only fifteen percent occupied; had rentals continued at the spectacular levels of 1980 the Mexicans would have made a killing, but now they faced disaster. 'I'm sure they have at least a hundred and seventy million dollars in the three towers,' Maggie had told her husband, but he was so involved with Roy Bub Hooker in their exotic-game ranch that he could not pay full attention to the interesting proposal she was making, so she sat alone and stared at the mesmerizing target.

One night as the moon shone on the shimmering glass she made up her mind, and early next morning she dressed in her best business suit and flew up to Dallas: 'The poor Mexicans have made this enormous investment, Mr. Rusk . . .'

'Never feel sorry for the other guy. If he's made an ass of himself, gig him while he's bent over.'

'There's no way they can diminish their debt, and they may be paying as high as nineteen-percent interest.'

'You're sure they have a hundred and seventy million in it? What would they listen to? If we bailed them out?'

'I have a gut feeling we could get it for fifty million, maybe even forty.'

'See what you can do.'

She returned to Houston with a tentative deal much like the one before, for Rusk had said: 'Maggie, I'll chip in as much as thirteen million if you add your two. But you must convince the Houston banks to lend us the rest at a decent interest.'

Her first job was to confront the Mexicans with their perilous situation and convince them that in bankruptcy they might lose everything. Wearing her gentlest and most feminine clothes, she minimized the staggering difference between the $170,000,000 they had obligated themselves to pay and the mere $40,000,000 she was offering, and quietly she assured them that they had no reasonable alternative: 'Besides, gentlemen, as you and I well know, a great deal of what you call your loss is paper money only. This is a drying out of the market, and if you'd had your funds in oil, you'd have lost even more.'

With the banks she was soft-spoken but relentless: 'What alternative have you? Your loans are bust, but so are the ones you have in oil. Help my partner and me to refinance this disaster and you'll get back more than you had a right to expect.'

Just when she had everyone on the edge of the chair, each ready to jump forward if the others did, Beth announced that she was going to have a baby, and so Maggie dropped her negotiations for about a week, leaving Mexicans, Houston bankers and Ransom Rusk dangling; she had not planned it this way, but it was the cleverest move she could have made, for by the time she returned to the bargaining table, all the players would be nervously eager to reach a decision. Said one banker: 'Trust a woman to play a trick like this. We could use her on our board.'

But Maggie did not engage in tricks. For several years now, she had been aware that she was a much stronger person than her husband, much more attuned to the pressures and responsibilities of Houston finance; although she would never express it in this arrogant manner, she had character and he did not. If these delicate negotiations regarding The Ramparts evolved as she hoped, she would back them with every penny of her small fortune, every minute of her working life. Her deal would be meticulously honest and as fair to each participant as the exigencies of the economic situation allowed. She wanted a just share of the profits, but was prepared to suffer her share of the loss if her calculations were in error. A

Michigan schoolteacher who believed in George Eliot had become a Texas manip-
ulator who believed in Adam Smith.

In growing into this status, she was conscious of how far behind she had left
her breezy, glib-speaking husband: he played at games; she juggled with empires.
He had been a good husband and a better father, but she could not escape
realizing that under pressure he had revealed himself as a shifty, small-caliber
man. She hoped he would stay out of trouble and hold on to some of the easy
money he had made, but on neither point was she confident.

And finally the tears came. Toughened in the brutal world of Houston real
estate, she had not allowed herself this indulgence since weeping with joy at
Beth's wedding to Wolfgang Macnab, but now that she reviewed her own life
with Todd, remembering how it had started with such love and mutuality, she
could not ignore the sad loss she had suffered: Oh, Todd! We should have done
much better! And in this lament she generously took upon herself, improperly,
half the blame.

While the Mexican politicians and the Texas businessmen fretted, she spent her
days with her daughter, talking about marriage, and children, and responsibility,
and one afternoon when Beth was visiting her mother, Maggie called her attention to The Ramparts: 'The buildings are not only beautiful, Beth. They're in
excellent physical condition. But they're only fifteen-percent occupied. Frozen
tears. Monuments to dreams gone wrong.'

'Mummy, why would you want to get mixed up with such a failure?'

'Because I'm convinced that Houston is the liveliest spot in America. Because I
know it's bound to snap back.'

'But if you know this, don't you think they know it, too?'

'Yes, but I'm the one that has faith.'

'Are you gambling all your money on these towers?'

The two women looked at the shimmering beauty of The Ramparts, admiring
the subtle manner in which the three spires formed a unit, with the curve of one
iridescent expanse linking with the other two and complementing them. They
formed a work of art, Houston modern, and Maggie would be proud to be its
owner if she could acquire it, as seemed likely, at twenty-four cents on the dollar.

'Are you doing this out of vanity, Mummy?'

Maggie pondered this. It was exciting to operate in what had been considered a
man's field and to perform rather better than most of the men; of course she felt
proud of her achievements. And it was breathtaking to gamble with such large
funds, hers and other people's, and she was prepared to acknowledge this to her
daughter, but at this critical time in both their lives she felt it improper to operate
from such trivial and almost degrading impulses.

'Beth, you really do like Texas, don't you?'

'I'm in love with it. I can't even remember Detroit.'

'Do you want to remember?'

'No! This is freedom, excitement, the future. Wolfgang and I see unlimited possibilities. I don't mean life in the fast lane, or any of that nonsense. But a man like Wolfgang, with me beside him, he can do anything from a Texas base. Anything.'

'I feel the same way, Beth.'

'But Daddy isn't at your side.'

'No, he isn't.'

They dropped that subject, and after a while Maggie confided: 'I'm gambling most of my savings.' Before Beth could reprimand her, she took her daughter's hands: 'But do you think your mother . . . you know me . . . how cautious I am. Do you think I'd take such a gamble blind?'

'I'm not sure I know you any more.'

'Look at yourself. The way you were when we came down here. Lady poet and all that. Then lady baton twirler. Now lady socialite. I don't know you.' Quickly she added: 'But I'm very proud of you just as you are. Resplendent transformation.'

'What safeguards have you, Mother?'

'Mr. Rusk is in this with me, and we'd be out of our minds to buy that turkey.' She flipped a thumb contemptuously at the towers: 'We could never make it pay . . . all that unrented space.'

'My conclusion too. All that glass with nothing behind it.'

'However!' And here Maggie smiled. 'I've found a group of potential buyers. Canadians. They have a hotel chain behind them. They believe that if they can get title at a low enough figure, they can install an operation that will pay out.'

'Why don't they buy it themselves?'

'Because they need someone like me to honcho the details.'

'If the second tier of deals works, do you make a bundle?'

'You always phrased things delicately, Beth. Yes.'

'And if you can't unload to the buyers and the hotel chain . . .'

'Now wait. The hotel chain puts up no money. Just a managerial contract, but a very enticing one, I must say.'

'How do you know about the contract?'

Maggie Morrison smiled softly: 'Oftentimes, Beth, a dumb-looking peasant from Detroit can learn things a billionaire like Ransom Rusk could never learn.'

'But if your clever plan falls flat? If your secret buyers drop out?'

'I lose everything.' In the silence Beth looked across to the glorious towers; they seemed almost to sway with the wind, and she understood why her mother would find exhilaration in this game of Houston roulette, and she understood her gambling everything on such a precarious toss, but then her mother said: 'I wouldn't lose everything. We'll be buying this for twenty-four cents on the dollar. If we did have to bail out, we could probably get back eighteen cents.'

When Maggie turned her attention from her pregnant daughter to the long-pregnant purchase of The Ramparts, she found the other players almost thirsting to conclude the deal, so she finished things off with a flourish. For $42,000,000 she acquired buildings worth $170,000,000, and she and Rusk had had to ante up only $12,000,000 between them, the banks being happy to carry the rest. Even the Mexican politicians showed relief: 'Only paper money, as you said. We feared we might lose it all.'

In July 1983, when things were looking slightly better in Houston, she sold The Ramparts to the well-heeled Canadians, who would convert the top floors of the buildings into superpenthouses for their wives. The price that Maggie was able to swing for this part of the deal was $62,000,000, which meant that she and Rusk had picked up $20,000,000 for about a year's work. Generously, he split this fifty-fifty with Maggie, telling her that it was the traditional finder's fee.

When the sale was completed—*finalized,* in Houston jargon—Maggie took Beth to a victory lunch: 'Why did I risk so much? I wanted to give you and Lonnie the best start possible in Texas life. I'm afraid your father will lose everything with his exotic ranch.'

'Mummy! Wolfgang and I earn a good living. Far beyond what I dreamed.'

'For the time being. Linebackers don't last forever.'

This meeting occurred in August of 1983 and as it ended, the television in the posh restaurant was broadcasting continuous alerts regarding the first hurricane of the season, Alicia, which stormed about in the Gulf, with winds exceeding a hundred and twenty miles an hour, presumably heading toward Galveston. The two women stopped to listen, and Maggie, who studied such storms because they could influence real estate values, said: 'Poor Galveston. In 1900 it was wiped out by a storm like this.'

'I've heard about it. Was it bad?'

'Are you kidding? Six thousand drowned. Worst natural disaster in American history.' When Beth gasped, she added, professionally: 'But they built a seawall afterward, and it's been impregnable.'

'I would hope so,' Beth said.

During the next two days Maggie followed the tropical storm, but only casually, for the winds dropped to a relatively safe eighty miles an hour, which the Texas coast had learned to cope with. She had almost forgotten the threat when the storm stopped dead, about fifty miles offshore, and whirled about upon itself, as if uncertain where to land.

Now those who understood the rudiments of tropical storms became apprehensive, for this stationary whirling meant that the eye of the storm was picking up terrible velocities, perhaps as much as a hundred and sixty miles an hour, and with such accumulated force the hurricane could be a killer wherever it crashed ashore . . . and it did head for Galveston.

By the grace of a compassionate nature, the wild storm veered off during the final moments of its approach to land and struck a relatively unpopulated area of the beach, so that instead of killing thousands, as it might have done, it killed only twenty. With a sigh, Galveston went to its churches and gave thanks for yet another salvation. The great storm of 1983 with its violent winds had passed inland.

Through a curious trick of the winds aloft, when it was well past the coast it turned back on itself and struck Houston, not from the east as might have been anticipated, but from the southwest, and as it came roaring in at velocities no architect or builder had foreseen, it began to whip around the tall buildings, creating powerful currents not experienced before.

Now the lovely architecture of Houston, those spires challenging the sky, those castles of glass so brilliant in the rising or setting sun, were subjected to a tremendous battering, and one by one the windowpanes began to shatter. Glass from one building would somersault through the air and smash into the glass of an adjacent building, which would in turn throw its panes toward another.

Maggie Morrison, hearing of the savage effects of the storm, went outside, against the advice of everyone, to see at close hand what was happening to The Ramparts, for which she felt a custodian's responsibility even though the buildings were no longer hers. Finding partial refuge behind a concrete abutment, she watched in anguish as the fantastic winds struck at the towers.

'Pray God they hold!' she whispered as the climax of the hurricane struck, and she drew breath again when she saw that although they swayed, as Beth had imagined them to do that afternoon, they behaved with grace and dignity, bending slightly but not surrendering. 'Thank God,' she sighed.

However, when the winds at this great velocity passed around the curved expanse of the three buildings, it acquired that capacity which lifts an airplane—a kind of venturi effect as when material of any kind is constricted and flows faster —and on the far side of the buildings, away from the frontal force of the gale, the wind began to suck out the windows, popping them outward from their frames, and as they fell to the streets below, they formed a delicate, deadly shower of glass, millions of shards little and big, clattering to the asphalt streets and the cement pavements, maiming any who stood in the way, covering the passageways with icicles that would never melt.

Oh God! Look at my buildings! She stood behind her refuge, her fingers across her face in such manner as to allow her to see the devastation, and as the glass showered down around her, missing her miraculously with its lethal chunks, she wept for the tragedy of which she was not really a part but for which she felt a personal responsibility.

Standing in the howling wind and the falling glass, she wept for the broken dreams of the oilmen she knew whose world had collapsed; she cried for all the recently unemployed, many of whom had given up everything in the North to move to the lures of steady work in Houston; she sobbed for the Mexicans who had gambled so heavily and seen the ground swept from under them; and she felt particular sorrow for the Canadians who had purchased these buildings three weeks ago. The Ramparts, with their empty rooms and shattered façades, were the responsibility of the new buyers—of that there was not the slightest doubt—but she had escaped this disaster by only twenty days, and had she been dilatory in her manipulations, she would have borne the full weight of this catastrophe.

In the storm she wept for all those in Texas whose great gambles came crashing down.

'This could be the most dangerous road in America,' Ranger Cletus Macnab said to his tall, hefty brother as they sped southwest from Fort Stockton toward the pair of little border towns which faced each other across the Rio Grande, Polk in Texas, Carlota across the rickety bridge in Chihuahua.

'Doesn't look too bad to me,' Wolfgang said, nor did it: a solid macadam roadway no narrower than most secondaries, bleak plains east and west, with cautionary white flood gauges at the dips where a bridge would have been too costly for the relatively little use it would have gotten. Looking at the black warning marks, foot by foot, Wolfgang asked: 'Can a flood really rise thirteen feet through this land? Looks bone-dry.'

'When it flashes up in those hills, fifteen feet in ten minutes, and if you're caught in this hollow, farewell.'

'Is that what you mean, "the most dangerous in America"?'

'No! Sensible travelers learn to beware when they see rising water. Those warning poles are for tourists . . . like you.'

'Then why the danger?'

The Ranger, a very tall, thin man in his mid-thirties, wearing Texas boots, a fawn-gray whipcord ranch suit and the inevitable Stetson, pointed to a car speeding south ahead of them: 'On this road I would stop that car only with the greatest caution, Wolfgang. And if I saw it stalled over on the shoulder, I'd approach it only with drawn gun, expecting trouble.'

'Why that particular car?'

'On this road, any car, watch out. Chances are it's been stolen up north. That one's from Minnesota, so what in hell is it doing on this road? I'll tell you what. Some goon has stolen it up there, late-model Buick, and is high-tailing it to Mexico to sell it for a million.'

'Is there a market?'

'Are you kidding? They caught the head of a Mexican police agency, fronting for an organization of hundreds, buying stolen American cars all along the border, changing numbers, repainting, selling them all over Mexico at outrageous prices. So if I try to stop them, they shoot.'

'If it's known, why don't they . . . ? Did they throw the police chief in jail?'

'What do you think? We're approaching northern Mexico, a world unto itself, a law unto itself.'

'So you steer clear of cars heading south?'

'And on this road, cars heading north, too.' He indicated a low-slung, modified Pontiac roaring north with Kansas plates. 'Probably loaded with marijuana or cocaine.' He studied the car as it whizzed past. 'If they are running the stuff, they'll give me a gun battle.'

'So what do you do?'

'I notify Narcotics farther along the line. They intercept them with machine guns.' And he cranked up his police radio: 'Vic, Macnab. Nineteen eighty-two Pontiac four-door. Kansas plates ending seven two one. Heading north on U. S. 69.'

'And I suppose many of the northbound cars carry wetbacks?'

'We don't bother with them.'

'Why not? If they're illegal?'

'Border Patrol has charge of that. So we let them handle it.' He hesitated: 'Of course, if a wetback commits any kind of crime . . .'

'They give you much trouble?'

'In the old days, almost never. Today, a more vicious element moving in. They rob. Now and then a murder. But we can track them pretty easy.'

Wolfgang, four years younger than his brother, a mite taller at six-seven and much heavier, reflected on this strange state of affairs, then said: 'Grampop Oscar would go out of his mind if he heard how you were running the show. Remember how he hated Meskins, how he ordered them around?'

'All that's changed, Wolfgang. I work very closely with Mexican officials on the other side of the river.' Before his brother could reply, the Ranger added: 'Couldn't do my job without their help.'

When they approached the dip that would carry them down to the Rio Grande, Cletus slowed the car and said gravely: 'Wolfgang, you sure you want to go the rest of the way? This isn't for fun, you know.'

'I asked to come, didn't I?'

'True, but once across that bridge . . .'

'That's the part I want to see.'

'So be it, little brother. Here we go.'

They dropped in to the American town of Polk, named after the Tennessee President who had fought so valiantly to bring Texas into the Union; it was a miserable testimony to a great leader, a town of sixteen hundred persons living for the most part in crumbling Mexican-style adobe huts. The town's chief fame derived from summer weather reports: 'And once again the hottest spot in these United States—Polk, Texas, down on the Rio Grande, a hundred and nine degrees.'

But to those who appreciated the Southwest, and the Macnab brothers did, this town, like its sisters along the river, had a persuasive charm: 'Reminds me of how it must have been in 1840. I love these dusty streets, the Mexican women peerin' at me through the shutters, the dogs chasin' their fleas.'

'I wouldn't be able to tell this was the U. S. of A.,' Wolfgang said.

'It isn't,' the Ranger said. 'It's something new. Maybe one day we'll call it Texico.'

'That's a gasoline.'

'No more flammable than this.'

Cletus did not stop in Polk, for he wanted as few people as possible to know he was on the prowl, and at the international bridge, a sorry affair, the customs people, American and Mexican alike, waved him through without an inspection or a question. This confidence in his trustworthiness was a tribute to the years of patient work he had performed along the border: 'I have never failed to accept the word of one of my counterparts here in Mexico. If they say a man I've arrested is a good citizen, in momentary trouble across the river, I drive him down here and kick his ass back into Mexico. They do the same with me if some college yahoo gets into big trouble down in Chihuahua. We live and let live, and they've never gigged me on a heroin shipment or anything like that, so I let their cattle cross, if there aren't too many and if they pick some spot well hidden and away from the bridges.'

Once safely within Carlota, he drove by circuitous back streets to the office of the chief of police. 'We have not seen the plane,' the jefe said in Spanish. He stopped, gaped, pointed at the Ranger's brother, and cried: 'Wolfman Macnab! Linebacker! Dallas Cowboys!' When his discovery was confirmed, all work in the office halted, as men and women gathered around to question the rocklike man they had seen so often on the American television shows transmitted into Mexico. They wanted to know what he thought of the Pittsburgh and Miami and Oakland teams, and they especially wanted to hear about that covey of wild linebackers which the press had labeled 'The Dallas Zoo.'

'Well,' he explained, always delighted to talk football with real aficionados, 'we are three pretty tough guys, but the league is full of men like us. What makes us different, our names. They call me Wolfman. Rumsey they call the Gorilla, and Joe Polar, you can guess his name.' Many of the Mexicans could speak English and they translated this jargon to those who couldn't, after which one woman asked in Spanish: 'Is it true, you take the Gorilla to away-games in a cage?' and he assured her: 'He could break your arm like this,' and for three days she would feel the pressure of his hands.

'All-American at Texas?' one of the officers asked, and he replied truthfully: 'One evening newspaper—Wichita Falls, I think it was—they nominated me for All-American. Nobody else, because in my junior year I weighed only two-twenty and opposing offensive tackles ate me up. But in my biography, circulated by the

Cowboys, it says clear as day "Consensus All-American," like as if all the papers in the country hailed me.'

'But in the pros? You have been All-Pro five times?'

'Six, and if I make it this year, maybe my last season.'

'Oh, no!' the men protested, but a woman clerk said in great admiration: 'You want to get on with your art, don't you?' and he nodded to her as if she were a duchess.

The men now asked: 'Is it true? You're an artist?' The Dallas management had made so much of this that his skill was known even in distant Carlota, and on the spur of the moment he reached for a pencil and a sheet of paper and completed a good likeness of the woman who had asked the question. As the men applauded the speed and dexterity with which he drew, he asked in English: 'How do you say "To a Beautiful Lady"?' and a would-be poet in the group said: 'A una princesa bellísima,' and as they spelled the words for him he wrote them down and handed the portrait to the woman, who began to sniffle.

'Shall we proceed?' the jefe asked, and when Cletus nodded, the Mexican indicated two assistants, who procured a veritable arsenal of guns and a load of ammunition, which they piled into a beat-up Land Rover.

Since it was some hours before darkness, they drove far south of Carlota to a small cantina, where they had a delicious meal of hot chili and freshly made tamales. As they ate, Cletus explained the situation: 'We got word two nights ago. Thieves in La Junta, Colorado, we have reason to think they're part of a cocaine ring, stole a Beechcraft, two-engine job, flew right down the New Mexico-Texas border, well west of detectors at Fort Stockton, and into Mexico, south and east of here to that field they've used before.'

'The one on the high plateau south of the canyons?'

'The same. From clues we picked up, they've got to be there, because their gas supply won't permit them to go any farther south. And we believe they'll try to make their return flight after dark tonight.'

'Do you want them, or the cocaine, or the plane?'

'Reverse order. Plane first, the drugs, whatever they are, next, them last.'

'So if we have to shoot?'

'We shoot. We do not let them lift that plane off the ground. My brother and I fly that plane north. This hijacking has got to stop.'

'Understood,' the jefe said. Then he asked a curious question: 'Macnab, can you assure me? I mean, these men are American citizens, not Mexicans?'

'I give you my word, the three airplane men are Americans. Anglo-Saxons, not even Spanish names. The ground men, supplying them, of course they're your turkeys.'

'We'll take care of them, the bastards. But we must not have Rinches killing Mexicans, not any more.'

'Compadre,' Macnab said, placing his arms about the jefe, 'my usefulness along this border is destroyed if I kill even one Mexican chicken, let alone a smuggler.'

'I know that, Macnab. So you promise not to shoot at the ground crew?'

'Promise.'

They drove slowly away from the setting sun, trying not to throw dust, and at about nine they dismounted, crept through the low grass, and came to a secluded field on which sat the stolen Beechcraft, shimmering, loading doors open in the moonlight. The three American smugglers, easily identified, were directing the loading of their plane, and it was apparently going to carry a maximum cargo of two types: large bales, probably of marijuana, and smaller packages, most likely of either heroin or cocaine. Cletus, watching the care with which they stowed the stuff, whispered to his brother: 'Like they always say, "with a street value of millions." This batch will not hit the street.'

When the plane was fully loaded, the jefe gave the signal and his men ran toward the field, firing high so that the Mexican suppliers could escape, but Cletus ran right for the plane, guns blazing but with no intent to kill. The American smugglers, frightened by the thunder of gunfire from what seemed all sides, started to fire back, then turned, dodged, and ran to a truck, which whisked them into the night.

As soon as they were gone—no one dead—the Mexican policemen ringed the plane to prevent counterattack while the Macnab brothers scrambled into the pilots' seats. The Mexican officer closed the door and waved, whereupon Cletus opened his window and shouted: 'Send my car to Alpine, like before,' and the officer saluted.

With a skill that amazed Wolfgang, his brother wheeled the plane about, revved the engines to a roar, checked the brakes, and took off into the night: 'Clean operation, kiddo. I could have killed one or two of those bastards, but I shot late. It would mean a lot of paper work for the jefe. We'll catch them up north one of these nights.'

'Are you disappointed?'

'We got the plane. We got the cargo. "Who could ask for anything more?" '

Their course back to the American airfield at Alpine required them to fly directly across those hidden, unknown canyons of the Rio Grande east of Polk-Carlota, and in the silvery night Wolfgang saw that marvelous display of deep rifts in the earth, tortuous river passages and sheer-walled cliffs that seemed to drop a thousand feet. This was the unknown Texas, the wild frontier unchanged in ten thousand years.

'That is something!' Wolfgang shouted, and his brother replied: 'I recapture about seven hijacked planes a year . . .'

'My God, why don't the police . . . ?'

'Who can protect all the American airfields? This plane came from La Junta God forbid. It's the new rustling on the old frontier.' He flew in circles so tha'

Wolfgang could catch an even better view of the great canyons: 'I like to check them out after each capture.'

When he landed the stolen plane at Alpine in the early dawn the Narcotics boys were on hand to confiscate the drugs and an insurance man was there to take possession of the plane, but Cletus was diverted from such matters by an urgent telephone call from the Ranger at Monahans, north of Fort Stockton: 'Cletus, woman clerk at the convenience store murdered. About eleven last night. Almost certain it was a wetback, headin' south.'

'Now take it easy. Before midnight? Get much cash? Peanuts, eh? But the woman's dead? Mack, my guess is he'll hitchhike to Stockton, catch that morning bus to Fort Davis, drop down to Marfa, then try to make it back to Carlota, like they all do. I'll intercept the bus.'

'We'll trail him to see if he made it to Stockton. We've got to catch this bastard —she was a good kid.'

'We'll alert Marfa and the folks on the bridge at Polk. I think we can close in on this paisano.'

In a car borrowed from the Narcotics men, the Macnabs sped to Marfa, where they reached the bus stop fifteen minutes before the arrival of the Fort Davis special. As they waited, Cletus asked: 'You want to go aboard with me? In case he tries to run?'

'Why are you so sure he's coming this way?'

'Averages. We play the averages.'

It was agreed that the huge linebacker would accompany his brother onto the bus, but behind, in hopes that his sheer size would cow the murderer. Cletus would keep his gun at the ready, but every precaution would be taken to avoid shooting.

'Here she comes!' Quietly, purposefully, the two Macnabs pushed aside those waiting for the bus, and as soon as the brakes took effect, sprang aboard like cats and moved immediately to the rear, where a very frightened wetback cowered in a corner of the back seat. Without touching his gun, Cletus said in good Spanish: 'All right, paisano. Game's up.' And when they frisked the man they found the murder weapon, the small amount of money from the store and two candy bars.

They were with the Marfa police for about three hours, making telephone calls back to Monahans and Fort Stockton, and as Macnab worked, rabid supporters of the Dallas Cowboys crowded about, and one man asked: 'It's confusin'. Sometimes they call you Wolfman, and other times it's the One-Man Gang.'

'Don't you see?' the star explained. 'They used both halves of my name. Wolf and Gang. Two for the price of one.'

It was obvious that the capture of a Mexican murderer on the main street was an event of some importance in Marfa, but to have a linebacker for the Dallas Cowboys in town, so close you could touch him, that was something to be remembered.

The sleepy brothers returned to Alpine to recover their car, and found that the Mexican driver from Carlota had delivered it safely; however, when Wolfgang inspected it he was appalled by its condition: 'Looks like a chain gang of sixty slaves had been ferried north,' and Cletus explained: 'The jefe down in Carlota, he probably loaded twenty wetbacks into this car. Cigarettes, sandwiches, tortillas.'

'For what?'

'To bring them up near the big road. The jefe probably got ten dollars a head, the driver five.'

'You allow that? Isn't that criminal?'

'Little brother, it's how we operate down here. Do you think I could go into Mexico, a Texas Ranger, and bring out a stolen airplane—no permission, no papers, no clearances—unless I gave them something in return?'

'But . . .'

'Little brother, you play a tough game, football. I play a tougher one, life and death, and when I go down there next time, it'll be the same. The jefe will shoot high so he doesn't kill any Mexicans. I'll shoot late so I don't muddy up the place with any American corpses. I'll get the plane, and the jefe will get twenty safe passages into the United States for his wetbacks on which he will pick up his usual mordido.'

'What's that?'

'The most useful word on the border. Means *little bite.* And sometimes not so little. It's the oil that makes Mexico run. Payola. Graft.'

'Isn't this entire scenario illegal?'

'Sure is, and if I spot my car coming north with those wetbacks, I'm supposed to arrest the lot and call the Border Patrol. But when the car comes through I arrange to be far distant. Never spotted it once.'

'That's a hell of a way to run a border.'

'It's the only way. Grampops would understand, and so would Old Otto. In fact, it's how they ran their border. And it's how my grandson will handle Polk and Carlota in his day. Because there will never be any other way.'

'To hell with Burma!' The speaker was Ransom Rusk sitting in his mansion in Larkin with a world atlas in his lap. He had been trying to determine what foreign country was a few square miles smaller than Texas, so that he could say in his next address to the Boosters' Club: 'Texas is a country in itself, bigger than . . .' He had hoped it would be some prominent land like France, but that comparison would belittle Texas, which had 267,338 square miles, while France had a meager 211,207 and Spain a miserable 194,884. No, the true comparison was with Burma, which had 261,789. But who had heard of it?

Rechecking his figures, he slammed the atlas shut: Hell, the men in our club would think it was in Africa!

Africa was much on his mind these days, for he had spent his last three vacations in Kenya collecting trophies for his distinguished African Hall: elephant, eland, zebra. Of course he knew that Burma was not in Africa, but it pleased him to dismiss it in that insulting way: Who could imagine Burma giving Texas competition? Kills my whole point.

Fortunately, he had devised another way of making it, and now he took out the mimeographed sheets his secretary had prepared, one page for each man who would attend, and this study pleased him. It was an outline map of Texas, with five extreme points marked. El Paso, for example, stood at the farthest west, Brownsville farthest south, and radiating from each point in Texas thus identified were dotted lines to cities in the other fifty states and Mexico.

His figures were startling. The longest distance between two points in Texas was 801 miles, northwest Panhandle catty-corner to Brownsville at the southeast, and if you applied this dimension to the rest of the nation, you came up with some surprises:

> If you stand at El Paso, you are much closer to Los Angeles than you are to the other side of Texas.

> If you stand at the eastern side of Texas, you are much closer to Tampa than you are to El Paso.

> If you stand in the Panhandle, you are closer to Bismarck, North Dakota, than you are to Brownsville.

> And always remember, if you stand on the bridge at Brownsville, you are 801 miles to the edge of the Panhandle, but only 475 miles to Mexico City and 690 to Yucatán.

As he finished these comparisons, which showed certain Texas points closer to Chicago than to El Paso, he received an urgent phone call from Todd Morrison at the Allerkamp Exotic Game Ranch: 'If you fly down right away, I might have something rather interesting.' Accepting the challenge, he called for his Larkin pilot and within the hour was on his way to the Pedernales.

During the flight he tried to recall whether he had met Todd Morrison through Maggie or the other way around. All he knew was that he liked them both, him for his custodianship of the large game ranch, her for her aptitude in handling big real estate deals: The way she masterminded that Ramparts affair! Remarkable. She got us in at just the right time, then out three weeks before the hurricane. I don't know whether she's bright or lucky, but she's better than most men in handling money. He could think of half a dozen situations in which he could profitably use a woman with her skills.

But he was more interested in Todd Morrison, for the man had shown determination in putting together the ranch and in stocking it with some of the best animals in Texas: I've never known how much that other fellow, Roy Bub Hooker, has contributed, and I don't care, because I don't feel easy with him. You pay big money to shoot one of his animals, and he looks at you as if you'd shot his cousin.

He thought that Todd had been wise in shifting his attention from real estate to ranch management: Anyone can make a buck in Houston, but it takes a real man to raise a buck in Fredericksburg. He chuckled: I like that. I'll use it sometime when I introduce him.

When the plane landed at the long paved strip which Morrison had built at the edge of the ranch, Rusk hurried out, called for his guns to be handed down, and joined the handsome graying fifty-two-year-old rancher: 'Hiya, good buddy. What's the big news?'

'Which animal—and maybe the best of all—have you consistently missed?'

'You mean the sable?'

'That's exactly what I mean.'

'You have one in the wild?'

'I do.'

'Your Mr. Hooker told me the sables would never be turned loose.'

'He doesn't run the place. I do.'

'And you've decided that your herd . . . ? How many have you?'

'We have eight now. And we can certainly spare one of the bucks.'

'Where is he?'

'In the big field. With the rocks. You may search two days without finding him.'

'That's the challenge.'

They did not go out that first afternoon, because the guides warned that the light would fade so fast that no shots would be possible, and at supper in the old house that the German Allerkamps had built during the middle years of the last century, Rusk noticed that Roy Bub Hooker was not present. Rusk decided not to ask about this, for the partners might have suffered a break, or maybe Morrison had bought the lesser man's shares.

Early in the morning Rusk, Morrison and two guides carefully opened the high iron gates protecting one of the pastures, then fastened it behind them. They were now in an area of about four thousand acres, completely fenced, in which a variety of African game animals existed in about the life style they would have followed on the veldt: the land was the same, the low trees were quite similar and similarly spaced, the occasional rocky tor was much like the kopje of South Africa, and the availability of water was identical. It was a splendid habitat, and splendid creatures roamed it, but to find them was extremely difficult.

'Believe me,' Ransom said, 'this isn't shooting fish in a rain barrel. This is work.' He looked askance when Morrison told him how many animals were in that huge enclosure: 'Sixty eland, I promise you. Big as horses, and we haven't seen one. And maybe we won't.' In fact, during the entire morning they saw only a few native Texas deer, and they were does protected from hunters except for a few days in late autumn.

At noon Morrison said: 'They'll be resting during the heat. You couldn't find a sable now with a magnet and a spyglass,' so the men went to the ranch house for chow, and in the afternoon they did see oryx and a couple of zebra, but no sign of the sable.

'You promise me he's in here?' Rusk asked, and Morrison said: 'On my oath. We checked him out before you came, helicopter. He's here.'

They did not find him that afternoon, even though they stayed within the high fencing till dusk, and when night fell they gathered at the lodge to swap yarns about hunting experiences in various parts of the world; it was the opinion of those who had been to the notable safari areas of Africa that the two big enclosures at Allerkamp provided both a terrain and a spirit almost identical with the best of the Dark Continent: 'Soil, hills, everything comparable. The fact that animals transported directly here from Kenya or the Kruger adjust with never a day's illness proves that.'

Rusk was especially interested in what one guide said: 'I wish Roy Bub was here to explain his idea, because I agree with him. It'd work and would teach us a whale of a lot about animal behavior.'

'Where is Roy Bub?' Rusk asked.

The guide ignored the question, preferring to continue with his description of the co-owner's plan: 'Roy Bub, he says: "Let's fix a field for our native whitetail deer. Less than a mile wide, five miles long. Good cover. Lots of rocky places. And we'll put a hundred deer in there, guaranteed, and we'll start you off, Mr. Rusk, with another gun at this end and let you two prowl that field from sunup to sundown, and challenge you to get one of those deer.'

'From today's experience with that sable, we'd have a hard time finding them.'

'That you would. Mr. Morrison, how about settin' up such a long narrow field?'

'Could be done. Take a lot of expensive fencing for a little area.'

'Let's talk about it, maybe,' Rusk said, and both Morrison and the guide glowed, for when an enthusiastic man with a billion dollars uttered that reassuring phrase, it meant that something might happen.

In the morning, Rusk, Morrison and the two guides stalked the big enclosure, and just as the noonday heat was becoming excessive, so that all animals but man would be taking cover, the guide who had spoken of the proposed deer test whispered: 'Movement, two o'clock!' and when Rusk looked dead ahead, then slightly to the right, he saw shadowy evidence that an animal of some size was moving there. The other three men froze as Rusk carefully worked his way into a more favorable position, and when he had done so he saw in the direction from which the wind was blowing one of nature's grandest creations, a large bull sable antelope, splendidly colored in the body, with a white-and-black-masked face and the majestic back-curved horns which were the animal's hallmark.

The sable was so perfect in both manner and appearance, that even an avid hunter like Rusk, lusting for his prize, had to watch in awe as it moved toward a patch of fresh grass: How did God fashion such a beast? Why spend so much effort to make it perfect? The horns? Who could have thought up such horns? He was sweating so copiously that if the wind had shifted only a fraction, the sable would have dodged and darted back among the deeper shadows.

'When's he gonna shoot?' the lead guide whispered to Morrison, for occasionally some Texas hunter would come onto the ranch and stalk an eland or a zebra for two days and then refuse to kill the animal when it was in full sight: 'He was too handsome. I don't want a head that bad.' Always the man would pay the fee, as if he had killed the animal—$3,000 for an eland, $4,000 for the zebra—and would return home exalted.

'Trust Rusk,' Morrison whispered back. 'In everything, he's a killer.'

And then the explosive shot, shattering the noontime air, and the swift rush of the three watchers to where the great sable lay dead. There was much backslapping, many congratulations, and then the guide calling on his walkie-talkie: 'Clarence, Mr. Rusk just got his sable. Field Three, by the small rocky outcrop. Bring in the large truck with the rack in front. No, the Jeep won't be big enough.'

In due course, after the animal had been disemboweled on the spot, the truck rolled up and four men muscled the splendid beast onto its rack, but as they left the enclosure, and the guide ran back to lock the high wire fence, they had the bad luck to run into Roy Bub Hooker as he returned unexpectedly from his trip to Austin, where he had arranged with Wildlife officers for the importation of two planeloads of animals from Kenya.

When he saw the dead sable coming at him, he recognized it as the specific male he had been cultivating to be master of the herd and whose semen he had been distributing to other American ranches and zoos that were endeavoring to keep the species from extinction. This was not some casual animal; this was a precious heritage worth enormous effort to keep it alive.

Roy Bub did not cry out; he screamed at the top of his voice as if he had been mortally lacerated, a beefy thirty-seven-year-old man, shrieking as if he were a wounded child: 'What in hell have you done?'

When he saw that the murderer was Ransom Rusk, he leaped at him and began pounding at him with his fist: 'You son-of-a-bitch! You murderin' son-of-a-bitch! Comin' onto this land . . .'

Rusk was more than able to defend himself, and with strong arms pushed the enraged Roy Bub back, but this did not stop the game specialist: 'Off of this land, you murderin' bastard! Off! Off!'

Morrison and the guides were appalled when they saw Roy Bub reach for his gun, which he carried regularly, for they could visualize a terrible tragedy. But it was Rusk, cool as a blue norther, who stopped him: 'Roy Bub! You horse's ass, put up that gun.'

The harshness of the words, their authority and the correct use of profanity stopped the big gamekeeper. Lowering his gun, he said quietly and with quivering force: 'Take your sable, God damn you, and get off this land. And don't never come back, because if you do, I'll kill you, for certain.'

Shaken, Rusk started toward the car that would take him to his airplane, but Roy Bub would not allow this: 'Take your sable with you.' When Rusk ignored him, the hefty man screamed: 'Take him. You killed him. Get him out of here.'

And when Rusk turned back to supervise the delivery of his sable to the taxidermist, he could hear Roy Bub shouting at Todd Morrison, his partner: 'You slimy son-of-a-bitch, I ought to shoot you,' and then Morrison's hesitant voice: 'Roy Bub, we're running a business, not some toy zoo.'

They did not meet at Allerkamp, because Rusk was afraid to return there, and besides, he did not want to discuss this important affair in Todd Morrison's presence. They met in a private suite at the Driskill Hotel in Austin, where Rusk had spread maps and real estate plats on a table. He was there first, and when Roy Bub arrived Rusk hurried forward to shake his hands, both hands at the same time, as if they were old friends: 'Roy Bub, I apologize,' and before the younger man could say anything, Rusk added, in a rush of words: 'You have haunted me. All my life I've admired men who stood for something, who were willing to fight. Roy Bub, you're my kind of people, and I apologize.'

They opened cold beers taken from the refrigerator in the suite, after which Roy Bub asked: 'So what?' and Rusk said: 'I love animals as much as you do,' and Roy Bub replied: 'You have a strange way of showin' it.'

'I think I was hypnotized. At Gorongosa once, that's in Mozambique, I saw a group of sables, and right there I vowed . . .' He stopped, bowed his head, and said: 'Shit, I pressured Morrison. But he did call me down when he knew you wouldn't be there. I should have suspected.'

'It was a very precious animal, Mr. Rusk. He was on all the zoo computers, father of the revived herd. He was . . .' His voice broke, and he lifted the empty beer bottle to drain the last few drops.

'I know. The man from San Diego called and tore me apart. So what I want to do, Roy Bub, and maybe this is what I've always wanted to do, I want to buy out Morrison, give him a hefty profit, and I want you and me . . .'

'I doubt he would sell his share.'

'Share? He owns it all.'

'Now wait, we bought this place . . . I found it. I did the deed search.'

'But it was bought in his name, Roy Bub. He owns it. You do have certain rights.'

'He owns it?' The big man's voice began to rise, so Rusk placed the documents before him, and there was a lot of gobbledegook about this and that, but it was painfully clear that where the actual ownership of the land was concerned, Todd Morrison had it all.

When Roy Bub finished reading the incriminating documents and listened as Rusk explained each twisting labyrinth, he did not shout or even swear: 'Mr. Rusk, in everything I've ever done with that S.O.B. he's gigged me. Buy him out and let's wash our hands.'

'In his real estate deals, I now find, he operates the same way. And I cannot understand it, because his wife is so completely honest. I've seen her turn back commissions when she's loused up some deal. She did it with me, voluntarily.'

'Todd Morrison!' Roy Bub repeated as he handed back the mournful papers. 'With land as important as ours, with him dependin' on me to keep it goin', you'd think . . .'

'How many acres do you two have? I mean how many does he have?'

'About ten thousand. The Allerkamp ranch plus the Macnab, dating back to the 1840s, I believe.'

'If you and I were to do something, we'd do it Texas style,' and he asked Roy Bub to study the plats he had brought along: 'I've had my men looking into the land situation out there along the Pedernales, and they think they could get us an additional thirty thousand acres, not all of it contiguous but we might make some trades.'

'There isn't that much money in the world,' Roy Bub said. 'We paid very heavy for the Allerkamp acres.'

'I think it could be managed,' Rusk said. 'If it could be, would you run the place? I mean really first class, everything.'

'I wouldn't be interested in no chrome motel, Mr. Rusk, like some of them others.'

'To hell with the customers. I mean the animals.'

Roy Bub thought a long time as to how he should reply, and then decided to share his vision of Allerkamp: 'Mr. Rusk, if you have the money, and they tell me you do, one of the best things in this world you could do with it is put together a real game refuge on the Pedernales. Sure, we'll rent out fields for hunters and charge 'em like hell for the shootin' of game that can easily be replaced . . . eland, elk, zebra. But in the back fields, where you only go with cameras, we could hide the animals that are in danger.' He stopped, walked about the room, then said: 'Helpin' to preserve an animal that might disappear from this earth, that would be a good thing to do, Mr. Rusk.' And before Ransom could respond, Roy Bub added: 'I thought that's what Morrison and I would be doin', not shootin' sables for a few lousy bucks.'

They spent the next two days in the Driskill, drawing maps and meeting surreptitiously with Rusk's lawyers and real estate men, and when they were through they found themselves with an imaginative design for a master exotic-game ranch covering 44,000 acres along the Pedernales, with a small contributory stream running in from the north. It was divided into seven major fields, each of which would be defined by game fencing eight and a half feet high. It would contain the old Allerkamp and Macnab buildings as lodges for guests, but a central administrative building just inside the gates would also be required. 'Low key,' Rusk said, 'like the best buildings in Africa.'

'How do you know Morrison will sell?' he asked Mr. Rusk, and the latter said: 'For money he'll do anything. Don't worry about his acres. We'll have them.' And he added: 'When the deal goes through, Roy Bub, I'll insist that he give you a share of the purchase price,' and Roy Bub said: 'You can try, but he never surrenders a nickel, especially if it's an Indian head worth nine cents.'

It was Roy Bub's job to figure the cost of the fencing, which Rusk proposed erecting right away, and when Roy Bub placed the figures before Rusk, he was apologetic: 'You see, we'll have to rebuild that fence along the Pedernales. Morrison wanted to use every inch of our land and he put the posts too close to the river. Floods wash them out. And we have to fence both sides of the creek. To do the job right, and I'm ashamed of these figures, almost eighty miles of fencing at about ninety-five hundred per mile, that means well over seven hundred fifty thousand dollars just for fences, let alone the animals.'

Rusk turned to his real estate men: 'Let the contracts right away, but get a much lower price than that ninety-five hundred.'

When the second day ended, Rusk and Roy Bub shook hands, after which Rusk's Austin lawyer said: 'Mr. Hooker, you'll have ten million dollars for the purchase of animals. Scour the dealers and the management areas, but get the best prices possible.'

'Ten million?' He gasped, but Rusk placed his arm about him and said: 'This isn't an ordinary ranch. This is a Texas ranch.'

Two nights later, as Rusk was at his Larkin estate watching the armadillos, his Austin lawyer called: 'Mr. Rusk! Have you heard?'

'What?'

'Roy Bub Hooker has just shot Todd Morrison. Three shots. Stone-dead.'

There was silence, then Rusk's quiet voice: 'Have Fleabait Moomer call me . . . immediately.'

In his historic defense of Roy Bub Hooker, Fleabait made several prudent moves. Claiming local prejudice, he had the venue changed from Gillespie County, in which the Allerkamp Ranch stood, to Bascomb, a more rough-and-ready county just south of Larkin where juries were more accustomed to a good murder now and then. Also, he employed two private detectives to trace every business deal in which Todd Morrison of Detroit—which was how the dead man would be invariably described during the trial—had ever been engaged, whether in Michigan or Texas.

The county prosecutor in Bascomb, having heard of these investigations, summoned his first assistant and gave him the stirring news: 'Welton, I'm not going to prosecute the Roy Bub Hooker case. You get the assignment. Now, don't thank me. Frankly, I'm running out because I have no desire to face Fleabait Moomer with the local press looking on. You're young. You can absorb the punishment.'

'What do you mean?' the Yale Law School graduate asked.

'You've never seen Fleabait in action? Suspenders and belt, both. Snaps the suspenders when he throws off some rural expression like "Of course bulls are interested in cows, but only at the right time." '

'I'm sure I can handle that. Besides, the case is cement-proof. Hooker did it before five witnesses, three of whom heard him utter threats at the killing of the sable antelope.'

'Welton, you miss the point. Fleabait is not going to defend Roy Bub. He's going to convict Morrison.'

'Not if I—'

'Welton, it doesn't matter what you do, or what the judge does. Fleabait is going to conduct this trial, and he is going to condemn Todd Morrison of crimes so hideous that your jury is going to commend Roy Bub Hooker for having removed him from the sacred soil of Texas.'

'But that won't be allowed.'

'Allowed? Fleabait determines what is allowed. Two bits of advice. Study up on Michigan and Detroit, because they're going to be on trial, not Roy Bub. And when Fleabait stops, sticks both hands under his coat and begins to scratch, hold your breath, because what he says next will blow your case right out of court.'

'I've handled exhibitionists before,' Welton said, whereupon the older man warned: 'But Fleabait Moomer is not an exhibitionist. He believes everything he does. He's protecting Texas against the Twentieth Century.'

Mr. Welton of Dartmouth and Yale Law required only one morning to nail down his case, and an irrefutable one it was: 'Ladies and gentlemen of the jury, I shall show you that Robert Burling Hooker, known as Roy Bub, threatened his trusting partner Todd Morrison with shooting, and I will bring three witnesses who heard the threat. I shall show you that two persons of excellent repute heard the argument between the two men on the day of the shooting, and I shall put five men on the stand who actually saw the shooting. Furthermore, I will bring you the gun that did the shooting, and an expert to prove that it was this gun that fired the bullet which killed Todd Morrison. Never will you sit on any jury where the evidence makes your vote so automatic. Roy Bub Hooker killed his partner Todd Morrison, and you will be present at the murder.'

Fleabait, scowling at his table, challenged none of this evidence, but he did go out of his way to show extreme courtesy to Todd Morrison's widow, who would sit every day of the trial in somber dignity, accompanied by her daughter, the famous baton twirler from the University of Texas, and her son-in-law, Wolfgang Macnab, the giant linebacker of the Dallas Cowboys; cautious members of the Cowboys' staff had deplored his association with a murder trial and had even hinted that he might wish to take a hunting trip to Alaska, but he said: 'If Beth's family is in trouble, I'm in trouble,' and sat stone-faced as Fleabait's plodding defense paraded before the court unsavory details of his father-in-law's life.

Mrs. Morrison's son, Lonnie, the electronics expert, also attended each day with his wife, to whom Fleabait was also unctuously courteous. Said one watcher: 'You'd think he was defendin' the Morrisons, not Roy Bub.'

Ransom Rusk did not attend the trial, even though he was paying for the defense; the state did not know that Roy Bub had also threatened to shoot him, and Fleabait was certainly not going to introduce such incidental evidence. But when the trial recessed for a long lunch on the morning of the third day, Fleabait jumped in his car and drove not to the restaurant where lawyers ate, but twenty-two miles up the road to Larkin, where he consulted with Rusk in the latter's mansion: 'It's possible I could be wrong, Rance, but from watchin' Mrs. Morrison closely, I'm convinced that if we could get her to testify, she'd support everthin' I've been tryin' to prove. She knows her husband was a jerk. She knows he hornswoggled everybody he ever did business with.'

'Leave her alone. She has a heavy enough burden.'

'Her son-in-law would testify the same way. He's a clever lad. He must know.'

'Fleabait! Don't touch the family!'

'I'm pretty sure we can win without their evidence. But it would be neat to startle the court with a request for a surprise witness.'

'You old fraud, you know you can't use a wife to testify against her own husband.'

'That's what the layman always thinks. There are a dozen ways—'

'Fleabait!'

'You want that boy to walk out of that courtroom free, don't you?' With Fleabait, an accused client was always a boy; his nefarious opponent, whether living or dead, a corrupt, evil man.

'I certainly do. And you're the man to do it.' At the door, as the lawyer started back to the courthouse, Rusk said: 'In my divorce trial, when you accused me of sodomy, sort of, that was just good clean fun. This case is real. Haul in your biggest guns, Fleabait, but leave the Morrisons out of it.'

On the fourth day of what should have been a simple trial, Fleabait spent the entire morning interrogating the other two members of the original Morrison-Hooker hunting quartet, the oilman who had transferred his affections to Scotland, and the dentist who loved dogs, and rarely did he have two witnesses who supported a case more handsomely. Each man in his own way proved that he was a dedicated sportsman, and each disclosed secrets of Todd Morrison's behavior which proved that he had never been. 'He was not a true sportsman,' the oilman said with a decided English accent. 'He never gave the game a fair chance.'

'You mean he would fire at a quail sitting on the ground?' Fleabait asked in horror.

As soon as the oilman replied 'He would,' the county prosecutor leaped up: 'Objection! Distinguished defense counsel is leading the witness.'

'Objection sustained. The jury will ignore that last reply.'

Fleabait stood apart, as if detached from the proceedings, and shook his head as if in pain. At the same time he muttered to himself, but loud enough to be heard throughout the courtroom: 'Shot a sittin' bird. I can't believe it.'

He then sighed, returned to the trial, and asked the oilman: 'And he shot a doe out of season, with no license to shoot one even in season?'

Again the charade was repeated: 'Objection!' 'Sustained.' And Fleabait brooding aloud: 'A doe out of season. I can't believe it.'

And then, patiently: 'Did Mr. Hooker, the man you call Roy Bub, did he ever do such things?'

'Oh, no! Roy Bub taught us all what sportsmanship was.'

'Now, as to the financial arrangements covering your lease at Falfurrias, I understand that when you pulled out, some rather harsh words were spoken.'

'I believe that was the dentist . . . about his dogs.'

'Yes, yes. Very harsh words indeed. We'll get to that. But in your case it dealt with money matters, did it not?' And in this patient way the sleazy shifts and dodges of Morrison's operations were unraveled.

The dentist was an admirable witness.

'You say you never fired a gun at the Falfurrias lease. What in the world did you do?'

'I trained my dogs.'

'You brought your dogs along so that the other three could profit from their skill, which I am told was extraordinary.'

'Yes.'

'You surrendered all your free time so that others could enjoy the hunt? I call that true sportsmanship. Was Todd Morrison a sportsman?'

'Didn't know the meaning of the word.'

'When you quit the foursome, I believe you had words with Morrison. About his financial dealings.'

District Attorney Welton objected to this line of questioning, charging that without any kind of substantiation, it was mere hearsay, but the judge overruled the objection.

'In my dealings with Morrison, he invariably tried to chisel me. He was not a likable man.'

'But you were his partner, so to say—in the lease, I mean?'

'At first I thought he had no money, so I sort of carried him. Later I discovered that he had more than I did. He was not a pleasant person.'

On the fifth day Fleabait practically destroyed Todd Morrison, proving much, intimating more, and then, after a dramatic pause, thrusting both hands under his armpits and scratching. The jury, having been alerted to watch out for this, smiled knowingly.

'Now, you know and I know, that people from Michigan do not adhere to the same high moral principles that govern behavior in Texas. They can be fine people by their own lights, and they can get along fairly well in the more relaxed moral climate of Detroit and Pontiac. But when they move to Texas, as so many do, they find themselves confronted by a much stricter moral code. Here a man is supposed to behave like a man. A sportsman has certain clearly defined patterns of acceptable behavior, which the newcomer from Michigan has a difficult time honoring.

'I have nothing against Michigan. I'm sure there are fine people in Michigan, many of them. But when they come into Texas they are held to a nobler code of behavior, and to tell you the truth, many of them fail to meet the mark. They are not ready for Texas. They are not prepared to face our more demanding standards.

'Todd Morrison was such a man. I do not want you to judge him harshly, because he knew no better. He had not been raised with the clean wind of the prairie blowing away the cobwebs that entangle human beings. He never rode a horse across the plains. He was not trained in the harsh lessons of honor and trust and sportsmanship. I do not want you to condemn this poor dead man who lost his way in a new and more exacting land. I want you to forgive him.' (Here he scratched again.) 'And I want you to understand why an honest, God-fearing Texan, born in the heart of good sportsmanship, felt that he had to shoot him. You surely know by now that Todd Morrison, this pathetic stranger who never fitted in, who could not obey our strict code of honor, deserved to die.'

The foreman of the jury asked the judge if it was obligatory for them to leave the jury box before handing in their verdict, and he said: 'It would look better,' so they marched out and marched right back in.

During Sherwood Cobb's first two years as a member of the Water Commission he could make no headway in his campaign for a sensible water plan for Texas, but now two natural disasters struck which awakened the state to the fact that it lived in peril, like all other areas of the world, where though the perils might be different, all stemmed from the inherent limitations imposed by nature.

Drought hit some portion of Texas about every ten years, but the state was so large that other areas did not suffer; however, about once each quarter of a century great portions of the state were hit at the same time. Farms were wiped out, ranches were decimated, and land-gamblers were reminded that there were definite limits beyond which they dare not go. In 1932 the Great Drought had struck in Oklahoma, reaching Texas in 1933 and converting large areas of both states into dust bowls, and 1950 had delivered a savage drought which lasted seven years. Now another crushing dry spell gripped the western half of the state. Water holes went dry, rivers that were supposed to be perpetual failed, and even a supposedly safe coastal city like Corpus Christi was forced to institute water rationing.

Now when Cobb moved about the state, seeking to generate support for his plans, people listened, and he told his wife: 'I used to say we'd have no serious approach to our water problems till the year 2010. A few more years of this drought and you can advance that to about 1995. But I want to see it happen in 1985!'

He went to all parts of Texas, pleading with farmers, ranchers and businessmen to devise a water system for their state, but in addition to talking, he acted, sometimes twenty hours a day, to rescue ranchers who were about to lose their cattle. He arranged for grasslands in the unaffected eastern half to truck in cattle from the arid areas and water them without cost till the emergency waned. He organized auctions at which ranchers with no water at all could sell their animals to buyers from other states whose fields did have water, for as one rancher who had to sell at distress said: 'I'd rather see my cattle live and make a profit for someone else than stand here and watch them perish.' And Cobb persuaded other Texas cattlemen to adopt the same attitude.

In short, Sherwood Cobb acted in this emergency the way his ancestor Senator Somerset Cobb had responded to the disasters of the Civil War and Reconstruction, and as another ancestor, Senator Laurel Cobb, had acted when great changes were under way in the 1920s: he rolled up his sleeves and went to work. Like Ransom Rusk gritting his teeth and bearing his enormous financial setbacks, Cobb accepted the challenge of the natural ones, but in the midst of his constructive work Texas was struck with a final assault of such magnitude that even Cobb reeled.

Folk legend said that once every hundred years snow fell in Brownsville, the southernmost city in Texas and a land of palm trees and bougainvillaea. On Christmas Day in 1983 the thermometer along the Rio Grande dropped far, far below freezing, and the results were staggering.

When Cobb arrived two days after Christmas on emergency assignment from the Department of Agriculture, he found entire grapefruit orchards wiped out by the excessive cold. Avocado trees were no more. Orange groves were obviously destroyed. And the famous palm trees of Corpus Christi and other southern towns were dead in the bitter winds. Hundreds of millions of dollars were lost in this one terrible freeze, so that communities who had watched their stores close because of the fall of the peso, now saw their agriculture destroyed by a fall in the thermometer. The Valley, staggered before, now lay desolated.

Cobb found in the distraught area one local leader who seemed to have as firm a grasp of reality as he, Cobb, had. It was Mayor Simón Garza of Bravo, who toured the Valley ceaselessly, organizing relief operations, and as the two men worked together, Cobb ten years the older, they formed a pact that would endure through the years ahead: 'Garza, you make more sense than anyone else I've met. People live on the land, the rancher out west, the citrus grower down here, the farmer up the coast. We're restricted by what the land will allow us to do, and when we forget that, we're in trouble.'

Garza said: 'I read an editorial the other day. It said: "God has gone out of His way to remind us that even Texans are mortal." These are devastating years, but we can build upon them.' And the two men, optimists as all Texans are required by law to be, went quietly ahead with their plans, however fragmentary, to save the citrus industry in the Valley, ranching on the high plains and water supplies everywhere.

But Cobb, like his valiant ancestors and like his aunt Lorena up in Waxahachie, was an ebullient man, and as he toured his state, proud of its ability to fight back, he savored the many hilarious behaviors that made Texas different from any other state he knew. And as he witnessed these crazy things he jotted down brief notes, which he mailed back to his wife so that she, too, could laugh.

. . . In Jefferson, I attended in the schoolhouse a lecture entitled 'The Heritage of Robert E. Lee,' and at the end the chairlady said, voice throbbing with emotion: 'Now if we will all stand, please,' and with her hand over her heart she led the singing:

'I wish I was in de land of cotton
Old times dar am not forgotten . . .'

Fervently we sang of a glory none of us had ever known but whose legends were etched on our hearts, and when we reached that marvelous chorus, one of the most powerful ever written, I was shouting with the others:

'In Dixie Land I'll take my stand
To lib and die in Dixie.
Away, away, away down South in Dixie.'

When the song ended, with some of us wiping our eyes, I said to the man next to me: 'If a bugle sounded now, half this crowd would march north,' and he said: 'Yep, and this time we'd whup 'em.'

. . . You and I have often talked about what our favorite town in Texas was. North Zulch always stood high. Oatmeal was good. You liked Muleshoe. The other day I drove through my favorite. Megargel, population 381, with a sign that says WATCH US GROW. As I drove through I saw a pickup with the bumper sticker SUPPORT JESUS AND YOUR LOCAL SHERIFF. Carry on, Megargel!

. . . At Larkin, where they have that famous statue you wouldn't let me photograph, I saw something I hadn't noticed before. On the courthouse lawn were two bold bronze plaques, one proclaiming that for three glorious years during the 1920s the Larkin Fighting Antelopes had been state champions in football, the other that one night in 1881 the notorious one-armed gunman, Amos Peavine, had slept in Larkin prior to his gunning down of Daniel Parmenteer, respected lawyer of the place, and as I studied the two memorials I had to reflect upon the mores of the small Texas towns.

I'm sure Larkin must have produced dedicated women who taught their students with love and constructive influence. It surely had bright boys who went on to become state and national leaders. It must have had brave judges who tamed the western range, and men who built fortunes which they spent wisely. And there must have been citizens of no wide repute who held the town together, perhaps a barber or a seamstress on whom the weak depended. I can think of a hundred citizens of Larkin that I would like to memorialize, but what do we do?

We erect monuments to a murderous gunman who slept here one night and to a football team whose coach and most of whose players came from somewhere else. Just once I would like to drive into a Texas town and see a bronze plaque to a man who wrote a poem or to a woman who composed a lasting song.

. . . Returning from the session on catchment dams, I had the radio on and heard the song I'm going to recommend as the official state song of Texas, because it honors the two noblest aspects of our culture, football and religion: 'Drop-Kick Me, Jesus, Through the Goal Posts of Life.'

. . . I grow mournful when I hold a water meeting in some little town that used to flourish but is now dying. There must be hundreds of such places doomed to disappear before the end of the century, and I've constructed Cobb's Law to cover the situation: 'If a town has less than four hundred population and stands within twenty miles of a big shopping center, it's got to vanish.' The automobile determines that and there's not a damned thing we can do about it. Texas, always dying, always arising in some new location with some new mission.

. . . I love the redneck songs of Texas, 'San Antonio Rose,' 'El Paso,' and the new one I've memorized so I can sing it to you when we're traveling:

> Blue flies lazin' in the noon-day sun,
> Dogies grazin' at their rest,
> Old steers drinkin' at the salty run . . .
> This is Texas at its best.
> Sleep on, Jim, I'll watch the herd,
> Doze on, Slim, fly northward bird.
> All the range is peaceful.

He had a chance to sing this ballad to his wife when she accompanied him to two water meetings held by chance in two of the truly bizarre places in Texas. The first was the schoolhouse in the little oil town of Sundown, southwest of Levelland. The feisty town fathers, discovering that the oil companies would have to pay for whatever the board legally decided, opted to have the finest school in America. So for a total school enrollment of only a hundred and forty pupils they built a seven-million-dollar Taj Mahal, featuring a gymnasium fit for the Boston Celtics, an auditorium finer than most New York theaters and an Olympic-sized swimming pool under glass.

'What staggers me,' Cobb told his wife, 'is that in the pool they teach canoeing. Yep, look at those two aluminum canoes, and there isn't any water within miles. When I asked about this, a member of the school board said: "Well, some of our kids may emigrate to Maine, where canoeing is real big." ' Mrs. Cobb preferred the miniature condominium built into the center of the school: 'What's it for?' And an official explained: 'We want to teach our home-ec girls how to make beds.' The superintendent's office was special: directly under it at a depth of thousands of feet, rested an oil well, drilled at an angle. 'It's how we get our petty cash,' an official said.

But what gave the Cobbs renewed hope for Texas every time they saw it was an amazing structure in the roughneck oil town of Odessa, where the oil rigs Rusk had been unable to sell even at a heavy loss rusted in the sun. There, years ago, a young woman schoolteacher without a cent had fallen in love with William Shakespeare. Driven by a vision that never faltered, she had begged and borrowed and scrounged until she had accumulated enough money to build an accurate replica of Shakespeare's Globe Theatre. There it stood in the sandy desert, full scale, and to it came Shakespearean actors from many different theaters and countries to orate the soaring lines of the master.

'We don't do many of his historical plays,' the director told Cobb. 'Our customers prefer the love stories and the gory tragedies.'

'I'll be sending you a check one of these days,' Mrs. Cobb said, for the Globe was kept alive by families like the Cobbs who felt that Shakespeare added a touch of grace to the drylands.

As Cobb left the meeting at which, speaking from the Shakespearean stage, he had pleaded for water legislation, he stopped and looked back at this preposterous building: 'I love the craziness of Texas. It's still the biggest state in the Union . . . without Eskimos.'

Maggie Morrison had been shocked by the murder of her husband, not by the fact that his shady behavior had resulted in the shooting, for she had anticipated something like this, but by the fact that it was Roy Bub who had done it. She knew him to be a man of intense integrity, and for him to have pulled the trigger added extra pain.

After the verdict was returned, a proper one she thought, she learned that she stood to inherit all of Allerkamp, a fair portion of which morally belonged to Roy Bub. With the honesty which characterized her, she flew to Dallas to consult with Rusk: 'I cannot keep Allerkamp. Much of it is Roy Bub's, but I can't offer him an adjustment because it would look as if we had conspired to have my husband eliminated.'

'Allow the will to be probated. Take Allerkamp and keep your mouth shut.'

'To do that would strangle me.'

'Maggie, I wasn't going to tell you this, but I've taken care of Roy Bub. What we call a finder's fee.'

'What did he find?'

'Allerkamp. Before Todd died, the scoundrel was preparing to sell me Allerkamp. He was going to quit the exotic business.'

'What about Roy Bub?'

'Your husband never gave a damn about him.'

'I'm not surprised. Houston ruined Todd. When we first came down we held family meetings: "Kids, Maggie, we're going into this deal and we could lose our shirts." We shared everything. Then, when he began to shave corners, we knew only the honest parts. Finally we knew nothing.'

'Your husband and I agreed on a fair price for the place. I'll show you the papers. His lawyer, mine will confirm their authenticity. You should allow the deal to go through.'

'What will it mean to me?'

'Four million dollars.'

The deal did go through, and on the day it was settled Maggie initiated three moves which symbolized her changed attitudes. She drove out to Allerkamp to inspect the manner in which Roy Bub Hooker had laid out the seven main areas that would make it one of the best exotic ranches in Texas, and when Rusk explained how it would be used, she told the partners: 'You're putting the place to good use. May it succeed beyond your dreams.'

The second thing of importance she did was surrender the family's fancy condominium along Buffalo Bayou. As she confided to her children: 'I feel uneasy sitting here and looking across the way at those three towers of The Ramparts, thinking how I bought them at distress from the Mexicans and sold them to the Canadians three weeks before the hurricane. It haunts me . . . seems immoral.'

She moved instead to a beautiful, dignified condominium well west of the center of town, The St. James, where she bought one of the smaller units on the twenty-third floor for $538,000 and spent another $92,000 decorating it. There, overlooking a park, she did the brainwork for her real estate business, driving to her office early each morning.

When real estate acquaintances in other cities called to ask: 'Did Hurricane Alicia destroy values in Houston?' she felt so defensive about her city that she drafted a thoughtful form letter:

> I know you saw the horrendous scenes on television, our beautiful buildings with their windows knocked out like old women with no front teeth. I assure you with my hand on the Bible that only a few buildings were so hit and not one of them suffered any structural damage.
>
> Houston has snapped back stronger than before. I am buying and selling as if there had never been a hurricane, for I know that if we survived Alicia, we can survive anything. If you crave action, come aboard.

But it was her third change that represented the most significant modification, because when she moved to The St. James she found herself conveniently close to Highway 610, that magic loop which encircled the central Houston she loved. Now, two or three nights a week after dinner when the intolerable traffic abated, she went down to her garage, climbed into her Mercedes, and drove thoughtfully eastward till she hit a ramp leading to 610. There she weaved her way onto the striking thoroughfare, one of the busiest in America, and started the thirty-eight-mile circuit of the city, ticking off her position on an imaginary clock.

Where she entered was nine o'clock, due west. Up where the airport waited, with its enormous flow of plane and auto traffic, was twelve. Three o'clock on the extreme east carried her into the smoke-filled, bustling commercial district that huddled about the Houston Ship Channel with its hundreds of plants affiliated with the oil industry; this area interested her immensely, for in it she saw many prospects for growth. Six o'clock was due south where the immense Medical Center and the handsome Astrodome predominated, and at the end of fifty minutes she was back at Westheimer, taking a last look at the city she had grown to love: What a glorious town! Spires everywhere glinting in the moonlight! God smiled at me when He brought me here. To help build and sell those splendid buildings!

Two nights a week, sometimes three, she made this circuit of her city, checking upon current building, predicting its future growth; sometimes male dinner companions accompanied her: 'Maggie, you mustn't do this alone. Six-ten is a jungle, worst highway in America. You know that during rush hour the police won't even enter it to check on ordinary fender-benders. They got beat up too often by enraged motorists, sometimes shot and killed.'

'But I stay clear during rush hours.'

'And for God's sake, don't drive with your window down.'

'This is my town. I love it and I want to check on it.'

One night as she was driving, with her eye to lands outside the circle, a full moon illuminated a section of the city she had never before studied seriously; it stood at ten o'clock, to the northwest, and it comprised about fifteen blocks of housing which could be torn down at no great loss, and she eased into an outer lane so that she could slow down and inspect the place. With imaginary bulldozers and wrecking balls, she leveled the houses, then erected a pair of soaring towers with all attendant shopping areas: Forty-eight floors to each tower, right? Six condominiums per floor? But save the first four levels for office space. We could get five hundred units easily, plus six gorgeous penthouses at $3,500,000 each.

Futura she dubbed her imaginary towers, and now when she circled the city at night she waited breathlessly for the approach of Futura, analyzing it from all angles. In the daytime, after work, she drove through the area and found that seventeen blocks would provide the necessary land area. Then she began to consult secretly with Gabe Klinowitz as to prices in the district, and with his figures in her head she started sketching plans for a major development. When she costed them, as the phrase in her industry went, she found that for $210,000,000 she could probably acquire the land, raze the buildings on it, and erect her twin-towered masterpiece.

As soon as she had a working budget in mind, she realized that there was only one source available to her for such a vast amount, so she flew to Dallas and placed her design before Ransom Rusk, who was recovering nicely from the shocks of the preceding years when he saw his net worth drop by nearly half a billion. He was deeply engaged in the election, sweating over whether or not Reagan would be reelected: 'So many damned blacks and Mexicans registering, a man can't make predictions.' He was also contributing vast sums toward the defeat of eight or nine Democratic senators around the country, because he felt, as he told Maggie: 'This is one of the crucial elections of our national history. If Reagan's coattails are long enough, we'll even regain control of the House, and then we can turn this sloppy nation around permanently. Reagan, a great patriot in the White House. His nominees filling the Supreme Court. A Republican Congress. And we'll start taking over the state houses.' With each potential triumph he became more excited: 'Maggie, we can put some backbone into this nation. Clean up things in Central America. End the disgrace of public welfare, and see America tall in the saddle again. We'll wipe out the stain of Franklin Roosevelt once and for all.'

As a lifelong Democrat whose parents had come from the working class, she was amused when Rusk fulminated in this way and did not take him seriously, but gradually he said things which astonished her: 'It's criminal for the Democrats to go around making Mexicans register, when they understand none of the issues. The vote should be reserved for the people who own the nation and pay the taxes.'

'Do you mean that?' she had asked, and his thoughtful reply surprised her: 'I calculated the other day that my efforts ensure the employment of nearly four thousand people. Counting four to a family, that's sixteen thousand citizens I support. Am I to be outvoted by two unemployed Mexican hangers-on who can't read English?'

When she pursued the matter, he confessed: 'Yes, I'd like to see a means test for the vote. Only people who have a real stake in society can know what's best for that society.'

She was not yet ready to accept this new philosophy which was sweeping the nation, but in August when Rusk invited her to join him at the Republican National Convention in Dallas, she had an opportunity to observe him as he moved among people of his own kind, and she was impressed to find that he knew all the leaders and was welcomed in the suites of both President Reagan, delightful man, and Vice-President Bush, a reassuring fellow Texan from Midland. She noticed that Rusk was warmly greeted by the famous clergymen who had swarmed into Dallas to prove that God was a Republican and America a Christian nation.

It was an exciting week, and once when she sat in a privileged seat she felt a surge of pride as she looked down upon the delegates, that endless parade of fine, clean-cut people from all parts of the nation: the bankers, the managers, the store owners, the elderly women with blue-tinted hair. And not too often a black or a Hispanic to confuse the pattern. It was at this euphoric moment that Maggie first began to consider seriously her partner's philosophy that the men who own a nation ought to govern it. The idea was crudely expressed and she knew that if the newspapers got hold of it, they would make sport of Rusk, but it did summarize a fundamental truth about America, and it was worth further study.

On the morning after the convention ended on a note of high triumph, Maggie placed before Rusk the plans for her master development, and was distressed when he seemed to back off, as if the project was too big for him to finance at this time.

'Ransom, are you turning me down?'

'No. But I am turning down Houston. Now is not the time to start new building in that town.'

She gasped, then said defensively: 'I love Houston. It gave me life . . . maturity . . . even happiness of a sort.'

'Time to be realistic. New buildings are standing empty.'

'But, Ransom, I've been mailing brochures assuring real estate customers that Houston is not finished.' She hesitated, looked pleadingly, saw the obdurate scowl, and asked softly: 'Are you suggesting Dallas?'

'I haven't mentioned Dallas. It's overbuilt too.'

'What do you have in mind?'

'Austin.'

She had never contemplated shifting her operations from a city with more than two million to one about one-fifth that size, but Rusk was adamant: 'Houston twenty years ago is Austin today.'

'Can it absorb something like Futura?'

He avoided a direct answer: 'That's a dreadful name. Sounds like a bath soap.'

'What would you propose?'

'Something classy. English. Like The Bristol or Warwick Towers. But they've been overdone.' Then he snapped his fingers: 'I have it. The Nottingham. Our logo? Robin Hood in outline wearing that crazy peaked hat. We'll make it the most fashionable address in Texas.'

Maggie, trying not to smile at the picture of Ransom Rusk offering himself as a Robin Hood stealing from the poor to aid the rich, kept her mind on the main problem: 'Where do we get the two hundred million?'

Without hesitation he replied: 'West Germany or the Arabs. They're itching to invest in Texas.' And while she waited, he called his bankers in Frankfurt and asked: 'Karl Philip, do your boys still have those funds you talked about last month? Good. I'm putting you down for two hundred and ten million.' There was a pause which Maggie interpreted as shock on the other end, but it was not: 'No, not Houston, it's marking time at present. And not Dallas, either, it's overbuilt. Austin.' Another pause: 'State capital, America's new Silicon Valley, our fastest-growing city. Hotter than an oil-boom town.'

When he hung up he gave Maggie a simple directive: 'Fly right down to Austin, locate the perfect spot, and get someone to buy the real estate in secret.'

With the design for her two luxury towers firmly in mind, she rode to the airport in Rusk's car, which delivered her to the door of the Rusk plane. In less than forty minutes she was landing at the Austin airport, and the next four days were hectic.

In a rented car she explored the unfamiliar beauties of this lovely little city, and by noon she had counted a dozen giant cranes busy at the job of erecting very tall buildings. 'My God,' she cried. 'This really is the new Houston,' and that afternoon she chanced on a young man, Paul Sampson, recently down from Indianapolis, who could have been Todd Morrison in 1969. He had the same brash approach, the same nervous eagerness, the same indication that he was going to be adroit in arranging deals. He worked for a large real estate firm but gave every promise of owning the outfit within two years, and by nightfall he had shown Maggie sixteen sites which could accommodate new buildings.

That night she called Rusk: 'Ransom, real estate is so hot down here that the place simply has to go bust.'

Very quietly he assured her: 'Of course it'll go bust. Everything does sooner or later. Our job is to get in fast and out first.'

'Then you want me to go ahead?'

'With German money, how can we go wrong?'

So early next morning she was at Paul Sampson's office with the kind of proposition cagey operators had brought her husband in the early 1970s: 'Could you quietly assemble about six city blocks for me? Standard commission?'

'I can do anything you require, madam,' he said, and she could see that his palms were sweating. 'Where do you want them? In the heart of the city?'

'Show me the possibilities,' and when he kept stressing an area which she distrusted, she said: 'You own a parcel in there, don't you?' and he protested: 'Look, madam, if you don't trust me, we can't do business,' and she said: 'If you try to sell me that junk you're stuck with, we'll never do business.'

Startled by her shrewd understanding, he stopped trying to peddle his third-rate property and started driving her to the eligible areas, and by the end of the fourth day she had found something farther out than he had expected her to go. It was a grand area west of Route 360 and atop a rise which gave a splendid view of both Lake Travis and the famed hill country.

'Will people buy this far out?' Sampson asked, and she said: 'When they see what we're going to build,' and with that, she gave him a commission to acquire four parcels of about ten acres each, and when the agreement was signed, in great secrecy, he said: 'Can I ask what you're going to build out there?' and she said: 'A hunting range for Robin Hood.'

When she saw the excitement in his eyes and his eagerness to get started, she thought of her former husband, and she wished the young man good luck. She hoped he would handle himself better than Todd had done, but she had a strong premonition that he was going to go the same way, because three weeks later, after he had delivered the forty acres to her at a price that was gratifying, she learned that he had mortgaged himself to the hilt in order to buy for his own account two small choice plots that would dominate any roads into or out of Nottingham.

'You'll do well, Sampson,' she said as she ended negotiations. 'Stay clean,' and he startled her by saying with great assurance: 'Mrs. Morrison, you'll bless the day you met me. That land will be worth millions, because this Austin thing can go on forever.'

That night she flew back to Larkin, and when she informed Rusk of her proposed land purchase in Austin, he congratulated her. Then, ignoring the two-hundred-million-dollar deal as if it were an ordinary day's work, he took his seat before two television sets as the first Reagan-Mondale debate started.

The next ninety minutes were a nightmare for Ransom, because he had to watch the man who was supposed to save the Republic fumble and stumble and show himself to be uninformed on basic problems. At one point Rusk growled: 'Maggie, how in hell did he ever allow himself to get tangled in a debate? He looks ninety years old.'

But soon his anger was directed at the three newspeople asking the questions: 'They shouldn't speak to him like that! He's President!' And then, as Maggie had anticipated, his ire fell on Mondale: 'Reagan ought to walk over and belt him in the mouth.' Toward the end, when Reagan confessed 'I'm confused,' Rusk shouted at the television: 'They didn't ask that question fair. They're trying to mix him up.'

The next weeks were agonizing, for the press, very unjustly Rusk thought, kept bringing up the question of Reagan's age and his capacity to govern. 'He doesn't have to govern like other people,' Rusk told Maggie. 'He has good men around him who look after details. What he does is inspire the nation.' Calling his friends in the administration, he advised: 'Keep him on the big picture. Patriotism . . . the Olympics . . . standing tall in the saddle.' And when Reagan did just this, smothering Mondale in the final debate, Rusk said: 'The incumbent must never allow upstarts to get on the same platform with him.'

On Election Day, Rusk would drive out to Larkin to vote while Maggie would have to remain in Houston to cast hers, but it was agreed that then Rusk's jet would ferry her to his place, where they would watch the returns together. As she approached the polling place she was still undecided as to how she would vote: I can't turn my back on eighty years of family history. I don't think a Svenholm has voted Republican since Teddy Roosevelt ran in 1904. But then she recalled the persuasive logic with which Rusk had defended his thesis that those who own a nation ought to be allowed to govern it, and she suspected that the time had come when dependable Americans like him should be handed the reins, since they had the most to win or lose. Also, like many women, she had some misgivings about Geraldine Ferraro.

Realizing that what she was about to do would have pained her hard-working parents, whose lives had been rescued by Democratic legislation in the 1930s, she willingly took the step that transformed her from a Michigan liberal into a Texas conservative. Stepping boldly into the voting booth, she looked toward heaven, crossed herself, and said with a chuckle: 'Pop, forgive me for what I'm about to do.' Then, closing the curtain behind her, she did what hundreds of thousands of other Democratic refugees from wintry states like Ohio, Michigan and Minnesota were doing that day: she voted the straight Republican ticket.

That night as she sat with Rusk, watching as the early victories rolled in, she agreed when he cried: 'Maggie, we're going to put some iron in this nation's backbone.' Toward nine o'clock, when the magnitude of the swing was obvious, he said with fierce determination: 'We have the White House, the Supreme Court, the Senate and enough right-thinking Democrats on our side to control the House. Maggie, we've captured the nation! For as long as you and I live, things are going to be handled our way.'

At a point when it was clear in the returns that all areas reporting so far, except the nation's capital, had chosen Reagan, Rusk growled: 'If that city full of niggers is so out of tune with national thinking, it shouldn't have the vote,' and Maggie said sharply: 'Ransom! You're never to use that word again,' and he grumbled: 'I'll watch myself when I'm in your hearing,' but she said: 'Never! And I mean it! A man in your position cheapens himself with such a word.' He turned from the television, stared at her as if he had never seen her before—or had not appreciated her if he had seen her—and then returned to his victorious watching.

When it was certain that all states except Minnesota had cast their votes for Reagan and proper American values, he said: 'That entire state should be sent to a psychiatrist. To be offered a choice between Reagan and Mondale and to choose Phinicky Phfritz . . . the whole place must be sick.'

In triumph, a man who had helped save a nation, he drove her primly to one of the Larkin motels, promising as he left her: 'Tomorrow I'll close the financing,' and she realized that all his life he had been able to throw his full attention into something like the election of a President, then start afresh the next morning on a new assignment that bore no relationship to the preceding one. In this regard he was a lot like Texas: the first settlers lived off cattle, the next off cotton and slaves, then came the big empty ranches, then oil, then computers, and what would come next, only God knew. She hoped she and Rusk would be able to unload their share of The Nottingham before Austin went bust.

. . . TASK FORCE

During the two-year existence of our Task Force we had often suffered snide attacks that were launched upon Texas, and always they seemed to focus on its wealth. Outsiders either envied our possession of it or resented the way we spent it. As our deliberations drew to a close in December 1984, I had the opportunity to witness and even participate in three typical explosions of Texas wealth, and I report them without venturing a judgment.

When it came time to draft our report, we encountered little difficulty, although Ransom Rusk did insist upon a minority statement, signed only by him, decrying emphasis on multicultural aspects of Texas history and calling for a return to the simple Anglo-Saxon Protestant virtues which had made the state great; Professor Garza submitted his own nonhysterical minority report defending Señorita Múzquiz's interpretation of bilingual education and recommending that it continue through at least the sixth grade.

When none of us would co-sign either document, Garza taunted us amiably for what he called our 'ostrichlike capacity for hiding from reality.' When Miss Cobb asked: 'What do you mean, Efraín?' he said: 'I want each of you to answer honestly, "How many illegal Mexican immigrants do you employ?" ' Rusk said: 'That's a fair question. Various projects, maybe forty.' Quimper said: 'I have about six each on my nine ranches. Four extra at the home ranch.' Miss Cobb said she employed two maids and two men, and I surprised them by saying: 'Lucky for me, I have a maid who comes in three days.'

But it was Garza who startled us: 'I have a husband and wife. Invaluable.' Then he smiled: 'And this committee, which depends upon Mexicans, thinks that the problem is going to fade away? So be it.'

On all other content we agreed easily; we recommended more careful structuring of the two levels of teaching in Texas history: 'The primary level, where the child first encounters the glories of Texas history, should depend less on fable and more on historical reality, which is miraculous enough to ignite young minds. And in the junior-high obligatory course, educators must remember that because of heavy immigration from the North, classrooms will be filled with young people who have never before studied the glories of Texas history and who will not be familiar with its unique and heroic nature. A most careful effort must be made to inform them properly before it is too late.'

Philosophically I supported Miss Cobb in a statement she proposed: 'We recommend strongly that in both primary and junior-high, Texas history be taught only by teachers trained in the subject.' But to our surprise, Rusk, Quimper and Garza refused to vote in favor, for, as Quimper pointed out: 'We have to have somewhere to stack our football coaches in the off season.' Miss Cobb wanted me to join her in signing a minority report, but I told her I would not, since I felt that it would be improper for the chairman to reveal that he could not hold his horses together. My real reason was that I did not want to stir up the football fanatics, for if I did, there was little chance that our report would be accepted. Texas history might be revered, but Texas football was sacred.

I was involved in the first money explosion. On the December day our report was to be signed, I announced that my temporary duty in Texas had proved so congenial that I was surrendering my job at Boulder in order to accept an appointment to the Department of Texas Studies at the university. My colleagues and our staff applauded my action, and when I was asked why I had made what must have been a difficult decision, I said: 'It was easy. Consider the things that have happened here since I took this chairmanship. The Mexican peso has collapsed, turning the Rio Grande Valley into a disaster area. Then Hurricane Alicia struck, threatening to wreck Houston, which had already been suffering from forty-three million square feet of unrented business space. Next the Great Freeze of 1983 destroyed the citrus crop, completing the wreckage of the Valley. The west didn't escape, either, what with that Midland bank going under for a billion and a quarter and the Ogallala Aquifer dropping precipitously, so that farmers out there are beginning to cry panic. The Dallas area got its share, with Braniff going bankrupt and TexTek dropping a billion dollars in one day. Farmers everywhere were hit with a drought. And to top it all, the Dallas Cowboys folded three straight years. Hell, the blows this state has had to absorb in one brief spell would collapse the ordinary nation.'

'What's your point?' asked Rusk, who had been rocked by many of the disasters.

'Point is, I respect a state that can spring back, pull up its socks, and forge ahead as if nothing had happened. And I like the way Lorena's nephew out in Lubbock is fighting for sensible water legislation.'

But Miss Cobb had a much simpler statement, and one that came closer to the truth: 'Texas seduced him to come back home, as it has a way of doing.' And I agreed.

But then Rusk released his bombshell: 'Barlow, even though you are a liberal and a near-communist, the three of us, Miss Lorena, Lorenzo and I, have put together a little kitty to endow your chair in Texas Studies at the university.'

'One million clams,' Quimper said as the research staff gasped.

Miss Cobb explained: 'Under the terms of grant, Barlow can't spend a penny on himself, but he can apply the yearly interest to the purchase of books for the library and fellowships for his graduate students—not generous, but enough to live on. So why don't you assistants enroll with him for your Ph.D.s?'

This unexpected bonanza had an interesting effect on our staff. I had been aware, as our work drew to a close, that they were growing apprehensive about their futures, and to have this sudden manna descend upon them was a boon. The young woman from SMU, seeing herself reprieved from a life of writing publicity releases, showed tears. The young man from El Paso sat stunned. But the young fellow from Texas Tech acted sensibly: he kissed Miss Cobb. What did I do? I remained gratefully silent, thinking of the tenured years ahead and of the endless chain of young scholars who would work with me and of the good we would accomplish together.

After mutual congratulations, we attacked the final agenda, and Garza, Miss Cobb and I suggested that we conclude our report with two vital paragraphs. Knowing that they would occasion sharp comment from the public, we wanted them to say exactly what we intended, and no more:

> Any state which acquires great power is obligated to provide outstanding moral and intellectual leadership. Although we believe that Texas has

the capacity for such leadership, we cannot identify in what significant fields it will be exerted. When Massachusetts led the nation, its power was manifested in its religious and intellectual leadership. When Virginia gained preeminence, it was because of the learning, the philosophy and the style of her citizens. When New York undertook the burden, it excelled in publishing, theater and art. When California led, it was through Hollywood, television and attractive life styles.

In what fields is Texas qualified to lead? It has no major publishing house, no art except cowboy illustration, no philosophical preeminence. Obviously, it has other valuable assets, but not ones that society prizes highly. It leads the nation in consuming popular music; it has bravado, and is wildly devoted to football. It runs the risk of becoming America's Sparta rather than its Athens. And history does not deal kindly with its Spartas.

When Rusk saw our draft he exploded: 'You sound like a bunch of commies, and frankly, Lorena, I'm amazed you would put your signature to such a document.'
'You have it wrong, Ransom. I didn't agree to it. I wrote it. The other two support it.'
'The Cobb senators will be turning in their graves. They loved Texas.'
'And so do I. I will not stand by and see it converted into a Sparta.'
'Quimper,' Rusk cried, 'help me kill this thing!' But to everyone's surprise, Lorenzo sided with us: 'Ransom, it's a proper warning. Hand it over, I'll sign it.'
'Is everyone going crazy?' Rusk bellowed, and Quimper said: 'I've been looking into the real Il Magnifico, that Medici fellow. And what do I find? In his day he led the Florentine Mafia, like my father led the Texas Mafia. But he's remembered for his patronage of the arts. He tried to make Florence think. I feel the same about Texas.'
'If you people insert that statement,' Rusk threatened, 'I'll blast hell out of it in a minority disclaimer.'
'You won't,' Miss Cobb said quietly, 'because if you did, you'd look foolish, and you can't afford that.' When he continued to bristle, she soothed him until he surrendered; he'd refrain from public dissent if we'd allow him to alter a few phrases. He changed *Although we believe that Texas has the capacity* . . . to *We know that Texas has the capacity* . . . He also changed *In what fields is Texas qualified to lead?'* to *In what fields will Texas lead?* And he changed *it has bravado* to something which we all preferred: *it still has the courage to take great risks.*
Then Quimper made his own good change, knocking out the condescending part about popular music and substituting *It has four universities which will soon be among the best in the land, Texas, Rice, A&M, SMU.*

When all was done, Rusk asked Miss Cobb: 'Was Sparta so bad?' and she replied: 'It was a flaming bore, and we must avoid that in Texas,' whereupon he growled: 'Only an ass would call Texas boring.'

The million dollars for my chair was the first display of obscene Texas wealth. Now to the other two. They focused on Ransom Rusk and came well after our December report had been submitted. The first was initiated by Lorenzo Quimper, the second by Miss Cobb, and each was quite wonderful in its own Texas way.

At the amicable year-end dinner celebrating our final session, Quimper said, as the wine was being passed: 'Ransom, you sit on all that money of yours, and you don't do a single constructive thing with it. You're a disgrace to the state of Texas.'

'What should I do?' Rusk asked, and this was a mistake, because Quimper had a proposal worked out in detail. He needed several months of telephone calls to flesh it out, but when he was done and all parts were in place, he produced a Lorenzo Quimper extravaganza which would be talked about for years to come.

'What we're going to do,' he explained in my Austin office, 'is introduce Ransom Rusk, secretive Texas billionaire, to the general public, who will be allowed to see him as the lovable and generous man we Task Force members have discovered him to be.'

'What will you offer,' I asked, 'a mass execution of Democrats?'

'No, we're going to put on a masterful Texas bull auction. Ransom is proud of his Texas Longhorns, some of the best in America, but few people get a chance to see them. What we'll do is sell off eighty-three of the choicest range animals you ever saw.'

'That could involve a lot of people, maybe three, four hundred.'

Lorenzo looked at me as if I had lost my mind: 'Son, we're talkin' about five, six thousand.'

'Why would that many come to a . . . ?'

Quimper put his arm about my shoulder in his confidential style, and said in a low, persuasive voice: 'Son, half of Texas will be fightin' to get in.'

Excited by the prospects of a really slam-bang cattle sale, he involved me in the wild festivities he had planned on Rusk's behalf, and I was staggered by what a Texas multimillionaire would recommend to a friend who was a Texas billionaire.

By sunset on the Friday before the auction eleven Lear jets were lined up on the grassy field beside the Larkin runway, and next morning at least eighty smaller planes flew in, including six helicopters that ferried important guests to the ranch, eleven miles away. On Saturday eighteen huge blue-and-white Trailways buses, each with uniformed driver, moved endlessly around the motels, hotels and guest houses, stopping finally at the airport to finish loading before heading for the Rusk ranch.

At four different barricades on the way armed security men in uniform halted us to inspect our credentials, and when we were cleared, the buses delivered us to a huge field prepared for the occasion. It was lined by thirty-six green-and-white portable toilets. 'Experience has taught,' Quimper said as he showed me around, 'that the proper division is twenty-one for women, fifteen for men, because women take longer.'

More than a hundred Rusk employees and high school students hired for the day were scattered through the vast crowd, each dressed in the distinctive colors of the ranch, gold and blue, and twenty of the more attractive young girls, in skimpy costume, manned that number of drink stands, serving endless quantities of beer, Coke, Dr. Pepper and a tangy orange drink, all well iced. What gave me great pleasure, a mariachi band of seven musicians—two blaring trumpets, two guitars, two violins, one double bass guitar—strolled amiably through the grounds, playing 'Guadalajara' and 'Cu-cu-ru-cu-cu Paloma.'

At noon four open-air kitchens operated, serving a delicious barbecue with pinto beans, salad, whole-wheat buns, cheese, pickles and coconut cake, and at one o'clock we all gathered in the huge tent, where a large stand had been erected behind a sturdily fenced-in area in which the Longhorns would be exhibited one by one as the sale progressed. Eighteen hundred interested men and women filled the tent as the two auctioneers appeared to considerable applause. They were a fine-looking pair of men in their early forties, prematurely silver-haired and possessed of leather lungs. 'The Reyes brothers,' Quimper said as they bowed, acknowledging the applause of spectators who were proud of them. 'Their father was born in Durango, northern Mexico,' Quimper said. 'Walked to the Rio Grande, that muddy highway to salvation, and found a job. He sired fourteen children and sent them all to college. The six girls became teachers, medical assistants, what have you. The eight boys all went to A&M, doctors, accountants and these two skilled auctioneers. Shows what can be done.'

The Reyes would be assisted, I learned, by four energetic young men who made themselves the highlight of the sale, for they remained at ground level, each wearing a big cowboy hat, and it was their job to excite the crowd, encourage the bidding, and wave frantically, shouting at the top of their voices: 'Twenty-three thousand here!' or 'Twenty-four in the back.' I asked Quimper who they were, and he smiled proudly: 'What I do, we establish a generous budget for advertising. Maybe a dozen major cattle publications. But before I give any magazine a bundle of cash, I make a deal: "I'll give you the advertising, Bert, but you must send me one of your editors to help." These are the men the magazines have sent.' They were an active, screaming lot.

The Reyes brothers were verbal machine guns, rattling off a jargon of which I understood not one word until they slammed a piece of oak wood against a reverberating board: 'Once, twice, sold to Big L Ranch of Okmulgee, Oklahoma.'

Since there were eighty-three animals to be sold, each one groomed and perfect, and since the average price seemed to be about $29,000, it was obvious that the sale was going to fetch more than $2,000,000, which explained why no bidder ever sat for fifteen minutes before one of the costumed Rusk girls appeared with a tray of iced drinks. 'We want to keep them happy,' Quimper said, but I pointed out a curiosity of the sale: 'Lorenzo, if you sell only eighty-three animals, and if the same bidders keep buying two and three each, there's only thirty or forty people in this tent who are seriously participating.'

'You're right. The rest are like you. They come for the freebies . . . food, drinks and entertainment.' He indicated the huge crowd of watchers, then added: 'And to see what Ransom Rusk looks like.'

He looked great. Tall, thin, dressed in complete cowboy garb, smiling wanly, nodding occasionally when a particularly fine animal was sold, he stood at the far side of the auctioneer's stand, saying nothing unless the manager of the sale halted the bidding to ask him: 'Mr. Rusk, this bull brought top dollar at the Ferguson Dispersal, did it not?' and then Rusk would say, with the microphone in his face: 'It did. A hundred and nine thousand dollars,' and the rapid-fire chatter of the Reyes would resume.

Quimper had a dozen surprises for the crowd. After the second bull had been sold, a roar went up, and when I looked about I saw that a remarkable man had taken his place in the middle of the screaming helpers. He was in his sixties and weighed about two hundred and sixty pounds. 'It's Hoss Shaw,' Quimper informed me. 'Imported him from Mississippi. Enthusiastic aide, best in the business.'

If the four young men were active, Hoss was volcanic. Chewing on a long black cigar, he leaped about, roared in bullfrog voice, wheedled shamelessly, and when he elicited a bid he went into paroxysms. Throwing both arms aloft, he kicked one leg so high, he looked as if he were a crow about to take off. Watching Hoss Shaw report a bid could be exhausting.

'He adds two, three thousand dollars to each animal,' Quimper whispered. 'Worth every penny of his commision.'

With his arrival the serious part of the auction began, and I was perplexed by the confusing variety of cattle items for sale. An expert beside me explained: 'We call it a bull sale, and as you can see, we do sell bulls. In various ways. You can buy a bull outright and take him home to your ranch. Or you can buy part of a bull— breeding rights and profits from the sale of frozen semen—but the bull stays here. Or you can buy a straw of frozen semen and impregnate your cow on your own ranch.'

But it was when the cows came up for sale that I really became bewildered. The expert again explained: 'First you have a cow, pure and simple, like this one being sold now. Then you have a cow, but she's certified pregnant by a known bull. Then you have a pregnant cow, with a calf suckling at her side . . . that's a three-fer, and you buy enough three-fers, you've got yourself a big start.'

'That sounds simple enough,' I said, but he laughed: 'Son, I'm only beginning. In the old days a great Longhorn cow like Measles, best in forty years, could produce a calf a year . . . maybe sixteen in her lifetime, each one more valuable than gold. But now we can feed her hormones, collect her eggs as she produces them in her ovaries, inseminate them artificially, and encourage her to give us not one calf a year, but maybe thirty or forty.'

'Sounds indecent!' Then I asked: 'But how does she give birth to them all?' and the expert laughed: 'That's where genius comes in. We place each fertilized egg, one by one, in the uterus of any healthy cow . . .'

'Another Longhorn?'

'Any breed, so long as the cow is big and healthy and capable of giving good milk to her young.'

'And that nothing cow produces a Longhorn calf?'

'She does. But it's the next step that tickles me. Experts can slice a fertilized egg in half, implant each half in a different recipient cow, and produce identical twins, three times out of ten.'

'Aren't you fellows playing God?'

'Son, we're doin' with Texas Longhorns today what scientists are gonna do with people tomorrow.'

But I was most interested in the next items, for into the auction ring came, one by one, six animals with the longest, wildest horns I had ever seen. They were steers, so in normal husbandry they would have been good only for the meat market if young or the dog-food industry if aged, but here, because of their tremendous horns, they were remarkable assets, eagerly sought by Texas ranchers. 'We call them "walkin'-around Longhorns," ' the man said. 'We buy them to adorn our ranches so women can "Oh!" and "Ah!" when they come out to see us from Houston or Dallas. They're also very effective if you're trying to borrow money from a visiting Boston banker.'

How grand those horns were! 'Real rocking chairs,' my informant said admiringly, and when a huge, rangy beast stalked in with horns seventy-seven inches from tip to tip, he started bidding wildly, and I cheered him on, for this was a remarkable animal. Finally I winked at Hoss Shaw, as if to say: 'You got a live one here,' and Hoss put on his act until my man bought the magnificent steer for $11,000. 'You got some real walkin'-around stock that time,' I whispered, and he said: 'Thanks for your encouragement. I might have dropped out.'

At one point I got the impression that more than half the bidders were medical doctors, and when I asked Quimper about this, he said: 'In Texas, never get sick during a cattle sale. Most of the doctors will be at the auction.'

It was a dreamlike day—the dust of the great buses, the noise of the helicopters, the aromatic smoke from the mesquite logs toasting the barbecue, the soft singing of the mariachis, the whirling about of the pretty girls in their short skirts as they passed out drinks, the rapid-fire cries of the Reyes brothers: 'Hoody-hoody

hoody-harkle-harkle-krimshaw-krimshaw twenty-six thousand,' the figure repeated eleven times before Hoss Shaw screamed, arms waving, one foot in the air: 'Twenty-seven thousand.'

But when the noise was greatest, there was a solemn moment, forcing even the rowdiest participants to come to attention as a splendid Longhorn bull was brought into the pen. An expert from Wichita Refuge in Oklahoma took the microphone and said: 'Ladies and gentlemen! As you may remember, in 1927 the United States woke up to the fact that the famed Texas Longhorn was about to vanish from this earth. Fortunately, thoughtful men and women of that period took action, and my predecessors at the Refuge scoured the West and Mexico looking for authentic animals with which to rebuild the breed. It was here in Larkin, at the ranch of our host's grandmother, Emma Larkin Rusk, that they found that core of great Longhorns on which we rebuilt.

'No name was prouder, no animal meant more to the recovery of the Longhorn than Mean Moses VI, the perfect bull that Emma Rusk sent up to the Refuge. Along with the sensational cow Bathtub Bertha, these animals launched the famous MM/BB line, and right now we're going to bring before you the living epitome of the breed—Mean Moses XIX.' As we cheered, the left-hand flanking gate opened and up the ramp came the stately bull, long, mean, rangy, not too fat but tremendously prepotent.

'Ladies and gentlemen,' intoned the auctioneer. 'Mean Moses XIX, top animal in his breed, is owned by a consortium. He lives on this ranch, but he belongs to the industry. Today we are selling one-tenth interest in this greatest of the Longhorns. One-tenth only, ladies and gentlemen, and the bull stays here. But you participate fully in the nationwide sale of his semen. Do I hear a bid of fifty thousand?'

I gasped, for if Reyes could get a starting bid of that amount, it meant that Mean Moses was valued at $500,000. The bid was immediately forthcoming, and before I could catch my breath it stood at $80,000, at which Hoss Shaw sprang into action, dancing and wheedling the bidders until the hammer fell at $110,000. Mean Moses, whose line had been kept extant only by the affection of Emma Larkin Rusk, was verifiably worth $1,100,000.

As night fell, six thousand bowls of chili were served with Mexican sweets on the side, and the visitors found seats about the place, facing the large stage which Quimper had erected for the occasion and onto which now came the first of three orchestras that would entertain till two in the morning.

It was a beautiful night, as fine as this region of Texas provided, and the music was noisy and country. People wandered about freely, locating old friends, making appointments and closing deals. Men running for office circulated, shaking hands, and some of the most beautiful women in America moved about, lending grace to the night.

I should have suspected that something was up when I saw among these beauties one who was especially attractive, a girl I had cheered when a graduate assistant at the University of Texas. She had been Beth Morrison then, premier baton twirler of the South West Conference and everybody's sweetheart. Now she was Beth Macnab, wife of the Dallas Cowboys' linebacker. She and her husband went to New York a good deal, the gossip columns said, where they were friends with various painters, who stayed with them when the artists had one-man exhibitions in Texas.

I could not imagine why Beth, who was now regarded as one of our Texas intellectuals, had bothered to attend a bull auction in Larkin, but I gave the matter no further thought, because Quimper took the stage to make an announcement which stunned the crowd: 'Our brochure said we'd have four bands. The mariachis, the dance band you've been hearing, and the Nashville Brass, who were so sensational. What the brochure did not say was that the fourth band which we'll now hear brings with it the immortal Willie Nelson!'

The crowd went berserk, because many of its members had known Willie when he was a voice wailing in the wilderness, adhering to a simple statement which seemed to lack the ingredients of popular acceptance. I used to listen to him in the small Austin bars and tell my friends: 'This cat can sing. He has a statement to make.' And then in the 1970s the world discovered that people like me had been right, and he became not only a roaring success, but also a symbol of that stubborn Texas type which clings to a belief, ignores snubs, and survives into a kind of immortality. Willie Nelson was basic Texas, and when he came onstage in tennis shoes, beat-up jeans, ragged shirt and red bandanna about his head, some of us old-timers had tears in our eyes. What a voice! What a presence! By damn, when Lorenzo Quimper threw a bull sale, he threw it just short of Montana.

But even Willie was not the highlight of the evening, for after he had given us a masterful rendition of 'Blue Eyes Cryin' in the Rain' Quimper took the stage, drums rolled, and Willie stepped aside. 'Friends,' Quimper said, 'my dear associate Ransom Rusk, who has arranged this celebration, has been just what the cartoonists pictured, a lonely, self-motivated Texas oilman of untold wealth. He was afraid of people, so I prevailed upon him to invite six thousand of his most intimate friends here tonight to share with him a moment of transcendent joy. Friends!'—Lorenzo's voice elevated to a bellow—'Ransom Rusk, that mean-spirited, lonely son-of-a-gun, sittin' in his office at midnight countin' his billions, he's gonna get married!'

As we cheered and whistled, Rusk, in a freshly pressed blue whipcord rancher's outfit featuring a pair of special gold boots provided by Quimper, came onstage and bowed. Taking the microphone, he said, pointing to Quimper: 'Loudmouth is right. I'm getting married. And I want you to be the first to meet the bride.' From the wings he brought in Maggie Morrison, forty-nine years old, one hundred and twenty-one pounds, and the portrait of a successful Houston real estate magnate. She wore, to her own surprise but at the insistence of Quimper, the Mexican China Poblana costume, complete with Quimper boots and topped by a delightful straw hat from whose brim dangled twenty-four little silver bells. She was a warm-hearted, smiling woman of maximum charm, and I thought: Rusk is lucky to land that one.

But Quimper was not finished—indeed, he was never satisfied with anything he did, so far as I could recall, for there was always a little something he wanted to add—and this time he added a stunner: 'Good ol' Rance is not only gettin' hisse'f a stunnin' wife, but he also gets one of the most beautiful daughters in Texas, Beth Macnab!' When Beth came onstage, Lorenzo signaled to the wings and a pretty girl of fourteen ran out with a silver baton.

'This is a surprise, folks, and I haven't warned Beth, but how about some of those All-American twirls?'

It had been some years since Beth had performed at the various half-times throughout the state—Dallas Cowboys, Cotton Bowl and the rest—and she could properly have begged off, but this was her mother's big night, so she kicked off her high heels and said: 'A girl doesn't usually twirl in an outfit like this, but if Mom is brave enough to marry Ransom Rusk after what the papers say about him, I'm brave enough to make a fool of myself.'

She threw the baton high in the air, waited with her lovely face upturned, and was lucky enough to catch it. Bowing to the crowd, she returned the baton to the girl, then blew kisses fore and aft: 'Never press your luck. Mom, this is wonderful. Pop, welcome to the family.' And she parked a big kiss on Ransom's cheek.

When the couple returned to Texas in August after a hurried honeymoon in Rome, Paris and London, Miss Cobb called me on the phone and asked me to rush immediately to Dallas, where our disbanded Task Force was to meet with Ransom Rusk and his new wife, and when we filed into the room to meet him, she spoke bluntly: 'Ransom, my work with you on our committee and my attendance at your bull sale made me appreciate you as a real human being. And the fact that you were brave enough to marry this delightful woman from Houston confirms my feelings.'

'Sounds like an ominous preamble,' he said, and she replied: 'It is.'

None of us knew what she had in mind and we were startled when she disclosed it: 'I think your good friend Lorenzo did you a great service when he prevailed upon you to throw that bash. Best thing you ever did, Ransom. Made you human. But it's not enough.'

'What else did you have in mind?" he asked gruffly.

'You're one of the richest men in our state, maybe the richest. But you've never done one damned thing for Texas. And I think that's scandalous.'

'Now wait . . .'

'Oh, I know, a football scholarship here and there, your fund for leprosy research. But I mean something commensurate with your stature.'

'Like what?'

'Have you ever, in your pinched-in little life, visited the great museum complex in Fort Worth?'

'Not really. A reception now and then, but I don't like receptions.'

'Are you aware that Fort Worth, which people in Dallas like to call a cowtown . . . do you know that it has one of the world's noblest museum complexes? A perfect gem?'

'I don't know much about museums.'

'You're going to find out right now.' And she dragooned all of us, plus Mrs. Rusk, whom she insisted upon, and we drove over to that elegant assembly of buildings which formed one of the most graceful parts of Texas: the delicate Kimbell museum, with its splendid European paintings; the heavy museum of modern art, with its bold contemporary painting; and the enticing Amon Carter Museum of Western Art, with its unmatched collection of Charles Russell, Frederic Remington and other cowboy artists. Few cities offered such a compact variety of enticing art.

'What did you want me to do?' Rusk asked when the whirlwind trip ended, and Miss Cobb said boldly: 'Rance, there's an excellent piece of land in that complex still open. I want you to place your own museum there. Build the best and stock it with the best.'

'Well, I . . .'

'Rance, in due course you'll be dead. Remembered for what? A gaggle of oil wells? Who gives a damn? Really, Rance, ask yourself that question, and let's meet here two weeks from today.'

'Now wait . . .'

She would not wait. Standing boldly before him, she said: 'Rance, I'm talking about your soul. Ask Maggie, she'll know what I mean.' And she started for the door, but when she reached it she reminded him: 'Two weeks from today. And I shall want to hear your plans, because in my own way, Rance, I love you, and I cannot see you go down to your grave unremembered and uncherished.'

No one spoke. Of course it was Quimper who finally broke the silence, for he did not like vacant air: 'She's right, Rance. It would be a notable gesture.'

Rusk turned harshly on his friend: 'What the hell have you ever done with your money, Quimper?' and Lorenzo said: 'Get your spies to uncover how much I've given to the university. Did you know that it now has a chair of poetry in my name?'

'And forty baseball scholarships,' Garza said, and Quimper laughed: 'Each man to his own specialization.'

When the meeting broke, Rusk asked me to remain behind, and this started one of the wildest periods of my life, for he wanted me to discuss with him in the most intricate detail what would be involved if he donated a fourth museum to the Fort Worth complex, but first we had to decide what the museum would cover. He arranged with the university for me to take a six-month leave, paid for by him, and patiently we went over the options. First he suggested a cowboy museum, but I reminded him that the Amon Carter had preempted that specialty, and then when he proposed an oil museum, I reminded him that what we were talking about was an art museum: 'Besides, both Midland and Kilgore already have excellent oil museums. And what's worse, oil has never produced much art.'

He asked me if a man like him could buy enough European art to compete with the Kimbell, and I had to tell him no: 'Besides, that's already been done.'

I shall never forget the long day we spent at the Kimbell, with him trying to discover what it was that justified such a magnificent building, a poem, really, for he wanted to know everything. I remember especially his comments on several of the paintings. The chef-d'oeuvre of the collection was the marvelous Giovanni Bellini 'Mother and Child,' and when he finished studying it he said: 'That's real art. Reverent.' He dismissed the great Duccio, which showed Italian watchers hiding their noses as the corpse of Lazarus was raised from the dead: 'That's a disgrace to the Bible.'

He paid his longest visit to a beautiful Gainsborough, a languid young woman in a blue gown seated beneath a tree. 'Miss Lloyd' the picture was titled, and I thought that she had awakened some arcane memory, for he returned to the portrait numerous times, in obvious perplexity. Finally he took out a ball-point pen, not to make notes but to hold it to his right eye as he made comparisons. After about twenty minutes of such study he said: 'She'd have to be eleven feet nine inches tall,' and when I restudied the delightful painting, I saw that he was right, for Gainsborough had elongated Miss Lloyd preposterously.

'Whoever painted it should be fired,' he growled, and I said: 'Too late. He died in 1788.'

But he did not miss the glory of this museum, its excellent structure and the way it fitted into its landscape: 'What would a building to match this one cost?' I told him that with current prices it could run to eighteen or twenty million, minimum, and even then, with far less square footage. He nodded.

At three A.M., three days before our scheduled meeting with Miss Cobb, my phone rang insistently, and Rusk cried: 'Come right over. I've sent my driver.' And when I reached his modest Dallas quarters in which the new Mrs. Rusk shared the lone bedroom and bath, I found both of them in nightrobes, in the bedroom, surrounded by a blizzard of newspapers.

'I've got my museum! I was reading in bed, running options through my mind, and I asked myself: "What is the biggest thing in Texas?" And this newspaper here gave me the answer.' It was a Thursday edition of the *Dallas Morning News* and I looked for the headlines to provide a clue, but I could not find any. Instead, Rusk had about him eight special sections which the paper had added that day, making it one of the biggest weekday papers I'd seen. He grabbed my arm and asked: 'What *is* the biggest thing in Texas?' and I said: 'Religion, but the cathedrals take care of that.'

'Guess again!' and I said: 'Oil, but Midland and Kilgore handle that.'

'And again?' and I said: 'Ranching, but the Amon Carter Museum covers that.' So he slapped the eight special sections of the newspaper and said: 'Look for yourself. The *Dallas News* knows what really counts,' and when I picked up the sections I found that the paper, in response to an insatiable hunger among its Texas readers, had published one hundred and twelve pages of extra football news: Professional, with accent on Dallas. Professional, other teams. Colleges, with accent on Texas teams. Colleges, the others. High Schools, very thick. High Schools, how star players should handle recruiting. Sixteen full pages on the latter, plus, of course, the customary sixteen pages of current football news, or one hundred and twenty-eight pages in all.

Rusk, having made his great discovery, beamed like a boy who has seen the light regarding the Pythagorean theorem: 'Sport!' And as soon as he uttered that almost sacred word, I could see an outstanding museum added to those in the park.

Neither he nor I, and certainly not Maggie Rusk, visualized it as a Sports Hall of Fame filled with old uniforms and used boxing gloves. Every state tried that, often disastrously. No, what we saw was a real art museum, a legitimate hall of beauty filled with notable examples of how sports had so often inspired artists to produce work of the first category: 'No junk. No baseball cards. No old uniforms.' Rusk was speaking at four in the morning: 'Just great paintings, like that Madonna we saw.'

I warned him that the art salesrooms were not filled with Bellini studies of football players, but he dismissed the objection: 'It will be American art depicting American sports.' And when dawn broke we three went out to an all-night truck stop and had scrambled eggs.

By the time Miss Cobb and the others reached Dallas that weekend, the Rusks had a full prospectus roughed out, but before they were allowed to present it, Miss Cobb distributed a glossy pamphlet that had been printed in high style by the Smithsonian in Washington: 'Before we mention specific plans, I want to upgrade your horizons. I want us to do something significant, and to do that we must entertain significant thoughts.'

Holding the pamphlet in her hand, she looked directly at Rusk and Quimper: 'You two clowns thought very big with your bull sale. Glorious. Real Texas. My two Cobb senators would have applauded. They said it was important to keep alive the old traditions, and I must confess, Rance and Lorenzo, you not only kept them alive, you added a few touches. Now look at someone else who has thought big.'

I was perplexed when I looked at my copy of the pamphlet, for it apparently recounted a gala affair at the Smithsonian in which a Texas oil and technology man had been honored by the President, the Chief Justice and some hundred dignitaries from American and European universities. It was a rather thick pamphlet and three-fourths of it was taken up by photographs; before I could inspect them, Rusk said: 'I worked with him. One of the best.'

What the rear two-thirds of the pamphlet showed were the twenty-seven colleges and universities to which the Texan had given either magnificent solo buildings or entire complexes. Any one would have been the gesture of a lifetime—a tower at MIT, a quadrangle at the University of Vancouver in Canada, a School of Geology at Sydney in Australia—but when I saw the two entire colleges, and I mean all the buildings, which he had given to Cambridge in England and the Sorbonne in France, I was staggered.

Twenty-seven tremendous monuments dug from the soil of the most barren fields in Texas, twenty-seven halls of learning. The total cost? Incalculable. But there they stood, in nine unconnected corners of the world, more than half in the United States, and more than half of those in Texas, centers of learning and of light.

'I want us all to think in those terms,' Miss Cobb said, and Rusk snapped: 'It's my money we're talking about,' and she said: 'My father always told us "Rich people need guidance." We're here to help you, Rance, because we love you and we don't want to see you miss the big parade. Now, what bright idea did you and Barlow come up with?'

'Sport,' Rusk said, and Miss Cobb asked: 'You mean one of those pathetic Halls of Fame? Old jockstraps cast in bronze. Old men recalling the lost days of their youth?'

'I do not,' Rusk snapped. 'I mean an art museum. As legitimate as any in the world. Fine art, like the Kimbell, but glorifying sport.'

Miss Cobb pondered this, and then said enthusiastically: 'That could be most effective, Ransom, but don't keep it parochially American. Be universal.'

'You mean art from all the world?' he asked, and she replied: 'I do. We Americans forget that our three big sports—football, baseball, basketball—are focused here. If you do this, don't be parochial.'

If there was one thing the new Texan, of whom Rusk was a prototype, did not want to be, it was parochial: 'You make sense, Lorena.' Then, turning to me, he issued an imperial ukase: 'Barlow, we'll make it universal.'

At the end of that long day she kissed Ransom: 'I have a feeling, Rance, you'll do it right. Make Quimper your treasurer. He likes to spend other people's money. And keep Barlow at your side. He'll know what art is.'

Early next morning Rusk summoned me to his office: 'Hire the man who built the Kimbell and tell him to get started.'

'Louis J. Kahn is dead. That was his masterpiece.'

'Get me the next man . . . just as good.'

'They don't come "just as good," but there are several around who design buildings of great beauty.'

'Get me the best and have him start his drawings this weekend.'

'Architects don't work that way,' I warned him, and he growled: 'This time they will,' and within a month, an architect from Chicago, noted for buildings of great style which caught the spirit of the West, was making provisional designs for a new kind of museum ideally suited to the Fort Worth site, and two months later, ground was broken, with no announcement having been made to the public.

In the meantime I had opened an office in New York to which all the dealers in America, it seemed, traipsed in with samples of their wares, and I was astonished at how many fine American artists had created works based on sport. With a budget larger than any I had ever played with even in my imagination, I put together a guiding committee of seven, three art experts, two artists and two businessmen unfamiliar with Texas or Ransom Rusk, and with the most meticulous care we began reserving a few pieces we would probably want to buy when we started our actual accumulations. Rusk flew in from Dallas to see if we were prepared to fill his fine new museum when the scores of builders and landscape architects working overtime had it ready. For when a Texas billionaire cried 'Let us have a museum!' . . . zingo! he wanted it right now.

Loath to accept personal responsibility for what he termed 'this disgraceful delay,' I assembled my committee and seven major curators and experts for a day's meeting at the Pierre, and there we thrashed out our problems. Rusk listened as a curator from the Metropolitan explained that in the case of a wonderful Thomas Eakins painting, 'Charles Rogers Fishing,' negotiations with the present owners could require as much as a year: 'The Sturdevant family is divided. Half want to sell, the other half don't. A matter of settling the old man's estate.'

'Then we'll forget that one,' Rusk snapped, but the Met man counseled patience: 'Were you fortunate enough to get that Eakins, it alone would set the style for your whole museum. Men like me, and Charles here, we'd have come to Fort Worth to see what other good things you have.'

'You're satisfied there's enough out there to build a topnotch museum?'

'Unquestionably!' and they all grew rhapsodic over the possibilities.

One man from Cleveland summarized the situation: 'Even we were uninformed as to the magnificent possibilities. In the short time we've worked we've come up with a dazzling list of how artists have portrayed men engaged in sports. Ancient Greek statues, Roman athletes, Degas jockeys, Stubbs' unmatched portraits of racing horses.'

'Never heard of that one. Who was he?'

'George Stubbs of England—1724 to 1806. No one ever painted horses better than Stubbs.'

'Can we buy one of his works? I mean, one of his recognized masterpieces?'

And that was the question which led to the explosive idea which got the Fort Worth Museum of Sports Art launched with a bang that no one like me could have engineered, because when these experts explained that to find a Stubbs or a Degas that might be coming onto the market took infinite patience and a high degree of skill to negotiate the sale, Rusk saw that his building was going to be finished long before he had much to put in it.

'The things you've been talking about are European. I understand why they might be difficult to find and deal for. But how about American art? Have we produced any good things?'

It was here that the experts became poetic: 'Wonderful things! But again, Mr. Rusk, all requiring many months of bargaining and cajoling.'

'Why can't we just find a good painting and say "I'll take that"?' and the man from Cleveland laughed: 'Mr. Rusk, if it were that easy, experts like us would lose our jobs.'

I now set up a screen, and with slides I'd been accumulating, gave a preview of the Rusk museum, with the experts gasping at the beauty of some of the artwork we'd located but not yet purchased, and several times some museum curator would sigh: 'I'd like to get that one!' at which a member of our staff would warn: 'Remember, we were promised that Fort Worth would get first crack.'

I showed a marvelous Winslow Homer, one of the finest George Bellows prizefight canvases, cattle-roping scenes by Tom Lea, Charles Russell and Frederic Remington, a masterful George Bingham which someone said we might get for $800,000 and a wonderful semi-hunting scene by Georgia O'Keeffe. But the one which brought cheers was a football scene by Wayne Thebaud entitled 'Running Guard 77,' in which an exhausted lineman sat dejected on the bench, his huge numbers filling the canvas.

Nineteen fine paintings in all flashed across that screen, and at the end the man from the Met said: 'Mr. Rusk, if you can land those nineteen beauties, you're in business. Add nineteen like them, and you have a museum.'

And then Rusk returned to his penetrating question: 'How long to buy them? Assuming we can find the money?' and the men agreed: 'Maybe three years. If you're lucky.'

'I can't wait three years,' Rusk said. 'Why don't we borrow them? Let people see the kind of stuff we're after?'

A hush fell over the darkened room as these wise men, who had assembled so many enlightening and enriching shows of borrowed art, contemplated this perceptive question, and finally the man from Boston said, with guarded enthusiasm: 'Mr. Rusk, if it were done right, and if you could establish a committee of

sufficient gravity to give the thing credibility with the foreign museums . . .
goodness!'

His confreres were less inhibited: 'It's never been done!' 'It's a capital idea!' 'I
can think right now of forty items you'll have to have . . . and probably can
get!' I had rarely seen a workable idea catch such immediate fire, and within the
hour we had put together recommendations for a prestigious group of financial
and publicity sponsors. Reaching for the list, Rusk began telephoning the well-
known men and women and received the consent of most. At the same time the
rest of us were drawing up a list of great works of art from various museums in
the world, and plans were launched to request loans for a huge show to open the
Fort Worth sports museum. When Texans dream, they do so in technicolor.

Then something happened which brought our meeting back to an equally
exciting reality. A New York dealer, who had sat outside waiting to present seven
good canvases for my inspection, asked if he could now come in, and I was
pleased to see that these world-famous experts were always eager to see whatever
the art world was putting forth.

He was a modest man, as were his seven canvases, but after we had been
soaring in the empyrean it was good to come back to earth: 'These are fine works
of museum quality and condition. I have wanted you to see what is immediately
available.' And he showed us a perfectly splendid painting by a man I had not
heard of, Jon Corbino, of athletes posturing on a beach, and then an exhilarating
oil by Fletcher Martin titled 'Out at Second.' It presented a baseball ballet, showing the runner coming in from first with a hook slide to the right, the shortstop
sweeping down with a tag from the left, and the energetic umpire throwing his
arm up in the hooking 'Out' signal.

When the man completed his presentation, Rusk said: 'Would you please step
outside for a moment?' and when he was gone, Ransom asked his advisers: 'I liked
them. But were they good enough for a museum?' and the experts agreed they
were.

'Call him in,' Rusk told me, and when the dealer returned, Rusk said: 'We'll
take them all.'

'But we haven't talked price, sir.'

'Barlow will do that, and I've already warned him to offer no more than half
what you ask.'

'With your permission, I've brought along a European painting I thought you
might want to consider. It's certainly not American and the sport it presents isn't
the way we play it today. But please take a look.' And he placed on the easel a
rather small canvas painted by the Dutch painter Hendrick Avercamp, 1585–1634,
showing a frozen canal near Amsterdam with lively little men in ancient costume
playing ice hockey.

It was the epitome of sport—timeless, set in nature, animated, real—and in addition, it was a significant work of art. The curators and experts applauded so noisily that I cried 'Accession Number One.'

But Rusk forestalled me: 'We want it, surely. That's just the kind of thing we do want. So old. So beautiful. But not as our first acquisition. I've already bought that, and it ought to be in Fort Worth ready for installation when we get back.'

This man Rusk never ceased to surprise me, for when I returned to Fort Worth two weeks later, I found that he had installed in the rotunda of his emerging museum a splendid antique Italian copy of perhaps the most famous sports-art item in the world, the dazzling Discobolus of Myron, dating back to the original Olympic games.

'Where'd you get it?' I asked, and he said: 'Old Italian palace. Saw it on our honeymoon and remembered it ever since.'

An art dealer from New York had come to Dallas with color slides of eight canvases relating to sport, including a Thomas Hart Benton of a rodeo cowboy trying to rope a steer, and I was concluding arrangements for their purchase when Ransom Rusk phoned urgently from Larkin: 'Come right over! Catastrophe!'

Since Rusk rarely pushed the panic button, I excused myself, hopped in the car Rusk provided when I worked in Dallas, and sped out to the mansion, where in the African Hall, I met Rusk and Mr. Kramer, the armadillo expert, in mournful discussion with a Dr. Philippe L'Heureux of Louisiana, a very thin man with beard and piercing eye. When I looked at his card and fumbled with his name, he said: 'Pronounce it Larue. Half my family changed it to that when they reached America.'

'Tell him the bad news,' Rusk said, slumping into a chair made from the tusks of elephants he and his partners had shot on safari, and L'Heureux, standing straight as if giving a laboratory lecture to a class of pre-meds, revealed a shocking situation.

'We have solid reason for believing that the armadillo not only serves as a laboratory host for the study of human leprosy but can also infect people with the disease.'

There was a painful silence as we four stared at one another. L'Heureux stood rigid, prepared to defend his accusation. Mr. Kramer, whose years in retirement had focused on Texas storms and the armadillo, looked mutely from one of us to the other, unable to speak. Rusk, whose walls bespoke his constant interest in animals, was confused, and I, whose only contact with the armadillo had been chuckling at the beer advertisements which featured them, did not know what to think.

Finally L'Heureux spoke: 'We're recommending that since the threat of leprosy is real, and since we have identified five documented cases in Texas in which

persons handling the animals have contracted it, all armadillos that might come
into contact with humans be eradicated.'
'You mean we're to poison them?' Rusk asked.
'Or shoot them.'
Mr. Kramer rose, moved about for some moments, then looked out toward the
former bowling lawn: 'I could not shoot an armadillo. I suspect your evidence is
nothing but rumors.'
'I wish it were,' L'Heureux said. 'But I assure you, the danger is real.'
'Actual cases?' Kramer asked, his white hair glowing in the morning sunlight.
'Yes.'
'And you're recommending extermination?' Rusk asked.
'We are. And so are the experts in Florida. And the epidemiologists in Atlanta.'
And hearing this verdict delivered with such solemn authority, Rusk said: 'As
responsible citizens we must do something, but what?'
'You have two choices. You can shoot them all . . .'
'I'd never do that,' Rusk snapped. 'They're my friends.'
'Or you can trap the lot and ship them to our research station in Carville,
Louisiana.' While Rusk considered this, L'Heureux added: 'You'd be doing us a
considerable favor. Leprosy is a terrible disease if left unchecked, only minor if
treated quickly. Your armadillos could help us to solve some of the mysteries.'
'We'll let you have them,' Rusk said, and I remained in Larkin with L'Heureux
for the remainder of that week while Rusk supervised a team of his illegal Mexican workmen in placing traps about the lawn. When the young armadillos there
had been captured and caged for shipment, the Mexicans were loaned to Mr.
Kramer, who was busy trapping other animals known to be at various spots
around Larkin, and when that task was completed, L'Heureux told us: 'I feel
better, and assure you that you are much safer than you were a week ago.' He
returned to Louisiana that afternoon, so that only Rusk, Kramer and I were
present when the improvised lights came on and we saw the old mother armadillo
come out alone, for her eight children were gone, and stand in perplexity in the
middle of the bowling green.
Mr. Kramer said: 'Don't trap her, Mr. Rusk. She knows she belongs here.'
Years back, when I studied geography, a professor drummed into us the fact
that we must never stumble into the pathetic fallacy, and I remember asking him
what it was: 'The sentimental attributing of human motivations to inanimate
objects like *angry clouds* or *the vengeful tornado*. It's particularly offensive to
attribute to animals such human reactions as *the mother buffalo was eager to fight
off the wolves* or *the collie obviously preferred the runt of her litter*. Things are
things and animals are not humans. Treat them dispassionately.'
Now, when Mr. Kramer was presuming to explain what the mother armadillo
was thinking, I rejected his assumptions. She was not *mourning the loss of her
children,* nor was she *recalling the good times she'd had on this lawn.* My scien-

tific training forced me to think of her as a dumb animal that might be carrying leprosy, and I felt no other emotion as I watched the workmen close in on her when Rusk signaled: 'Edge her toward the trap.'

But she had always been a canny creature, and now some instinct warned her that with the disappearance of her children, she also was in peril, so, evading the trap, she scurried toward the entrance to her underground sanctuary. Normally a nimble man can run down an armadillo, and since there were three Mexicans ready to chase her, they should have nabbed her, but she made a dive between their legs and escaped.

'You'll have to shoot that one,' someone said, 'I've seen old-timers like her fool the best trappers.' So Rusk asked a servant to fetch from the African Hall a high-powered rifle used normally on elephants or Cape buffalo. Handing it to Mr. Kramer, he said: 'Take care of her,' but Kramer refused to do so. Rejecting the gun, he told Rusk: 'She's your responsibility, not mine.'

I thought it appropriate that Ransom, who had in a sense sponsored the armadillos in Larkin, should eliminate the colony, and when the mother of them all came out of her hole to investigate the ominous silence, he drew a bead on her.

But he could not pull the trigger. Looking at me pleadingly, he said: 'I can't do it,' and I found myself with the rifle . . .

Pinnnggg!

The armadillos of Larkin were no more.

The next months were some of the most exciting I have ever spent, because into our temporary offices in Fort Worth came a sequence of cables which caused us to rejoice: THE LOUVRE IS PLEASED TO INFORM YOU THAT WE SHALL BE SENDING THE DEGAS 'HORSE RACE AT ANTEUIL' THE CÉZANNE 'WRESTLERS AT THE BEACH' AND THE LA TOUR 'DUEL AT MIDNIGHT'

From Tokyo came word that a museum would ship nine Japanese prints of the most glowing quality depicting the greatest of the ancient sumo wrestlers, Tanikaze, who flourished in the late eighteenth century. When they arrived I decided that they must have a small room of their own, for they were bound to be one of the hits of the opening show: this massive human figure, more than three hundred and fifty pounds, with its sense of controlled power, all shown in high style by four different artists of world class.

The cable from the Prado in Madrid caused both jubilation and fracas, because we were being sent a precious first printing of Goya's remarkable series of etchings on bullfighting, plus a glowing canvas of same, and our Mexican population showered encomiums upon us for paying this tribute to Hispanic art, but a dedicated women's group opposed to bullfighting warned that they would picket our opening if it included the Goyas, and a wild brouhaha erupted in the press.

Less provocative was the cable from Scotland promising a rare series of prints depicting the development of golf; Rusk appreciated that. And another cable from London completed our foreign loans: WE SHALL BE SENDING YOU A NOTABLE COL‑ LECTION OF RARE PRINTS AND CANVASES BIG ENOUGH TO FILL TWO ROOMS, SHOWING THE WORLD'S MOST POPULAR SPORT, IF ATTENDANCE ALONE IS THE CRITERION, HORSE RACING

I was delighted with the prospect of hanging that part of the show, because I like horses, and so did Rusk.

It was now apparent that this opening show was going to be not only a spectacular success, with art of the highest quality from unexpected corners of the world, but also the first-ever of its kind, and as I studied photographs of the three hundred items that would comprise the exhibition and began to allot each to its probable location in the building which was being rushed to conclusion, I became aware that I was making decisions that ought to be the prerogative of whoever was going to direct the museum over the long run, but we had no director, and I took steps to correct this deficiency.

'Mr. Rusk, you really must get your top man in position . . . and soon.'

'I have that in hand, Barlow,' he assured me, and the next day as I sat in his office I overheard two of the strangest phone calls of my life. My close contact with Rusk over the past years had made me appreciate the man; I had watched him grow in courage during the disasters and in wisdom as he reached out to embrace a larger world. Before my eyes he had matured, as I hoped I would mature in my new position; I not only liked him now, I respected him. However, he could at times do the damnedest things, and these two calls ranked high on the roster of Rusk improbables.

'Get me Tom Landry,' he told his secretary, and shortly he was speaking to the coach of the Dallas Cowboys: 'Tom, this is Ransom. Yes. Tom, I need your confidential advice. Is Wolfgang Macnab what you would call manly?'

I could hear Landry sputter as he defended his linebacker, after which Rusk said: 'I know all that, Tom, but you must have heard the stories that are surfacing. Defensive tackles kissing each other at the end of the game.' Again Landry sputtered, so Rusk put it to him straight: 'Tom, can you assure me that Wolfgang is manly? You know what I mean . . . not queer?'

Apparently Landry wanted to know what in hell Rusk was talking about, and he must have given Ransom a dressing down, because Rusk said: 'Of course he's my son-in-law, but a lot's riding on this and I have to be sure. Any man who studies art, you've got to suspect him.' Landry made some comment, and Rusk continued: 'You ought to see some of the so-called experts up in New York who've been spending my money. Yes, for my new museum. If you ever visited Fort Worth, you'd know about it.'

Assured by Landry that Wolfman Macnab was a macho terror, Rusk now called his trusted friend Joe Robbie of the Miami Dolphins and asked me to listen in:

RUSK: Hiya, Joe. Your old buddy Rance Rusk.

ROBBIE: You fellows showing anything this year?

RUSK: Always enough to beat you bums. Joe, I want to ask a very personal question. Most important to me.

ROBBIE: Shoot. I owe you one for your help on our boy Martínez.

RUSK: In your opinion, is Wolfgang Macnab manly?

ROBBIE: Hell, Don Shula's been trying to get him for three years. Shula doesn't fool around.

RUSK: I know he's a good player, the One-Man Gang they call him. But is he . . . you know what I mean?

ROBBIE: How would I know anything like that. All my players are Democrats.

RUSK: You know those rumors about football professionals. That bit about defensive tackles.

ROBBIE: Forget it. Macnab's the best.

RUSK: Thanks a million, Joe.

That afternoon Rusk summoned Wolfgang Macnab to his office, and when the All-Pro was seated, Rusk said, out of the blue: 'Son, I want you to be the director of my sports museum. Don't speak. You've got one, two more years of professional ball. Good, stay with it. But at our big press conference Friday, I want to announce you as our director.'

'I love art, Mr. Rusk. I know something about it . . . but director? A major museum?'

'If you can handle those Pittsburgh running backs, you can handle a bunch of paintings.'

'You know, sir, I take art far more seriously than I do football. I'm not kidding around.'

'I wouldn't want you if you were.'

They discussed salary, and Macnab almost fell out of his chair at its proposed size. So did I.

And then the young man showed his maturity by asking a penetrating question: 'As director, would I have a small budget for acquisition of new works?'

'You sure would. As of today, assuming you take the job, you have thirty-two million dollars on deposit.'

When Macnab blanched, no more stunned than I, Rusk rose and put his arm about his shoulders: 'Never forget, son, when you represent Texas, always go first class.'

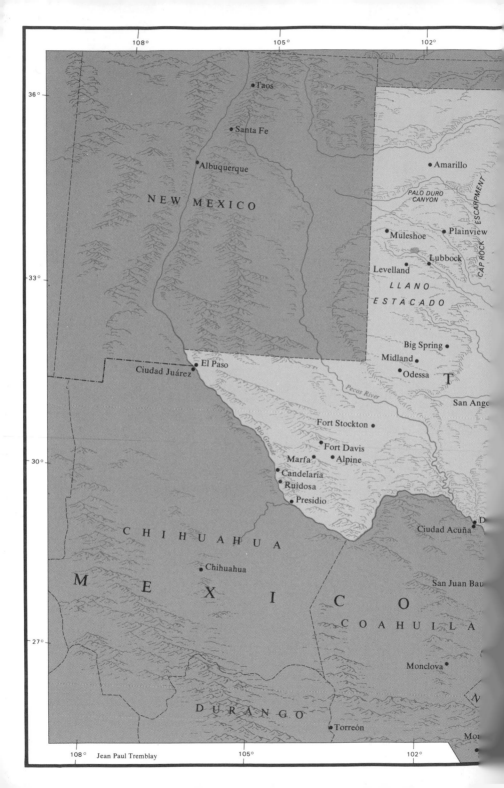